GANG

MAN'S

GALLOWS

Carroll John Daly

THE COLLECTED

OF RACE WILLIAMS

INTRODUCTION BY

STEEGER BOOKS

2020

GANG MAN'S GALLOWS

HARD-BOILED STORIES

VOLUME 6

BROOKS E. HEFNER

CARROLL JOHN DALY

"Introduction" copyright © 2020 Brooks E. Hefner. All rights reserved.

Published by arrangement with Steeger Properties, LLC, agent for the Estate of Carroll John Daly.

ASSOCIATE EDITOR

Ray Riethmeier

ACKNOWLEDGEMENTS

Walter Behnke, the Estate of Carroll John Daly, and Brooks E. Hefner

Cover photo © Mark Krajnak | JerseyStyle Photography

ISBN

978-1-61827-563-9

xi INTRODUCTION
BY BROOKS E. HEFNER

1 A CORPSE ON THE HOUSE
DIME DETECTIVE • MARCH 1938

39 A CORPSE FOR A CORPSE
DIME DETECTIVE • JULY 1938

76 MEN IN BLACK
DIME DETECTIVE • OCTOBER 1938

113 THE QUICK AND THE DEAD
DIME DETECTIVE • DECEMBER 1938

152 HELL WITH THE LID LIFTED
DIME DETECTIVE • MARCH 1939

189 A CORPSE IN THE HAND
DIME DETECTIVE • JUNE 1939

224 GANGMAN'S GALLOWS
DIME DETECTIVE • AUGUST 1939

265 THE WHITE-HEADED CORPSE
DIME DETECTIVE • NOVEMBER 1939

306 CASH FOR A KILLER
DIME DETECTIVE • FEBRUARY 1940

346 VICTIM FOR VENGEANCE
CLUES DETECTIVE STORIES • SEPTEMBER 1940

384 TOO DEAD TO PAY
CLUES DETECTIVE STORIES • MARCH 1941

Introduction

BY BROOKS E. HEFNER

HISTORIES OF HARD-BOILED detective fiction—that American blend of tough-guy action, vernacular narration, and a hint of deduction—love to celebrate the genre's founding figures. Dashiell Hammett provided the sophisticated model; his Continental Op stories showed a world filled with corruption and violence, a world managed only by the efforts of a laconic, slangy, wise-cracking, and nameless narrator. Raymond Chandler provided the world-weary polish, first in his finely wrought Carmady and John Dalmas stories in the pulps, and then in his renowned Philip Marlowe novels. Marlowe's private detective loner—one deeply indebted to Hammett's other pulp creation, Sam Spade—combined the right amount of weariness and wit, of dangerous dames and colorful metaphors, perfect for a world where surety appeared to be slipping away and powerful forces—for Chandler, usually the wealthy and elite—seemed to be pulling everyone's strings. This genre—or perhaps this style or attitude within a genre—has had such an influence on crime fiction that it is difficult to find any example of the genre in contemporary American culture that doesn't exhibit some trace of the hard-boiled. Innumerable adaptations since Chandler's heyday have included such diverse variations as the work of Chester Himes and Mickey Spillane, James Ellroy and Sara Paretsky, not to mention countless film noirs modeled on the attitudes and postures of hard-boiled fiction. For all intents and purposes, American detective fiction is almost inevitably hard-boiled.

Such truisms about the genre nevertheless obscure a more complicated truth. Hammett's first hard-boiled stories appeared, as many crime fiction fans know, in a pulp magazine named *Black Mask.* Chandler's first stories appeared there as well. From the mid-1920s through the mid-1930s, editor Joseph T. Shaw all but made the hard-boiled style the house style of *Black Mask,* emphasizing action over deduction and spare narration over gratuitous detail, placing the magazine in contrast with the classic detective fiction of the Arthur Conan Doyle and S.S. Van Dine model. During Shaw's sometimes tumultuous tenure as editor, he introduced a number of other talented purveyors of the hard-boiled style: Paul Cain, Frederick Nebel, Raoul Whitfield, Horace McCoy, Lester Dent, George

Harmon Coxe, and others. In 1946 he collected these writers in the first anthology devoted to hard-boiled fiction, *The Hard-Boiled Omnibus*. If anything, *The Hard-Boiled Omnibus* both created the first canon of hard-boiled writers and emphasized the collective nature of the enterprise. After all, many writers worked together to produce the style of these stories in *Black Mask,* and, with Shaw's editorial suggestions, the "hard, brittle style" associated with the hard-boiled became a product of the publishing culture that was *Black Mask.*[1] A glaring absence from Shaw's volume, however, was a wildly popular *Black Mask* writer named Carroll John Daly. There are many reasons Shaw may have excluded Daly: Daly's star had fallen by the mid-1940s, Shaw never really liked Daly's cruder style, and Shaw had not really "discovered" or cultivated Daly the way he had done for so many of these other writers. In fact, Daly began publishing in *Black Mask* four years before Shaw entered its editorial offices. And Shaw's omission is a crucial one, for if any one writer can claim to be the originator of the hard-boiled style, it is Carroll John Daly.

Daly presents a curious problem for historians of the hard-boiled. His name is briefly mentioned in many of the standard narratives of the genre's emergence, and he is often credited with originating the style, but then quickly dismissed as some kind of evolutionary Neanderthal, a writer who somehow invented something without realizing what he was doing and went on to see others perfect it while he remained in a state of arrested development. For example, William F. Nolan, in his excellent collection *The Black Mask Boys*, called Daly "an artificial, awkward, self-conscious pulpster" and described his writing as "impossibly crude, the plotting labored and ridiculous."[2] Ron Goulart called him "a somewhat embarrassing founding father."[3] Others have made equally broad judgments. In one of only a couple of academic articles on Daly, Michael S. Barson called him "a third-rate word-spinner who hatched a second-rate protagonist who did his thing in these fourth-rate productions best left on the broom-closet's top shelf in the back."[4] One must, however, balance these harsh words with praise for Daly, and such praise often came from *Black Mask* readers and writers. Daly's greatest champion was Erle Stanley Gardner—fellow *Black Mask* contributor and creator of the Perry Mason series of novels that began in 1933. Nearly every significant effort to write Daly out of hard-boiled history was met by a Gardner response. Not long after Raymond Chandler published his famous homage to Hammett, "The Simple Art of Murder," in *The Atlantic Monthly* in 1944, and when Shaw was about to present his canon in *The Hard-Boiled Omnibus*, Gardner lauded Daly in Howard Haycraft's *The Art of the Mystery Story*, a documentary volume by one

---

1   Joseph T. Shaw, *The Hard-Boiled Omnibus* (New York: Simon and Schuster, 1946), vii.

2   William F. Nolan, *The Black Mask Boys* (New York: Mysterious Press, 1987), 35.

3   Ron Goulart, *The Dime Detectives* (New York: Mysterious Press, 1988), 32.

4   Michael S. Barson, "'There's No Sex in Crime': The Two-Fisted Homilies of Race Williams," *Clues: A Journal of Detection* 2.2 (Fall–Winter 1981), 110.

of the great historians of mystery fiction. Gardner's contribution, "The Case of the Early Beginning," argued that "Daly did as much, or more, than any other author to develop the *type*" of what he called the "action" detective story.[5] Throughout his career and even after Daly's death, Gardner was insistent on the importance of Daly as a foundational figure for *Black Mask* and for the hard-boiled model of writing. In a 1965 contribution to *The Atlantic Monthly*, Gardner resolutely claimed, "Carroll John Daly helped to originate the hard-boiled school of detective writers when, some forty-odd years ago, he created the character of Race Williams."[6]

Despite the efforts of writers like Gardner, traces of Daly have remained scant; he still appears a kind of ghostly forbearer, unseen and unheard, rather than one of the most successful and popular *Black Mask* writers of the 1920s and 1930s and one of the best known writers of pulp crime fiction in his heyday. His work has only occasionally appeared in crime fiction anthologies, often with headnotes and introductions apologizing for his inclusion, but by and large Daly's short fiction and serialized novels remain hidden away in the pages of rare pulp magazines. This volume—the second in a series chronicling the adventures of Daly's most successful character, Race Williams—seeks to correct that by providing a definitive edition of Daly's work, documenting the untold history of the emergence of the hard-boiled detective. For the first time, readers will be able to assess Daly on his own terms and to read the stories that captivated pulp magazine readers and provided the basis for Hammett, Chandler, and the rest of the American crime fiction canon. Of course, the stories here show Daly's innovations in language and action, as well as his penchant for pulp melodrama. But one thing is sure: with Race's two guns blazing, this is hard-boiled history.

As is the case with his fiction, Daly's biography also remains little documented; a handful of sketches present just a few (occasionally contradictory) details about him. Daly's grandparents emigrated from Ireland in the wake of the 1840s Irish Potato Famine; his paternal grandfather, William Daly, set up as blacksmith in Manhattan, living in the diverse Ward 20 on West 34th Street. His maternal grandfather, a liquor dealer, settled in Yonkers, New York, just north of the city in Westchester County. Daly's father, Joseph Daly, studied law at Cooper Union and soon moved to Yonkers to set up practice with John F. Brennan, a classmate. After rooming with the Brennans for a time, Joseph would soon marry John's sister, Mary. With a successful law practice and a strong connection to the Tammany Hall political machine, Joseph Daly would soon build an enormous Queen Anne style home in Yonkers, which the society pages took great notice of in 1894. Carroll

---

5   Erle Stanley Gardner, "The Case of the Early Beginning," in *The Art of the Mystery Story: A Collection of Critical Essays*, ed. Howard Haycraft (New York: Simon and Schuster, 1946), 205.

6   Erle Stanley Gardner, "Getting Away With Murder," *The Atlantic*, January 1965, 72.

would have been about five when his family moved into this mansion. Seven years later, on June 27, 1901, tragedy struck the family as both of Daly's parents died of heart failure on the same day, a freak occurrence that garnered significant attention from *The New York Times*, given Joseph's prominence in New York Democratic politics.[7]

Daly spent the rest of his youth living with his uncle John Brennan, who willed Daly nearly $40,000 on his death in 1925.[8] For the years between his parents' death in 1901 and his emergence as one of the most popular writers in *Black Mask*, most of the details we have appear in an autobiographical statement in *Black Mask* from 1924:

> I was born in Yonkers, Sept. 14, 1889; attended half the prep schools in the country with a fling at the American Academy of Dramatic Arts; a little known school devoted to the study of the human body; a short period at the study of law and a longer one in stenography.
>
> My first business venture was the opening, with another chap, of the first moving picture show on the boardwalk at Atlantic City—came theatres at Asbury Park, Arverne, and a stock company at Yonkers. After that the deluge—stock salesman, real estate salesman, manager of a fire-alarm company, and a dozen or more other jobs.

Daly was quite honest about his peripatetic working life: his first business venture was The Criterion Theater in Atlantic City, which Daly briefly owned with John Child in 1911 before selling his interest in the theater back to Child within six months.[9] In 1916, he took over the Warburton, a theater in Yonkers, and recruited a stock company before shutting it down within a month.[10] Despite his patchy work history, he did manage to settle down in one respect. Daly married Margaret G. Blakely—known familiarly as Marge—in 1913, and their first and only child John Russell Daly was born in 1914. Daly's World War I draft card shows that he was then serving as a law clerk in his uncle's law office, but by 1920 he was working as an independent real estate broker, possibly following in the footsteps of his father-in-law Samuel Blakely. It's clear, however, that this was around the time he began to seek publication of his fiction.

Daly began writing in earnest in the early 1920s, publishing in a handful of general fiction pulps like *Brief Stories*, *10 Story Book*, and *People's Story Magazine* before breaking into the pages of *Black Mask* in 1922. This relationship became absolutely central to Daly's success over the next decade. While he continued publishing in other pulps—includ-

---

7   "Died Almost Together," *New York Times*, June 28, 1901, 5.

8   "John F. Brennan Left $174,150.82 Estate," *New York Times*, May 13, 1925, 23.

9   I.B. Pulaski, "Atlantic City," *Variety*, March 18, 1911, 24. I.B. Pulaski, "Atlantic City," *Variety*, October 21, 1911, 30.

10   "With the Press Agents," *Variety*, October 20, 1916, 10. "Shows Closing," *Variety*, November 24, 1916, 13. "Stock Repertoire," *The New York Clipper*, December 6, 1916, 13.

Carroll John Daly

ing *Argosy All-Story Weekly*, *Top-Notch*, *Action Stories*, and others—Daly's strongest affiliation was with *Black Mask*. Above all, Daly's creation in 1923 of the first undeniably hard-boiled detective series character, Race Williams, is his greatest legacy as a writer of pulp fiction. This new style of detective fiction, however, wasn't a sure thing; the *Black Mask* publication of Daly's first hard-boiled stories was nearly an accident. As he reflects in "The Ambulating Lady," a piece published in the *Writers Digest* in 1947, *Black Mask* editor George Sutton was on vacation when these stories were submitted and associate editor Harry North accepted them. On Sutton's return he expressed his dislike for Daly's hard-boiled characters, but the characters drove circulation numbers up. North became a central figure in the direction of *Black Mask* during the years he was associate editor—cultivating Daly, Gardner, and Hammett—before taking a position at the newly founded magazine *The New Yorker* in 1925. Daly and Race Williams quickly became synonymous with *Black Mask*, and his name on the cover—especially in the early years—could mean "a 15 percent rise in sales for that issue"; a 1924 Readers' Poll listed Daly and Hammett as the two reader favorites.[11] By the time Joseph T. Shaw arrived at the magazine in 1926, Daly was central to the magazine's identity; indeed, at that point his name had appeared on more covers than any other contributor. It was also around this time that Daly started to move toward longer novelettes, producing his first Race Williams novel-length serial, *The Snarl of the Beast*, in 1927.

As Daly's pulp successes increased, he found himself both settled and established. After living far uptown in Manhattan (at 620 West 190th Street) following his marriage, he purchased a newly constructed home at 37 Concord Avenue in White Plains in 1923. Three years later, in November 1926, he was the subject of a brief news sensation when he was mistaken for a swindler named John J. Daly, arrested by U.S. Marshals, and imprisoned in Manhattan's notorious Tombs for a night before clearing things up.[12] Despite this case of mistaken identity, Daly was at his professional peak. As the pulps thrived, so did Daly,

---

11 Nolan, 39. *Black Mask*, October 1924, 40.

12 "Innocent Novelist Jailed as Swindler," *New York Times*, November 11, 1926, 1.

and his greatest successes occurred between the introduction of Race Williams in 1923, and the beginning of the decline of the pulps in the late 1930s. His Race Williams serials began to be collected in book form in 1927, supplementing his primary income from the pulps. And when magazine pay rates were cut—sometimes in half or more—in the early 1930s as a result of the Depression, Daly responded by churning out more fiction and new characters, tripling his published output from 1931 to 1933, and still receiving top rates for his work. During the 1930s, Daly introduced new characters—Satan Hall (1931), Vee Brown (1932), and Clay Holt (1934) were the most popular—and published regularly not only in *Black Mask*, but also in *Dime Detective, Detective Fiction Weekly*, and other crime fiction magazines. Race Williams continued to sell at high rates, even after Daly left *Black Mask* over a shakeup in editorial strategy under Joseph Shaw in 1934. In the late 1930s, the popularity of Daly's characters almost translated into film—a transition that other *Black Mask* writers like Hammett and Gardner had made—as he had a couple of contracts for the film rights to the Race Williams character nearly executed.[13]

For a number of reasons—possibly including the Hollywood potential of his characters and his son Jack's interest in an acting career—Daly and his family decided to relocate to the west coast, and, after a brief stay with Erle Stanley Gardner at his Temecula ranch in 1938, rented a house in Santa Monica in 1939. Like many other pulp writers, Daly was chasing new forms of entertainment in the face of declining pulp sales: film, radio, and, later, television. However, he never broke into the business and continued writing for the pulps as they declined precipitously throughout the 1940s. As the decade wore on, Daly found it harder to place stories in a contracting pulp market that demanded shorter stories, not the serials and novelettes that had been his bread and butter. When he was able to place these shorter pieces, the rates were among the lowest he had ever been paid. Squeezed out by a real estate boom in Santa Monica, the Dalys soon moved, first to a desert home in Coachella in 1944, then to a small house in Montrose, California in the Crescenta Valley north of Los Angeles in 1948. When he wasn't writing or reading mystery fiction, Daly was pursuing two of his beloved pastimes: mentoring teenagers and young adults in the neighborhood, and studying and practicing hypnotism, a hobby that only turned up in one of his late stories. Meanwhile, Daly's son Jack, back from the war, pursued a career as an actor, and by 1950, began receiving work in both motion pictures and television. Daly would publish through the mid-1950s, but by then most of the magazines in which he'd regularly appeared would be long gone. While pulp writer and historian Frank Gruber writes that "[t]oward the end of his career he had become reduced to writing for the comic books," there's only evidence in his correspondence with Erle Stanley Gardner that Daly tried his hand at comic strips, and that, as Stephen Mertz describes, his focus in the later

---

13   See David Wilt, *Hardboiled in Hollywood: Five* Black Mask *Writers and the Movies* (Bowling Green, OH: Bowling Green State University Popular Press, 1991).

years was on attempting to sell to television.[14] After his move to California, and especially by the late 1940s, Daly regularly touched his friend and admirer Erle Stanley Gardner for loans to carry him over between increasingly rare and small payments from magazines and Marge's inconsistent work opportunities. Meanwhile, as pocket paperback novels filled with ever more sensational content began replacing pulp magazines as escapist reading material, Daly was eclipsed by writers like Mickey Spillane, who found astonishing success, in part, by introducing heavy doses of sex and sadistic violence into the hard-boiled pulp formula. As many critics have noted, Spillane was a huge fan of Daly's work and wrote a well-known fan letter to him in 1952, admitting that "Race was the model for Mike" Hammer.[15] Such praise troubled Daly, who remained conservative about sex and felt distraught over Spillane's astonishing success, considering his own virtual poverty in the early 1950s. The final pulp publication under Daly's own name—fittingly, a Race Williams story billed on the cover—appeared in *Smashing Detective Stories* in May 1955, just two months after Marge died.[16]

The final trace of Daly is a bit of cruel irony. His obituary notice, published January 15, 1958 in *The New York Times*, begins, "Carroll John Daly, who wrote the 'Race Williams' series for The Saturday Evening Post, died Monday in Los Angeles."[17] Neither Daly nor Race Williams ever got close to the pages of the high-paying, culturally-authorized *Saturday Evening Post*. If Daly had not spent the last fifteen years of his writing career attempting to get published in a magazine, any magazine, such a mistake on the *Times's* part might be merely funny. But to glance over Daly's record of submissions and rejections, a copy of which is held by UCLA, is to witness Daly's desperation as he sent dozens and dozens of stories to one magazine after another, only to see the vast majority of them rejected. He would almost always start with the high-paying slicks, like *The Saturday Evening Post* or *Collier's*, but the rejection notices from these magazines came far quicker than those from the numerous pulps he would submit to afterwards. This evidence makes it clear that Daly's moment had passed, that both he and Race Williams were—for a time at least—relegated to the literary historical dustbin.

Unlike Hammett, who shifted to the slicks in 1932 with his Sam Spade series, or Gardner, who transitioned to *Liberty* in 1934 and *The Saturday Evening Post* in 1937, or Chandler, who reluctantly published one of his last short stories in *The Saturday Evening Post* in

---

14   Frank Gruber, *The Pulp Jungle* (Los Angeles,: Sherbourne Press, 1967), 141. Stephen Mertz, "Carroll John Daly: The Post War Years," *Race Williams' Double Date and Other Stories* (Normal, IL: Black Dog Books, 2014), 14.

15   Mickey Spillane, *Byline: Mickey Spillane* (Norfolk, VA: Crippen & Landru, 2004), 215.

16   Daly's final pulp appearance was under the pseudonym John D. Carroll in *Double-Action Detective Stories* #4 in 1956.

17   "Carroll J. Daly, Wrote Mysteries," *New York Times*, January 17, 1958, 25.

1939, Daly never quite managed to straddle the cultural divide between the low-paying pulps and the high-paying slicks, even if he routinely tried to sell (or "slant" in writers' slang) his work to outlets like *The Saturday Evening Post* and *Collier's*. Had he done so, his name might be better remembered today. But in some ways, the case of Daly's disappearance from the critical and historical radar makes collections like this more exciting: to read Daly's Race Williams stories is to follow a long obscured path of hard-boiled history, winding through the desolate highways of Westchester County and the dark alleys of New York City, surrounded by tough-talking figures and explosive action. Few writers embody the energy of the pulps like Carroll John Daly, and this republication of his Race Williams stories, in the signature two-column format of the pulps, is the first time most of these stories have been available since their original publication. It is a long overdue triumph for one of the most influential and successful figures of the pulp era.

THIS VOLUME TRACKS the adventures of Carroll John Daly's Race Williams from 1938 to 1941, a period that saw a rather significant reversal of fortunes for Daly as an author and Williams as a character, an abrupt change after their successful move to *Dime Detective* in 1935 (documented in Volume 5 of this series). During this period, Daly left his native Yonkers, New York and moved to California, while his signature character remained firmly ensconced in the familiar environs of Manhattan, the Bronx, and neighboring Westchester County. As the Great Depression continued to impact the pulp magazine marketplace, driving many magazines to fold and others to reduce payment rates for even the best-known names in pulp writing, Daly found himself less of a draw in the waning years of the 1930s. His name still appeared prominently on the cover of many magazines, but editors were increasingly likely to see his work as outdated, representative of an older and more old-fashioned model of pulp writing increasingly out of place in a magazine marketplace far more willing to exploit social taboos of violence and sexuality. Although *Dime Detective* poached him from *Black Mask* in 1935, advertising this as a major pulp coup, they soon started to cut his pay, and finally to reject his Race Williams stories altogether. Frustrated with his interactions with editors, Daly hired agent Sydney Sanders around the beginning of 1940 and left the placement of his stories to Sanders's office. This arrangement resulted in two more Race Williams stories appearing in Street & Smith's *Clues* in late 1940 and early 1941, after which Race disappeared from the pulps for over three years and Daly himself published sparingly.

During this time, Daly expressed his exasperation over his relationship with the pulps in correspondence with fellow pulp writer Erle Stanley Gardner. In January of 1940, he wrote, "I felt things were not right with *Dime Detective* when they cut me—from four cents a word—then to three and the last one they bought to—two cents. Now they have just turned down a Race Williams." [18] This change in attitude toward Daly's work was rather swift: after publishing Race Williams stories for eleven years in *Black Mask,* he spent less than five years placing these tales in *Dime Detective* before the magazine abandoned the character. [19] Williams had always been Daly's premier fictional creation, and after *Dime Detective* came calling, he wrote Gardner that he started to consider his relationship with the magazine as something relatively exclusive. As a result, he didn't seek as many other publishing opportunities, especially if they offered significantly less than *Dime Detective:* "I tried to get them to take as much work as possible as I didn't think it was exactly right to sell my stuff to other markets under three cents—you see I always expected a cent a word more for Race." [20] Regardless of Daly's sense of the relationship or of the value of Williams as a character, *Dime Detective* soon soured on Daly's work, especially Race Williams. "I guess I told you that Race is out of *Dime,*" he wrote Gardner, "*Dime* suddenly seemed to get an idea that my stuff is juvenile [sic]—and I placed the Race Williams elsewhere—again a sickening rate." [21]

When Race Williams moved from *Black Mask* to *Dime Detective,* there was an almost immediate darkening of Race's fictional world: deaths became more detailed and gruesome, and his female characters took on more complexity. No longer simply innocent heiresses with corrupt guardians, the women in Race's *Dime Detective* adventures—from his first appearance in that magazine—often had real criminal pasts and struggled to escape from a world of crime that seemed deeply imprinted on their experience. However, one line that Daly refused to cross in his Race Williams stories was the depiction of sexuality. Across his fictional career, Race would consistently declare "there's no sex in crime." Race's experiences in these stories certainly draw him somewhat closer to a world of pulp sexuality. In "Hell with the Lid Lifted," Race's sometimes partner, sometimes nemesis, and always love interest the Flame actually arranges for Race to be married—to another woman! And in "A Corpse in the Hand," a wealthy young woman outfits Race's penthouse with "modernistic furniture" and tells Race her "greatest pleasure" would be "to spend my time doing things for you," suggesting the possibility of a torrid affair in this modernist love nest. True to form, Race dodges her advances and escapes from the apartment. Ultimately, Daly's presentation of sexuality would lag far behind the median of the pulp magazines, especially those in publishing combinations like Harry Steeger's Popular Publications, the home of *Dime Detective,* which imagined Daly's relative prudishness as "juvenile."

18   Carroll John Daly to Erle Stanley Gardner, 31 January 1940, Erle Stanley Gardner Papers, Box 143, Harry Ransom Center, The University of Texas at Austin.

19   Race Williams would return to the pages of *Dime Detective* in a handful of stories in the late 1940s.

20   Carroll John Daly to Erle Stanley Gardner, 1 March 1940, Erle Stanley Gardner Papers, Box 143, Harry Ransom Center, The University of Texas at Austin.

21   Ibid.

Undeterred, writing to Gardner, Daly claimed that the "sex stuff is killing" the detective magazines.[22] He believed the genre's obsession with more explicit sexuality was a phase that would soon pass away. Daly's difficulty to adapt to new pulp norms explains much of his struggles to remain relevant in the last decade or so of his career.

Still, the stories in this volume show Daly both experimenting with new ideas and reworking many of his familiar themes. The inheritance plot—a signature of the Williams stories since their beginning—features prominently here across a number of stories, including "Hell with the Lid Lifted," "Cash for a Killer," and "Too Dead to Pay." Called in to protect the interests of young women with sinister guardians looking to murder them and take control of their inheritance, Race always delivers. Additionally, the first four stories in this collection—"A Corpse on the House," "A Corpse for a Corpse," "The Men in Black," and "The Quick and the Dead"—represent a loosely organized serial, a form Daly gravitated toward in the late 1930s. Like the serial that concludes Volume 5 of this series, these stories also feature Jane Blake/Iris Parsons, an orphan reared among the criminal element who has come into an inheritance and reinvented herself as a Manhattan society heiress. Across these four stories Race becomes caught up in a large-scale battle for the soul of Manhattan: a group of anonymous, wealthy, and influential men style themselves as "The People Versus Crime" (also known as "The Men in Black"), personally funding efforts to combat organized crime across the city. This serial has Race tangling with a variety of gunmen, racketeers, and shady politicians, as well as his frequent nemeses Police Inspector "Iron Man" Nelson and the detective Gregory Ford.

Other familiar faces in these stories include Sergeant O'Rourke, Race's influential friend in the New York City Police Department, and the Flame, who shows up in two stories that have Race moving outside the familiar confines of New York to a corrupt small town "seven hundred miles away from New York" ("Gangman's Gallows") and to a gruesome scene on a train from the remote "Homestead Junction" ("Hell with the Lid Lifted"). Daly's stories from *Clues* include some innovative elements as well. The final story in this collection, "Too Dead to Pay," has Race making a rare trip to "Bay City, Long Island" to protect the rightful heir to a major fortune. And the first Race story after finding himself out at *Dime Detective*, "Victim for Vengeance" seems to take on the question of Race's pulp reputation directly. In a likely reference to his rejection from Steeger's magazine, a prominent gossip columnist and friend of Race writes that the public thinks Race is "washed up." As if responding to these accusations, "Victim for Vengeance" features a particularly memorable scene at the Silver Slipper nightclub where the columnist sees Race in action.

The specter of World War II, which the United States entered in December of 1941, eight months after the final story in this volume, also looms large in these tales. In "Cash for a Killer" (February 1940), Race looks to escape the violence of the New York streets in

---

22   Carroll John Daly to Erle Stanley Gardner, no date (May/June) 1940, Erle Stanley Gardner Papers, Box 143, Harry Ransom Center, The University of Texas at Austin.

a "news-reel theater," but finds no relief in the news. In a mirror image of the violence of Williams's own stories, he says of the newsreels, "I saw nothing but guys shooting other lads all over Europe." And "The White-Headed Corpse" (November 1939) sees Race in a "government job" working on some "espionage business," finding the head of a spy ring. This wasn't the first time Race took employment with the government: he collaborated with the Feds against an international crime syndicate in the stories comprising *Murder from the East* (1934, featured in Volume 4 of this series). Admiring Race for "shooting down your daily dozen," one government agent in "The White-Headed Corpse" muses, "Sometimes I wonder if it wasn't you who started off the G-Men."

Ultimately, the stories in this volume find Carroll John Daly and Race Williams navigating new realities: the financial contraction of the pulp market, the exponential rise in sensational violence and sexuality in the detective pulps, and the imminent arrival of World War II for the United States. While Race does experience a few changes—in "Victim for Vengeance" he says, "I'm changing a bit. I'm using my head, now"—Race still represents action first and foremost for his readers, whether readers of the late 1930s pulp magazines or these reprints. His characteristic bravado and tough masculinity come through strong in lines like "I never needed any school to learn my finishing." And though editors like Harry Steeger may have found these later stories somewhat "juvenile," outdated, or melodramatic in comparison to the increasingly sexualized norms of the pulps, Race had a few words for that, as well: "A little melodramatic, you think. Well, melodrama or no, lead kills just the same."

A Corpse on the House

CHAPTER 1

DEATH NOTICE

CHAPTER 1

DEATH NOTICE

UNDERSTAND NOW, I'M not saying it was anyone else's fault. I've always said the unexpected can never happen to me because with my way of living there is no unexpected. I'm always expecting anything to happen. But there was no excuse for this. I'm not a guy to make excuses, but I'm not denying the truth either. The girl, Jane Blake, was with me—and she was gripping my arm—and she was pleading. And I was listening—whether I wanted to listen or not.

I hadn't wanted to see her, and I was telling her so now, and talking to her like a Dutch uncle while we hopped it along the street.

I was saying: "You're Iris Parsons now. Just past twenty-one and a very wealthy woman. Only a few people know that you were jerked out of the underworld to inherit a fortune. You mustn't go back to being Jane Blake—though I'll always calls you Jane. And don't look at me like that. Sure, I've been ducking you."

"But your promise." She squeezed

1

my arm. "It was you who made me Iris Parsons. It was you who fought for and obtained my inheritance. And you promised that you would use that money of mine to fight crime. Use it to wipe out the breeding places of criminals—the slums such—"

"Forget it," I told her. "Even the government hasn't done that job." And when she talked about using the money to salve her conscience I said: "Take a trip around the world—and I'll keep my promise and call on you for dough whenever I need it. Listen, Jane"—I stopped in front of a store there on the crowded sidewalk—"I'm no Robin Hood looking for people to save. I'm a cold-blooded private investigator who hunts criminals for pay. You hired me out. I got my money. There is nothing more I can do for you."

"All right," she said a bit grimly, and I looked down and saw the hardness in her face. "But there is a lot I can do for you. I know plenty of criminals—I know plenty of their hide-outs. I know my way about. I thought it would be a fine gesture—a fine ending to your hunting of men and my atonement for my past. One big sweep of the vicious criminals— one helpful hand to the beginner in crime who'll turn into a vicious criminal without such help. Then—that trip around the world together." A pause and then, "You love me, Race."

It wasn't a question. It was a statement of a fact. And if it was meant to embarrass me into an admission, it didn't work. I gave her a fair answer.

"I don't love any women," I told her.

She wasn't knocked over any. She said simply: "Well—I love you. It's only fair you should know from the start." And with a smile that would knock your eye out, "You shot yourself straight into my heart."

It was then that it happened.

I saw the man's face in the glass of a jewelry-store window. I saw the scar high up on his forehead. I saw— But that wasn't what happened.

The thing that happened was the sudden blast of a gun, Jane's scream, and a hot stab straight through my back. I was on my way down when the second shot came. It pitched me to the sidewalk on my face. But my gun was in my hand. Instinct that, for I don't know what use it was. Try as I did—and damn hard—I couldn't swing my body around.

Things I know and things I don't know happened. I don't know that I gave my gun to Jane, but I do know that she threw herself to the sidewalk and it slapped into her hand. And I do know that she must have fired it, for gunshots blasted straight into my ears, and the hard, cold, twisted face of a young girl swam before me.

People were running. A crowd was forming and my left hand was clutching my other gun almost beneath my chin. Then there was a man with a small bag and a short quick step who was saying: "I'm a doctor, I'm a doctor, I'm a doctor."

No one else but this efficient guy was doing anything. He told Jane to keep people back, knelt down quickly, turned me over and the sneer went out of his face, and the gun he held hidden nearly fell from his hand.

2   **CARROLL JOHN DALY**

That's right. My death was planned well. Personally I thought that the first bullet must have split my spine and I didn't have long to live. But the killer wanted to be sure, so he had another lad ready. Yep, the sneer went off the fake doctor's face all right, for as he knelt and swung me over he looked straight into the nose of my forty-four.

Maybe he was a doctor—maybe he wasn't. As a rule doctors don't stick guns into patient's stomachs. But doctor or no doctor, dying or not dying, I still had enough strength to press the trigger of my gun.

There wasn't any scar on this lad's face—at least for the split second I looked at him there wasn't. Did he fire and miss me? Did he fire and hit me you wonder? Neither. He didn't fire at all. I just closed my finger once, and his face was gone. He didn't flop dead over me. No such mess as that—not with a forty-four when I use it. This lad just picked himself up off his knees and was doing a back dive—when someone pulled down the curtain.

Things went black. A moment here and there of semi-consciousness. A stifling crowd, a cursing cop, the siren of an ambulance, a white coat and a voice that said: "By God, it's Williams—Race Williams—and he's dead!"

A woman screamed. The white-coated ambulance interne said something I couldn't hear, and a girl dropped beside me. Hair was against my cheeks, something wet was dripping into my face—and Jane was saying over and over: "Race! Race!"

And me, I couldn't speak. But I could think. I don't believe I was afraid of death except that I thought it was a hell of a way to go out—on the public street with a girl holding your head and crying all over your face. Besides, there was the lad with the scar—and I just couldn't believe I was going to die before I ran a little lead up and down his face for him.

Funny death maybe—funny thoughts. No squawk that I hadn't led a better life. No thoughts but about those who were alive and I who would be dead. There was Pete Slocum's face—and I wanted to get him before I went out. There was Joe Massiani whom I hadn't seen in ten years—and I wanted to get him. Yep, that's right—unfinished business. Guys who were living and should be dead, guys that I always thought I would meet again sometime and had neglected. Guys who—

I was in the ambulance screeching along the street and soft hair still brushed my cheek—then total blackness.

LIKE THE MOVIES there was a little white bed—and I was in it, and I moved my hand and opened my eyes—and a nurse was there at once. I suppose I should have used the gentle, pleading voice and all that stuff, but I didn't. I said without thinking, and without giving the nurse a chance to answer: "This is a hospital, isn't it? Then what the hell are those guys making all that noise for outside the door? All that hollering."

"That's the doctor whispering—so as not to disturb you."

"Hollering, not whispering," I told her.

"I'm here to get well." I paused a moment there, for I had a feeling my spine was broken, though she said nothing about not moving.

I asked the nurse how I was and she said: "*Shs—*"

So I tried: "Keep them quiet! I've got to get well—got to get well quickly. I've got to get out of here."

She turned a smile on me and started fixing the bed and talking softly and finally she piped: "We're going to make you very comfortable. Why should you want to leave us so quickly?"

And I gave her the answer that bounced her right back from the bed. I said: "I want to get out and shoot a man to death."

She didn't like the crack, and she took it hard. Then she settled on her heels and looked straight at me. Color out of her cheeks, shaking inside, perhaps, but she stood her ground. She was even ready to move forward in case I got violent. But I didn't get violent, and I didn't pop the question that was on my mind. Would I live or die?

She smiled the reassuring smile that she had been smiling for years, then she went to the door and opened it.

A soft voice said in answer to her long whisper: "There's nothing strange in that. Don't you read the papers, Miss Evans? He probably meant what he said."

"About—about killing—about shooting a man to death?"

"Yes, exactly that."

The door opened further and a loud voice spoke—a domineering, confident, authoritative voice. "If things are as you say, doctor, my talk can't hurt him any."

"But I don't think you should tell him that."

"Come, come, doctor. If it can't hurt him— But there, you wait in the hall." The door opened more, huge shoulders loomed, and the voice spoke just before closing the door. "Five minutes when a man is about to die may serve the State and save the lives of others."

The rumbling voice of the doctor outside, the closing of the door, and the man turned. He was my worst enemy on the police force, inspector Iron-man Nelson.

I didn't yip as he walked toward the bed. I would have preferred Sergeant O'Rourke, my friend. He was Inspector Nelson's superior, in fact, if not in rank, for O'Rourke worked straight from the commissioner.

Inspector Nelson came forward and took me by the wrist. His voice was low now, with sympathy, perhaps even sentiment in it, which made it ring false as hell. Nelson could never produce something he didn't have, and that something was sentiment.

He said: "We've had our rows, boy. You saved my life once. I saved Jane Blake's reputation. Saved her from scandal—perhaps even imprisonment. You haven't liked my ways and I haven't liked yours. But after a fashion, we are both the law."

"What do you want?" Maybe I wasn't pleasant.

He seemed to be taken aback. Then he sat down on the bed and said: "I want to know how you feel."

"I feel fine."

He got up, stood looking at me, turned suddenly and walked to the window. It was a big room—three windows, a bath.

Nelson didn't speak for a full minute, then he said without turning: "You've been a great lad in your own way, Race. Asking help from no one—giving none. A lad that can take it and give it—and settle his own troubles as the criminal settles his. You don't think of the laws of the State—"

I snapped in: "Are you going to make a speech or offer me a job on the force?"

"Neither." He swung suddenly and faced me. "You got it as every copper, every newspaper man knew you'd get it. You've got to count on me now. This time you can't be your own law. I want to know who put those bullets in your back. The one in—er—"

"Why?" I tried to sit up in bed. Something gripped at my shoulder, reached down my back and damned near tore me apart. I lay back on the bed. "Come on," I said, "spill it. What do you mean?"

"I'd like to know it in your place," Nelson said grimly, "and I think you'd like to know it." He came closer to the bed. "Good God, man, do I have to tell you more!"

"No," I said. "I guess you don't." Then after a minute, "I know you want something out of it—but thanks just the same. There are certain things a man has to know."

"I thought so." Nelson nodded. "And I thought you'd take it exactly like that. Now—I want the name of the man who shot you." And quickly, "Or a description of him."

I shook my head. "I don't know his name. I just glanced at him. That is, I saw a figure—his face in a window."

"His face." Nelson was eager now. "Describe it."

"I simply glanced at it in a window—I can't describe it." So there were big things in the wind. Nelson wasn't often stirred.

I said: "I'd like to see O'Rourke—you know—before I push over."

"O'Rourke's out of town. I tried to get him. Now you saw his face. Were there any identification marks—anything you'd notice?"

"And Jane—I want to see her," I told him.

"She's downstairs—sick, hysterical. The doctor handed her a jolt of dope. She'll be up before you die."

Now that's putting it rather straight. I didn't feel so bad. Oh, I don't want to squawk—not me—but I felt as if I couldn't move now.

"That's nice," I said. "I suppose you had the doctor give me something to jazz me up so I'll talk. There—don't deny it. I've had the same thing done to others. Tell me who I shot."

"Billy Frank—a lad called Billy Frank. At least, that's who we think he is. You messed up his face considerable. But that's not the point." He was talking fast now. "This time your death was well planned, Race. No chance for you to turn and shoot. Just a man with a gun who intended to empty that gun in your back. He didn't because you went down on the first shot according to witnesses. You see, he planned to let you have it at a certain point, step into an office building and disappear. Well, Jane—rather Iris Parsons—picked up the gun and opened up. So the killer went through his arrangements and disappeared into the office building."

"And the other lad—Billy Frank?"

"That was to make certain if anything went wrong. Frank shouted he was a doctor, so he was the first to reach you. You see, these killers knew the psychology of how people act at a street murder. Those nearest run away—those at a distance who don't see the actual killing run toward it. Billy Frank could have killed you and gotten away."

"Except," I said, "he entered too much into his part as a doctor and not enough as a killer and got his face punctured."

"The point is—the great importance someone placed on having you killed. Now, there must be some reason for it. Of course it means you've just had a client, or this client can disclose the killer's identity to you, and—well, you always were pretty handy with a gun."

I didn't like the past tense but I said: "Just at present I'm as free of clients as a bluefish is from wings. Why do you think I saw the man? What about other witnesses on the street? Wouldn't they see his face—any mark on it?"

"The mark—if there was a mark—was on the right side of his face."

"What's that got to do with it??"

"He stayed close to the building. Then he slipped into the entrance. You might have seen a—well, a deformity on his face."

I might and I had. Because I saw it in the window—the scar on the right side of his face. I tried thinking. It was hard to die—much harder than if I had fallen over the man's dead body.

Nelson horned in. "Hell, Race—you're a killer, but you're not a criminal. You wouldn't die a gangster's death—your lips sealed. It's not vengeance now—it's justice. If I could get this guy with the mark on his face. Just say there was a mark—describe it." And then he tossed his bomb. "Not for me, then. Not for the law—but for the girl. For Jane Blake. Maybe she didn't see him. But he'll think she did—and with you dead, he'll kill her sure. How can we protect her if we don't know. Come on, boy, you haven't got much time. You—"

"All right," I let him have it suddenly. "The man was slightly bald on the forehead. His hat went back when I…. What's that!"

CHAPTER 2

THE GIRL WITH THE GUN

THERE WERE LOUD voices in the hall—a body jammed against the door. Some hospital! And damn it, there I was, a dying man, and Nelson wanted me to talk through all that rumpus.

He kept saying: "Come on, Race. Come on—tell your old friend, Nelson, before it's too late."

It was too late. The door banged open. A small crouched figure shot into the room with a backward leap that would have done credit to a jungle tiger. And that small figure was flashing a gun, flashing a pair of black eyes that held the jungle in them. It was no Iris Parsons, frail child of society and wealth now. It was Jane Blake—the Jane Blake that had pulled herself up through the years from the bottom of the underworld.

There was a crooked twist to her mouth as she straightened near the window and spoke to the man who followed her in, who held a gun in his hand—a gun that hung down by his side. Then she straightened, spoke, her voice harsh, cold, steady.

"Raise that gun an inch, flat foot, and I'll—"

"Jane—Jane!" I sat straight up in the bed and called to her.

A lad with specs, a white coat and a blank look stepped into the room. "Gentlemen, gentlemen!" And turning to the girl, "Miss Parsons, how dare—how could you!"

The girl laughed. Nelson spoke to the detective.

"You were in the room off the office with her downstairs. You were to keep her there. Now—where did she get that gun?"

"Hell—" The detective turned sulky. "I was supposed to detain a young society girl, a sheltered flower of wealth. Well, the sheltered flower pulled that gun out of her bag like it was a powder puff, then asked me how I'd like all my teeth shot down my throat. Who am I to—"

I had my say there. "She's got a license for that gun. And Nelson—why damn your hide, Nelson, I'll—"

And I was out of the bed and onto the floor and after him. Funny—if I had any

pain then I didn't notice it. Nelson had grabbed the girl around the neck—and placed a hand over her mouth. She was struggling furiously and trying to talk.

The doctor said, as I sprang at Nelson and tried to tear him away: "Come, come, there's been enough of this. I demand—"

And the girl freed her mouth and shrieked: "They're ridin' you for a talk, Race. You won't die—you're not even badly hurt. You're— Take your hands off me!"

I couldn't seem to get my hands up, but I stuck an elbow in Nelson's ribs that he felt. Anyway he tossed the girl loose, swung and faced me.

There was hate, disappointment, vengeance—everything in his eyes when he struck out and got me clean on the chin. The blow hurt all right, lifted me off my feet or staggered me back, I don't remember which. But my landing-place was O.K. Right back in the center of the bed.

There was hell raised all over the place after that, and I'll admit the doctor had guts even if he was an ass in grabbing Nelson. At first, I thought Nelson was going to let him have it—then he seemed to get control of himself.

"Get out—go downstairs," he said to the detective. And to the doctor and nurse, "Stay if you will." He stiffened, eyed the doctor, and became the efficient officer he really was. "I am sorry, Doctor Gaumont. It is police business that you can't understand. Shall we forget the incident?"

"Forget it!" The doctor was doing his stuff now, and his dignity reached up and overshadowed Nelson's. "That man on the bed was shot. His recovery may be set back a week—a month even—from your brutal and unwarranted attack. Why, if he's the nervous type he might be permanently affected for life!"

I'M AFRAID I grinned as Jane and the nurse came and tucked me into the bed. I was hardly the nervous type. The pain wasn't so bad. My head—well, Nelson had knocked some sense into it. Why should I be worried?

"I shall most certainly not forget the incident," the doctor went on. "I shall report it to the Board of Directors—to the Commissioner of Police himself, the District Attorney."

"Why not write a thesis on it?" Nelson put his hard jaw close to the doctor and hammered a finger against his chest. "What I did in the beginning was with your sanction and permission. The young lady was detained in your office." He turned suddenly and jerked Jane from the bed. "That gun, young lady."

"I haven't got it," the girl said as he snatched the bag from her hand and tore it open. "That detective took it."

Nelson grumbled as he shook everything from the bag upon the floor, and no gun fell out. He looked at her—shrugged his shoulders and started toward the door, said: "Don't turn on the loud-speaker all over your face, Doctor—and don't look so sour. Your patient won't complain. And perhaps I forgot to tell you that I am simply an individual—Inspector of Police. I don't know the ethics of your profession, but the action you permitted

me to take is entirely outside the law—I mean from your side of the fence."

"But you said the lives of many people hung on his talking, that a moment's fright to a strong man would save others. You made a mistake then."

"The only mistake I made, Doctor, was in not belting him a few times in the chin before I started to talk to him."

"Don't you worry, Inspector Nelson," I said. "I didn't even see the man who shot me."

"That's too bad," Nelson said easily, then turned at the door. "Don't forget, Race, when you leave this hospital you'll still have a back—a back to shoot at. Well, no hard feelings, Williams. You'd do the same thing yourself."

"No hard feelings," I told him as I rubbed at my chin. "Yes, I'll do the same thing myself."

He looked at me with hard gray eyes, shrugged his great shoulders—and bumped squarely into O'Rourke as he left the room.

Jane said: "I telephoned O'Rourke from downstairs, Race. Oh, don't look surprised. The dick just sat there with his feet on the desk while I opened my bag, took out the gun and shoved it almost down his throat."

I shivered slightly. It wasn't the cold. I was glad the nurse had left. I wasn't in love with Jane—not me. But somehow I didn't like to hear her talk that way.

I said as O'Rourke and Nelson passed a few unfriendly words in the doorway: "Don't talk like that, Jane. That's your environment for most of your life cropping out. It's the heredity you have behind you that counts. Fine people—fine background."

She grinned, stood up and faced O'Rourke as the door closed on Nelson. She said: "Ah, Sergeant O'Rourke. Isn't it just too, too fortunate to find our friend so comfortable after the little accident." She made a flourish with her hand. "I mean the artillery attack on the street, of course, not Nelson's swinish foul blow. I've got to go now, dear fellow." She smiled at me and left the room.

O'Rourke nodded his head. "She's a fine girl, our Jane, Race. Money hasn't spoiled her, but associations have given her a certain air of culture—background."

I CUT IN there and got to talking about the shooting. I told O'Rourke everything about Nelson's pretense that I was dying, for I wanted to find out if there was anything big stirring—and if Nelson was in on it. But I didn't tell him about the blow on the chin. I knew he'd go right downtown and poke one on Nelson, and I knew that Nelson, though past forty, was the strongest and hardest-hitting man in the Department—also the toughest to take it. But let me tell you straight, right here—I'm a trained athlete myself, and Nelson would never have put that one on my button if I had not been so damned unsteady on my pins.

O'Rourke shook his head. "There're things stirring, of course. That banker shot dead with the peculiar visiting-card in his hand—*Crime Versus the People*. Nothing in his past—no motive—no women. Weren't interested in that were you, Race?"

"No." I shook my head, "But Nelson wanted to know badly if I recognized the man who shot me. What the hell did he have to tell me I was dying for? Damn it, O'Rourke, he had me believing it—I could hardly move. Then when I learned the truth—*bing*—just like that, I was out of bed. Nelson could simply have asked me in a fair and honest way."

O'Rourke laughed. "You wouldn't have told him. I know you saved his life and he saved Jane's money. Then you went back to hating again." And suddenly, "I can tell you this though, Race. Nelson is making a record lately. He's bagged some pretty big guys. Someone has been giving him information."

"A poor hop-head he's been beating up." And I added with disgust: "Why he'd beat women and children if he thought he could get information. There—don't tell me he's honest—a straight man-hunter." I snorted, then said: "How long am I here for?"

"About two weeks." O'Rourke looked down at me. "There was a hunk of lead close to your lung—another in the muscles under—oh, something about the left clavicle—you know, the shoulder. It'll bind you up for only a short time "

I laughed. Yes, I felt pretty good. I said: "We'll call it a week then." And after a bit of thought, "The man who shot me in the back was pretty close. About abreast of the door to the office building he dashed into. He was walking close to the buildings. So close that no one could pass him on his right side. Witnesses, then, saw only the left side of his face. But me—I was close to Trainer's Jewelry Shop. There was a silver plate in the window that shone like a mirror. I don't know if I saw him in the window or in that plate. There was a scar up on the right side of his face when his hat jarred back.

"Go play with Nelson for a bit. Act wise on everything but that scar." And just before O'Rourke left me for the night, "And remember this—no arrest if you find the man. I don't intend to wait any twenty years for a lad to come out of stir for me to kill."

"Damn it, Race! I wish you wouldn't talk like that. I know you, and others don't. You're a swell guy, but you talk like a killer—a common killer."

"Please, O'Rourke." I smiled as the nurse entered with one of those "scram" looks. "Please, O'Rourke—not common…. O.K., nurse, I'll be leaving in a week. Give me all that comes with the room. I can take it." And O'Rourke was gone.

CHAPTER 3

DEATH'S DELEGATE

JANE SHOWED UP that night and proved a regular guy. She didn't talk about love and trips around the world, but got right down to business. We tried to play guessing games about who the lad was that shot me—and why the fake doctor—and why someone wanted me dead pretty fast.

We talked about ourselves after a while. Outside of a couple of slugs in the back, there wasn't much wrong with me. I planned to pop over Mr. Scar-on-the-

Forehead the first time I saw him. Jane told me she was spending her days being Iris Parsons, and an aunt was coming back from London to chaperone her in society. But at night she'd often sneak back to the old life as Jane Blake.

"I want you out of it—out of crime forever," I cut in bluntly.

She said: "I'm glad I wasn't out of it when your gun slapped into my hand. I began shooting wildly. He might have emptied the rest of his gun in your back if I hadn't blasted away."

"You mean—he did step out of the doorway." I gulped. "And that I owe my life to you!"

"I'd never claim your life that way. But don't you think that if—" She paused and came to her feet. "I won't take advantage of your weakness and make love to you now." She pointed to the little phone on the table by the bed. "You can call me any time you wish—if you can't sleep."

"And how about you—your sleep?"

"I'll dream on while I talk to you." She leaned forward, straightened the pillows, bent her head even closer as she pulled up the sheet around my shoulders. Then she suddenly bent down and kissed me full on the lips. After that she was gone. And so was I—well, to a certain extent. She was a peculiar kid and no mistake.

The nurse came in and I got information. My whole room, flowers, different pictures, books on the table—everything had been arranged by Jane.

"You're really quite a person, Mr. Williams. You can use the phone or have visitors any time of the day or night."

"Sergeant O'Rourke fixed that?"

"I don't think so." She was doubtful. "I think Miss Parsons arranged that too. May I give you fresh pillows—or just let me take those and plomp them up a bit."

"No," I told her flat and a little hard when she was getting ready to insist. "That's something Miss Parsons already attended to." She didn't get the point or got the wrong point from the way she smiled knowingly. "Give me a book—oh—that detective story there. I'll—"

Just then the phone rang.

The nurse beat me to it, "Oh'd" and "Ah'd" a couple of times, then turned to me.

"It's Mr. McGrath," she said, and her voice was hoarse as she held her hand over the receiving end. "Timothy McGrath—the district leader—a powerful politician and an evil man."

I guess I was just as surprised as the nurse, but I said: "Give me the phone. He's a ward-healer and a cheap one."

"Don't speak to him, Mr. Williams—what do you suppose he wants with you?"

"I'm quite a person as you say. He probably wants to know that I'm treated properly or he'll tear the hospital apart. Give me the phone."

"But he isn't on the phone. He's downstairs, and wants to see you—and it's nearly midnight."

I just grabbed the phone and said into the mouth-piece: "O.K., sister, send him up in the freight elevator."

The nurse looked shocked. I didn't blame her. "Dirty" McGrath had power in that district, but everybody was onto him. He made no pretense about being honest, but he spent money freely, bought the votes, and you got what you paid for. His grandfather and father before him were district leaders. It was said that his grandfather introduced really dirty politics into the district, and passed the name he had earned down to his grandson. Anyway the name had stuck. Jokingly, perhaps, at political headquarters, scathingly by his opponents, and only whispered in his own district by those he ruled. But Dirty McGrath was his rightful heritage.

I told the nurse to leave—take her supper or dinner or whatever she called it—and she was at the door when McGrath entered.

"Good evening, nurse." He made a motion with his stomach which some years back might have been a bow. "Good evening, Race. It is an unhappy thing to hear that you met with an accident—but a happy occasion to find you so fit."

"Good evening, Dirty," I said loud enough for the nurse to hear, and with enough feeling in it to make his big eyes flash up and down like a neon sign. "Sit down—the room reeks with disinfectant anyway."

The door closed. Dirty McGrath pulled up a chair, placed a huge bag on the side of the bed and said: "That was quite unnecessary, Race. You and I have never really crossed. Why make a bad friend in this neighborhood? You don't know why I've come."

I stretched my arms up, my hands under the pillow and said: "I know why you came all right—and I don't like it. I was shot in the back today. I thought it was big stuff—now it turns out to be gutter work. Don't tell me, Mac, don't tell me. If it didn't stink of the sewer, you wouldn't be here. How do you think it makes me feel to be shot at by a common hood? Yes, I know why you're here. You want to know if I recognized the man who shot me."

"That—" McGrath nodded his fat head—"is part of it. But you don't need to tell me if you don't wish."

"The hell I don't." I guess I raised my voice. "That's damned white of you." I jerked out my left hand and damn near tore my shoulder apart, but I snapped open his bag and got a look inside before he could grab it back and shut it tight again. I had seen enough—money, many tightly packed lengths of bills. Those on top, at least, were hundred-dollar notes. It floored me for a moment and gave Dirty McGrath a chance to talk.

"Ten grand—ten thousand dollars right in that bag. It's a lot of money, Race."

"Not a lot for a bag that size." I shook my head. "There's room for a bomb in that bag."

"Oh, they're not all hundreds," he said as he lifted the heavy bag from the bed and getting up crossed to the window and set it down there. "You know, Race"—he was talking as he came back and sat on the side of the bed—"lawyers are smart men—smarter than you are. In many instances I have known the highest public officials to hire a big lawyer not to take a case. He can't use him, but he wants to be sure that the other side won't have him. That, I think, is a great honor to pay a man."

"Go on—you interest me." And smil-ing pleasantly, "I'll take a lot, Dirty, but I won't be compared with lawyers."

"Well," he said abruptly, "I'm a politi-cian. Most of my work may not be pleas-ant, but tonight it happens to be. You can have that ten thousand dollars to refuse one case. I know your word is good."

"Just one case—and no strings to it?"

"None whatever. You might not even be offered any case. If you are, you refuse it."

For a while I lay still. There was no harm in what he suggested—nothing unethical about it. Still I didn't like it. Yet, ten grand was a lot of money. I did a lot of get-thee-behind-me-Satan thinking before I strung the conversation out a bit longer.

I finally said: "No strings—nothing at all?"

"Nothing at all—except, of course, if you know the man who shot you, you won't tell anybody."

I set my teeth. "It won't cost you a cent to be assured that I won't tell anyone."

"And won't—well, you won't seek vengeance against him."

My jaw set a little harder and my lips a bit tight. He must have seen it under the light.

"I don't know if you'll call it vengeance or not, but I'll shoot him to death the first time I see him. Yep, even if we meet in Police Headquarters."

McGrath took on a sad look, ran his hand beneath his stiff linen collar, wobbled his chin with huge pudgy fingers.

"And you'd let that stand in the way of ten thousand dollars—your own personal feelings?"

CARROLL JOHN DALY

"I wouldn't take a million," I told McGrath and meant it. "And don't shake your head like that. If you want him alive, let him hide in sewers or any other of his familiar places. If I see him he takes the dose."

"He's a dangerous man, Race. I'm your friend. The least threat—even breath of a threat on your part means your death. So think of it that way. You just take ten thousand dollars and live—you refuse it and die. What choice can you have in the matter?" And half musing, "He was wrong then. You did recognize him. He was sure you wouldn't know his face again."

He was right. I didn't remember anything but a scar. But if he wanted to try and kill me again I wasn't the lad to stand in his way. So I went the whole hog with Dirty McGrath.

I said: "I did see his face. I saw it in the shining silver plate in a jeweler's window." And when McGrath's eyes closed and he studied me carefully and unbelievingly, I let it go, lie or no lie. I said: "I'd know him even without the scar on the right side of his temple."

It stunned McGrath—at least it jarred him erect. His face did more tricks than the midway of a county fair.

"No, Race—no— God, you didn't!" He was backing away. "I didn't want it this way. I thought you'd take the money." He looked toward the door—the bag at the window. "Take the dough, Race. Swear you won't touch him. I didn't want to. I had to come."

"Take your dough and get out, Dirty.

Don't you worry about yourself. I won't be looking for you unless I can't find my man. You tell him what I just said."

"Not me—not me. I don't know him." McGrath's eyes bulged like little round marbles sticking out of his head. "They made me come. You've got to do certain things—you know. I—I'll get the money from the bag." He hurried toward the window and the dim side of the room. "Come on, swear it."

"I'll swear," I said slowly, "to shoot him on sight!"

McGrath straightened in the darkness. I could see him turn, lean slightly out the open window as he sucked in great gulps of air. It must have been a bad moment for McGrath. Someone must have told him: "You fix it with Williams—or else." Yep, I heard his breath, the whir of it. The whir—hell, it didn't sound like his breath, but it was a whir all right.

He turned then and came quickly back to the bed. I saw him reach up and toss the cord the call-bell button hung on to one side. When he spoke his voice shook, and the white hand that didn't grip the bag trembled.

"It's tough, Race—to come through an expected sure death, then face a surer one all in the same twenty-four hours."

I put both my hands back under the pillows and lay there on the bed. I didn't holler, didn't lurch for the phone. McGrath was in the way of that. I didn't speak either.

I just watched the man who climbed in the window. No one had to tell me then. The whir I heard was the unwinding of a cleverly made rope ladder—strong silk more likely. I knew then. A killer was coming into the room.

The man had a slouch hat on the side of his head—the left side—and I saw no scar on the right. He held his hands in both jacket pockets as he approached the bed. If ever a gunman, a killer, had stepped out of a movie, this was the lad. He even twisted his face as he came nearer to the light.

"O.K., McGrath." He jerked an elbow at the now trembling ward-healer. "I was expecting the ladder. Williams always thought he was a smart guy. So now I get the ten grand. Go on—and don't let yourself get robbed or you'll have to dig it out of your own bank account. Hurry now. You've got your car and fifteen minutes to establish an alibi."

"But," McGrath stammered, "they know I'm here. They might not find the body for—well, until morning—or even if he has a private nurse, they must establish time of death." And with almost a plea in his voice, "I can mark the time of my departure downstairs. If you'd use a gun, Harry, it would establish my alibi—my safety."

"Sure, it would," Harry agreed. "But it wouldn't establish my safety. Get out."

Yep, there I lay and listened and watched Dirty McGrath half stagger to the door with his bag, tell his friend, the killer, that there was no key in the lock, hear the killer say that he had one that would fit.

It was great stuff. Live and learn—die and learn, for that matter. But I felt sorry for Dirty.

I called to him: "Don't you worry, Dirty—and don't talk. Whatever happens I won't say you were here."

"Shut your face!" Harry locked the door after McGrath, turned and faced me in the light of the lamp by the phone. I whistled softly. In a way I was being entertained by class. I knew him, of course—Harry Morgan. He did most of his work with a knife.

"Well—" I said to him. "So the man behind this racket picked a classy killer. Or were you the only one in the city who had the nerve to kill a man helpless in bed?"

He leaned down close, drew his left hand slowly from his pocket, and flicked the end of his fingers across my face. Maybe I did see a little red—the boys have a way of doing those things that draw blood.

Harry cocked his head, squinted his eyes. "There was another guy today who didn't mind taking a shot at you on the public street."

"It wasn't you, was it?"

"Now"—he lit a butt—"what put that into your head?"

"Oh, I was shot in the back."

"So—" He didn't get it for a long time, then he did. He held his temper well. "Want a butt?" he asked. And he shot his hand suddenly forward shoving the lighted end against my lips.

He laughed then, but I saw that half-lifted gun showing from his pocket, and me there flat on the bed. I didn't holler—he wouldn't simply shoot me then and make for the ladder. Besides, we had some time to kill—no pun intended—

CARROLL JOHN DALY

before the fifteen minutes were up. Harry wanted to talk and I wanted to hear him.

"Ten grand for this job—what a laugh! You're a great guy, Race, and honestly, no lad around at the time wanted any part of it. Ten grand. In a way, Race, you're a lucky bloke. I could sit around and hack you to death slowly." He bent over. "Yeah, and enjoy it."

My eyes widened. I remembered now. But Harry was telling it.

"What the big lads don't know and what you don't know is that I'd have done the job free. I'm going to die some day from a bullet that sits right on the edge of my brain—nicks into it a bit. You put it there…. So you do remember. Yeah, I was the chopper in the death car three years ago. You threw yourself flat on the sidewalk. I stuck my face up when you lifted your gun. I might have opened up the rattler and killed you, but that bullet of yours was marked straight for my forehead. I turned my head and took it—took it right into the edge of the brain."

"Is that so, Harry?" But his subject didn't interest me then. "Now this guy who shot at me. Why is he so big? How can he be so important if he had to try to do the job himself?"

"He was brung up that way. Besides"—Harry parted mean lips, but kept his facial expression the same—"it ain't so easy to get guys to do a job on you."

"But you"—I got sarcastic—"big, brave fellow."

"No"—I guess Harry was honest enough—"it was easy money. The doctors do it to guys here every day and beat the rap."

"But this fellow—the man with the scar?"

"Well—"

Harry Morgan produced, with the ease of long practice, a large knife that he snapped open. It was a vicious-looking, sharp instrument. My eyes were glued on it. "Well, Race, the fifteen minutes are about up. I don't see how you can lie there and chin. On the level, if I knew my way around this hospital I'd give you an anesthetic. It's a break for me, but you certainly can take it."

"That'll be a nice message to take to the boys. I've got the guts, all right, because I don't believe you're going through with it." And in a louder voice, "Your fifteen minutes aren't up. Think of Dirty McGrath."

"I got to think of myself. And the boys ain't going to hear how you died game. I'm going to tell them how you crawled and begged and tried to scream for help. I'll be the number-one man. I'll show up every killer on the Avenue. They'll give me a dinner." And as he worked himself into a fury for the kill, "That's how you'll take it, you dirty rat."

It was in his blood. There was no way of stopping him—no way of threatening him—no way of buying him off then. I hadn't really expected the suddenness of it—the fury. Steel glittered up—and down.

It was to be a sudden and an awful and a sure death, and I did my best to avoid it, but all too late.

I hollered: "No, God no, Harry!"

Then I jerked my hand from under the

pillow and shot him straight through the center of his forehead.

I suppose I should have closed my eyes from the awful sight, but I don't go in for that sentimental stuff. He might have a friend who'd come up the rope ladder, so I watched him. Sickening? Well, maybe if you're built that way and not used to seeing lads die. Harry Morgan died easily. Burnt powder, a great hole, and his face was gone even before he ever hit the floor.

A young doctor broke the door down after a lot of running around. Some hospital! Just a fine fraternal organization. I guess I'm the guy who should have written the book, *Fun in Bed*.

As for the gun. It was a thirty-two caliber automatic, the one Jane told Inspector Nelson she gave to the detective. Only, of course, she hadn't. She just slipped it under my pillow. I'd be a fine chump to entertain such characters in my room at midnight unarmed.

Men in white now—plenty of them. And a big lad saying: "That man's dead. Who is he? He's been shot. What—what will— God, what'll we do about him!"

Me—I turned over on my pillow. They had pushed on the lights and it hurt my eyes. But I managed to say before I feigned sleep: "A hospital—plenty of lads being—er—plenty of lads dying all the time. And you ask me what to do with a stiff."

They sobered down then, got over their fright, talked of the reputation of their institution and began to lay it onto me. I sat up in bed, spun around, grabbed the phone and called O'Rourke's number.

"Listen," I told them while I waited for the connection, and I wasn't too nice about it either. "What kind of a hospital do you think you're running? Isn't there a scandal in the papers about you now? First you let a cop walk in and tell me I'm dying. Then just to prove it's so, you let another lab climb in the window and try to stab me to death. The whole thing is simple enough. I—" A voice buzzed in my ear. "Oh, O'Rourke," I said into the mouth-piece. "I want some protection down here…. Hell no, not from outsiders—from the guys inside. Come down and tell them…. Yeah—thanks." And to the doctors, picking up where I left off, "He tried to stab me and I shot him to death."

"But how—" one of them chirped. "Why did he threaten to kill you?"

"He said"—I pointed a finger at them—"it was because I hadn't paid for this room a week in advance."

I was a sick man, a very tired man. I turned over and went to sleep.

CHAPTER 4

I SLEEP WITH MY PANTS ON

I felt good when I woke up next morning, but almost immediately took a turn for the worse. At least I pretended to while Nelson was there, and the D.A. and a few Headquarters experts who wrote down on little pads the evidence they'd like to find but couldn't.

They even brought Dirty McGrath

into the room, though the D.A. wasn't anxious to have him connected up with it. But cruel or mean, Inspector Nelson was an honest man. So honest that there were times I thought he was just dumb—and other times when I thought he was the slickest man on the Force. He had a way of putting things to the D.A. that completely tossed that worthy gentleman.

The D.A. said: "Williams here has exonerated Mr. McGrath. After all, Mr. McGrath is a gentleman and one of our leading citizens."

This was just the D.A.'s way of saying Dirty could get out the votes.

Nelson's answer, for lack of politics, and tactlessness, was a classic. "Not drag McGrath in!" He fairly bellowed the words. "He was the last one to see Williams before Race blew this punk's head off. Hell, a rookie would know enough to drag him in. God A'mighty, Mr. Jeffries, there are times when I wish you'd keep your face out of police business."

Understand now, this was from an inspector of police to the district attorney of the city, and what's more, they were friends—close friends. So perhaps Jeffries was used to it. Anyway, he wasn't angry, didn't shout, didn't even reprimand.

Jeffries said simply: "If you believe it's for the best interests of your office, my office, the people of the great city we both serve, by all means ask him to come over." And with a smile, *'Ask*, Inspector—not drag Mr. McGrath in."

Nelson said: "I'll get him." And he did.

McGrath came, and his legs were trembling in his pants. He had the same baggy suit, the same collar slightly soiled—and he wasn't shaved. He looked at me and expected the worst.

I said in a low voice, as if I was too weak to talk: "Hello, Dirty. I told you you'd have nothing to fear from me."

Nelson started in, and if it wasn't for the D.A. he'd have given McGrath the same arm-twisting and ear-shouting he gave to any common crook. But Jeffries prevented that.

McGrath knew his way around. He looked at me a couple of times, wondered why I didn't blow the works, decided I wasn't going to and answered Nelson simple and direct.

"I came to see Mr. Williams on private business. That business is not yours. I'll thank you to show more respect in talking to me. Williams is not a friend of mine. That he exonerates me is quite enough."

"Tut, tut." I looked at McGrath. "We're good friends now, Dirty, old pal."

He winced at the "Dirty" but let it ride. He didn't understand my game—and maybe I didn't either. Though he had planned my death—at least had orders from someone to plan it—I knew that I couldn't put the finger on him just then.

The D.A. said: "All right, Williams. Here's your story. Things were quiet when Mr. McGrath left. Sometime later—ten minutes or so—this Harry Morgan came in the window by a ladder which he later planned to carry away. He came to the bed, pulled a knife and—and—" He played dumb as if he couldn't remember, then added: "What did you do then?"

"Why then I pulled my gun from under the pillow and shot him to death."

"All as simple as that?"

"All as simple as that," I repeated.

SUDDENLY THE D.A. tossed his head in his best courtroom manner, leaned down, worked his eyes like a drunken sailor, pointed his finger at me and shouted: "The gun—where did you get the gun?"

I drew my lips up as if in pain and answered: "From under my pillow."

"I don't mean that! I don't mean that," he stormed. "You know what I mean."

I looked sort of hurt, half raised my right hand and swore: "As God is my judge, I got it from under the pillow."

"But—damn it, Race—I won't be fooled with! How did you get the gun?"

"I always have a gun."

"Not this time. Your clothes were taken away. Both your guns are downstairs locked in a desk." And when I started to tell him I always carry a gun anyway, he exploded: "You don't use that kind of a gun. You never use an automatic. This was a thirty-two caliber automatic."

I grinned at him in admiration. "Jeffries, you certainly have me there. I was as surprised as you seem to be. I generally carry a—"

"Who gave you that gun!" I was about to say a little bird when Inspector Nelson chimed in. There was a funny look in his eyes, and I knew he was thinking of the girl—of the detective she said took the gun from her, and that Nelson was planning to ask her.

He said thoughtfully: "If you give me a little time, Mr. Jeffries, I think I can tell you where he got that gun."

And I thought fast, and spoke faster—or maybe it was just a natural. But I said: "Well"—and looked straight at Nelson— "you'll find out or you'll guess, so I'll tell the truth. McGrath brought me the gun."

"Him?" from Nelson.

"Impossible!" from the D.A.

"Ask him." We all looked at McGrath's face as even the unwashed neck took on a gray sort of pallor. "He'll tell you the truth. That's why he was here. I rang up and asked him to bring me a gun. I did him a good turn once. You know the slogan—'Dirty McGrath who never lets a friend down.'"

McGrath stuttered and stammered and let his eyes pop up and down trying to decide whether to deny it or not, and thinking that if he did, I'd put the bee on him and stir up such a smell that they wouldn't even let him in City Hall.

"Well—" Nelson was at him now. "You heard his story. Come on. He must be mad. You—bring him a gun! What a joke! What a—what— By God, you did bring it to him."

McGrath fought himself out of the corner like the rat he was. Oh, he didn't face Nelson. He didn't try to stare the Iron-man down, for he might get his face caved in if Nelson blew up. But McGrath laid it on thick. And his words were fast—and sharp, and I could see then how Dirty had managed to rise in politics.

"I won't be shouted at by any second-hand, smart-aleck cop, Mr. Jeffries. This is my district. Williams has a license to carry a gun. He was shot cold-bloodedly in the back—taken to this hospital. He was lying here in danger of his life. I came personally to see if he was capable of handling a gun. He was—decidedly he was."

"That's right." I came in before McGrath could get to floundering. "I told him I'd been threatened, that—well, Nelson, do you want me to tell all of it?" And I sat up in bed and let them all have it. "Iron-man Nelson. Yes, when he has a guy in bed he beats him up." Nelson jarred back then, so I hit in heavy at the D.A. "You're trying to hang something on me. Well, I got witnesses. Do you want to see the bruises on my body? Do you want the doctors and nurses to go on the stand? You let it slide—and I'll let it slide."

Nelson went higher than a captive balloon. He roared: "He's a damned liar. I never put any bruises on his body. He was trying to prevent me doing my duty—with— Well, do you want to make any more of it, Race?" And I didn't want the girl's name in it, so I didn't speak as Nelson finished. "Go on, Mr. Jeffries, ask him what you have to ask him."

And me? I decided Nelson didn't think my story about the punch in the jaw would be funny, so I said nothing—just collapsed on the bed as I rang the bell for the nurse.

JEFFRIES WAS SORE as hell then. Whatever he asked me I rolled my eyes, talked with my lips, but made no sound.

"Damn it!" Jeffries felt like shaking me, but he had more control over himself—at least while others were there. "Damn it, Race—you're not that badly hurt."

I stretched a hand out from under the covers and clutched Jeffries' wrist. My voice was a dull whisper, but he heard me this time.

"Jeff, Jeff, old boy." I gave him the old melodramatic pathos. "Jeff—I'm dying."

"Dying—nonsense!" He seemed surprised though. "Why the doctor said—Who told you you were dying?"

"He—he did." I barely let the words slip out and made Jeffries ask me several times. Finally I closed my eyes, struggled out the words. "He—Inspector Iron-man Nelson."

The nurse came then, but Nelson cursed just the same, and the D.A. whispered in a voice as loud as if he'd shouted, that he was district attorney—he wouldn't be talked to like that.

McGrath was saying: "Gentlemen—gentlemen!" as they disappeared from the room.

The nurse came and fixed my pillows and gave me a butt and acted as if she thought I'd shoot her to death.

She nearly passed out when I said: "Bring me my pants."

"What are you going to do with them?"

"I'm going to put them on," I told her.

"But—where are you going?"

"Where can I go?" I took a good drag on the butt. "But one thing is sure if I have to leave here in a hurry, I'm going to have my pants on, and that's that."

After that was settled and I was back in bed, I said: "This is a hell of a hospital."

She looked disturbed, said: "It has been lately." And after a pause, "We have never had a patient before who stayed in bed with his trousers on."

"I'll bet you never had a patient before who had to protect himself from outsiders killing him instead of the doctors."

"Is—is there any danger—any danger of anything happening to you again?"

"Not after Sergeant O'Rourke arrives. He'll get me both my guns. I am feeling better now—and I'll shoot their heads off for them when they pop over the window sills. What is your name?"

"Miss Carmen," she said. "Miss Gladys Carmen."

"Well, Gladys, it's your job to keep an eye on the window so I won't be cluttering up the room with a lot of dead bodies."

She smiled, neither sad nor pleased nor nervous. Then she shook her head as if many thoughts were going through it. Finally she piped: "We've never had anything like this happen as long as I've been in the hospital. You must be a famous man, Mr. Williams."

"Must be!" I gave her a hard eye. "I am! You can bet your life savings on that."

Whether she bet or not I never did find out. But her life savings must have been considerable. She was no giggling school girl, not by thirty years she wasn't—and sometimes I wondered if Jane had attended to that. But Gladys was worth the two or three extra century notes I threw her way.

It seems like a lot of money for doing nothing and saying nothing. But I kept my pants on and two guns slid into straps just under the bed springs.

CHAPTER 5

I HEAR FROM MY CLIENT

No ONE KNEW the guns were there except O'Rourke who brought them and Dirty McGrath. I invited Dirty down to see them. I wanted him to know, to spread the word up and down the Avenue to whomever wanted me killed, so that the man with the scar could strut his stuff.

He couldn't strut his stuff now, if I lived—not if he had to make public appearances, he couldn't. So that's why they wanted me dead—dead now. But what about before? I didn't know him then. I didn't have any interest in his activities then. So why the attempt on me now?

And I thought I had the answer to that. I was going to have a client. And the man behind the man with the scar wanted me dead before this client hired me.

And that was where Jane and I had our fights—most every day. Just pleasant little battles, but she was certainly persistent.

"Now look here, Race," she said when the first week had passed, and I had come to keep my pants under the mattress, "I'm not going to take advantage of you and force you into a marriage while you're flat on your back. But you need a rest. You're going to be shot to death the minute you leave the hospital. Don't tell me it can't happen to you. I very nearly saw it done."

"Listen, Jane. I don't even know who wants me dead."

"That won't help you. You didn't know before, and went down and nearly out. You can't stall around any more that death can't happen to the self-admitted great Race Williams. Think of me. What will I get out of being in love with a dead man? I don't go in for unhappy endings. I'll meet you half-way—a Mediterranean cruise."

"But my client—there must be a client."

"Where is this mythical client? Your boy Jerry's been sitting in the office for the last ten days. You've been waiting in bed with two guns and your pants ready—as if you expected to dash out any moment. Me—I'm playing two parts—Mrs. Doctor Jekyll and Mrs. Hyde. That's right. I am driven here in my car as Iris Parsons. Then I slip back into the underworld as Jane Blake. There—don't stop me. There's nothing doing in your line. Just a great upheaval underneath the surface. The old racket guys being pushed out—a new and high-class crowd taking their place. McGrath is in it some place. Would you like to have the old gang as your clients?"

"Client or no client, this scar-faced lad laid me on my back. I'm a fighter in training. I've stayed here to get in good shape—not by the doctor's orders any more. They'd be glad to see me out." And with a laugh, "They expect a bomb to explode in the center of the building any day I guess."

"That's no joke, Race. One of the biggest detective agencies in the city is guarding the place day and night. But this client or no client business, I don't like. That's vengeance—that's your own pride. That makes an amateur out of you, not a professional. It's not business."

"Not business!" I guess I jarred erect. "Why every rat, every murderer, every punk that ever carried a gun knows that I was shot down on my face right in broad daylight. Me—Race Williams! It took years to create fear of my name—and some punk shoots me flat in the street. Why I've got hundreds of enemies whose names I have forgotten. Now what! Word

that I'm slipping. Guys thinking maybe I never was so hot, taking shots at me. It isn't the lad who shot me I have to fear—it's the others—the numberless others. No, kid, this *is* business. Scar-head has got to die. It's not simply my reputation, it may be my life. Just find out where he is, and I'm back where I started ten days ago—maybe higher."

"You'd kill him in cold blood?"

"Cold or hot, he takes the dose."

She shrugged her shoulders. "You're right, Race. I've lived long enough below sunlight to understand." She leaned eagerly forward. "What will you do for me, Race? What will you give to me if I find this man with the scar and set him up for you?"

And there you were. Heredity forgotten, environment slipping in. And all of a sudden she was arguing my way—and I'm arguing hers.

"Jane—Jane!" I started to holler piously. "You've got honest money, honest position, honest background—a long list of classy ancestors behind you. I like you coming here. I'd like even coming to see you. But if you talk of going back to that life, meeting that crowd again I'm through with you—washed up. Be Iris Parsons to the world, and if people must see us together, let me be the man who saved your inheritance. Not Jane Blake of the crooked side, but the girl who crossed the ocean from England to become heiress to a great name—a great fortune."

"Baloney." She leaned back and laughed. "I like the excitement of it. No one in my new life has connected me up with the past. No one out of my old life connects me up with my future. I can disappear in a moment—and establish a new identity."

And there I was. There was no talking to that girl. And yet when she left I wondered if I hadn't just talked her back into her old life. I had shown her why the man with the scar must die, and she— God, it was an unpleasant thought. She had looked on me as a gunman, and on herself—well, I might as well say it right out—looked on herself as a gunman's moll—my moll.

THE DOCTORS SAID I would have to stay in the hospital two weeks, and I said I'd be out in one. But I didn't leave there for three weeks. Oh, I was in fair shape to leave in one—in great shape in two, and in three—well, I was just like a fighter who has been in training and primed himself to perfection for the biggest fight of his career.

Three weeks—and it might have been a month. I was waiting for my client—and it turned out I was right. At least a client showed up at my office late one afternoon, saw Jerry, and told him there was big money behind him.

Jerry sauntered in to see me that evening. I liked Jerry ever since I had picked him up in the underworld and made an honest man out of him—well, as honest a man as you can be in my business. He wasn't a kid any more, but he knew the life, could do things with a gun or a knife, for that matter. Jerry came in just after I finished dinner.

"It's eight o'clock now, boss." He came right to the point. "Your client sports a cane, gray-white waxed mustache, wears clothes that cost money, but don't look it. Puts fifteen-dollar shoes on his feet. Real class not the fake kind. His home is— well, you're to meet him at nine tonight at this address.... I don't think he'll shoot you to death, but he might. He's big business—honest or crooked. He didn't give me his name, but I sat down on his tail and slid to his home. His name is Richard Daniel Havermore—head of the brokerage house of Fenman and Clark. Says it's the biggest thing you'll ever get a chance to handle. Wanted to know if you were well enough to take it on. Said he'd judge when he saw you tonight." He leaned into his pocket and tossed my gun-harness on the bed. "There's the shoulder holster," he said. "You got your rods."

"Did you tell him I had been waiting for him?"

"I did. And you're right about him coming to you because of the shooting. I wove it into the conversation and— Hell, boss, he didn't say it exactly, understand. Maybe he didn't even hint—but I ought to tell you—"

"Cut out beating around the morgue, Jerry, and give it to me straight."

"Well, he said, 'Yes, yes, I knew he was shot in the back. We were just about convinced at our last meeting that Mr. Race Williams was invulnerable. Now'— And he shook his head, boss—'now—I have my own personal doubts—the Board may not wish him. We have been unable to discuss it. But assure Mr. Williams he will receive a thousand dollars for just making an appearance.'"

"What the hell, Jerry! Did you tell him

they were damn lucky if I even considered talking to anyone. Did you tell him I'm big money—expect to be treated as such—and even if they have enough dough, I don't take cases I'm not interested in?"

"I told him. Now, in my opinion, boss, he didn't seem impressed. He said there was no question of money involved. If you lived long enough you could collect a hundred grand—only he said a hundred 'thousand'—maybe more, but this time you'd have to work for it."

"And what does he think facing hot lead is, just plain fun? My pants are under the bed. I'll get the bill on my way out."

AFTER I RANG for the nurse I had her call the office and tell them to get my bill ready. "Funny," I said to her. "They never even sent me a weekly bill."

The nurse turned from the phone.

"They wouldn't have permitted you to stay here, only the commissioner of police himself requested it. As for collecting each week"—she let her teeth show in a smile—"I guess no one wanted to present the bill—certainly I wouldn't, knowing about those guns."

I slapped another century into her hand. She had developed what was pretty close to a sense of humor.

Jerry went first, then I sauntered into the hall, ignored the elevator and walked one flight to the floor below. The girl on the desk checked up and said my bill had been paid until the end of that week. I started to speak, then let it slide. It was O'Rourke or Jane, and I felt pretty sure it wasn't O'Rourke.

I took myself leisurely to the front door, walked down the steps, skipped quickly to the right, avoided the path and ran across the plot of grass toward the high spiked fence. Jerry would have a ladder there for me, and I could leave the old brick dump without being seen. Understand, I hadn't forgotten the boys who tried to kill me. Not that I feared my friend with the scar, but I wanted to meet him face to face—not a lot of hired gunmen.

I had forgotten the detectives who had been hired to guard the place, and I damned near shot one of them to death, having a nervous gun-finger at the time

"God in Heaven, Frazer!" I said when he popped up before me with the order to "Stop!" "Is that the way your chief gives out instructions? It's a wonder that half the Gregory Ford Agency men haven't been killed."

"So it's you, Race." He put away his gun that would have been useless. "Were you questioning the bad guy?"

"What bad guy?"

"Don't kid me," Fraser came back. "We've been watching this place to see that some mob don't come up, walk in and machine gun some lad to death like they did uptown at that other hospital." And suddenly, "Cripes, I forgot! This is where you were parked." He guffawed all over his face. "We've laughed our heads off about it. Some punk shot you in the back."

I didn't like it, but I grinned. So they were laughing around about my nose dive. I knew it. And I knew the answer to it. The answer was a corpse—a corpse with a scar far up on the right side of its forehead.

Frazer was saying: "Hell, Race, we're all glad you didn't take the dose. But you—above all guys to be laid out on your face. I bet you've laughed yourself sick. That's why you been in the brick pile so long." He tossed a thumb at the dirty brick building behind. "Where are you going now?"

"I'm going out to give that guy a chance to repeat. Nix on your mush, Frazer." This as Jerry pushed the ladder over the fence.

"O.K., Race. I won't say a word—not even a word to the boss, Gregory Ford. Nope, I won't even say you climbed the fence in the dark so as not to meet him out front and kill him too soon."

"Fine." I stepped toward the fence when Frazer caught my arm.

"I'd do anything for a lad like you—you're a great guy, Race…. Say, the missus ain't been well. I spent a lot sending her away. Guys hounding me with bills. Could you lend me a couple of hundred?"

I shook his hand off my shoulder. "Would a hundred keep you from worrying and making you apt to talk?"

"All right—all right." He took the money and not at all sheepishly said: "You know as well as I do, Race, you only get what you pay for in this game."

After that he steadied the ladder for me, and helped toss it back over the fence. So I saw Jerry drive off with it as I sauntered slowly down the dark side street. Pleasant thoughts I had then. It's great being a detective—nice, clean, wholesome sort of a career!

CHAPTER 6

A GRAND'S WORTH OF TALK

THE HOUSE OF Richard Daniel Havermore, the broker, was on a swell street, had a respectable, old-fashioned front and a butler to open the door. But Richard Daniel Havermore was right behind him, and never gave me a chance to give my name. Richard Daniel was all Jerry had said he was—quick of wit, too. Listen to the crack he pulled—an original guy.

"Come right in, Mr. Jones." He gripped my hand, shook it, gave me one of those athletic grips that men like to pull when their stomachs begin to protrude. I guess he felt a bit surprised when he nearly lost the fingers of his right hand for being so smart. But he carried the Jones through, led me to his library and let me toss my hat on the mantel.

"I didn't want the butler—don't want anyone to know your real name," he started the conversation. "That's why I called you Jones."

"Really?" I took the chair he offered. "I was wondering why you called me Jones."

He jerked at his little waxed mustaches, eyed me a moment, and not being sure I was riding him, let it slide. But he was a guy who didn't ask about your health or how business was or if you wanted a cigar. He just sat down and looked at me until the butler brought in a bottle of brandy and the set-ups. Then when the butler left he got down to his own business.

"I'm in a predicament, Mr. Williams—quite a predicament. I am, because of circumstances, the voice of a great organization—not great in number, perhaps, but great in the things they will accomplish—have been accomplishing." And after a pause, "And great in wealth."

It was a good time to pause. I liked that—so I waited for him to go on.

"Now these men—gathered together, employ private agencies, detectives and other means to attack the criminals that the proper authorities cannot or will not prosecute—or will not or cannot locate. Do I make myself clear?"

"Not exactly. Is it a brokerage protective organization, a jeweler's protective organization, a bankers' protective organization or something like that? Such organizations serve a good purpose." And when he put up his hand, "If it's a Ku Klux or vigilante organization—not so hot."

"It is not any of those. There are bankers, brokers, lawyers, men of various professions in this organization. They represent no one but the people. We like to call it *The People Versus Crime*. We have shown results. We have found evidence that the police could not locate. We have turned that evidence over to the proper authorities and seen our efforts bear fruit. But—several detectives working for us have been killed. At the last meeting—a month ago—your name was brought up most forcibly. It was decided to engage you."

"Engage me for what? To go out and shoot people to death—people you name? A sort of list to be murdered?"

That stiffened him a bit, and the hand that held the brandy shook. As for me, I didn't drink until I knew what was in the wind. I don't like to be in a tough spot with a snootful of brandy.

"There is no list. Indeed, we do not even know the names of the criminals we wish apprehended or killed if necessary. For instance, we say to you, 'Mr. Williams, there was a bank held up on such-and-such a date. The police have no clues. Two bank employees were shot to death—and a small child killed in her mother's arms. Now, Mr. Williams, find those men—bring us the evidence that will convict them.'"

"Listen, Mr. Richard Daniel Havermore," I gave him all of his name, "I hold no brief for the honesty of some of our officials. I'm in trouble plenty with the police at times. But they're a ninety percent straight outfit. I'm rough, and I'll shoot it out with any lad at the drop of a hat—or no drop of a hat maybe. Also, I'm no dumber than any other private detective in the matter of clues. Only I tell you the truth. I can follow a trail if I find one. But I don't run up big expense account feeding you baloney."

He leaned forward. "So you wouldn't know a way of going about finding those men?"

"None but the usual police methods. Witnesses, stool pigeons, guys spending heavy dough they shouldn't be and can't account for. Just go over ground that's already cold turkey."

He leaned back and laughed. "It took our little organization—only one member of it, too—to discover what a simple matter it is."

I grinned politely, said: "You should have the idea patented. Let's hear what it is."

"It's money," he snapped quickly. "All crime is the desire for money. We permit you to offer anything from five thousand dollars up to a hundred thousand dollars or more for the evidence you want. Don't you understand? Won't crooks sell out even their friends for enough money?"

"Mister," I said, "you've got something there. I've been around criminals for years. One hundred thousand dollars—why the best of them would turn on their own mother for that amount of money."

I LOOKED TOWARD the ceiling. Boy, what a game! It took my breath away. An old game played in a new way. Nearly all crimes are solved by the police's use of stool pigeons. A little something to hold over their heads, and a few bucks now and then. Why with a hundred grand—

"I see that you are interested." He read my thoughts without much trouble. "And I am glad that you agree with me."

"Agree with you! Why, I'll have all the crooks in the city running right out in the street for a new cover in no time. Just drag them in and shoot them down and—"

"Not so fast," dear old Dick cut in. For the moment I was thinking of him in a friendly way. "I have told you what I was told to tell you. That is, what was agreed upon at our last meeting. We meet again tomorrow afternoon. You will attend that meeting and be looked at. You will be given a thousand dollars for your time, and since your honor has never been questioned by any client—we will expect your silence. We will expect you to forget us as we will forget you—if the committee of ten vote not to use you."

"Hell!" I said. "They voted to use me— isn't that what you said?"

"Yes, yes, but that was before. May I speak frankly, Mr. Williams?"

"Sure—let me have it."

"It's this unfortunate shooting of three weeks ago. I was hesitant about calling you here tonight, but I was forced to follow the dictates of the committee. We never speak outside of our meetings. Remember, you were shot in the back by an unidentified gunman—shot in broad daylight. Others read the papers. All ten men must know. They may question the advisability of engaging you."

"Why you—" I started and stopped. "You mean they question my courage?"

"I didn't say that." He was real stiff now. "But if you can be shot down so simply, why—well, two detectives disappeared never to be seen again. Three others were shot to death—their bodies mangled. One of them must have been horribly tortured. He knew little about our organization—did not know the names of anyone in it but myself. Yet, though he could not have divulged the name of any member, one of our committee was killed. He was a banker—Byran Courtney—you recall reading it in the papers."

"But—how do you know they guess the name you call yourselves by?"

"Because," he said slowly, "in the dead hand of the banker was slipped a small visiting-card. On it was printed, *Crime Versus the People.*"

"I don't remember reading that."

"No, no, it was not reported in the paper. It was found by a police officer we trust. You see, we send him the evidence when we collect it. Our organization is never mentioned in the papers. We are satisfied that the police get all the credit."

"But does he know the name of your organization?"

"Certainly." He opened a drawer and drew out several visiting-cards, handed them to me. On each was written in a fine, distinctive hand, *The People Versus Crime.* "Some day," he went on, "we intend sending such cards to gambling-houses, places of ill fame—to known crooks. We hope to establish our name well enough that such cards will—will— I thought I had four, but no matter." He put the three cards back in the drawer. "Such cards will drive them from the city without the necessity of taking action."

"A reign of terror—honest terror against criminal terror. I think I like your job, Mr. Havermore. I will be glad to face your meeting."

"Without prejudice—for I strongly favored using you—I must truthfully tell you that I will vote against you tomorrow noon."

"Because some punk missed killing me?"

"Yes. If that can happen to you, you can hardly imagine how quick and sure would be your death. After all, it might be better to bring in the whole Gregory Ford Agency. We had favored a one-man campaign. Now—"

"Now," I cut in, "did it ever strike you that the lad who shot me knows that you were to hire me for something and wanted me out of the way? Don't shake your head. That's what I expected—that's why Jerry told you I was waiting for you to call."

"You are a very clever or a very gullible man, Mr. Williams. You do not understand the complete secrecy of our organization. The members who sit around the dark table do not know each other. I am the third man to be the outside contact— the other two are dead."

"Ah, some criminals guessed that you were going to hire me. Is there some big—"

"Enough." He held up his hand. "I have done my duty. I believe you will be voted down as not fitted for the tremendous task. Perhaps we were foolish to believe that one man—even one with a name like yours was—would be sufficient. But if you wish to present yourself, take a thousand dollars for your trouble and forget, why—it is my orders to invite you to stand before the committee of The People Versus Crime."

I never wanted a job so much in my life—that kind of a job. And now my courage was questioned—if not my courage, my efficiency, which was just as bad. I didn't push his face in. I said: "I'll accept on one condition. There is to be no one thousand dollars."

"Very gallant." He was on his feet now, and bowing slightly at the waist as he handed me ten crisp one-hundred-dollar bills. "If you do not accept the money, you cannot come. No more." He raised his hand. "I am simply carrying out the will of the majority. No one man dictates."

So I took the thousand berries and listened to the instructions he gave me.

This was one time I listened and the other man did all the talking. Was I tamed? No, I was mad, but I think I hid it.

They had a nice way of doing business. Bankers and lawyers and brokers, all right! They put entire trust in my honor—yet listen to how I was to find the place. I was to go to the Astoria Hotel, take a seat in the lobby, be always smoking a cigarette until I received instructions. Then I was to follow those instructions. I was to be in that lobby at exactly three o'clock the following afternoon.

Now I wasn't suspicious of what this man told me. Yet—well, you know how it is in my business. I would have gone, of course, if ten gunmen were waiting outside that hotel for me. I don't take talk from any man—without showing my stuff. I wasn't at all suspicious. I just asked one question.

"You wish me to be there unarmed?"

He waited a long moment.

"That's an odd question, Mr. Williams. A very odd question. Many men want your life—a man shot you down on the public street. We entertain no suggestion of your possible dishonesty. We want you to travel as you always travel—and with as much self-protection as you always afford yourself." And with a slight curve to his lips, "We hardly expect that you will force us into hiring you at the point of a gun—or is it two guns?"

"It is two guns," I said. "Good-night."

CHAPTER 7

GOOD AND DEAD

I DIDN'T GO to my own apartment that night. One reason—I wanted to duck Jane if she came there. Another—I wanted to face this strange organization before I attended to my own pleasant little duty of shooting my friend with the scar. Sure, I'd know him if I met him—and I'd certainly take a shot at him—and I don't make a habit of missing.

I copped myself a room in the Astoria Hotel, rang up Jane to see if she was all right, refused to tell her where I was, then had a first-class sleep.

I had a combination lunch and breakfast, read my papers in the morning, and cursed the announcement that I had left the hospital. It wasn't much, but it was there, and an enterprising columnist had added color to it.

Race Williams, who says it with bullets instead of with flowers, sneaked over the fence surrounding his hospital asylum of the last three weeks. Is it feared that the man who shot the notorious Williams on his face may repeat? That is the story—but it wouldn't surprise us one bit if Williams flat-footed the same street. You know—as old-time fliers used to hop into their planes and fly directly over the spot where a companion was killed. Not bravado, but fear that they might lose their nerve and never fly again.

So—all I had gotten for that hundred bucks I gave Frazer was the steadying of a ladder. As I said, it's a nice clean game.

At two forty-five I hit the hotel lobby,

picked out a seat that would face the door and had a pillar behind it that would hide a Mack truck. As for smoking cigarettes, that wasn't hard. I killed the butts and waited.

Three o'clock was rather a dead hour, yet a plain clothes man or two passed through that lobby. Neither one of them looked at me—so, of course, I knew they spotted me. But there was one lad I wasn't quite sure had spotted me—nor was I sure I spotted him. Yet I thought I saw Nelson slip from the bar around back of the telephone booths. I didn't turn and look, but I thought—

An old gentleman with a party of three stopped. There was an unlighted cigar in his mouth. He said: "Would you be so kind as to give me a match? There—don't get up. I'll light it myself." His voice was fairly loud as he took the match fold from me and returned it with a pleasant "Thank you" as he joined his party in a spurt of smoke.

The thing hadn't taken a whole minute. Though the old man's hands seemed to shake, his fingers must have been remarkably steady. I knew the second that the returned match-fold touched my fingers that there was a bit of paper tucked beneath it. I read it—held tightly in the palm of my hand—as I walked toward the door.

Go directly to the cigar store on the corner of—it gave the corner of a street-crossing at Broadway—and damn it, if I went direct it would take me over the exact spot I was shot down three weeks ago.

I had decided to let that little walk go for later. I mean I wouldn't purposely look for trouble until after I kept my appointment. But I don't avoid trouble. Sure, I had read the column, and it was possible that the fellow who shot me had read the column too. Now—any man who could shoot me down twice at the same spot was entitled to do just that. I was on my way.

There was a bit more to the note—after it gave the street corner. It said simply—*At the tobacco store you will accompany without delay the man who addresses you by the name, Mr. Dough.*

Dough—I liked the sound of that name. Whether it was meant for humor or not, it screamed out loud for attention. I wondered if his first name would be Heavy.

I TURNED THE corner and hit Broadway. It was wide at that point, but narrowed down a bit as I approached my late Waterloo. The jeweler's shop would be about four blocks further on—the cigar store another five blocks. Believe me, I was riding high as I hung close against the wall, stepped over the last curb, and was on the block where I had taken the lead like any bumb rooky.

Hope! Yes, I hoped that history would not only try to repeat itself, but have to rewrite itself. There was a thrill walking along that block—approaching the doorway of the office building where the lad with the scar had ducked. No girl clinging to my arm now—no one tailing me along the broad sidewalk. No death car approaching slowly and getting ready to pull to the curb and spray lead into me.

This time if anything happened, it was going to be played my way. I had a tiny mirror strapped about my left wrist just about the size of a wrist watch—and it looked like one too. The kidding was over. There would be no one shooting at me. As soon as I spotted a lad with a rod I'd shoot first. Oh, I know. But it would be just too bad if some innocent chap planning a little hunting started cleaning his gun on dear old Broadway.

I was humming to myself when I hit that office-building doorway. And I'm telling you I stared into it—got a good look. No guy was coming out of there— or going into it, for that matter. And, by God, it happened again!

Not from the doorway, but just as I turned my head back and started on. I won't say I heard the bullet pass by my face, but I will say I heard the bang of the gun, the tinkle of glass—yes, and even the feel of a stray splinter as it nicked off that same jewelry-store window and sprinkled my cheek.

I dropped to one knee and turned and faced the lad with the gun. Faced him and saw him just as I felt my hat jerk on my head.

Yes, I looked straight into his face— and the distance was exactly the width of two sidewalks, and the street between us. He was almost directly across the street. I fired once and saw him jar erect. Then his legs gave slightly. I closed a finger again and let it loose as a running woman passed between me and the gunner—well not exactly passed, but rather dropped between us. The dirty louse. No wonder he was willing to shoot it out with the street between us. Look at the advantage he had. He never hesitated to fire because

he didn't care if he killed others or not— while I had to wait for an opening and—

God, I'd got him! He didn't like it either, for he was moving toward the corner and the open door of a big sedan there at the curb—about fifteen feet down the side street. He was clutching his stomach with his left hand—still shooting with his right.

And me—I was coming toward him. I was ducking through the milling people, ducking speeding cars and passing taxis that had stopped dead and whose drivers, used to the ways of a great city, had parked themselves on the floors of their cabs.

He had an eye all right. A bullet dusted the hood of a cab and took a chunk out of my forehead. Still he didn't like it. He was dragging his right foot and holding his stomach and was shooting from a half bending position.

And I had him—until another frantic woman ran straight out of a store smack into my line of fire, kept in it, dashing toward me—her arms flung out—as if she expected me to save her.

He was a rotten beast all right. He let go a hunk of lead that drove the woman sprawling to the pavement. Then he made his way along the wall, reached the corner, was about to turn that corner as I hurdled the woman's body and made the curb not twenty feet from him.

And he pulled another trick. This time it was a young girl who had been moving along with her back flat against the wall of the tall building. Yep, he grabbed that girl to him and used her as a shield—just as he was on the point of vanishing around the corner.

He would make good his escape. I couldn't just shoot him through the girl. Although everything had happened in a few seconds, police sirens were already screeching. A cop was dragging his bruised body from beneath a car from which the driver had jumped, and which had run the police officer down in the confusion.

No, I wouldn't get him. That girl that he held so tightly would help him clear the corner. Then I almost jarred to a stop. The thing was unbelievable, impossible, yet it was happening plainly before my eyes. He was not trying to drag the girl around the corner. He was trying to shake her free. And I knew then, even before the girl shouted, that she had slid along that wall and grabbed the killer.

Now SHE THREW him back against the wall. His hat went off and the scar was plainly visible. And the girl— He hurled her against the wall, drew his left hand up very slowly and crossing it over his chest, pushed the gun in it smack against her throat.

Yes, you guessed it. I knew her then beneath the short veil: The girl was Jane Blake. She had been fighting desperately to keep him from gaining the corner and freedom. And now—now she was going to die for it.

I never did things faster in my life. I heard plenty, but saw only one thing— that dull scar high up on his right forehead. My finger closed. The dull scar suddenly became a vivid purple. Then I didn't see it any more. I couldn't. The man was a twisted mass of flesh, doubled up

on the sidewalk—and the girl was leaning against the wall, tottering slightly as I dashed across the sidewalk and the cops came.

I meant to grab the girl, but found myself thrust aside so that I stumbled to one knee beside the corpse and his peculiarly clutched left hand from which the gun had fallen. I gripped that closed left hand and turned him over to get a good look at him.

At the moment it seemed natural to talk to O'Rourke as he knelt beside me and looked down at the dead man's blood-streaked face.

"It's Georgie Bent," O'Rourke was saying. "Don't know him, eh, Race? I knew he was in the city. He showed up at all the night-clubs—plenty of dough, but we never had anything on him. Now you guys stand back." O'Rourke was addressing in particular a well-known crime reporter.

The reporter said: "He's got something clutched in his left hand—the writing on it don't make sense or does it."

But I didn't hear any more. I caught up to Jane as she was hurrying down the street.

"Race—Race!" I thought there was a little hysteria in her voice, and that the hand that clutched my arm trembled. But if it was hysteria she hid it at once. "I thought you'd be angry—my interfering with your business. But I couldn't get you last night. Then I read that column. I knew you'd come. I knew he'd be waiting for you. O'Rourke and a few special marksmen with rifles were up two floors. But you see, he was on our side of the street—and they were of no earthly use. I hope—I hope I didn't endanger your life."

"Endanger me! Hell, kid, you were superb. Just the pal a guy like me should always have around and—"

And I pulled a zipper across my mouth. Here I was encouraging her in the very thing I was trying to drive her out of. Then I thought of the meeting and of Mr. Dough.

"The key to my apartment, Jane." I handed her the key. "Go there and wait for me. There's no danger now," I finished as I jerked a finger back a block to where the stiff was.

No, I can't say I understood things then. But I didn't care much. I was taking it on the run to meet Mr. Dough—Mr. Heavy Dough. Sure, I was curious why that lad Georgie Bent wanted me out of the way. But why worry about him. He was dead, damned good and dead the last time I looked at him.

CHAPTER 8

THE PRICE OF A CORPSE

Mr. Dough nailed me almost the minute I got into that cigar store. I had hardly gotten my hands on some cigars when he leaned over and said: "You don't remember me, sir, but I'm Mr. Dough."

I felt pretty chipper, looked easily up at him and said: "Sure, I remember you. I have used you a lot. Now you want to use me."

He didn't speak nor did I until I was in his car. I said: "Have you any influence?"

He answered: "None at all—and very little knowledge."

So I leaned back in the car and smoked in silence. I like to talk to guys who can talk back—and know what they're talking about.

"What was the commotion down the street?" he asked, just before we stopped at a house on a side street.

"A fire," I told him.

"Was anyone hurt?"

"One man was burnt down…. Is this the place?… Oh, so I go down and in the house by the basement." This as he took my arm and watched me down the stone steps beyond the iron fence. I stood before the door to my left and waited for him to join me.

It was a cinch he wasn't going to join me yet—at least until he made sure I wasn't followed. It turned out he wasn't going to join me at all. A slide in the outside steel door grated open, there was a creak of hinges—the door opened.

Mr. Richard Daniel Havermore, white waxed mustache and all, said: "Come in." And hardly before he closed the door behind me, "I have sounded out the feelings of a few and they are against you. However, you must be present at a full committee. This way, please."

"Well, you welcome me anyway." I tried to be cheerful, but his answer didn't help any.

He repeated, as he led me through the hall, the kitchen, and to the elevator in the rear: "I simply said, 'This way.'"

I rode to the next floor, stepped from

the elevator, looked at the great plush curtains that led to the room beyond. Then I sat down in the empty chair in the empty room. Inwardly I thought, "To hell with it." I had vindicated myself. What difference did it make what these birds thought? But I'd tell them where they got off—or would I? I had my pride, but these guys had dough.

It wasn't that. No money can buy me. It was simply that these guys had an original idea—something brand-new to fight crime, and I wanted in on it.

Folding-doors slid back. I saw them moving as Havermore pulled aside the curtains. "This way," he said again.

I passed through the curtains, down a dimly lit hall and stood at the entrance of a large black room. I could make out the long table. I could make out dully that figures were at that table. Before each figure was a tiny electric bulb, fastened in some way to the table. Just a pad and pencil were completely visible—and occasionally a white hand with a pencil in it that wrote rapidly, tore off a sheet and passed it along toward the opposite end of the table where two white hands collected it, read it beneath the little light—and nodded or didn't nod. I couldn't be sure, yet something white, like a face beneath a cap, bobbed in the darkness.

Richard Daniel Havermore introduced me to the shadowy figures with their flickering lights as a protruding dark arm or two would, for the space of a few seconds, hide the lights.

Havermore said: "It was your wish to have Mr. Race Williams present here. It was your wish in writing. I have brought him—despite my understanding that you cannot use him."

THE MAN AT the end of the table spoke. "I might," he said, "reprimand you for not realizing that it was unnecessary. But at another time you might deem something unnecessary which it was not your right to judge—as it was not your right to judge this time—though your judgment is in accord with this committee's. There is but one vote that we use him. As is usual we do not know the member who voted. You may pay Mr. Williams and retire him."

Havermore gripped my arm, but I held my ground and opened my mouth. Oh, not to tell them that I had wiped out what they considered a stain on my courage. I wasn't in any apologetic mood. I spoke to let them know where they got off.

I said: "I took the thousand dollars. Maybe I'll give you some talk in exchange. Don't try to talk me out of this room." This as the figure at the far end placed two white hands flat on the table giving the impression he was about to rise.

"I know more about crime and criminals than any of you do," I went on, "and I don't care what books you've read. You haven't read my book—the book of life and death and lead. Gentlemen, I am not here to explain or excuse anything that has happened to me to make you change your mind. Personally, I wouldn't be interested in what you thought—and it isn't any of your business. I am here because you've got some money and a real idea. Other lads take your money and get spilled over. Even some of you have taken the ride. I don't need you and the money half as much as you need me. You're fighting the underworld with money not bullets—at least you think you are. I know my way around better than anyone you ever had or ever can get. I'm here tonight. I've taken the insult, but you boys are getting a break, and only one of you knows it."

The man at the end of the table said in a low but clear voice: "And just what would you do for us, Mr. Williams?"

"If you mean in the long run—what you want done. If you mean something of the moment—the immediate moment—I could knock over the lad who has killed a few of you."

"You mean you'd commit murder?"

"Call murder by any other name and it smells as bad. I like to call it killing. You fancy gents call it murder when one of you get knocked over—and call it killing when some criminal takes the dose. Well—that's right. There's no law says it's murder to kill a rat."

There was a lot of writing after that—and collecting and reading of papers at the end of the table—a sort of gasp or two. Then his voice again.

"Number Five wishes to speak, wishes to tell this Race Williams a story. Mr. Williams' honesty and silence is beyond question. Number Five may speak."

If Number Five stood up or not I couldn't tell. There was no white face in the darkness. He spoke as if he was down in a tunnel. But before he was half through I knew why. He held a handkerchief to his mouth. I didn't care. His identity meant nothing to me.

The figure in the darkness was saying: "Mr. Williams, we have built up a system which we believe will wipe out organized crime. We have gained stupendous knowledge of our public officials' private life. We were ready to strike—and things slowly changed. This great criminal organization was slowly disappearing. Something—someone, perhaps was taking its place, until we felt that our acting against this crime ring would only make it easier for a new and a greater organization to arise against the interests of the people.

"This much I can tell you. A man who not only controlled our city and state, but much of the country, fled the United States just before the repeal of prohibition. Since then he has been preparing for his return and is clearing up—or has cleared up—every charge which might be brought against him here in our city. Now he is ready to act.

"His brother has come here from South America—his brother who has never been accused or associated with criminals. He meets our best people, and also our best—or worst—criminals. He is preparing for his elder brother's return, preparing by building a new foundation for a far greater criminal combine. If the old underworld figures are already suspected by us—they die. If they are not, he uses them and jockeys them into positions where we must start all over again. This organization is almost ready to take over the city. They await only the arrival of this elder brother to take the reins, give to it the brains and money which it needs. Now—since there is no evidence against this younger brother, there is little we can do. He is not an ordinary sort of man. I understand—simply understand without legal evidence—that he has personally removed three of our group. Mr. Richard Daniel Havermore may be in immediate danger."

He paused a long time. Then he said rather solemnly: "There are many things all right-thinking men abhor. I suggest that Mr. Williams be given a trial—a really difficult trial. He must eliminate this younger brother before the older brother can arrive and take things over."

"You mean he—that he must die?" A voice spoke across the table.

"He means," said the head man at the end of the table, "that Mr. Williams is a clever man. He must find his own way to eliminate him as a great danger both to society and to us who have taken it upon ourselves to represent society. This man has murdered. The law cannot convict and punish him. We here must be our own judges, our own jury—and at times our own executioners."

There was a long silence, and I spoke.

"Who is the man?"

"That I can't tell you until all have voted. There must be seven assenting votes. But this man can be seen at any time—any hotel—any night-club. He goes openly about the city. We will see what the committee wishes now. Shall Race Williams have this chance to serve society."

Immediately all the little lamps were extinguished. We were in pitch darkness. The voice spoke. "We will vote, gentlemen."

Almost at once his own light clicked back on upon the table. Then another, another and another. I knew that they meant votes, but I didn't know whether they were for or against until five lights were lit. There was a long moment and a sixth light went on. Nothing exciting about that you think? I knew what the lights meant then—and it was exciting. One more light—just one more and—and— No seventh light appeared.

"I am sorry," said the voice, "but there must be seven. Mr. Williams, I thank you for your interest and bid you good-night."

With my sinking hopes there was a blast of light like a great flood light—at least to me. But to the others, and in a second or two to me it was really just another tiny table-light—the seventh.

"Good." The speaker was looking at a sheet of paper. "We are to give you a picture of the man, his name—the best places to locate him. He does not suspect that we are engaging you."

There was a short wait after that. Someone walked across the rear of the room. A door closed, opened and closed again. Curtains swished and white hands moved quickly all along the table.

I received the picture, and at Havermore's suggestion looked down at it. It was a good face—a little sharp, rather cruel—with steady, penetrating eyes. But there were other things that made me gasp. Yep, I certainly caught my breath as I looked at the man's name, then back to the picture and straight at the scar up high on the side of his face.

I didn't speak at once—I couldn't. This was my baptism of fire—and damn it, I had killed the man they wanted dead less than half an hour before. Extras must already be on the street. So he was one of the two brothers—Georgie Bent.

"Well"—and this time the voice was pitched higher and came from a place where the light remained dark—"you have looked at him, found the face hard and cruel. You don't like the job?"

"On the contrary, gentlemen." I bowed low. "The price will be exactly ten thousand dollars for his body. Cash on the line—now."

"But"—the head man this time—"this is simply a test of—"

"I know, I know." I was myself again now, rather enjoying the situation. "Ordinarily"—I tapped my finger on the picture—"I'd produce that corpse for twenty-five hundred or three thousand at the most." And when a couple of them started to talk in shocked surprise, "Surely, gentlemen, you don't expect charity. But enough. I have the man's picture and his name. If you wish me to assist your organization permanently, I must have ten thousand dollars in cash delivered at my door before six o'clock this evening. No, no—no more talk. If I am not wasting your time you are most assuredly wasting mine." I looked down at the picture again, tapped it again and said just as I turned and walked out of the room: "If you don't wish my services, don't bother about the money. Just consider this corpse one on the house."

I WAS TAKING a laugh when I left the building. Mr. Dough drove suddenly to the curb, and very nearly got his head shot from between his ears, though I didn't quite pull a gun. He was to take me wherever I wanted to go.

"Back to the same corner," I told him. "I think you're going to live up to your name, Mr. Dough."

As I stepped from the car a boy was hollering, "Extra!" I grabbed two papers and gave one to Mr. Dough. The headline read—

GUN BATTLE ON BROADWAY
Race Williams Shoots Attempted Killer To Death—Mystery Card Found On Dead Man Message Reads—"People Versus Crime"

I folded up the paper and walked leisurely down a side street. Then I grabbed a taxi, stalled around until I got a later edition, gulped when I discovered one of the women who'd been shot would die, but that the other wounded would recover. And this paper did me proud. My picture was spread across the front page. I shook my head a little. The publicity wasn't bad for my business—but with all the pictures the papers had of me, why pick one where I looked such a mug?

As to the mystery card, there was no mystery about that. I had put it there myself. Havermore had been right about taking out four and only returning three to his drawer. I'd snitched the other.

I remembered Jane at my apartment, let my taxi double on itself and shoot back across town. It wasn't long before I reached my apartment house.

Sure, I was feeling good. Why wouldn't I be? When that committee of hidden lamp-lighters read the papers they'd realize who they were doing business with. I took myself to the fifth floor in one of the automatic lifts, started toward my apartment door when I remembered that I had given the key to Jane. I raised my hand to tap, and got a feeling like a young colt. She was a good kid. I'd give her the surprise of her life—do one of my magic tricks. So I walked down to the door of the apartment just around the corridor, stuck the key in the lock and entered.

That's right, I have only one lodging-place, but it's two apartments—just in case I have to leave in a hurry. Two exits—in this case two entrances. The thing was simple. I went to the end bedroom, stepped into the closet and opened the door I had cut through the wall to the closet of my regular apartment beyond.

I was in my own bedroom now and killed the humming in my throat. Down the hall, in my living-room, I heard talking and sobbing. Or was it sobbing? It sounded more like an angry gasp.

Reporters, I thought, or maybe a photographer or two. But I sneaked down and took a look in that living-room.

Jane was on the floor on her knees. There were finger marks on her white throat. And so help me God, the man who held her there was Iron-man Nelson, the cop who'd do anything to get information.

He was just finishing with: "You know—you gave Race the gun. You know about that card. Who are they? Who are the people behind that card, *People Versus Crime?* Why, I'll wring your neck if you don't come across."

Yes, I knew all the excuses that the district attorney, and even O'Rourke made for Inspector Nelson. His whole life—day and night—was the hunting of criminals, and he didn't care how he worked as long as he got results. He was the law.

Jane was not sobbing now. She was saying, and her voice was rasping: "You beast, you dirty beast! It's your kind that cause crime. I don't know. I don't know! I wouldn't tell you anything Race told me if I did. Not if you killed me. You filthy, yellow coward who'd strike a badly wounded man in a hospital room. If he was here now you'd—"

He slapped her across the mouth with his huge knuckled fingers, said: "When he comes you'll think I'm gentle as a lamb. I'll—"

"Good-afternoon, Inspector Nelson," I said—and I didn't have any gun in my hand either. I couldn't have had. My right hand was too low to the floor, and my fist was clenched too tightly.

His eyes sort of turned, and he saw me. That was all I wanted. I pulled that right fist of mine up from the rug, and let it drive. Iron-man Nelson took it right on the button.

It was rather pleasant to watch. He picked himself up and tossed himself straight up in the air, then landed on his back on the floor. Pleasant dreams for Nelson!

I dragged him into the hall, took him to the basement in the elevator, dumped him out and rolled him into some soiled laundry. Then I lifted the cellar phone and put through a call to Headquarters.

"The Greenway Apartments," I said, disguising my voice. "A police officer is lying disgracefully drunk here in the basement."

WHEN I GOT back upstairs Jane clung to me like twisting ivy to a wall. She kept at me to give it up. I was a right guy now. Why not leave the old town while I was on top?

I said: "Jane—I had a big chance today. Big stuff—steady work." I rubbed my hands. "Nice work, too. I think I talked myself out of it." I felt a bit glum for a minute—then I was high again. Where the hell did those rich guys get the nerve to give me the thumbs-down? As far as I was concerned I'd—I'd—

"Listen, Jane. Maybe I'll take that trip around the world with you. You know, simply on the same boat. Look—I'll let you know by six o'clock. But it's almost certain those bums won't—"

And I stopped and turned. The doorbell was ringing.

I untwined Jane's arms from around my neck, swung a gun into my hand and looked through the little slide in my own front door. My cannon went back in my pocket and the door went open.

Mr. Dough was there—and dough was correct. I counted the money close to his face, and ten grand was right. He didn't look like a lad you'd tip a hundred or two, so I closed the door and went back to Jane.

"Listen, kid," I told her. "I'm going to see them again." I shook her by both shoulders. "Money, kid—money. No hunt-'em-up and drag-'em-out business. Cash—just cash. Cash that sets them up for the kill."

I know Jane didn't like it. Anyway she turned toward the window. But me— *People Versus Crime. Race Williams Against the Underworld.*

It was hot stuff. I liked it. Yes, I liked it a lot.

A Corpse for a Corpse

CHAPTER 1

CRIME VERSUS RACE WILLIAMS

I WAS MAKING plenty money these days—and most of it was easy money. I bought information for certain people and got paid to turn it over to them. Once in a while things got a bit tough, and a little shooting took place—but not too often, and not too tough. During the last few days, however, I had not seen Richard Daniel Havermore. I passed by his brokerage house, laid around a bit for him, but that was all. He was the outside man for the organization I did business with, the greatest bunch of clients in the world. Some guy had had a brilliant idea—and I don't mean he'd invented light bulbs either—though light bulbs were certainly mixed up in it.

I didn't think much of it when I was first taken before that unknown tribunal of ten who had set themselves up to wipe out crime—even dished out little cards which read, *The People Versus Crime*. But I didn't laugh when I heard the brand-new scheme they had to eliminate crime in the city. Those boys who sat back of a long table, hidden in the darkness except for those little lights, had something they should copyright.

It was simple enough. In plain words they'd mention any given murder and I'd spend a few hours—or at most a day or two—and lay my finger smack on the killer's shoulder. Was it done with mirrors? Not at all. It was done with cash.

Sometimes a century note to a little punk would steer me toward a bigger punk. Then a single grand to the big punk'd steer me toward a guy within the criminal circle they were after. And that guy— But here's the truth. If a name and evidence was wanted on a lad really worthwhile, why this organization would pay as high as a hundred grand in cold cash for that information.

You know the underworld. You know the big-time criminals. Name me one who wouldn't sell out his own mother for that amount of money. Why the meanest killer in the city would damn near sell himself out for a few bucks more.

It was a big thing—an easy thing, if you didn't get yourself killed off. And now I was worried about the one man who had to work in the open—Richard Daniel Havermore. Not because he was the man who had contact with the outside world and so tipped me off to the heavy dough, but because in a way he was my client. That was the way it worked. Those men at the table did not know each other, but they all knew Richard Daniel Havermore, and he, of course, knew most of them.

ON THE WAY to my apartment the feeling crept over me that I was being followed—and I remembered how I was shot in the back on Broadway in broad daylight not so long ago. Later, of course, I had killed the man who did the shooting—Georgie Bent who'd been straightening out things for his brother, Orrey, to return from South America and take charge of a big crime machine.

No, I didn't see this guy riding along my heels, and I didn't hear him. There were too many people on the Main Stem. Yet I knew he was getting my smoke just the same. I tried to place him in a street window, but I didn't look directly back. I knew I'd only lose him then. As a rule such things wouldn't bother me at all. This time though it took guts, for as I said a lad had shot me through the back on a crowded street. Now—if I turned, I'd lose my little lamb—and if I didn't turn— Which is where the guts come in—or sometimes, literally, get shot out. But that's the way I earn my money. Anyone can shake off a shadow, but anyone can't turn that shadow into substance—then make that substance talk.

I did one more crowded street to see if he'd open up with a gun. The last time I shot it out on Broadway I broke all the front pages wide open—and that's not bad advertising in my business. So I threw a swagger into my walk, got no results, and turned another corner.

The side street was pretty well deserted at that time of the evening, yet not enough to turn, grab my shadow and beat him to his knees. That's right—I was sure of him now—but he was too far back to be sure of me—at least sure enough to try a shot.

All this wasn't anything new to me. I've done it a dozen or more times, I guess. I just looked up at the row of houses that had been made into apartments. Soft feet were gaining on me now as I spotted a brownstone with the outside door open just a crack.

Things were brightening up. I swung up the steps, waited for a split second till I plainly heard hurrying, running feet—then I was inside the vestibule facing the inner door—half crouched as if putting a key into the lock.

So far everything had gone as I wished it to go. Now I'd suddenly swing and face him, knock the gun from his hand or the teeth from his face with my own gun—or even reach up and grab the hand that held the blackjack. And I did neither. The man had been too fast. Here was something clean and neat, and I made a mess of it.

As I turned, his body had already lurched toward me. His right hand was coming down. It did not have a blackjack in it. Instead there was steel—long, sharp steel, shimmering down from a white background. Near death! Do I need to ask you?

My left arm shot up to protect my face as the finger of my right hand closed once, twice to put two slugs in his body. It was unpleasant work—two slugs from a forty-four. They ripped him apart!

I straightened as he tossed himself all over the vestibule. There wasn't any chance to get him to talk—no lingering, dying words to send a message to the old folks back home. He didn't die any movie villain's death either—with words that righted some terrible wrong he had done

mankind. Let's just say that he took the two slugs—and was dead.

There wasn't a soul in sight as I put my flash on his face—Les Rankin who liked to do things nice and quiet. I hadn't set eyes on him in over two years. He had been working Chicago where there was little interference if a lad wanted to kill someone. I had no kick—no apologies either. Les was first-class stuff. Les knew who he was after. He took his chance—and now look at him.

I TOOK OUT one of my little *People Versus Crime* cards. In the beginning it seemed silly to stick these on lads who jumped in front of a spitting gun. But my clients were right. It certainly advertised their business in the underworld. Crooks may not fear the law, the long trial with a chance to beat the rap, the political strings they can pull, the buying off of witnesses, the fixing of alibis—all the stuff that goes to make the city safe for murder. But one thing every criminal does fear—at least he isn't pleased with it—and that's a belly-ful of lead. They fear exactly what they dish out.

I picked up the knife, realized what the white background was. It was a card like mine. Only this card read, *Crime Versus the People*, and the word people had been scratched out and in its place two words written in so that it now read, *Crime Versus Race Williams*.

I didn't search Rankin, I didn't have time. I remembered his name on the list of my organization as a wanted man. He was good for five thousand dollars dead or alive.

As for searching professional killers, it's mostly useless. And I might add that when you kill a man it isn't good business ethics to hang around until someone comes along and takes a look at you. If the police didn't question me, I never blew about such things.

I do give myself a bit of protection, however. I stepped into the drug store on the corner and called my best friend, Sergeant O'Rourke, the closest man to the commissioner in the entire city.

"Listen, O'Rourke," I told him. "This is Race Williams talking. Les Rankin is back in the city." And when he started to splutter, "Don't worry. He's lying dead in a hallway." I gave him the street and number. "It's not a nice job, and if no one thinks of my being in on it, don't you think of it."

I wish I'd hung up then, for when O'Rourke started talking he nearly turned my stomach. I hated Inspector Iron-man Nelson—and Nelson hated me.

Sergeant O'Rourke said: "Inspector Nelson knows that Rankin is in town—and he knows he's out to kill you. There was a flash out to all the scout cars to find you and give you warning. Don't curse, Race. Nelson's fast becoming the big guy on the force. I used to pick up most of the bad guys, but Nelson's turning them in fast lately."

"How?"

"I don't know how."

"Well, he's been on the force for nearly twenty years. He should make an arrest once in a while."

"Yeah," said O'Rourke. "Well, he's making them now—plenty of them."

"Well, I—" And I put my mouth close to the phone after taking one look through the glass door. I said: "So long, Honey—the evil face is at the window." I dropped another nickel in the slot, made a quick call, then opened the booth door and faced Iron-man Nelson. He was dressed in a plain blue suit—nothing of the comic-strip detective about him.

"Hell, Nelson!" I told him in shocked surprise. "I'm damn sorry—I never guessed it was you. I saw you outside and—"

"The hell you saw me." He pushed his slouch hat back on his forehead and put hard eyes on me. "Where did you come from?"

"The telephone booth," I told him innocently.

"I don't mean that. I was outside when you passed. Did you see anyone—did you hear anyone?" He gulped a bit. "Did anyone follow you?"

"No." I shook my head. "What's the beef?"

"Well"—he grumbled out the words as if he begrudged them—"it is my duty to tell you that Les Rankin is on from Chicago to kill you."

"Kill me—why? I don't even know him." And then, walking toward the front of the store and stopping to buy a mouthwash, I said: "Yeah, I remember Rankin now. Thanks for the tip. I'll knock him over for you the first time I see him."

His HAND SHOT out and fell upon my shoulder. His face turned a dull purple. "You leave him alone," he fairly sputtered in anger. "You and I have crossed too often, Williams. Don't let us cross again. Rankin is worth money alive—money to me. Understand? Rankin can talk."

"Yeah," I said as he faced me, his back to the store door, "and money to me—dead."

"What do you mean—you—" He seemed startled, surprised.

"Well, *I* wouldn't be worth anything to myself dead." I kept my eyes on the door and I was ready. I just nodded my head, clapped a hand on Nelson's shoulder. As I shook myself free I bellowed: "I have a good mind to bust you in the nose—trying to maul me!"

Nelson was really surprised now. He saw my hand turn into a fist. Saw it start slowly upwards. There was nothing of the coward about Nelson. He didn't know the meaning of that moving hand, but his own made a fist, started up—and two cops and a dick shot through the door and were on his back.

Nelson cursed in a way it was a pleasure to hear until one of the cops got a hand over his mouth. The dick walked around, gave me a friendly smile.

"Thanks for the tip, Race," he said. "We're glad to see you're not working your own law now. This is—"

He looked up and saw Nelson's face. He started to talk, then recognized the inspector, stopped dead, slunk back a bit.

I said: "Sorry. Sorry! But he did follow me into the store—and I didn't recognize him at first any more than you did. So I called the police."

Two burly coppers shot to either side and landed on the floor. I stepped through the side door wearing a grin. I didn't stay for the fun.

I'm a strong man—damn strong—but both cops were six feet of beef and muscle, no fat on them. And I had a disturbing thought. It was that if Nelson ever laid his hands on me I'd kill him. I'd have to.

As I slipped out the side door I saw a uniformed officer hurrying back to the prowl car across the street—the one that Nelson must have been waiting in. He had taken a look-see into that drug store and must have seen the two cops go into their act, but I chanced it anyhow. I didn't know him, so I walked right up to the car, opened the door and climbed in beside him.

"Nelson said to take me home, Joe," I said simply.

He screwed up his face nasty without getting a good look at me. "My name ain't Joe, Buddy," he said.

I raised my head and looked straight at him. "My name ain't Buddy, either," I said easily. "But that's beside the point. Iron-man Nelson's name is still Iron-man Nelson. On your way!"

He put the car in gear and ten minutes later I climbed the stairs to my own apartment.

CHAPTER 2

THE RAT, THE TRAP, AND THE CHEESE

ONCE AGAIN I was followed and this time you'll have to admit it was once too often. A head ducked back around the turn in the hall near my own apartment. I swung my gun loose, walked silently toward that corner—and very damned near blew the top of the girl's head off.

It was Jane Blake—alias Iris Parsons—brought up in the underworld before I discovered her and brought her back to her right name—society debutante, and heiress to more money than you and I like to think about.

"What's the matter?" she asked. "You look pale. Race, Race—" Both arms went around my neck.

"Nothing the matter, kid," I told her. "I just nearly shot you to death. Don't play Little Bo-Peep with me again."

"I wanted to surprise you."

"Well, you did." I took her arm. "Come on down to my apartment." And as I dragged her in and bolted the door, "I told you not to come, but you're here—so what?"

"So I'm keeping my promise about helping you. Don't laugh. I know the racket. The People Versus Crime. Nice organization."

I gripped her wrist as I led her from room to room, tossed up a couple of steel shutters, searched the apartment thoroughly—even looked in my little closet with the fake back which led to the empty apartment beyond.

Seated in my living-room I said: "What do you know about this organization?"

"Well"—she made a face at me, and she had some face—"I read in the newspapers that a man you killed had a card like that on his chest. Then there have been others. Oh, don't look so mysterious. A good many lads below the line believe you are in it."

"It's silly." I took off my coat and chucked it on the couch. "Imagine putting cards on stiffs!"

She shook her head. "It's a great advertisement, Race. Criminals are beginning to fear it. No one knows exactly who hired him, but a killer—Les Rankin—has been offered a load of money to kill you."

"Fine! I'm cashing in on his corpse for five grand. But it was rotten shooting."

"You mean you—you—"

"Oh, he's dead enough." I got to pacing the floor. "But I'm worried about the whole business. I haven't heard from—oh, anyone for the last few days. I—" And I snapped my face shut. I was leaning down on the table looking at a card.

Mr. Doe will call for you—up the street from your apartment—six prompt.

I turned the card over and read on the other side of it, *The People Versus Crime*.

Mr. Doe. I rubbed my hands together. Maybe Mr. Heavy Dough, for I always spelt his name that way, and thought of him in dollars and cents. He was the bird who generally took me to the meeting place of the ten in black. Then it hit me like a carload of brick. How did that card get there? Had it been put there while I was out? If so, how did Mr. Dough get in? And I didn't remember seeing the card there when I first looked at the table. For I had looked at it, and I—

The girl said: "The card again, eh, Race? How did it get there? Only you and I were here in this room. Did someone slip in the door behind us?"

I shook my head. "It must have been there earlier."

"No." Jane was emphatic. "That card was not on the table when we went—or rather you dragged me—through this room."

I LOOKED AT her—the narrow burning in her eyes, the forward lean of her body, the listening cock to her head. She was Jane Blake now—the girl who had crouched in alleyways, had lived among criminals, had jerked up a gun, and on more than one occasion used it. I walked straight over to her.

"Jane—Jane!" I damn near slapped her face, but I dropped my hand to my side again. "Snap out of it! Remember your heritage—your—"

"Forget it! Tonight I'm just plain Jane Blake. Here's some news for you. You killed Georgie Bent who was laying the groundwork of an organization for his older brother. Now—well, this older brother, Orrey Bent, is in town."

"So that's why the Hidden Faces want me. I understand he's the underworld's smartest organizer. How the hell he cleared up all the things against him I don't know."

"No?" she smiled. "Did you ever think of McGrath?"

"McGrath—Dirty McGrath?" I took a laugh. "Oh, he's a good ward-heeler up in his own district. His father and grandfather before him were political heelers— all nicknamed 'Dirty.' He isn't much out of his district. Besides, I don't think he knows Orrey Bent."

"Bent was big in his time—it's hardly more than five years ago. If McGrath didn't know him, he knew McGrath—

used McGrath as his fixer, and since he has been away McGrath has grown very rich. I think it was Dirty McGrath who straightened things out for him."

I laughed again, couldn't help it. It struck me funny.

"McGrath," I said disdainfully. "He's a shake-down artist on a small scale. Sells a little political patronage, gets out the votes, and I suppose has made a few bucks over the years. Whoever heard of him in anything big! You don't hear the name McGrath in important political circles hardly at all."

"And you do hear the name of Race Williams? Don't you understand, Race, that men can be as smart as you—perhaps smarter—by sitting tight, keeping out of the limelight, by growing great in another man's shadow. They advise, dictate, even rule, but never push themselves to the front. Don't you see, Race—you can't all be walking down side streets shooting each other to death."

"You've been listening to a lot of cheap talk, kid." I patted her head. "McGrath's business is getting lads out of jail for stealing milk bottles, keeping pickpockets in his neighborhood from being sent up the river, protecting small gangs of hoodlums, straightening out tavern licenses, and what-not."

"That's right." The girl nodded. "That is his outward life. Inside, above that dirty neck of his, is real brains—big brains. Special juries, special city investigators sent by the Governor ignore him. His activities—his outward activities—are too small to bother with. But I am telling you, Race—big guys in trouble go to McGrath."

"They've been feeding you baloney. Maybe the crooks suspect you and don't trust you any more. McGrath is and always was simply a ward-heeler. Make him a district leader, and he's still a ward-heeler. Make him—"

The phone rang—the one connected to the switchboard downstairs. I swung the instrument into my hand and said easily: "Williams on the wire, Jessie. Let me have it."

She did, and no mistake. She said: "Mr. Orrey Bent and a friend—tough friend. Let 'em come up?"

I slammed a hand over the mouthpiece, said to Jane: "After all, there are some thrills in life. The older brother of the man I killed wishes to see me." And before she could answer, "All right, Jessie, send the gentlemen up. I am quite alone."

Jane didn't want to go but I finally persuaded her to take the out through the closet to the next apartment, and so down to the street and home.

"Now, listen, Jane—be Iris Parsons from now on. I don't want you in the underworld."

"Will you marry me?" she said suddenly. And when I stared blankly at her, "Very well then, I'll go—but only my husband can order me to stay home."

I saw her flash down the hall, into the bedroom, heard the closet door close, then I looked my living-room over. It was always set for visitors—it was set now. They would occupy the low couch on the other side of the long table. I would sit with the table between us.

My fingers felt of my gun, my blood tingled slightly—like an itch inside my body that I couldn't scratch. Yes, there are times in my life when the big thrill comes. Rare they are, but this was one of them. I was going to meet the man who, at one time, was within inches of controlling the entire city. The biggest man in the biggest rackets—and the man whose brother I had killed.

THE BUZZER SOUNDED off and I went down the hallway to the door. I had a real kick as I slipped the little slot aside and peeped through. Two men stood there. One was a big bruiser—the other my man, the dead Georgie Bent's brother, the lad my hidden clients felt was the new leader due to take over organized crime. Number One man on my list.

The price on his head was high. Sure, I'm human—the temptation was great. I could raise my gun and put a bullet just below the neat part in his black shiny hair that was pasted back on his forehead.

He was dark and handsome in a greasy sort of way. He stood there leaning on his gold-headed cane, both hands showing. The plug-ugly with him had both hands plainly visible too, and plainly empty. They didn't know I was looking at them. Yet they didn't know I wasn't. They wanted in, and a couple of guns in their hands would have saved me a lot of trouble and filled my pockets with money.

Maybe my fingers did tighten a bit, maybe I did lick my lips a bit, but don't think the worse of me for it. My business was killing rats, and here were a couple of juicy morsels. But I dropped my gun back in my side pocket, patted the other that showed plainly under my left arm, and opened the door. I've never resorted to murder—yet.

Orrey Bent of the soft, slick hair and the dead brother, bowed low. His tough friend walked straight and stiff behind him. None of us spoke until we were in the living-room. I brought up the rear, of course. I motioned them to the couch, watched Orrey light a cigarette, then he spoke.

"Mr. Williams. Mr. Race Williams," he said very slowly. "I never met you. And I wanted so much to see the man who killed my brother."

I said: "Here I am then. Take a good look at me."

"Yes, you are well built." He glanced over my body. "The newspapers said that you shot it out with him—the width of a street between you. Knowing my brother it seems impossible."

"You can't believe all you read in the papers." I shrugged my shoulders. "It's a simple but a gay little story. The first time we met he put me in the hospital. The next time—I put him in the morgue."

"You jest." His mean eyes narrowed slightly.

I said: "No, I don't jest. The plain truth, Mr. Bent, is that your brother had it coming to him—and I gave him the dose."

"So—so." He took one of his hands off the gold-headed cane and stroked his chin. "As simple as that, eh?"

"Just as simple as that."

He cocked his head now toward the bruiser whose coat swung open and whose gun showed. He said: "Mr. Williams, this is my companion, Harry. He can do many things with his guns. Do not excite him. You are fortunate that you are in your own apartment, and that the telephone girl below knows we have come up."

"Hell!" I wasn't so pleasant now. "Why bother about her? Why not simply stick a knife in her stomach when you go out?"

"Just what do you mean by that?" He jarred to the end of the couch.

"I mean"—I leaned far forward on the table now—"I mean don't think of her— don't think of me. I won't complain. Just let your friend there go into his act."

"You mean you—"

"I mean that if Harry's so fast with a gun, let him do his stuff. I'll shoot you both to death." And smacking the words through my teeth, for I like a little melodrama of my own, as I came to my feet. "Harry's a dope—you're wasting your money. Look at that!"

Harry was showing his stuff in slow motion. He thought he had a new trick. He kept his right hand in full view upon the table, didn't move it toward his left armpit, but instead he was bending his body forward so that the gun would fall into his hand—instead of his hand grabbing his gun.

I had to do it. I saved Harry's life. I just swept the nose of my own heavy gun out and down on Harry's fingers, then I jarred it up against his chin. Then I simply turned, swung my hand and shoved about two inches of my gun into Orrey Bent's stomach until, seeing he didn't mean business, I dropped easily back into the chair again.

Harry had passed out on the couch.

Blood was trickling from his chin. Orrey Bent was staring at him in wide-eyed amazement.

I chirped: "Listen, Slick Hair. There's no reason I should do you a favor. But if you can't use a gun yourself, you'd better shake Harry. I don't know what you're paying him, but if it's half as much as I think you're paying him, it's ten times more than he's worth. Have you any other business here with me?"

"So it's all true what I've heard about you. I could handle you myself, but I'm not built like my brother—I'm not built like you. He was a show-off, a strutter—you are the same. Me—I wait. Yes, Mr. Williams, there is other business. I understand you warn people, threaten their lives. Most laudable, I assure you—and in that way you are like me."

"You wish to threaten my life?" I grinned. "I hope you have better luck than today's attempt."

He had complete control over himself now. I couldn't tell if he knew about the dead Les Rankin or not. His voice was even, cold and steady.

"Yes, I have come to threaten you. I'll give you time to leave the city—leave it forever. South America is not so bad. Perhaps some day you too will find it all right to come back."

"And I hope I won't walk into such a mess as you have. Your start is not auspicious. So I guess I won't go."

"My start," he threw at me suddenly, "is better than you think." He ducked his hand into a vest pocket and tossed a card on the table. It read, *The People Versus Crime*.

"Do you know where I got that?" He smashed out the words, for after all, his emotions inside were just like any other guy's. "Well, I got it from Richard Daniel Havermore. See?" His face was close to mine and hatred was in it too. "I'll leave you now, Mr. Williams. Later I'll tell you where Havermore's body is—so you can go and place the card on it. Ah, you don't laugh now. That's right. We knew about him for some time, and I picked him up. He'll die many times over because of my brother's death."

I held the table tightly, made sure of his words.

"Am I to understand that you have taken Richard Havermore prisoner, and that you know personally where he is, and that you intend to torture him to death?"

"That's it exactly," he said slowly.

And that was all. He'd made his own trap, put the cheese in it, then stuck his face in for that cheese. My gun was out again, up and down—and his lean body crashed upon the table. There was a long cut over his forehead now. I fastened both my hands upon his throat and dragged him over the desk.

I guess I laughed as I beat him to his knees, hollered the words in his ears that would never be heard past the walls of my sound-proof apartment—my steel windows and doors.

I didn't give him a chance to talk at first, though I wanted information from him. Once he tried to get a gun, and I banged his head hard against the table. Then I gripped his throat, his tongue hanging out, his lips showing purple, and said: "Your brother died an easy death, Mr. Bent."

Afraid he would die there on his knees I chucked him across the room, followed him.

It did me good, and I guess it did Bent good. Anyway, when I went for him this time my heart wasn't in my work—and the courage of the rat to fight back had gone from Bent. He had felt that death was coming when I knocked him up and down the floor. Now he breathed out words as he clutched at his throat.

"I will tell you where Richard Daniel Havermore is—for my freedom." Then he added: "And without further harm to me. I know your word's good, Williams."

"Fine!" I stood with legs far apart, guns parked again. "There's the phone, do your stuff." And as he climbed to his feet and struggled toward the phone, "As soon as Mr. Havermore reaches this apartment, you can go—go in the same condition he's in."

Bent stopped by the phone just as he grasped the instrument. "I intend to be honest with you, Williams—since I know you'll be honest with me. You see I still have a gun in my right hip-pocket."

I took a laugh. "That's all right. Any time you feel like using it, just pull it out and start shooting."

That may sound foolhardy, but it wasn't. I could cop that gun any minute I wanted to, but the very fact that I let him keep it would always be in his mind. And my indifference to that gun would be strongest in his mind whenever he tried to use it on me. You'd think pretty well yourself of a man who knew you wanted to kill him, yet let you cart a cannon in your hip-pocket. Sure, you would—and you'd think twice before using it—and likely if you did use it, your hand would tremble.

At first, with his trembling voice and shaking hands, Bent didn't get very far on the phone. I knew that from the way he pleaded. Then he made a quick recovery, snapped words out and got action.

I heard him say: "Damn your thick hide, I'm telling you. My—er—the life of our entire organization is in danger. Havermore must come to Race Williams' apartment at once. Understand—at once."

I sat down and smoked then. Harry got conscious and looked sillier than ever. I walked over and snapped his guns, chucking them in the waste basket. He just sat there and nodded his head up and down like it was on a wire. I started to caution him, then let it go. He took a good look at Orrey Bent and got the idea.

There was little conversation. Bent wanted to go to the bathroom and clean himself up. I shook my head.

"How will I explain my appearance downstairs?" He put the question as if it were important. Maybe he had someone waiting outside, and wanted to make an impression.

"Tell them you yapped to the wrong guy for once, and got yourself messed up," I said. "Try the mirror to the right. Do your best with your handkerchief. Don't argue. It's immaterial to me how you look."

He stared into the mirror for a minute then turned and looked full at me. His eyes had something new in them. Vengeance? Yes. And hate too, a real hate.

He spoke very slowly. "You did this to me"—his fingers touched his face, his neck, ran along his bloodstained forehead—"and now you—you would leave me so. Why?"

Maybe I didn't know why, but I gave him the first answer that came into my head. I said: "Because I don't want to have to begin all over again if Havermore doesn't show up. I want to start on you where I left off."

If it wasn't the right answer at least he believed it. He turned, and moistening his silk handkerchief with his tongue began to wipe the blood from his face.

Silence then. And grim determination and boring hate in the eyes reflected in the mirror. There was a dumb, uncertain look on the face of the huge bodyguard, Harry, who sat stiffly on the end of the chair—both his hands plainly visible. Harry, poor fellow, had had a shock. He wasn't a sneering gunman and killer any more. He looked more like a great bull going to the slaughter. I turned and spoke to him suddenly.

"Don't you worry, Harry," I said. "I'm not going to kill you. You're really a harmless sort of fellow." Believe me when I tell you that he wasn't even insulted. Believe me when I tell you his breath just shot out of his mouth as if a pin had been stuck in a balloon. And his words when he spoke nearly knocked Bad Boy Bent right off the chair he was kneeling on before the mirror. His words knocked me a bit too.

Harry said: "Thank you, Mr. Williams—thank you. I—" And then he closed up.

Get the psychology? Get the pride I take in my name and my record? Harry had been almost certain of death in his own mind before I spoke. That's the stuff that makes the boys hesitate to even take a shot at me. And that's the stuff that makes them miss when they do.

CHAPTER 3

MR. HEAVY DOUGH

THE PHONE RANG. Jessie gave me the man's name—all of it. It was Richard Daniel Havermore. "All right," I told her, "send him up—alone."

"Oh, he's quite alone, Mr. Williams." And her voice lowered. "Quite harmless-looking in a distinguished sort of way—seems depressed."

I let it go at that. To Jessie I was a detective, and she liked to splash a little of the Sherlock Holmes into her conversations with me. She was right though, about Havermore's looks. He's a big guy in the business world and likes people to know it—gray-white waxed mustache and all—though he didn't seem very old.

When he came in his eyes were restless, his clothes not so neatly pressed—and though he'd twirled one mustache into a point the other one that he was working on now seemed to go sour on him.

"You know this man?" I asked Havermore as he leaned rather heavily upon his cane, and I pointed out slick-haired Orrey Bent. "Maybe you can't tell him from his new looks—had his face changed by a plastic surgeon—at least, his face has been plastered." And when

Havermore shook his head I put a bit of feeling into my voice. "He's the lad who so kindly telephoned to have you released—and what's more I'm the guy who taught him some brand-new tricks. O.K., Orrey, get out and take Charlie McCarthy with you."

I watched them go toward the door. The dummy would have taken Orrey Bent's arm, but Bent shook him off. The two of them almost fell. I took a laugh as they collided going out the door, then turned back to Havermore.

"The sleek-haired guy is Georgie Bent's brother." And enjoying the bewilderment in Havermore's face, "That's right—Orrey Bent—the big shot who came back from South America to run this city."

"But he—he looked rather—odd."

"Odd? That's a new way of putting it, Mr. Havermore. He just passed through the information booth. That's what they intended to do to make you talk. You see, this Bent got threatening me, and to show how smart he was he told me what they intended to do to you to make me a good boy. That's where he slipped up."

"You—you do that to people?" He seemed paler now.

"I did it for your life. You'd pay good money for him dead—you or those boys in the dark room. I offered him his life for yours. After all, you got me into this business."

"Did—did he talk at once?"

"By God!" I said to him. "You're free— what do you care? But if you must know, he didn't talk at once. I didn't figure a guy like him would." And after a thought, "Maybe I didn't give him a chance to talk.

You were really my boss, and hell—I was mad."

He tried to steady himself, sank into a chair, rubbed a handkerchief across his forehead, opened his mouth and closed it again. I brought him a drink of brandy then, watched him sip it.

I said: "Did you know this man Orrey Bent before?"

"No, no—of course not. My business is a respectable one. But through the system of the organization we learned that he was coming back to take over and build up the crime ring we were tearing down." He put a hand to his head as if in thought. "Terry Macon went to the chair last week. Tony Frisch a short time before."

HE RATTLED OFF the names of quite a number of big guys who had taken everything from the hot seat or the book on down. I nodded, for I had worked up their cases.

"Many of them came from Dirty McGrath's district," I said.

"Timothy McGrath, yes—he has helped us at times."

"If he did," I said, "there was something personal in it for him or—"

"McGrath," Havermore edged in, "has made money, and has kept a great deal of it. I do not care to discuss him—in fact, I am not permitted to. I would simply advise you not to trust him too much."

"Thanks," I said sarcastically. "I never would have expected Dirty McGrath of a dishonest act."

"He dislikes the name 'Dirty.'"

"He should. His father and his grandfather before him introduced dirty politics into his district. The McGraths have kept it dirty ever since. It is nearly time for that meeting I was ordered to attend."

"A meeting—yes, there is to be a meeting, but I was to inform you." And he told me about a gun being thrust against his back right in front of his own building downtown, and how he was shoved into a cab. He went on about his imprisonment, the threat of his death by torture, masked men waiting for someone to appear—and then how he was taken away and dropped from a car and told to go directly to my office. Then he finished with, "How did you get the message?"

That needed a long explanation, and led to too many mystifying events. I had been wondering how that card got into my apartment. So I just said: "Mr. Dough telephoned me. He's to pick me up."

"Doe, Doe?" He seemed greatly surprised. "Well, perhaps when they missed me—yes, that must be it. One of them must have come to my office."

"Mr. Havermore," I asked him bluntly, "do you know every one of these secret ten?"

"I don't see any harm in telling you that. I know most of them—I must, for I am the outside contact. But one or two—no, exactly three of them—I don't know. They have come in through our finest channels—our biggest and original organizer."

"And you, Mr. Havermore, who must go about to contact others, are known to the criminals. You are suspected?"

"Yes. I thought that I was some few months back. After today there is little doubt." And sticking out his stomach with the innocent idea that it was his

chest, "I shall be more prepared in the future, and I will travel armed. There, Mr. Williams—others have suggested that I drop out and go abroad. But it is my duty to stay. Each one who has accepted outside contact has stayed until the end." He was getting prouder now, "And that end was death."

Boy, he struck a pose like George Washington crossing the Delaware! And me, I took the pose right away from him. I said simply: "I wasn't thinking about you, Mr. Havermore—but the others. You might be followed, and those whom you meet secretly suspected and murdered."

"I am most careful," he said, "to think of the others first."

"Well, that's laudable—but the problem still remains."

We were downstairs and out on the street ready to separate when he suddenly grasped my hand.

"I forgot. I am upset. I wish to thank you, Mr. Williams. I do thank you for saving me from a fate worse than death."

Spoken like an honest woman, I was about to say, but didn't. He was too serious. I didn't laugh either. Any way you looked at these birds—serious or in comic relief—you had to admit they were doing a lot with their money, a lot for the citizens, a lot for me too.

"Don't bother to mention such a little courtesy," I said, and then the mercenary side of me creeping in, "Your name doesn't happen to be on the list of cash prizes, does it?"

He got stiffer and stuck out more in front than a pouter pigeon. "I am sorry,

Mr. Williams, but I do not think that I understand your question."

I didn't drop the subject there—not me. I put it to him straight. "I mean," I said slowly and distinctly, "does your name figure in the cash awards for men—living or dead?"

"Certainly not!"

And that was that. He shook hands with me when he left. Shook his head as if his work stood above all monetary consideration. And maybe his did, but not mine.

Mr. Dough met me up the block from the apartment. When we started off in the car I got some information out of him.

I said: "You take some chances smack out in the open—you must get pretty good pay for it."

I expected silence, but he said: "Yes— one hundred dollars a day."

"Saturdays?"

"Both Saturdays and Sundays—and on Leap Year an extra hundred." So he did have a little sense of humor. Then, "Big things will happen tonight. Have you read the papers?"

"Every word."

"Julius H. Vanderberg is dead."

"Yeah," I nodded. "Heart attack."

"That's what the papers say. The police haven't mentioned that the disease was caused by a knife through his heart with a bit of paper attached to that knife which read, *Crime Versus the People*."

"He was—"

"Yes, he was one of us. Number Nine at the table. He contributed over half a million himself to our society—and had three other people donating a hundred thousand a year apiece. Who do you think killed him?"

"Les Rankin?" I just tossed out the name.

"Hardly," said Mr. Dough. "It was Vanderberg who first picked up the information about Georgie Bent, whom you killed. Vanderberg furnished the society with his information through a South American agency. He also knew the time of the arrival of Orrey Bent—the biggest, most dangerous and most—"

"Cut it," I told him, and I was burning too. I understood now why Dough talked so much now, and his cheeks were red. "Don't tell me how bad Orrey Bent is. I just finished cleaning up my office with his face."

"He'll get you next, Williams." Dough let all his manners go forgetting even the Mister. "You'll get this Bent—you'll kill him. You'll—"

"We'll see," I said soothingly, but I liked Dough from then on. Before he was so placid, so unreal. Now the spirit of the thing gripped him—not forgetting his hundred bucks a day.

I tried: "How do you know Orrey Bent killed him? That's only a guess."

"No, no." Dough shook his head. "He didn't leave the knife in the body. He brought it—brought it—" He suddenly drew the car to the curb and I leaned over the front seat, saw the long, pointed knife, the card upon the end of it. Dough went on: "Bent seemed in a mad rage. His face was covered with blood. He tossed the knife on the seat beside me. He said, 'Give that knife to those who want it, or to Race Williams himself. Tell them I stuck it into Vanderberg's chest and turned it around.' Then he was gone."

"You recognized him? When did it happen?" I lifted the knife carefully, examined the blade under the flash of the trouble-light. The blood was dry.

"Yes, I recognized him after he left. I was stunned. He's a monster. It must have happened this morning, for the papers had—"

"No, no," I cut in. "When did he give you the knife?"

"Him?" Mr. Dough was trying to think, to clear his fogged brain. "Ten minutes ago—fifteen at the most."

How, I wondered. Certainly he gave Dough that knife after he had left my apartment, and while I was talking to Havermore. But he didn't have it on him in my apartment. Or did he? No, that was impossible. So—and the answers were many and simple. He might have left it carefully wrapped in a box down at the desk—or just beside my door—or under the seat of his own car, if he had a car.

But I only said: "Do you want me to drive or—"

"No, no." Dough set his teeth tightly. "I'm not frightened. I'm not even nervous. It's inside of me—I just want to find him, kill him—strangle him—"

"That," I told him, "is my part of the job. Don't you worry, Dough. I'll lay the finger on him. After you take me to the meeting place, take a week off for yourself."

"I am to take you to the Vanderberg home first. Then I keep driving around a couple of blocks below it, until you come out. I made a quick phone report—after the knife business. Those are my orders. Then to the meeting."

CHAPTER 4

A KNIFE—TURNED AROUND

THE VANDERBERG MANSION was a big place. I didn't know if O'Rourke was there, but I got in by shoving a few harness bulls around, telling them I wanted to see the commissioner who had sent for me, and asking if O'Rourke had turned up in answer to my call. Of course they knew me, and no one was ever surprised to see me where a lad had just been murdered.

The body was still there, and would be until the burial. You hear of the police taking bodies to the morgue for post mortems, but they don't run off with corpses who bear high-priced labels such as Vanderberg.

The commissioner wasn't there, but the district attorney was. He let his eyebrows lift a bit, started to scowl down his nose, then said: "Have you seen Inspector Nelson today?"

"Sure," I said. "He was knocking a couple of cops around. Isn't here, eh?" And with a grin it struck me. The district attorney's worried look was a fake. Nelson was prowling around outside.

"I guess he's hot on the trail." The D.A. seemed to be nervous, damn near knocked over a lot of flowers a lad was photographing. They were photographing or looking through microscopes at every article in that room.

The D.A. saw my smile, went into his act. "We're covering this case thoroughly," he said. "We'll have every fingerprint in this room examined."

He knew as well as I did that such an examination was a waste of time. A lad beside us was going over the back of a chair. He had cards in his hand. He cursed and the D.A. turned around.

"Well?" he said. "Prints?"

The print man said: "Yeah—three of them—a maid and two cops." And to me, "Come on there, buddy. Slip your fingers on a card. The more cops, the more prints. Why don't those guys keep their hands in their pockets."

I turned and muttered something about seeing the body.

"Business?" The D.A. grabbed my arm. "Who paid you to come here?"

"Maybe the lad who killed him." And stiffly, "D.A. or no D.A., you'd better see Mrs. Vanderberg before you refuse me permission to see the body."

He didn't like that one. Murders are generally duck soup for district attorneys. They strut around, give orders, shake their fingers in relatives' faces—nearly tear sudden visitors apart. But those murders are among the poor, among frightened people who have something to fear from the police—or imagine they have. With the name Vanderberg it was different. You don't go around shaking fingers, even in a maid's face. It mightn't be good for you. Besides, big shots object to seeing their friends murdered. Such goings on must be kept to the lower levels of society.

The D.A. unbent, said: "Well, Mrs. Vanderberg has been hysterical. I think the doctor has given her a sedative. She can't be disturbed."

"How about Mr. Vanderberg?" I said. "He got his sedative." And suddenly as if giving in to a point, "Very well, I won't see Mrs. Vanderberg unless she insists on it."

With that I swung to the stairs, shoved the two cops aside and went up. A cop at the top started to stop me, and O'Rourke leaned out of a door down the hall.

"All right, Simons," he said. "Come on in, Race."

A chosen few of the sacred cows of the Press were in Vanderberg's den. The coroner was sitting on the arm of a low chair. A body was lying on the couch, a sheet over it. A couple of men in black suits hovered around the couch.

The medical examiner was talking. He broke off in the middle of his speech, said: "Greetings, Mr. Williams. I was just telling the boys. But the whole thing is summed up in a few words. Someone stuck a knife in his chest and turned it around."

"Why around?" a newsman asked.

"Why not?" said the amiable little doctor. "Why do you drink every night—even after you are drunk? If I could solve those idiosyncrasies of human behavior, I would not be running out to look at stiffs day and night."

The M.E. came to his feet and motioned to the reporters gathered around. "That's all, gentlemen. The undertaker's men have work to do. You wanted to see the body, Mr. Williams?"

I did want to see the body. I took down the sheet and looked at the wound. It was a smooth job. I needed a long steady look to tell that the knife had been twisted around.

"Neat, Williams—very neat," the little M.E. said. "If you went in for the knife it's just the sort of job you'd do. There, there, don't be huffy. I've been hustled out before breakfast many a time to look at a corpse you made. And I must say I've gone back home to breakfast most times without even a bad taste in my mouth. I admire your work." He shivered slightly. "Les Rankin was killed today. You should have seen the job—a novice or a maniac." He poked me in the side. "I took one look in that little hallway and you were exonerated at once."

"Listen, Doc—Vanderberg's dead. I'm pretty late on the job. What did they tell you?"

"Well," he stroked his chin, "I understand that someone spoke to him on the phone, made an engagement to meet him here in his den. The maid had orders to let the visitor come right up. The murderer came right up, stayed perhaps ten minutes, then left. The maid heard the door close. Now the Rankin murder—"

"I'm not interested in that," I told him.

"You should be." He didn't resent my sharpness. He turned and went out.

As I slipped out into the hall, O'Rourke put the mitt on me. "Vanderberg had visitors, Race," he said. "Visitors that came up unseen or with their hats over their faces. At least one visitor. He was killed by someone he knew or thought he knew. Mrs. Vanderberg doesn't know, but she said he was doing some 'great good.' We may discover what he did with a lot of money. Still, he was a secretive man. But the point is not that, Race. I've stuck to you for years. Played your hand even against Nelson. Right?"

"Right." I was a bit surprised. "And when I had a kill that needed a police label on it, or some evidence that would give you a push with the commissioner, you got it. You—"

"Listen," O'Rourke said. "I beat Nelson to this murder tonight. He ain't here yet. But the commissioner isn't looking on me as the fair-haired boy like he used to. Evidence I should have is coming straight through the district attorney's office."

"I can't help that," I told him.

"No? What about the Massey case, the Richards kill—the triple murder with the bodies taken to Jersey. Don't tell me, I know."

"So"—I looked straight at him—"you traced them back, eh? Where the original information came from. You recognized my hand in it. You're pretty slick, O'Rourke."

"Yeah, I am. I could have been an inspector—a deputy-commissioner—most anything. But I get the largest salary on the force for staying a sergeant and taking orders from no one but the commissioner himself. I like to stay close to the cops—the people. That's what made me worth more. Now—I'm not getting the stuff from you. I'm just covering you up at times."

"Old boy"—I ran a hand through what was left of his hair—"you'll have to cover the Rankin kill for me, too. Oh, I may never be suspected, but—" And when he would have cut in, "Yeah, I know it was a mess."

"A mess!" He almost bellowed out the words. "What did you use, an axe? No, Race, you're not giving me the breaks. Things get into court and I might—"

"They've come straight from clients," I told him. And I held his shoulders and looked into his honest, straightforward, and slightly angry eyes. "You know I wouldn't double-cross you."

"That's right. That's right. But I'm not getting any younger, Race. A man like Nelson comes along, snaps the big jobs." And suddenly, "I'm even afraid I can't talk up to the D.A. any more."

"You're not afraid of anything," I told him flat. "You're just worried about your family and your prestige."

"Big things are happening. The criminal organizations in the city are changing. The old days were better—when McGrath ran the city."

"Imagine," I said, "a mug like Dirty McGrath in charge of crime."

"Well, a cop was treated right. Maybe political jobs were fixed, men who didn't get in line left the city, vice and gambling and everything went—but the citizens didn't have to see it if they didn't want to. To the honest citizen, ours was the cleanest city in the world." And suddenly, "You know who murdered this lad Vanderberg. It'll be the biggest scoop in the city. It must have been well planned, Race. If I could break this case— Have you any idea who—"

"I know who did it," I told O'Rourke. "I can give you the name now. No evidence maybe—but the name is Orrey Bent."

"Bent—Bent. Hell, Georgie Bent's elder brother! He used to be the biggest shot in the city. Fled to South America. Two-hundred-thousand-dollar bail. That must be several years ago. Now—"

"Now—nothing," I told him. "It took a long time, but things have been cleared up for him. He's back in the city. I'll let you have his corpse—later."

"You're—going to murder him."

"You can call it what you will, O'Rourke. And I don't think you'll call it murder. You see, he'll be your body—self-defense. There, don't hang your mouth open. I'll give you the gun I kill him with, and let you have the corpse. Does that satisfy you?"

Some people won't be satisfied with anything. O'Rourke had been crabbing a moment before, and when I offered him the biggest danger to the city, stiff on his back, he just looked stupid. That's the law for you.

Of course, I knew the whole racket. The People Versus Crime were turning the evidence I collected for them over to the district attorney. Otherwise, he couldn't have got so many convictions. Yet he seemed nervous. Why? I guess that's easy enough to answer. Any D.A. would feel nervous if he had a murdered body of a man like Vanderberg on his hands—and a murderer to find. Murders make good news stories and put the cops in the limelight and make them shine. But murders of lads like Vanderberg make a much bigger story, put the cops in the spotlight—and don't make them shine either.

As I passed out of the house the commissioner was coming up the steps. He was worried too. I greeted him and he didn't recognize me, at least it didn't sound like it.

He said: "Good evening, Lieutenant— the days are longer now."

"And the nights too, Commissioner," I tossed back over my shoulder. "Tonight especially will be a good sight longer."

I felt that his little body turned around and that his eyes followed me. But if he spoke again I didn't hear him.

I walked up to the corner and started down the block. I was keeping an eye out for Dough. There were a lot of parked cars, and maybe Dough had parked with them, for I'd been longer than I had expected.

I did some thinking. This wise guy, Orrey Bent, wasn't so dumb. Things had happened since he hit the city—and to show that he hadn't lost any of his old-time skill, he'd done a bit of killing.

It didn't make any difference what he said to me about being too big for that stuff. He was impressing the boys—the big boys in the racket, and impressing them plenty. Though to me he hadn't seemed so hot, nor the cheap punk he brought with him.

I stopped thinking—for there was Dough's big car at the curb. The key was in the lock, but Dough wasn't behind the wheel. I opened the door and looked in, put a flash into the back of the car.

Then I snapped the light out again, swung from the car and almost had a gun on the two men who passed by, their canes swinging, importance mapped upon their faces. Nervous? Well, I won't admit to nerves. Just say I was apprehensive— nothing more.

Mr. Dough was dead in the back of that car—just like Vanderberg. Someone had stuck a knife in his chest and turned it around. I got back in the car, took out my handkerchief and leaning over jerked out the knife and laid it on the front seat. Evidence? Well, perhaps.

I liked Dough. I was sorry he was dead. You can't do anything for a dead man except avenge that death. So with the knife on the seat of the car beside me, I drove away.

I didn't need Mr. Dough to take me to my destination any more. I had been there several times to deliver evidence I had collected, or a list of the guys I had had trouble with and placed on a slab. I had a list for the money men now. I looked down at the knife once before I wrapped it up carefully and tucked it in my coat pocket.

I set my lips very tightly. Orrey Bent had soon shaken off his fear of me. He was a man, apparently, who meant business.

CHAPTER 5

MEN IN THE DARK

I DREW UP before the basement entrance to the big house. Richard Daniel Havermore was at the little door around at the bottom of the steps.

"I'm a bit shaken up, Williams, but I

came down to admit you. I know you can come alone now—but wasn't Mr. Doe sent for you?"

"Mr. Dough is outside in the car dead." It's all right to let widows and orphans down easy, but these lads played at a dangerous game. Havermore was paying me to give him the news. "Mr. Dough was stabbed with the same knife that killed Vanderberg. Well, am I to come in?"

I came in all right, let both doors shut, then put it straight to him.

"The body's in the back of the car. Do you want me to dump it some place, report it to the police? Or do you make arrangements to handle your own dead?"

"I—we will make arrangements."

"Good." I was all business, too, for I was late. "I'll want the car myself when I leave, Mr. Havermore. If there's blood, a new mat on the car floor will do—but I must leave here in Dough's car. You have a phone here?"

He stared at me, gulped, then said: "Why?"

"Why?" I gave him the high-and-mighty. "You, or rather the people here, thought enough of me to hire me. Your friend, Mr. Orrey Bent, will think enough of me to plan my death. He knows now he takes the dose in the front or in the back—depending entirely on what way he's facing when I meet him. Now— isn't it natural for him to plan to kill me tonight? And isn't it natural for him to expect me to drive off in Dough's car?"

"Then, then—" Havermore's eyes widened. "You will be playing into his hands."

"That's it," I told him as we started for the automatic lift. "I want to play into his hands. I want to see how fast he can move those hands."

"You will enter the room alone tonight," Hawthorne told me when we left the elevator. "Light Nine at the table was Mr. Vanderberg. We never allow a chair to be vacant—the effect is bad. Someone will fill it permanently later, but for tonight I shall take Chair Number Nine."

He left me then and I entered the door of the outside room. I nearly went flat on the floor and did half draw my guns. But one of the men spoke to me, and I took a laugh.

"Four of us here with machine guns, Race." I recognized the man who spoke to me as the best from a certain detective agency. I more or less recognized the others with the Tommy guns over their knees. He went on: "Well, it's lucky for you, big boy, that we didn't have orders to fire. What a sieve you would have been."

I said as I looked at the heavy sliding doors across the room: "Four of you—that would make it easy for me."

None of the men liked me. None of them disliked me, for that matter. They were rough and ready guys who were all right as private detectives went. Their boss was a big guy, and there was little chance of them blackmailing any client later. Their boss didn't allow that, and what their boss didn't allow, they didn't do. No, not even if they left the agency. Maybe it was fear of sudden death. Maybe he had enough on each man to roast him before he hired him. As I say, they were good, as private dicks go, and that's why I call myself a Confidential Investigator.

I lit a butt and waited. They didn't ask my business, and I didn't ask theirs. I knew they were a guard. I guessed the black figures in the darkness knew they needed to be guarded, and when they did things, they did them in a big way.

"How long am I—"

A bell rang above the door. The head guy, Eddie Reed, spoke.

"That's your cue. Open the door, close it, and do your stuff. I don't know the racket, but if they don't like your stuff, they holler, and we shoot you down." And as I went toward the door, "Only kidding, Race—we ain't to guard against you."

"I know that or you wouldn't be here." I opened the door, closed it behind me and faced the thick drapes. I knew, too, why he told me he was only joking. Four machine guns or ten, Eddie wouldn't like the job of hunting me down in that house.

I was in the room I had visited several times before when I made my reports. Curtains were thick across from me. A man who had been sitting on a chair got up. He was young and strong and eager-looking, and his face was slightly familiar. Then I recognized him. He was young Johnny Crawford—the boy wizard of Wall Street.

"I know you won't talk, Mr. Williams—and all that. But I don't mind so much. I've chucked a million into this thing for the thrill of it. Just think of walking down the street, expecting a bullet any minute."

"You think of it," I told him. "Do I go in?"

"Yes, after me. I have my seat—Light Number Three."

"Light Three? Is he—is he missing?"

He nodded. "They've talked more freely than usual tonight—when I think they should talk less. I think Number Three was—well, the man Vanderberg brought in with him." He placed a hand on my shoulder. "I've put into this organization for some time. But I never before got the opportunity to sit in with the ten who offer their lives. They need you tonight, Williams. Be easy, be assured, be above all, calm. There's our signal now."

The room became dark, curtains parted. A light immediately went on above my head. The room beyond the curtains was in blackness. Then the man at the end of the extremely long table called numbers.

One, two, three—and right on through to ten. Each time a number was called, a single electric bulb was supposed to light beside each white hand—or each dark sleeve. Then pencils moved rapidly as white fingers appeared.

Two lights remained out. Light Nine and Light Three, as the voice above Light One spoke.

"Our lights," he said slowly, "never fail. Number Nine Light is temporarily filled tonight. We all know this new light and respect him, for it is he who hides behind no darkness, creeps carefully into no building. It is he who makes our outside contacts. The enemy more than suspect him." And in a deep, solemn voice, "We pray for the dead and welcome the living. Number Nine. Light!"

A bulb snapped lit. Another moment of silence, and I guess every head was turned there in the darkness to where Number Three Light should be.

"Friends of humanity, The People Versus Crime." And Number One big shot was talking again. "We filled at once the vacancy made by Number Nine. It is our newly recommended friend who now holds the Number Three chair. That vacancy was not expected tonight." He waited a moment, and as Light Number Three snapped alive, "Its original owner has—" He paused and then directed his words to me.

"Mr. Williams, we welcome you again. Not perhaps with the same enthusiasm, the good cheers—the advancement of the work which so rapidly you have pushed along. Number Nine, Mr. Williams, has been murdered. Number Three, perhaps, too. And maybe another who served us well, and whom it may be hard to replace. We mourn our dead." And after a moment of silence. "Well, you do not speak."

"That's right." I let them have it. "I don't want to offend you lads—er—gentlemen." And then I laid it out. The words I spoke I felt. "I'm sorry, too, for anyone who got the dose. But I think these memorials are stupid. You're playing a game with death—sudden and violent, just as I play it. When you don't get the breaks, why squawk? I'll admit two or three in such a short length of time is tough going for a secret society. Get the point? Your society is not so secret any more. If you're asking my advice—"

Number One cut in like a falling icicle. "But we are not asking your advice. You are here to report—and claim your rewards."

"My pay, you mean. Well—" I tossed a lot of papers on the table, saw white hands grab them, move them along to the end of the table. "There's your evidence. There should be ten thousand dollars left out of the money you gave for petty cash, but I used it up myself—take it off my pay. Since then I knocked over Les Rankin which was just a bit of luck. I think he's a five-grand job."

THE NUMBER ONE guy was going over the stuff I brought to him. "Very good—remarkable what a man like you can do."

"Sure." I nodded. "Increase the ante, put up plenty more dough, and I'll raise the roof off the City Hall. Not in your line, maybe, but you could start a scandal rolling, and some newspaper would take hold and finish the job free."

"Please, Mr. Williams, let us not talk like thugs. Understand, I am not giving you orders—just a suggestion. We wish to place ourselves above—"

"Above me?" I cut in. "Listen. It's not how we put words together—it's not even our simple understanding of them. It's what you do with those words after they are spoken. We're all on edge a little tonight. No doubt you made a few mistakes, and so did I. But the thing to do is to polish up a slab in the morgue and reserve it for Orrey Bent. Now don't draw deep breaths. If you're going to uphold your reputation, you've got to put a card on Orrey Bent—the dead Orrey Bent."

"You think that is necessary at the moment—an actual killing, or rather complete evidence against him for murder?"

"Forget the evidence in this case." I leaned forward now on the table. "The cards struck me as silly at first—*The People Versus Crime*. Then I saw the worth of them—the fear they would throw into others—the only fear the criminal knows—death. An eye for an eye, a tooth for a tooth, and a corpse for a corpse." And when the man behind Light Number One would have cut in and even tapped on the table, I went right on.

"Don't let us talk about murder and self-defense. You started out a big advertising campaign. Now what? Vanderberg is killed, someone else on this board is missing—another lad gone. They'll be killed. Why? Because you've blown up on your ads. Hell, one guy walks into town and makes your ad worth nothing. He kills where he pleases and makes your organization look like a bunch of punks.

"Don't you see? You're big guys. You've got money. Look at me. I've got pride. I don't let anything be put over on me. I wouldn't even let a gunman—and I mean the best in the city—threaten my life, kill someone in my office without settling it up quick. I—I—" And damn it, I was stumped. I just waited. And then, "Orrey Bent is probably holding out for a while."

"No," said the Number One Light. "He's not exactly holding out as you put it. He is going to torture the man who sat behind Number Three Light for our names which he cannot give, for information he does not have. This Bent wants your information that comes to us. We have passed our word that each member must stand alone—die alone—before he gives any information damaging to our cause."

"And the other missing member?"

"I did not say member—and I'm not sure if another is missing. Mr. Havermore whom we all know—and who tonight takes the seat of Number Nine Light—has received those phone messages, hardly twenty minutes ago. Under the circumstances don't you think it wise to wait—to be sure to find out where he is?"

NUMBER FIVE MOVED restlessly. I got the impression that he rose. It was Number Five who had actually first talked this organization into hiring me, and I wanted to listen. Again the handkerchief covered the mouth of the speaker as it had the first time I heard that voice. I could see the white end of it flutter, as the husky voice spoke.

"I think I could send Mr. Williams to a place where he could find out for himself just where this Orrey Bent is. I think it would probably be a trap for his death—if he wants to go. There he could kill or be killed."

"Fine," I started when Number Three, the boy I had met in the hall, spoke.

"Let me," he said, "cast one vote for Race Williams and go on record as one vote for murder."

That started them off! But these men stuck to their rules.

Number One said: "We will have a vote. Number Five promises to furnish the information to Mr. Williams' satisfaction. I am against the word 'murder.' Let us vote 'yes' if he goes—'no' if he does not. Knowing Mr. Williams, I presume he wants the sanction of this committee, nothing more."

I pulled in my chin, spoke deeply, imitating Mr. Number One Lamp.

"I want nothing but the votes of this committee, not by lights, but by papers—papers so no one can tell how his friend votes. I want these papers handed to me—now."

WHY DID I want those votes on ballots? Why did I want them myself? Because a man with a number on him may speak from his head, from the thoughts others may have of him—from the fear that someone will find out and call him a killer—even worse, a murderer.

I was right. Every one of those papers but one read, *Yes,* and that single sheet had written on it, *Yes. I vote yes even to murder.*

Every one wrote as he believed—straight from his heart—straight back into his conscience. Get the significance of it? Ten out of ten votes "yes," and Number One was one of those voters.

"Gentlemen, I thank you," I said. "I have ten votes for murder."

Then on one sheet I saw the word, over. I turned the small slip, read the writing on the back.

This is the promised information. Mr. Timothy McGrath can tell you if he wishes. Make him wish.

It hit me all right—hit me hard. McGrath had been in this thing before. Oh, in a small way, perhaps, but when I was shot and in the hospital he came and gave me warning that I must take a long trip or be killed. He was wrong, of course, and later when I could have stuck

the attempted killing on him, I gave him a break. That doesn't sound like me you think? Well, maybe he got a break because I wanted to help someone else. But Dirty McGrath didn't know that—and he did get the break.

No more business was transacted after that. To have criminals killed, to supply evidence that gave them long terms or even a seat in the hot chair, these ten men took as a solemn act of justice performed by them in doing their duty. But when a couple of their own associates were grabbed off or knocked off in a single day or so, it put them into a flutter. Here they were talking about a couple of men when they were in the business of saving an entire city. And they were sure that Orrey Bent was the man behind it, the hand that now guided crime. Certainly Orrey was showing these wealthy executives quick action. They needed those machine gunners outside, needed twice that number.

What's more, at first they wouldn't give me the name of the missing Number Three Light. He was useless now, so I finally got it. Havermore told me. And it was a big name—at least a wealthy one. James Duncan, scion of a wealthy Philadelphia family.

Havermore said as we reached the ground floor: "The car has been attended to, the body removed. It's at the door for your convenience."

"Not mine." I shook my head. "I won't need it now. Find me another way out of this place. I won't be wanting that car tonight—now that I have information where to go."

"Oh, yes," he said. "But Number Five is gone. I must— Damn my soul, Williams. Number Five is one I don't know. He put in a great deal of money and now—"

"I got the information," I told him. "Guess you didn't see it reach me. I'm sorry I don't know Number Five. Is this the other exit?"

"Correct." He nodded gravely. "Take care of yourself, Williams. You heard Number Five say it will be a trap. You'll take the police with you, of course."

"Of course not," I told him. "I'll do this job alone." And as he followed me to the stone steps and stood half back in the deeper darkness, I added: "It's you who need protection."

He smiled wanly. "I carry a gun, and I have done a little practice with it. But I'm afraid it wouldn't do me much good. However, my car is calling for me. You wish to go alone?"

"That's right." I went down the steps and straight to the corner. There I turned, dropped into an areaway and looked back at the house and Richard Daniel Havermore standing on the steps. He moved forward now, lit a cigar and held the match ablaze a moment. A car moved down the street from me.

The big car drew up before Mr. Havermore. There was a chauffeur and a footman who got out to open the door, and inside I saw the form of another man and caught the flash of a gun.

Maybe I grinned, but certainly not derisively. Havermore needed protection all right—more than any man in the country, I guess. And he knew it, and was hiring it. Well, he was entitled to it all right.

As for me, I walked across town a way and took the subway uptown. Yes, I went straight to Dirty McGrath's house. Or rather, I went to Timothy McGrath's house. I didn't know yet. It was "Dirty" if I intended to get rough. "Tim" or "Tim, old boy" if I wanted to turn on the oil, and thought he'd take it.

CHAPTER 6

DIRTY McGRATH

I WAS STILL in that uncertain frame of mind when I rang the bell of that huge old dilapidated-looking house. I was practising one of those kid tricks with my face. You know, rubbing the hand over it bringing a smile—rubbing the hand back down and bringing a vicious look in its place.

That's exactly what I was doing with my pan—only I wasn't moving my hand over it—when a slovenly-looking maid opened the door. I asked if Mr. McGrath was home. She beckoned me in, showed me to a room where worn furniture was set up like the back room of an old-fashioned saloon. Maybe there weren't so many tables, but there were lots of chairs.

"I don't know if Mac is in or not," she said with easy informality. "Do you want me to take your name to someone who'll know, or do you want to write it on a piece of paper and seal it in one of those envelopes." And when I looked at the ink, the small oblongs of paper and the envelopes on the table, she went on: "Most times I can tell by your face—you'll be the writing kind I think."

It was all new to me, so her idea should be better than mine. That is, if I had an idea. So I wrote my name on a paper, started to write a message under it, and hesitated. I was going to say—Race Williams. It is important that you see me—important to you.

But I shook my head. If he didn't believe me or didn't want to see me, I couldn't chase him all over the house. And he might guess what I meant by important to him, take it as a threat. So I appealed to his curiosity.

I wrote—

Race Williams. It is important that I see you—important to me.

I sealed it, and the dirty-uniformed maid crept out of the room with it. She was a slow mover. I heard her feet in the hall. It was five minutes, maybe longer, for I had begun to pace the room, when feet came back. They shuffled, but they moved faster.

The old woman stood at the door. "Follow me," she said. "Don't be afraid. Himself has nothing ag'in you."

"I'm not afraid," I told her. "And I may have something ag'in Himself."

She snapped back: "I only say what I'm told to say. If you ask a question what I ain't expecting, I have no answer for you. Look out for the step."

I did look out for the single step. We went down a dark hall, stopped before a door, broad and heavy. The woman rapped on it. It was opened at once. A butler in full regalia greeted me.

"Come in, sir—come in. That will be all, Mrs. O'Toole."

And that was all. Just the closing of the door and a different setting. Lights shone brighter, though not too bright—and I was in a hall decorated in the finest of taste. By that I don't just mean money. Oh, money had been spent on it, but you didn't notice that. The picture of the old boy at the end was a masterpiece of painting. Yeah, I know. I don't know much about art, but I know class when I look at it. This part of Dirty—no Timothy McGrath's home was the real kind of class—not the lavish million-dollar home that spits gold in your eyes.

Another trot, another turn—and an open door, and I took a shock. Yep, McGrath could have raised a gun and shot my head off without batting an eye.

Oh, it wasn't the largeness, yet seeming cosiness of the library that got me. Or the fire before which McGrath sat with the pictures of his father and grandfather above his head. It wasn't even the leather-bound book in his hand. It was McGrath himself.

Damn it, he was wearing a dressing gown and slippers. He was clean-shaven and washed. There was a pipe in his mouth and an ease of manner about his whole attitude as he beckoned me to the chair near him.

"Sit down, Race." He looked at the tall drink beside him. "A little Irish Whiskey? No? Very well, O'Hara, you may go." And when the butler had disappeared and I took a look-see around that room, noting the balcony that surrounded it, the narrow stairs from that balcony above that widened out at the bottom, McGrath said: "No liquor. That means, Race, that you intend to kill a man tonight. There,

there, I know your habits—and you—at least tonight—are surprised at mine."

I WAS SURPRISED and admitted it. But I simply said: "Yeah. And they talk around as if you can't read or write. This must cost you a lot of money."

"A lot indeed. But you want something. You put your note quite correctly. If you had said it was important to me I would have taken it as a threat." He lifted his fingers to his neck, and for the first time I saw McGrath was wearing a soft collar instead of that stiff one he always wore outside. But his fingers played with his flabby chin just the same. So this was the lad I thought everybody was onto. Maybe they were outside. He made no pretense at being an honest man. He would fix anything for any man who voted right or brought out the votes. McGrath's district had grown bigger and bigger—yet it was always known to be in the bag—reckoned on long before any election.

He went on: "This is my night off. This is when I live as I want to live. See few people—and none who say it is important to me." He took the pipe from his mouth and pointed it at me. "I won't say you were unexpected, and I won't say it was a sudden whim to bring you into my inner sanctum. I shall expect, of course, that you do not speak of it to the outside world."

He didn't ask for any promise, didn't make any threats. He just said that as if it was understood. And before I could pound home what I was after, he continued.

"We shan't have a scene of violence, Mr. Williams. Certainly you could not shake me around as you did a certain party this afternoon, not because of weight only. You see, I give myself protection here."

"I could shoot you to death before any help would reach you. Don't tell me I couldn't escape in time—and don't make a movement toward a button or—"

He laughed. "There, there, Williams. I like the way you do things. Yes, right up to your threats of death. Tut, tut, there is no use to threaten me. My grandfather, my father—and myself, talked man to man with everyone who wished or dared to talk that way. They carried no guns, and I—well, I seldom carry any." He grinned broadly. "Except, perhaps, the one I admitted giving you at the hospital."

"I am afraid, Dirty McGrath, that you have made a mistake." I came to my feet, was very close to him, my gun out. "The information I want is very important—important enough to—"

He was on his feet suddenly. His great right hand came out and knocked my gun away from his stomach. His eyes narrowed and blazed, his lips trembled. I could have shot him dead, of course, but I didn't. One reason, that men just don't do those things when I go into my act. Another that I had stepped aside and still had plenty of time to blow a hole in him. He was a fool, had plenty of courage—or maybe I— But he was talking, and I was gaping—yep, my mouth was hanging open when he crashed through tight lips his reason for even risking his life.

"Don't you dare—killer or no killer! Don't you dare ever use that name to me in this part of the house. I introduced you here as a gentleman."

"Sure, sure." I tried to quiet him now. I'm—I'm—" Hell, I wouldn't apologize to him, not me—and then I half looked toward the stairs. "I'm sorry, Tim old boy." I put real feeling into my words.

"That's all right—that's all right." The red went out of his face, the pipe went in. "I'll give you what information you wish if it pleases me to give it." He broke off there, pretended that it was the first time he looked toward the stairs. There was no pretense on my part. I had heard the steps, seen the tiny pumps, the evening gown folded about the lithe young body—then her throat, face—and she was a knockout.

McGrath hesitated, my gun dropped from sight, and the girl came slowly down the stairs. She stood at the bottom of the steps. McGrath didn't speak, and neither did I.

Then the girl crossed the room, speaking as she came.

"I'm sorry, Father, but I didn't think you had company." And turning straight toward me with chin tilted and eyes blue-bright, "I know you, of course. You're Race Williams. I'm Ione McGrath. I have always wondered, Mr. Williams, if you are as bad as—as the papers describe you."

She didn't put out her hand, so I didn't put out mine. I said simply: "I'm bad enough."

After that I guess she stood there a bit, and I guess she talked. I know she explained recognizing me from my picture in the papers—and I know that I was looking straight down at her golden hair. She was a pip—there were no two ways about it. And she did throw me for a minute. Not because of her beauty—I've seen too many dames for that—but because she was McGrath's daughter. And all at once I knew why McGrath was dressed up—and I knew why he had such swell diggings—and I knew why he had actually risked his life rather than have his daughter hear him called "Dirty."

The girl's hand slipped out from somewhere beneath her evening wrap and gripped mine. She said: "It is thrilling to meet you, Mr. Williams—the notorious Mr. Williams."

"The word is famous—if anything." I let her have it straight back.

Her hand was soft and white like an advertisement come to life, but McGrath took her from me, led her to the stairs, kissed her on the forehead. I didn't object. McGrath was the referee, and he saw that we broke clean in the clinches.

He stood and watched her up the stairs to the balcony above, where she paused and called down to him. "I just wanted to know if you liked my dress. You generally want to see me before I go out."

"You look elegant," McGrath snapped, and I nodded a silent agreement. Then she was gone.

I said: "She's a fine-looking girl. I heard somewhere that you had a daughter, but never—"

"That's right. That's why I grew so angry. She's everything I've got to live for—and living for her I must hide most of my life from her. That's why I have the rooms outside so that my—" he put his finger to his neck and wiggled his Adam's apple—"well, my constituents won't see me living in such a grand style." And when I waved a hand toward the filled bookcases, "Yes, the books are fake, Race." He pulled out a leather-bound volume of Shakespeare, a first edition of Thackeray, Shelley's poems in hand-tooled Morocco. He tossed them all on the table, said: "They're to impress her. I wouldn't give a hoot in hell for any book in this library— that is, any one you can see."

"She's class, Tim—real class. I won't spoil things by talking about her." I walked up and down a bit, finally said: "I've got business, Tim, and the death of one man—perhaps two—may rest on minutes, even seconds."

"I understand, Race. We won't go into details. You'd never gain anything by threatening me—no, nor even making that threat good by killing me. And I'm glad you didn't, though somehow I knew you wouldn't bring my daughter's name into it. I'd have torn you apart if—" His chest seemed to swell, his great neck thicken, and his huge hands raise. No, Dirty McGrath in the finery of his own home was not the ingratiating ward-heeler he appeared before big shots in politics.

HE DIDN'T SPEAK again—or maybe he couldn't. He was bloated up with his own wind, and couldn't get it all out the little hole in his face. I helped him out by putting a finger hard against his chest and saying: "Maybe some day I'll do a good turn for your girl, Tim."

"Don't get the idea I'm doing you a good turn, Race." He got it out and the breeze with it. "I know what you're after and am giving you the address you want,

and perhaps sending you to your death. Not a bad thought at other times. But tonight—somehow I'm not so anxious to see you killed." And with a sigh of great resignation, and in a voice that left me with the feeling that McGrath wouldn't lose much sleep over anything that happened to me, he said: "You asked for the information, and you got it. You must go alone. A police escort will be useless. They'd be spotted before you could enter the house. It's inside they'll trap you."

"How is it you know so much, Tim? You were mixed up with these same people not so long back when you offered me ten thousand dollars to get out of the city."

"That's right." He nodded. "What I know I have learned through forty years of—well, you'd call it crime. I'd call it politics. What you know is bought by others. Look out you don't find out that your secret society has bought your death."

"You have nothing personal in this matter. Yet it is understood you fixed it for Orrey Bent's return—a slick-haired gent."

"Nothing at all personal, Race. I make my money fixing things for—well, perhaps, a slick-haired gent. That is my business. He has paid me well. He has seen my daughter. Let me know if you shoot him out of the picture. I'm a little old for killing, Race. Yes"—he looked up at the pictures on the wall—"great men both my father and my grandfather. Yes, I could kill if necessary. Good-bye—good luck."

At the door he said: "I don't believe you appreciate what I permitted you tonight."

"In reference to my death?"

"No." He was very solemn. "In reference to my girl. I permitted you to meet her."

"I did—and do appreciate it, Tim," I said, and meant it. No man could not mean it if he stood as I did with Timothy McGrath. Yep, the same Dirty McGrath who robbed the city, stole money from the private citizens, favored criminals at a price. Yet he had the largest list to which he gave charity, a list that topped even the biggest politicians'. Some said it was not his heart, though they never knew where his money went. The big boys just thought, "Tim spends the money. Tim gets out the votes."

There was no understanding McGrath. I had always looked on him as small-time stuff no matter what was said. Now I began to think of the talk downtown— that some day Tim would be mayor of the great city. There wasn't anyone who had anything worthwhile on him. He had gotten things straightened out for Bent though—but now he had gotten Bent straightened out for me. At least I hoped he had.

CHAPTER 7

ON THE KILL

THE CAR DREW to the curb so suddenly when I turned the corner that I chucked myself flat on my face and swung my body around, was closing my fingers on two guns.

The girl laughed. "You certainly know the tricks, Race. If I had had a machine gun I would have gotten you on the roll toward the gutter. What's this diving all over the street going to get you if—"

"Never mind that. What are you doing here anyway, Jane?"

"Just obeying orders," she said. "Jerry stepped out for a minute to get some sandwiches. So I took the call."

Jerry was my right-hand man—boy rather. I had picked him up in the underworld, trained him—and he always obeyed my orders.

"You mean you sent him out for sandwiches—and I didn't call the apartment at all."

"Oh, someone fooled me then," she said in mock surprise. "Where do you want to be driven to?" And suddenly, "Did you come from Dirty McGrath?"

"It doesn't matter if I came from Mr. McGrath's or not."

"Oh"—she was sweet as cream gone sour, but which still looks sweet—"it's Mr. McGrath now. After all, it was a girl's voice on the phone asking Jerry to come here for you. Did you meet the refined Mr. McGrath's daughter?"

She was driving now in the direction I had given her.

I said in feigned surprise: "Has he got a daughter?" And remembering that most of Jane's life—in fact, nearly all of it—had been lived in the underworld, "Has this daughter—I can't think of the color of her eyes. Were they blue now? The girl I saw there had red hair—or was it golden?"

The brakes jammed on, and I nearly went through the windshield.

Jane said: "So you met her then. You

did meet her. Why the dirty little tramp who—"

I stuck out my hand flat, pushed it against her mouth. Jane was the girl of the underworld again, the little wildcat I had known. But I gave it to her straight.

"Open that door and hop out before I bounce you onto the street. I picked you out of the underworld and gave you a real name with money back of it. I've let you haunt me, toss your stuff in my apartment. Now get out of my car—and get out of my life. No half-brained doll—"

She cut in then. "I'm sorry, Race—really sorry. There's got to be a woman in your life. There's a woman in every man's life. I love you—I'm jealous. I'm—"

"You're a damn nuisance." I was telling her the truth now. "I've got a job that recognizes no sex line."

"I—I could kill someone tonight," she said as if she weren't listening to me.

"You can, and I'm going to, but I don't blame you for that. If it does you any good, here's the truth. Do you think I'm in love with you?"

"No, no," she said. And slowly, "But I think you're going to be."

"The 'no' part is right," I said. "We'll get things straight for tonight anyway. I'm no more in love with the McGrath girl than I am with you—and I saw her once. Now beat it."

But she had changed at once.

"You'll need me tonight. I can guess where you're going—what you intend to do. I read the papers." And she turned hard, even slightly tough—the way I didn't like her to be. "Listen, Race, you'll need this car for a get-away. You'll need

a driver if you have to shoot. I have a rod with me that would poke a hole through the Statue of Liberty—or even Orrey Bent."

"You win." I looked at those slits of eyes. Jane had come through before, and I could use a car. "Drive to—" And after figuring out how far the house was from the place I wanted to park, I gave her the directions. I said also: "Now give me your gun."

The car started again. Jane said, and there was cold hardness in her voice: "I haven't got any rod. I was kidding you, Race." And turning sharply as I put an arm behind her. "I don't mind being suspected of lying, but I don't like being pawed over—"

I let it go. She was tough to handle—all that refinement had slipped off her like whiskey down a drunk's throat. I said simply: "My life depends on the way you act tonight."

"How about mine?" She took the corner neatly, hit forty to the next block, and swung to the curb. "Will I cruise around or wait right here?"

I looked up at the house, looked too at the clock far distant. It was not yet eleven o'clock.

"If I'm alive and make it—and have to get from under—I'll come over the back fences."

"And if you're dead—what am I to do?" Her voice was cold as steel.

"If I'm dead," I said, "go haunt slick-haired Orrey Bent. Maybe you can confuse him so that he'll take a dose of lead later."

She was out of the car, grabbed me by both arms. Her slender fingers were strong—and bit like thin strips of steel.

"You don't mean that, Race. You don't mean that I hurt you—more than I help you. You don't mean that!"

"What else could I mean?" I tried shrugging my shoulders. "Having a woman hung around my neck for—"

"You don't mean it. Answer 'yes' or 'no.'"

Jane was the stuff all right. I had seen her turn sharply and put a gun on a lad and make him spring back—not because of what was in her gun or her steady hand, but because of what was on her face. It was on her face now.

"You don't mean it," she said again.

And she got me. I looked down at the beautiful little face all distorted now with hate, with vengeance—call it what you will, perhaps even the lust to kill. Understand, I only say maybe. But I answered her. I couldn't help it. I said: "No, no, Jane. I don't believe that."

And hell, there on the side street she did it. Just threw both arms about my neck and pecked me on the ear. Surprised? Well, I'm telling the truth, I was holding a gun against her chest—but I don't think she knew that.

Then she was back in the car. Simple words, cheerful words—but the same hardness in her voice.

"I'll be waiting for you, Race. I'm sure you'll come through. I only wish I were on the kill tonight."

At least that's what I think she said as I went down the block in the opposite direction from the lighted drug store on one corner. I rounded the corner, made the short block—then headed straight down toward the house—the number McGrath had given me. It was of worn red brick with stone steps, just like the others on that block.

Fear? No, I don't think I know the meaning of that word. Thrill? Yes, I got that. This was big stuff. I walked steady and straight with my hat pulled down, but I could see—and I could hit anyone who popped out of an areaway that was in front of each building. McGrath might have lied to me. He might be sending me to my death.

How to get in? I simply turned up the steps of the house, pressed the bell on the outer door—and when no answer came at once, I went to work.

I knocked out the glass with my hand, took a long reach and opened the outer door. All in a few seconds. I tapped once at the inner door, started to kick hell out of it, then to hurl my body against it and as I got ready for the final entrance—a few bullets through the lock.

Unexpected? Don't ask me. This was no job at all—or it was a killing job. I had no intentions of hiding my presence.

Anyway I got action. A light went on, feet pattered, and the door opened.

I WALKED STRAIGHT in and set the Japanese servant back about ten feet with my chest. He caught his balance, went into a Donald Duck monologue. Then I cut him off sharp.

I twisted two guns into my hands. He looked blank and chirped in a bird-like voice that could be heard all over the place: "You police—no?"

"No is correct." Then I stepped forward, lifted my gun up and down. It was the blow with my gun that knocked him to the floor, but it was his own idea to hit it with his face.

A voice called: "That sounds like you, Williams." And with a slight laugh, a nervous laugh, I hoped, "At least the body hitting the ground had that familiar touch of yours. Come down the hall, turn at the door that is slightly open and enter. I've been expecting you—though not by the front door."

"I was coming anyway," I called.

The voice was somewhere there in the back of the house beyond the stairs. As I passed those stairs, I swung back quick and laid two bullets into the darkness.

Had I heard anything? Well, I don't know. Had I seen anything? Well, I don't know about that either. But I had felt something—yes, my shoulder had brushed against something stiff, and hard.

I'm always complaining about the breaks in life. I won't any more. I just let my mouth hang open as the man tumbled down the stairs, rolled over once still clutching the Tommy gun. Now if that isn't hauling something out of the grabbag of life, I don't know what a lad wants.

A voice hollered—and it was Orrey Bent. "Good God, Race, let this be a harmless visit. Are you hurt?" I didn't answer at once because I had seen the light down the hall. Someone, and from the sound of the voice, Bent himself had opened the door of the room he was in just a tiny bit—and him telling me it was slightly open before.

I said as I went down the hall: "Peace-ful mission is right. A mad dog fell down the stairs with a Tommy gun and broke his leg. It was only charitable to put him out of his misery." And was he out! One bullet had gone through the side of his head just as if he had pointed out the place to me.

Someone in that room whispered: "That was Pete—he should have been in the back. Now no one is in the—"

"Shut up," Orrey Bent said. "This Williams always likes to do his own work."

I was at the door that was open a sliver now. Standing before it, ready, I said: "Orrey, you had your chance to skip town today. I have come alone tonight. I want you to understand the full significance of my visit. I'm on the kill."

There was a moment of silence, and then, "Really?" Orrey kept his voice pretty steady, but there was a tremor in it just the same. "I thought you wanted to make a deal—about some chaps you were looking for. You know me, Race. You got in—if I'm in a tough spot I'll talk."

"Your spot," I told him, "is too tough to talk. I'm opening the door—a few seconds now—then have your guns out—and use them if you can."

"Fine, Race! Well, that's downright nice of you. Come in. Come in gently. I think my little set-up will take this talk of death out of you. Oh, you're in the house now, Race. You can't go out again. There are two men in the front. They were to let you enter—but not to exit."

I don't know if I believed him or not. But if he was telling the truth, my words must have jarred him. "Those two men are both dead. I'm coming in. I'm bringing death with me."

I won't say I heard him chuckle. But I do know he was ready for me. And I do know, and he didn't that I was ready for him. Sure, there are more ways of entering a room than gripping the knob and opening it slowly. I'd give Bent something new in death, though he'd never use it.

I COVERED THAT hall with my eyes as I took one long, soft step forward. Then I lifted my knee high, pulled it close back to my body. After that I stretched back my left hand, let the gun in it hang from my thumb as I braced my hand against the wall of the staircase. And, bang! I let my right foot go.

"Surprise!" I yelled, and shot the gunman dead who knelt beside the desk behind which Orrey Bent sat. Oh, I saw the rest of the picture, the horrible picture in the far right-hand corner. I saw the great curtains that covered the entire back of that room, and I saw, too, the man at my left who lay stretched out upon the floor, a gun in each hand. His face was mashed up considerably—and there was a great cut, a gap rather, in his forehead. When I kicked that door open I knew what I was facing. Knew it just as well as if I had had a look-see.

I didn't more than glance at the horrible sight to the right in the far corner. But I saw enough. A man was standing right upon a closed trap door. On his shoulders were huge feet—a big man who had trouble supporting himself. He had trouble because his hands were bound around his back and a circle of rope was pretty tight around his neck. A movement of that man below, and the man above would drop.

Yes, he would drop to death. For that noose was only short while he stood there. It gave him no support except his pressing hard on the man below and so forcing his own head against the huge beam above it.

And I saw, too, in my split-second glance, that the rope around his neck was really long—not short, for the rest of the rope was coiled neatly upon the plank.

The room was high, the fall might break his neck before he reached the floor, but certainly the longer drop through that trap door, if it were open, would snap his neck as surely as though it were a tiny bit of dead branch.

The man who held him so I knew to be the missing Number Three Light—James Duncan. That man above had a heavy towel wrapped around his head. There was no doubt that he saw me through the slits.

But the main attraction was Slick Hair—Orrey Bent. He sat there with two guns in his hands, his elbows resting on his desk. I said to him: "Well, you've got the guns. Why not try them out?"

"You watch my fingers too closely, Race. You watch for the white upon my tightening fingers that will mean my death. No, Race, at this time I have no desire to match my physical skill against yours." He tapped some papers on his desk. "But I have already matched my mental skill against your client's—The People Versus Crime. These documents were gathered by you—evidence that will burn certain men—send others away for a long stretch—a simple memorandum where dead men can be found. Your work—delivered by you to The People Versus Crime—documents that were to go to the authorities who prosecute. Well, I have intercepted the messenger who delivers them. No, he was no member of your organization, but he shall carry no more information to the authorities—dear gentle souls."

"He is dead." It was more a statement than a question.

"Perhaps not quite dead—but he hasn't much longer to live. His death is slow—and horrible."

He looked up at the men, the under one beginning to sag at the knees, looked down at his own left foot, said: "I am holding a board in place with my foot. If you shot me it would slip. The man below whom you must recognize as James Duncan, the Number Three gentleman of your unpleasant organization, drops through the trap to the floor below. But the man above—he has nothing to offer me but curses. He dies at the end of the rope. Shall we make a deal?"

"No deal, Orrey." My fingers were burning on my gun triggers, but I could also see the board waving up and down as his foot moved to the side of his desk. "Your death is worth more than their lives. Don't be foolish."

Orrey Bent said: "Well, I don't doubt your word there, and I appreciate such flattery coming from you. Let us say that the man on the top is worth more than my life. Let us say that your organization may wish them to live rather than to have me die. I shall not appeal to the mercenary end of it, but I will let them both

go safely for my life. There, you take your orders." He nodded at the phone on his desk. "Call up Mr. Richard Daniel Havermore—you see, I know quite a bit about your organization—and—"

And I did it. I dropped to one knee as I fired—once—twice. Under ordinary circumstances it wasn't a hard shot—that bit of rope between the planking and the toweled man's neck.

OF COURSE, I fired at Orrey Bent at the same time. Oh, I didn't expect to hit him. It was just a wild, blind shot. To split that rope was the thing.

I think the strands parted. I don't know. But the board was gone—and the trap had dropped.

The man who held the other upon his shoulders disappeared into the black hole below. The man above had guts. Instinctively he knew what had happened. He tossed his body, swung it to avoid the trap that he must have thought meant death. And he stopped suddenly. I watched the rope snap, and saw the man spread out over the edge of the trap and lay upon the floor. His acrobatics were good, but my shot helped considerably.

And Orrey Bent? He was on his feet. He fired twice—once from his left hand and once from his right. They were close, I guess, or maybe they weren't. But I turned and faced him. Yep, faced him with a gun in each hand. I didn't shoot then. I put the old smile on him as I spread my legs far apart.

He fired again, plaster hit the floor and I simply laughed. I wanted Orrey Bent to know the truth when he took it. Maybe I wanted him to kneel upon the floor and beg for mercy. Maybe—but a shadow entered the door. Had I waited too long? Certainly not too long to kill Orrey—but perhaps too long to save my own life.

There was stark terror in Orrey Bent's eyes. His arms shook, those eyes bulged, his mouth hung open. And that was all of Orrey. He took my slug like it was a lead pill—just swallowed it. At least it disappeared in his open mouth.

Nothing from the door as yet. I turned, jerked up my gun and said: "O'Rourke! What—how—are you alone?"

"That was the condition under which I came, Race. Do you want me to take care of this shambles? God in Heaven, man, you can't keep your name out of this!"

"Who sent you here—McGrath? There, don't stare like that. I said McGrath."

O'Rourke finally laughed. "Does Dirty McGrath talk like a woman or am I—"

"Jane." I said the name under my breath. "Well, I'd have sent for you now anyway." I gave O'Rourke quick orders. "The man in the cellar—let him go unless—" And I stopped. A voice came from below. "I am perfectly safe. I will report your actions to The People Versus Crime."

"Now what the hell was that?" O'Rourke rubbed at his head. "He talked like—like some of those cards I sort of think you sprinkle around. You know, with the reading matter— *People*—"

And I was at the desk. Looking over the papers—papers that astounded me. They were my affidavits, my reports on criminals for the police to raid.

I turned and knelt beside O'Rourke. The man on the floor was struggling now. I cut the cords off his hands, tore the towel from around his head, took the gag from his mouth. He tried to speak, took the water O'Rourke gave him—and I held the knife—then didn't cut loose his feet. He was in a roaring rage.

"Give those papers to me. They are mine. Bent took them from me. I am the man who—"

I placed a foot gently on his mouth, handed the papers to O'Rourke.

"Look, Sergeant," I said. "This is the sort of evidence that you'll get. It'll make you tops again with the commissioner. You take it. From now on you'll get all of it."

So I lifted my foot off the mouth of Inspector Iron-man Nelson. He could talk now—and did.

Men
in
Black

THE GIRL IN
THE ROLLS

I STOOD IN the doorway killing a butt—thinking. Well, maybe. I don't generally go in for heavy thinking. It doesn't get me far in my business. And my business just at present was the softest job I had landed in years. I mean soft if you don't mind getting a bullet in your head any time of the day or night. But here I was, paid high—damn good and high—because lads wanted to shoot at me. The funny part of it was, lots of guys always wanted to shoot at me, whether I was paid to prevent it or not.

From a rough and ready lad who had a permit to carry a gun and the itch to shoot it—I had turned into a slick, quick thinking private detective who could lay his hands on anyone in the city.

At least that's the way the boys on the police force and the crooks along the Avenue looked at it.

"Say it isn't true, Race. Say it isn't true," was the kidding I got from the right guys. And it wasn't true. That is, the thinking part of it. But it was true that I could let you name any criminal in or out of the city that the cops couldn't find, and I could lay my finger on him or tell you where he was in twenty-four hours.

If you want to make the bet a big one, I'll make it twelve hours.

The scheme was new—and the setup was simple. Big, influential men in the city had raised a fund of several hundred thousand dollars and it was mounting daily. They called themselves, P.V.C.—The People Versus Crime. When they wanted to find some particular tough criminal who was interfering with their business or with Society in general, they just gave me the word to find him. And they gave me with those orders any amount of money I asked for.

I could find a little criminal for a few hundred bucks—bigger ones for a few thousands—and the best in the business from ten grand right on up to a hundred grand.

Easy? Hell, any criminal would give up his own brother for that amount of money. Why, I just slipped the good news that I had jack for information—then sat down and waited for the information to roll in.

Why hadn't anyone ever thought of it before? Well maybe it wasn't altogether new. The government sticks up the picture of a five-time murderer in the post offices, lets you look at a face that would scare your whole family stiff, and under it the offer of two hundred and fifty dollars reward. Why, as a matter of fact you'd spend twice that money avoiding a meeting with the deadly killer. But if they offered fifty thousand reward they'd have to install a new telephone switchboard and hire ten or twelve more girls to take the calls that would come in.

This bunch of millionaires started their racket to wipe out rackets. And there was one big racket they especially wanted to bust. That of the Bent boys who had just come back in the city—and who were foolish enough to start gunning for me. It is not enough to say that they didn't shoot right, and it may sound immodest to say that I never shoot wrong. Let's put it that they both were dead—and I was alive and you can form your own opinion.

But now it seemed that the Bent boys were not exactly as big as—

THESE THOUGHTS, OR ramblings, suddenly turned to business. The girl was coming out of the office building, hitting it straight toward the big car at the curb—and the chauffeur who wasn't in it. A nice job—I mean the car—it was a Rolls. And the girl was a nice job too. Not the girl I expected— not the girl I was there to meet—Jane Blake—but an entirely different girl.

I had met her only once, but I recognized her—trick hat, blue eyes, blonde hair. And the tiniest feet—at least the tiniest shoes anyone ever got feet into.

But this was no time for descriptions of dames.

I stepped out of the doorway, saw her reach her car and look up and down for her chauffeur. Then I saw the finely dressed young gentlemen I had been watching. Two of them sauntered from the street, from behind her car, and one from the car ahead. She seemed about to cry out, then she didn't. I couldn't see the gun. I couldn't know that the men were anything but friends, for the man facing her tipped his hat and did the talking. No, I couldn't know as she faltered, moved toward the big black car ahead that these men were threatening her.

That's right—I couldn't know. But I did. Ione McGrath, daughter of Dirty McGrath was being kidnaped right on the public street. Few men knew that Dirty McGrath, the uptown fixer and apparently small politician, was blowing himself up to control the entire city.

She might have screamed and died. She might have screamed and gotten away with it. But she was near the car now, one of the men swinging open the rear door when I reached the little party, and before any of them saw me I spoke my piece. I didn't know if they knew who the girl actually was, so I didn't make a social error.

I spoke simply.

"If you guys want your bodies smeared all over the public streets, why turn around with guns in your hands. Race Williams speaking," was what I said.

I always like to add my own name to an unknown situation. No one can claim then that his friend didn't know he was going to get his head blown off if he tried gun tricks.

Only one guy turned. His face wasn't much in his favor. He showed no rod, but his mouth opened like a sixteen-inch gun and the words that came out of it were as foul as his breath. He said, without quoting the adjectives: "Mr. P.V.C. Williams,

this dame is going to go with us. And you take orders from me. O.K." He swung open the rear door wider, turned and glared triumphantly at me. "So—you got orders—what are you going to do about it?"

I didn't really kick him. I just raised my leg and pushed him. He was sort of leaning forward, bent nicely for my foot to fit into his stomach. No, I didn't kick him, but I shoved him so quickly into the car that he nearly went out the other side.

I said to the girl without turning my head: "Go back to your own car—stand almost in the middle of the sidewalk. Holler—if you have reason to holler." And when the girl was gone I said to the men: "And I don't want any of your guff—that goes for the driver too. I want to speak to the man on the floor."

He was able to talk and was cursing me out. Making threats of future violence and others of retribution or vengeance—everything but what he was going to do right then. He'd never have talked to me like that unless he had lost his head or didn't know me—or had someone behind him, someone he thought had authority over me. Anyway, I stopped his yelping.

I leaned against the door and said: "What do you mean by P.V.C.? Come on, before I blow a hole in your stomach. Come on!"

He wasn't so tough any more—and the others had left him. I saw them go. The man behind the wheel shut off the motor and slipped away—and the others started up the street in the opposite direction from the girl. No, they wouldn't get in some doorway and plug me—but just in case they would, I climbed into the car.

The man on the floor said: "P.V.C.—you know."

I sat down on the seat and looked at him there on the floor. I let a gun from my left shoulder holster drift easily into my right hand.

I said rather lazily: "Cars, whistles, people—a hundred chances that the shot won't be heard. Tell me more."

He squirmed at my feet.

"It means People Versus Crime."

I SHOOK MY head, took out a card with *The People Versus Crime* printed on it and dropped it on his chest— the death notice.

"Come on, fellow," I encouraged. "I left that notice on a few stiffs myself. It won't be hard to find. Who sent you? Name the real people—or out you go."

I could see his face grow white down there in the dimness. It was a tough racket, working for those hooded figures who gave me orders. No one likes to kill—just kill. But here was a man who would use our cards of warning—my cards of warning. No, it wasn't safe to let him live. I half closed my finger on the trigger—then had the thought that I might frighten him enough not to try that stuff again. But he spoke before I had a chance to raise my gun. He thought I was going to kill him.

He said: "The men in black. They sent me."

Yes, you could have knocked me down with a wagon load of brick. I got up, climbed over him to the door, and out of the car. I slammed the door and walked down to where the girl should have been. She wasn't there. And then I saw Jane Blake, the girl I had expected to meet. She was coming out of the same building.

"I'm late, Race. I'm sorry, but—"

She stopped dead. A voice called. It came from the Rolls at the curb. There was a chauffeur at the wheel now. The blue eyes of Ione McGrath sparkled. I turned to explain to Jane—and a cloudburst of wisdom struck me—one of my sudden inspirations. I ran to the Rolls, heard Jane call, swung open the door and slapped myself down beside the girl. I had the door closed before we were in traffic. I looked back once and saw Jane Blake standing there in the middle of the sidewalk staring after us—and I saw the middle-aged, kindly looking man who unavoidably bumped into her. But that wasn't the point. The point was the jar she gave that man in return—and the hardness of the Avenue that was in her eyes—and not Fifth Avenue, where she now belonged.

Ione McGrath said: "It was fine of you to do that for me—risk your life." And then in surprise, "Why you're the man I met at father's for a minute one evening. You're Race Williams. You did this for father."

I turned and took a good look at her. Pretended or real surprise, I didn't care. But people don't travel around this city misunderstanding me. I gave it to her flat.

"Kid," I said, "your father may be all right to you—and I'm not saying he didn't do me a good turn once—but I did him one first. At the same time I wouldn't raise a hand for him—unless it was for my own interests."

"Oh." She seemed rather gentle and timid. "So it was to your interest to save me—you thought my father being such a big man might do something to help you."

I COULD HAVE laughed in her face, but I didn't. "Lads help me sometimes," I told her the truth. "But I'm a lone worker, and I wouldn't raise a hand to help your old man for any reason of any kind."

"Then you think my interests will be your interests—so that's why you helped me."

I shrugged my shoulders, then said: "All right—have it your way. Your father hasn't any use for me. I don't care. Probably you haven't any use for me, and I don't care about that either."

"And you haven't any use for me?"

"Not a bit. But you were like a kid in the wilderness. It just struck me that if you were—er—my kid, I'd want a guy to give you a break."

"I think," she said slowly, "that's a very nice feeling, Mr. Williams. At least I hope it is. But I was born and brought up in the city—and the wilderness seems—"

I said to the chauffeur: "Turn here at the corner and stop at the first place you strike down the block." And when he did, "Now get out—come on, get!"

"Listen"—the chauffeur turned and looked at me—"I don't take orders from you."

"Brother"—I put a gun in his back—"take it on the run. If I let you go back McGrath would— Shut up! Now get out." And when he opened the door reluctantly, "Come on, or you'll fall out dead. I don't know your story. If you think it's good enough, let me know where McGrath can find you."

He stood on the sidewalk now—his hard, sharp face and his mean eyes staring out from under his chauffeur's cap.

"Tell McGrath that he'll find me in Brazil." He turned and was gone.

The girl said: "We've had him for nearly two years. I know he's pretty crude, but—"

"You could have his kind for seventy years, and if someone offered him a piece of jack he'd— But there, climb in the front and drive. I should know what you can do with money. Loyalty is counted in dollars and cents." And as she dropped behind the wheel and made the silent motor do tricks, "I can't see how your father ever let you get into such a mess."

She raised her head.

"People would think twice before harming Timothy McGrath's daughter."

I was about to give her the horse laugh when I took a good look at her soft skin, the deep double blue of her eyes, the finely shaped mouth. I said seriously: "Certainly, I would think twice about harming Ione McGrath."

And as we neared McGrath's home, a huge, sloppy, dreary house on one street, and an elaborate and freshly painted one on the other, I asked: "Which side?"

"Why the front." And slightly perplexed, "There is just the one entrance."

So she wasn't on to the rear entrance—indeed, the rear part of the house where Dirty McGrath entertained his political friends—crooks and what-nots, and, if I do admit it, fed the poor. Either she was not aware of it or she lied. But she took me into the terraced driveway. I hopped around and opened the door for her with a flourish.

"I'd like to borrow the car, Ione." I had hard work dropping her hand. "But for you—for Tim McGrath's daughter—that buggy is dangerous. He has enemies, kid—enemies that would hurt him through you. A Ford is your meat—a tired little man to drive it—a little man who can shoot at any speed. I know that man and— Good-bye."

She held my hand.

"Come in and have lunch with me. I eat alone—always alone at lunch and most times at dinner. But do come in. I'll tell you things about myself."

CHAPTER 2

DIRTY McGRATH

WE HAD LUNCH in an open room off the terrace—a long stretch of grass to the high iron picket fence. We talked and she sure did tell me things. Her head was held high as she talked of her father.

"I know he's a politician and they don't think much of politicians at a girls' school. At least at first they didn't. I used the name of my aunt—Ione McBane—and someone said"—her head went higher—"that my father—that Mr. McGrath was a crook. I told them the truth then, showed the newspaper clippings I always kept. The picnics for the poor kids—the trips up the Hudson River twice a year—the many things he had done. But I went to another school— the Norwood Seminary. It's the best in the country. And I went under my own name."

She paused a long time.

"I wasn't liked by the other girls at first. The teachers made them like me— and afterwards, they just liked me." She leaned over the table, took my hand, "Is my father a very bad man?"

I ducked on that one a bit, muttered something about finding him all right around.

"Oh, I know he goes out a lot—that he visits some unsavory people," she shot in. "And I know that they see him here at times. But that's politics, isn't it? He gives plenty to the poor, takes care of many families."

"He does all of that," I agreed, but I didn't tell her that was just his racket.

Then she pulled her bombshell, and gripped my wrist tightly as she pulled it. Catch a load of this.

She said: "Mr. Williams—Race— believe how I mean this when I say it. Is my father a man like you—is he as bad as you?"

Silent? Sure, I was stunned to silence. Twice I tried to get the words out, then had to change them altogether. Finally I gave it to her rough anyway. Good God, I had to!

I said: "You read nothing but good things in your papers about your father, and bad things about me if you believe killing bad." More I didn't want to say— less, I couldn't.

She said: "What you do is different. I look upon you as a friend. But my father— all that I have heard outside is bad. All that I see of him is good. I'd—" She put her hand across her mouth suddenly and screamed: "Father!"

And I saw him too—saw him in the mirror across the room. He was coming straight toward me—toward my back. His hat was slammed on his head, he was unshaven, his coat was none too clean. He was the McGrath that his immediate outside world knew. Dirty McGrath— district leader with the few dollars he made—shared with the poor. But he was not playing the outside role now—nothing meek and ingratiating. He was the big boss who gave orders in his district, and if what I had heard lately was true—the big boss who gave orders downtown.

Yes, it was Tim McGrath, the last of the three great McGraths. And he was in a towering rage.

I was on my feet, turning and facing him as he came—great hands stretched out toward my throat—powerful hands that could easily crush a man's neck and probably had, earlier in his career.

"What are you doing here? What do you mean by taking advantage of my daughter because I showed you a kindness!" And his hands moved and clutched my shoulders, bit into them like iron fingers—just as my gun slid into my right hand. He didn't see the movement. His hands held my shoulders, and he spat his words out through half-broken teeth.

"Father—Father!" I don't think the girl could rise from her seat, facing him. "You—like that—I never saw you when—"

His right hand moved, closed into a fist. It swung back from my shoulders, was poised as his left hand shifted and gripped at my throat.

"She's your kid, Dirty," I said, and the name, "Dirty," just came out without my meaning it. As his hand hesitated, I added: "I'm willing to let this incident slide for her sake. She's never seen you like—"

He muttered unintelligible syllables and then the words came.

"I start things and I finish them, Race." And his right hand swung.

There was no talking, no ducking, no trying to reason with him. I just had to do it, and I did it. I let him have it with my gun.

McGrath was a big man—a strong man, and I wasn't fooling when I struck. My hand jerked up—a short, quick jolt. My gun landed flush on his chin with a speed and viciousness that nearly tore his great head from his shoulders.

McGrath was a strong man—and I guess a fearless one. I don't know of any man who wouldn't have smacked his face down on the rug after that crack. But Mac stayed on his feet. Oh, he was jarred back. His eyes swam, but he was swaying on his feet there before his back had even struck the wall. Yes, swaying—and lumbering forward again.

"You're a strong man, McGrath," I told him as I heard feet running somewhere in that house. "It's your house. You've got friends. If you can't control your rage—I'll have to make it a kill."

I side-stepped then as the girl came from around the table. I have learned to trust no one in this business. But the girl was on her father, clinging to him, crying out: "You must be mad! Race Williams just saved my life. Perhaps from a terrible death by enemies of yours. They—four, five— Oh, I don't know how many. I was kidnaped."

"Where?"

He stepped back—straightening his tie as men in the soft black of servants, but with the hard pans of gangsters began to appear.

It was Ione who ordered them away. McGrath nodded reluctantly before they went. He wanted details and Ione gave them to him. She had come from the building, been suddenly surrounded and bewildered. I had rescued her.

"Where's Morse, the chauffeur?" McGrath demanded.

"Gone," I told him, and before he could argue, "It was a busy street. The car is bullet-proof. They could not have tied him in the back of the car without a fight. He's either yellow or in on the snatch."

"Yes, yes." Ione seemed to understand now. "It was simple to untie his hands and feet—and the tape across his mouth—hardly tight."

The girl didn't want to leave the room when her father ordered her, but after a look at me and my nod, she started to leave. At the door she spoke.

"I have never seen you like this, Father—old clothes and unshaven. And Mr. Williams saved my life today."

"Yes, yes." McGrath's anger was toning down. "Just circumstances, child—my way of visiting the poor without embarrassing them."

"I wish I could believe that," she said as she left the room, closing the door.

McGrath spoke half to me, half to himself.

"She has never doubted me before. You—" Anger flashed and died. He fingered his loose flabby chin and stiff dirty linen collar. "I suppose I should reward you, Mr. Williams, not seek— Well, I didn't want her to find me like this."

He looked toward the ceiling, then spoke very slowly. "I have talked with men this morning who gave me orders, men who borrowed a few dollars with almost a threat, men who— Well, men who would kneel and pray for mercy if they knew the truth." His fist clenched. "Some day I will rule the city of New York. Understand that, Williams—the entire city." And as if he wished he hadn't made his mystic speech, "Where were you earlier this morning? Did you come directly from your own home to the office? Were—were you at your home this morning?"

"As a matter of fact," I said, "I wasn't home all night." But I didn't add that I was in an obscure family hotel grabbing off some peaceful sleep.

"It doesn't matter. It doesn't matter." He spoke quickly. "Perhaps I should let you meet my daughter—but you must not be seen driving with her. There, there, we'll call her and you can finish your lunch. I'll dress up a bit."

"No, you'll give her my excuses." And I hummed softly, "Your excuse is my excuse," as I walked toward the rear of the house.

McGrath led me through narrow hallways and between the dirty rooms with the bare floors, the barroom chairs and a dozen or more ordinary saloon tables.

"I am not unmindful of the good you thought you did in saving my daughter."

"Thought!"

"Yes." He nodded gravely, then pulled his chin out of the dirty collar. "I am going far, Williams. I've been moving slowly over a great many years. I am about to move faster. Yes, I could have lifted a telephone and freed her."

"You might have found her dead. Bye-bye, I'm on my way to a board meeting."

"The men in black—the wealthy citizens who furnish you with money. There, don't look surprised. Richard Daniel Havermore, the distinguished gentleman, heads it openly. Your reward, Mr. Williams— Well, the next name on the list is Tasker. Oh, don't look so surprised. Orlin Tasker has been working for fame—much as I have. He, to do harm— I, to protect the citizen."

I grinned. Let McGrath have his little joke. Three generations of McGraths had all been in politics—had all systematically robbed the citizen. Dirty McGrath—the name "Dirty" had started with his grandfather, not for his appearance, but for the dirty deals he handed the taxpayers—was the fast-disappearing old-time politician. It didn't seem possible now that he could hold great influence. But he did. Never outwardly to the citizens, but within the magic circle. Why? I can only guess as you can guess. Over those three generations he may have gained a great deal of knowledge. As the youngsters say today: "He knows where the body was buried."

But back to Tasker.

I said: "The ride finished him, McGrath. The five-year jolt up the river broke him." And after a little thought, "Yet, he was a hard man to break."

"You've told the story in those few words," McGrath said. "A hard man to break, and he was out in eighteen months, and, like me—he's a patient man. He'll wait—he has waited. He let the Bent brothers—others—build up the racket again—build it up for him. Well, you killed the Bent brothers—you'll have your orders to kill him. Then—then—just one more."

"One more?" I looked directly at him.

His teeth showed as he grinned back.

"It doesn't matter so much to you who that one is. You'll be dead. But today, tonight—you're marked for death. Take care of yourself, Race. You know I'm honest. I think a lot of my girl. Few in this neighborhood—at least this side of the house—know I have a daughter. A girl who's been to the best school." He bit his lip, and then I guess he spoke the truth. "The highest-priced school in the state—and I paid four times the tuition to keep her there. Sure, she's graduated from the highest-priced school in the world."

"Me too," I told him. "But I never needed any school to learn my finishing."

His laugh was pleasant enough, though he seemed to be thinking of something else.

Finally he said: "Don't ever cross me, Race. I'm not saying I minded you meeting that kid of mine once."

It was something to see McGrath then. Not the conciliating, ingratiating McGrath who had trembled last time I threatened him. But a McGrath who would fight back viciously like a dog on his own property.

I stood there by the door as he held his hand on the knob ready to open it, and said my little say.

"You're mysterious, McGrath, and all knowing and threatening. Me—I'm innocent like a lamb. But the double cross works both ways. You strike quickly with political power—I strike much faster with a forty-four. Anyway, we're getting along swell."

"Yeah, that's it—swell. But for one thing. A woman—Jane Blake—who played the underworld for years. What became of her for a while I don't know."

I didn't wise him up that she became Iris Parsons of wealth and position.

"But she's back in the criminal world again. I'm giving you the once now that if she works with you much longer she—"

His hand went off the door knob and I laid my gun against his chest.

"McGrath," I said slowly and meant it, "you'll swear right now that no harm will come to Jane or—or—yes, by God, I'll bust you wide open right here on your own floor."

I GUESS McGRATH was without fear—his timidity a pose. I'm telling you he took a belly laugh right there with my gun in the place where the laugh came from.

"Race," he said, and his voice was not even unfriendly, "I'm a great deal older than you are. Yet I'd never be alive today if I took the chances you take. Ever since we've been talking three men with rifles have been covering you. Oh, they didn't hear us. Just little slides in the room that

flash up on a single switch. It's rather thin glass, but sound-proof." He moved to one side of me as my gun followed him.

I said: "It's O.K. by me if you want to make it a double killing."

"You'd lose on the deal. You're a number of years younger than I am. Again, one shot mightn't kill me. But those men would lay bullets in your head. Come, give me your gun. I have moved so they can't see you."

"I want to know about this Jane Blake, McGrath. She's a pest, but what she does she does for me. You'll have to leave her out of it or—" He was moving away from me and I cried out my warning. "Right in the stomach if—"

And a voice interrupted me—cut in like a knife. The voice of a woman. No culture nor finishing school in this one. It said: "Call off your gunners, McGrath—or I'll plug your kid."

McGrath didn't smile then. He stretched a hand out over my shoulder very quickly, but in such an attitude to insure me it was a harmless gesture. His finger touched a button on the wall. The sharp voice from the corridor spoke again.

"O.K., Mac. Lift your gun to his head, Race. McGrath is from the old school. He's carrying twenty-six pounds of steel across his chest and body—yep, a bullet-proof vest. But I might put a bullet in his back."

A girl screamed—another one laughed. A door closed sharply and Jane Blake trod down the hard wooden floor. She held a long purse in one hand—a thirty-eight in the other. I don't know about the purse, but I knew that Jane could use that gun.

"Followed you in the front, Race,"Jane said. "Thought I was part of the luncheon party." There was a slight—well, something to her lips. I don't like to call it a sneer. As McGrath faced her as she placed her hand on the door knob, she said: "You should be proud of that kid of yours. I stuck a gun in her back and she wouldn't move, for she thought it meant your life."

McGrath looked at Jane Blake. Even though she held the gun in her hand he stretched out his left hand, lifted her chin, looked at her.

"You're as pretty as ever, Jane—and just as hard. If it wasn't for my daughter I'd marry you today—no fooling."

"Still the big-hearted gentleman." Jane shook her head. "If those trained rats of mine had died, why I might have married you—Dirty McGrath."

McGrath's eyes went up.

"I don't like that word, Jane. You shouldn't use it to me—not you. I did you some favors when you were a kid—a wild kid."

"O.K., Tim," she said. "You give me the breaks now. I don't know how Race stands with you, but I know how he stands with your girl. You were on the kill, but your daughter wasn't."

"What do you mean?" McGrath's eyes grew wide.

Jane threw open the door, said: "She wouldn't move when she thought it might be your life, but she moved quickly enough when she thought it might be Race Williams'. You see, she wasn't afraid to die for you. But she wanted Race to live—for her."

McGrath's eyes bulged—his lips set back. Quick, vicious words hovered on his lips, but they never got through. Suddenly he threw back his head and laughed.

"And you want to know if I'll harm Jane, Race. She'll tell you later I offered her about everything—and so did many others. Today they'd double the offer. It's too bad, Jane, you never liked me. I wouldn't want you otherwise, but if you did—did—" He hesitated and then, "You can have the city."

Jane's smile was—well, like a glorious sunset, if you like the poetic. But me—I don't. So we'll say it was like the opening of a new and gay night spot.

McGrath took both her hands now and looked hard at her.

She said: "The city, eh? I think I'm beginning to like you, Tim." She drew back quickly as his hand started up her arm. "Oh, not the whole city, Tim—say the Borough of the Bronx."

And I stood there like a dummy while McGrath took the words right out of my mouth.

"When you ran with a mob you were like something that didn't belong. Something that even a hardened official recognized—and now you return. Not the same—not that touch of beauty back of your eyes. Not that sparkle of youth. You were a happy girl then. Now you're a woman with a purpose. You'd better go now."

CHAPTER 3

MONEY TO BURN

I PULLED HER down the steps and when we reached the street I started in on her.

"Let go of my arm." She jerked away from me. "In the old days it was real—now I'm playing a part."

"A part!" I led her down the block to where her car was parked. "You're sure one of the world's greatest actresses."

She clutched my arm, said: "And, I suppose, also the world's greatest pest."

I sat in the car and talked to Jane—perhaps gave it to her harder than I had ever before.

"Jane," I said, "I took you out of the underworld and put you in Society—and laid a lot of dough in your hand. Kidnaped at three and an heiress at twenty-one. Yep, I was paid for the job, but I've got more pay coming to me. I wanted to know which would win out—environment or heredity. Your heritage was of the best—your environment of the worst. Now—you're not playing the game right. You're forcing yourself back into the old environment." And when she would have spoken, "Oh, I know it's to help me. To help rid the city of the poverty and suffering you have seen because of crime—and I promised to let you help with money but not—"

"Come out of your trance, Race." She snapped the words at me. "I know as much of the Avenue as you do. I can pop up any time and the boys and girls think I've been in stir. Now—here's a message. Yeah, People Versus Crime." And she handed me an envelope.

I didn't say anything, but before I opened the envelope I noticed it was carefully sealed—and the seal had not been broken. It was a cinch she hadn't seen inside of it. But she guessed, I suppose. I read the note. It gave the time and place of the next meeting—and it was that night. Havermore would meet me personally, earlier, to discuss a few details.

"O.K., you made a fair guess, Jane. Now take me to my office."

"Home." Jane nodded. "Your apartment. I've got eats for you. You didn't have any breakfast. Your lunch was disturbed. I know because I followed you in. And don't tell me you protected that girl for the knowledge she might give you."

"Well, she was McGrath's daughter. It wouldn't be bad to stand in with a man like—"

"Blue eyes and blonde hair—and she thinks you're a great guy," she said, and before I could get in any words, "Well, I think you're the greatest guy in the world, too." The car hopped from the curb and made a complete turn.

Women have surprised other people I guess, but women are always surprising me. It seemed as if I had to make an answer, and I did. It wasn't a good one.

"So you're jealous," was the best I could do.

"Yes, jealous." She turned and looked at me. "Jealous enough to let Ione McGrath know where she stands. Oh, don't tell me where I get off, Race." She shrugged her shoulders, suddenly jumped the subject when she thought I was a little sore, and said: "Orlin Tasker—a tough boy—a killer. But I can't see him leading a mob—leading a city-wide racket."

"A killer always has influence." I, too, was glad to get off the other subject. And I, too, couldn't see Tasker as the big brains of crookdom.

"He's one man though who isn't afraid of anything, Race—isn't even afraid of you."

I nodded at that. Our paths had only crossed once. Tasker was a man without fear—a shrewd, vicious, stocky little man who looked somewhat like a prosperous broker—and could draw a gun as fast and as surprisingly as a magician could produce rabbits from a hat.

"I wonder," I said to Jane, "just how fast Tasker can shoot."

"I think," Jane spoke slowly, "that you may have a chance to find out. I knew him, Race. He didn't take much talk from any politician—and the police knew of at least seven murders he committed. He shot it out with the Massey twins and killed both of them. He was free—always free. There was never evidence, but just that once. If he hasn't changed, Race, he's a better shot than you are. Faster and cleaner."

I just grinned.

"They're all good, Jane, until they face a man who's going to shoot back—shoot fast. There's where I have the biggest edge. A living, moving target—a target that returns a bombardment and shoots to kill."

"He won't be afraid, Race. He's got cunning and courage—if he can't use the cunning."

I shrugged my shoulders as we reached my apartment house. It was all in the business. Tasker would have a chance to use both.

We climbed the stairs and entered my apartment. Jerry, the boy I had picked up in the underworld a few years before, met me at the door.

"Inspector Nelson," he said quickly. "I let him in and—"

I moved quickly down the hall and to my living-room. I was not any too soon either. Inspector Iron-man Nelson was over by my table examining the mail. I jerked it out of his hand, noted the letter on the top. It was long, heavy. It had Timothy McGrath's name in the corner. I motioned Jane and Jerry to another room. Then I slapped the envelope down as if it didn't interest me and gave it to Nelson straight.

"Nelson," I said, "despite all your hints about my aide, Jerry, he is straight and honest. I even teach him respect for the police. That's why he let you enter—and I catch you reading my mail."

"Reading it! God almighty!" Nelson gasped. "That boy watched me like an eagle. I was just skimming over it—killing time."

"Have you any other reason for being here?" I looked at the blazing logs in the fireplace.

"Yes, I have." He stood flat-footed before me. Nelson, the hardest man who ever hit the force. Iron-man Nelson who could break a man's arm with a twist of his powerful hand—at least that was the claim, though he never broke mine. Yes, I knew my rights and I knew Nelson's disregard of those rights. But he knew also if it came to a showdown, I'd pelt him with lead.

"Well," I said after he waited. "Why the visit?"

"It's this." Nelson glared belligerently at me. "There is a certain man who heads a certain organization. That organization buys up, or obtains in some way, evidence on criminals. And up until lately that evidence has been handed over to me."

"So what?"

He stepped forward and pounded a finger hard against my chest.

"So I get convictions. I get my name in the headlines. I'll be the commissioner of this city some day. Now—I don't receive that information any more. I haven't received that evidence since you found out I was getting it—and since I guessed that you collected it for these people."

"Is that all you've found out?"

"No, not quite all. Your friend—Sergeant O'Rourke—who has the commissioner's backing and doesn't take orders from me, is now being pushed into a lieutenancy. Maybe he doesn't want it, but it's being pushed on him. And why? Because he's getting convictions all over the place."

"Just as you did."

"Just as I did." Nelson nodded.

"Well." I tried to look at Nelson as if I were the commissioner and he was a stupid—a very stupid—rookie. "It seems fair that O'Rourke should receive a bit of that evidence. Especially since you mixed things up and gave me the unpleasant duty of saving your life."

His FACE GREW red—then blotches of purple showed on it. He'd have liked to strike me then—and maybe I would have welcomed the blow. I trained well for my business. I could shoot straight and fast. I could be in the ring today as a professional boxer. I can do better work than many of the highly paid wrestlers—and I can hold my own in a back-room brawl with any man or men—on or off the force.

Nelson finally gulped the words. "It's O'Rourke—your friend O'Rourke. You see that he gets the gravy."

My shoulders moved again.

"O'Rourke always did well. He is an honest, efficient officer. If I had any information in a criminal way I would feel it my duty as a citizen to turn it over to the police. Now that you mention it—I can't think of a man more capable of receiving and handling it than my friend, Sergeant O'Rourke.

"Tut, tut—and couple of more tuts, Nelson," I said as he moved toward me. And quitting the levity as I saw the whiteness of his face. "You're big, Nelson. Maybe you'd be bigger with that evidence. Time may give you breaks, but you won't get any place if you're dead."

His right hand lowered from his left armpit the least little bit.

"That's a threat of death." He was using the old cop stuff, but he meant it just the same. Only this time he got a different answer.

"It's a threat of quick and violent death." And when he still hesitated, "It would look better for me if you had the gun in your hand."

"All right, Race." He dropped both hands. "You're in an organization to wipe out crime. You're hired by them—sometimes to kill. Now—don't tell me it's for the good of the people. The police—the law attends to such things. You're through—your organization will be wiped out. Big men will be arrested unless—"

"Unless you get dough, eh? Unless you are bribed." I was smacking these accusations at him fast to get him off his guard. If you liked Nelson or didn't like him, he was a straight cop. He was a—

We both stopped talking. Stood silently as Jerry walked through the room and out to the door. The buzzer had sounded its warning of a visitor.

In a minute Jerry was back. Dirty McGrath followed him down the hall. In fact, passed by him at the living-room door.

"Field day, boss." Jerry was never impressed. "You wanted open house. Will I stick around?"

I shook my head and Jerry left. McGrath and his ingratiating manner was there as soon as he saw Nelson.

"Ah, good afternoon, Inspector. There, don't go. I just came in to give Race a tip."

Nelson said: "Don't worry about me, Dirty. I have no intention of leaving."

I said: "The inspector means he has no intention of leaving unless he is asked to leave. If you wish to see me alone why—"

"No, no." McGrath spotted the letters, stepped toward them. "My letter to you, Race—haven't read it I see." He took it in his hand, juggled it, looked at it. "My, my, looks as though it might have been opened."

I set his mind at rest on that by saying: "Nelson had no opportunity to open it. Important?"

"Not very, and yet—" McGrath caressed his chin with the envelope. "Yes, I'll read it to both you and the inspector. I think perhaps he should read it. Ah, Inspector, I see suspicion in your eyes. Always the detective, the born sleuth!" He moved over toward the fireplace, put his back to it, tore open the envelope.

McGrath's lips set grimly as he held that long thick envelope in his right hand. He tapped it once or twice on the palm of his left hand, said: "Perhaps Mr. Williams should read it alone as I had intended." And as Nelson stepped slightly forward. "No, no, it was a silly thing to write from the first."

McGrath turned suddenly and thrust the envelope into the crackling flames. I stretched out a hand to grab the paper, started to push McGrath aside—and Inspector Nelson was pushing me aside.

Yes, I wanted that paper. It was meant for me. McGrath didn't want Nelson to see it—perhaps didn't want either one of us to see it. And so it was I who turned and kept Nelson from getting the very paper I had rushed for a moment before.

A minute—two—three, and the last ash was gone. McGrath had little to do with it. Jane Blake had suddenly dashed into the room, grabbed up the wrought-iron poker and pushed the whole thing deep down in the bed of fire.

"By God!" Nelson straightened himself and quit the roundhouse dance we had been doing. "Didn't you see that envelope, Williams—didn't you feel the weight of it? There was money in it."

"Money!" McGrath laughed. "Tim McGrath with money to burn. Did it look like money to you, Jane?"

"No, no." Jane shook her head. "I just saw paper—thick paper, folded sheets like a legal document. If there was money I would have seen it."

AND WE HAD another visitor—Sergeant O'Rourke. Jerry just grinned as he ushered him into the room. Three to one against Nelson now, for certainly no one would accuse O'Rourke of liking Nelson—and everyone knew that Nelson hated O'Rourke—mostly because there were times Nelson had to take orders from the sergeant. That those orders came directly from the commissioner did not lessen Nelson's dislike for Sergeant O'Rourke—who was only a sergeant because he wanted that rank. It kept him close to the "men in blue," he said.

"Well, well, well." O'Rourke came into the room. "Sounded like a barroom brawl from the door. Hello, Nelson. Howdy, Race—and you too, Mr. McGrath."

"Mr. McGrath," McGrath repeated the name. "That sounds better, Sergeant—much better than some servants of the city have been in the habit of addressing me. You, too, Sergeant, if I am not mistaken."

"Our habits change, Mr. McGrath."

"It would seem"—McGrath looked directly at Nelson—"that Inspector Nelson keeps his habits." There was a hardness in McGrath's voice. He did not like the name, "Dirty." Nelson knew that when he first spoke to him. But McGrath was considered small-time stuff.

O'Rourke spoke quickly.

"I am sure Inspector Nelson meant no harm." And walking close to Nelson I heard him whisper: "Friends or enemies, we're both cops, Nelson. Some rather big people would prefer 'Mr. McGrath.' Things are changing downtown."

As if he had heard, McGrath said: "Perhaps the inspector wishes to change his form of address—or perhaps apologize." It was the McGrath I had once seen in the dressing gown and luxurious library who was speaking then.

Nelson said: "It was Dirty McGrath before—and it's Dirty McGrath now. Good day."

Nelson's feet pounded down the hall—a door slammed.

McGrath said: "There's an honest officer of the law—so straight he bends backwards. You would do well to watch him as an enemy."

"I've watched him for years," I said. "He can't harm me with his honesty."

"Honesty?" McGrath rubbed at his chin. "Yes, I think open honesty is sometimes our greatest fault. Now—I'll be trotting along too."

"But your message—or did you simply come to destroy it?"

McGrath smiled.

"I'll wait. Sergeant O'Rourke has business with you. Might I sit far over by the door and—ah, Jane—she will entertain me."

Jealous? I had thought that of Jane and now— McGrath would laugh and pat her arm. She would smile and— Hell, I got down to cases with O'Rourke.

"I've got some small stuff and a few big fish for you," I told O'Rourke, and with enthusiasm, "One that Nelson would give his right eye to have."

"Who, Race?"

"Jimmy O'Connor." And I liked the way O'Rourke's chin set. "Stopping at the Robson-Plaza Hotel. Name of Alexander H. Paterson. He got protection some place—though it isn't McGrath." I went to the little wall safe and opening it took out the papers. "These are your witnesses—and here are a few affidavits."

O'Rourke said: "You're a wonder, Race. Nelson has wanted that lad for years. And these other papers?" as I slapped a bunch into his hand.

"Regular stuff. One escaped murderer—two boys in the policy racket who'll confess if the D.A. makes a bargain—a guy named Larnigan who's running reefers up through Harlem—oh, lots of small stuff, all on paper—hangouts, witnesses and so forth."

"You're a real friend, Race. I— What's the matter? Why watch McGrath? He can't hurt Jane here."

"No, no. Do me a favor, O'Rourke. Beat it along. Jane might cut his throat. That's a good fellow."

WHEN O'ROURKE HAD left I jerked a thumb and Jane left the room. Then I said to McGrath again: "Now, Tim—why the burning of the envelope and its contents?"

McGrath said: "I think, Mr. Williams, I simply changed my mind. But I have got a tip for you. Orlin Tasker is not the simple soul you think. He's got a great deal of you in him—a swaggering, assured sort of fellow. I don't know if he's faster than you are, but I want to warn you not to hesitate when the moment comes. I think I know how it will end—providing you meet on equal terms."

"And how will it end?"

"It will be a matter of courage and confidence and a sense of appreciation. There is no doubt that you both have the courage—and both the confidence. But I think Tasker has the greatest sense of appreciation."

"I don't get the appreciation."

"Tasker will. He will appreciate—despite the men he has fought it out with—that he is meeting the fastest man on the trigger he has ever met. He will allow for that and won't do any swaggering."

"And me?"

"I'm afraid you'll do your swaggering without any appreciation of Tasker's ability. He's trained, mechanical—while you're emotional, and your ability is a natural one. You shoot on impulse. Oh, I don't mean you haven't got fine timing and headwork. But you don't jockey for position."

"That's me," I agreed with him. "The time and place mean nothing. Tasker or any other guy can take the dose when he asks for it."

"Tasker will not ask for it." McGrath moved toward the door, and as Jane came back lifted her hand, said: "You are as beautiful as ever, Jane, but with Race Williams in the running I'll forget the pleasure of asking you out for dinner. Later, perhaps, you'll forget the younger man for the older one. It's too bad. But

Tasker's plans make it positive that he'll kill Race—without Race even seeing him do it."

McGrath laughed as he moved down the room, crossed the hall: "Good-bye for a bit, Jane—and to you, Race—good-bye. There, don't laugh at death. Do as I would do. Put your house in order. If Tasker felt the need of it he'd come with his own little army. His is the business of death—you are on that list. A single tip. Tasker never swaggers when he's on the kill. He's deadly in his purpose then."

McGrath spoke solemnly enough, but the minute the door closed I was out in the kitchen grabbing off some of the morning coffee. Nothing seemed ready to eat.

I said to Jane as she came in: "A real lunch, kid. We'll go down to—"

"No, no." She grabbed my arm. "Not now—not until after. Don't you understand. He's waiting—he'll kill you."

"Nonsense." I put an arm around her shoulders. "McGrath may mean well or he may be just trying to bother me. Come on. Stick up your chin. Killing me on sight is an old game—not over a dozen have ever tried it. I've heard too much about Tasker already."

"Don't joke about it, Race." And suddenly her arms were about my neck. "I've got plenty of money. Why continue in this work? I don't care what you get paid—it can't last—it can't last."

She put her head down on my shoulder—or rather up on it. I used force to tilt back her head. Her eyes were wet. I know there should have been a choking feeling in my throat and maybe there was. I know I should have dripped sentiment—

and maybe I did inside. Outside—well, I pushed her off, said sharply—and meant it: "I don't like women hanging on me—and as for crying women—that's too much and—and—"

I stopped dead. She was grinning up at me. Real or imaginary I don't know. But she said: "O.K., Race. Let's go out and kill someone."

She went into the bathroom, and I looked around at Jerry. Jerry liked to snoop. Jerry knew everything. He even knew about women.

I said: "Well, since you took an eyeful, what's the answer—a fake or the real thing?"

Jerry missed the sarcasm and dished out the advice.

"She's kidding ya, boss. Guys like it sentimental—and she's crazy about you. But the blubbering was turned on to soften you up. It nearly did, but she missed the look she wanted to see on your pan and turned it off. Don't you worry about her going soft, boss. She totes that thirty-eight in her bag for one purpose—to use it."

"Thank you," I said as the girl came out daubing at her face. "Your opinion, Jerry, has been most enlightening—I won't worry further."

"Right." Jerry's eyes glowed as he looked at Jane. She had taken him for a loop, all right.

As we left, Jerry finished: "Take good care of the big boss, Miss Jane—and bring him back alive."

Nice little household, you say? Well, you're right. You could always count on some good clean fun.

CHAPTER 4

ENTER—AND EXIT—
THE VILLAIN

ONCE WE GOT seated in the side booth of the restaurant the blue-eyed Ione was forgotten—forgotten as soon as Jane turned her glims on me and went to work. I'm telling you.

"Look here, Race." She leaned across the table and gave it to me straight. "You and I made a bargain. I was to play the Society dame and you were to use my money to help wipe out crime. Now—since I knew the underworld and was part of it—I came in to play along with you. I'll admit I butted in too much—told you where you got off far too much. But from now on—you make me a full-fledged assistant, and I'll stick it anyway you please."

"But there's too much I can't tell you, Jane."

"All right—don't tell me. Take me along when I can help. I've got to stick by you."

"But why?"

"A sensible woman studies the man she intends to marry—and don't shake your head. Some day I'll marry you."

"And Ione—your threat about her?"

"Silly talk. I'm twice the girl she is and—" She was opening her purse. Now she dropped it in her lap. Her face went suddenly white, then red—and white again. But her voice was clear, though low—and there wasn't a tremor in it as she said across the table: "Don't look now, Race, but Orlin Tasker is coming toward our booth—swaggering across the room."

Swaggering.

I remembered McGrath's saying that when Tasker swaggered he wasn't on the kill.

The girl leaned forward.

"He's coming to kill you, Race. He's—" And suddenly changing and raising her voice, "It's really quite marvelous to be having lunch with the great Race Williams."

"Isn't it?" a voice said close beside me. And I looked up, let my eyebrows tighten. Then I said: "Well, what do you want?"

Tasker was a fine-looking chap. Eyes clear, shining. Hair black with a touch of gray in it. Tiny mustache over a cruel mouth. I looked at his hands—strong, muscular, yet his fingers were long, slender like a musician's.

"Don't remember, eh Williams? Take a good look."

I took a good look.

"Face is familiar, but I can't say that I remember you."

"That's right," said Tasker. "You can't say that you don't either. Well, the kid there will tell you. Jane—Jane what?"

"Jane Blake." Jane nodded. "I remember you quite well. You're Mr. Finch, aren't you?"

Tasker's eyes tightened. I guess he wasn't used to that kind of kidding. I pulled a belly laugh. He cut his words sharp.

"Laugh this off. I'm here in the city to kill you. Understand, Race Williams—the great Race Williams—to kill you."

I didn't reach for my gun, but I remembered McGrath's "appreciation." I turned sideways, let my right hand half rest on the table and turned my body so that a shoulder gun would drop right into that hand. Then I slowly drawled out the words.

"Killing, eh? Why not! There's no time like the present. Let me see how you go about it. It will be interesting to the young lady."

"Why, yes." Jane fell into my line to make Tasker lose his head. "It would be interesting. I've never seen Race Williams killed, you know."

THERE WAS ANGER in the man's face now—grimness to his lips, and a movement of his hand. So—it was coming. If it had to come, this little restaurant might be just as good as another place. My gun slipped into my hand, and the anger went out of Tasker's face.

He said: "So you know—and you fear. Race Williams who is always glad to give first draw to the other man is not glad to give it to me." He was pleased now. "And you, Jane—ratting out on your own kind. Don't you remember?"

"Yes." Jane nodded. "I was young then—very young. There were some big shots there when I struck you."

"That's right," Tasker agreed. "They were big then—most of them are dead now. You slapped people then. Now—I saw the bag. And Williams with a gun in his hand. So you're afraid and don't want any part of Tasker."

I should have shot him dead then, but I didn't.

Jane said: "Pull up a chair and sit down. What have you been doing? Race and I have a little business. He takes his enemies to lunch. Sit down."

Tasker shook his head—half bowed to me.

"I know you wouldn't just kill a lad in cold blood, Williams—but the dame. It's the way of dames. She's grown up. She used to slap guys who tried to kiss her or make an offer. Now I guess she shoots them when they don't. I—"

"Tasker—" I started, but Jane cut in quickly.

"Where have you been—what have you been doing there, and why the sudden bounce back to Broadway?"

"I was with the Bent boys—you know, the two who were killed. Killed by your friend, Williams. They were a wash-out. They never were sent up to head a racket—never came back from South America to gain control of the one big city mob—or rather build one big city mob. They and some others just knocked off a few guys. The big lad—the lad who takes over the city is here. Maybe it ain't me. But when I'm finished I got an offer—a big guy in a big racket or one hundred thousand dollars in cash—exactly one hundred grand for pushing you over."

"You're going to be quite a business man—if you live," I said.

"I'm going to be quite a business man if you die, Williams. And the girl—Jane Blake. Does the Avenue know that she's traveling with a cheap dick, that she's probably ratting out on the boys who have forgotten her. But I haven't forgotten her any—the lousy two-timing little tart who—"

Perhaps it was lack of appreciation, but if it was, it was on Tasker's part not mine. But truth is truth. I didn't think of a gun then. I didn't think of Tasker, the great Tasker, or if I did I thought of him as I would of any other punk. What did I think of? I didn't think of anything. My emotions ruled my head though my head couldn't have thought it out better.

I just came up from that seat and clapped my left fist into Tasker's stomach. If he reached for a gun or not I don't know. He bent forward with a groan as my right hand bounced toward the ceiling. It didn't reach the ceiling because Tasker's chin was in the way.

As for Tasker—he shot straight into the air and spread himself out on his back. To the hurrying waiters and manager I said: "Apple pie—for two please. This fellow annoyed me."

Which was the truth beyond a doubt. And goes to show you that every man should speak the truth. For Tasker got the air and I got the apple pie.

Yes, the waiter was so stunned he walked right out and right back and laid the pie on the table. If it wasn't for the customers across the room that got hit with a few tables that Tasker crashed when he took his nose dive, there wouldn't have been any trouble.

But a couple of women screamed, a man cursed, and the folks up front must have run for a cop.

I WAS EATING my pie anyway when Big Mike Farley strode in. He had a pad and pencil in his hand ready to report an accident. The manager said things were all right. Big Mike scowled, looked at the man on the floor who was lying on his face now, then looked at me. I hung my head down and kept right on with the pie.

Big Mike scowled again, said to the manager: "Is this the lad who—who"—he looked down at the floor and seeing no blood figured it wasn't a stabbing—"the lad who hit him?"

"Fooling—just fooling." The manager tried to smooth things over.

"Fooling!" said a woman customer. "I saw it all. That man at the table struck him so hard that he stood straight up on his head."

"You, eh?" Big Mike put a great mitt under my chin ready for one of those quick jerks that nearly tear your head off, but I beat him to it. I nearly put my fork through his elbow as I turned and looked suddenly up at him.

"Hello, flat foot," I said. "The pie's fine. Oh, was that your arm."

He rubbed at his arm and stared with wide eyes at me. Of course, he knew me—and he didn't know his next move.

He said in kind of a hushed voice: "Is he dead, Mr. Williams?"

"How do I know? That's between you and the coroner. I only knocked him there."

"With lead?"

"No, my fist. Didn't you ever hit a man with your fist?"

"I did that. I mind the time—" And Mike stopped suddenly. "Well, even you can't be knocking folks around."

"He insulted a lady."

"Even so it's— But he's coming to now and can make his own complaint."

Tasker was coming up from one knee. He held so, his back to us, his hand on a table. Then he pushed himself erect, turned slowly around and looked squarely at Big Mike.

Tasker swung back and without a word walked straight to the door and disappeared in the crowd that had gathered outside.

Big Mike didn't follow him. He just looked from Tasker to me. Finally he said: "Tasker—Orlin Tasker and Race Williams." And half aloud, "There'll be death at the end of it, I suppose."

"I suppose so." I nodded.

"Now that's something." Mike shook his head. "They have the two fastest horses in the country meet. They have the two greatest fighters. Tennis and golf and what-not. Now it's you and Tasker. I'd give my life savings to be there when it happens."

"Who will you bet on?"

"I like you better than him, Race—much better—but mind you the city would be better off without either one of you. Still—still—Tasker's the one I'd like to see get killed."

"Who do you bet on?" I almost demanded this time.

"If I was younger—if I was a betting man—I'd bet on Tasker. You're fast, Race. Tasker is faster. You shoot straight. Tasker shoots straighter."

"The hell he does." I came to my feet and shoved against Mike as I left the booth. "Why do you think I poked him around if I wasn't sure of myself?"

"Oh, you're sure of yourself—that's the whole damn trouble," the big harness bull said.

I was mad. I didn't speak. I just took Jane's arm and spun her around. But just before I left I had to say to the big smiling cop: "Any time Tasker wants it—he can come and get it."

Where the hell do people get that idea? I was pounding it at Jane after we climbed into the car.

"I'm alive, ain't I?" I said. "The others are dead. They had first draw—any number of the best in the city and they're dead. Me—I'm alive. Tasker! Where do guys that know me get that stuff? Why I'll blast him clean out of his conceit and— What did you say, Jane?"

I damn near ran down a cop.

"I said"—Jane spoke slowly—"that you're like a little boy talking his courage up—or a man whistling in the dark."

Me—I could have burst. I fear neither man nor devil nor Tasker. But I didn't speak at first. I just leaned over her and opened the door. Then I said: "Come on, get out! Get the hell out before I push you out."

Jane looked at me and the smile went off her face as if you'd yanked a mop down over it. And she got out—got out and walked.

As for me I was blue, yellow and pink. Tasker, eh? Why I'd bury so much lead right in the center of his head that it would take two men to hold that head up straight when the police came to photograph the body. That's me. I was only sorry that Tasker wasn't twins.

CHAPTER 5

THE RIGHT TO DIE

THINGS BOTHER YOU. At least they do me. Here I was being paid big money, and the boys in black had not even laid a price on the conviction or death of Tasker. And me—I was driving around places looking for Tasker. That's how I'm built. I wouldn't sleep now until we had it out. Sounds silly? Maybe it is to you folks who just read your morning paper and don't believe half of it. But men go out in the city and gun for each other every day. I was doing it now. If Tasker could shoot me to death he was welcome to it. But I had no luck.

Maybe I was still steamed up a bit when I met the head outside guy of The People Versus Crime. He was waiting for me at his club—Richard Daniel Havermore—to give him his full name. He wore high-class, but not flashy clothes, sported fifteen-dollar shoes, and was just a little on the pompous side. He was doing a good deed, and lucky to be alive, for he was the only man who actually knew the names of the members who met around that dark table to fight crime. Sure, I give him credit—but it was hard to go his gray-white waxed mustaches. Somehow that outfit under a man's nose gripes me. But this was business.

He always shook hands when we met and being of the athletic type showed the powers of his grip. Generally, I had taken his squeeze, shook my hand afterwards as if it hurt and looked at him admiringly. That was good business. But tonight I wasn't in a good mood. When he gave me the tough squeeze, I squeezed back and nearly broke all his fingers. He kept looking at them and wiggling them all through dinner.

I started with: "I don't like the way things are going, Mr. Havermore. Oh, I don't mean the small fry I pick up—the evidence I get by just sitting down and spending money. What we want is the leader."

"Mr. Williams," he said, "I am known as a broker, but my hobby is crime and the study of crime. You live too close to the picture. I stand far off and see it from a distance. If I knew the big man who is trying to get control of all rackets, dominate all crime as the mayor dominates all departments of the city—I would go after him, of course, for any army without a general is a sorry sight."

I coughed, said: "That's the stuff!"

"But"—he pointed a finger at me—"an army without a general is immediately given another leader. So which would you rather meet on a battle field—an army without a general or a general without an army?"

I nodded.

"Good," he went on. "I am driving at just that. I suspect who the leader is or who will be the leader. We are cutting off his lieutenants. We are sending many of the riff-raff—small political crooks, even known gunmen to jail. Or to their graves—as we did the Bent brothers. So—when we strike down the last man close to the leader there will be no one to take his place. The leader must stand alone—and perish alone. The gap between himself and the nearest man he can trust will be too great for him to leap. Then we will have the leader removed, and the criminals who were an organization—highly efficient, richly financed, politically protected—will disband and drift alone upon the streets. After that—"

"After that, the mopping up," I helped him out. "You certainly have the head for it, Mr. Havermore—and the men in black the money." And I leaned forward now. "But it is no secret organization either to the crook or to the police or to—well, at least one politician."

"McGrath," Havermore slammed in quickly. "We will reach McGrath in due time."

"But," I kept driving my point, "one of our men in black was killed—another nearly killed. Surely in some way these criminals or this leader you hunt must be in on the know."

"Mr. Williams, since the deaths—and violent deaths—of the other men who had the outside contact, I am the only one who knows who sits at that table—and none of them should talk."

" 'Should' is not a very good word," I told him. "Others must know—must talk. Yes, talk themselves right into death. You know—even hints around."

Havermore shook his head. "I can't believe it. I have been threatened, shot at and even hit—yes, struck twice by bullets. But the others should be safe."

"And what's more," I was giving it to him straight now, "you discuss at these secret meetings what you are going to do. What criminal of importance I am to—to discover." I didn't like to say "kill."

Havermore felt himself a sensitive soul. "Well," I popped it, "I hear from outsiders whose number is up before I even attend the meeting and listen to the ten black unknown figures vote."

"Impossible!" He made use of his wax mustaches for the first time. I had never seen him so abuse the twisted ends.

"O.K.," I told him. "Orlin Tasker."

Havermore seemed to think a long time.

"Funny. Very odd. We have been busy on other things—McGrath for instance. But it's true that Tasker is in town. A detective I hire occasionally—oh, not for big things—and entirely beyond your duties, brought me the news. But how did you find out?"

"Me?" I grinned. "Why Tasker came up to my table in a restaurant and stood straight on his head."

Havermore made his mustache do tricks without the use of his fingers. It sort of twisted in and out across his lip—or anyway gave that impression—something like a barber's pole.

"I don't understand you," he said.

"No, you don't." I leaned across the table. "I've heard nothing but Tasker and how fast he is with a gun—and how he would kill me. And as if that wasn't enough of outside talk, he came right up to me in a restaurant and told me he'd kill me. Don't you understand now? I belted him. Yeah, knocked him up in the air—and he came down the wrong way."

Havermore's eyes bulged.

"I hadn't heard of that," he said.

"How would you? Tasker wouldn't be

apt to blow about it, and it's not likely you'd run across him unless he—he—"

I stopped dead. Dead is right. Havermore raised his head, stuck out his chin.

"Say it! I'm not afraid. I know it has to come to me some day. I became the man in the open, knowing that. I may not be as old as the others, but—" He laughed. "I have a bad heart and no family. That's the reason I took the job."

There was no use in going into that. There are all kinds of bad hearts. He might have a bum ticker that would kick him out any minute, but certainly it wasn't the kind of heart that stops beating from excitement.

The rest of the dinner was rather a speech. Havermore had to laud the people, the great work the men in black were doing—and how much they had been helped by my assistance.

"It would be a terrible catastrophe," he said, "if outsiders—the big brains behind this attempt to control the city's crime, knew who these men were. Such a knowledge would mean their deaths or at least the death of our mission. Do you know, Mr. Williams, to what heights our People Versus Crime has risen?"

I didn't—but he didn't care. He went right on talking.

"One man alone has given himself, and raised among his friends, over eight hundred thousand dollars. We see a future with a—well, perhaps a ten-million-dollar organization, willing to help the police destroy crime. My own fortune which is considerable goes to our organization at my death. I am a bachelor and all my relatives amply provided with worldly goods.

But these men offer their lives. They can't be known, for once they are known—they'd die—be shot down like common hoodlums who—"

"Well, you'd better watch out. Their names may not be known, but their planned attack on the criminal is known."

"Certainly." Havermore beamed. "The criminal must know and fear. Must know that once the stretching hand of the men in black reaches him—no political influence can save him. We want criminals to know—that's the reason for the card. That's the reason the greatest criminal lawyers in the city are hired to assist the prosecutors—yes, and watch some of them."

"Great stuff," I agreed. "What's the price on Tasker?"

"We will know that tonight. We will leave together for the meeting."

He was finishing his meal when to waiter brought the note extended him on a silver tray.

Havermore excused himself, said: "I was sure that all of our members knew the meeting-place. We are changing our habit of hiding out in dark buildings, but tonight meet in the executive offices of Meredith and Stone in the Hudson Building. We think that better. They do not know why—but they were glad to accommodate certain influential men who made the request."

He opened the note and started to read swiftly. There were two pages to it. I thought he would never get to the second page. And he didn't until he had read the first page over and over. There was little on the second page.

100   CARROLL JOHN DALY

"I am sorry, Mr. Williams." He dropped a match in the ash tray, started to hold the note over the flame, changed his mind and replacing the note in his pocket beckoned to a waiter.

"Bad news?" I showed an interest, for his hand shook.

"Very bad news—the worst news possible for me to hear. I guess my heart must be better than— Ah, waiter—plug in a phone by the table please."

He just shook his head when I would have spoken, thanked the waiter when the phone was brought, and speaking softly and distinctly called a number. I guess my eyes widened, for the number was that of the Gregory Ford Detective Agency. When he got it he asked for Ford—the head of it. I don't know what answer he got, but I heard what Havermore said.

"I am not interested in Mr. Ford's being busy or not being busy. Now listen and do not talk. This is Mr. Richard Daniel Havermore. It is imperative that Mr. Ford get in touch with me at once—at once. For your own information, so you will bend every effort—it is a matter great importance to me—and worth thousands of dollars to Mr. Ford. Yes, yes, call me back. I am at my club. Mr. Ford knows."

There were instructions to the waiter about the phone call he expected and silence between us as we smoked. Havermore made use of his time by carefully adding up our bill, signing it after making a correction and at last saying to me: "You will excuse my apparent rudeness, Mr. Williams, but the lives of our entire organization are at stake. I can say no more until I consult with the committee

of ten—the brainiest men in the country today."

"Maybe you don't need brains," I told him. "And maybe you don't need—" But I never got a chance at knocking the Ford Agency, for the waiter was bringing back the telephone.

I listened to Havermore and tried to get the drift of the phone conversation.

Havermore was saying: "I will want extra men—a dozen or ten dozen. The number I leave to you. There must be enough men to prevent even a police raid. I think some should have machine guns…. Yes, machine guns. They must surround the entire Hudson Building— fill the ninth floor—both outside and inside the offices. I know we have six, but there must be more—and not too many to attract attention. As for myself I am here at my club. Have four of your best men call for me—to escort me to the meeting."

A short pause and Havermore again, "I am not interested in how you work it on such short notice—nor am I interested the price you charge…. Yes, certainly double price is perfectly satisfactory. Don't argue—those are orders…. No, I expect nothing to happen."

He jammed up the receiver.

I said indignantly: "You have me here tonight to escort you to the meeting."

"I will be glad of your presence, Mr. Williams. If the responsibility was my own I would not order other men." He tapped his pocket. "I have a note to read tonight that will throw panic into courageous men. That note must be protected until it is read." And as we arose from the table and went down the great, old-fashioned staircase to the main floor, "I can tell you that the whole organization is in danger of annihilation tonight. More I do not feel free to say until others have listened and spoken. We are ten—all with equal right. Equal right to choose life or death."

CHAPTER 6

MEN IN BLACK

OUTSIDE, UP AND down the block, and inside too, especially the ninth floor of the Hudson Building, was lousy with private dicks. The boys in black had the money and Gregory Ford could give them what they paid for. But he wasn't there in person, for I recognized his head man, Sam Pierce, a little fellow with sharp eyes who was a damned sight brighter than he looked.

"Good evening, Mr. Havermore." He went right to work on the lad who paid the dough. "It was impossible, of course, to give you proper protection to the extent you wished it without my men being conspicuous. You see, this time of night there are few people in the building and—Ah, Williams—Race Williams." He took my hand. "It can't be that all this protection is for you."

"Sure." I took his mitt. "You're to keep me from knocking over too many guys tonight. The four in the car who came with us, for instance."

Havermore cut in.

"We will dispense with the levity. Mr. Williams is our very valuable man. Now, Mr. Pierce, I do not know nor do I care how much you may suspect our meetings You are here to protect influential and prominent men. Let me impress you with the importance of my message to Mr. Ford. I think I may say without fear of contradiction—that if the contents of a letter I have in my pocket tonight became public property—your numerous and I am sure very capable men would not be enough to guard these offices."

Sam Pierce winked aside at me, but he spoke very seriously to Havermore.

"We appreciate your position, Mr. Havermore—will render the best service possible—and have facilities for obtaining at a moment's notice any number of men you may require."

Havermore turned and looked at him steadily.

"If things seem—if there is even the remotest possibility of it getting beyond your control, the police must be notified. You cannot overrate the danger."

Sam Pierce didn't smile this time. Neither did I. I'll give Havermore credit for putting real meaning into his voice.

Sam said: "Yes, Mr. Havermore. Every stairway is guarded. The building is completely surrounded. The hallway of this ninth floor has seven men. The reception-room over there"—he pointed with his thumb—"contains ten men—all heavily armed."

"Machine guns?" Havermore demanded.

"Why—er—no, no," Sam Pierce almost stammered. "We never find that necessary in cases where—"

Havermore broke in sharply.

"No more, Mr. Pierce. The telephone operator is on duty at the switchboard. There is a phone on that table. Have these men in the office armed with machine guns. I don't care about the price."

"But you should," I told him. "Tommy guns are no good to men not trained to use them. You'll only—"

"My men are trained to use anything," Sam Pierce snapped in.

And as Havermore started toward the reception-room, Sam whispered to me: "There'll be some jack in it for you, Race—don't talk him out of it. My boys can handle any guns—at least some of them." And after a second or so, "Is it very bad?"

I looked at him now, leaned down and let it come through the side of my mouth.

"So bad," I fairly snarled the words, "that sixteen-inch guns mightn't help you." Then I hurried after Havermore. Of course, I wasn't in on the show, but then neither was Sam Pierce. I had given him something to think about.

I PASSED THROUGH the men in the large reception-room, trotted behind Havermore into a small office. He turned and said to me sharply: "What did you tell that man—I mean Pierce?"

"What do I know?" I gave him as sharp an answer, and when he puffed up and was ready to blow, I added: "Maybe you will tell me in your own good time—if you're alive in your own good time."

"Mr. Williams," he had his hand out reaching for the knob of a door, "you will take orders from me—obey me. I'll—"

"You'll what?" I was tired of the high hat talk. I don't take it from anyone—never did and never will. "I've been hired by the vote of the men in black—your vote was not for me."

He turned and came toward me.

"Come into the room," he said. "The committee is ready. You'll excuse my jumpy nerves."

"O.K. You'll excuse mine too."

"Yours?"

"Sure, mine." I told him the truth. "The People Versus Crime hires me—pays me good prices when big jobs are needed. You have me tonight. What you want with that carload of bum dicks outside? I've got some pride."

"Race." He laid a hand on my shoulder. "Upon my word you are a remarkable man. But ten minutes from now you will understand that perhaps the entire police force of our entire city will be helpless to save our organization. Come with me!"

He opened the door. Beyond it were heavy curtains evidently hastily put up. We passed between the curtains. This was the library of Meredith and Stone—and an electrician must have worked fast—though the job didn't amount to much. Ten figures in black sat around an extremely long table. Before each figure a tiny light burned and hanging from the shade was a bit of cardboard with a number on it. Beside each bulb was a pad and a pencil.

I didn't see the figures very clearly—not at all at first, just a hand gripping a pencil before the light—a black-robed arm upon the table—white fingers tapping.

The first light I looked for was Number Five. It was Number Five's vote which had made it possible for me to have my job. But someone was speaking. The Number One Light at the end of the table. His voice was clear.

He was saying: "Perhaps I am the oldest man of any of you and should now be in Mr. Havermore's place—but I am too old to get around. Tonight we are near the completion of our great work. Our files are filled. Hundreds of crooks, and dangerous criminals and murderers are ready for the police net. Lawyers and detectives and even criminals themselves have given us all the evidence the police will need for convictions. Mr. Williams— to whom, tonight, each one is thankful for his great work—has risked his life, pushed himself into danger, fought his way out, killed if necessary. We have found him invaluable."

When he stopped for breath I felt like hollering: "Hear, hear! Let's give the little man a big hand."

But I didn't—and the man behind the Number One Lamp didn't get started again. Havermore spoke from beside me.

"Gentlemen, I am sorry to interrupt. But my message is of such importance that minutes—even seconds are too long to wait."

I heard him scrape a chair, then a light flashed. Havermore sat down at a little side table. The white of his features stood out plainly. He leaned forward and unfolding some paper laid it on the table beneath the light.

THE OTHERS DIDN'T know then, but I knew. It was the letter Havermore had received from the waiter at the club. A long moment of silence and Havermore spoke.

"We who took upon ourselves the terrible task of ridding the city of crime were brought here tonight to discuss how close we were to the end—our files complete— our single man still suspected, for we do suspect Timothy McGrath or it would be to our best interest to first take care of one Orlin Tasker, though we never quite placed him alongside McGrath. At least in the last few years.

"But we were to discuss Tasker and perhaps give Mr. Williams a huge sum of money to uncover him, get the evidence against him or—" He paused, cleared his throat and went on. "Now, gentlemen, let me warn you against a most serious catastrophe—the ruin of all our plans. My head alone is not big enough to solve this problem. We need each other's council. Let me read you a letter. Permit me not to comment on it now. It begins simply 'Listen!' May I have your attention, gentlemen?"

Havermore began to read very slowly and distinctly.

"Listen!

"You or I, gentlemen, are going to retire from business. Me with one million dollars in cash to travel about the world, or you—all of you—to travel from a cold slab in the morgue to a colder grave in the cemetery.

"You—The People Versus Crime—are prepared to strike at many criminals. They fear you because they do not know you—do not know how to protect themselves. I do not fear you, gentlemen, because I know you."

CARROLL JOHN DALY

Havermore stopped reading, raised his head, spoke.

"Much as I would rather cut off my tongue than tell you this, I must. After that passage in his letter he names you all—one by one in two columns. In every single instance he is correct. Please do not start questioning me how he knows—none of us can tell that. It is impossible to even consider one of our number betraying a great trust. Some of you may guess who your companions are, but I alone *know* your names. Let me finish the letter."

Havermore continued reading aloud.

"I understand, gentlemen, that you have nearly completed a great plan to wipe out crime. You have spent plenty of money—you are willing to spend millions. Here's your chance to save your purpose—your opportunity to keep your names from being known—to someone else. If that someone else lays his hands on these names, well—

"Gentlemen, there is only one condition. Race Williams must bring me this money. He must first be searched by my men. He must come unarmed. He can go in safety. There is no other copy of this list, but the names are planted deeply in my head.

"Gentlemen—one million dollars cash on the line!

"Yours against crime, Orlin Tasker."

That room had held silence, but when the final name of Orlin Tasker dropped upon that group, the silence seemed to be a living thing. Something that rose unseen in the darkness, yet gripped you by the throat. Every light was out; no voice spoke. You could have stretched out a knife and cut yourself a piece of that silence.

Suddenly a flash of light. Number Five lamp was burning. I could see a figure move, then the whiteness of a handkerchief that Number Five always held close to the mouth. It made the voice sound different.

Number Five said: "If there is any thought here of paying the money—I'm against it. We have no assurance now that each one of us may not be blackmailed separately. I vote *No*."

Now you would think they'd all vote *No*, wouldn't you? Well, they didn't. Lights popped on and off. Speeches long and short were made. Tasker would leave the country with so much money. Tasker would be silly to expose them and leave himself open to any charge—even extortion.

Once he was in jail they could work up a murder charge against him. Surely Tasker had killed many men. From the murder charge they went to Tasker confessing the name of the head man behind the whole racket. Tasker would do that for his freedom. So they settled down to a different train of thought. It was worth a million to keep Tasker silent—and perhaps worth a million to get him to talk. Yep, there wasn't any talk about raising so much money, but there were several suggestions that the price be cut—as business men they just couldn't help bringing that up.

I sat there and listened. Their arguments for paying the money weren't bad.

They couldn't start over again with new people—and if they could that wouldn't save their lives—though I don't think it was their lives they considered so much as they did their "mission." Indeed, they concluded, and rightly so, that each one of them could have a bodyguard or several bodyguards.

Remember, money meant little. They hated to spend it, but as the old duck under Number One light said: "A million—if Tasker leaves the country—it's worth it. If we catch him and make him confess the identity of the real boss, it's worth it. If we can send him away for life or to the chair, it's worth it." Anyway they started to vote—started to vote *"Yes."*

Then I came to my feet.

"Boys," I said a bit sarcastically, "you are great, big-hearted fellows. You're willing to spend a lot of money to help your fellow citizens. You're willing to take a little chance on death. Now—let me talk. In the first place Tasker will leave the country, perhaps, and blackmail you through someone else. In the second place, he will still have the information in his head which will be worth something to the lad who's really grabbing off things."

And when I paused the lad at the end of the table simply said: "Each light that goes on means *Yes.*"

Then I chucked in my big argument—one that the greatest minds in the whole country couldn't beat.

"In the third place," I said, "I won't go with the money. Play with your lights or argue that one out anyway you wish. I'll be honest about it. I like you. I like work-ing with you, but I'm not the sort to die for dear old Yale. Unarmed—don't you understand? Tasker intends to murder me. Now vote on that."

And that was something to chew on. Why there was indignation that I would even hint that they would send me to my death. One said Tasker wrote I'd be safe. They felt terrible that I should think they would even entertain such a thought.

"Don't worry your heads, gentlemen," I told them off hard. "I'm not going. Tasker has either lost his nerve or is thinking of that crack I gave him and wants to torture me to death."

Sure, I had them stumped. A lad with a piping voice, Number Two, came to his feet and said: "We were misinformed about you—by you. We understood you would do anything for money."

"Not suicide," I told him, and then, "Stall him off and I'll knock him over for you the first time we meet."

Number One was in again.

"You talk, Mr. Williams, as if we were an organization of criminals—murderers."

I shrugged my shoulders.

"You're big men and you like to feel you're doing big and fine things. I'm only a little guy, and I just call things by their right names. There isn't one of you who wouldn't sleep better tonight—if I put the finger on Tasker."

I TURNED THEN and walked out of the room. Havermore followed me. He said: "I'm expecting a telephone call, Williams. We may be able to change things." And after a pause, "Yes, from Tasker. He's got to know how they took it tonight." And suddenly gripping me by the shoulder, "You'd be a fool to go. And I guess you're a braver man than Tasker."

I said: "You gave him the phone number—that's why so many ops are here."

"No." Havermore shook his head. "I didn't read the end of the letter aloud. It was a P.S. He knows where we are meeting, and the telephone number already." He looked at his watch. "I'll have the call any minute now—if you wish, go out and talk with the detectives."

I took the hint and walked out the door. Then I got another idea. It was a big office. Wouldn't there be a switchboard, and couldn't I make use of it?

A dick directed me to the switchboard. He said: "The switchboard operator is in a little room by herself. The room is glass half-way up. The operator is reading a book. She looks class, but she won't look when you tap on the door. I guess she sees that the right lads get their calls."

And as we stood before the booth-like room at the end of the hall and before he left me, "She won't pay any attention to anyone, but you're so big and handsome maybe she'll take a peek at you."

Maybe she would. Maybe she wouldn't need to. I walked up close to the glass, looked at the door, found it a plain lock, stuck a skeleton key into it and got ready.

No, she wouldn't look. She kept reading a book, phones over her ears. Good. I spun the key, turned the knob and closed the door softly behind me.

She heard me all right but not in time. I took two quick steps, clapped a hand over her mouth.

"Sister," I said close to the earphones, "how would you like to make a couple of hundred dollars extra tonight?"

I wasn't afraid of her screaming now. But I was afraid of her struggling. I was afraid of the attention she might attract if that army of detectives, who kept bumping into each other came down that hall again.

That someone was coming I was sure of. Yep, I saw the advancing figure in the mirror across on the wall. I tried to make my strangle hold look like a caress as I lifted her earphones playfully and whispered in her ear:

"Three hundred dollars, sister—and steer this bloke off."

Sam Pierce pushed open the door and walked into the room.

"What are you doing here, Race," Sam said sort of hard. "And—"

The girl turned, looked squarely at him with hard blue eyes. She said: "You detectives have orders to stay out of here. Mr. Williams has orders to come in. Mr. Williams and myself attend all executive meetings of importance. Mr. Havermore wouldn't like your interfering."

"That's all right. That's all right." Sam Pierce backed toward the door. "I know Race is close to things, but I just keep my eyes open. No offense." He backed out of the room and closed the door.

Me—I hadn't spoken to the girl. I hadn't spoken to Sam Pierce. I just stood there and looked at her.

It was Ione McGrath.

She said: "I don't want the money, Race, but—" And suddenly, "Why not come around the other side of the desk and sit on the floor? You want to hear the call Mr. Havermore expects, I presume. There, don't stare at me. I work for Meredith and Stone—at least tonight I do."

SHE HANDED ME a French phone from her desk as I sat on the floor behind the big switchboard, invisible from the door. Fascinated I watched her plug the loose cord in. Then I spoke.

"Why are you here—McGrath's daughter? Don't they know?"

"No," she snapped. "I was put in here tonight and Mr. Havermore met me as the regular operator. I will expect you not to talk about me. Don't be worried. This firm of Meredith and Stone is owned by my father. Nice, eh?"

"You're—you're in this thing!"

"What thing? I'm just taking an interest in you, Race. For the first time in my life I spied on my father. That's why I'm here. I heard that your heroic saving of me from those kidnapers would cost you your life, so I'm—"

She pointed to the hand set and I put it to my ear. Then she adjusted her own head set, leaned toward the speaking tube on her chest, and said as if she had been at the job for years: "Good-evening—Meredith and Stone. Whom do you wish? ... Mr. Havermore? Your name please.... Very well, he's expecting that call. One moment please.... Mr. Havermore? ... Here's your party now."

This time I was getting both sides on the conversation. I heard a gruff voice and I heard that voice say: "Never mind the name. It's the call Havermore expects."

After that the voice which must have been Tasker's and Havermore held a guarded conversation like this—

Havermore: "We can't make a decision at once. It's a lot of money. And—well, the party you wish won't go."

Voice: "Won't deliver, you mean. Yellow?"

Havermore: "Sensible. The man is not a fool. Besides, I would—yes, I would advise against it."

Voice: "So what? Where is the money? How do they feel about that?"

Havermore: "Agreeable, but it will take some time to raise the money."

Voice: "I want to talk with you now. Hell, you've got nothing to fear. You're the money bags." And as Havermore hesitated, "Come down to the Barton Park Hotel, Room Seven Fifty-one. I'm registered there under the name of Norton Lasker."

Havermore: "At present I couldn't possibly—"

Voice—sharp: "Start in five minutes or I'll sell you all out down the line. Come alone. You'll be watched every inch of the way."

A very long silence.

Voice: "Well?"

Havermore: "Very well—I'll come."

After that a double click.

"Great work, kid." I came to my feet. "I'll be on my way."

"What are you going to do?" She grabbed at my arm.

"I'm going to shoot Orlin Tasker to death."

CHAPTER 7

LAST LAUGH

I WAS ON my way. Most of the detectives knew me—even the one who grabbed me when I slipped out a side door. Once I was held for identification, and if that identification had been one half-minute longer, there would have been a dead detective lying there on the side street.

It was a run against time. What was I going to do? I was going to enter Room Seven Fifty-one. This was a straight kill—no two ways about that. No appreciation on my part—no chance for any on Tasker's. I'd just walk to the desk and say: "The gentleman to see Mr. Lasker, please."

I felt good. I liked it. I sort of tingled. It was his life or mine. He wasn't apt to give me a chance—I wasn't apt to give him one.

As the taxi sped uptown I had a kindly feeling toward Havermore. A man in his position willing to go and face that killer. Yes, mustaches or no mustaches he seemed a good guy then—and what's more he had told Tasker right over the phone that I was no fool and sensible not to go.

Things were hot. This was going to be action. O'Rourke was getting evidence from me that brought convictions. O'Rourke was as close to the commissioner as any man could be. Anyway, who would want to arrest a guy for knocking over Tasker. The police had wanted him for years.

I handed the driver five bucks, jumped out and ran through the theatre crowd,

back to the side entrance of the hotel. There was a cocktail lounge there and a long hall which led to the lobby of the hotel. I'd make time that way.

Few people were in that dimly lighted corridor as I hurried along toward the huge palms just at the entrance of the main lobby. I'd be close to the desk then, and could send up my message without anyone who was watching the front of the hotel seeing me.

It was a swell dump this Barton Park Hotel. I slowed down my pace now. The voices and laughter of men and women floated into the hallway. I was walking slowly when I hit the palms and started out into the lobby, started out under the brilliant lights. Yep, started and stopped. It was as if the marble floor had suddenly become a swamp and I was bogged down in it—standing there, leaning half sideways.

Something had hammered itself against my shoulders. Someone had come from behind a huge palm. A voice spoke, spoke the words I used so often—and now might never speak again. Sure, it was Tasker. And even in death he was stealing my own stuff.

He said, his gun held firmly in his right hand, pressed hard against my right shoulder: "It's me—Tasker—and I'm on the kill."

Did people see us? I didn't know. Some must have, of course, for I was half in the brilliant light and Tasker was plainly visible in the shadows.

It was seconds not minutes, of course. Terrible seconds when I wondered if I was trapped by that phone call. Had Ione—

had she— And why didn't Tasker shoot? Why hadn't he shot? I knew the answer to that. He wanted to be big—real big along the Avenue. He wanted me to die with a gun in my hand. He pressed his gun against my right shoulder so that when my right hand reached my gun, he'd blast my right arm.

Appreciation. Appreciation. The word rang in my ears. And then—nothing but action.

He was watching my right hand hard, of course, when I crossed my left to my right armpit. Appreciation. He knew I carried two guns, but he didn't think I'd chance him with a left hand.

Of course, I took the lead—of course, I expected death. I didn't expect, but I hoped, that perhaps I'd take him with me.

Tasker fired without moving his hand or his gun up to put a bullet in my head. And why didn't he lift his gun up? I liked the reason for that. He didn't have time— not even a split second of time. And he knew it.

Luck? Maybe there was a bit of luck in it, but I always say a guy makes his own good or bad luck—and I've had plenty of bad. Yep, he made his own luck when he fired that shot into my right shoulder.

I wasn't facing him, you see—and didn't think—or we'll say maybe I wouldn't be able to swing in time. But I did swing in time.

IT WAS HIS own spitting gun that crashed a slug some place along my shoulder. It hit me and it spun me and I closed in finger on the gun in my left hand. Yet he had shot me into a position where I faced him. My gun exploded in my left hand, exploded so close that it ripped up his chest and staggered him back against a potted palm.

He hit the floor like a thousand bricks, sprawled out on his stomach, his legs and arms grotesquely spread out before and behind him like a frog. Me—I swayed there and looked at Tasker. Looked at him as one might look at an object through the wrong end of a telescope.

He was looking at me too—and there was blood on his lips, and a certain glassiness to his eyes. There was his gun still in his right hand. Well, he had his chance, did Tasker—all the chance he was going to get in this world. Yep, his great chance and he wasn't fast enough to take advantage of it.

I brought up my left hand and shot him again—straight through the top of the head.

People were screaming. Peculiar the way people act. Those who were in the hotel and had seen the death, fought to get out—those on the outside who didn't know what had happened, fought to get in.

There were cops there now—and Havermore—and a girl. Yes, it was a girl—Jane Blake.

Havermore kept saying over and over to me: "You met him, Williams—you met him and he's dead."

I agreed with that. He was dead enough.

Then Havermore got a grip on himself and began to talk big and Jane Blake was holding me. And the manager was saying: "Right in my lobby—and what can I do?"

It seemed hazy to me, but Jane told me later that I told him exactly what he could do.

I said: "Get a sponge and a pail and a bit of soap—and you'll never be bothered with Tasker again."

The house doctor had a flower in his lapel and a black ribbon on his glasses, and I could have cracked him down. Yes, I'll bet I fought my way out of the damned hotel, and Jane drove me straight home.

I didn't tell her how bad it was. I was losing a lot of blood and no mistake about that. I did tell her how I listened in on the phone, and that a girl let me—and about the conversation I had overheard.

"The girl," Jane said. "She let you listen, knew you'd come—and tipped off Tasker. But what a place for him to—attempt murder."

"It was a good place," I told her. "Why the streets were jammed with people. He could have skipped right back down that hallway. No, better than lonely streets, Jane. You can escape in a panic-stricken crowd. You can mix with them. None of them could ever identify him."

"How bad is it, Race?" She had got me up to my apartment and Jerry had called my doctor.

"Just a shoulder wound," I told her. "I've learned to take most of my lead there."

Doc came—my own doc—a specialist on removing bullets and fixing up gunned and knifed men in the underworld.

He put Jane out of the room after Jerry had brought the water. And after he got busy he stood back and looked at me for a moment.

"It's not the shoulder this time, Race—and you must have known it. You must have been bending or he tried for a crack at your spine. The bullet ran down back of your shoulder—along your side, has nicked two ribs I think—then turned peculiarly and trotted out just between your thigh and your knee. Different terms if you want medical testimony."

"God!" I said. "As bad as that."

Doc smiled.

"Good—especially fortunate against a man like Tasker. He must have sported a high-caliber revolver. If it had been different he'd have shattered your clavicle to pieces. No, you're very fortunate." And with admiration after he had fixed me up, "Half-price for this job, Race. The boys have been talking about it—and making bets around. Well, just stay quiet for a few days."

And just before he left, "I don't mind telling you I made an even three grand betting that Tasker would die the first time guns blaze. Nice work, boy." And he was gone.

I DIDN'T TELL Jane that Ione McGrath had let me hear that conversation, but I did say: "Jane, I've got a feeling that Dirty McGrath put me on that murder-spot."

"No." Jane shook her head. "And I'll tell you why. Dirty McGrath didn't want you to mix it up with Tasker. You thought you saved Ione McGrath from a kidnaping. And maybe you did as far as she was concerned. But I think she's been butting into her father's affairs—and the kidnap was a fake."

"A fake—you mean he had his own daughter kidnaped?"

"That's right." Jane pounded right through the disbelief in my words, on my face. "You see, McGrath mailed you a letter asking you to save his daughter. That he had secret information that she was being taken to Canada. Don't talk yet, Race. McGrath mailed you that letter before the actual kidnaping. It reached here even before the kidnaping. That's why he wanted the letter back. You see, I knew something fishy was in the wind—that's why I asked you to be outside the building to protect me. Don't you understand? He sent you a letter and five thousand dollars. He wanted you and that blonde daughter of his both out of the way for a time."

"And—and he let five thousand dollars be burned up like that!"

"He did." Jane smiled. "Or thought he did. You never asked how I knew all this. Why, I opened the letter, took out the money, filled it with paper—and that was what he burned. So perhaps he wanted to save your life."

"Or save the life of Tasker," I said, and what's more I straightened up a bit in bed. I had a pleasant feeling toward Dirty McGrath.

I said to Jane: "Down in his heart—his black or white heart—he thought me the better man of the two. And crook or not—murderer or not—the lad who wants to control the city or not—McGrath was right. For Tasker is dead."

Jane played the nurse and put a bag of what she called ice on my head, though it slopped around like jelly.

She said: "We should both chuck it, Race. The doc said you nearly got it this time. Sometimes I wonder how much you must hide—what you must really feel inside. What thoughts must have run through your head when you shot a man—so horribly to death."

I leaned back, put my hand under my head with a great deal of difficulty, but also with considerable satisfaction. I looked out the window at the last touch of the sun.

It may sound silly, it may even sound poetic, but I said to Jane: "There wasn't time to think then—but now—I never heard a sound so soothing as that first shot of mine when it pounded into his body. Somehow I knew then—no matter how I came out he'd be dead."

Hell, I know that's a laugh. But just like other fellows I suppose I have a touch of sentiment in me too.

The Quick and the Dead

THE DANCING MURDERER

I WAS FEELING pretty good. As a matter of fact, I'd never felt better. I was sitting pretty, taking things easy and raking in dough from the Men In Black—those men of position and wealth who had raised millions to wipe out organized crime. Ten men who sat around a table and put the finger on the criminal they wanted. And I always landed him easy—simply by letting it be known in the right places that for information leading to his whereabouts, cash would be laid on the line. It was so simple it was almost laughable—the way friends wanted to squeal on buddies for that heavy dough I paid out.

Yes, I was feeling good. Two of the Bent brothers and a so-called rapid shooter, Orlin Tasker, were dead. Nothing better could have happened to them, for they had come back to the city to start their criminal activities again with the idea of controlling, finally, the whole underworld. A younger Bent brother was somewhere around the city—but he was a weak sister and not to be taken seriously. The eldest Bent brother had not been heard from in years. The talk on the Avenue of his having been the brains of the Bent outfit years ago—and of a quarrel between himself and his brothers that made those brothers flee the country—I took as plain bull. But there was someone—one powerful figure, in or out of politics, and I don't mind saying I suspected who he was—who had brought the two Bent brothers to the city for me to pop them over. He was the one we were trying to get now and if I—

The phone rang. I quit shaving, opened the bathroom door, listened. My eyes widened. Jerry, my assistant, whom I had picked up in the underworld some years back, was not answering the phone. A girl was taking my call. It was Jane Blake, born Iris Parsons of the upper crust, kidnaped at three to become Jane Blake of the criminal world, and rescued by me at eighteen to become Iris Parsons again. Now she'd turned Jane Blake once more with a crazy yen to help me fight crime.

SHE WAS SAYING, as I strutted out of the bathroom, soap on my face, and a suds-laden brush in my hand: "I'll have to have the name. I'm Mr. Williams' confidential secretary. He has no secrets from me so—"

I jerked the phone out of her hand and slapped the brush into it. I said: "Race Williams talking. What's on your chest?"

I heard a gasp at the other end of the wire and a small voice that grew louder and more dignified as he got the mouthful out. "How can I be sure I'm talking to Race Williams?" And then, "But of course, your voice and your manner should tell me that."

I didn't mind the "voice" part of it, the "manner" didn't set so well. But I only said: "All right—now you know, talk!"

And he did talk.

"You'll be paid well for your time, Mr. Williams. I must see you at once."

"Sorry"—and though I said it lightly, I meant it, for he sounded as if he had dough—"but my time is fully engaged."

He went right on like a guy who didn't take "No" for an answer when he could buy "Yes."

"My name is Norman B. Philips. I am vice-president of the Second State Bank. There—don't refuse me. My life may be at stake." And just as I was going to tell him to notify the police, he added: "And my business is the one your time is fully engaged in. I am the Number One Light."

"What's that?" It was my voice that was soft and doubtful now. But I got wise quickly. I snapped in ahead of him: "Never mind telling me your business. Do you want me to come over?"

"No, no." His voice was low and excited now. "I'll come to you. No one will suspect that. And Mr. Williams—be near your door. I'll slip quickly to it—and scratch."

"O.K. Right away then." I didn't kid him along or wisecrack about the "scratch." He must have read that in a book—or maybe they do it in banks. Certainly he seemed to think that if he rang my bell a siren would blow from the top of the building.

Jane handed me the brush, said: "You

look cute—in your undershirt, your face covered with lather and two guns in your shoulder holsters."

I grinned down, said: "What's wrong with two guns? Get wise to yourself, Jane. The shaving soap on my face is not bullet-proof. I knew a dick once who—"

"Now don't tell me you knew a dick who got killed shaving."

"Yeah, that's right. And I've known of a dozen guys who took lead while kissing a pretty girl." With that I leaned down close, smeared soap on her cheek, and—

Jane threw both her arms about my neck and kissed me. She laughed when Jerry came into the room and I walked nonchalantly back to finish my shave. Her words followed me.

"Race, don't be so proud of your indifference to women. At least this one woman—who loves you very much." And shouting as I closed the bathroom door, "You kissed me back, you know."

I didn't answer. I wasn't mad either. Women will always bring trouble into the sort of life I lead. But whether I kissed her back or not—truth is truth, I liked it.

My thoughts changed as I shook the soap from the razor. Norman B. Philips—vice-president of a bank. Sure, I knew who he was. And I knew more. Number One Light was the chairman of those Men In Black who sat around that table of ten with their tiny lights. The P.V.C.—People Versus Crime.

I was curious who these men were, but not overcurious.

Often I took orders directly from them as I stood at the end of the table. But just one man—their outside man, the broker, Richard Daniel Havermore—knew who each one was. Havermore was the man who faced death every second that the society functioned. It was from him I got my outside orders. How he'd managed to live so long, I don't know. He was a most courageous man. Of course, I faced death from the enemies of the society too—plenty more than Havermore. But facing death is my business—and dealing it out is my business too. And that last part of my business, which was hardly up Havermore's alley, protects me from the first—if you get what I mean.

Conceited? Maybe. But if you sell a better line of goods, you advertise so the other lads know it. I sell a better line of goods. I hit what I shoot at, and I always shoot at any lad who needs it.

The doorbell rang and I heard Jane going to the door. But it didn't matter. It couldn't be my man of the Number One Light yet.

There was a chain on my front door and the door was made of steel. There was a slit-like steel grill you slip back and see through without a bullet coming in. Jane knew her stuff. She'd be sure before she opened that door.

I was almost ready for an eleven o'clock breakfast when I heard Jane coming back through the hallway. A man was with her. He was talking and his voice was not pleasant. His words were taken right out of some old-time melodrama. I was tucking in my shirt when he started down the hall, and was tossing my shoulder holster back on by the time he hit the living-room. I stopped just as I finished the last jerk on my tie. The guy was shooting off rough stuff.

"It was lucky you put the hall light on, Jane, when you let me in. It was to be a silent and a quick death. Just a knife—vengeance for the Bent brothers—my brothers."

"Your brothers? Why I thought your name was Charlie Morse."

He laughed. "It was, while the Bent name smelled up the whole city. But my right moniker is Bent. Plain Ike Bent—the baby of the family. The man who saw you shoot and run one night. The man who kept silent because you were a woman—a beautiful woman. You're a little harder-looking, a little cruder perhaps, back in the eyes, but that's your beauty. It held me then. It holds me now."

I CAME OUT into the hall to hear better, took a look through the curtain. The lad was tall—broad and heavy from the chest up. His shoulders stuck out with strength, but the rest of his body was slim—almost to thinness.

Jane said: "I'm glad you feel that way, Charlie—er—Ike. But then I always called you Charlie. I'm glad you find me beautiful—your brothers wouldn't have cared."

"No, no." He looked down his hooked nose at the girl. "But my brothers didn't know what I know about you, the reason you permitted me to come in. The reason you told me you were alone in this Williams fellow's apartment. I cannot kill beauty." I leaned closer and got a good view of the room. "But I can first destroy beauty." A knife flashed into his left hand and a gun into his right almost simultaneously. "The knife is to destroy beauty—the eyes, the ears, the pretty mouth. The gun is to kill what is no longer beauty."

For the first time I saw the surprised look on Jane's face. It wasn't because of the knife. Her eyes were glued on the gun, making it useless for her to rip open her handbag and tear a hole in his chest from her own weapon. But no fear showed in her face—just cold calculation. I knew. She didn't dare call out. She was counting on me—and time.

At first it was funny. It looked like the Apache Dance as he stalked her around the table. Maybe he was good with a gun—maybe he wasn't. But he held it as a defense weapon and not for offense. The knife was his attack, and damn it, if he hadn't had the gun in his hand, he'd have ripped the girl more than once when he leaned across the table and let the knife swing. Yes, he was good with a knife.

Me, I've got no respect for knives—not even to eat with.

And so on they went, stiff-legged about that table. Then they'd stop just like a real dance. Then he'd lunge and Jane would step back. Serious? I suppose so. Tragedy if I hadn't been there. It was my presence behind the curtain that put comedy in it. If he ever made a real dangerous swipe with that knife I'd pound his stomach up under his wishbone on my first shot.

Then I got thinking and I got mad. I had a client coming who didn't expect a floor show for his money. I pulled back the curtain and stepped into the living-room. I was directly behind the knife dancer when I spoke.

"Jane," I said sharply, "you'll have to entertain your friends elsewhere—try Roseland Dance Hall."

I won't say his act was expected, for no man but a fool would have turned with the idea of pounding lead in me. And, of course, I could have shot him to death. But he was small-time stuff to me.

I simply threw my body forward when I first spoke, so I was inside his gun and slightly below his knife when he swung. My gun was hard against his chest and my voice rasped into his face—his startled, but I can't honestly say terror-stricken, face.

Yet he spoke quickly as he felt the nose of my gun beginning to bore a hole in one of his ribs. He said: "Do you know that I can send her to the chair if—"

"If you live." I added words he wasn't going to speak.

I stopped. Not a scratching on my door but a pounding, and almost the very moment that my gun shot up and the nose of it drove Ike Bent's chin up and wrapped it some place back behind his ears, the shots came.

I know this Baby Bent tossed his head back and then forward, for I hit his chin again when he came forward. Then I was dashing toward the front door. My man, my client, the man who was going to tell me something about the Men In Black. They were shooting him dead by my front door. Or were they? Was it a trap to have me dash out in that hallway and get it— maybe from a Tommy gun? Maybe my client was a fake—but if he wasn't, if he was there, he was dead by now. I was willing to bet my bank roll on that.

CHAPTER 2

ROUGH ON RATS

I swung right, nearly pounding my face on the floor as the little rug Jane had bought to improve my apartment refused to take the turn with me. But I didn't go down. I hollered to Jerry to watch over Jane. He hollered back something about my grabbing a machine gun from our five-foot trap door in the ceiling.

No time for that. I skidded to a stop at my bedroom door, went through it and across to the closet. There were two doors in that closet. One that led into it from the bedroom, and a hidden door in one end which opened on the bedroom of the apartment beyond. That's right. I rented that other apartment in case I needed a surprise entrance or exit. This time it was an exit and would bring me out in the side hall so that I would be completely hidden from the main corridor where my regular apartment door was, and where the killers would be.

I reached the hall door of my extra apartment, tossed it open, dashed out. And that side corridor was not deserted. There was a figure standing there by the curve in the hall.

He saw me all right, but I saw him too. I think he jerked up his gun and fired, but I didn't know then and he never told me later. I cut him down before he even got his mouth open to yell.

Jumping his dead body, I landed smack in the main hallway and was facing the door of my own apartment.

Death trap? Yes, it was all of that. A

figure was crumpled there against my door, down on his hands and knees, blood seeping out upon the marble floor. It must have been my client and he must have taken the dose as he pounded on my door.

They had laid their death trap well. They must have come down from the roof, for they would have had hard work passing through the lobby below with its little shops, besides the trip they'd have to make up the stairs to my floor.

Six men were there in that hall. Two, far down, close to the stairs and facing me as I came forward. Another lay on his stomach a little up from my door to pop me off if I peered cautiously out. A fourth I nearly knocked over, running into him—and the one I'd just killed. That was five.

The sixth man, a squat, heavily built, evil-eyed rat had his back against the elevator shaft. He directed a Tommy gun straight at my door. He turned it toward me as I blasted the lad who was between us out of the picture.

The machine gun spat lead, but the man who held it wasn't half as anxious to deal out death then as I was. Just a few scattered shots that went harmlessly up the hall somewhere before I shot him dead.

They all had a chance, of course. All of them were armed. They fired as they ran, fired back over their shoulders as I went to work, mad with a fury I'd never felt before. But I was deadly accurate with my guns and they were blinded by terror.

I remember the guys turning and running down those stairs. I remember the man on the floor coming to his feet

and making a run for it as he fired back— with no chance of hitting me. I could see his gun shake as he cut off my fire at the disappearing men and died for his trouble.

I tore the machine gun from lifeless hands and went in pursuit.

Doors were opening and closing, people were shouting as I reached the stairs. Four flights to go, and I was gaining on them every foot. Once one of them stopped at a landing and shot back—at least he fired a gun—and I dropped half a ton of lead in him.

There were shots ahead of me and I jumped the body of a woman—fainted or dead, I didn't know. There was a cop leaning against a rail, hanging on with his right hand—his left close against his stomach. He recognized me and spoke as I passed. His words seemed to glide down the stairs after me.

"Never mind me. He killed the woman. It's Lance Markey—and he fears nothing."

The cop fell then and I heard his body hit the stairs behind me. He was a brave man, but he didn't know the truth. Lance Markey feared something—and what he feared he was going to get. He was the last man.

People now—cops shouting in the lobby below as Markey avoided the main stairway and, running along the little balcony, dashed for the side stairs that would pass the inside jewelry-display window of the shop that faced on the street. There were people even along that balcony, and in the small lobby that the cops fought to get into, and frantic men and women fought to get out of.

People, too, had sought safety on those narrow stairs, figuring we'd come straight down the main stairs instead of skidding along the balcony. Give the police credit. One of them jumped from a rail and tried to take Markey in a flying tackle.

I tossed away the rattler and tried to spot Markey, but the place was a mess. Twice I thought I could pick him off, but once the white face of a woman and next the small, round, bewildered face of a child blocked my fire. Such things didn't bother Markey. He took cracks back over his shoulder at me, even knelt once to fire. Then he was on the run again, for I was moving fast now.

More police were outside—some in. Plainly I saw the face of my friend, Sergeant O'Rourke, and over his shoulder I recognized Inspector Nelson, who was no friend of mine. It was no coincidence either that they were there. Nelson dogged my apartment hotel most of the time, for it was I who'd set him in bad with the D.A. and other officials. The Men In Black had been giving all evidence collected against criminals to Inspector Nelson, but I had changed things, and now O'Rourke got it all.

Markey was trapped now, jammed up with the frightened people above and below him. He had two choices. One to shoot his way through helpless people and land in the hands of the police. Or to shoot his way through other helpless people up to me.

That was some choice. I smacked my lips. I'd open up and bounce him clean over those stairs and through the jewelry-store window.

I cursed that thought the moment I had it. For as if Markey read my mind he vaulted the stair railing, landed on a packing case hidden beside the stairs, and continuing his leap tossed himself right through that jewelry-store window.

I tried for a shot, saw the uselessness of it and took the same leap myself, landed on the packing case and, jerking my jacket up over my head and hands, made the hole in that glass bigger. Why? I don't know why. Wild horses couldn't have made me quit now. Just one thing burned in my head—that not a man would escape alive.

Markey had scrambled to his feet, started to run to the back of the shop and perhaps freedom on the street beyond, when he must have heard the second crash of glass. The clerks were standing like soldiers on parade with their hands held high above their heads. And they were right. They were paid to sell stuff—not to be killed.

Markey turned and faced me. He started to lift his right hand, the gun still in it, then the hand dropped to his side again.

"No, no—no, Williams!" He shrieked my name and the final "no" at the top of his voice. "I'm not armed. No, no—" He was screaming now. "There will be hundreds outside to see it. It's murder!"

Murder—well, perhaps that might be a legal term for it. He was certainly helpless, unable to lift the gun in his hand in his own defense. He was sinking slowly to his knees—Lance Markey, who feared nothing.

A clerk was moving toward the iron-grilled door which must have been locked when the shots started.

I said out of the side of my mouth: "If you open that door for the police I'll kill you. Don't move again."

It happened to be the manager, but I didn't know that then. He said: "You're—you're not going to kill him like that!"

"Yes," I said slowly. "I'm going to kill him—just like that."

Maybe you don't like my ethics, maybe I don't fancy them myself at times. But nothing could stop me then. The dead man at my door, the woman on the stairs, the falling body of the cop.

I raised my gun, said: "Raise your head, Markey—and take it."

His head fell lower on his chest. His knees began to buckle. His eyes swam—yet they raised and saw the gun. I couldn't help it—I'm built that way. I squeezed the trigger slowly.

I heard the shouts outside but I didn't care. I knew that Nelson was watching, but I didn't care. I knew O'Rourke was there, and still I didn't care. And—my finger hesitated.

It was a girl's voice that spoke. The voice said: "That isn't the way, Race. That isn't the way."

Things sort of broke in my head then. Both my guns smacked home into their holsters. I was conscious of the cries outside—the clubs of cops upon glass. I don't exactly know what happened. I don't know if I dragged Markey along the floor. I don't know when I lifted him

above my head. All I remember is that I stood by that glass window, that O'Rourke cried out and Nelson cursed—and figures in blue hollered indistinguishable words. Then I hurled the fear-inspiring Mr. Lance Markey through the glass into the arms of the waiting police.

The girl had me then and I was running fast. We didn't dash out the back of the store. We turned at the end, went along a narrow passage, down steps into a cellar, up more steps and finally into an apartment.

"Thanks, kid." I clutched the hand of Ione McGrath, the big politician's daughter. "You gave me a break, then. I'll rest a bit, and go back and face it. Bring me a glass of water—or a pail, I guess."

"You can wash inside."

I laughed, said: "I'll wash later. Right now I'll drink a pail of water."

"I think"—she went and poured a double brandy into a tumbler—"that this is what you need."

"Not me, lady." I went for the water. "I don't want and don't need any kind of courage that comes through the neck of a bottle. Liquor is only for pleasure with me. On business it's water."

"But"—she was washing my face with a wet towel big enough to bathe a Great Dane—"I thought gunmen even used dope to build themselves up for the kill—to make them vicious."

I took a laugh. "Maybe—some of them, when they want to shoot a lad in the back. But dope doesn't make for good marksmanship. Look at those birds—they didn't even hit me. Rats—just rats." I was thinking of the dead woman on the stairs.

THE COLD TOWEL felt good across my forehead. I leaned back for a bit. Then I came to my feet, smacked both hands upon Ione's shoulders and looked down at her. Blue eyes faced me squarely. Golden hair— But me—I was business.

"Listen," I said, "I don't know if you came in handy or not, but I don't believe in coincidences. Why were you in that jewelry shop. Did you know something might happen?"

"My father owns the shop."

I snapped: "Your father owned the brokerage firm where the Men In Black met a month ago. You were on the switchboard then—and let me listen in on a conversation that nearly cost me my life. Oh, I know"—and the word "Dirty" hovered on my lips, but I said—"I know Tim McGrath is big politics. You look up to your father and you should, because—because—"

"I know what you're thinking." The girl was close to me now scraping blood off my vest. "I'll tell you as much as I know. My father bought this store only last week."

"Ione"—I had hard work getting the words out, her face was so innocent—though with real expression, real character. But I wondered if inside her was the foul soul of her father, Dirty McGrath.

"Ione," I tried again, and this time pushed it out, "you must know something. Did your father—does your father want my death?"

She let her blue glims get sort of hard and I think she spoke the truth. "My father does not want your death. But if it weren't for me he might sacrifice your life toward a great end."

That jarred me. Was Dirty McGrath's great end the leadership of crime. Was he the head man behind the new criminal combine that the Men In Black hoped to block, and whose leader they hoped to kill? Havermore thought so. I thought so.

Dirty McGrath in his old clothes, making his trips to the poor uptown. Dirty McGrath with the great house that posed on one street as cheap living quarters where the poor—yes, and the criminal—met him. But those who entered that same house on the street beyond found huge gates, a beautiful driveway, and terraces leading down across grass as smooth as a putting green.

Sure—to the outside world there were two McGraths. But few people knew him in both characters. Wealth and position met him in his sport clothes, his evening dress. The poor and the destitute and the petty criminal met him in his shaggy Prince Albert that had seen a generation of wear.

I said to the girl: "Did you come here for your father? Did you fear I would hurt him?"

"I came here," she said simply, "because I love you." And damn it, if I had not been quick I'd have had two girls hanging to me in the course of a single hour.

"I've got to get back," I said suddenly.

The girl led me downstairs, across a rear court, showed me a fence.

"Beyond that's another street," she told me. "Now you're on your own." And just before I left, "Race, see Father, ask him—ask him anything. Something terrible is going to happen—soon."

"I think something terrible has

happened already, Ione. I don't know what people want for their money—though a jewelry store like that must cost a pretty penny."

"But, Race"—she gripped my arm—"make it dinner tonight. You need never fear anything again. I am going to tell my father that I—I—I'm going to tell him."

"Hell, no." I started and stopped. Crooked as the McGraths had been for three generations, Dirty McGrath was mad about that kid. She had been sent away to the finest schools—now he had brought her back. But the girl was seeing the life he led, and damn it he must know it.

I said: "No, don't tell him about me, Ione. You won't feel the same in a few days." I was wondering what she'd think when I put the finger on him.

She laughed. "You don't think—really think my father would harm you."

"Ione," I said, "he'd shoot the dinner right out of my mouth." And when her eyes opened like twin Ferris wheels. "There, don't mind. I'd do the same for him, too."

"No, no—" And as I pulled away, "You'll come for dinner—you must come for dinner tonight. Promise."

"I'll come," I told her. "Don't get me wrong, kid—I'm not afraid of your old man."

But as I hopped the fence and hurried around to the front door of my own swanky apartment hotel, I was pondering if even Dirthy McGrath would want to be rough with me after he read his paper. The massacre should have a soothing effect on him, on a hundred or more killers who planned my death. Maybe it wasn't a clean job, but it was a nice one—a damn nice job any way you look at it.

CHAPTER 3

WITH A KNIFE IN HIS HEART

YOU'D THINK IT was a policemen's picnic when I entered the lobby of my apartment house. You never saw so many harness bulls and plain dicks at one time who weren't trying to hide their profession.

A cop grabbed me by the arm, said: "Come on! Take it easy, big boy. Where do you think you're going?" Unimportant cops become very important under such circumstances.

I handled him quickly and went toward the elevators. I said: "One side, fellow. I'm the mayor's brother. I live here."

He wilted and a cop standing behind him who was listening in gave me half a salute as I passed. But I was nailed before I reached the elevator. Lieutenant Donovan gave me the office.

"Howdy, Race." He grinned. "Inspector Nelson said you'd be along soon and for you to go right up to your apartment." He shook his head as I grabbed off an automatic elevator. "I figure they came to kill you—then got into a gang battle among themselves or—"

I nodded pleasantly and shot the car to my floor. A young dick, a bright lad, met me in the hall. There were other cops there, a doctor bending over the machine gunner I had split open.

I said: "Don't tell me there's been shooting right where I live!"

"Guns and mouths, Mr. Williams," the young dick said. "The boys out here are speculating how it happened. Me—no one asked my opinion." And in a whisper, "Inspector Nelson, Sergeant O'Rourke, the commissioner and the district attorney are in your apartment."

"The mayor isn't here yet?" I grinned.

"Not yet." The smile came off the dick's face. He leaned closer. "I think the mayor is coming. They're wise men in there, Race. They'll be figuring. I have always admired your—"

My apartment door banged open. Nelson stuck out his head, shouted: "We've been expecting you, Race. Come on in."

For the first time I looked at the condition of that door. They must have broken it down with fire-axes.

I said to Nelson: "Where do you get that stuff—breaking and entering? No warrant. I'll—"

Nelson's grin was ugly. "Why not complain to the police about it? There's enough of us here. Come on in."

I didn't like Nelson wisecracking. He never went in much for that sort of stuff, didn't have the imagination for it.

I went in, nodded at the commissioner, grinned at the D.A. I noted the fire-escape windows were closed and one curtain askew. No one spoke as I walked through the rooms, made sure my apartment was empty, took a look in the closet that led to the apartment beyond. But I didn't look in the apartment. Footsteps were close on mine. No one spoke.

When I'd finished my prowl I said: "Gentlemen, I've had a—er—a rather vigorous morning. I am about to take a shower."

"That's all right, Race," the D.A. said. "Our time is unimportant. You had nothing to do with the killings here, of course—a number of deaths. Just happened to meet Lance Markey on the stairs, eh?"

I looked straight at him, then at Nelson, then at O'Rourke who was behind them and mugging. At least his face was screwed up as his eyes went up and down me. I got the point, half turned and took a quick glance over my clothes, the blood on my pants and jacket. Hell, they didn't think I'd deny a job like that just because I ducked out with Ione. I had seen Nelson as plain as he had seen me.

But I kidded them along, said: "You figure it out. I'll toss the bloodstained garments from the shower. I've been downtown giving a blood transfusion. The surgeon wasn't very clever."

I DIDN'T CLOSE the bathroom door. I let them look at my suit and stand in the bathroom and question me as I made a monkey out of half a cake of soap.

"The truth is," I finally told the D.A., "that a client with information was coming to see me. The boys ganged on him. Surely you didn't take him for one of the mob. He was lying by the door and—"

The D.A. said sharply: "There was no body by the door and—" He stopped. I couldn't see through the shower curtain, but I knew that Nelson had grabbed his arm before Nelson spoke, for Nelson said: "The body has been taken away. No one has identified him yet. Of course, you must protect clients. What was his name?"

"I was kidding about a client." I guess some cold water splashed out, for there was scraping of feet on tile. "The boys trapped me. I walked into that trap with a gun in each hand. They didn't have the guts for it and—" I grabbed a towel and came out of that shower with a jump. I was suddenly mad again. You'd be too. I let them know how I felt.

I said: "Listen! You've listed those lads' names—every one of them is better dead. And me—me— You men stand there with tragic pans. Why? Because I knocked over boys you couldn't get? Every one with a record. I've got a license to carry a gun. I never pretended I wanted it as a souvenir. A cop would get a medal of honor. Me, I get long faces. Yep, I killed them. Want to make something out of it? I got a lawyer. The city's got newspapers. It was in self-defense. Come on, Nelson. Take your dirty foot off those clean socks."

The commissioner, O'Rourke's boss, was a brainy little man, and must have known of the tie-up between O'Rourke and me, though outwardly, and I dare say even to O'Rourke, pretended ignorance of it.

He said, and his voice was soft and gentle: "Self-defense, Mr. Williams. But the district attorney makes the point that you followed these men, shot them to death on the stairs and endangered the lives of others."

"Baloney," I told the D.A., and meant it. "Anyone in their way as they sought flight would have been killed. I kept them busy looking back, that was all. Protectors of the citizens! Why, you men should be ashamed of yourselves. I don't ask for any protection. If I did, I wouldn't get it. And what's more, I don't lay on my belly and spend an hour or two shooting around corners at guys who want to kill me. Those murderers came on an errand of death. They knew when they came that I don't play with firearms."

The D.A. hesitated a long time. He spoke to Nelson in a low whisper, then to the commissioner. There was doubt in his face. In his words too, I guess. O'Rourke tossed in the towel at the right time. He spoke with authority, too.

"Gentlemen," he cracked straight out, "the papers will make something big out of this. The law-enforcement heads will have to take an attitude if not a definite stand. As for me—just a lowly sergeant"—he stepped forward and gripped my hand—"I think Race Williams did one grand job. I think the law should recognize that. He hasn't got a mark on his body. All those men were desperate men."

The commissioner stepped forward—then the D.A. It had been a long time since the D.A. put his hand in mine.

I heard myself saying: "It wasn't much. I was just mad, I guess, and let my temper run away with me. They were yellow when I began to open up. I'm sorry if I gave you boys any trouble. It's the way I'm built. Rats that come in gangs for a single man get in my hair."

They were leaving now. Nelson stood

on one foot, then the other. But he finally said: "I don't like you, Race. I don't like your methods. I think you're as bad as the, the— But hell, man, it was some job."

"You'd like to have done it," O'Rourke finished for him.

He closed the door on the three men and stayed behind with me. "The man," he said quickly. "The client you thought dead. Was he in this millionaire society to fight crime? Was it part of that?"

"It was," I told him. "And he was there—lying dead in front of my door."

"Are you sure he was dead?"

"Of course, I—" And I stopped. I wasn't sure by any means. The man had lain there by the door. Shots had started before I went into action. No, I couldn't be sure. Maybe he was only stunned. Maybe only hit on the head. Surely, the killers had lined things up for me. Those shots might have been to trap me. But certainly the body wasn't there now. Yet it had looked real. His position—the blood. And then, "What happened to the lad I tossed through the window?"

"Search me." O'Rourke shook his head. "Not a scar on you, yet there was blood all over your clothes. I've known you a long time, Race. I know how you can hit the ceiling at times. But until an hour ago I never thought you, nor any other man, could carry such hatred so far, so viciously—make death so certain." He paused a moment and then, "I've killed men, Race—quite a few in my years on the force. But afterward—when I got home—I'd have the jitters."

"Good old O'Rourke." I patted his back. "No one would suspect it to see you carry on afterwards."

"But the old lady knew—after it was over and she put me to bed. God, I wonder how you feel now!"

I lit a butt and sat down in the easy-chair and looked toward the ceiling. Perhaps I had given it thought before, but not very serious thought. Now, I tried to look into myself. There had been fear, abject horror, on some of those faces. I remembered it then and I remembered it now. But to O'Rourke I said simply: "I feel fine." And O'Rourke winced when I added: "I never felt better in my life."

Things snapped back on me though when O'Rourke had left. Here was something big. My death would have been a sure thing if I hadn't come out that side door of the other apartment and started the fireworks myself. Who had been behind the set up? Dirty McGrath? Perhaps, if he was the head crook The People Versus Crime were getting close to. The young Bent brother—the Apache dancer with the knife? But I couldn't believe that.

And I sat up with a start. What had become of Jane? The younger Bent never got her. Jerry was there too. I nodded in satisfaction. They had bolted up the fire-escape to the roof. Jerry's orders were to duck out before cops came to question him in anything like this. I guess Jane went with him. But the other lad—Bent.

I shrugged my shoulders. He'd have made the roof ahead of them. Besides, he didn't seem such a dangerous man at that.

I passed through the closet door,

carefully examined the clothes there, especially those which hid the door to my other apartment—the door which had no knob and no appearance of a door. It was locked—so Jerry must have attended to that.

I unlocked it, pushed it open and went into my unoccupied apartment beyond. That room was a bedroom. The shades were down. I looked toward the bed, stepped back, jerked out a gun, then let my mouth hang open.

But I did my job as I always do my job. I went through that apartment from one end to the other. It was five full minutes before I came back and stood looking down at that bed.

The man lay stiff and straight and his arms were folded across his chest. His head was set carefully upon the pillow, and his feet were up with his heels touching and his toes in the air. He looked as if an undertaker had laid him out—except for one thing. Someone had stuck a knife in his heart and forgotten to take it out.

You guessed it, of course. It was Ike Bent, the Apache dancer. It was a nice job, too. And that's a real compliment coming from me. I never did fancy the toad-sticking fraternity. I just looked at him and thought—and my thoughts were not unpleasant. This man had had information in his head that would harm Jane. I have often said that you can shoot information right out of a man's head, but it had never occurred to me before that you could cut the information right out of his heart.

Sure, it was a good job no matter how you look at it. The manner of his death did not matter now. I leaned forward. That white spot held there by the knife was not part of his shirt. It was an oblong of cardboard the size of a visiting card, and on it were the printed letters, *The People Versus Crime.* Now who could have put that there?

Jane? Hardly. She wouldn't know to begin with, and besides Jane wouldn't— wouldn't— Well, I wanted to think she wouldn't go in for a knife.

Who else? Jerry? You could count on Jerry for almost anything but—but— And that was entirely too much thinking. Besides, it was time for my lunch engagement with Richard Daniel Havermore.

You've got to admit that I'd spent a very active morning—and I was hungry. I left the corpse on the bed and went back through my own apartment. One of the triple-thick steaks they served at Havermore's club, that and a mug or two of ale—I went whistling out of my apartment and down in the elevator.

CHAPTER 4

HUNDRED-GRAND KILL

AT TEN MINUTES to one exactly I met Havermore at the club. He held a folded paper in his hand. "We'll be rather conspicuous, Mr. Williams, I'm afraid." He led me quickly to an elevator. "The news is already in the papers. And—you weren't hurt!"

"Not me," I told him. And when we had entered the booth at the back of the club dining-room, "You mustn't mind the papers. It was really a cinch job. They were on the run before they really got started. Killers aren't killers after the first one or two take the dose."

He handed me the paper and I looked at the picture and headline. The headline was O.K. *Race Williams Does It Again!* But the picture! Some enterprising retoucher cooperating with the cameraman had shoved a gun into each of my hands, pulled up my jaw so that my nose almost rested in it, stuck a cap on my head and gave me about the meanest slit-like eyes you ever looked at.

I shrugged my shoulders. It was good advertising for other boys who might have the urge to kill.

Since Havermore was the only outside connection of the Black Knights of the Heavy Dough, I told him of the telephone call from Mr. Norman Philips telling me he was the man who sat by Light Number One. I told Havermore of his death and the disappearance of his body.

"I should not have let Philips come. That's fact. I made an error," I finished.

"You say he telephoned you? Told you his name was Mr. Norman B. Philips, that he was the Number One Light, and was afraid and wanted your help, that others guessed his identity?"

"That's about it."

Havermore closed his eyes as if he were thinking. Then he said: "You say Philips lay there dead. Did you recognize him?"

"Recognize him? How? I never saw him before in my life. He was just a crumpled body. But the killers knew somehow that he was coming and set their trap. The

shots that killed him were to bring me to my death."

"And when you came back—after killing these men—the body of Philips was missing. Is that it?"

"That's it."

"You found no trace of his body anywhere?" He leaned across the table and stared at me intently.

"Nowhere—and no police report on it." I stopped. "There might have been men upstairs though, men who could have grabbed the body and rushed off with it before the cops came." I hesitated and then, "But it's hard for me to swallow that one. What would be the reason for it?"

"No reason—no reason at all."

I said: "I feel like hell about losing a client." And perhaps to blame myself less, "But I never really had one."

I went at the steak then and Havermore finished up his bit of sweetbread and lit a cigar. He looked at me for a long time. Then he said: "You may set your mind at rest, Mr. Williams. Mr. Philips is quite well—and quite alive. I talked to him less than fifteen minutes ago. He will preside at the meeting tonight."

"What—what are you trying to tell me?" I gasped.

"I am telling you that you were completely fooled. It is quite evident that Mr. Philips was not there, that he never telephoned you. Don't you see? They used his name to trap you. They hoped you'd rush from your door, see the body and—"

"Shoot them all to death."

Havermore smiled. "In that respect they erred. Though how you lived I don't understand." And since I hadn't mentioned the extra apartment I can see how it puzzled him, but he was talking. "After you dashed downstairs this man at the door got up and fled to the roof. I know—I know. The blood was simply counterfeit. You understand now? The head of this murderous combine we hunt is desperate. He sees that his time is short. If he doesn't fear the evidence that our organization is collecting he fears death. He fears you."

"By God!" I said. "You're right. I thought of the fake, but I didn't have it figured as completely as you did. The simplicity of the thing got me. So it was all a plant to blow me out." I didn't know Havermore had it in him and I told him so.

HE LEANED FORWARD, tapped a finger on the table, said: "Simple, Mr. Williams. But remember—the one who called you on the telephone knew Philips' name, knew he was vice-president of the Second State Bank, and knew, too, that he sits by the Number One Light."

"That's right." I was startled. "How could he know that? No one knows that. Only you."

Havermore nodded. "Therefore someone in the organization—one of those ten men—has betrayed his trust."

"But why? They have money—position. They went into this thing because—"

"Fear," said Havermore. "Philips of the Number One Light will not be afraid. He'll be there. But how about the other man—the one who knew or recognized Philips after so many months of close contact? Don't you see, Mr. Williams?

Our enemies—the criminals—this one desperate criminal—might in some way have discovered another of our members." Havermore's eyes brightened. His hand stretched out on the table. "He might—by threats, say to his family—force this man to divulge our secrets, force him to let this head criminal—let us say it's McGrath—take his place at our council table—tonight."

"Dirty McGrath? He is the man?" The words bounced out on me.

I won't say that I'd actually known, but certainly I'd more than suspected it. So things were getting near the end of the racket. McGrath's racket—our racket, for certainly ours was a racket to break all rackets. After the top man was dead—well, it wouldn't be so hard to smack the small fry down before they ever got started.

The whole planned organization would collapse then.

I said to Havermore: "Since Mr. Philips' name is known—he should have protection."

"No." Havermore shook his head. "There is no reason for his death or he would have been killed before. Somehow I know that things will break tonight. How—or what I can't guess. But you will be with me as usual at the end of that room. McGrath will be there. That, I do know."

"You're the boss," I told him, and forgetting sentiment I slipped over on the mercenary side. I said: "I took a chance with a lot of lead this morning—and nothing in it for me."

"You have been paid well. You knew

your life was in danger when you came to work for us."

I nodded at that, and didn't pull my next punch. "What's in it for me tonight?" I asked bluntly.

Havermore answered just as bluntly. "Exactly one hundred thousand dollars in cash."

"For getting McGrath?" I put it daintily.

"For killing the man who shouldn't be there tonight."

I KNEW THAT ten Men In Black sat at the table with lights beside them so they could jot down notes, pass them from one to another as they formed opinions and voted on the price paid me for finding certain criminals. But these men were big shots. And me—well, the amount mentioned sounded all to the good.

I said without much sense: "What do you mean?"

"I mean"—and Havermore was very serious—"that someone of our number is a traitor to our cause and will not be there tonight. He will give his seat to another—with instructions how that other may enter. And that man will be there."

"If you know he's to be there—why let him come?"

Maybe I thought that was a tough question to answer. But Havermore only smiled—a determined sort of smile. Maybe he had the same hatred for criminals that I had. Maybe he had the same indifference to their deaths. But I didn't think he could give it the same simple expression, though he did and no mistake.

He said: "How is it I let him come?"

His voice was soft. "So you, Mr. Williams, can make one hundred thousand dollars. Yes, you needn't say it. We want him dead."

"And it's Dirty McGrath."

He looked at me a full minute, got up and stood over the table. "I must leave you now. My business is important. The check has been attended to." And just before he left, "One hundred thousand dollars cash, and the man is Dirty McGrath."

Then Havermore was gone. I ordered up a fifty-cent cigar and some more coffee. Dirty McGrath, eh? One hundred thousand dollars. That wasn't so hard to think about. Then I sort of started. I had forgotten to mention Ike Bent to Havermore. Well, after all, he wasn't so important. I could tell Havermore the first time I saw him. A guy as melodramatic as Ike Bent had been, with me in the next room, must have been a half-wit.

I thought of the dough again. I could use it. And I thought of Dirty McGrath, and things went just a little bit sour. I was to go to his house for dinner. Imagine having dinner with a man, then shooting him to death before he had fairly digested it!

I WENT DOWN to my office in the afternoon, but Jerry was not there. And Jane—no word from her. Jerry should have showed up at the office or at least made a telephone call. I had more than a dozen different ways of communicating with him—and I tried them all—from asking for a Mr. George Fairchild Carlton at the ritziest joint in town, to calling Mike Lannigan in a Bowery saloon. This was Jerry's idea of the proper association of places and names—not mine. I even walked around the corner and found that the little box in the post office for just such an emergency held no mail.

I was on my way back to the office when I saw Inspector Nelson. He was hurrying into my building so I took three guesses what for.

The rest of the afternoon I spent at a movie—running from my seat in the rear to the telephone booth to drop in nickels. I must have dropped twenty-five nickels, but I got them all back but one.

That was when I called O'Rourke, got him and told him I wanted to know what Nelson was doing.

"Putting up your new door. At least he's attending to it. He's got an idea, Race, that big things are in the wind."

"And he's right."

"Straight? The big lad behind the show?"

"The big lad behind the show."

"And me, Race—you're dealing me in?"

"I'll give you credit for the mess."

"A mess?"

"Yeah—a mess not a massacre. Sit at the phone at home tonight. Have a fast car at the door, and—" And as he jammed in on me. "And good-bye."

Until the time came around I'd had no real intention of eating at Dirty McGrath's. There was too much to think about. Jane was missing. Jerry was missing—and McGrath was the one who wanted to control the city's crime ring.

Now he had become desperate. His leaders had been cut off one by one. His own turn was coming. He'd anticipate

that and would strike at once. Big guys in the city had been getting it lately—bigger guys than McGrath—at least bigger in the public eye than he was. McGrath saw the right people—but one at a time and alone. He'd never been labeled the "Big Boss." Though he'd been in politics since boyhood it was only a short time back that I realized his real power.

Maybe the dinner was a coincidence and maybe it wasn't. Maybe it was a trap, to prevent me going to the meeting that night. Then all of a sudden it struck me. After all the years was McGrath going into action—going alone? Could a rat have guts? And I got an idea that cost me one more nickel—and which might cost me my life. I called McGrath's house.

"Hello, Race." He answered the phone himself and talked before I could. "I was afraid you'd try and put off your date for tonight. I tried to get you on the phone. I wanted to make sure you'd accept my daughter's invitation. I want her to see more of you."

"That's nice." I thought I saw the idea at once. He'd try and keep me from that meeting tonight. "But I'll have to leave so early. I called up to tell Miss McGrath I can't come. Some other night when—"

"Tonight," said McGrath, and his voice snapped, "I'll expect you at seven in the interests of others."

As I have often said there isn't any use in hanging onto a phone and talking to yourself—and there was no use in calling him back and making threats. I knew what he meant. Jane and Jerry. Their silence was explained.

CHAPTER 5

A PROMISE OF MURDER

I WAS IN a plain business suit when I walked up the stone steps, looked out over the terraces and the water beyond, and gave my name to the pompous butler at the door. There was nothing of the gangster about this lad. He was the real thing.

He looked disdainfully at the bulky but nicely folded bunch of newspapers in my topcoat pocket and spoke his piece. "I'll take your coat, sir. Mr. McGrath is not down yet. But Miss McGrath wishes me to show you to—to— Not up the stairs, sir."

But I was making time up those stairs, chucking back over my shoulder: "I'll just put my coat in the room reserved for the gentlemen. There, there, this is not a foot race."

Sure, I had something in mind as I slid my hand along the perfect smoothness of that staircase, turned the corner and grabbed the banister of the second floor. There I stopped—for two reasons that later turned into three or even four.

Number one reason was the sudden nick in the banister. Number two was the thing I stepped on and, leaning down, picked up and put in my pocket. Number three was when I straightened up and saw the shadow on the wall just where the stairway curved. It was the shadow of a Thompson machine gun.

I turned back quickly to the stairs, met the butler. He was winded and indignant, but his words were polite enough.

I said to him: "Where's the room, and—"

"I am afraid, sir," he said, "that you are mistaken. Mr. and Miss McGrath are dining alone with you. It is not"—he looked at my business suit—"a formal or even a business dinner, as I understand it."

We went softly down the stairs together. I sized him up from the rear now. He was not a fake. If he had been he wouldn't have let me walk behind him.

At the bottom I asked him point-blank: "Where do you come from? I never saw you here before."

"I come," he said very solemnly as I slipped a newspaper from my coat to my jacket pocket, "from the Leroy family. The Massachusetts Leroys, not the Louisiana Leroys. I have arrived a week ahead of time." He waited as if for me to question him further, then said when I didn't: "And maybe I shall be forced to leave before I was supposed to arrive."

Now that was an earful for me—and perhaps, to give Butts credit, a mouthful for him. I decided to play on his dignity, his importance—and his greed.

I said: "Look here, I'm not up to the proper etiquette like you. I guess you sort of awed me." He liked that "awed." "So act as if I just came in and didn't pull a social error by going upstairs. Now take me to Miss McGrath." I slipped a bill into his hand.

Maybe he didn't look at the bill, maybe he did—or maybe he just had a way of feeling it. Anyway he smiled and led me to the drawing-room. The bill was a twenty and somehow he knew it. I'd debated five, ten, fifteen, twenty over in my mind as I looked at him. Yep, I felt positive he wouldn't pretend my respectability under a twenty, much as I wanted to give him a finif—and a push in the mush.

But he announced me to Ione McGrath—and if a king were meeting a queen he couldn't have done it better. My twenty and her poise. High-class finishing schools had given Ione all the poise that Jane had inherited.

BUTTS CLOSED THE door. The girl moved across the room, took both my hands and dragged me down on the couch beside her.

"You mustn't mind Father's high-hatting you. The butler is ahead of time and hardly fits with the other servants. However, he'll have his own firing and hiring after tonight."

"Why after tonight?"

"I don't know." She shrugged her shoulders. "Big things are to happen. Respectability, society, safety. It all sounds so silly, but it's for me—at least Father says it is, and I must pretend. They'll like him though."

"Who?"

"Society. Don't laugh. He—"She came to her feet, pulled curtains aside before a door and disclosed a little dining-alcove. "Tonight we three eat alone. I will serve. I want you to feel perfectly at ease."

No poison, I thought, but I didn't say it. I let her talk for a moment.

"It will please you, Race, if Father can convince Jane Blake that she should take up her normal life—back in society as Iris Parsons. He will see that all her past is buried. Her taking him—or rather me—

with her to meet the better people, will be her return for Father's wiping out any of her past. The safety will"—she looked straight at me now—"will come from you if I need it."

I didn't argue that point. I said: "And the respectability?" And could have bitten my tongue out from the expression on her face.

"I shall try and make that come—from me," she answered. "But a big change is to take place. I don't know how. I don't know why." She jerked up her head. "There will be no more—Dirty McGrath, because—because—"

"Because why?" I thought I was making it hard for her.

"Because people will not think of him that way. No, not even you."

"Ione"—I took her hands now—"you're a swell kid—a damn fine kid—and you're going to have money and maybe get a break in life." I gulped and let it go at that. I couldn't tell her the truth—about this very night. "But you and I are—well, we won't be seeing each other."

"No!" She came to her feet. "I helped you today, Race. I helped you once before. I—I won't—" She paused and then, "I can't lie to you. I'll go after my man just as Jane goes after hers."

"It's not that." I decided to give it to her straight. "It's your father. He doesn't think much of me and I—I think he's a—" She put fingers over my mouth, said: "Some day you'll see eye-to-eye—he said so himself."

I started to shake my head. Then my eyes widened. Her old man was right. We would see eye-to-eye—and he would die.

Not such a bad epitaph at that, I thought, as Timothy McGrath entered the room.

McGrath was a remarkable man. I had seen him at times, slipping through the night like any common hood. I had seen him in his own library, in a dressing gown and slippers—the night I first saw his daughter. Tonight, he was different again. Gray suit, plain blue four-in-hand tie, a blue shirt with a soft collar, and shaved clean as a whistle—as if he had just come from his barber's and his tailor's. Even his chins seemed to have disappeared, and although his old habit of playing with those chins caught up with him at times, he had to content himself with straightening his tie. He fairly breezed across the room and gripped my hand.

"We're going to be pretty swanky around here, Race. Ione has heard too much that is wrong about me. But we're starting fresh."

We sat down at the little table and Ione kept going in and out of the door serving the meal. Sensible meal, too. None of this soup to nuts business. Broiled chicken—plenty of it, French fried potatoes—then apple pie with ice cream on it. Nothing elegant—maybe I don't know proper food. But me—that's what I call eating.

McGrath talked.

"My girl Ione wants you—so you come. The butler was not a bit of light comedy for your sake. I tell you, Race, he's going to stay. The back of the house is going to die. That is, the old street entrance. It's to be the servants' quarters. I'm going to let James—if his name is James—have full swing on what it costs. He thinks we don't know things, but I'll have him eating out of my hand. We'll give him a butler's paradise, and if we can't make a home out of it afterwards we'll live across the street and entertain here."

"Did you see the afternoon papers?" I interrupted.

"No, no, just a glance. But I heard the talk. It didn't seem like you, Race. You must have been mad. The paper I saw said—*Race Williams on the Kill Again.*"

I grinned. "They haven't seen anything yet." And as he frowned I finished my coffee and nodded at Ione. She took my cup and left the room.

I came to my feet, spun the key in the lock behind her, walked over to the only other door and turned the key in that. I was watching McGrath all the time. He said nothing, lit a big cigar and put the box on the table. The girl was trying the knob.

I called to her: "Your father wants to talk privately with me, Ione. It's all right."

She called back in a frightened sort of voice: "No, no." And then, "Father—your word. Race will be all right."

Dirty McGrath took out his cigar and laughed. It was a real laugh—a belly laugh. The girl heard it all right. Then he said: "It's all right, Ione—absolutely. Wait in your room. I'll call you on the house phone. So be there."

We both listened. Five—ten—fifteen seconds passed. Then we heard her feet moving from the door.

"Well," McGrath said. "That's a funny one. It's a threat, of course?"

"Yes," I told him. "A threat of death. One more or less wouldn't bother me much tonight." I let my coat flash open, my guns show. Then I tossed him the paper. "Read that before we begin to talk. Understand, I want Jane and that boy of mine—at once."

He turned over the paper and shook his head. He was not the McGrath I was used to meeting—and I don't mean simply dress and front now—I mean inside.

He said: "That sort of stuff never bothers me. I know your record too well. Personally, it seemed a messy sort of job for you to be mixed up in. A corpse here and a corpse there—and blood all over the damned place. No, no, there is only one saving grace about it. You did accomplish your purpose."

"That's right. I accomplished my purpose."

HE TOOK THE cigar out of his mouth and leaned forward. "We won't go into what you threaten or don't threaten. To begin with, don't forget I hired that jewelry shop—maybe to watch you, but Ione was there when you needed her. Oh, you needed her all right, for you were half mad then because your client Norman Philips had been killed. I was talking to him last night. He said he was going to see you. I tried to get him. Tried to stop him and—"

"You stopped him all right. He isn't dead."

"Don't kid me, Race, I know better. You'd never go berserk like that just for your own amusement."

He was right. I told him. "I thought he was dead at the time. Now—"

"I'm a busy man—especially busy tonight," McGrath shot in on me. "My daughter has taken a fancy to you, wants you to stay alive. I'll ask you to hear my threat first. I wouldn't be fool enough to sit alone here with you unless I played a sure thing. So—my threat. You spend the evening here with my daughter—until twelve o'clock—or you'll never see Jane and Jerry again. There—I'm not going to match fast draws with you. I've placed them such a distance away that it would be physically impossible to bring them here tonight anyway."

"Until after the meeting, eh?"

"What meeting?"

And I let it go at that. I shouldn't have mentioned it at all. I shouldn't have put him on his guard. But I thrust my hand into my pocket, pulled out the thing I had found on the stairs.

"Come, come," he said. "Make your threat sharp—and quick. I don't like to beat around things."

"That's all right by me." My temper was rising, my back was against a wall, so there could be no surprise. I jerked a gun into one hand and tossed the thing across to him with the other. He picked it off the table examining it carefully. It was the heel of a woman's shoe.

I said: "Deliver to me in this room within three minutes, the shoe that belongs to that heel, and see that the live foot of the girl is in it. That's right—" I leaned toward him now. "The answer is a hole in your stomach big enough for your fancy butler to walk through."

His eyes narrowed as he looked at me. "Getting to be a sleuth, eh—clues and all that."

"She kicked the banister while she was being carried upstairs. It knocked the heel off her shoe. No one bothered—but me. She's not far away. She's in this house now."

His features took on a very grave look. His upper teeth clamped down hard. His face was slightly ashen. Then he shook his head. His words were no more than a whisper.

"You wouldn't dare. You wouldn't dare."

"McGrath," I told him. "I've built up a reputation among crooks, murderers—the lowest scum of the night. It took years to build it. You must know, too—of the many times I nearly lost my freedom because I wouldn't talk. I couldn't talk and keep my word. You'd take that word, wouldn't you?"

"Yes." He thought a long time. "Yes, I'd take that word."

"Then," I said, "I know you, and know Jane's chance for life—or even torture. If you don't produce her, I give you my word—my word of honor that I'll put a slug in your stomach—or enough slugs to make you dead."

HE GOT UP, shrugged his shoulders, pounded his waist line once, then said without any mirth: "Race Williams, raise your right hand. Do you solemnly swear to commit murder by shooting one—" He stopped suddenly, said: "You'll take my word, of course."

"No," I said, "I won't."

He laughed at that.

"I've built up my reputation by breaking my word, lying to the people and torturing women and children, eh Race?

Well, I'll make you a proposition. You owe more than you think to my daughter. Oh, I won't ask you if you'd feel the same about her under the same circumstances. But she likes you. Youth of today is peculiar. There is a sort of glamor about your—this killing of criminals—this defending the citizens. We'll put it this way. Jane and your boy—your dear boy, Jerry, who by the way, takes after you—will have their freedom. But you will not see them until after midnight. There's a phone there on the little table. You can talk to Jerry—and no doubt you have some way of understanding whether he's being forced to talk or not. But you can't talk to Jane—and you can't leave here before twelve o'clock."

"I don't have to see them," I agreed. "But I do have to leave here."

"All right," McGrath said. "You're a stubborn fellow—have it your way."

"Good," I told him. "Now what?"

He turned and faced me—and his words set me back on my heels.

"Now shoot," was all he said.

Stunned? Sure I was stunned. I guess I gasped at him.

"But I gave you my word—"

"That's right—your word and one hundred thousand dollars in cash for my dead body. Go on—earn your money. Not even the Bent boys were offered so much money for a single murder."

I set my teeth. McGrath knew more than I thought—more than anyone could possibly think.

I said: "I won't touch a penny of it." I guess my face was white now. I could feel the blood drain from it. "But I'm going through with it, McGrath. You've seen the papers. With you dead—the others in this house— Yes, by God, I'll shoot my way to Jane on the floor above."

McGrath clapped his hands.

"Bravo, Race—my word against yours. I don't think you'll make it." And suddenly, "Time passes. We can't have you breaking your word. I'll make a deal with you. You stay here with my daughter until twelve o'clock—unless she gives you permission to leave. You can even try my supposed method on her—torture."

I looked at my watch, saw the seconds ticking off, raised my gun, waited for McGrath to speak, to sink slowly to his knees.

And he didn't. He put his cigar back in his mouth and waited too. I got a bright idea. I tried to hide my smile, but it slipped through as I said what I hoped was grimly: "All right—you have my word again. I'll stay here until Ione gives me permission to leave."

"Good." He lifted the phone on the desk and did his stuff.

CHAPTER 6

ALL'S FAIR IN LOVE AND DEATH

McGrath was right. Jerry and I did have a system and twenty minutes later McGrath gave us a chance to use it. He handed me the phone from the desk, said: "Your assistant Jerry is on the wire. Jane and he were upstairs in this house as you said. They are both free. He was told to call you here an hour after he was freed.

Jerry can assure you of their safety—nothing more. If he tries to give you other information he will be cut off." He took a hand phone and plugged it in the wall. "Satisfactory, Race? Satisfactory for this word of honor of yours?"

"Satisfactory," I said.

McGrath spoke through his own phone which he had plugged into a socket and put to his ear. "All right," he said. And to me, "I'll be listening, Race."

Then the voice of Jerry came. "It's like this, boss. Jane and I are free. We picked up our own taxi and she drove off in it when I come in this drug store to telephone you. She gave me a little dope on where—"

And as McGrath frowned at me, I cut in. "Where are you now?" I asked.

"Now, boss—ain't guys listening? You know that Apache dancer whose name had better be secret? Well, he and me did a dance and—"

McGrath snapped his plug out of the wall. Jerry's voice died. But I didn't need to hear any more. I had seen what Jerry had to tell me, on the bed in my extra apartment.

McGrath said: "Fair enough?" And I had to nod. "Now for Ione. You're on your own, Race—just her permission." He laughed and the girl came into the room.

She was beautiful then—just enough of a doubtful look in her blue eyes to make them seem to swim. I looked her over well—throat, neck, the softness of her arms, the peculiar light in her hair. Women are bad stuff in business sometimes, but tonight— I had real business to attend to. The business of women—or at least one woman. Ione loved me or thought she did, which is the same thing while it lasts. And me— I have made killing a business—why not make love a business?

Her father put both hands upon her shoulders. He spoke to her very slowly and made each word count with a seriousness and earnestness which impressed the girl deeply. Me too—until she put her glims over on me—and those blue lamps had melted. They even glistened now.

"Ione," McGrath said, "Mr. Williams is to stay here with you tonight until you give him permission to leave. He is a very brave and a very courageous man. He would kill for what he thinks is right— and has. He would die for a principle or to protect someone." He laid that "someone" on thick. "I am leaving now. I may be back before twelve. But without your stated permission he can not leave this house. Let me impress upon you—let me assure you, Ione—that if you give him that permission he is going straight to his death." He leaned down and kissed her. "I hope we may see more of Race Williams—that you may see more of him. So mark my words, child. If he leaves here—you and you alone send him to his death."

And McGrath was gone.

He'd laid it on a bit thick, but McGrath had his rights, I suppose. I stood there and took it. Maybe it bothered me a bit as I watched the girl and her eyes turned toward mine. They were more than wet— they were filled. She turned away.

I said: "Don't be silly, Ione. Your father was exaggerating things. Why, you're crying."

She swung back and faced me—no handkerchief to her eyes—just the tears dripping over the lids. Oh, I know women turn the water works on or off as the fancy suits them. But they bury their heads and sob—or sink them on your shoulder and try to grab some dough—or even pretend they're not crying. But Ione just faced me and cried silently.

It was tough, but I was going to work when she beat me to it.

"What does it matter?" She nodded and wiped away the tears. "I'd never let you go. I guess it's just that I have the power of life or death over you that makes me cry—when I really should be happy."

I went to work in earnest then. I just took two steps forward and held her in my arms. Maybe she tried to draw back— maybe she didn't, when I chirped like a Clark Gable: "You have more power than that over me, Ione." I could feel her hands come up and press against my neck. "Funny, I didn't seem to know, but then I guess it's my way with women."

But I'll cut out the sentimental stuff. I won't lie. I liked it, of course. She was young, her lips and her young body were very close to mine. Yet I didn't lose my head.

"There is Jane," she said once.

I grabbed her tighter and laughed. "There was Jane, you mean. Jealous already and me just finding out that for the first time in my life I—I— Ione, I'll do anything in the world for you—make any promise you ask. Just as you would if I ever—"

"Yes, yes," she said. "Any promise—any sacrifice—"

"No matter what I might ask now? Your word?"

"Yes, yes—anything that wouldn't harm you or—"

I looked at the clock, cursed under my breath, started in all over again. I was doing well, too—doing fine, liking my job, when suddenly it happened.

"Yes, anything." She pushed me from her and stood looking straight at me. "Even to sending you to your death." I backed away. Her eyes flashed and I didn't feel any too good.

"Go, Race," she said. "You have my permission to go." And as I started toward the door deciding against any explanation, she added: "All's fair in love and death and the hunting of the criminal, I suppose. Women do it to men—why not men to women?"

She was helping me with my coat there by the front door, holding it open for me. I'm a convincing talker, but I kept my mouth closed then.

She said: "I hope nothing happens to you. I hope that I am big enough to look on it in the right light—as a part of your business. I hope that I am a fool, and you are not—not—a—"

The door closed. I didn't hear her final word. I don't know if she even spoke it. And I didn't try to figure out what it might have been. But I felt mighty cheap. Yeah—damned good and cheap.

I had kissed her and lied to her and—

For once in my life my stomach turned over inside. I had kissed her and lied to her so that I could be free to shoot her old man to death.

Lousy. Yep, maybe it was lousy. But it wasn't the money. Not that I don't like the heavy dough as well as the next fellow, but anyone who says it was money in this case lies in his teeth.

I didn't know what was in the wind. Evidently Havermore didn't know what was in the wind. McGrath— It seemed as if he did know. It seemed as if he knew the impossible and would be at the table—at the secret meeting of the Men In Black. But they were reputable, reliable, big men in business. No money could influence them. No threat—

And I drew in a deep breath as I remembered Havermore's words. A threat—yes. To his family. To a wife, a daughter, a young child perhaps. Under such circumstances rich and poor—courageous and cowardly are all one.

Ione—of course McGrath figured the girl wouldn't let me go to my death. And he had my word. He impressed the girl with the importance of keeping me there. Yet he might have been telling her the truth when he said I would go to my death. At least what he thought was the truth.

A lousy trick? Well, I looked at it this way. I was paid by these Men In Black. Havermore was their mouth-piece and risked his life—day and night—for he was in the open. These men expected me to be there. Tonight their lives might depend on me. Anyway, I didn't think Ione would be onto me. I was just going to get her to release me from my promise with some song and dance. She just wasn't dumb enough, that was the trouble. I'd make it up to her later by carting her around town a bit. Conceit? Maybe.

But that's what she wanted, wasn't it? O.K. Have it your way. She'd hardly pal around with a guy who blasted her father apart.

CHAPTER 7

THE COUNTERFEIT LIGHT

IT WAS A little early so I took it easy-going to the building where the meeting was scheduled—a brownstone front this time, instead of a great office building.

It was after ten when I walked down that dark side street—practically deserted, too. An easy walk, you think? Well, it felt like the most dangerous walk I had ever taken.

I saw some of the men—call them shadows if you wish—crouched down in the sunken courts before the buildings. And ducking shadows that moved down an alleyway between two houses. And across the street a couple of huge cars.

Those would be the guard—the private detectives hired from the Gregory Ford Agency to watch over the Men In Black. At least they should be—and I hoped they were.

I spotted the house before I reached it or saw the number. The building beside it must have been torn down, for a car dashed into a driveway—which is not the way with most brownstone fronts.

I walked on eggs to the right house, turned up the steps and nodded at the men in the darkness who were leaning to each side of the stone balustrades.

The man to my left said: "Come on, brother. No one goes in here tonight."

"Really?" I started and stopped as a light flashed from inside and the door opened. My friend spoke to the man silhouetted in the doorway.

"This man wanted—" He swallowed the words and said instead: "Whatever you say of course, Sam."

I stepped into the vestibule, waited while Sam Pierce, the right-hand man of the Gregory Ford Detective Agency tapped on the inside door to gain admittance to the dimly lit hallway beyond. I nodded. This was real business. If Sam had refused me entrance I couldn't have forced him to open the door. But now inside, the door locked, the man gone, I asked: "Those your men outside, Sam?"

"No, they're cannibals from the South Seas. One of them bite you?"

"Not me." I shook my head at his smirking grin. "But they'll bite you."

"What do you mean?" He seemed disturbed. "Gregory got extra men tonight."

"Then you don't know them?"

"Who said I didn't? They took orders fast enough." And when I looked sadly at him, "Well, who'd you think they were?"

"Strangers to me." I shrugged. "I wouldn't know their names, but from long experience—both with the police and against them—I'd be laying better than even money that they're quiet clothes men from Headquarters."

"You must be off your nut." Sam turned back, however, and looked at the door. "The big boss here hires a guard of his own—you know, Mr. Havermore."

"Police guard, Sam?"

"No, not a police guard." And facing me squarely, "I'm not dumb, you know, Race. I'm not even curious. If I was, I might guess about these meetings of big financial interests—and the heavy guard they need. But the agency is not paid to figure things out. In fact, we're paid not to figure things out." And eyeing me carefully, "You should know cops. You know O'Rourke pretty well."

"Yeah, I know O'Rourke pretty well," I said. "I know Nelson, too—too damn well."

"Inspector Nelson? Why he—he—"

"He what?"

"He was questioned by a couple of our men tonight. Down by the corner. The damn fools didn't recognize him. And he nearly knocked their heads apart after he'd identified himself. You don't think—"

"Yeah, I do think," I jammed in. "I think those two men out there work for Nelson." With that I turned and started toward the stairs which led above.

"Stop!" Sam said suddenly, his voice harsh. It sounded like an order from a man who meant business. Then his voice softened as he followed me. "I want to ask you a question, Race." His voice was casual now—yep, too damn casual for a man who'd first spoken that "Stop!" order.

I JUST SWUNG and did it before he could jam a gun into my back. Surely, his gun was in his hand when I turned, but I was inside that gun close against his body. And right into the pit of his stomach was the nose of my own forty-four dug deep. I gave him the horse laugh. "So you read your paper, eh Sam? And wanted to be sure? What's on your mind? And don't call for help." I shoved the gun tighter. "It's nestling pretty close, Sam—you wouldn't want me to press the trigger and let it lay a lead egg."

Sam didn't sneer. He didn't step back even though I crowded him. He said: "You can't go upstairs tonight. That's orders."

I stretched up my hand and twisted his gun free. Then I stepped back and digging a paper from my pocket gave it to him.

"It's my lucky day, Sam." I handed him his gun. "Who gave you those orders?"

"Ford," he said. "Gregory Ford himself."

"In person." I made a face. "Things must be big if—"

A door opened across from the dining-room. A figure squeezed through it—a big man with massive shoulders, a massive frame. He had a large open face, and one extra chin since I had last seen him. His eyes were wide and staring. He walked toward me tilting the black felt hat on his head. He ducked a hand into his vest pocket and producing a half-smoked cigar shoved it into his mouth. He hadn't changed any, except the derby hat was gone. Yep, Gregory Ford was a detective who looked exactly like one. He'd played that part for years until he really lived it. He always said: "When people want a detective they want a detective to look like a detective—as they picture one."

Now he was holding some papers in his hands and moving his feet quickly.

"Hello, boy," he said to me. "I see great things in the paper about you. I want a talk with you. There, don't stand like an idiot looking at me. Sam Pierce isn't the only man in the world who can manage my business. Either shoot him to death or leave him alive, but come and have a talk with me."

"It will be worth my time?" I asked.

"Sure, sure—at least it's worth mine," Gregory said. "Come on." He turned and I followed him across the dining-room to the door beyond, but over my shoulder I warned Sam: "Any false move on your part and I'll plug Gregory in the back."

"By God," Sam muttered, "if I could be sure of that I'd make a dozen false moves!"

Gregory opened the door, waited for me to pass into the little room and when I nodded for him to go first he whispered: "Don't start any argument. Don't get a desire to just shoot people. Take it easy— you're one under par now."

Then we were in the room with the door closed. I looked at the dignified gentleman on the edge of the chair in the corner. He leaned heavily on a gold-headed cane.

Gregory waved a hand, said: "The gentleman will speak to you, Race. He has an idea he is going to be killed tonight. You are to see that he isn't." And before he went back into the dining-room, "And for the love of Pete don't kill everyone in the building to avenge his death! He won't like that."

GREGORY GONE, I waited for the man to speak. He didn't, so I took the lead. I said: "Well, what's on your chest?"

The man opened his mouth to speak. The cane slipped to the floor and he seemed suddenly to slip inside his clothes.

They didn't seem to fit him any more when he sat up.

He said: "I am the Number Four Light." Then he walked across the room, took down a bottle of whiskey and poured himself a glass with shaky hands—a full glass. Then, damn it, he only took a sip, shook himself and turning added: "I am also the president of the Second State Bank."

"Got anything to identify yourself?"

He waved that question aside, said: "Mr. Ford will do that—should have done that. Now, Mr. Williams—liquor has given me strength. I may or may not hold a terrible secret. What happened to Mr. Norman Philips—my friend—vice-president of my bank? Was he killed when he went to see you?"

"No, no, I thought he was, but he wasn't. I was told that—"

"Enough." He raised his hand. "I expect death tonight—death if I sit by the Number Four Light."

"Good." I leaned forward and got down to business. "This is a purely private transaction. You consider it very serious?"

"So much so that I hesitate to— to—well, not to go myself. We have all sworn—"

And damn it, I had to talk him into the idea he had in his mind.

"Hell," I said. "Suppose I had a big banking deal on. I'd be a fool to try to pull it off. I'd come to a man like you to do it for me—pay you well for it. Now, you face a big deal—a deal in death. Death is my business. I face it one way or another every day. You think you're going to be popped off beside the Number Four Light—and you will if it has been planned that way. You'd sit there with no way to prevent it. Now—put me there! That's right in my line. Here, look at the evening paper."

He looked over the headlines and shuddered visibly. "I saw it. But this—this might come so suddenly that you wouldn't have a chance."

"You consider it extremely dangerous even for me?"

"The truth is that I consider it sure death for anyone who sits by that Number Four Lamp tonight."

I rubbed my chin and looked at him. Then I said: "Very well, in that case I'll expect more money. There, don't seem surprised. You figure bonds in dollars and cents. I figure life and death the same way." I gripped his hand. "Certain death, eh? In that case I'll charge five thousand dollars."

Sure it got him. I wanted it to get him. Four times he tried to make out the damn check with his trembling fingers, and then we had to have Gregory Ford in. I didn't tell Gregory the exact agreement, but I think he more than suspected it. Anyway, I let him fill in the check and we finally got a satisfactory signature on it.

With that Mr. Number Four Light staggered from the room. He gurgled before he left: "The rest—all of it—is in the hands of Mr. Gregory Ford, but these few instructions only—you must read them, tear them up—all but the single card."

The instructions were simple—a few words, an excellent sketch of the room the meeting was to be held in, the position of the lights upon the table—the little side door down by the Number One Light through which I would enter. Also, the far end of the room—the card table that held a light, and where at other meetings, I could sit—or Havermore, who usually stood in the back with me. Beyond that—folding doors, the usual thick curtains. He even had the outer room in—just beyond those folding doors—where I usually entered, where sometimes dicks stayed on guard. House, office building, hotel or what-not, the set-up was just the same each time.

Gregory Ford and I had it out then. He was to give me instructions just how to work things—and damn it, he wouldn't open his mouth until he got his ten percent. He said he was my agent. He wanted his cut. Agent? Sure. Agent of death. But Gregory Ford was not like the rest of the boys. You couldn't just stick a gun down his throat and settle matters.

I said: "I'll pay you tomorrow. This is supposed to be certain death—and I can't cash his check if I'm dead. Suppose I gave you my check for five hundred and then got killed—what good would it do me?"

"The law," Gregory stated very slowly, "does not permit the cashing of checks if the maker is deceased. That's clear."

It was clear. I gave Gregory the check, watched him produce the cigar and gave it a few twirls.

"Now, boy"—he held that cigar as if it were a dart and he was about to hurl it at me—"back you go to the hall, out the front door, and step into a taxi that will catch up with you as you start down the street. That taxi is fixed. It will take you to a chauffeur-driven private car. Two men will be in that car. They will both carry guns in their hands—across their knees. They will drive you back to this house. You will enter the driveway, be whisked into the cellar. Lights will be dim. Your hat must be pulled far down and your coat collar turned high up. You will be Number Four Light—and use the formula you have on that paper which you are burning."

He was right. I had touched a match to it. The little card that was in the envelope, I kept.

I didn't hesitate this time. I looked at the name on the five-grand check, whistled softly, for it was a big name in the city. Then I handed Sam another newspaper when I left. I believe strongly in advertising—especially when it's free.

I walked down the street, entered the taxi and sped away. When I returned it was in a high-priced boat. I thought the license number on such an expensive car would easily give the owner away. Later I discovered that none of the Men In Black came in their own cars.

I had my hat down all right, had my coat collar turned up and certainly was hustled, if not "whisked" down steps into the lower floor of the house. No, I wasn't afraid of a trap, not with Gregory Ford in it. But I was afraid—or rather suspicious—that whoever had suddenly identified all these men who had never had any trouble before night, might spot me, too, and the attack on Number Four come sooner than expected. It was just a question of how far things had gone—and whether the attack would come upstairs or down. For I knew

as well as Number Four that there was trouble brewing—and much more trouble than just his own death.

CHAPTER 8

LIGHTS OUT

I STOOD IN the closet-like room with the door I had entered behind me—and the door I was to pass through before. I just watched and waited in the darkness. Then light, as the grill in the door slid back and an opening like a bank teller's window appeared.

The man behind that window was young. He smiled pleasantly, said calmly: "Good evening, sir. Your number, please."

I handed the card through the window. He looked at it, held it to the light, turned it around. After that I handed him the twenty-dollar gold piece with the queer little hole in it that the banker had given me, and also spoke the passwords that I had memorized from the paper I had burned.

The young man said: "I am sorry to be slow tonight, Mr. Four." He pushed a mask through the window to me. "But I have been ordered to be overcautious. Thank you, sir."

There was a small elevator, and I took that instead of the stairs, though the man sitting on the stairs with the machine gun over his knees offered me my choice with a motion of the gun. The show was about to begin.

I was late. All the seats at the table were taken—every light but one was lit.

I could not see Havermore at the back of the room. There was a dim light that disclosed the folding doors—mostly hidden by thick curtains. No lamp was lit where the card table should be.

I passed in back of the chairs. My mask was carefully adjusted. Number One Light was at one end of the table—Number Six at the other end. On my side were Numbers Two, Three, Four and Five. Across that long table Numbers Seven, Eight, Nine and Ten. Plainly on each lamp shade was a number.

It wasn't hard to pick Number Four. The light was out, and my instructions were explicit. I reached the chair, pulled it out and, while pulling it quietly back to the table with one hand, sought the light-switch at the end of the pencil which lay beside the pad by the lamp, with the other.

I made a noise pulling my chair in when I touched the switch. It sounded simply as if I sat down and lit the light at the same time—which would give an air of long familiarity with my surroundings.

Almost at once the lights went out one by one. There was a dead darkness. Then lights flicked on and off. After that one by one they lit and went out.

A moment's pause and a light across the table went on. A white hand appeared and wrote hurriedly. The light went out. Another light went on. Then beside me Number Five Light snapped on. A slender hand with long delicate fingers scratched quickly on a pad. Number Five Light went out. Almost at once a hand touched mine—there was paper in it. It came from my right—a note from Number Five.

Now I understood—notes went back and forth among these people—people who did not know each other—would not recognize each other on the street.

I slipped the note under my light, read—

Number Four:
You always voted with me—voted the night we took in Race Williams. Is he here tonight? Havermore is out in the reception-room. I think it's going to be McGrath. I don't believe he finishes our job. I hinted to you once before that there was another Bent brother. Vote with me against going after McGrath—despite what evidence is brought up until we're sure.
                    Number Five

I remembered Number Five had voted me in—yet I wrote back—

McGrath it is. I'll vote to get him.
                    Number Four

I hadn't seen Number Six below me at the end of the table writing until I got his note.

It's to be McGrath. Did you see the papers? With Williams it will be a vote for murder. They say not. I don't know how to vote. I think it's McGrath
                    Number Six

I answered that one.

It's McGrath. Williams is an upstanding man. He'll do no wrong.
                    Number Four

I felt like adding that there was a hundred grand in it for Mr. Williams, but both modesty and caution forbade it.

But you see notes came from all over. When I got the note from Number Six, it passed through the hands of Number Five who gave it to me. Yep, there was some frenzied writing about. I picked up a note from Number One. It read—

Something happened to Race Williams. Do not fear no blame is attached to you.

Number One

I picked up at that and took a real interest. Mr. President had been afraid there would be something happen to him, and Mr. Number One Light was lulling him into the idea of safety. And who was Mr. Number One Light? Why the man who was Mr. Bank President's friend—Norman B. Philips. I gulped. Or had Philips given his place to Dirty McGrath?

I picked up a note that was a beaut. It read—

Number Four:
You're picked for death. Get under the table before it happens. I can't save you. If you know any way out—take it. I was wrong. My gun was taken from me. Unless they always search the Committee, and I believe you told me they didn't, why watch for death. If I thought there was a chance I'd strangle him with my own hands, but I can't reach him. Do not try to escape by the door. It has been bolted.

There was no number signed to that. But what a warning! And where did it come from? And who was in cahoots with who?

I TRIED TO figure things out and I drew it this way. Mr. President of the Bank had sold out to Dirty McGrath. McGrath had told him that his vice-president, Philips, would die unless he arranged for him to take Philips' place at Light Number One. So he arranged it. Then in some way he also arranged for someone—some member of The People Versus Crime—to be there armed and kill McGrath before he was killed.

And he had evidently lost his nerve, heard that this certain person couldn't get a gun in, felt death was certain for him, and let me take the rap. But who'd stop the lad getting a gun in? Surely that would mean others at the table or someone crooked below. Yet, no one had taken a gun from me. And if I may say so myself, they're damned good and lucky they didn't try it. But my thoughts were twisted ones. I didn't know what was breaking. It was just my belief that Dirty McGrath was at that table.

Who that note came from I didn't know. But he must have been surprised at my still sitting there—that is, if he could still see me sitting there. For my light was out.

The Number One Light arose. He said quietly: "All lights on. I must speak to you most confidentially. Something very serious has happened."

Lights popped on and the man behind the Number One Light spoke. His face was covered by the mask, his mouth deep in some cloth. A muffled voice, a hidden voice, but I was positive it was not the voice of the Number One Light I had listened to before—though the thoughts behind it in the beginning were the same, that "old man" stuff he always pulled.

"Gentlemen—" He leaned upon the table and his dull outline was clear enough—I mean clear enough to take a shot at if either of his white hands should suddenly turn black clutching a gun.

"Gentlemen, my thanks to Mr. Havermore who has risked his life for us. I am an old man and have least to lose. Tonight I have ordered Mr. Havermore to stay away. In turn, we do not have Race Williams with us. I have not given these orders as your leader, for we have no leader, but because in cases of grave danger I am permitted through your trust to act for you. Tonight we face a grave danger. Two of our number have turned traitors."

And with that statement he stepped suddenly back in the darkness. The crowd was dumfounded all right. His words didn't help them any. Every figure was clearly defined there by the light. Yep, I was sure it was McGrath now. He was going to kill those who knew or who had any evidence against him. I would be one because he thought I was the Mr. President who had evidence on him. The vice-president would be the other whom he had prisoner, if he hadn't already killed him. Havermore— And sweat broke on my forehead.

God in Heaven! He had already killed Havermore. McGrath suddenly backed far into the shadows—into the darkness. Yes, he'd kill the evidence in the minds of two men who had it. Myself, alias Mr.

President—and the man who had sent me the note. The other evidence if written, he would have taken from Havermore or Philips, the vice-president.

And then what? He'd walk out that small heavy door I had entered, lock it behind him and escape. The end? The rest at the table would cover up his crime since they'd think it was their real associate— never suspect it was McGrath.

The figure was talking in the darkness.

"When it is over the darkness shall turn to light. Gentlemen, these men have betrayed a trust that may mean the death of many. I am old—it does not matter about me." I was trying to pick out something to shoot at while he talked. "No one of our many guards will even suspect. Gentlemen, I correct a wrong— with perhaps another wrong. These men must die. All sit quiet. It is given to me to kill them. Number Four—lean forward— your face close to the lamp."

DRAMATIC! YOU COULD have heard a jug of gin drop. That voice still carried command. Five thousand dollars to save another man's life less ten percent. There was command in the voice all right. McGrath did his stuff well. An old man— about to kill. To kill to save a great cause. It sounded hot stuff. Yep, I leaned forward peering into the darkness—knowing nothing had moved. Dramatic—sure it was. Yep, I leaned forward and as I leaned forward I tore off my mask. Maybe that saved my life—maybe it didn't. But he saw my face plainly—and a cry of surprise— yes, and I think of terror, jumped from his throat.

"Darkness and light," I said. "One shot, Dirty McGrath—one shot."

And the Number One Light put the match to the store-full of fireworks.

He fired, all right—fired just as I pressed the catch on the flashlight in my left hand. He fired and shot the lamp shade right into my face. Darkness and light—and the pencil of light from my pocket flashlight shone smack upon the black hood that hid his entire head.

He didn't fire again. There were two slits in that hood for his eyes—before he had even finished crying out my name in fear, there was a third hole in the hood—a hole right between the other two. It rocked him, all right. He tossed himself against the wall like a car full of drunks missing a curve.

"Sit tight, gentlemen," I said. "It was Dirty McGrath and he had it coming—and I gave it to him." I let them digest that then I added: "Mr. Richard Havermore speaks through your mouths. The man I just killed was on the books for exactly one hundred thousand dollars in cash. Do I hear any objections?" And when I didn't, for they all sat stiff and straight, I leaned over and knocked the shades off the lamps on Three and Five.

"Gentlemen"—I was talking to them like a Dutch uncle now—"there will be no secrets from now on. There will be no one in this room that the others won't know. It's a showdown now."

I tore the mask off Number Three and two voices said in unison: "Good God, it's Jim Hastings!"

I turned to Number Five. He ducked on me, started down the room, was close to the little door when I grabbed an arm and tore the mask from his face too. His face? Her face! It was my turn to gasp. "Jane—Jane Blake!" I said. "You— How did you manage to get here tonight?"

She said: "Every night. I helped start The People Versus Crime, Race. I said I'd use the money you saved for me to eliminate crime. I was here at the first meeting. I was here at the last. I—I—"

And that room was no longer sound-proof. The pounding at the doors sounded like axes. Someone hollered: "The police!" Someone else must have opened the door.

I heard the voice of Mr. President whose seat I had taken screeching: "I couldn't help it. I knew he was there to kill. I—I—called the police—your friend O'Rourke, Mr. Williams."

And me, I was standing over the body looking down at the dead hands that flopped back when I grasped them.

Nelson was there beside me. O'Rourke too and—hell, there was a cough that jarred me and meant trouble. It was the commissioner of police.

He said, and his voice was slightly awed in the beginning when he used the names: "Mr. Hastings, Mr. Conroy, Mr. Gerthstein, Mr.— Well, upon my word I never saw such—" And turning to me as I knelt on the floor, "What, again! What's all this, Williams?"

"This," I said, as I grasped the dead man's hood-like mask, "is the end of the party. Take a look. I have pretty high-class witnesses that it was both self-defense and to prevent murder. Take a look-see, Commissioner. Dirty McGrath." I started to give a quick jerk at the hood when a voice spoke behind me—calm and low.

The voice said: "Not Dirty, Race. Timothy J. McGrath is the name."

I DROPPED THAT hood, straightened and swung. I couldn't speak at once. McGrath was grinning at me. I finally said: "You were the man who was searched and had your gun taken away, and sent me the note thinking I was the man who always sat by the Number Four Lamp." And forgetting all that, "But then who is this man?"

"That dead man," said McGrath, "is the fourth Bent brother—and the most dangerous, for he had a brain as well as a gun. He even arranged to have his own brothers killed so in time he would control things. There, boy—don't look so surprised. I have been for a clean city for a long time. Since the police got the cases and the convictions I let Gustave Bent have his own way in killing off the enemies that would interfere with his own private ring of cut-throats. Once other criminals were eliminated he would be ready to go into action. How easy it would be to start on these Men In Black—these men of millions." He placed a hand on my shoulder. "There, I'm not a leopard changing his spots. A clean city has always been in my mind—and I had to roll in the dirt a bit—to make things clean."

"So"—I knelt down on the floor again—"a stranger has to walk in at the end. I never heard of anything like that before. Damn his hide! I'll take a look at him anyway."

"It'll be hard work," said Nelson stupidly, "to prove he's Gustave Bent—and committed all the crimes he's wanted for."

"Good God!" I said back over my shoulder as I tore off the hood. "Who wants to prove anything against a dead man who—who—"

And that was that. McGrath didn't seem surprised. But I was. For the dead man was Havermore—that's right, Richard Daniel Havermore—spats and all!

McGrath crossed the room and brought the still shaking and perspiring President of the Bank, Mr. Francis X. Vance over to our little group of O'Rourke, Jane and myself.

"Mr. Vance," McGrath said, "has been my friend for years, handled all my private money matters—and knew that those money matters were for the best interests of the people. He believed in me. So much so that he came to my house one night and told me that I was suspected of heading the city's crime—and he feared my death was planned. It was then that I told him everything and we made our plans."

"Not everything." Vance was still a bit nervous. "You never told me then who Havermore was. You just said you were fighting crime as we were—and that I should arrange your attending one of our meetings—this particular meeting. That you would make a speech, that you would point out that one of our number was a traitor to our cause. I never even knew who that member was. Though when I think how quickly the former men who held Havermore's job as outside man died, I should have suspected him.

Instead I felt as we all felt, that he bore a charmed life."

McGrath said: "I didn't want to give you too sudden a shock."

"You mean you thought I'd be afraid. Well, I was—that's why I got Williams to take my place. Yes, I was afraid, but I thought, too, that Race Williams could face death better than I. Havermore had been to the bank to see me—and I read something in his eyes—something terrible in his eyes. You see, the man under Number Seven Light had promised to stay away. Number Seven—that was your light tonight, McGrath. Havermore had not been able to locate the real Number Seven Light—who is George Frederic More, Chairman of the Atlantic Plant and Power Works—in over a week. I was afraid Havermore suspected me. He was clever enough to know that you kept More away so you could take his place. But you insisted on going through with it."

"That's right." McGrath nodded. "I had a gun and—"

"You expected to use it," I cut in, "much as I used mine. Havermore suspected you all right. He told me as much. So he let you come anyway—and had your gun taken away. He intended to shoot both you and Mr. Vance. But Mr. Vance—how did you come to know who the Number Seven Lamp was?"

Mr. Vance said simply: "I didn't know everybody there, of course, but some of us knew each other, rubbed shoulders during the day." He raised his head. "I'm glad Havermore's dead. He had my friend Mr.

Philips shot down before your apartment door. Philips received a note, grabbed his hat and coat and started from the bank. Then he came back and sitting down in my office wrote hurriedly. He handed me a sealed envelope, said, 'Open this if I should die. I am going straight to Race Williams.'"

Mr. Vance coughed and continued. "I opened the envelope as soon as he left me. It contained a letter from Philips to me, and the note he has just received. The letter read—

" 'Dear Vance:

" 'I don't believe a word of this, of course. I don't wish to alarm you without cause. If it is a plant and I am killed, do not go near that meeting tonight. Something is terribly wrong. I know you have been very friendly with McGrath. Since he is the man—guard yourself well. But you will have the proper protection from now on. Shun McGrath.' "

I said: "And the enclosure?"

Vance who had been reading from the letter handed me the enclosure. It was addressed to Mr. Philips, and read—

Dear Light Number One:

McGrath and your friend Vance are working together. McGrath suspects your knowledge of their relationship. There is not a moment to spare. Telephone Race Williams. Do not let him come to the bank. Go see him. Above all, not a word to Vance.

There was no signature.

"There you are, Race." McGrath spread his hands far apart. "Havermore, whom I knew was Gustave Bent, sent the note, of course. He didn't want you at the meeting and used Philips to set the trap for your death at your door. Mr. Vance opened the letter at once even while Mr. Philips was telephoning you. He rang me—read me the note, and I was on your roof and—"

"And caught Jerry and me when we were leaving," Jane broke in. "I thought those were real detectives with you—"

"They were real detectives." McGrath nodded. "I never suspected you were in this thing, Jane. I simply hoped by holding you a prisoner and threatening you with bodily harm I might keep Race away from the meeting that just ended—ended forever. Jerry was with you, so I had to hold him too."

Then I had my say.

"But the body? Was Philips killed or wasn't he? If he was, what became of the body? I should have thought the police would have searched every apartment." I knew they hadn't because young Bent was dead on the bed when I got back.

McGrath smiled, shook his head.

"They didn't search for the body of Philips because they found it right before your door. It was at my suggestion that the body was dragged into one of the smaller automatic elevators. Don't look at O'Rourke, Race. He didn't know." McGrath leaned toward me now. "I knew how close O'Rourke was to you. I knew you had an engagement with Havermore. I knew that Havermore suspected I was planning to be at his meeting tonight. And I knew that he would take the place of the Number One Light, for after Vance called me I realized Philips was to get the dose. But Haver-

more couldn't tell how his friends had turned the trick, since none of the killers were alive or able to advise him."

"That's right. That's right." I remembered Havermore's surprise there at lunch and admired too, the quick way he took advantage of that disappearing body, even if he didn't know if the man were dead or alive.

McGrath continued.

"When they took my gun away from me and let me pass on, I thought it was curtains. There I sat facing death with half the police and private detectives in the city waiting to help me outside. And there beside Havermore was the little door that would lead him to safety. And every one in that room would swear that the man known as the Number One Light had killed two men and departed. They didn't search you, Race, because Havermore had no idea you were there at the table. He thought all along you were the terror-stricken bank president who— who—" McGrath reddened slightly as he looked at Vance, then said boldly: "There's nothing to be ashamed of in knowing fear. I knew fear myself tonight. Race is just lucky they didn't take his guns from him—which they probably would have if he had come into that room as himself, and not as Number Four Light."

I said and meant it: "You mean the guys are lucky they didn't try to take my guns from me."

"Well, that's the way it is." Dirty—I mean Tim McGrath put his arms around my shoulder. "My little girl failed me and saved my life. I don't know how you worked it, Race, but maybe you'd better come and see her—sort of fix things up. Yes, and have some good beer."

"That's fine." I grabbed Jane by the arm. "Come on, Jane."

McGrath's eyes widened, but he only said: "Jane is welcome—what, you too, Sergeant?" This as O'Rourke followed us out onto the street, down toward McGrath's big car.

Jerry was there. He ran up and grabbed my arm, pushed me back.

"O.K., boss? Good?" His face was kind of white. "You ask Jane and she'll tell you the truth. I was just as nice about it. Then he caught me with the knife—like to cut my neck apart. Look!" I looked under the street light at the tiny line of red on Jerry's neck. "Then—you know, boss—the other room. I—Jane gave me the card— The People Versus Crime. I did the best I could for him. Crossed his arms over his chest like when I worked for the undertaker and—"

"Jerry." I shook his shoulders. "You have too much imagination. Nothing at all has happened. No one even knows that extra apartment of mine exists. I don't want anyone to know about it. Listen." I bent down close and said: "If you want to pretend some guy fell on a knife, all right, but pretend the thing happened right on my living-room floor." I shoved him toward my car. "You've got five minutes to get home and pretend he's on my living-room floor. After that go out for the night—and never mention such a silly thing again." I pushed him into the car and followed the others.

"Sergeant," I said to O'Rourke, "with-out you this whole affair—the Men In Black—The People Versus Crime could never have been so satisfactory. It was you who collected the evidence that reached the district attorney." And turning to McGrath, "You'll remember that, Mr. McGrath, when you speak to the mayor—to the papers."

McGrath said he would, and my voice lowered as O'Rourke took both my hands and said he'd do anything for me.

"Sure—me for you too, pal." I pushed the key to my apartment into his hand. "If other guys can cart bodies around, you can too. I got a stiff for you by the name of Bent—Ike Bent."

"What do you mean?" he demanded.

"I mean," I told him, and I told him flat, "there's a stiff on my living-room floor that fell down on a knife. I don't care what you do with him. But I don't want any part of him. Good-night." I jumped in beside McGrath who drove.

For some time we traveled in silence. Then he said close to my ear: "You're pretty wise, Race—more brains than I thought you had. Trying to make peace with one woman and bringing another along seemed stupid at first. There, don't explain—and don't lie. I understand. You'll look much better in Ione's eyes if Jane's along. Women are that way."

"Come on," I said climbing into the back seat with Jane, "let the boat make time. When I want action—I want it."

Jane put both her arms around me.

"Just action," she whispered.

I felt her soft lips against mine and had but a single thought. "I could go for a bottle of beer right now—'Good beer.'"

Hell with the Lid Lifted

CHAPTER 1

CROAKER WILLIAMS, M.D.

COLD, RAIN, FOG—AND me at the world's loneliest railroad station just after one-thirty a.m. ten minutes before the through express was due to stop and take on Doctor Gordon—whoever he might be. Florence Drummond—The Flame— that strange and beautiful creature who was with the law at times, as often against it—had given me just enough information to interest me. No talk of money— just an invitation to death. And not even an *R.S.V.P.* requested.

I shivered—it was the winter weather, I haven't any nerves—and looked up at the waving sign beneath the small light— *Homestead Junction.* I lifted a station lantern and moved toward the road in the blackness of the storm. Then I saw a pair of lights. A car was coming through the dirty weather. I didn't know whether it was the station master or the doctor. I took the lantern from beneath my coat, held it ready, and waved it just before the car reached the open circle which was the approach to the station. The car braked, and a window came down.

I took a chance and came fairly close, said, "You're the gentleman for the train—the doctor?" and got a nod. "It's flooded bad around the grounds—muddy too," I went on. "Pull your car off to the side of the road here. It'll be safe enough, I guess."

I LET HIM drive the car half off the road, heard his curse as the wheels sank almost to the hub caps in the mud. Then I walked around the other side of the car and opened the door. I was a different man when I climbed in beside him. He started to say something about "station master" and "mud" and my gun dented his heavy raincoat, brought out a grunt when it hit his ribs.

"Doc," I said, "you don't know how good I am—and I don't know how bad you are. Do something that I don't appreciate and I'll know you think this business is worth a belly full of lead. That's right. Now you talk."

"Talk—talk?" he half blustered and half stammered. "So it's a hold-up, eh? The urgent call to meet this train and take care of a patient was a fake to rob me. I have nothing but my bag and a few dollars."

"Doc"—I kept my hat pulled low and didn't let him peer under it—"your urgent call to meet this train was planned far ahead. Don't squawk all over your face. I know some word must have reached you within a few hours, but that was just for the benefit of the railroad. They don't stop trains here unless it's an emergency. Tell me something about yourself."

"Why—there is nothing to tell. I'm on an errand of mercy. Surely you won't stop a physician in a matter of life or death."

"That's just how I'm going to stop you," I told him. "Life or death—according to how you talk."

"I can say nothing. I know nothing." He turned and sprayed me with an alcoholic breath that would have made a barfly blush for shame.

A train whistled in the distance and the doc got a surprise. I grabbed him by the throat, yanked him over and sat on him while I handcuffed him to the steering wheel. Then I frisked him and tucked the heavy bearskin blanket around him to keep him warm. I climbed out and lifted the hood, tore loose the wires. No power, no lights, no horn now.

"Listen, Doc," I gave it to him at the car window, "I'm giving you a break, for I'm not sure where you stand. So wait around without hollering. It's almost two now. You can keep warm if you don't twist the covers off. Don't shout. Someone might hear you, but that someone might be a friend of mine and— Be sensible, Doc. Here comes my train."

I grabbed his bag, dashed back toward the station as steam and cinders and blazing lights blasted by to the tune of grinding brakes. I knew my car was the rear one, and I ran toward it. There was a porter's white coat to guide me, so I made a springboard out of his stool, and almost knocked the conductor off the platform above. The train was moving as the conductor spoke.

"I can assure you the train would not have stopped for the president of the road, Doctor—"

The door of the rear car swung open and a rough voice said: "Doctor—come in."

I pulled my hat down even lower, shook off the rain, and stepped into the dimly lit corridor of the private car. The door closed, a bolt shot home.

"O.K., Doc. Move down to the rear. You don't seem shaky." The man sniffed. "I don't smell liquor either. I'll fix you up with a double whiskey right away."

He was a big guy and kept shoving me down the hall while he talked. I kept my head lowered. The first part of that private car was like any car—staterooms or compartments—anyway closed doors to the left of the narrow hallway, windows to the right. At the end of the corridor the car opened up like an ordinary club car, except that the chairs were not pushed back against the sides. There was a rather elaborate writing desk. At the far end of the car I saw another narrow passage— more staterooms, I guessed, or perhaps one big compartment. I didn't know.

Somehow or other the whiskey crack riled me. I like my liquor as well as the next fellow, but I never need the kind of courage that comes through the neck of a bottle. When I sat down and he spoke again of a drink, I said: "Drink it yourself if you need it—what's the liquor idea?"

This part of the car was fairly well lighted and the shades were tightly drawn. I let my gaze run up my host from the polished tan shoes, over the snappy gray business suit to the man's face. He was twenty-eight or thirty—not bad to look at, but his mouth was too big and his nose too flat, and his eyes set too close to that nose.

He tore my dripping hat from my head, said: "You don't look too bad." And when I stared and didn't answer, "I don't know you either, Doc, so we'll let it go that way. But I heard tell it was liquor that tossed you from top surgeon's job at Mount Elmira Hospital, and later out of the office of Doctor Benjamin Burton. And now no liquor. Let me see your hand."

I stretched out a hand and it was steady. I didn't know the game, but he had tipped me enough to make me cover the whiskey angle.

I said: "There are other things besides liquor to steady a man."

He laughed. "Dope, eh? Well, you look all right—seem all right. However, Doc, you're not doing any business with me. The other doc's the man to help you. We want this job to look exactly like Burton's work."

I put my hands together and wriggled my neck a bit. "He's good then, this other doctor? I can count on him?"

"No." The big mouth cracked wide open. "He'll assist you—nothing more. I don't want him to lay a hand to the girl—let alone a knife. He understands that. You'll talk with him." And putting his hand in his pocket, "There's nothing cheap about this job." He tossed me a roll of bills; it counted up to fifteen hundred dollars. "You got the other thousand yesterday," he added, seeing my surprise.

"That's right." I put the money in my pocket. "You trust me implicitly?"

He took a grin on that, leaned over and laid a finger against my chest. "I trust myself implicitly." He didn't leave any doubt that he believed what he said. "I'm tough, brother—damn good and tough when I'm mad. You don't get around now, Doc—at least around Chi. They know me. When I'm mad I could tear you apart with my two hands. Yeah—that's why I trust you."

I stayed seated. I was afraid if I got up and faced him I'd queer the game, whatever it was, by knocking his head clear through the side of the steel car.

The doctor came then. He was a dapper little vandyked guy in a neat dark suit, glasses with a ribbon, and a carnation in his button hole. I watched him down the length of the car. I didn't know him, and he didn't know me, but I was ready—the moment things started—to electrify the atmosphere with a gun or two.

Did I expect I'd have to do some shooting? I didn't know then. But ten minutes later, when I had finished my private talk with Vandyke, I could have put a dozen bullets in his back and eaten a hearty breakfast afterwards.

Vandyke pulled up a chair and sat down before me. "So. Whiskey and dope got you. But me—I'm going places."

"Never mind that." I tried being surly. "Get down to business."

"No liquor, eh?" He stretched out a hand, to feel my pulse I guess, but I drew my arm away. "Well"—he smacked his lips—"I've got to admit twenty-five hundred dollars is high pay for such a simple job."

"And the job?"

"Nothing—hardly anything. You'll enjoy it. There's a kid on this train—a young girl—almost twenty-one. You're to take her leg off just above the knee."

"Which leg—left or right?"

"It doesn't matter much," he said indifferently.

"Doesn't matter? What's wrong with her legs?"

"Nothing—nothing at all, Gordon. In fact, they are very pretty legs. I have never done much surgery, but I'd find pleasure in the job." His thin lips parted. His grin was evil. "Let me see—you're right-handed, of course—there will be more room for you to work. We'll say the right leg then. I suppose it'd be safer that way anyway."

"Nothing wrong with her leg, yet you—someone wants it amputated."

"You're paid to do a job—not argue a point of professional etiquette." He actually chuckled.

"Professional etiquette!" I was trying hard not to explode, but I finally got my words out. "Why, if there is nothing wrong, do you wish to deprive her of a leg?"

"She runs around too much." The doctor grinned, removed his glasses and stared straight at me. His eyes were small and shifty now. "You look anything but mad, my friend, yet they called you 'the mad surgeon,' said that you took pleasure— Well, it was more than hinted around that Doctor Gordon's surgery was not his main interest. That you had a queer sadistic quirk and often operated with an insufficient—even, at times, without any—anesthetic, so that you might study the effect of pain. Study it—not enjoy it, Doctor." He leaned forward, placed a hand upon my knee. "Or do you enjoy watching others suffer pain?"

So I was a doctor. I had been good. And I liked to see people suffer. Now I was talking with a kindred spirit. It was hard, but I played my part—as best I could. At the other end of the car was the big tough guy, his coat thrown open. I couldn't see the gun, but it was there all right. I felt it.

The story Vandyke told me then almost turned my stomach. I don't understand how I took it without wringing his scrawny neck, or shoving down his stinking throat the glasses he kept taking off and putting on.

The germs and bacteria that he spoke of I didn't understand fully, but I did understand that after the girl's leg was removed he planned to inject a tube full of them into the wound, causing an infection which would slowly destroy her body. He gloated over the ingenious method, telling me how quickly gangrene would set in.

I got my stomach settled and objected with: "But it will be my job, and I'll be blamed."

"No, no, it will be Doctor Benjamin Burton's job, and he'll be blamed. We have attended to that. If anything should happen later it would be most unfortunate, but who would suspect the eminent Doctor Burton's best intentions in removing the girl's leg?"

"Then there has already been surgery? The leg's off? Burton did—"

"Ah, you grow curious." He glanced up toward the big man who was sipping a tall drink. "I'll tell you, Gordon. It's rather a clever idea—a credit to the man who thought it up. You see, it—"

THE BIG MAN was coming toward us. There was good-natured banter in his voice—a grin on his face. He stood before us, his legs far apart, said: "Have you two croakers got things cooked up yet?" And smiling at Vandyke, "Understand now, she's not to die here on our hands."

"She won't—she won't." Vandyke nodded. "She's not as frail as you think." He came to his feet and steadied himself against a chair as the train swung. "And she can scream her head off without a soul hearing her. Maybe you'd like—" The big man laughed. "There wouldn't be room for me. Bring us good news now. Barney is waiting."

"He should hate her enough. She caused him all this—"

An arm went around the doctor's shoulder, a hand clapped over his mouth. The big guy still smiled, but there was a hardness, a curve to his lips that Vandyke couldn't see when he said: "We want to give Doctor Gordon a real break. Oh, I know he's too deep into it—or will be—to ever want to talk. But if he don't have anything to talk about, why his mind will be at ease? That right, Gordon?"

"That suits me." I lifted my bag and followed them down to the rear end of the car to what proved to be two rooms and a bath.

Vandyke said as he grabbed the knob of the door: "I'll go in and see if things are ready." And when I started to follow him, "You wait, Gordon. We'll have to use the couch. We'll have her strapped down for you—plenty of sheets."

That was my biggest moment. The "we" meant there was someone else in that room besides my "patient." So far there had been no one to identify me. Would it be the person in that room? I was evidently there to save that young girl. Was this my cue to turn and clout the big guy on the head with my gun, bust through that door over Vandyke's body and shoot down the "we" inside? Was it time for the slaughter to begin?

As usual I got nowhere by thinking. Vandyke had slipped through the door closing it after him.

Plainly I heard screams coming through that door. Shrieks that would start and die—and start and die again. But they seemed far distant, and stepping back from the door they seemed to stop entirely.

The big man shrugged his shoulders. For a moment his face changed. It grew hard and set. He spoke to me.

"I can hear her already." And after a pause, "I don't know how much our doctor told you—or if such an operation without an anesthetic will affect her mind or not."

"It might—it might," I told him. "You don't want that?"

"Sure, sure. That'd be O.K." He nodded vigorously. "But I don't want her to die on us. After we reach New York City we're taking her to Florida. I mean—you won't let her die while you're operating."

"No, no," I said. "If I find her in good shape, I'll leave her in good shape."

CHAPTER 2

MAJOR OPERATION

The door opened and Vandyke beckoned me in. The big man gave me a gentle push and whispered: "If the job is done to—our doctor's satisfaction—there will be another thousand in it for you, Gordon." And as I entered the room, "She's given us a lot of trouble. I'll be listening."

I stepped into the tiny room and saw the girl on the couch. Three leather straps held her there. Her mouth was gagged and her large brown eyes were terror-stricken. There was a sheet covering her body, but her right leg was exposed up to the knee. A nurse in white held her head.

Vandyke said to me: "A pretty leg."

I said: "Rip that gag off her mouth, nurse."

Vandyke cried out: "No, no—she'll talk—waste time." But I bent forward and tore the gag loose.

The girl tried to speak, couldn't. I raised my head as the nurse raised hers and our eyes met.

She was The Flame.

She didn't smile a greeting but she tried to send me a message, I think, when she spoke. "Better get to work, Doctor. There isn't much time—*much time.*"

I turned, bent far down toward my bag as a figure slid from the washroom and, pushing a little three-legged stool into the corner, sat down and faced me. He made no noise as I swung completely around, away from him, as though I wanted to speak to Vandyke.

I knew what The Flame's message meant now. There was to be another man present—a man who, perhaps, knew Doctor Gordon. And that man had held something in his hands—something I had only glimpsed briefly but had recognized beyond a doubt. It was a heavy, long-nosed revolver and it had been pointed straight at me.

"Hello, Doc," the man said, and I remembered that voice, though I couldn't place it, not until he told me.

"I'm Tim Slattery," he went on. "I haven't seen you in years, Doc Gordon. You look healthy—very healthy for a lad who was supposed to be all the way down. Come on, Doc. Come on, Doc Gordon! Turn around and let me see your face. If it's not your face, I'll shoot it out of the picture. But why the hell should you mind—if it's not your face?"

He was sure, and he wasn't sure. Maybe he thought I wasn't Doc Gordon, and didn't know who I really was—but he'd know the minute he got a look at me. Yes, my face would be plenty familiar to him.

I was playing on my name alone now, counting on the shock of recognition to make him hesitate. I jarred erect, spun suddenly and faced him, faced the long-nosed revolver too. And the split second of indecision was there.

He cried out: "By God, Race Williams!" And me—I shot him straight between the eyes.

After that things went mechanically. Maybe Vandyke reached for a gun, maybe he simply wanted a handkerchief to rub the sweat from his forehead. He muttered something that sounded like my name as the hot nose of my big .44 swung in a looping arch, caught him beneath the jaw and sent him crawling like a spider along the wall before he dropped to the floor unconscious.

The Flame said as she unstrapped the girl: "I knew you'd make it, Race. I didn't think they'd know you. Then they pulled Tim Slattery onto the car at the last minute. It was nice work."

"Get the kid dressed," I said and looked into those wide, childish eyes as The Flame helped her from the couch.

The girl said—her voice soft, low: "What has happened? What is going to happen to me now?"

I said: "Not a thing. You're going to do just as you please from now on."

She broke loose from The Flame who was helping her toward the other room beyond the open door across from the washroom. She looked like a slim boy in her silken pajamas, the dressing gown tight about her. She said: "You're Race Williams, the man who does so much good for people—for everyone."

"Well, not those boys on the floor," I cracked wise, then wished I hadn't as I held her so she wouldn't fall. "I do good for good people." And trying to take her mind off things I'd just put that mind on, I held up her chin and asked: "Are you good?"

She looked at me a long time, said very seriously: "Yes. In my heart I am very good."

I believed her, too. I had never met a girl just like her. Oh, I know a lot of guys say that about a lot of dames, but they don't mean it my way. She was slim and pale and beautiful, and when she took both my hands and looked up at me I couldn't just swagger and say: "It was nothing."

She said: "I am very grateful. Those men were horrible. I don't know why you risked your life for a poor little nobody—nobody to you." And damn it all, there I was blushing like a school-boy while I tried to hide the corpse from her view, when I should have jumped all over that "poor little nobody" for I like cash on the line for my work.

The Flame led her to the adjoining stateroom, told her to dress, popped back through the door and said to me: "I never saw you so bowled over by a girl before, Race—except me. But she's real. It seems so horrible that a child like that could be chosen by Fate as the instrument of such destruction."

"Drop the fancy talk, Florence," I snapped. "Just what is the racket? Why amputate her leg? And why her death? Listen!" There was a knock on the door and we both swung.

I TORE OFF my coat, parked my shoulder harness on the couch, rolled my right sleeve and grabbed a saw from the bag. Then I slipped back the bolt, twisted up my face, opened the door and looked out. The big guy was there. He had a gun in his hand, but it was held down low.

I said, "What the hell do you want? The damn girl's fainted," and slammed the door.

He took it, and I turned back to The Flame. "Come on, Florence, I want the answer."

She said: "It was very clever, Race. They had Diane McKay—that's the girl—a prisoner in Chicago. One of their gang who looked like a benevolent old gentleman visited relief bureaus until he found a girl who needed a leg amputated. It had been broken and set by a bum surgeon, was in bad shape. They got her a private room, registered her as Diane McKay, and Doctor Benjamin Burton removed her right leg. Then they arranged for a private ambulance to take her to the station—and onto this private car. Don't you get the idea yet? The ambulance simply ran her off to a nursing home and another one with Diane McKay and me as nurse arrived at the station. They carried her aboard this train, then arranged for Doctor Gordon to come aboard and take off her leg. Gangrene or something would set in shortly and she'd die in Florida. But the record would show her operation at the Chicago hospital by Doctor Benjamin Burton. Everything would be regular."

"And she—Diane? What has she done? Is it money? Where do you fit?"

The Flame's smile was rather hard. She said: "I've been hired by these crooks who know I used to be a criminal. They think I'm working for them. But I'm for Diane, all the way, of course."

"But what's behind it all? Why not the police?"

"It's outside the law, Race, or we wouldn't be in it, either of us. Greed, hate, love—but mostly greed, as it always is. No more now. We've got to get her out of here. No one but Slattery knew you're Race Williams." She looked over at the dead man still sitting comfortably on the stool. "The big man—Jerry Finn—thinks I'm merely pretending friendship with the girl."

She started to see if Diane was ready, nearly fell over the unconscious Vandyke, then turned to me as pounding came upon the door.

"Finn is suspicious," she said. "Or he wants information. He'll have to be taken care of. Do you want to slip out through the door in the other room, or do you want to handle him in here? It's a bit crowded."

THINGS WERE CROWDED all right. I was getting my own feet mixed up with Vandyke's, and the outstretched legs of the dead Slattery, and the bag by the couch. But I nodded my head to The Flame, tossed the doctor over near the door she was closing behind her and finally, straightening myself, turned to the corridor door and slipped back the catch.

The quarters were tight but I like tight quarters, and things were still boiling inside me. That's right. You can't let off much steam just by shooting a man through the head and crashing a runt along a wall with a single wallop. Now a big guy, a tough guy, a man who tore others apart "with his two hands," wanted in—at least he seemed to think he wanted in.

The door burst open. Jerry Finn, the giant killer, hurtled into the room. I let him slip by, cracked the door closed, and snapped the bolt. He was standing there swaying with the motion of the train, his eyes smack on the glassy glims of the dead Slattery. There was a gun in his right hand when he turned and faced me.

"What's the mess? Who—" and he knew things weren't right.

I stepped forward, knocked the gun from his hand and smacked him a right cross that staggered him back between the couch and the wall.

"The mess is mine, brother," I said. "Now do your strong-man act."

He tried to fight, and once he did get the fingers of his right hand onto my neck, closed the fingers too. Power? Yes, he had power, but he needed more room to use it. The fingers hurt, but I upped a right from the waist that nearly tore his head off his shoulders. He tried to stick his knee in my stomach, but my own leg caught his and drove it up to his own chin.

Elbows, chin, head—and driving uppercuts. I fought his way and he didn't like it. Fast? Maybe he could be fast. But a guy isn't encouraged to put on steam when he has to keep jerking his head back out of a dent in a steel wall, only to have it knocked back in that dent again. And he made his fatal mistake. He lowered his left hand and reached behind him for another gun.

I don't think I ever hit a man harder, for the sudden swing of the train was with my blow. My left caught him on the side of his head as he was bending. He crashed down on the floor, skidding along it on his neck, his feet in the air, and wound up against the door in that same position.

Yep, there he was, two hundred pounds and six-feet-two of solid beef and muscle. And I ask you! What the hell good was he to anyone now?

The Flame said emotionlessly through the crack in the door to the next room:

"We'll go out through the stateroom beyond, Race. Diane is ready. We haven't much to fear from Finn, I gather."

I grinned across at her. "No, I don't think we have much to fear from Finn."

She reached for my hand to steady me as I stepped over Vandyke, and whispered through closed lips before we stepped into the stateroom beyond: "You're as good—or as bad as you ever were, Race. You know all the clean and all the dirty tricks of the game, don't you?"

"Clean." I took a laugh. "Are there any clean tricks? It's not a game, Florence. Crime's a tough, sordid business. And it's the dirty tricks that make the boys appreciate you. Personally—" I saw Diane and stopped.

She was dressed in a dark-blue tailored suit. There was a dark-blue hat on her head and a ribbon that went under her chin. Her little feet were close together—like a school girl at attention. When I stepped forward she held out both hands to me.

"I have just escaped from something terrible, Mr. Williams. I know that. Now you are going to take me away. I am not afraid. Should I be afraid?"

Hell, I just took those hands and pulled her toward me. It was nice the way her head settled on my chest. "Diane," I said, "you're right every time. And you've got nothing to be afraid of—absolutely nothing."

I heard The Flame make a sort of snapping sound with her lips, but I paid no attention—not me.

"I'll go first," The Flame said. "I have been trusted absolutely. With my record why not? But there are more of them on the train, in the private car I mean. We may meet them in leaving the train or we may not."

"Hurry, then," I told her. "I'll watch at the door. The boys may come to life and get frisky again."

The Flame opened the door, stepped into the corridor and I heard her breath whistle.

A man said: "Nurse! Is there anything wrong? Everything is so quiet."

"Everything is fine," The Flame said. And as if anticipating his coming question, "Mr. Finn and the doctor are resting. I'll call them in time. You had best rest too, Mr. Gibbons, and don't worry."

"Thank you, Nurse—thank you. You've been a great comfort to me. Good God, how can Barney sleep! He'd kill me if things went wrong." With that he turned, walked along the corridor toward the open part of the car.

The Flame pushed open the door and said: "Now's our chance, Race. Only Barney is dangerous—far more dangerous than any man you ever met. He even sleeps while he believes Diane is being viciously maimed in preparation for death. He's a tall man, Race—very tall with slightly bent shoulders. If he appears kill him without warning."

"That's more like it." I nodded as I let The Flame and Diane pass me and hurry across the open space to that other corridor that held more staterooms—and led to the door I had entered.

We struck a little trouble when we reached the corridor. Diane wouldn't go ahead of me, wanted to hold my hand, and while I'm not one to chuck cold water on such beautiful sentiment, it does interfere with gun-play. But she had her way. Her hand was warm and didn't tremble—and we reached the door that led to the platform and the cars beyond. Then we were across the platform and into the dimly lighted sleeper forward.

The Flame and her white uniform hadn't much more than appeared when a screech came, and far down at the end of the sleeper a man tumbled or jumped from his berth.

The Flame said: "That's the signal. We won't be noticed now."

A stateroom door opened almost beside us, and we three slipped inside.

A voice said: "Yes'm. Thank you, ma'am." Then a white coat pushed by us. The door closed. The Flame snapped on the light. I snapped over the lock.

THERE WAS AN upper and lower berth—a couch across from them—a washroom in the corner. Diane sat down on the couch and gripped my hand.

The Flame said: "It was all a question of timing. The man I hired did his stuff. It will turn out he had a nightmare. Besides, if the conductor finds us here, what of it? We're through with the private car. We've got tickets for three—and you're booked under the name of William Flemming two cars down. I have everything arranged. The train stops at Harmon to change from steam to electricity. An auto will meet Diane and me there. You can cover us. But I suppose you want to hear something about Diane—and what's back of it all."

"If you're in the mood," I said sarcastically. "So far I haven't seen one penny that—that—" And I stopped, stuck my hand in my pocket. Fifteen hundred bucks. Even I had to admit that was a start, even if it did come from the wrong side of the fence.

Diane moved to the edge of the couch, sat very erect.

"Let me tell it." Her lips moved like a mechanical doll's. "My father was Louie McKay. He was a hard, cruel man. When my mother left him she took me with her. His friends were such men as Tim Slattery, Jerry Finn, Doctor Beasley—that's the little doctor who would have cut off my leg." And she didn't bat an eye when she said that. "And most dangerous of all—Barney Hale. These men, by threats, made my mother's life one of terror. And my father egged them on by telling them my mother had taken a huge sum of money with her when she left. That was a lie. My father hated me, but he hated my mother more and wanted me back with him so he could torture her through me. But she knew his secrets—secrets of his criminal past—and would expose them if he took me away.

"Then my mother died and my father took me to live with him. He treated me cruelly—vengeance against my dead mother. He had made a great deal of money during prohibition, and he had hung on to it. But his friends, criminal associates, had not kept their money and wanted his. They argued that they had all been partners and should share his fortune. They threatened him, even tried to kill him once. So he sent for the only friend he had in the world, the man to whom he had entrusted the money he had saved. I don't know how much it was. His name was Thomas F. Rockland."

I blinked in surprise. I knew Rockland. He was wealthy, had political power, lived as an honest man. But there were rumors that he had not always been honest.

"Go on." I was getting interested.

"My father had a heart attack. I was just past eighteen. Before these men and myself, he had Thomas Rockland—I called him Uncle Thomas—swear a solemn oath. If I lived to be twenty-one and was married, Uncle Thomas was to give me all the savings my father had given to him in trust. If I were dead or not married, then Barney Hale was to receive this money—to divide among himself, Slattery, Finn and Doctor Beasley—as he saw fit. But if my father were to die a violent death, under no circumstances would they receive any of his money."

"Rockland didn't have to give them equal shares?" The Flame asked.

"No." Diane shook her head. "And what a hatred it bred."

"But the police—you could—"

"No police. If any one of us appealed to the law, Uncle Thomas must strike that name from his list. The game must be played as Father always played it— outside the law."

"Don't you see, Race?" The Flame came in. "Diane already loved a young man whom she hoped to marry some day."

"Let me finish," said Diane. "Father did not die then. He lived almost three years longer. Then when he died, Uncle Thomas notified us that the agreement was in force. They wanted to kill me so they worked out a plan—the one you just saved me from."

"Why didn't you just skip out and marry this boy?"

"They found him, told me they would kill him, told him they would kill me. Randy didn't want any money. I told Barney he could have the money, and I'd marry Randy after I was twenty-one. But they didn't trust me."

"Yet they could watch you, keep you prisoner without killing you."

"No. Barney said I was my father's daughter, said that once they had the money I would no longer be tied down by the terms of Uncle Thomas' agreement, that I knew too much and would blackmail them or go to the police."

Then she stopped and I talked to her just like a Dutch uncle. She could give me Randy's address. I'd bring him to her. They could get married. When she said the money was bad money I told her all the good she could do with it.

"No, no." She shook her head. "They hate me. Money or no money, their final act will be one of vengeance. They'll kill Randy. He is willing to chance it because of—our love. Our love—" She half shook her head. "I am not so certain that I love him—now." She turned and let those brown eyes look straight into my eyes. Smack—just like that!

I couldn't pretend I didn't get her point. It was like getting hit in the face with a ripe tomato, and pretending it never happened. So I jumped quick back to Randy.

"This Barney Hale may get to him," I said.

"You're right," she agreed. "Don't let Barney reach him before you." With that she popped out, "Randolph H. Philips," and gave me an address in the Seventies. "I can see his danger," she finished. "He doesn't like it, but he's hiding there under the name of Fred Barrington. It's an empty house that his aunt owns."

The Flame said: "Barney is our most dangerous enemy. He wants this money. He's determined to get it. He knows by now something has gone wrong. How much he knows about you and what happened, we can't guess. But he'll know Harmon is the first stop. And this much is certain. He'll try to stop us when we get off there."

"I won't worry," Diane said. "I won't even think about things. I'll just count on you."

The Flame grinned—at least she twisted up her lips and looked peculiarly at me. But what the hell. I didn't care. I liked it. Yes, damn it, I liked it!

CHAPTER 3

PARDON MY GLOVE

It was a cold gray dawn when we pulled into Harmon. We left our stateroom and walked through several cars, The Flame first, Diane second and me third. Four cars along we found a vestibule door open, a porter with a stool and a fat man trying to climb down, hold his own bag and button his vest all at the same time.

He made the platform and the girls followed him, took up their trek down the long platform to the high stairs.

I talked to the porter as I looked back toward the private car in the rear for the fearful Barney—and he came. A tall, lean figure, ignoring the absence of steps, opened a vestibule door and jumped onto the platform.

I said to the porter: "I'll take a little walk and come back. I'm staying on to Grand Central Terminal."

Barney did not run. He did not even seem to walk quickly, but he made time—enough to send me half skipping along the platform. He hit the stairs, jumped them two at a time, and got Diane by the arm. I saw The Flame try to turn, and knew that Barney had a gun.

"The girl comes back to the train," he said harshly. "You—"

If he was going to be friendly to The Flame or not I didn't know. I just stuck a gun in the center of Barney's back and said: "Stiffen, rat."

Barney knew his stuff. He stiffened, then said: "So you're the man of the train—'Doctor Gordon.' Well, you can't shoot me here, that's certain. There'd be a disturbance."

"You won't be disturbed," I told him, and to The Flame, "Go ahead with your patient, Nurse. Get moving."

Barney talked fast while I leaned against the stair-rail and picked out a nice place between his ribs.

"I'm Barney Hale, you fool," he said. "I could swing and kill you." I could feel his body quiver. I could tell by the twist of his elbow that he was feeling for a gun. "Men are coming, workmen at the top of the stairs," he went on. "It's only a moment, but the biggest in your life." He had a way of putting emphasis in his voice, a deadly earnestness and an apparent lack of fear.

He was right—men were coming down the stairs. I said simply: "The big moment is all yours, Barney—and it's your last. Turn and march back to that train…. All right—take the dose."

He turned and he marched—and what's more he was right. Barney knew. He walked straight back to the train and climbed aboard, and I walked with him, chatted with him a bit. I asked him if he wanted to bet a century or two that I couldn't stand on the step of a moving train and shoot a man to death if he jumped for it.

Did I win my bet? Barney never gave me the chance to try. He was on the train and it was moving when I swung aboard two cars down and gripped the porter's arm.

A five-spot fixed me up with a nice stateroom. I locked the door and lay me down to rest. I got to thinking of Diane—and how, if I ever had marriage in mind, she'd be the sort of girl I'd pick. I got to thinking of Randy too—the simp—and the money—and—

Someone was hollering, "Grand Central Terminal!" and I woke up. One look convinced me that Barney and the boys had departed at 125th Street.

I HAD RANDY Philips' address and I thought I'd better get up there and look the boy over. Some dough going to waste! But that's young love. Me, I know this love-and-marriage racket, that's why I've stayed out of it. In a few years Diane and Randy would want that money—need it maybe.

First I dropped a nickel in the slot and called my office. It was early, but Jerry was there.

He snapped in on me: "Business, boss—big business. I got in a few minutes ago and a lad was standing in front of the door. He wanted to see you in a hurry. Said he'd come right back. It's important. Name of Hale."

"I've a call to make first, Jerry. They all think they're important, but—" I stopped dead, then said: "What—what name did you say he gave?"

"Barney Hale. I—"

"I'll be right over."

I hung up, grabbed a taxi and hit my office in record time. What's more I cooled my heels there waiting. A little after eleven I sent Jerry out for a paper. There was an upstate item at the bottom of the second page. The engineer of a freight had seen the body of a man on the track, but the train hit it before he could stop. That would be Jerry Finn, though they couldn't identify the body. How did I know it was Finn? Because when the crew climbed off the train they found another body with a bullet hole in his head—and that one was identified as Slattery. So— the other man must have been Finn. I shook my head. I hadn't thought I could hit a man hard enough to kill him.

When twelve o'clock came and Barney Hale didn't show up, I grew suspicious. Then I decided that was silly. Barney couldn't know I was thinking of visiting Randy Philips. I puffed a bit, decided he had watched across the street, seen me hurry into my office, then lost his nerve.

A second later Jerry came to my private office door, stuck in his head and said: "Barney Hale."

When he came in he wore gray suede gloves and held a cane over his arm. There was no threat in his voice, no uneasiness in his manner. He took off his topcoat, placed it over a chair, leaned his cane against it, then put his hat on top of the coat. He kept his gloves on.

"Not thinking of fingerprints?" I asked as I leaned a bit sideways so my jacket hung open and a gun could slip more easily into my hand.

He laughed, pulled up a chair and sat down. "Kill you in your own office—not me, Mr. Williams. These gloves are simply an assurance to you that I can't draw and shoot quickly enough—and an assurance to me that I won't let my temper ride me."

"I missed you at the Grand Central Terminal this morning," I said.

"We left the train at One Hundred Twenty-fifth Street." He nodded. "I suppose the girl told you all about our little plan."

"Do you mean by 'the girl' Miss Diane McKay, my client?"

"Yes, I mean her." His lips grew thin, his whole face seemed to tighten. He leaned forward. "The plans for her death were mine. And being your client won't help her. Understand, Williams, I've come here to see you because I am not afraid of you. I fear no man. I'm warning you— you're out of this mess from now on or your number's up."

"You mean"—and my teeth showed now—"that you won't travel on trains anymore—at least while I'm on them."

He turned a blotchy sort of white and pulled at his gloves, but he didn't take them off. He finally said, and his voice shook: "It's my money, Williams. Her father wanted me to have it. But I guess he wanted me to kill the girl for it. He was a devil. 'Barney,' he said to me the night he died, 'I hate Diane as I hated her mother. But if she's alive and married when she's twenty-one she gets that money—all of it. Torture her, kill her, hold her in chains to prevent that marriage—but be careful she doesn't fool you.' He wanted me to have that money, Williams. Warned me against the girl. Don't you see?"

"He hated all of you," I said. "Deliberately tossed you all into a maelstrom of hatred and death. And he was right. She will fool all of you at the end. He knew well his own flesh and blood."

"I'll kill her first. I hate her. There is something about the way she looks at me."

"Any child could look at you now and see what's inside of you," I told him. "She's decent and good—and she's entitled to some happiness. You've spoken your piece, Barney. I'll speak mine. She'll get that happiness if I have to kill you to give it to her."

"Don't think you're dealing with any hoodlum now, Williams. I am fast with a gun only because that sort of thing was necessary when I started in business. But I am not a stupid man with a conscience. Now I would prefer to do things the easy way and shoot you through the back of the head."

I let my gun slip into my hand, tossed it on the desk.

"Barney," I said, "a man like you is capable of anything. I'm going to believe your threat of death, and I'm going to stay on this case. My gun and my fist were busy this morning and two men died."

"You flatter yourself, Williams. Finn was alive when I tossed him from the train. I don't need him anymore, and I can use what he thought would be his share of the money." He came to his feet. "I'll speak plainly to you. I intend to kill the girl, of course. You must warn her and—"

"Warn my client that she will be killed? A fine business man you must think me."

"No, there is no need to warn the girl that she will be killed. She's like her father in that way. I damned near strangled her but still she wouldn't tell me where this boy friend of hers was hiding. Tell her now that he is to die—die horribly—if she doesn't return to me. Tell her I'll put Doctor Beasley to work on him."

Barney Hale put on his topcoat and tossed his cane over his arm.

"I have warned you about your own life—no matter how things turn out. I've already got political connections here. I'm ready to take over some New York stuff. But I have got to show the money first. I need that cash. I'm a man who gets what he wants, Race Williams—remember that."

"My dear fellow," I told him. "The girl didn't want a cent. But now that she's my client, she takes my advice. She'll take all she's entitled to—every penny of it."

"So that's how it is."

"That," I said, "is exactly how it is."

"I'm a man who never loses."

"There's always a first time." I shrugged as I tossed my gun back beneath my left armpit. "I don't like guys who torture women." And as we reached my outer office I called to Jerry: "Open all the windows. We've had some dirty company today—and the place stinks of him."

Barney turned in a single spin. His face was red, his eyes crackling coals. His right hand half reached up under his coat.

I said: "It would be a pleasure, Barney. Pull it out."

It didn't last long, but Barney was right. He had a temper. Then he stretched out his gloved hands, turned and walked from the office. The temptation to put a bullet in his back was strong, but he was right about the gloves. They had saved his life—or mine. I know it isn't a nice thought, but somehow I wished that Barney Hale had never owned a pair of gloves.

CHAPTER 4

MR. AND MRS. RACE WILLIAMS

I WAITED ANOTHER hour or so for The Flame to telephone. Then I left word with Jerry to tell me if she called and started to go and see the boy Randy. Three minutes later I was in a taxi and on my way to the address in the middle Seventies. I was about Fifty-ninth Street before I even thought of a plot—and I didn't like my thoughts. Had Barney Hale stalled me in my office while Randy Philips was kidnaped or murdered? Was I being followed now?

That thought made me do tricks. It's mighty easy to shake off lads that follow you. I jumped a couple of taxis, passed in and out of a hotel or two, popped up and down some subway stairs and wound up on the street next above the one I sought. I had decided on an unexpected entrance from the rear.

I went through the delivery entrance of the house that backed up to the one I wanted, hopped the rear fence behind it, and ran straight toward the rear of Randy's hide-out—an old four-story brick affair.

No one saw me—at least no one opened a window and hollered or took a couple of shots at me. But Randy couldn't watch both the front and the back of the house. I didn't waste time. I stuck close to the house as I dropped down to the barred cellar window sunk into the ground.

One, two, three—and the third barred grill came off in my hands. I kicked open the window, prayed for three seconds of safety and dropped to the hard floor below.

I USED MY flash, snapped it out at once and moved quickly along the wall, my gun ready. For my light had shone on the face of a kneeling man behind a round iron upright.

He did not shoot, did not move. And then he did move. At least his body made a sort of sinking noise as though he had slid down from the iron pole and lay upon the floor. Again I let the flash go. This time I was across the floor to the man, supporting his head that had fallen over the rope that held it—the rope that was strangling him. The pressure relieved, he breathed—the gasp of an old man. He had been strapped to one of the iron uprights, and left to die there.

I cut the ropes, tore the gag from his mouth and carried him over to the laundry tubs that were faintly visible in the dull light from a window buried below the ground level.

He drank and choked and at length came around to tell me he had worked with the Philips family for years, seen the boy Randy grow up, and had hidden out with him in this house owned by Randy's aunt.

"So they got Randy and killed him and—" There was a sound from above. I stopped talking, and darting my flash about found the stairs and started toward them.

"No, no." He grabbed my leg. "There are three men there. There were five. Miss Diane and another lady are bound—by the front door. I saw it all—before they found me."

"But why bound by the front door?"

"I don't know. I should have run for the police, but I had Mr. Randy's orders. Now he has been dragged away to die. Two women left behind."

"Listen"—I gave it to him fast—"if you could watch them, I can watch them. Give me the lay of the house—from the cellar stairs up."

The old servant told me what I wanted to know and I went up to the kitchen, took the back stairs from there to the second floor, found the front stairs and started down them.

Half-way down I crouched low and could see the two chairs and, plainly, the two girls strapped in them. Gagged and bound they sat straight and stiff. Diane McKay was sideways to me, but The Flame was directly facing me and the stairs. I saw the legs of men too, and heard the voice of Barney Hale.

"You understand now, boys," he said almost pleasantly. "You simply slip the wire back over the knob of the door when I leave. Remember as soon as that door is far enough open the bombs go off. They are well made. There will be little noise. The acid eats slowly but is deadly. Williams will have to close the outside door then he'll start to open this one carefully, see the girls bound, and dash in to his death. As soon as you put the wire in place, skip out the back way."

THE DOOR SLAMMED shut. Another, with just a distant thud, closed too. The men were stepping forward and The Flame was looking into my eyes. I just sat side-saddle on the smooth banister and let go.

The Flame's signal had been correct—as it was always correct. One man was lifting a bit of wire. Another was moving a chair with Diane on it. The third stood with his gun in hand, but all had their backs to me.

I left the banister. My weight carried me over the couple of remaining steps, and I hit the floor with both feet. I spoke my piece as soon as I landed.

"Race Williams talking. I'm on the kill."

All New York boys these—all familiar with my name. No general in the army had ever given a command that was obeyed more quickly than mine. The man with the gun in his hand dropped it without my telling him. All three reached for the ceiling.

One of them cursed softly—the others did not speak. I had them turn around one by one—and I knew two of them by name. Big Freddy Fay, Ike Gillman—and the third just a face. There are few real gunmen in New York I don't know. Ike Gillman was the best of this bunch. They didn't have any special rackets, just took on killings and such at a price.

The old servant came in from the kitchen and I watched the men while he cut the girls free.

Diane said: "Randy! They got him. We came to warn him. They traced him through the house which they learned belonged to his aunt."

The Flame said: "Race, Race—you're the same as ever. I remember how you used to—"

I leaned close to her and whispered in a voice for the three men I had driven into the large shuttered living-room to hear: "Then I'll get my job over. Now boys, take your choice. Come on. Back or front to the wall—either way. But you've got to die."

"You can't get away with this, Williams," Gillman had the guts to bluster.

The stranger said: "We were just paid—never knew it was you—we meant no harm and—"

"I heard it all from the stairs," I told them. "You first, stranger. If anything goes wrong—I'll know where to find the others."

Tough guys? The stranger was on his knees before I got fairly started talking. Big Freddy was crying all over his face. Ike Gillman's legs were trembling in his pants as The Flame pulled down my arm. But not one of them thought of fighting for his life.

The Flame pleaded with me. "You can't do it. You can't just line them against a wall and kill them as if you were a common hood yourself. There's a law, Race."

I raised my voice to a pitch of fury. "There is no law for their kind. It's only death that counts. They'll know it in the underworld. Other killers will know they came—and they'll know that their three bodies are stretched on this floor. Now's the time for it!" I swung up my gun again and—

Gillman broke then. He screamed out not to shoot. The Flame grabbed my arm, and the show was over. Three men marched from that house one at a time and each one carried the fear of death—the fear of me—carried it to every paid murderer in the city.

I turned to Diane who was leaning against the mantel.

"You're a brave kid," I told her. "But I couldn't just murder men, of course. The Flame and I have put on that act before. It's great personal advertising. You were not afraid?"

"Yes, yes." She took a long time getting the words out. "I was afraid they would not die." And when I opened my mouth to speak, "You will not think unkindly of me, Mr. Williams. I have seen so much, lived so much that was terrible—know so well how much better this world would be if good men like you killed bad men like them. I could gladly have seen them die."

"Why did you come here?" was the best I could get off then.

"Because of you. Because you told me I should not let this money go to these men. Because you told me I should be married."

"And what did Randy say?"

"He said, 'All right, Diane—go ahead and marry him then.'"

"Who?" The girl had me dizzy.

"You—you." She was close to me now. "Don't you see? Don't you understand? I told him the truth. It is you I love. You I want to marry."

I looked at The Flame, but she didn't help me any.

Diane said: "Randy was the love of a young girl who met someone of another world, someone who worked and slept each night without the fear of never awakening. He did not keep a gun under his pillow. I thought I loved him. I was mistaken."

I was stupefied.

"I love you, Race," she said again. "I knew it when I saw you. For years I have dreamed of your helping me. When you are my husband I will make you care—and the money shall belong to my husband."

"It's not a question of money, Diane." I tried to come out of my fog. "I'm not a marrying man. The Flame can tell you that."

THE FLAME SAID: "You marry her—or the money goes. You can get a divorce afterward if you don't care for the money or the girl."

"He will not want that—but he may have it." Diane put those eyes on me.

It didn't seem so terrible all of a sudden. I said: "We'll see what comes up in the next few days."

"No." It was The Flame who spoke now and her lips twisted. "We forgot to tell you, Race, that Diane's twenty-one tomorrow. So—she has to be married today—or before twelve o'clock tonight."

"Hell." I felt relieved. "We can't do that. The law of New York State won't—"

"I have attended to that." The Flame jumped in. "We use another state. I have already arranged for a special license. You have nothing to do but get married."

I tried to be tough. "Anyone will marry her with that money."

"But no one—not even Barney's hired thugs—would dare kill the wife of Race Williams." And as I shook my head, "So you won't marry her?"

"We're all talking nonsense," I started. "Why the idea is—"

And the girl Diane was in my arms. When I raised her head and looked at her— Well, I kept my head. "Remember, Diane," I said. "We are just pretending until—"

"Until you will never want to pretend anymore." And suddenly, "They won't—Barney will let Randy go after we're married?"

"Good God!" It hit me like that. "You're not marrying me because—"

"I'm marrying you," she said slowly, "because I love you. It is natural that I don't want Randy to die because of me."

I pulled her close—and The Flame spoke.

"Come on, Race, we've got to move. I can't stand the cow-like look. You'll 'moo' in a minute."

WE HAD BEEN riding for over an hour before I began to realize all I'd let myself in for. There had been a time when The Flame had more than hinted that I retire from business, get married and travel around the world. But I didn't feel like retiring. I didn't intend to retire.

I looked at the girl who was determined to be my wife—then at The Flame who drove. Nervous? Sure, I was nervous.

Diane drew close to me.

I said: "Diane, I don't know how I got mixed up in this marriage or you got mixed up in it. Understand, you're a swell kid, but my life—it's one bullet right after another. It isn't the kind—"

She put a little hand over my mouth. "Barney, Doctor Beasley, Finn, Slattery—my father. They all killed people, but none so slowly and horribly as they killed my mother. They never laid a hand on her. But they saw her, and they saw me—and they told her what they planned for me." Those great, deep eyes of hers were on me now. "I have lived in hell ever since I can remember. I am not afraid of anything that may happen with you. I will help—" And when I started to talk, "Or will not help, as you wish."

"Well"—I'll admit I was beginning to hedge on a deal for the first time in my life—"The Flame has made our marriage possible—snap like that. The divorce can be the same way."

She parted generous lips, smiled, started to speak and—we were there.

I didn't see the sign *Justice of the Peace* until we were right close to the door.

The J.P. himself was hard to describe, because you didn't know if he wore whiskers or just needed a shave. His wife looked us over, and two or three dirty-faced kids kept jumping in and out behind the curtains. It was going to be a hell of a marriage—like a lot of others, I guess.

The old boy had a room with a desk littered with papers, and finally produced some which I signed, Diane followed suit.

He wanted to talk. "You know the right people to get things fixed so quick," he said, but I interrupted.

"Never mind that. Get started."

"But there's only the one witness. My wife acts as witness often without charge. No more than you force on her. But this here lady—"

"He's right," said Diane. "I have someone coming. Someone I have known a great many years. A few minutes won't matter."

"No," I started in. "Why—"

The J.P.'s wife was by the curtains. She parted them and a man walked through.

I spun like a top, jerked out my gun—and Diane grabbed my arm. The man in the doorway was Doctor Beasley.

His erect little figure suddenly cringed. His eyes popped, and his voice squeaked like a mouse when he said: "She promised—she—"

Diane said: "It's all right, Race. I promised the doctor that no harm would come to him. I want him as a witness. You'll admit he'll make an ideal one." That justice of the peace must have seen plenty of queer marriages, but I'll bet he never saw a bridegroom search the witness before like I did. I went over Beasley with a fine-tooth comb. The most deadly thing he carried was a bunch of keys.

Beasley grew cocky after a bit. He finally said: "You know the consequences of your act, Diane. You know the danger you subject this man to for—"

I took a step forward. Doctor Beasley remembered the single loop of my gun on the train, or maybe he didn't. But his words came to the end of his tongue, stopped, jarred back and he swallowed what was left of his sentence with a single gulp.

"Ready?" The J.P. took his place behind the desk, glanced once at his own double-barreled gun in a corner and began the show.

His words were short and to the point. Just a few stood out. I think we all gasped, excepting the J.P. when he said: "Until death do you part."

After that—the ring which The Flame produced, and the J.P.'s words—"Kiss your wife."

That was the time I should have grabbed her in my arms, but I didn't. I was out of my class—lost—lost until she pulled my head down, smiled and kissed me. Her lips were cold as ice.

There was an old book to sign, a certificate to be made out. I remember reaching for it—and the J.P. handing it to Diane.

"It's hers. Always keep it, my dear." And killing the sentiment promptly, "Certified duplicates will cost you fifty cents apiece."

Diane turned to me. "Race," she said very calmly, "pay the justice—and then

I would like five minutes in this room—alone with Doctor Beasley."

I gave it a minute's thought. Then I handed the old bird a hundred bucks. His face didn't change, so I guess he was pleased. But I wasn't pleased about leaving Diane alone with dear old Beasley. I told Diane that, flat.

"Please, Race." And when I still objected she led me aside and whispered: "You may watch through the curtains then." And turning and raising her voice, "Doctor, come over here behind the desk."

We went out through the curtains, damn near fell over the kids who ran up the stairs. The Flame, Mrs. Justice and the J.P. himself went into the dining-room.

Me, I watched through the curtains all right. The doctor was half facing me, but he couldn't see me. He spoke plainly and quickly.

"As soon as Barney knows, you'll die—Williams will die. You're a fool, Diane. I had no intention of harming you on that train. I wanted to frighten you. I—" He was leaning forward when I pulled my gun, and Diane saved the doctor's life when she knocked the tiny metal needle from his hand.

"The time for that is past," she said. "You'd have died if—" And her voice lowered. I knew that she was talking, for sometimes I heard the buzz of her voice and sometimes I saw the changing expression on the doctor's face.

Once he said: "You'll be dead by morning." And later, "No, no—he'd wait—even if it took years, and kill you anyway." A long minute after that while Diane spoke rapidly. Then the doctor said: "You must

be mad—mad. He'd kill me like that." His fingers snapped, but he still listened to the girl, and the expression on his face was changing. His head began to nod up and down as he agreed with her.

The doctor started to talk, said: "That would be murder and I don't think—"

Diane put a hand across his lips. She pulled her chair closer to his. I had my gun ready. Personally, I considered Beasley the most dangerous of all her enemies. At least at a time like this. I was wondering if I had searched his sleeves well, felt of the lining of his jacket. A quick movement, a thin surgical instrument—the skill to use it—and Diane would be dead.

Then suddenly I wasn't afraid for Diane any more—though I didn't relax my vigilance. No, I didn't hear another word of what they said. I didn't need to. The doctor was not only nodding in agreement now, but he was evidently adding to what she said. Then it was over. The doctor held out his hand. Diane hesitated, then taking her handkerchief she lifted the doctor's outstretched hand, rubbed at it. After that their hands met.

Me—I just had time to move back into the hall before they reached the curtain. Sweet? Yes, the word seemed to fit her. Good? Yes, that word, too, still fitted her. But I also had a sudden feeling that I had married a very dangerous woman.

Diane called The Flame and myself into the room. This time she had the J.P. close the folding doors.

She said: "Doctor Beasley and I have had a talk. He is no longer my enemy. He has convinced me that he only wished to frighten me on the train."

"Frighten you," I gasped. "What about the other girl? What about the hospital arrangements? The two ambulances and—"

She said very softly: "I am afraid, Race—afraid I have made a mistake. Doctor Beasley has convinced me that he meant me no harm. So you, too, and Miss Drummond must be convinced." She turned to the doctor. "I will hear directly from him then?"

"Yes," said Beasley. "Mr. Williams, Miss McKay—rather Mrs. Williams and myself—have reached an understanding—a pleasant understanding. I shall in no way harm her or attempt to harm you. You—in return—are not to shoot me to death."

"That's a blunt way of putting it."

"You, Mr. Williams, have a blunt way of doing things. May I wish you a pleasant honeymoon and a long life." He held out his hand, but did not press the point when I kept mine at my side and puckered up my lips. Then he was gone.

"You bought him off, Diane?" I asked.

"I bought our happiness."

"You shouldn't have done that. I have protected others for years. I am capable of protecting my own wife—yes, capable of killing for her."

"But our happiness—our chance of happiness is better my way."

"You promised him money—and his life," The Flame said when we were back in the car again. "You could have threatened him with your husband, Diane. It was fear of Race that made Doctor Beasley agree to anything you asked."

But Diane remained silent.

CHAPTER 5

LITTLE KILLER

I SAT WITH my wife as we drove into the setting sun—if you like your stuff that way. Me—I didn't know what to think, if I did think at all. Where the idea got into my head that somehow I was sucked in, I couldn't understand. I guess it's what every married man feels when he takes the first jolt.

I looked at Diane. Beautiful? She was more than that. Young—twenty-one. Class—a lad could cart her any place and maybe have to take a tuck at his own poise and assurance to match her. Money? Plenty, but I didn't know the amount. Romance? Hell, a divorce could cure all that at any time. Romance wasn't up my alley. Or was it? This kid had come along and put the finger right on me. Maybe the years had mellowed me.

The biggest surprise came when we hit the apartment hotel on Park Avenue. We were in the swanky duplex on the tenth floor before The Flame explained.

"I sub-let it in my name, Race—people away until spring. Look." She waved a hand around at the modernistic furniture, the drapes across the high windows, the piano in the far corner. "Furnished to the hilt," she finished. "Even to a bottle opener in the kitchen, and a bottle of champagne in the ice box."

We killed the bottle before I even looked over the place, or made any comment. Then I looked her straight in the eyes and said: "In one morning, eh? You arrange for a special license for marriage, pick out a swanky apartment, and—"

"I know people." The Flame shrugged her shoulders. "The license was a snap—just a telephone call. This place"—she moved away from Diane, and whispered while the girl looked out the window—"I had friends looking for it a week ago. You see, well, I didn't think the honeymoon would be yours then."

I saw her point and let it ride.

Diane came over in that way she had, and placed tiny hands in my big mitts.

"I am going to lie down, Race. I'm going up to rest. You will stay on guard here below. It will be my first untroubled rest—in as long as I can remember."

I went through the apartment then—every room, every cupboard. It wasn't so large, though I got the impression that there were more baths than bedrooms. But it was safe.

"Florence," I said after I had closed the door on my—my—on Diane, and went below with her. "We're alone. Tell me."

"What?"

"How—well, about the money, and Thomas Rockland—and if you're positive that it's true. How will the money be paid?"

"It's true. I know Thomas Rockland, and so do you. He's the only reformed criminal I do know. Too much money—too easy a life. Oh, not that he isn't above lending money occasionally to finance a big job, but that's all. He and Diane's father were great friends. He's a peculiar man. But tonight at midnight we all meet in his library."

"All—who's all?"

"Barney Hale, Doctor Beasley—the other two if they had stayed alive. Diane, you and myself. Don't look surprised, Race. Proof of her marriage, proof of her age which he had—but most of all proof of her life. It's tonight at midnight—things move fast."

"Yes," I agreed, "things move fast. You and I here, and—"

"And once I wondered. But I wouldn't have picked this place for—us. It would have been older, far out in the country. It—Race"—she laid both hands upon my shoulders—"after the years, you've taken the dive just like any other man. Do you love Diane?"

"How could I, I met her only yesterday. Hell, at two o'clock this morning. Why the thing's impossible."

"Do you love her?"

"I don't know. There's something almost—I don't know."

"Be careful, Race. Remember it is only for a little while. It would be a pity if after all your years, your distrust, indifference to women, you finally fell in love with Diane."

"Yeah," I said. "That would be a joke. No, Florence." I lifted her arms that were creeping about my shoulders. The Flame was a young girl again. The sparkle of youth was in her eyes, the hardness was gone. Her soft hair brushed my cheek, and—the phone rang.

I TURNED MY head suddenly. Diane was coming down the stairs. She smiled as she lifted the phone, said, "Yes," very softly. Then her voice changed. "Yes, yes—yes," she said over and over, and finally dropped the phone back in its cradle and sank gently to the floor.

I crossed the room, picked her up in my arms, carried her up the stairs and eased her down on the bed. She was real, this frail little girl who needed the protection I could give her. And that was the first time I knew—or did I know?—that I loved Diane.

She came around then and I asked: "What made you faint? Who was on the phone? What did he say?"

She put up her arms and pulled my head down very close to her. She said: "It was Barney Hale, Race, and—and he said money or no money—marriage or no marriage—you are to die. Race, I'm afraid for you."

"For me?" I was both pleased and mad if you can figure the connection. "Why, Diane, you must be out of your mind."

"For your sake and mine I hope so. Remember, Race. I am only afraid now for you."

We let her sleep while The Flame put some food together. That ice box must have contained everything. It was quite dark now, and the living-room glowed pleasantly with the indirect lighting. Since there was a chain across the front door I spent my time in the kitchen with The Flame.

"We've got a ride tonight, Florence," I said. "It will be a long fifteen minutes. Understand I wouldn't mind if Barney Hale called out the Marines, but it's the girl and the money. I think I'll telephone Jerry and get the machine gun set up in back of the touring."

The Flame laughed. "Now that would be nice for the respectable Thomas Rockland. A couple of cars and half a dozen men blasting each other apart in front of his house. No, that's neutral ground, Race. Eleven forty-five is the hour of safety. Thomas Rockland must be called then by Diane. From then until she reaches his house she is safe from attack. That is the play."

"But Barney Hale and even Beasley don't seem to be guys who'd play it as a game."

"They must. If Diane telephones and fails to get there, why Barney gets no money—nothing. They all understand there is to be something given the loser."

"A booby prize, eh?" I started and stopped.

We listened. The Flame said: "What was that?"

Someone was talking in the living-room. The voice was very low. My gun was in my hand when I soft-footed it across the kitchen.

It was nothing but the voice of Diane. She was at the telephone again. I caught a few words, would have caught more if I hadn't slipped on the rug trying to hold back my prepared jump—and threat.

The words I caught were "—I won't forget what you've done for me, Doctor Beasley. Someone listening? Did you—" That was when Diane turned and saw me. She didn't faint this time. She placed the phone carefully back in its prongs, though there seemed to be a sharp, distant cry when the broken connection clicked home.

"Race, Race—" she was across to me. "I don't want to rest any more. I want to help—be gay."

We talked of many things but we avoided crime, avoided the business of the evening. And, since The Flame hinted it to me, avoided talk of our marriage until the hands of the clock crept toward the zero hour. Finally The Flame's voice.

"Eleven forty-five, Race. I've got Rockland's phone number here."

A moment later I was talking to Thomas Rockland and he was saying: "Glad to find you in on the show, Race. Of course, come right over. I'm not playing any favorites, understand. I'm just paying off the winner with my congratulations. But I've got to speak to the principals when they call. Put on the Little Killer."

"Who," I asked, "is the Little Killer?"

"Diane, dear boy—Diane. Just a pet name her father gave her. I called her that too. Haven't seen her in years…. Yes, yes, I know. I'm satisfied with the proof of her marriage. Now I want to know she's alive."

Diane went to the phone, said simply: "Uncle Thomas, I'm coming for my money."

If he said anything in reply he was talking to himself, for my—yes, I'll get it in this time—my wife slammed down the phone.

CHAPTER 6

THE POISON AND THE CURE

THOMAS ROCKLAND'S HOUSE was a pretentious affair with a great iron fence around it, and huge doors that opened almost the minute we pressed the bell.

The old butler was dignified and pompous, and stood aside for us to pass. There were other servants—three men and two women—standing at attention in the hall. My eyes widened slightly. I knew one of the men. He was from the State Detective Agency. He grinned as my eyes widened.

There we three stood. The Flame, Diane and myself as the butler disappeared entirely and Rockland came slowly out of a room, closing and locking the door behind him.

Thomas Rockland was well into his fifties—tall, stout, his chins laying out over his collar. He was in full evening dress and his little eyes twinkled, his mouth opened. His pleasure at seeing us was plain. It even shone far back where the baldness of his head finally picked up some foliage.

"Diane, my child—and Florence—The Flame. You haven't changed a bit, my dear. And Race—Race Williams. Ah, my dear boy, you didn't know our little affair was formal. One other guest has arrived. He is now in the library. Evening dress, of course. You—Forbes—forward"— he beckoned the detective I knew—"will take Mr. Williams to the front room. We have clothes there for you, Mr. Williams." And he came over close to me. "Change, understand. I'm not going to have my home turned into a shooting gallery.

"As for you ladies. These women here will take you above, show you where to leave your wraps—and things. You may continue to wear beautiful jewelry, but will dispense with all other—hardware."

I looked at Diane, looked at The Flame. They nodded and I went into the room with Forbes. He grinned all over when the door was closed, and I saw the evening clothes on the bed.

"A new kind of frisk, Race," he said. "Sort of genteel. You must take your clothes off. I got to see that no artillery goes into the library."

The system was not a bad one even if the dress suit was a little tight. But standing there in my shorts I couldn't very well hide a gun. He did his job well.

He discovered with ease both my heavy guns beneath my arms, waited patiently until I removed the clip from my sleeve and let him have the little automatic.

"Didn't think you went in for automatics, Race." He watched me put on the stiff shirt, gave me a help with the tie after my things were stowed safely away in a closet.

I said: "I don't like automatics. Both my regular guns are revolvers. Automatics aren't rough enough for my business."

"No?" He grinned. "A matter of opinion. We use them. The cops use them, your boy friend ahead of you sported one thirty-eight automatic. You beat him out on the sleeve gun, but he carried a knife and a blackjack. There's your pants. What's the big pow-wow tonight? Never saw that other bird before. But I got orders to see that neither you nor the other guy carried anything. Surly and mean he was."

Doctor Beasley, I thought, would be the "other bird," but to Forbes I said: "How about the girls—are they being searched? Pretty far-fetched procedure with a couple of girls."

"Yeah." Forbes laughed. "It may be with the little one who hid her face. I never seen her before. But Miss Drummond—

The Flame, I know. I bet she drops guns and knives just like the Marx Brothers."

I shrugged and went out into the hall and waited for the girls.

They came. The Flame with a gesture of resignation. Diane—just a smile. Neither one of them seemed to be embarrassed.

We entered the library, looked at the long table, and Barney Hale who sat unsmilingly tapping its polished surface. His face was white and drawn, and hate was in his eyes. When we three sat down and our host took his place at the head of the table, one leather chair was vacant.

"Doctor Beasley's place." Thomas Rockland nodded at the empty chair. "The papers informed me that Slattery will not be here, and I guessed that swaggering Jerry Finn was distributed too far along the railroad tracks to be put back together again in time for our meeting. However, he was identified—by a ring that remained upon one finger—one whole finger."

"To hell with that, Tom," Barney said. "What about this dough? You know me. Where do I fit? That money should be mine. Talk straight."

Thomas Rockland's chest went up like a pouter pigeon's. His shirt did tricks. His big cheeks grew red. He waited to speak, and when he did there was no emotion in his voice.

"Barney Hale," he said slowly. "Tonight you will listen. Don't vent your hate on me. I have the birth certificate of Louie McKay's daughter, Diane. She is twenty-one—and she is here. You know the terms of the agreement. Tonight I shall talk. Beasley has not come. It is after twelve. Now—all of you—listen to me.

"Louie McKay was my friend. His deeds or misdeeds, his brutal treatment of his wife and daughter, his courage in facing you, Barney Hale, Slattery, Beasley, and Jerry Finn—the murders and bloodshed, the evil thoughts of him do not matter. He saved my life and he was my friend.

"I made money, retired from all activities with Louie McKay. It was then he started to save his money. Saved for a day that you didn't save for. None of you. And when you wanted Louie's savings you were told I had them—for an arranged purpose when he died—if he died a natural death. That's why none of you shot him in the back. And he hated you all—yes, and his young daughter who came to live with him when her mother died.

"Then, over two years ago—Diane was eighteen at the time—he got his death warrant. Remember that night he thought he was going to die? You were all there, and Diane was there, and he cursed you all even as he thought he was about to go out.

"It was then that he made plans for his money, put it in my hands. But you remember all that. Just a mad idea of a greater hate between you all. Diane"—he reached down and with some effort lifted a bag and put it upon the table—"your father was my friend. This money is yours. His instructions to me were that the police must not be called in by either side.

"Your father said you had a brilliant mind. He hated you, but he admired in you what he thought was his own blood—but perhaps was the blood of your mother. He had one pet name for you. I give it to you tonight." He opened the bag. Stacks of bills bulged there—thousand-dollar bills, and larger. "Little Killer, the money is yours," Rockland finished. "Two hundred and fifty thousand dollars. A quarter of a million."

Barney Hale came to his feet. He fairly took the polish off the table with his foul language. "It's mine—mine." He had to hold himself from grabbing at the money as his eyes grew red, his breath like the panting of some animal. "You're crooked, Rockland—yes, crooked as hell." And when Rockland stood up and faced him, "You're not living up to the spirit of your contract with your friend Louie McKay. Maybe he didn't say it, but he meant it. We have only fought off one man—Philips—the man he hated because the Little Killer loved him."

Thomas Rockland spoke slowly. "I have lived up to the letter, to the intent, even to the spirit of his wishes. She is married. She is twenty-one, and she is alive."

Barney turned toward Diane—and me. He was ready to make his threats when I spoke.

"Barney," I told him, "you've got two guns—and only one mouth. So far, lots has come out of that one mouth—but nothing out of those two guns. I won't be hard to find."

Barney opened his mouth again. No words came. Thomas Rockland handed him a plain sealed envelope. It was very thin.

"And this"—Thomas Rockland looked Barney straight in the eyes—"is for the loser. Just as Louie McKay wrote it. He took a long time to write it—at least he played with the pen a long time before he put down the words."

Barney tore open the envelope. Plainly I saw the words on the smaller envelope inside. *For Barney Hale.* It didn't take him a minute to read the note he snatched from that inner envelope, but it took him a good three minutes to gather himself together, then toss the note down and walk rapidly toward the door. I stooped and picked up the note and read it—first to myself—then aloud.

"I think it will be you, Barney. I think the Little Killer will plan it that way.

Louie McKay."

And Barney was back leaning over the table, talking to the girl.

He said: "Plan it that way. There was Gibbons, the lawyer. We knew him for years. You were always different to him— and it was Gibbons who saw that we met Florence Drummond—The Flame, whose reputation as a criminal seemed safe to us. And today I found out that The Flame and Williams were very close—at one time. You stuck close to the ranch, too, after your father's funeral. You knew, with the servants there, that if we simply killed you we'd be caught." He was shaking his head now, trying to think. Then he had it. "By God, you were in no terrible danger on that train. The Flame was armed. Race Williams came aboard. Slattery dead. Jerry Finn dead. No, Gibbons

kept you informed of every move we made. Little Killer is right. You planned it all."

Diane looked straight at him without the slightest expression.

"No," she said slowly. "I did not plan it. I willed it that way."

"Then"—and there was viciousness in his voice when he said it—"then will my death at once, for I have plans for you that will make Doctor Beasley's operation seem like a pleasure."

Barney turned and without another word walked out the door.

Thomas Rockland sat down and laughed. "Diane," he said. "I'm glad you won. You must visit me before you start on your honeymoon and tell me everything. Tonight my part in this little comedy-drama is over. It would be best to leave this money with me. Meet me at the Twenty-second Street Bank tomorrow, or rather this morning, at nine o'clock sharp. We will arrange for your account. So you willed it that way."

"Exactly, Uncle Thomas," she said seriously. "For years I lived on my father's ranch among murderers and criminals of all kinds. Their minds were deformed and their plans never simple. I was not supposed to know that they even intended to harm me—yet through suggestion I put into their minds many things which they did to cause my death. Naturally, since I prepared the poison, I had the cure ready."

CHAPTER 7

WITH A .38

I SAT DOWNSTAIRS, back in our high-priced apartment with a gun across my knee. So what? Was I going to spend my life sitting up with a gun all night—every night?

Diane was sleeping above. The Flame in the other bedroom. I went up the stairs, turned to Diane's—my wife's room—tried the knob. Though I had told her to lock it, the door was not locked. I went in and looked straight down at her asleep beneath the light. I sat on the edge of the bed and her breathing broke slightly. She was very beautiful, very innocent-looking. I couldn't figure out this Little Killer business. How this young girl could be accused of being a master-mind among criminals. There was not a line on her face, no circles beneath her eyes, yet she had gone through so much. I touched her hair, brushed it back. She half turned and her face rested on my hand. For a moment her eyes opened. She smiled very sweetly.

She turned, clutched my hand, held it close to her lips, kissed it.

"Race, Race," she said softly. "I am so tired, so happy. Barney won't bother us any more."

Her arms suddenly shot out around my neck and something white seemed to jump from beneath the pillow and land upon the floor. I saw it when she held me then, saw it plainly beneath the light. It was an envelope. It was addressed to Henry Trojan, and there was a street and number well uptown.

"It's all right, Diane," I told her. "Sleep now." I ducked down and getting the letter, crammed it into the side pocket of my jacket.

I put her head back on the pillow, leaned down and kissed her on the forehead. Then I snapped out the light and left the room.

Downstairs I opened the letter and read it. It was short. The Henry Trojan on the envelope was really Barney Hale. The letter read—

Dear Barney:
The game is over—life begins for both of us. I enclose check for one hundred-thousand dollars. Race Williams must live.
Diane.

I cursed as I read that letter, looked around to see if I had dropped the check. Of course I hadn't. I knew why the letter was unsealed. Diane would enclose the check when the money was deposited in the bank and mail it to him. I read the letter again, wadded it up and threw it on the floor.

What kind of a guy was I? Why I was paid by people whose lives were in danger. My business was protecting others. My business was to take guys like Barney, dump them over or chase them out of town.

Now—damn it to hell! It was like a nightmare. My own wife was paying money to protect me from a rat out of a Chicago sewer.

With that thought I was out and into the night.

BARNEY HALE was not a New York killer. He had said himself that he wanted that money to go into business—lay it on the line. The chances were that he didn't have any friends there at his apartment with him, and if he did, the pleasure was mine.

I spotted the name in the hall of the five-story, walk-up apartment. *Henry Trojan. Apartment 5C.* I looked at it a long time.

There were plenty of bells to press that would give me admission to the apartment house, as the owner of any bell I rang could press the button in his own apartment which would open the front door. So I gave Barney a break. I pushed his own bell. I'd let him know he was going to have a visitor, and that visitor's name might be—Death.

I waited for the answering click as I held my hand on the door knob. There wasn't any click. The rat! He'd run out on me. Or maybe he didn't want a visitor. Or maybe he was expecting me. Someone could have tipped him off when I left my place.

But this was a business trip. I didn't wait around. I picked a button on the ground floor, never bothered about the time being close to three—and gave it a push.

I got fair service. The buzzer snapped. I turned the knob, passed through the dimly lit hall and bounced onto the stairs. A door opened in the back, but whoever opened it was too late to see me. I lulled his suspicions with the same old gag I'd used on many such occasions.

I said in a thick, whiskey-hushed breath: "Sorry, brother. But it's a hell of a lot better to wake you up than the wife."

Before his door slammed I was up to the second floor. After that I took things a bit easier. Probably Barney had this place ready for him to use whenever he came to New York. The top floor would naturally be his meat. There was a square block of apartments in that neighborhood. A lad looking for an out could run to the roof, hop a few other roofs, and come out on another street.

There was light in the halls. Dim—but enough. I cased each landing up and down the hall, then dashed for the next flight of stairs. I wasn't any easy-going guy now. I didn't expect to blow my name in Barney's face and scare him stiff like I had those lads that afternoon. He wasn't the kind for that. I chanced death on every flight I made, chanced that he might be lying flat on his stomach at the top of each new floor. But I made those steps on my hand and knees. Hand is right—just my left hand. My right hand held a gun. Yes, I realized I faced death, but so did Barney.

I'm fast with a gun. Barney was fast. But that wouldn't be what counted at the end. It would be the sureness of the man. A guy's got to be more than fast to shoot at me. He gets one shot only. Killers fear one thing above all law—even the prospect of the chair—for they can so often beat that rap. But a stomach full of lead or a bullet in their head can't be beat, can't be fixed.

And I made the fifth floor. I squirmed on my belly as I looked up and down that floor. 5C was in the back, away from the stairs, so I was safe from a shot from that direction.

With my back flat against the opposite

wall, and my gun covering the shining knob of 5C, I made the trip down that hall. I meant business now.

No sound, no movement, not even a draft down the hall, though it was a little chilly. I reached 5C, crossed the hall, covered it up and down once more, then raising my head and watching for some trick panel, I clutched the knob with my left hand, turned it and leaned against the door slightly.

Surprised? Yes, I guess I was. The door gave beneath pressure. It wasn't even locked.

Some guys open doors carefully, and get their heads shot off, if a killer hides back behind the door. Me—I let the door stay open a fraction of a slit, held the gun in my right hand, my flash in my left, and raised my foot. The door was heavy, understand, and I was kicking against weight, so I pushed more than kicked it.

I figured on one of two results. If there was anyone behind that door he would be knocked cold. If there was anyone in that hall—and that anyone happened to be Barney and he had a gun—why he'd be shot cold.

The door bounced back, then slowed down and finally stopped moving. Nothing happened. I moved into a narrow hallway, white walls, a turn at the end—just a few feet down.

And I stood there alone.

My light covered the entire hall, and my eyes followed the light—so did my feet, for that matter. I watched the raw white plaster there by the curve. Surely a hand would come out and a gun would blast away—that is, it would if I didn't shoot all the fingers off that hand first.

But no hand came. The dirty rat! A run-out, you'd think? Well, I didn't. Somehow I knew Barney would be there, and somehow instinct tells me when another human is present. Somewhere in that apartment men, or a man, waited. I was certain of it.

I reached the end of the hall. The turn was a two-foot one. There were no curtains. Plainly I saw into the room beyond. There wasn't much furniture—a couch, a table, one lamp, a couple of chairs and a rug. There were windows almost straight before me, and beyond them the fire-escape. To my right a door, and to my left another door. I bent back, covered the door to the right with my flash, and leaning in—gun rather loose in my hand—I found the light switch and pressed it. Four brilliant lights in the center of that room flashed on as I jerked back my hand and looked quickly toward the door on the left.

Then I jarred back on my heels. I knew now why Doctor Beasley had not attended our midnight gathering at Thomas Rockland's. He couldn't. He lay there flat on his back.

There was a knife stuck squarely through his chest.

Of course, my reaction was to spring forward and examine the body. And I did start to spring, but prevented that by stretching out my hands, gripping both sides of that broad open doorway and holding myself back. It was a trap, of course, and I had been about to spring into it.

I could have laughed at my own stupidity. Then I couldn't laugh. It was a trap all right—a real trap and I was caught in it.

The gun jabbed into my back—and Barney spoke behind me.

"Freeze—or 'stiffen' if I may quote a famous gunman. Simplicity is the thing, Race. I was on the stairs leading to the roof when you went in. It was easy to follow you in my stocking feet, push open the door a bit and make my run when you first saw and admired the late Doctor Beasley."

And when I didn't speak, "Go on—move across the room—by the blank wall there. Hands high, Race. You wouldn't kid with me—not over a few seconds you wouldn't. There—that's better."

My hands were up, his gun against my side close to my heart. He moved with great ease, long familiarity and rapidity. His left hand took one gun from my right hand, slipped the other big revolver from beneath my armpit. He tossed them on the couch. But the gun still remained in my sleeve. I tried not to raise my arm too high, the sleeves of my coat—the right sleeve at least—might slip back too far, but I don't think the gun would show even then.

Like all his kind he had to talk, and there was fury in his voice while he emptied his rotten soul of its hatred. While he waited and while that gun was held close to my back I still had the gun in my sleeve.

Yes, and death in my soul.

Barney sneered his words.

"So she willed my death this morning. This time I did the willing—and it's you that die. I'm going to kill you, of course, Race, then I'm going to get her. And get this Randy and let her watch him die—first."

I hoped for time, said: "Randy—he's alive then?" I moved a little closer to the wall, twisted my right arm. I'd have to curve my arm down to snap that sleeve gun into my hand.

"Yes, alive for a while. Diane willed it. Diane planned it. Little Killer, her father called her, and he was right. We kill with guns. She kills with that mind of hers. Let me tell you what she did. Doctor Beasley went to see her marry you. She bribed him. Promised him fifty thousand dollars if he'd set Randy Philips free.

"Beasley double-crossed me and let Randy go. Then what? Randy telephoned her that he was safe—and she immediately called back to this apartment. To thank Beasley, and to let me know Beasley had double-crossed me.

"Strange but true. Yes, she let me know, so Beasley would die. And you. I don't say you wouldn't have come yourself, but I think she had a hand in it. She—"

He stopped suddenly and laughed, then grabbed at my right hand, dragged it to my side. With a single slap of his gun he knocked at my arm. The sleeve gun fell to the floor.

He kicked the gun across the room, said: "Forbes, the dick at Thomas Rockland's house, told me you had it when he gave me my stuff back. Put your hand up again, Williams. So you don't like it. You try and climb through the wall, eh?" He sunk his gun deep into my back. "I'd like to see you die slowly, but you bear a charmed life. I'll count ten, give you time to think if she sucked you into coming here. I'd like to know how—but at the count of ten I'll blow a hole through your back."

I knew he was counting. I knew I was going to die. And what was I thinking about? Why that louse Forbes! What the hell did the stupid dick tell him that for? Forbes had told me—told me— Yes, by God, I didn't think of Forbes as a louse then. Forbes had said that Barney sported a thirty-eight automatic—understand, a thirty-eight automatic.

I think that Barney said "Nine" or maybe it was "Eight." I don't know. I simply went into action. I didn't leap away from that gun that was lightly pressed against my spine. But I did back into it. Backed hard against the nose of it as I dropped both my hands and swung around.

I heard the dull click, and Barney's curse as he pressed the trigger, and no bullet went into my back, no explosion shook the room. His damn gun wouldn't go off. I helped the illusion along too, as I pressed harder back and he tried desperately and unsuccessfully to send a row of slugs into my spine.

I shouted: "It's jammed, you fool! Jammed—" I swung my elbow, knocked his arm, spun like a top and tore the gun from his hand. It wasn't very difficult. Once he got the idea that his gun was jammed he didn't want it. He slugged me with the blackjack that jerked into his left hand.

I went down, knocked to a sitting position against the wall. Dazed? Yes, slightly. I was on one knee. His automatic was in my hand pointing directly at him when he grabbed the knife from the mantel and roared down on me. Just a beast he was then, and my words of warning went unheeded.

"Drop that knife or I'll shoot," was the best I could get off.

His answer was an upward and downward leap in the air, a flash of the knife down at my throat.

There was nothing else for me to do. I closed my finger four times in a split second and laid four slugs from his own gun—yes, his own thirty-eight automatic—right in the center of his chest.

He didn't stab me and he didn't fall on me. He was very close when I shot. The slugs almost tore him apart as they threw him back across the room. I grabbed up my sleeve gun, whisked my two revolvers from the couch, hopped out the window and fled up the fire-escape to the roof above.

One thing was certain. Diane hadn't willed that little trick of mine with the automatic. But no more of that now—I was a busy man.

It was three minutes of four when I tapped at the cellar door of the Turkish bath.

Oscar let me in.

I said: "I want the works, Oscar. Here—" I gave him my money and my guns. "Put them in the safe upstairs and book me in at two o'clock." And after he had taken me into the quiet of the bath itself, but before he went above I said: "And see that I leave here no later than eight."

That was all. I took the beating Oscar gave me, the alcohol rub, a bit of steam and even a dip in the pool. Did I think? Well, perhaps. Certainly Diane had received and made a telephone call. Certainly a letter had popped surprisingly out from beneath her pillow. Certainly she had been afraid for my life—

Or had she just managed to make me believe she was?

CHAPTER 8

MONEY, MONEY, MONEY

FOUR HOURS OF sleep was enough. I felt good and I went straight back to our Park Avenue apartment house. I told the clerk to telephone up to Miss Drummond.

"Tell her," I said, "that I have come from the home of our friend—who just died."

I turned and walked into the dining-room. I felt funny. I felt funnier than I ever did in my life. I set my lips tightly. So the whole thing was a mistake, eh? Don't you believe it. Marriages are very serious things in this part of the country, and not easy to break. Was I mad—damn good and mad—or was I mad in love—hell, in love with my own wife?

But I was hungry and I ate. The shadow was close to my table. I half reached for my gun, and didn't. I looked up at the eager-eyed young man who stood looking down at me. He was about twenty-five. His eyes were blue and shining—his cheeks red and healthy. He was a nice-looking boy.

I said: "Well, what's on your chest, son? Yeah, that's right. My name is Race Williams."

"I knew it. I knew it. I've seen your picture in the papers." He pulled up a chair and sat down. "I know you won't think me a coward. I just never got the chance to fight back. Diane was right. Don't stare at me. I'm Randy Philips, of course—you know. Is there any danger to her now?"

"None whatsoever," I told him. "Everyone—everything is settled."

"She's a wonderful girl, Mr. Williams." I had to shake both his hands from my hands. "I didn't care about the money—but our trip abroad now—it will be a real honeymoon. You've made everything possible. I shall never be able to thank you enough."

I stared straight at him. He didn't know then. Didn't know I had married the girl. He was a straightforward honest-looking boy. If he had been through hell when they held him prisoner he didn't show it, didn't speak of it. He talked more—but it was all about Diane—and me, and how brave I was.

I bit my lip and stared at him. I wondered how I'd feel in his place. The answer was I'd want to know the truth before I kept on making a fool of myself as he was, talking about "Paris in the spring."

He said: "And you, Race Williams—the swellest guy in the world, who made it possible."

"You don't know the whole of it, Randy." I looked him straight in the eyes. "Sometimes a girl—"

I stopped dead. He wasn't listening to me. But I was listening to him. My eyes popped. The coffee had a bitter taste. I didn't understand what his words meant at first, yet he was driving that meaning home with a meat axe.

He was saying: "Diane was just eighteen, and I just out of college when we got married. It was very sudden. She took me by the hand and looked into my eyes and said she—"

"She willed it?"

"No, not that. She said she had an intuition that something would part us if we didn't marry at once. Why—what's the matter, Mr. Williams?"

And my coffee went down the wrong way just as The Flame and Diane entered the dining-room.

I hate sentimental slush, and the way Diane and Randy went on was disgusting. But I took The Flame by the hand and led her to the elevator. I didn't talk until we were back in our apartment. Then The Flame spoke first.

"Does Randy know?" she asked casually.

"No, but I do." I gripped her wrist. "The justice of the peace—his wife—the three kids. All actors. A fake arranged by you. Come on Florence, tell me the truth. You knew it wasn't real. Didn't you? Didn't you?"

She jerked her hand free, her head came up, her chin shot out, her eyes flared into mine.

"Race," she said simply, "I have always loved you. If I had thought it was real, I wouldn't have let you go through with it—not for a million dollars."

And there I was ready to bawl The Flame out—instead I turned and walked to the window. She followed me, took my arm.

"She's a brilliant girl, Race. She's made everything click into place—even you, and perhaps me, though—"

"She didn't make the automatic click into place when I killed—er—shot Barney Hale."

FOR A FEW minutes then it was like old times. I forgot Diane—just The Flame and me together and I was telling her of my trick with Barney's automatic. I had her get her gun out of her bag—a thirty-eight automatic too, for The Flame never went in for toy guns. But she did insist upon unloading it.

"Look, Florence." I handed her the gun. "Stick it against my back—so. You press the trigger and I'm dead. Now try it."

She stuck her gun against my back. I pressed back suddenly, pushed my weight against the nose of the gun.

"It won't fire," she said.

"Of course, it won't. No thirty-eight automatic will if there's hard pressure against its nose. It isn't because an automatic jams, shoots too low or too high at any great distance that I'm down on it and always carry a revolver. It's because I nearly lost my life as Barney Hale lost his tonight—when a lad backed up against my automatic, and the damn thing wouldn't shoot."

"But don't—don't—didn't Barney know that?"

"He should have." I nodded. "And maybe

he did. But the point is, Florence, that he didn't think of it at the time—and that I did. You put pressure against the nose of a heavy automatic—and the gun is useless. Hell, I remember—" I stopped short.

Diane Philips had come quietly into the room.

I said: "Good morning, Mrs. McKay Williams Philips. You'll hardly wish to talk to me." And as she started to open her mouth, "And if you do, I hardly wish to talk to you."

Diane smiled, pushed an envelope into The Flame's hand.

"I just came from the bank, Florence. That's for you. Please leave me alone with Race. If he doesn't care to talk I do. He can listen." And when The Flame had gone and we were alone, "I'm not going to ask your opinion of me, Race—or even explain myself. I thought perhaps we might say good-bye—be friends, and—" She put her right hand upon my shoulder, let her eyes grab mine, hold them tightly, draw the resentment out of them. But before she spoke she put a piece of paper into my hand.

And, damn it, her smile was very lovely. Her face very sweet.

"Once," she said, "you looked into my eyes and said I was good. Now look at that piece of paper."

I opened the check, sort of sucked in my breath.

"Yes," I said. "You are good."

After all, there are more girls in the world than there used to be, but not nearly so much money.

CARROLL JOHN DALY

A Corpse in the Hand

CHAPTER 1

BANKER'S HOURS

I'M NOT EXACTLY what you'd call a nervous citizen. I sleep quietly and respectably even though I do have two apartments, except when the jack runs out. Then I have to drop the Park Avenue penthouse. The money had run out now, a more or less regular occurrence, and I was parked in my walk-up—third floor of five—with its steel door that could hardly be bashed in without awakening me as well as half the people across the Hudson River in Jersey. No "soft as a feather" business would work, either. I'd be onto the sound of that floating feather before it ever crashed to the floor.

Sure I've got good ears and eyes—and a couple of good hands, too. The right one was caressing the trigger of a forty-four revolver beneath my pillow. My other gun was in its shoulder holster, hung carefully over the chair, all of six inches from the bed. Two good reasons why I'm alive—and why some others are dead.

The fire-escape was outside my bedroom and now that proverbial feather was coming down it, and doing pretty well. It wouldn't wake up anyone else, but my ears are tuned to silent feet. The feather was followed by great tons of coal. Two pairs of feet, both heavy, but one expert, that paused to help the other. My trained ears told me the story. I had gone to bed after midnight and the blackness outside my window marked the time now as still a long way before dawn.

I was going to jump out of bed and pull the steel shutters across the window and go back to sleep, but I'm of a curious turn of mind and decided to wait and see just what the hell. One figure was already by that window. It stooped beneath it, raised that window with its back and darted across the room toward the dim light.

I was sitting up in bed now, leaning comfortably against the pillows with my gun in my lap. Of course, I could have called out my warning and shot the prowler to death, but I didn't. It was surprise that tied up my tongue.

There in the darkness of the early morning, a jockey—yellow-and-white checks, riding boots, peaked cap and all— had made the turn under the light and disappeared in the room beyond.

THERE WERE OTHER things now to attract my attention. Two more men entered my room through the open window. One— an athlete—vaulted right in. The other foundered through, cursed softly.

As they hurried toward the living-room the last man said: "Be careful. You can't tell who lives here, Joe."

I joined the conversation then. "Why be careful? I've got nothing to hide." I used a low, gentle voice, and as both men swung and faced me, added: "Stiffen! You with the rod—drop it!"

The tall younger man hesitated for a full second, half lifting his gun. I didn't speak again. I had given him all the protection he was entitled to. And some-how, though he could only make out my shadowy figure in the darkness and I could see his twisted, angry—yes, and surprised—face, he knew the truth. He dropped the gun.

"I'm sorry," he said as he partly tried to shield his heavy companion who looked like a typical business man. "We are looking for someone who dashed in this window. We had no idea the apartment was occupied. She seemed so certain, though. Perhaps you are her friend."

His voice put over the impression that being a friend of "hers" was as good as being dead.

I thought that one over, remembered the mysterious phone call a few days before, and decided to give the girl a break, whoever she was.

I said simply: "I couldn't sleep. I was awake when you guys rattled down the iron ladders. No girl came into this room—no one at all. You must have been seeing things."

"That's a poor excuse, sir." The portly shadow spoke now. I could get a slant of his bald head, his bland face, the glasses with the black ribbon he was placing on his nose.

I wasn't so polite. "Listen, brother—I don't have to make excuses in my own home. Come on—make your trip back up the fire-escape."

CARROLL JOHN DALY

"But surely"—his voice was deep, commanding—"you're not going to object to our searching your apartment. We—I might insist upon that."

"Of course. I don't object if you insist on it. Your point of view is as good as mine. I'm just arguing that dead men don't search apartments. I'm willing to be convinced if I'm wrong."

While he blew up like a firecracker—sizzling and blustering—the other lad talked. He got smooth now—too smooth. He started off like the world's great liars always do.

"To be perfectly frank—and why not be frank with a gentleman like your-self?—the girl is Mr. Stockbridge's daughter. There, I didn't mean to divulge the name. She is a—er—not exactly a mental case—a borderline case perhaps. Surely now, you must know Mr. Benja-min Stockbridge." And when I didn't say anything, though I knew of the banker all right, "You know, the banker. His daugh-ter—"

"To be perfectly frank," I cut in on him, "I never heard of Mr. Stockbridge, banker or no banker, and if this is the way he solicits new depositors, why—" And when both would have come in together, "I tell you no one came through that window but you two. Both of you get out—or I'll call the police."

The word police seemed to puzzle them. They whispered over it. I wasn't sure if they were for it or against it. But the big fellow with the hard face, hard chin, hard strong hands, moved toward me.

"There are two of us here. You're a stranger—and a fool to be mixed up in this thing. Your gun trembled in your hand. You're—"

I swung out of bed. Of course he didn't know who I was or he wouldn't creep up on my gun like that and collect himself a mouthful of lead.

"Come on!" I jammed my gun into his ribs. "Get out the window and get out it fast!"

I've got the voice for it. I've done it enough. When I give orders over the end of a gun they are always obeyed—or if that's not true there's no one alive to make a liar out of me. Anyway this guy almost crowded his friend through the window to make his out.

THE PORTLY GENT said—and his dignity was shaking like tar-paper shakes in a high wind: "You have been most ungracious to a distracted father. I shall not forget it—nor shall you."

And then, as I moved around the corner of the bed, he too got himself out onto the fire-escape—but he turned and said: "I was doubtful that she came in here, Joe. I am afraid, sir, we took you for someone else. There will be a disturbance going up the fire-escape. Can't we leave by your front door?"

I hesitated on that one, then said: "No." I had good reasons for saying no, but I added: "If you go down instead of up—the people above will forget about the racket you made coming down."

I know that he said something about no lights in the apartment above, but I didn't tell him that the apartment just above me was vacant and that the loving couple on the top floor would be gloriously drunk and asleep at this hour. I just jerked over the steel shutter, laid the bar across it, and finding a lounging robe, trotted out into the living-room and turned on the light.

Almost at once the light down at the end of the long hall which led to the apartment went out.

"All right, young lady," I called. "Come back here and let me have a talk with you. There's no use in trying to get out. That door is locked from the inside as well as the outside." I didn't tell her that was why I wouldn't let the two men out the front door. They would have seen her struggling there.

She was fixing her hair and tilting her jockey cap as she came slowly back into the room. She sort of tipped her head up sideways and grinned at me.

She was neither excited or embarrassed as she said, almost impishly: "Well, are you satisfied with me?"

I didn't let her get too close. I looked down at her little figure, tried to put an age on her and figured twenty-one to twenty-five might do the trick.

I said finally: "That's a hot outfit for an early-morning visit. What's your name?"

"It was considered a hot outfit at a masquerade. My name—" She gave that a little thought. "Would you consider Dolores Divine a clever name?"

"And would you consider me clever if I guess your name's Miss Stockbridge?"

"Not very clever." She pouted a bit. "You have gotten rid of those two horrible men, I suppose?" She looked at me steadily. "I know you, of course. What a coincidence it was that I should flee into the apartment of Race Williams."

"I don't believe in coincidence. I am thinking of the young lady who telephoned me, refused to give her name and said that she might see me very suddenly."

"You're a remarkable man, Mr. Williams." Again that impish twist of her head. "You discover my name—and connect my visit with my telephone call."

I took her by the shoulders, said: "You're a nice kid—a lad needs only one look to know that. I may have some trouble getting you home in that outfit. You have a case for me, haven't you?"

SHE TURNED AND looked straight at me now. The turned-up nose was even cuter than I thought. "By that do you mean money?" she said.

"Yes," I told her flat, "I mean money. I don't work for nothing. But I'm a specialist in my line and like all specialists I have my public duty. If you're a charity case—why I'll see you safely home—free, gratis, for nothing."

Thin lips quivered. Her eyes flashed into twin black-brown pin-points in the center.

"There will be men on the roof—men on the street." She snapped out the words. "Detectives maybe—even deadly criminals. How about charity then?"

I shrugged my shoulders. "Private detectives aren't much trouble. If the police are out of it we can make the grade all right."

"And criminals—men who'd kill for a hundred and fifty thousand dollars?"

"One hundred and fifty grand!" I gasped. "You've—but your father is worth plenty of money. Listen, Miss Stockbridge, no one can harm you—no one can take that money away from you. Why—your father and—and— Where did you get the money?"

"I haven't got it—yet. I own it, but I can't explain. I'll give you fifteen thousand dollars to keep me alive until I can cash in on it."

"Fifteen thousand now?"

"I haven't got it—now. A sort of—well, call it a fee of ten percent if we get it—nothing if—"

I turned and picked up the ringing phone.

Sergeant O'Rourke, my best friend on the force, and to whom I had chucked a lot of first-page criminals, blurted right out: "If you're entertaining Elinor Stockbridge, the banker's daughter, get rid of her. Inspector Nelson is coming up to your place for her. He just telephoned a newspaper man for her picture. I don't know what it's all about, but you're in for trouble."

"Has he got a warrant?"

"No—but you know Nelson."

"Yeah," I said. "And you know me." I jammed down the phone and turned to the girl. Inspector "Iron-man" Nelson hated me, yet he was a straight, honest, courageous cop.

"You're in for trouble. Your father is sending the police up here. He's a big shot, I guess. I'll get you out by the roof."

"No. They'll be waiting for me there—at least until the police come. Why can the police touch me? I've done nothing. How can they come into your apartment? You've done nothing. As for my father—he won't come. You can be sure of that."

I said: "Kid, we haven't much time. That's a lot of money you talk about. Can you raise twenty-five hundred dollars—now?"

She had a nice laugh. At least I thought it was nice until her words followed it.

"I couldn't raise twenty-five cents. I'm going to borrow a couple of dollars from you—then I might get a hundred or so." I began thinking. She had talked of big money. She looked honest, which is no reference at all. The best swindlers I know can look you straight in the eyes, have wide-open childlike, innocent faces. But I lifted the phone and made my call to Maxie, the best criminal brains of any lawyer in the city. Maxie could spring you from stir before they even closed the doors on you.

His voice was pretty sleepy when it came, pretty much like Maxie, too. He said gruffly: "Well, what are you in for?"

"Race—Maxie." And going on quickly, "I'm in a jam. I want you to come here to the walk-up. Bring your own secretary or any dame that looks pretty tough but hasn't got a record. You've got to make time. It may involve a hundred-and-fifty-grand case."

"May?" Maxie's voice grated. "Is there five grand to lay on the line when I get there?"

"Ten if things go right and the girl—"

"That's enough, Race. I could send you a hundred tough girls but not bring them. I'm a respectable lawyer and expect a respectable fee. No money, eh?"

"No," I said hard.

"Good-bye then. I'll see you in jail."

"All right, Maxie," I told him hard,

"you'll be buying new false teeth and they'll be digging lead out of your mouth when I see you again."

THE GIRL HAD my arm when I turned and told her: "A great guy, Maxie. He'll do anything for a friend who can show cash." And with a shrug, "We'll manage. You can't be in so bad." On second thought I added quickly: "Come on, I'll take you through the boys out front."

"No—no!" She clutched at my arm. "You asked that man on the phone to bring another girl with him. That was so you could hide me and pretend that girl was here. You wanted to fool the police, the others. Well, we can still do that. I can pretend to be the—other girl—your secretary."

"My secretary?" I took a laugh. "But the idea you had was right. Here— listen!" This as she began to disrobe— take off the jockey suit and cap. And then things were all right—or were they? Anyway she was wearing a sweater and skirt—and she was an eye-full. I just stood there with the jockey suit and cap in my arms and looked stupid.

"Well—" She looked at me. "Go put those away. Won't ten percent of a hundred and fifty thousand dollars help?"

"If you had the money." I shook my head. "If it wasn't for your father's wealth I'd have laughed at your story. Now I'm mixing in with the police, Miss Stockbridge—and the toughest cop on the force. I'll take you out before they get here, take you home or where you want to go—even lend you ten bucks."

"Further—you won't go for char-ity, eh? But I'm nice-looking, Race. I'm good company. We could have some fun together. Surely—I'm worth that."

I grinned at her. I rather liked such spunk from a dame who had always had dough.

"This is business," I said. "On an off day I'll wine you and dine you—if something better doesn't turn up. But I never let women interfere with business. At least I never have to my advantage."

"If I told you something about the money—the chances?"

"Yes, but it would have to be a good story. That's a lot of money, even for you."

"Suppose I told you it was to—" And suddenly the doorbell rang. "It's the Irish Sweepstakes, Race…. Ah, I see you lost on it." She must have read the truth in my expression. "Well, I held the ticket on Andover—"

"The forty-to-one winner? One hundred fifty thousand dollars!" I gasped it out. "And now—"

"And now it's worth all that money if I can find it before someone else. I'm the unlocated owner in the papers. You must have read about it. Look straight at me." And when I did, "I signed that ticket *Twin-Colored Eyes.*"

"Get in the bedroom," I told her. "I'll give it a thought."

CHAPTER 2

"IRON-MAN" NELSON

I WALKED DOWN the hall to the front door. There was pounding on the door now—the next thing would be fire-axes. Inspector Nelson was not a very patient man.

I sprung the little circle in the panel of steel and looked out at Nelson's glaring eyes, red face—listened to his cursing lips.

"This is no old-time speak-easy, flat foot," I told the inspector, and then added, as I saw the two cops behind him: "You're not the man you used to be."

"Those two men are not coming in," he said.

"And neither are you." I talked tough now. Nelson liked it that way. He wasn't impressed by logic or law, though I gave him a bit of law now. "If you've got a search warrant, O.K. I got nothing to hide."

"O.K." Nelson turned to the two cops. "Get a fire-ax and—"

I said before they could turn: "You don't need that. You can push the door in with your shoulders." While I talked I took off the chain, unlocked the great gadget, slipped the long steel rods out of the back of the door and put my thin piece of wood across and into the steel sockets, after lifting the heavy steel bar out.

Then I gave him the law suit. I said: "I'm telling you, Nelson, it's breaking and entering—illegal search or attempted search. A man's home is his castle, you know."

His sudden blast of words nearly blew the door down. "I've busted into more castles than King Richard the Lion Hearted," he went literary on me. "And what's more, I know this is a steel door. If it doesn't open we'll hack it into a ball of tin. Come on, boys—all three of us."

They couldn't have axed in that door—not for hours—but I didn't want the entire fire-department brought out while Nelson sent a cop over to wake up a friendly magistrate for a warrant.

I clicked out the light, stepped back, let the three of them follow that heavy steel door into the foyer hall and dashed back down the hallway.

Nelson fairly blistered that steel with foul words as he climbed to his feet and tramped down the narrow hall toward the curtain at the end, the entrance to the living-room. Me—I was planted flat against the wall inside that living-room to one side of the curtain. His pounding feet stopped when I spoke.

"If you come through that curtain, Nelson, I'll drop you like any other hood."

Maybe it was the "any other" got him—but he stopped dead. He spoke very slowly and he wasn't cursing now.

He said: "Mr. Benjamin Stockbridge, the broker, telephoned me that his daughter was in your apartment. I've come for her and I'm coming in."

"I have never met the young lady."

"Race, I'm coming in."

I was getting nervous as hell. If Nelson said he was coming in he meant just that. He was one copper who didn't kid around and he feared no one—not even me, I guess.

I said quickly: "Miss Stockbridge is over twenty-one. She's of age, has a right to go where she pleases."

"I thought you hadn't met her," he snapped back.

"I read the papers—and I read about her birthday party." That was one on

Nelson. He hadn't read about the birth-day party, either.

I saw the curtains move slightly and sensed, rather than saw, that his huge figure was straightening. I almost cried out my warning.

"I'm not bluffing, Nelson—I'm going to give it to you!"

"Bluff or no bluff, shooting or no shooting, I've never been backed down by any gunman. You, Flaherty, come to the far side of me with your gun in your hand. You, Masochelo, jump my dead body and get Williams as he falls back from my bullet. I'll get one shot at him sure."

There was a cop for you. He spoke of his own dead body. He knew that I wouldn't miss—yet he was coming.

The curtain moved and I shouted: "Don't, Nelson—for God's sake, don't! I know my rights."

The curtain parted and my gun went up.

THE LIVING-ROOM LIGHTS snapped on and a voice spoke—a girl's voice. Nelson and I were both looking at her. Her sweater was held tightly about her waist with my belt. Her skirt was so short that it came just below her knees. Her hair was brushed hard down and her eyes were penciled to a thin, black line. Her lips were just as thin but a brilliant scarlet, and curved almost into a sneer at the right corner.

The nostrils of her turned-up nose were wide and dark. The twin color of her eyes was mostly hidden by the droop of heavy, mascaraed eyelashes. It was a good job of make-up, but I would have known her because of my belt if she had turned into a movie queen.

Understand the job was good because she had no disguise except her own make-up for the kind of tough girl I wanted. Poor kid—she didn't know Nelson. He'd recognize her from her picture. She could only get by if someone were not looking particularly for her.

She said: "Sorry, Mr. Williams, but I thought we were going to work some more." She tossed a pad and pencil over on the couch. "I didn't know you went in for flat foots."

"Who is this dame?" Nelson was in the room now.

"Miss Stockbridge." I gave him the truth—why hide it now? "So what? She wants to stay here."

The girl smiled coquettishly. "Not if the inspector wants to take me out," she said. "His face is unfamiliar."

"Yours, too." Nelson glared at her, then turned to me. "Come on, Race, where's this Stockbridge girl. By God—I'll arrest you for kidnaping."

So he didn't recognize her, then—didn't even try to identify her through some picture or description he must have had. Surely he couldn't have seen her before and not recognize her now. Or could he, with just that quick glance, make a slip? Nelson started to swing suddenly toward me. The cops were in the room, too, standing by the curtain.

I stopped his swing by saying: "The picture hasn't changed any, Nelson. I still mean business." But the picture had changed—and I was glad of it. Certainly Nelson would have come into that room before—and certainly I would have—

But the threats and show and everything were over. I didn't hear the footsteps come down the hall. I didn't even know the man was there until the little unshaven figure was pushing the cops aside and stepping into the room.

MAXIE, THE CRIMINAL lawyer, said, all in one breath: "Good evening, Inspector—and you, young lady. Come Race—what's this? Door broken down—people gathering in the hall. Damn it, Race, I won't have a client forcibly resisting the law. The law is the backbone of—"

I took my cue and cut in: "The man's without a warrant, Maxie."

Maxie swung and looked at Nelson. "Impossible, Inspector—not a man of your standing. Surely—"

"I've got all the warrant I need." Nelson turned surly. "The break-in is a fake so you, Maxie, you dirty little shyster, could—"

Nelson stopped. Maxie had turned to the girl and said sharply: "Take that down, Miss. Just as he said it. That was libel, Inspector—expensive libel made before two officers of the law, and Mr. Williams, a client of mine. A financial loss there, and after breaking and entering—" Maxie was jotting down notes in a little book of his own—notes that Nelson knew he would use.

Nelson said: "I have a warrant." He half shoved his hand toward a jacket pocket, withdrew it at once. "But I'll just keep that with the date and time on it."

"And the complaint? Who made the charge?"

"Mr. Benjamin Stockbridge," Nelson said with some viciousness, then spoke to me. "Stockbridge is big-time, Race. Even you can make a mistake. If you want to correct that mistake, I'll be at the precinct. You know the number."

"Going, Inspector?" Maxie said sarcastically. "I'll run along with you. Good-night, Race." And as the inspector went down the hall, "He'll fool us on the warrant, Race, find a magistrate to sign it now, and he'll date it ahead." He looked sharply at the girl over his thick glasses. "You didn't do too badly on the tough end—" And his mouth hardening, "She's not been talking any hundred and fifty thousand bucks—or if she has, I'll take my share for fifty cents cash in advance."

"You turned down the case," I told him. "And how the hell did you happen to come over?"

Maxie winked. "The name of Stockbridge worked wonders, gave me insomnia. Tut, tut, Race, we have a way of finding these things out. Just a jingle gave me the dope that Miss Elinor Stockbridge was supposed to be here. After your frantic call—well—if I remember correctly, Miss Stockbridge's father has not applied for relief."

"You turned me down, you little shyster." I gave him the glassy eye. "I'm not paying you a cent."

"Me—dear boy—my friend? I would not think of taking money from you. I've got a little personal libel that I may forget. You've got real cause for action against Nelson—but we shan't attack the force. That leaves us the man who made the complaint—Stockbridge. Nelson properly played may—but there—"

"That's enough, Maxie." I was still down on him. "I've got big things under way myself."

"Don't worry, Race. Leave everything to your lawyer." Maxie lifted the girl's hand and I saw him rub his fingers over it as he bent low. "Your face is quite familiar, my child. Good-night."

"Perhaps," I said to Maxie at parting, "you know Miss Stockbridge."

"I have met her, of course," Maxie said back over his shoulder. "And I know her father quite well—a very shrewd man. Well, boy, I'm far too familiar with you to ask questions. Good-night—I'll be working for you."

"You're no lawyer of mine," I told him as I went to slam the door in his face. Sure I forgot. His face was still there, but the door was on the floor.

I think a couple of heads popped up over the distant stairs as Maxie went down them, but I was busy. The steel sheeting on the door was light enough, but the wood itself was heavy. Once I got the door up, the rest was easy. Everything fitted perfectly. The iron bar was across, the chain was in its lock, and the three long pieces of steel ran again through their little slots which made the hinges of the door. Then I trotted back to the living-room—and the girl was gone.

I WENT THROUGH my apartment pretty fast—no one was in it. I hit the bedroom last, jerked my pants on, threw my shoulder holster over my pajama top, put on a jacket, and jamming on a soft hat was out

the window and making tracks up that ladder.

Miss Stockbridge or no Miss Stockbridge, the girl had played the fool. Nelson would have sent a cop to the roof—and if he didn't, the other guys would have someone waiting there.

I was onto that roof with gun in hand, crouched low in the darkness, for the moon was doing its stuff. And I saw her—saw them rather. The roofs were flat. There were tiny walls between each roof and the one beyond. Sometimes, in this type of apartment, the jump from roof to roof may be a foot or so—sometimes more. But back to the girl. I knew now. She was struggling with a man two roofs down from where I stood—struggling there in the moonlight just before the door that led from the roof to the inside stairs.

So she'd got herself caught, would be dragged into that apartment house and down the stairs to another apartment, or even the street.

I started across the roof, got up enough speed to make the first little wall, and hit the roof beyond—and stopped short. I twisted to one side and slapped my gun against the figure crouched beside the chimney before he could even turn, let alone raise a gun.

"Stiffen, brother," I said, "Stiffen or—" And that was all. He simply stiffened, rolled from against the chimney and went down on the tar-covered roof. He wasn't dead. From the way he flopped his head from side to side, I knew that. But there was blood on his forehead, running down his face. I felt for his gun, then let it go. I saw the flash of the shield inside his coat.

So Nelson still suspected something and had left a dick to cover the roof. And now—damn my stupidity!—I'd never make the second apartment house down in time to save the girl.

I swung quickly from the chimney, then swung back again, crouched there as the unconscious dick had been. Only I wasn't out. I was plenty conscious—plenty excited, too. The girl had broken loose and was darting across the roofs, the villain in the piece in hot pursuit.

A race of death? Yes, the girl evidently thought that. Maybe I thought it too when she made her first hurdle and the man, missing her by an inch, jerked up his gun and fired.

I was on my feet then against the chimney. I could see the two figures plainly in the moonlight. The girl was running gamely and the man carried his gun low in his hand now as he turned slightly to the left. He was almost running beside her when she started down the home stretch toward me.

I smacked my lips—got ready to step out. But I didn't step out—and there was a mistake. I was watching the gun hanging low in the man's hand when the two flashes of orange-blue flame cut the night with almost a single sound. Yes, the running girl—the poor, defenseless, little thing—had opened up on him. She had turned sideways to do it, too—staggered slightly as she half fell, perhaps twenty or thirty feet beyond the chimney beside which I was hiding—lost her balance entirely and sprawled on the roof.

But she was up again immediately and going straight by the roof entrance to my house and the jump beyond—a good six-foot jump there. I couldn't watch her—my eyes were on the man.

He was kneeling there on the roof, his elbow braced on one knee, and he was drawing a sure bead on the girl. Broad, evil face, curving lips, and a steady hand—I saw it all in the moonlight and knew that here was a killer who didn't miss what he shot at when he had the time for it. And he had the time for it now—or thought he had.

I heard his quick sigh of triumph—and my finger closed once. He didn't shoot—he couldn't. There was a hole in his face. I saw it just before he jumped over on his side.

Was he dead? I didn't know. That job was for the city medical examiner. Besides, I was looking the other way, looking into empty space—the wall where the girl must have leaped—the deserted roof beyond and slightly below me. Poor kid! She didn't know about the space between and had crashed five stories to the hard walk below.

Then I almost cried out, "Bravo!" She had taken the hurdle. I could see her little figure spurting across that roof toward the entrance and the street below. As for me—well, it was a bit of a mess just after Inspector Nelson's visit. The shots would have been heard, of course. I might beat them to my apartment, for people don't generally stick out their heads when there's a bit of gun-play in New York. They know better.

CHAPTER 3

THE GIRL WITH THE ICY EYES

I TROTTED BACK to my apartment; tossed my clothes out in the living-room, and got Nelson on the phone. "Williams speaking," I said sharply. "I heard noises on the roof after you left, went up to investigate and found a quiet-clothesman of yours knocked unconscious. Then I was attacked—and in defending your unconscious detective's life and protecting my own I shot a man to death."

"Good God, Williams!" Nelson's words choked in his throat. "You ringing up to plead guilty to murder?"

I went on slowly and unexcitedly: "There was another man who attacked me and got away. I am making no confession of any kind. I'm making a complaint. I'm calling on the police of this city to apprehend the other man who attacked me—"

The phone clicked down at his end. But I know my law. I wasn't admitting or confessing or even explaining—anything. I was just making a complaint—and that's how I'd put it through in court if they arrested me, which wouldn't be likely.

I was going to call O'Rourke and a bondsman I knew, but the phone rang. I lifted the receiver and took the earful.

"Race—Race!" I knew my sweep-stakes-girl's voice at once. "I can't talk long. I— Oh, God, I just killed a man on your roof. Go to Apartment Five-C—three roofs down. There are heavy curtains at the living-room windows by the fire-escape. They're going to torture a—my friend there. She doesn't know anything. Should I come? Murder is so horrible, and I've lied, Race. I was acting all the time. I'm frightened and scared. My whole life, until I won on that ticket, has been horrible as long as I can remember." She was crying, I think. "I've been acting—just acting all the time."

"You're a damn good actress," I told her. "Don't worry. Keep under cover. Good-bye. I'll take care of your friend."

With that I turned and walked easily to my front door. I was fully dressed now in a neatly pressed blue serge suit, black slouch hat and gray suede gloves. When I opened the door the landlord and a little crowd of people backed away.

"You're the great detective, Mr. Williams. We thought you'd sort of tend to things." A fat guy in short trousers was spokesman for the crowd—self-appointed and very nervous. Yes, and he had threatened three times to leave the building if I remained as a tenant.

"Quite right, Mr. Feltman." I half bowed. "I have telephoned Inspector Nelson—and will now proceed to the roof. I imagine you allude to the shots."

"Allude to them!" The owner of the apartment, wrapped up in his bathrobe, shook a finger at me. "What do you think? I called the police. The people above are locked in their apartments. I don't care if you do pay double rent—if this is your doing I—"

"So." I turned and started to go downstairs. "If you don't appreciate my offer to investigate— Damn it, Mr. Johnson, ordinarily I'd charge a thousand dollars to go above and perhaps walk into a crowd of gunmen bent on tearing your apartment to pieces and murdering your overcharged tenants in their beds."

He coaxed me then. So did the others, who hadn't returned to their rooms below and locked their doors. They begged me to go. And I wanted to go in a hurry. Plainly I heard the scream of the siren. I told the little crowd that no one must follow me, which was a waste of time. Then I went straight up to the roof. I did a bit of hurdling and running myself until I reached the apartment building three roofs down. The shots could not have been heard there, of course.

THE DOOR FROM the roof into the building was open. I ran quickly down the stairs with the intention of finding Five-C, then going back to the roof and entering it by the fire-escape, much as my visitors had done a short while before. And my intentions worked out fine. After I returned to the roof, I simply skipped down the iron ladder one floor. The bedroom window was closed but not locked. I opened it carefully and crawled in. The bedroom was dark and unoccupied, but there were voices and the sound of pacing feet from the room beyond.

With a flash in my left hand and a gun in my right, I did my stuff. Just a pair of curtains separated me from the room beyond. I caught the faint glimmer of light as I moved toward those curtains, gripped one and listened. A girl was speaking. Her voice was clear and there was no emotion in it. It came from deep in her throat.

"There are times when I do not care to answer questions. But you can't make me lie to you. I know where that ticket is. I won't tell you. Pain will not bother me. I am a Stoic."

A rough voice without humor said: "What the hell's a Stoic?"

A bantering voice answered: "Where's your education, Laskey?"

A third voice spoke solemnly: "The girl means she has steeled herself against pain and suffering—both mental and physical. She's right to a certain extent, Laskey. I have tried both. It might be self-hypnotism or—"

"It might be a good ripping up and down the chest with a knife she needs." That was Laskey's voice—and it was then that I looked into the room. Just a slit through the curtains.

This girl had jet-black hair, a stocky figure, but by no means beefy—just athletic. She was taller than the jockey girl who had come into my apartment, and her hands—crossed on her lap—long, slender fingers steady—were as white as marble. It was her face that got me. As stony and cold as any statue you ever saw in a museum. Her eyes were black, staring, glistening crystals, and although they didn't look at me, I could imagine they were freezing the lad she was gazing at.

There was a little rat who stood in the corner—and rat is sufficient to describe him. You can pick his kind out of any police line-up, any morning in any city. He wasn't worth much. The man who did the talking I couldn't see very well, but I could see Laskey, and he was a beaut. Great, sensuous mouth, flat nose, ears—

what there was of them—driven and twisted into his head, and eyes that were holes of hatred. You might say the crudest, meanest face that ever topped a human body. You just looked at him and saw him torturing animals when he was a kid. He was a big man, too.

He was saying to the rat: "You, hood—beat it to the roof and see what became of Al Davis, and if he located the girl. If he didn't he can telephone her and tell her what we'll do to her friend unless she returns to our little party." Laskey waited until the rat had gone down the hall, and the door closed behind him.

Then the other man—a big-chested guy, clean-shaven, rolling with fat—had his say.

"That letter, Laskey. The one addressed to the district attorney that will prove her guilty of killing Worth, proprietor of the Aladdin's Lamp Club. Did you tell her about that?"

"Yes." Laskey was sulky. "I showed her that. She chucked it back in my face."

THE SUAVE FAT man said to the girl: "I don't know the contents of that letter to the district attorney, but I do know it will certainly send you to the chair. It carries the names of witnesses, people who know that—"

The girl stopped him. "I know," she said simply. "They'll go to jail, too. They'll know Laskey sent them. I'll see to that. I'll remember Laskey's ugly face easily."

"We only want part of the money from the ticket," the man went on softly. "We know your friend didn't get away with it. You're smart, but don't be too smart. Don't you know what happens to little girls who get too smart?"

"Yes," she said. "They make men like you and Laskey squirm and threaten."

"Why not be sensible?" the persuasive voice went on. "They'd put you through hell in court. Be a bright kid."

"Don't kid her along," Laskey cut in. "She won't live to reach any court." He came close to the girl. "He's giving you a stall, kid, painting a soft picture of death up the river. You'll tell me where that ticket is or I'll be my own executioner." He paused for a long time, then said: "I work with a knife."

The other man spoke. "Look, kid"—his words just dripped out—"Laskey has that letter, stamped and ready to mail." The girl seemed to hesitate as Laskey turned indifferently and leaned on the mantel. Then she said: "He'd tear the letter up? But no—he'd lie about it and keep it."

"No, no." The soft voice was eager now. "He'll give it to you. You can tear it up yourself." And when Laskey turned furiously the fat man pushed him across the room toward the curtains. I raised my gun, lowered it and listened. He was whispering to Laskey: "Let her tear it up. You can write another. She's too dumb or too frightened to think of that."

"Yeah." Laskey pushed the stout man aside, walked over and stood directly in front of the girl. His voice was sharp, hard. "Listen, sister—" He spread his legs far apart and looked down at her as he swept a long, unsealed envelope from his inside jacket pocket. "I'm not a guy to play *Letter-Letter-Who's Got the-Letter?*

If I give you this and you tear it up—you talk. Is that right?"

"That's right." She looked straight at him. "If I tear it up, I talk."

"O.K." Laskey smacked the letter across her face. She reached up and took it in her hand. There was a sort of triumph in Laskey's voice when he spoke. "You got sense—I'd have cut you to ribbons. Well, don't be afraid. It's yours to destroy. I guess you're a bright kid after all. Hell, what are you doing!"

The girl had suddenly lifted the long envelope to her lips, and running her tongue across the flap, sealed it between her fingers.

For a full ten seconds there was silence. Then the girl spoke as she turned the envelope over in her hand. "The envelope is properly addressed." She looked down and read aloud, "*To the District Attorney. You have not bluffed me with threats of death. Here is your letter. I don't think you'll mail it. You are not very convincing, Mr. Laskey. You have killed people, of course, but you want money. Until you get that money, I believe I will be quite safe. Don't forget your letter—all ready to be mailed now.*"

Laskey reached out slowly and took the letter. Just as slowly he put it back in his pocket. For a long moment he looked at the girl, then he led the stout man toward the hall.

I was enjoying the show. Here was a girl who was hard as nails, as cold as ice, too, and with a sense of logic that was damn near perfect. I'll admit I was tempted to step in and spoil the last act, but I was learning things. Who was this girl? Where did she fit in with Miss Stockbridge? In some way they must have been friends—from the telephone call I received.

I decided to wait as the stout man waddled toward the door. The story about the sweeps ticket didn't sound so screwy any more.

The door slammed outside and the man called Laskey turned back, buttoned his coat and stood flat-footed before the girl. "A word with you, sister. Women are peculiar creatures. I want it all."

"Well—" Those hard eyes faced him as she sat straight in that chair.

"Do you mean to sit there and tell me that you know where that ticket is, but won't tell me?"

"Yes." She nodded her head. "I know where the ticket is."

"But why do you say you do? Why don't you say you don't? What's the big idea?" He was puzzled and so was I.

"I don't believe in lying—and since you can't obtain your precious ticket without my help, I see no occasion to lie to you."

"So it's like that." His beady eyes were closing.

"Yes," she said very solemnly. "It's exactly like that."

"And"—a softness was creeping into his voice now, a softness that I understood as a deadly thing—"you could lay your hands on it, if you were free?"

"Yes, that is correct."

Laskey's words quickened now. "And you don't mind pain—you're a Stoic? Well, you don't know the meaning of pain yet. It would be a pleasure to work on you.

For the last time—and you fully realize what I'd do for so much money—will you tell me where that ticket is?"

She didn't even stiffen in the chair. She just said calmly: "No."

I'LL ADMIT THINGS happened too fast for me then. Laskey's hands shot out and grabbed the girl from the chair. He swung her and her body hurtled across the floor and landed almost at my feet.

Laskey came after her, his great hands stretched toward the girl's throat. He was like a jungle animal about to pounce upon his prey. Nothing could stop him now—at least, so he thought.

I think he saw me. Not my face, of course, because his body was half bent, but I think he saw my legs or my shadow, for he made a queer noise in his throat.

There I was, standing almost over the girl—a foot on either side of her head—when I swung my gun down and up. And what's more, I missed my mark. Yes, things happened so fast that my sweeping gun didn't catch him on the chin. It would have killed him, of course, broken his neck like you'd snap a match, and I was striking hard and viciously.

Yes, I missed my mark—the death mark, that is. But I caught him some place along the body, and I caught him hard enough to stop him where he was. Peculiar, these things sometimes. There he was, resting on my gun and hand, as if he were simply suspended there, held up by invisible wire. But it didn't last long. His body twisted and he hit the floor like a thousand of brick.

The girl was on her feet now, moving about the room. I saw her grab up hat, gloves, a coat—then she had me by the arm.

"The police," she said. "We mustn't have that."

Laskey lay on the floor, breathing heavily and twisting around. I took a good look at him. If I had not missed my mark he wouldn't be writhing in such pain now. I'd be willing to bet I hadn't even caved in a couple of his ribs—probably just knocked the wind out of him.

The girl was for going by the fire-escape and I was agreeable. Then, as we crossed the bedroom toward the ladder, I thought of Laskey—the letter in his pocket—and I reached out to grab the girl's arm. But she was already back from the window, crowding me. She didn't give me a chance to explain and it wasn't till she had pushed me through the front door that I got my thought over.

She said: "I should have had the letter a second after you struck him. I must have hurt my head when I hit the floor. I forgot about it. But it's not the police coming down that fire-escape. It's one of Laskey's men and—"

We were outside in the hall now and the door was closing on its spring. I stretched desperately for it and it clicked closed—locked. What did I care for one of his men—two or three, for that matter? But the door had changed things. The letter remained in Laskey's pocket. I didn't like such carelessness, but I followed the girl down the steps.

WE BEGAN TO meet people about the second floor—people coming upstairs.

Just before I reached the bottom I knew why. A cop there was chasing them back. I stopped dead, turned toward the hall which led to the back—and the cop called: "Hey you! Where do you think you're going? Fully dressed, too—"

I recognized the cop's voice, spun quickly, knew that his quick step forward changed to a back step when he recognized me.

I got in my crack first. I said in some heat: "What the hell do you think you're doing? Where's Nelson? Don't stand there with your mouth open. Damn it, I telephoned for him, nearly got killed and— What about the dead cop in the rear court who was just hurled from the roof?"

After that I waved once to the girl to try a get-away, saw her draw her coat tightly about her and start down the rest of the stairs. Then as the cop hesitated I pushed him forward and we were both on the run out into the rear court.

There were two cops out there. Nelson had pulled his old trick and the block was covered. My cop spoke to the others about the body and when he got a blank look, turned on me. But I blasted his story before he got fully started.

I said in amazement: "I never told you there was a dead cop in the back yard. I asked you what about him falling from the roof. How do I know? People were talking of it on the stairs. I thought you knew. I'm looking for Nelson."

A dick stepped forward. He was very close to the inspector. He said: "Inspector Nelson is looking for you, too. Race. I must warn you that anything you say—"

"Will be distorted—mixed up—added to—and finally convict me of juvenile delinquency for talking to a cop. Come on, Haddock."

He was an old-timer. He bit his lip. "The name is Fish," he said.

"O.K. Come on, anyhow."

With that we went back to my apartment to confront Nelson, Sergeant O'Rourke, Maxie, who had been shoved out into the hall, and half a dozen reporters who were listening to Maxie and kidding him along—at least they thought they were—but no one kids Maxie, not by a damn sight, they don't.

Maxie was waxing eloquent outside my door. He was saying: "And there's a story for you boys. Race Williams protects city detective from certain death and Inspector Nelson wants him arrested, wants him 'picked up.' Picked up! You print such a term about Mr. Williams. Why, a man of his reputation, his honor, his—" And suddenly seeing me, "They're laying for you, Race, and Nelson wants to make a mess out of it."

"No autographs tonight." I grinned at the reporters while I pushed past the two flat-feet at the door and went down the apartment hall to my rooms. Nelson and O'Rourke were there and a quiet clothes man or two. I pretended I didn't see the man lying on the floor as I crossed hurriedly to the other lad with the bandage on his head who was leaning back in my easy-chair. He was the detective of the roof. Hell, he couldn't be anyone else. I grabbed up his hand and went into my dance.

"No argument, boy—no thanks! I

never saw a braver act in my life. You were reaching for a gun and you practically unconscious and him about to shoot you." I knitted my brows as I jiggled the surprised dick's hand. "It nauseates me to kill people, but it was his life or the life of a courageous young detective. I can't bear—"

"No." Nelson took me by the shoulder and swung me around. "That's your corpse—there. Right through the side of his face."

The newspaper men were crowding in the door now. O'Rourke was shaking his head at me. A great guy, O'Rourke—only a sergeant though he might have been Nelson's superior if he'd wanted to be. But he was a man who worked directly from the commissioner and even Nelson had to respect his orders, though O'Rourke never gave them as orders.

HEAD-SHAKE OR NO head-shake from O'Rourke, I gave Nelson what I had on my chest—and I gave it to him loud. "What do you mean by dragging that stiff in here?" I bellowed. "Where do you think—"

Purple pinwheels appeared on Nelson's face while his words sizzled through his teeth. "I don't need any warrant this time. I'm arresting Race Williams for the shooting of this man—on the roof."

"Murder, eh?" Maxie had reached for my phone. "It's my right, Inspector," he said as Nelson reached for his arm. "I've got a bondsman for any amount—yeah, and a judge up and ready to sign his release. Come on, do your stuff."

"Why not let us hear Mr. Williams'

story, Inspector?" O'Rourke drawled softly and when Nelson glared at him, "I was simply suggesting, Inspector, that you might—that the commissioner might agree with you if you waited a bit. Now, Race, what do you say?"

"What do I say, Sergeant?" I looked blankly at O'Rourke. "Why, I was here dictating my autobiography to a young lady when Nelson broke in—started to talk about a Miss—" I paused and let the name go, as both Nelson and O'Rourke frowned. "Well, I saw Nelson out—Maxie out—came back to go on with my literary endeavors—and heard feet shuffling on the roof."

"Two floors up, eh?" Nelson sneered.

"O.K., then—the truth." I covered that quickly. "I wondered if Nelson would leave someone on the roof and went to investigate and saw his man being beaten to death. I jumped that corpse there hard. He pounced back—" I was going to throw in a few shots then but didn't, not knowing how many they'd found in his gun. "That's it," I finished modestly. "I shot him dead. What more is there to tell?"

"And the girl?" Nelson was of a curious turn of mind tonight. "The owner of the apartment saw you go to the roof—others also—but no girl."

"Oh, she went up the fire-escape. You know, Inspector—simple, home-loving folks—they might misunderstand. I took her down a few doors and put her in a taxi. Now, get that corpse out of here. Don't ask me about the girl. I thought her action most unconventional. She's discharged. I don't know where she lives—but her name is Jennie. Go—get out."

CARROLL JOHN DALY

They took the stiff all right, and though I was dying to look at his face, I showed no interest. I gave O'Rourke the wink and watched him follow Nelson and the two cops to the door, watched, too, Maxie slipping along with them.

Maxie was so crooked he could only walk straight on a circular staircase. But he was a good lawyer if you were floundering around dizzy on that staircase. Look at his quick action tonight—bondsman and judge ready. Yep, Maxie could spring you before the jail doors opened to receive you.

O'Rourke came back. He was pretty serious. "This Stockbridge girl, Race. Was she here tonight?"

I looked hard at him. "Nelson saw the girl and can tell you that."

"That's quibbling, Race." O'Rourke shook his head at me. "Things have been happening. Oh, the lad you shot doesn't matter. He was a killer, all right—but I want the truth. Nelson saw only one girl. He didn't search your apartment."

"I'll give it to you straight, O'Rourke. Nelson saw the only girl who was in my apartment tonight. Or if you want to be technical"—I looked at my watch—"he saw the only girl who was in my apartment, either last night or this morning. Could you go for some beer and cheese?"

O'Rourke could, and we did.

"About this biography of yours," he said in parting. "I'd like to see it first. The opening chapter should send you to jail for life. Well, if anything big comes out of this mess, let me in—remember."

"Sure," I said with a laugh. "I won't forget. There'll be a corpse for you, too."

CHAPTER 4

TWO WRONG PEOPLE

WHAT DID I expect to happen? I didn't know. I didn't know enough about sweepstakes tickets, either, except that you buy one and never hear about it again. But I did know that once someone had tied up a winner's dough with a law suit. In this case, though, what was wanted was the ticket itself. I closed over the iron window and went to sleep.

Did I dream of dead men all night? Not me. I dreamed of horses and women and money—yep, and a cruel face that a little better timing on my part would have caved in entirely. Then I slept like a baby.

And like a baby I woke up suddenly— that is, like a baby all except the gun I had in my hand. The ring came again—the telephone beside my bed. The clock said ten minutes of noon.

I lifted the phone and chirped: "Well, what do you want?"

Maxie's excited voice said: "Come on, get up, Race, and meet me on the corner by Stockbridge's house. I think we've got a libel suit if he started Nelson busting into your place." And when I started to ask questions, "No, I can't say he was cordial to me, but when I mentioned your name, he pepped up a bit. I said I had to go out and get some pipe tobacco and would be back."

"That was clever, Maxie—quick thinking, too." Maxie had never smoked a pipe in his life.

"Sure," he disregarded my sarcasm. "He'll know that's a lie and he'll have time to think. But get up here quick." He gave me the corner and the Stockbridge house number. "There will be money in it, Race."

I started to say something about not being mixed up in any shake-down, but Maxie hung up.

I took my time shaving and dressing. Was it simply the name Stockbridge that had put Maxie on the job, or did he know more than I thought? I couldn't answer that one.

I gave O'Rourke a buzz but if he had heard anything he didn't tell me. One of my questions, the important one, he did answer, though. There had been no other arrests in my neighborhood. That meant the girl, Dolores Divine, had gotten away. It meant also that Laskey had gotten away. But it left things wide open. None of the crowd knew yet that they were dealing with Race Williams.

Benjamin Stockbridge had a good address. Maxie was on his way to meet me before I passed the house and reached the corner.

"You took a long time," he said petulantly. Then eagerly, "It looks like Stockbridge is worried. Of course I can't tell if he used his phone or not, but his lawyer hasn't gone in. You let me handle it and there'll be some dough coming our way."

"Blackmail or extortion?" I shook his arm free of mine.

"Right in the courts—or we can settle out of court. He entered—or caused your apartment to be illegally entered. The police were his agents. It's like false arrest, Race. It's the guy who causes the arrest who is later sued. This is illegal

entry… Mr. Stockbridge was expecting me back." This last to the butler who opened the door.

The flunky said: "Yes, sir—and the other gentleman, too. This way, sir."

I nodded as we went down the hall and the butler opened the door of what turned out to be a sort of office-library.

A man sat behind a desk. I could see the baldness of his head, running into the hair behind. Mr. Stockbridge was in for a surprise. His dignity, his position in civic and social affairs, his presidency of the bank. What a bum I could make out of him—climbing in my window at two o'clock in the morning.

The butler closed the door behind us and the banker raised his head just as I said: "Mr. Stockbridge, we meet again."

"Again—" His eyes narrowed, opened, and peered at me. "Again," he repeated. "How interesting, Mr. Williams. I don't recall ever meeting you before." He came to his feet and stretching out his hand, finally shook the one I managed to raise.

He was right. I had never seen him before in my life! Certainly he was not the chunk of flabby beef that had entered my room the night before. As a matter of fact, now that I looked at him, there was no resemblance but the bald forehead.

"You seem surprised, Mr. Williams," he went on slowly. "This lawyer here is making veiled threats, with you as his client. I know Mr. Maxie Rice, and I can't say that I can pin him straight down to extortion—but he's very close to it."

Maxie said: "You called up Nelson and told him your daughter was in Mr. Williams' apartment and—"

Stockbridge raised his hand. "I never called Inspector Nelson or spoke to him about my daughter. Now, Mr. Williams—and let me warn you, but for one thing I would have the police here now—if you will dismiss your lawyer, you and I will talk."

"And you didn't telephone Nelson?" I gasped.

"Hardly." He snapped his fingers on the desk lightly. "I am not a fool. If your lawyer—"

"He's no lawyer of mine." I denied Maxie flatly then and there. "He's been horning in on my work and—and—" I turned to Maxie. "Come on, Maxie—on your way or I'll blow the top of your head—er—"

But that was enough. Maxie was gone.

Benjamin Stockbridge lifted a pencil, tapped the rubber end on his desk. His mouth was firm but pleasant and his false teeth done by an expert.

At length he said: "I have talked to Inspector Nelson, Mr. Williams. It is true he received such a call purporting to come from me. He was careless in not checking up on it. But then, earlier, I had called him to locate my daughter."

"Did he locate her?"

"I think that he did—but he did not know it. You are very clever, Mr. Williams—but not quite as clever as you believe. I might have had you arrested for this strange appearance of Maxie Rice today. I admit—and you'll admit—that I have strong influence in the city. I might have something I wish you to do."

He was seated behind the flat desk now and I went straight forward and leaned heavily upon it.

"Mr. Stockbridge," I said slowly, "surely you know better than to threaten me."

"And in what way would you retaliate?" And when I just grinned at him, "Would you strike through my daughter—here—" And suddenly, "Would you?"

"Your daughter," I said, "happens to be my client."

"Ah!" He seemed quite pleased. "You are a man of honor, then. My daughter told me that you were the only man she has ever met—only young man, I hope she means—that is really a man." And, growing more serious, "Her mother died when she was quite young—I have done my best—" And catching my eye on the picture he was twisting about in its standing frame, "Yes, this is a recent picture of her."

He turned the picture around and I took shock number two. The first one was in being wrong about the father. Shock number two—well, I was looking at a stormy countenance that might have been chiseled out of granite. That's right, Elinor Stockbridge was the last girl I had met, not the first.

Mr. Stockbridge was saying: "There—don't try to hide good, honest embarrassment. She's got odd ideas, Mr. Williams. I thought perhaps I might wheedle, cajole or even threaten you to insist that she go away for a trip. Some mutual friend of the family, or her Aunt Bernice, as chaperon—you as a protector. I believe she has studied life sufficiently to cause herself plenty of trouble. You see, Mr. Williams, she has always complained that things were made too easy for her, that she should have been born poor—suffered as thousands of other girls suffer—felt physical and mental pain and conquered it. She calls herself a Stoic."

"I know," I told him. "Has she been to a doctor—you know, a psychiatrist?"

"Yes—yes—the best in the city. But she fools them—or fools me. She does not act the same. The worst report I have ever received on her is that from my description of her actions—and I doubt that the doctors believe in my descriptions—she over dramatizes herself. Now is she acting for them? Acting for the world—"

"Or simply acting for herself," I said. "She's not a client of mine exactly. I won't divulge any secrets of hers—but I'll help you straighten her out if I can."

"Fine—fine!" He came to his feet and went to the side door. "You're the sort of man your friends say you are, Williams. You wouldn't even threaten me—if my daughter had committed murder."

I was rocked again but not as hard. I told him stiffly: "I have killed men, Mr. Stockbridge—many men. I do not—nor has the State—called it murder."

"I'm sorry, Williams," and there was real contrition, a sort of hurt in his eyes. "You and I have been brought up differently. We have lived differently." And before I could crack in with a wise one, "You see, she is my daughter."

HE JERKED OPEN the door, stuck his head through, then stepped back quickly. The marble girl came into the room—but she wasn't marble now. Her eyes were bright, her hair fluffed back, and both her hands that took mine were warm. The door closed and we were alone.

"Race—Race—" she started, then stopped. She stiffened. I could swear the hand she dropped from mine was getting cold. "Mr. Williams," she said stiffly, "I am worried. What has become of Dolores Divine, the girl who came to you, and whom you quite evidently took for me?"

"Listen, Miss Stockbridge"—I planted a hand hard upon her right shoulder, loosened my grip as I saw her face twist with the pain—"this Stoic business may be all right for everyday problems in life—but to put it on with a bunch of criminals is not so good."

"It worked all right." She kept the stony face on me.

"Sure," I agreed with her. "It surprised them. But if they actually put you to the test why—why—"

And I stopped talking. She just swung her right hand across and loosened her dress by the left shoulder. The wound of the knife was deep and fresh—and she must have felt it. Must have felt it plenty.

"Who did that?" I asked.

"Laskey," she said. "When he first showed me the letter that he threatened to send the district attorney."

"And—there was—your father knows, too—I mean some frame-up or threat to spread a story that you killed a man."

"It was Dolores Divine, a name she has assumed hoping to become an actress. I cannot believe any man would have such a feeling toward me. I am not easily thrown into a panic. I know the law. I attempted to escape. I did cry out. There was no escape. Then I recalled the law of self-defense and I shot him to death. I know the truth coming out would embarrass my father. Remaining hidden, it embarrasses these other men—" Her lips curved then. "Laskey is a desperate criminal. It was rather funny how he and his friend let me go in the taxi when I opened my bag and they saw the gun again."

"I can appreciate their embarrassment," I said with a grin. "Now, Miss Stockbridge, since you always tell the truth, is this Spartan attitude the real McCoy? Is this Stoic business an act or the real thing?"

"That's a fair question, Mr. Williams. It's a hard one to answer. I have asked it of myself so many times. You see I started acting it a few years back. It has become a part of me now. I am not quite certain that it has become my real character. Sometimes I hope so—just sometimes."

"I hope so, too," I told her. And when she started in on the essential evil of being born rich and how man was made to suffer, I snapped in: "But you weren't made to make other people suffer. There's your father—a nice lad in the home and on the golf links. If you want to help others, why not get him to go easy on some poor lad's foreclosure. Go out and help the poor with money and food and clothes—not with a gun. You'll feel pain then all right—not yours, but another's pain—and that's worse."

AFTER A BIT she nodded very seriously. "It's the criminal I want to save. Or someone on the verge of becoming a criminal.

Take Dolores for instance. She has spunk and hope and the will to go straight."

"Yeah—and what about Dolores? This winning ticket on the sweepstakes. If it's her money, she has a right to it— and can use it, I'll bet. If it's yours, cash in the ticket. If it belongs to this criminal—it'll mean a law suit. Only the name and address and the holder of the ticket will count. Otherwise you've got to file a claim. Those sweepstakes pay off on the level and fast."

"Laskey could cash in quietly if he had it—and I didn't talk."

"You know where it is?"

"Yes," she said. "I know exactly where it is."

Maybe I showed a little inclination to twist her neck then, but I held it back gallantly.

"Are you afraid of anything?" she asked me, and stared hard into my eyes.

"I'm afraid of neither man nor devil— or women," I added after a pause.

"I believe that." She studied me. "And you are much like Dolores Divine. She dives headlong into things, had to leave her apartment before the ticket arrived. I took it. You have a reckless courage—but more of the emotion than of the brain. Don't forget, Mr. Williams, that the brain should guide all emotions."

"I deny it emphatically." I gave it to her straight. "If I had stopped to think things out this morning when Laskey sprang, you'd have had your throat torn to pieces."

She came close and put her hands on my shoulders.

"It was just your brain working too fast for you to understand. I admire you greatly, Mr. Williams. I think I could trust you. I won't ask that you betray any trust. I will simply guess that someone asked you to guard me—perhaps to aid in sending me—away somewhere. I want to know if you would go into any such thing as that—for any amount of money."

I shook my dome back and forth, said: "There's nothing the matter with your head. There's plenty in it. You'll can this Stoic business after a bit and do a lot of good in the world. Me, I'm meant to be hard—was born to be that way. Now—how about telling me where the ticket is. I have a client who wants me to get it."

"I can't tell you," she said. "But I may help you—if I think that so much money won't hurt Dolores—or cause this Laskey to kill her."

She was softening up a bit. She even gave me her hand at the front door and said: "You can be sure I will do what's right by Dolores—and you. And you can be sure that Laskey will never collect the money. I'll close down on him first."

I squeezed her fingers. It was if I was handling the ice cubes for a highball. But I said: "That's the kid. Maxie is a shyster, but he'll tip me off. If the D.A. is going to start something I'll know ahead of time—and we'll jump in with a complaint before they can make any charge. If this Dolores gets a break I'll remember you—Elinor."

I went a long way throwing the 'Elinor' at that marble statue and what did I get for my pains? Just a stony grin. As she closed the door on me she said: "The name's Miss Stockbridge, Mr. Williams."

CHAPTER 5

ANYTHING FOR DOUGH

I DIDN'T SEE her old man again before I left. But I did see the lad who was following me. He was taking terrible chances. I was in an awful mood to be followed and if I hadn't had so much trouble with the police I'd have turned around and shot him to death, smack on the street.

I turned very slowly as he paused to look in a shop window. I didn't hurry when I went back to him. I wasn't even mad when I tapped him on the shoulder. I was just bored, I guess. I was soft-spoken when I looked at his surprised, mean face.

"Sir," I said, "did you see a man following me? I thought that I did. I'm going back down the street now. When I cross that corner again, you watch—then telephone for the morgue wagon. Not the ambulance, understand, but the morgue wagon. I'm frightfully sorry I troubled you."

He was a bit sorry, too, for when I passed the corner the little mirror in my hand showed me that he was disappearing around the corner one block back.

I went up the stairs to my apartment, shoved in the key, turned the lock, entered and stood still in the hallway. My nostrils quivered. I can feel an alien presence, but this time I smelled eggs—that's right, frying eggs.

I walked down the hall and straight into my living-room. There she sat, stiff and straight at a card table, just dunking a big hunk of toast in her coffee when she looked up and saw me.

"I know I shouldn't dunk," she said. "Miss Stockbridge wouldn't approve of that." And pushing back her chair, "I'm sorry I said that, Race—she's been very kind to me."

I went up to her and jerked her out of the chair. "Why did you lie to me last night, tell me you were Miss Stockbridge?"

"I didn't tell you." She winced. "You just assumed—insisted that I was. I told you my name—Dolores Divine. Please—I'm not a Stoic and you're hurting my shoulders…. There—thank you." She sat down. "I told Jerry you said to come back—and I was hungry."

"Gangway for the sausage—straight from the farm around the corner!" and Jerry, the boy I had picked up in the underworld some years back, stopped with the plate in his hand. "Good morning, boss. I came back early. Read the papers, you know— Hell, you look sore! Did the dame lie about my letting her in and feeding her up?"

"No—no—" I pulled a chair to the table. "Now you can take care of me, Jerry, and—"

"Coming right in for you, boss." Jerry moved that expressive face of his around. "The young lady—er—the young actress—said you'd be right along and I've got more sausage ready."

"Did she tell you to eat, Jerry? Did she tell you she was an actress?"

"I et myself—and she put on her act. Sweet little thing coming in—tough as blazes when I brought the eggs—now—just like that." Jerry made one motion with the plate that slid the sausage to the edge, another that brought it back on the plate again, and set it down before the girl.

In a couple of minutes I was cutting into the eats and swallowing coffee.

Just before I dismissed Jerry he said: "She's got a gun in her bag over on the couch. Want it?"

"No." When Jerry left I said to the girl: "Tell me about it."

SHE KEPT ON eating. Then, "There isn't much to tell. I haven't had any parents for a long time. I was just a cheap little crook and used to case places for the boys. I could act. You know, a maid in this house—a nurse in another—a waitress—even a cashier at times. Then along came Miss Stockbridge to show me the error of my ways. I tipped off the boys and they proceeded to take her over."

"For much?" I asked.

She grinned. "Not a nickel. She told me they were rats—and that I had good stuff in me and only thought I was a rat—and that you could be whatever you thought you were. She was just a dumbbell at first, I thought—then I didn't know. I'm peculiar, I guess. Anyway, I kept myself clean and she made me believe I had the stuff and she got me a job. And I bought a ticket under another dame's name—because Miss Stockbridge didn't believe in gambling. You saw it in the paper. Her name came out. She gave me the ticket. This Laskey came for it and Miss Stockbridge came. It's hard to tell but—well they were not nice to me. They—well, she took the ticket and walked right out of the room."

"Leaving a dead man on the floor," I said.

"Yes." The girl's brow knitted. "She shot him like you might have shot him. He had a gun in his hand and was laughing when he held her in his arms and—and—she just pulled out a gun and shot him—and followed me out of the room.

"Not a man moved, Race—not even Laskey. Remember she was Benjamin Stockbridge's daughter. They wanted to get something on her—fake blackmail—anything to shake her down. And they had got it with a vengeance—it stunned them. They caught up with us. I made the roof and your apartment. I thought she'd slipped safely inside my flat, but they must have known. Two followed me—Pop and Davis. Davis is the man I thought I killed until I read the early afternoon papers. I telephoned you a few days ago because I thought she might need your help."

"Who is Laskey?" I asked.

"I don't know. He's big—from out of town, I guess. But Elinor Stockbridge says no one will use that ticket. I telephoned her this morning. She says she knows where the ticket is—and that it will cause Laskey's death if he finds it."

"Kid"—I tossed a hunk of sausage on her plate as I hollered to Jerry for some more java—"forget the whole business—these crooks—Miss Stockbridge—all of them." And when she started to harp on the Stockbridge girl being so good to her, "She'll take care of herself. She's found real good in you—so have I. You've got to start over. Have you any ambition?"

Her eyes sparkled. "I want to act," she said. "I want to go on the stage. I have even written a play. But I just want a chance—just a start—any—I just want to be an actress. It's hard to get started, isn't it? But you saw what I can do and Jerry saw, too."

"It's not hard, kid." I told her the truth. "Maybe a little harder than picking up a job as Secretary of State, or president of a bank—" And seeing the look on her face I picked up the phone, spun a number and soon had Jake Monty's theatrical agency on the wire. I had done things for Jake.

His secretary told me he couldn't answer the phone and then I gave my name.

You could have knocked me off that chair with a ten-ton truck when his secretary cracked back: "Sorry, Mr. Williams, but Mr. Monty's in conference. He says he may call you back in a day or two. Any message?"

She had one of those irritated voices and it burned me up, but I held my temper. I said in the same silly monotone: "Any message? I guess not—oh—wait a minute! Yes—tell Mr. Monty that there is to be an attempt on his life later in the day. I thought he might want me to protect him."

I snapped down the phone, let it ring and ring for about five minutes and finally answered it.

Jake Monty had plenty of time—and plenty of excuses. He couldn't think of anyone who would want to harm him. Then he began to name people. If I had let him go on I'd have gotten a list of all the people Monty had gypped in a deal but who didn't know it yet.

I finally cut in: "I'm too busy now,

Monty—I've got a find here—a hit for a new show—any new show." And I wound up by telling him I'd shoot him to death on Broadway if the girl didn't have a job by the middle of the week. "Understand, Monty," I told him, "I'm the guy who will be shooting you to death."

He was so relieved that it was a joke that he promised her a job at once. Then he was so sure it wasn't a joke that he wanted my protection, anyway.

"Just get this girl a job—and you're safe." I hung up then, said: "It's as easy as that, kid. Sometimes, if there are partners, you have to kill one to convince the other. Now—I'll write you a letter. Jake will get you a job—a small one. Do your best. Then it's up to you."

I wrote her a short note identifying her to Jake.

"O.K., kid—I can't help you with the critics—you've got to shoot them first or they aren't convinced. Since they haven't got hearts they're hard to kill. As for protecting them from death—" I shrugged my shoulders. "They're used to being threatened—they're Stoics like Miss Stockbridge. Now forget the big money and start with the small."

I OPENED THE door, let her go. Then I wiped the rouge off my face before Jerry could crack wise—and the phone rang.

That would be Miss Stockbridge, of course. I lifted the phone, said: "Well, what do you want?"

"Bad-tempered this morning, eh? This is Dick Maloney, Race."

"Oh, Dick—" I thought that one over. Dick was a ward-healer, had pull along the Avenue, was a big-time crook before he took up politics to protect other criminals.

"Well," he went on, what with your running up and down roofs and saving a detective's life and nearly getting locked up by Nelson—I don't suppose you do feel good."

"Oh, I feel good enough," I said. "Peeved, is all—no dough in it for me."

"If it's money that bothers you, Race. I'll take that peeved feeling away from you." Maloney had a pleasant laugh. "Take a taxi and come down to Phil Jordan's Young Men's Athletic Club. You know across from the post office. We'll be in a private room upstairs and— Don't hesitate. There'll be five grand in it for you if things turn out right."

"And if they don't?"

"Hell, man—we've all got to take chances in life. I'm doing this for a friend of a friend."

"I haven't got any friends," I told him flat. "I'll come down and talk it over for half a grand. If I don't like it I'll give you four centuries back."

"A hundred bucks for a ride, eh?" Maloney chuckled. "That's fair enough. You won't need to be armed."

I took a laugh there. "I won't need to be, but I will."

"How's it for coming right away?"

"Fine," I told him. "How's it for the money?"

"You don't trust me—" Maloney started off indignantly, then came down to earth. "I'll have a boy with five new bills right up there, if you're so particular."

"I'm not particular, Maloney," I said softly. "Old bills will do."

He hung up and I waited.

It wasn't much more than five minutes when a bell-hop from the hotel down the street showed up with a sealed envelope. Maloney was right. Five new hundred-dollar bills. I wasn't even surprised. Maloney could easily have telephoned the manager to send the money over. I tipped the boy and wasn't much behind him when I grabbed a taxi and rode downtown.

Five grand had a pleasant sound.

CHAPTER 6

LASKEY LIKES THEM TOUGH

PHIL JORDAN'S YOUNG Men's Athletic and Better Government Club looked all right from the outside. As a matter of fact, it was a political club. There was a bar in the back and a gymnasium in front so the members could have plenty of room to stagger before they reached the street.

Phil was there when I walked in. He had on a dirty white sweat shirt and duck trousers. I could smell his breath as soon as I opened the door. No—he wasn't drunk. That much liquor hadn't come out of bond since prohibition ended.

"Hello, Williams," he said. "I'm pretty busy. Having a basketball game here tonight. That's why I'm laying off the liquor—and I could go for a good drink. But Maloney said nix."

I smelled his breath and reeled back. "Take that good drink now, Phil," I told him. "It'll freshen that old liquor up a bit. Where do I go?"

"Just up them three steps. Here, I'll show you." He took me up three steps, turned into ten feet of dirty hall, and tapped on a door. "It's Phil, Frank," he hollered at the top of his voice. "The bloat from uptown is here."

The door swung open and there was Maloney. He had a wide open face and plenty of freckles grazing in the fields. His smile was like the opening of a new tunnel, his voice soft, friendly, and there was a youthful sparkle in his blue eyes, though the gray of his hair—turning white in the front—took much of the youth away. But he was still the same old Maloney.

He was saying: "Come in, boy—come in. When I saw a little money was to be made, I said 'It's for Race Williams.'" He had closed the door and was leading me into a comfortable, furnished room— big easy-chairs, cigars and cigarettes on the table, *your* brand of liquor over in the corner.

"Boys," Maloney said, "this is Race Williams. You've heard about him. If anyone wants to pull a gun on him why it's O.K. Eh, Race?" He patted me on the back.

"O.K. for me." I smiled. Maybe I should be shy and modest about my gun work. But guys might get the wrong impression—not understand I was kidding.

And the boys were three.

Big John Halleran, Maloney's personal bodyguard. The other, who nodded to me, a surly little machine gunner. I think his moniker was Graften. The third man was leaning against the fireplace. Maloney introduced me to him.

"Victor Monroe," he said. "The man with the deal. He has come well recommended."

I looked at Victor Monroe and damn near shot him to death. Yep, he was the flat-faced, cruel-mouthed lad who less than fourteen hours ago was going under the name of Laskey. The lad I batted the wind out of with my gun. But he didn't know me—and he was speaking.

"Race Williams this—Race Williams that. He don't look so tough to me."

"What do you consider tough, sister," I said easily.

His eyes grew uglier, his lips twisted, and his whole face looked more cruel and vicious, if that were possible. He leaned forward and stuck his pan close to mine. Then he spoke.

"Look at me. Look at me," he fairly bellowed. "How do I look?"

You have to admit he'd left himself wide open and I took advantage of it.

"You look," I said very slowly, "as if you had tried to crank a car with your teeth and it back-fired on you."

His RIGHT HAND shot out with great speed, grabbed at the lapels of my coat and snatched me to him—real movie stuff. His jacket flew open, too, and I saw something that glittered. It was the silver handle of a long-nosed gun that he carried stuck down through his belt, slightly to the right of his stomach.

I held my temper and without changing my tone, said to Maloney: "Call the big goat off, Maloney—or I'll scatter him all over the room."

When Laskey only gripped me tighter I slugged him. I brought up a right jab that should have flattened him but only rocked him. For a moment I was stunned by what he could take, but I wasn't worried. I knew where he kept his gun. Then Maloney and Halleran had dragged him off and cursed him out in low voices.

I said to the machine gunner who stood beside the fireplace, empty handed: "If a rattler should happen to bounce into your hands, Graften, you'd never use it."

"Yeah—I know, Race." His mouth twisted and maybe he smiled. "I understand it's to be a peaceful party. This guy Victor is bad—I'm mostly to protect him from himself."

Maloney was talking to me. "Don't ride Victor, Race. He's a big shot where he comes from—Western stuff. He won't let any lad get away with anything—at any time."

I started to say that someone must have got away with a lot on his face, but instead said: "He might as well know the truth— the next time he wants to play, he takes lead."

There was a lot of laugh-when-you-say-that stuff but finally Victor—or Laskey, as I knew him—wanted the dough so he got down to business.

He said: "These men who are highly recommended sent for you."

Oh, I kept listening to his story, but I was thinking at the same time. Some coincidence that Maloney should send for me. Sure—I know such things do happen, but they don't to me, and I don't believe in coincidence.

He was talking about wanting the lost ticket and said: "Mr. Williams, these other gentlemen said that you knew Stock-bridge—did some work for him—and they suggested you might handle it. But you are not so tough."

I turned to Maloney, shrugged my shoulders, said: "What does he want? All his teeth shoved down his mouth as a sort of reference?"

Maloney shook his head. "It's just his way of doing things, Race. It's a lot of money. He wants to—well, he'll give you five grand for that ticket." And when I straightened back my shoulders Maloney came close to me. "I got you to come here, Race—and I won't have you knocked around—but quit kidding this guy. They don't come any worse—right here in New York."

"So I tremble, eh?"

"No." Maloney's voice was low now. "Not yet—but he hasn't seen the papers yet—and won't. But he's talking about killing the guy who shot his friend and nearly tore him apart. Understand, I only know you shot a guy on your apartment roof. But I know this Laskey bird from people in Chi. I've got ten grand against one that says you're the only lad who'd knock him around—and did. If he ever suspected you, it would be—" Maloney spread his hands far apart.

I said: "It would be what?"

"Curtains."

"Curtains for whom?"

"For you, Race. Laskey's the boy who pays. You're the boy who gets paid. Now which side do you think I'm on?"

I was boiling up a bit.

"I didn't ask for your protection, Malo-ney—and I don't want it and damn well don't need it. I just think the guy's a heel."

"We might," Maloney said easily, "throw you out on the street and let it go at that."

I shook my head, said: "No, Maloney—you couldn't do that. It's not my dignity but my reputation along the Avenue. I couldn't permit it."

"Perhaps"—Maloney's voice was even lower now and I saw Halleran across the room—"perhaps, Race, we mightn't think of your reputation—nor ask for your permission."

I looked Maloney full in the face. "Do you mean that—that you'd try and throw me out?"

"Not try. Just throw you out. Yes, Race, I mean it."

"O.K." I spoke loud enough for Halle-ran to hear. "I believe you—so be looking for a bit of gun-play—and rather a mess."

"Good God!" said Maloney. "You wouldn't—" I was looking at Maloney now and, what's more, he was looking at me. He didn't finish what he had to say. He didn't need to. He put a gentle hand on my shoulder. His voice was friendly.

"Good-bye, Race." And when I started to take money from my pocket, "That's all right, boy. You won't take the case?"

"No." I shoved four centuries into his fist. "Not with that punk aboard." I stuck a finger at Laskey, then stepping around Maloney I spoke before Laskey could get his foul words rolling.

I said: "As for you, Laskey—tough, eh? I'm the guy who belted you around last night—yeah—knocked all the fight out of you. You cheap woman-torturer."

I CROSSED A left, gave him a straight right, watched for him to fall. But he didn't. He simply rocked on his heels again, lurched forward, and drove his whole huge body against mine. His right hand jerked a snub-nosed automatic from far up under his left armpit. It was not the gun I'd been watching.

Oh, my gun was out—out quicker than his was—spat quicker, too. But someone had jerked my arm, knocked the gun from my hand. Laskey missed me as I pounded back from the wall close against him, and wound my left hand around his neck. I twisted as he fired again—twisted with the feel of his gun—but I felt the stab of cold ice as the bullet cut across my body just above the hip.

It looked like curtains then. A guy dragged at me from one side—another guy from the other. I knew the second pull. It was Halleran, and he had strength in it.

My head went up once, bounced against Laskey's chin, and he spit blood. His face was ugly—red running down from his lips—but there was triumph in his eyes. Yeah, he was a killer all right. Fast or slow—anyway you liked it. Now it was slow, as light appeared between us and he brought up his gun, pushed it tight against my stomach.

Maybe I thought then—maybe I didn't. Call it instinct—call it anything except blind luck. I don't believe in luck. Anyway, he was too slow. My right hand shot just inside his jacket clutched the long-nosed gun that was stuck in his belt, twisted and pulled. There was a single shot. He was a powerful man, this Laskey—powerful

even in death. He didn't pitch forward and he didn't fall backwards. Nor did he give at the knees and sink to the floor.

For a single second perhaps he bent slightly, clutched at his stomach, then, straightening, swung like a whirling dervish, spinning on his heels and clutching for me with those great hands. It was then that I ducked, and just as I ducked Halleran fired. Yep, shot Laskey straight through the face. This time Laskey didn't do any tricks. He staggered slightly before he crashed to the floor.

It was nice work on Halleran's part—seeing he must have meant to kill me.

As for me, I did a complete turn and landed smack up against the wall. I said to the man in the corner, "Drop that rattler, Graften," and to Halleran, "You can keep your gun—if you want to use it."

The machine gun fell to the floor and Graften grinned. Halleran—well, I'll give a little credit to Halleran for he didn't drop his gun until Maloney told him to. Then it thudded to the floor, just before he would have thudded if Maloney hadn't saved his life.

Maloney said: "A fine mess, Race." And the other two followed him to the windows. All three peeked out between the curtains. Me—I was over Laskey—a hand beneath his jacket—and my sigh of relief was real. The envelope addressed to the district attorney was in his inside pocket. I had it in my pocket and was picking up my own gun and tossing the other on Laskey's chest when Maloney turned.

He said: "It's Nelson, Race—Inspector Nelson." And after a look at Laskey and a quite expressive shrug, "It's too bad—but you didn't have any more sense than the big thug. Nelson didn't hear the shots. He must have known you visited Stockbridge's house this noon—just as we did. Well, get going."

Halleran swung and his face was vicious. "If I ever see you again I'll kill you," he said—which remark should let you in on the set of brains he was sporting around the city.

I ignored Halleran, said to Maloney: "You'll take care of the body?"

"That's right. You lead Nelson off the trail, Race. We'll dump the body. He doesn't suspect anything—only saw you come in here. Go on, Race. You've got no part of this body."

I said: "Fine," and being a timid soul backed out the door, shut it behind me, and was down the three steps.

CHAPTER 7

A CORPSE IN THE HAND

THERE WERE INNER and outer doors. Both had glass in them, but the glass wasn't clean enough to see the street through both doors. I lifted the chain, went into the little vestibule and looked out.

I spotted Nelson. He was about twenty five feet down from the post office. He was hiding in a cigar store entrance—at least he thought he was. Now there were two things to do. Either dash for the post office or ease out carefully as though I were trying to keep under cover.

I smacked the door open and closed, walked directly across the street, right to the threshold of the post office door. Then I took a step or two toward Nelson and the cigar store. He had faded from view. I liked that. I walked into the post office, got myself a big envelope, six cents' worth of stamps and going to one of the desks, pulled out my fountain pen. I'd stopped trying to write with post office pens when I was ten years old.

I stuck the letter addressed to the D.A. in the big envelope and wrote Miss Stockbridge's name and address on the outer envelope. I looked toward the door, blotted the letter easily, glanced up at the wall and damn near dropped the letter.

You know the artistic display of wanted guys that are pasted on the walls of our U.S. post offices. Well, I was looking at a face with many aliases under it. One of those aliases was Victor Monroe—another was Jake Laskey.

There was his ugly puss, done justice to as only a police photographer can. Under that cruel face I read—

ESCAPED CONVICT 23897KX
WANTED FOR MURDER
$2,500.00 REWARD
DEAD OR ALIVE!

Maybe I froze at the desk, but not for long. I ripped down the "wanted" poster, ran across the floor, dropped the letter in the Local slot and was out of the post office speeding across the street.

I didn't think of Nelson now. I didn't think of Miss Stockbridge or the other girl. I thought of the dirty louses—Maloney—all of them. Laskey was dead and I had killed him and there was twenty-five hundred bucks in it for the lad who got him—dead or alive. Well, he was dead enough. Maloney had copped my corpse—my dough—my bird in the hand.

I smacked open the doors to the Young Men's Athletic Club, the inner one knocking Phil Jordan stiffer than—well, stiffer than he generally was. I made the stairs, crashed the door just in time.

Halleran and Graften were carrying the body of Laskey toward the door in the rear of the room. Maloney was holding the door open and giving the directions. I burst in, a gun in my right hand, waving the reward notice in the other.

I said: "Drop that—or I'll plug the three of you. Come on—the corpse is mine."

THEY DROPPED IT and turned and stared at me. It didn't strike me until afterwards that probably none of them knew what I meant—or were even thinking of the reward money. But I thought of it and I went right on.

"You dirty scum, to do an honest dick out of twenty-five hundred bucks. Tell the cops you weren't here. Say we met here. Say what you want." And with that I grabbed Laskey by the collar, dragged him across the room, out that door, down the hall and to the top of the three steps.

And there below was Nelson—Nelson and two cops. I licked at my lips—two cops—two witnesses.

"Look out below, Nelson," I hollered and hurled my body down. They had to jump back to avoid Laskey—then I was at the bottom standing guard over him.

"He's mine, Nelson!" I guess I must have shouted. "You wanted to catch me with a body I just killed. Well, there he is—Victor Monroe—alias Jake Laskey—alias twenty-five hundred dollars in cash, dead or alive!"

One of the cops said: "For God's sake, stop shouting, Williams. You're bleeding like a stuck pig."

"Who's a pig?" I could hear my voice ring through that hall. "It's my dough—"

My head began to whirl and Nelson took my arm. "Easy does it, Race," he said. "It's Laskey, all right. Catch him!"

But I didn't go down. At least O'Rourke said I was swaying there when he came in answer to a telephone call from Maloney. He told me, too, that I made such a row about getting in the ambulance that they had to take me to the hospital in a taxi.

"But the worst," said O'Rourke when they had me sitting up in bed, "was when you spit Phil Jordan's whiskey right back at him and threw the bottle at the wall."

I smiled at him when the nurse patted up the pillows.

"I couldn't have been delirious then, Sarge," I told him. "That poison would be the last straw."

After finding out that I'd been there for three days, and the baloney about the bullet being next to my heart, and that I'd be able to leave in ten more days, I called Jerry on the phone.

"Listen, boy," I told him, "I see I'm rating plenty of pictures in the papers. Fix up the penthouse again while the credit's good. I'll shake down the bank for a grand and—I'll be out of here and in good shape Monday."

When O'Rourke said no and the nurse looked quite severe I swung a leg out of bed. I'll admit I staggered a bit toward the chair by the window, but I told them the truth—that I knew more about my own body and what it could take than any medico.

Was I right? Of course I was right. I was out of that joint—and headed for my penthouse Monday morning.

THE PLACE WAS changed. Understand, to me it was only a penthouse because the movies called it that and it said so in my lease—and it was on an apartment roof. Now it was a real penthouse—modernistic furniture, a chair in the hall that you couldn't sit in unless you were a contortionist, a costumer that lads spent hours to put in the shape it was in, when one good saloon brawl would have done the same thing.

Jerry came to meet me after I was in. He had a stupid look on his face and—yes, by God, wore a dinner jacket! At first I thought he was working on the side as a waiter. Then I spotted the living-room—at least half of it. The spirit of Belasco had run riot in my penthouse.

I said to Jerry: "Take that monkey suit off and get the hell out of here."

"Yes, sir. Quite, sir. Damn it to hell, sir."

And he was gone and I was looking down toward the Venetian blinds, the blinking sunshine, and the girl, Elinor Stockbridge, walking across the room toward me.

"No Stoic outfitted this," she told me and her blue eyes were soft. Her face—well, the marble was gone and her arms were slender and moved gracefully, instead of acting like two sticks moulded for a museum piece. "It's my present to you. There, don't shake your head. You'll like it when you see it. Everything is for a he man—comfort in all the chairs you will use—the beds you will sleep in—the books you will read." She waved a hand about. "I don't want to be mercenary, but the rug cost over three thousand dollars. After you see the bedrooms you'll understand that I have worked hard. Sit down."

I did sit down and the chair was soft and deep. It was comfortable, but you were so close to the floor that you'd have to be an acrobat to get up without crawling along the arm.

She was talking.

"I have been selfish—very selfish. I have wanted to run other people's lives so that I neglected my own. Laskey's accusation has been torn up. I haven't any desire to fix it with the district attorney. Do you know why, Race?"

"Mr. Williams to you," I said without much thought.

She smiled, said: "My father's position and money would have gotten me out of that fix. Your kindness saved my life. You're—well, Laskey has carried his information about me to his grave. You see, I did nothing for myself. Only thought I did."

"I want to telephone," I said and started to my feet toward the white phone in the corner across the room.

"No—not that phone. That will be our private number. It will never ring unless I am calling. The phone there by your elbow." She moved half a dozen books and I found the phone, called Jake Monty, the theatrical agent. I was bothered about Dolores.

"Race Williams speaking," I said, "and if Jake is in conference—"

Jake's voice cut in. You could hear his teeth clamp right through the cigar. I said: "Did that girl get her job?"

"Don't kid me, boy," Jake said.

"I'm not kidding. I mean business. What does she do—what—"

"What does she do? With her talent?" he came back. "She plays the lead of course. Why wouldn't she? The part fits her. She wrote it for herself and—"

"You're putting on the play she wrote and she's playing the lead?"

"Sure, sure. It's a great job. Stop your kidding. Race. She insisted you have half-interest in the show. Thanks, boy, for shooting her over."

"You mean—she's backing the show? Where did she get the money?"

Jake laughed loud and heartily. "As if you didn't know. Don't you read your papers? Her horse in the Sweepstakes. That lost ticket."

"So I'm backing a play."

"Why not? Come down and see a rehearsal. It's colossal."

I STARTED TO put the phone down, but Miss Stockbridge took it from me and placed it on the hook.

"So you're backing a play," she said.

"Yes. You gave her the ticket, then?"

"It was the least I could do for you when you sent it to me." And her smile wasn't stony now. It was glorious. "Race, Race—" She leaned down close to me. "When Laskey first showed me that letter before you came, it was easy to slip the ticket inside the letter and back in the envelope. He hardly watched me as I read it. It was after, that he had me searched by a woman— every part of me gone over. You were there when I fooled Laskey into giving me the letter the second time. The ticket was inside it then, and I sealed it, sealed up the very thing he wanted, right in front of his eyes. That is, the girl that I was then did it."

"Is that so?" I moved sideways in the chair as she bent over me, lit a butt and tossed away the match. I made a dive forward—landed on the match. I had thrown it onto the three-grand rug.

"Race"—she came up very close to me—"don't worry about that. I think from now on my greatest pleasure will be doing things for others—maybe just for one other. There are plenty of rugs, but only one Race Williams. I would like to spend my time doing things for you."

Boy—those hard glims had melted as if an electric blow torch had worked on them! Her hands and arms were moving up! No kidding—a million dollars' worth of beauty was tossing itself my way.

If there was any Stoic then, I was it. I slipped under her guard—hurried toward the door—was almost running. But she didn't follow me.

I turned then and said: "I've got to go out. I don't know when I'll come back. Don't wait."

She just stood there and looked at me. "I'll wait," she said slowly, "forever."

Which was a lie, for when I staggered back into my penthouse three nights later she was gone.

Gangman's Gallows

CHAPTER 1

INVITATION TO KILL

IT WAS SUPPOSED to be a tough town. Anyway, my job called for a tough role, so I played it that way right from the start. I was dressed smart enough, and maybe I swaggered a bit when I walked.

The Casino was lighted up like a New Orleans' Mardi Gras—all honest and aboveboard-looking. The doorman—a big lad who looked more like a general than any real general could possibly look—stretched his hand out in front of me.

"Where's your invitation?" he chirped. "It's special tonight."

I slapped a ten-spot into his hand, and said: "That's my invitation."

He looked at the ten a while, hesitated, then turned quickly and opened the door wide.

Lights, music, respectability—if stiff shirts make it so—entertainment, if you can stand for a "great discovery" brought from Brooklyn, who was trying to tear the house down. The bar was cut off from the long hall and the main room by a huge partition that looked like a green cardboard sea. I went to the bar and leaned against it.

I saw the pompous little duck who filled the description I had received of the proprietor. He nudged a big hulk who followed me.

I knew the racket and braced myself for it. It came—a heavy hand upon my shoulder which was supposed to swing me around. "Supposed to" was right. My body didn't budge. I turned my head slowly and he spoke. His voice was high-pitched for so big a man, and I marked him as a former whiskey tenor in a cheap joint until someone noticed his strength. He said, as he looked down at me, for I was leaning on the bar: "I don't remember seeing your face before."

"Nor me yours," I gave it to him straight. "But I don't squawk all over the place about it."

It didn't throw him. He just stood there—his right hand on my shoulder. "So it's like that," he said.

"Just like that."

I thought we were at a dead-end street—but no. He lowered his voice slightly, said, "Go peacefully to the door and leave," and when I didn't move, and when he couldn't drag me from the bar with the attempted nonchalance of his great strength, he tried: "That would be better than being thrown into the alley."

I SWUNG THEN and straightened. His hand went off my shoulder and he staggered back. No one had seen the knee I stuck in his stomach. Not even Squeak Voice himself saw it—though he felt it.

I didn't give him a chance for a come-back. I did my talking first. I said, "Put your hand on me again, and I'll spray all your teeth down your throat," and to drive my meaning home with a meat axe, I added: "Don't kid yourself about being tough, Charlie—you're small-town stuff to me."

His face changed colors like a kaleidoscope—blotches of purple and yellow, pink and white, all at once. Sure it was in his heart to jump me. It was in his heart to slip a blackjack from his sleeve and let me have it, too. I won't say he was afraid—maybe just puzzled. Besides, a couple of stuffed shirts at the bar were beginning to notice—just listlessly. This time he squawked his words with a rattle like a bird who had a mouth full of buckshot.

"Tough boy." He glared at me. He half turned and nodded. Two bruisers got up from a table near the bar. They wore tux, but you can't dress up a gorilla, even in a circus, and make a man out of him. These lads were gorillas. I pressed my back against the bar. The pompous duck left a party he was speaking to—came half around the edge of the imitation green sea.

I said, loud enough for him to hear: "Two aren't enough, Charlie—you're in for a surprise."

Charlie didn't speak. The two men were leisurely coming toward me when the owner came up, stood right in front of me.

He said: "I am Mr. Alfred Latimer, the manager. We do not wish your presence here. You are at liberty to leave quickly and quietly."

"Thanks." I took in the little crops of hair scattered over his head like a desert growth. "I'm not going."

Very white teeth showed. Mr. Latimer smiled and said: "We dislike scenes, but they do occur, even in such a refined atmosphere as the Casino's, with people of your type." His voice grew slightly sarcastic. "You may be a very rough man indeed—but there are twenty men here to eject you, and just behind the bar— another room—an alley. They might not be too kind to you after—" His shoulders moved up and down. "It is not for me to know what happens in an alley, but I recall a truculent gentleman—bigger and stronger than you. I forget if he recovered. Now will you go? Speak up, my man, before I order you thrown from the place."

His eyes flashed. Mine didn't. I stared straight at him, raised my right hand and unbuttoned my jacket. I leaned slightly forward so for a moment he got the flash of the two guns—one under each arm. Then I spoke my piece.

I said simply: "When you put Race Williams out of a rat trap like this, you'll put him out in a cloud of smoke."

THE THREAT AND the guns got him— but I like to think it was the name that got him more than either. Yep—seven hundred miles away from New York as the crow and air-liners fly, and he knew my name.

"Race Williams," he said, and again, "Race Williams."

I'm quick to take advantage of a point, and I took advantage of it then. There was a hardness in my voice when I said: "Chase the drunk-tosser away and we'll talk. Come on—before I take your place apart."

He stood there for a long moment before he waved the boys aside and motioned me to a table. Motioning me to a table was on the level—the waving the boys aside was strictly a gesture— they had already started to sidle down the bar.

When we were seated he leaned across the table, spoke. "Mr. Williams, I have heard of you. If you have come from New York to play a bit, we welcome you. But your methods are so—"

"Mr. Latimer," I cut in, "we won't beat around the cuspidors. Do you know why I'm here?"

"I might guess if I desired." And after a pause, "Suppose you tell me."

"Fair enough," I agreed. "You won't question the fact that upstairs you run the biggest gambling house in town. You won't deny that Harvey Price has been a prisoner in your place for the past three days. Frankly, I am employed by his uncle, Duncan Price, to bring him home, tonight. His father is outside in a car. It's kidnaping, of course."

LATIMER SPREAD HIS hands far apart, said: "Then why not the police? Surely a man so prominent—so well known and influential as Duncan Price—could get any judge to sign a search warrant. Why not have the place raided again? If he were here, the police would find him. Or is that the reason there has been no police raid?"

"There would have been a police raid tonight—but I prevented it. I know the scandal and all that—but Mr. Duncan Price was quite willing to face it!"

"Really?" Thick eyebrows went up and

down. "And why, Mr. Williams, did you object to the police?"

"Business only," I told him. "I earn my money by keeping the police away."

"I appreciate your frankness, Mr. Williams—and in return will be quite frank with you. Mr. Harvey Price is here. He has gambled and is in debt to the house six thousand dollars. He is staying here as my guest until he can raise the money."

I gave Mr. Latimer a shock then. I put my hand in my pocket and pulled out the bills and slapped them on the table—twelve five-hundred-dollar bank notes.

"That's for his I.O.U.s," I told him. "Produce the paper and the boy."

He set his teeth grimly and said: "He can't leave tonight. He will accept no money from his uncle, and—"

"What do you mean?" I leaned on the table now. "You're peddling his I.O.U.s about town—with the wrong people."

"The right people would pay more."

I gave him a laugh. "You're lucky to get your money at all. Everyone knows Harvey Price. He's no good. Why not take the dough? His I.O.U.s are worth nothing."

"Indeed? I know someone to whom they are worth a great deal. Those I.O.U.s will be paid in full tonight. They will never appear to blacken the fair name"—a chuckle there—"of young Harvey Price or his Uncle Duncan. It's a gala night. People have been admitted by invitation only—and because of the respectability and high social standing of our guests this evening the suggestion was made that you, simply as a strange face, should

depart. I am sorry I cannot do business with you but you may stay and see the new star of the Casino. She unmasks at two o'clock exactly." He came to his feet. "For your own peace of mind, Harvey Price will have paid his debt, and be free to leave here—in the morning."

I grabbed at Latimer's arm, pulled him back to his chair, said: "Harvey's father is waiting outside to take the boy out of town. I must deliver him before one o'clock. Come, Latimer. Quit making faces. Bring down that boy—or I'll go up and get him."

"You must be mad!" Latimer gasped.

"Why not? There's a thousand dollars in it for me." And when he bit at his lip and put his hand in his pocket, I added: "An honest thousand dollars—the only kind of money I take."

Latimer said: "The district attorney is out front—several of his most trusted detectives are with him. You know the political set-up. The mayor is there and—"

I cut in: "Sure—and the sheriff—and Senator Rhoden. You have something up your sleeve all right. Friend and foe alike are at your tables tonight. And Senator Rhoden is the man who will supersede your friend the district attorney as soon as the Governor acts. I may raise some hell—I may spoil your special show—but I'll get that boy."

"Impossible—my help—those men you saw—and others. Williams, you talk like a fool, and I understood you were a clear-thinking, determined man." And slowly, "The reform newspaper published an article that men were killed in the gaming rooms above and their bodies taken to the outskirts of the city. It's a hundred to one against you."

"O.K." I was on my feet talking to him now. "A hundred to one. You're a gambler, Mr. Latimer," and I suddenly slapped the six grand into his hand. "There's even money that I take the boy out before one o'clock. Cover it!"

It got him. He went through all the expressions of an amateur actor who has forgotten his lines. Money talks. It talked to him. For the first time he was doubtful of himself—of me—of the whole business. He was a gambler—I had offered what he no longer felt was easy money. His eyes did tricks again but he finally shoved the money back into my hand.

Just before he left me, he said, and his voice choked slightly: "I never bet in my own establishment. Sit down, Mr. Williams. I would like you to talk to Mr. Malcom Brickner."

I sat down.

Mr. Malcom Brickner was the district attorney.

For a few minutes I had a chance to think back. I was a fool to be sitting there threatening the entire district attorney's staff as well as Latimer, who was supposed to run the D.A. and the whole town, for that matter. This town was on fire. The commissioner of police was on the level—so were some of the cops—though most of them didn't know where they stood. It was a political upheaval, and with the mayor in with the D.A., things were rough going all around.

But look at my position—I had been paid by Duncan Price, who wanted to drive all the crooks out of that town, if he had to spend every nickel he had. And he had plenty. At first he was a laugh—then he hired outside dicks, became a nuisance before the D.A. got onto himself and bought off most of them—maybe killed some. But Duncan Price had gathered his information—and Duncan Price had gotten a paper behind him—and Duncan Price had made such a squawk that the Governor had to listen, and was now about ready to step.

The crooks, like all crooks, had made their mistake. Duncan Price's car was machine gunned. A pineapple was tossed through his front window. His daughter's life had been threatened—and all the trimmings gangsters use on one another had been worked on Duncan Price, the town's big name.

Yes—that was where the boys made their mistake. Racketeers are used to the law of the night—the law of the gun—the law of violence and sudden death. They respect that law and fear it. But Duncan Price was not used to having pineapples tossed into his living-room—nor having his car explode in his face—nor threats against his daughter.

It didn't strike him with fear—at least the kind of fear the D.A. and his crook crowd expected. It surprised him—stunned him, and shocked him. He didn't believe such things could happen to a man of his position, his dignity. No, damn it, he didn't even believe it could happen after it had happened.

At all events, he went personally on the stump to clean up the town. He made speeches, he shook his fist—and he put up money. Duncan Price's single-handed crusade against his home town even made the front pages of the New York papers and jarred the governor of his own state smack out of his chair.

I remembered my first words with Duncan Price. He was a little man with a finely chiseled but determined face. He had walked up and down the room with jerky steps.

"It's a rotten town, Williams, but it's my town. Understand, if they can threaten Duncan Price—throw bombs at my house—no man is safe. I'm after them now if I have to indict the whole damned Grand Jury because most of them have been planted there by this Malcom Brickner. Why, I helped Brickner get his start. Understand, for once in your life you're not telling others—you're not telling me, that you may have to shoot someone to death to protect your life. My money is standing behind you—my name is standing behind you, and behind my name stands the governor of the state. If you were to shoot to death the district attorney himself, nothing could be done about it. I have evidence that this Alfred Latimer, owner of the Casino, has strangled people with wire right in his own establishment. At least twenty bodies of men and women—yes, one a young girl—have been found in different parts of the city—their necks twisted and broken. You say you are able to protect your own life. Other detectives I have used have said that—and have died."

I shrugged a shoulder and grinned. "That's O.K.," I said. "Meet violence with violence. That's the way I like to play." And being a careful man, I added: "You're sure of the Governor?"

"Absolutely." He nodded emphatically. "He hasn't wanted to interfere so near the election. They want things rough—they want things tough. So I brought you here from New York. I have them on the run. I expect the Governor to act any hour now—day or night. I'm pushing him damned hard to appoint Senator Rhoden as special prosecutor."

He showed me a picture of his daughter Dorothy, a pretty, slim bit of a girl, with dark hair and bangs—a profile like her father's, and eyes that— But he was talking.

"I am no blue-nose with a high hat, as some of these crooks have pictured me. Dorothy's a concert singer—sings at the Fenimore Hotel occasionally—just down the block from the Casino. A decent, respectable place. Latimer even had the gall to ask her to sing in the Casino. As I said about Brickner, the district attorney, I'd stand behind you if you shot him straight—"

And my thoughts vanished—my mind jumped back to the Casino. Malcom Brickner was entering the bar, walking straight toward my table.

He was tall, handsome—an open, honest face—bright blue eyes—eyes that were capable of a direct look. They were steady as he smiled, pulled up a chair, sat down and extended his hand.

"I am Malcom Brickner, the district attorney, Mr. Williams. I've heard a lot about you." And after a pleasant laugh, "You've heard a lot about me, too. I hope you won't refuse to shake hands with me."

I gripped his hand and said: "I'm not fussy. I shook hands once with a lad who killed his mother and father with a meat axe."

Brickner bit his lip. I read his mind like an open book. He was thinking how easy it would have been before to raise his hand and clap me in the cooler to be forgotten. But he smiled, showed great white teeth, and said: "I'm afraid Mr. Price has been a little hard on me. Given time I'll clean this city up in my own way—and thoroughly."

"There were two attempts on Mr. Price's life," I said simply.

"Good God—Duncan Price can't think I had the least suspicion that such a thing was going to happen! No matter what he has said about me—I'll find those men and see that they are punished. Lord, man—Duncan Price put me where I am today!"

"And he'll put you where you're going," I said solemnly, and wiped the smile off his face as if I'd run a vacuum cleaner over it.

He didn't speak. He couldn't. And I think for the moment the smell of burning flesh was in his nostrils. Then he said: "To the point, Mr. Williams. I'm here to convince you that it would be foolhardy to try and get Harvey Price out of here tonight. Besides, he wouldn't go with you."

Get the wording. Not, "I'm here to *order* you," nor even here to "tell" you—just the word "convince." I liked that. I was holding the cards then.

I said: "If he won't go with me, I'll drag him out."

That got Brickner. His mouth remained partly open and his teeth smiled—but his eyes didn't. They had turned a misty sort of blue—with a couple of single points of lead back in the center of them.

He choked before he spoke, said: "Why not watch the entertainment, Mr. Williams? It will interest you. In half an hour I will come to your table. If you still wish to take Harvey Price with you I will see that you go above and speak with him."

"Thank you."

I came to my feet and followed him around the screen to the great curtains that gave on the main room. The curtains parted immediately and stepping aside for me to enter, Brickner said to the head-waiter: "Mr. Latimer's guest—see that he has the best table."

"But, sir—Mr. Brickner, sir—every table is occupied. There—well—I might move the young Grants and their friends—they never spend much—but their names, you know, lend prestige to the place."

I said: "Don't move them—you need all the prestige you can get here."

The headwaiter didn't get it. Brickner frowned, tried to smile, and said: "You may take Mr. Williams to my table." He stretched his head and looked into the room. "I see the young lady is alone—you will introduce Mr. Williams. She will understand and see that he is properly taken care of."

So I went down the room in style. It was a mixed crowd. The fast set and I guess some society folks—but the fast set were not cutting up tonight. The only way you could tell the gambling crowd and their like was because of their superior poise and ease. The society people had an air of having come up an alley to hear a dirty joke and were surprised to find how many people they knew had come also. It was a queer set-up and no mistake. Something strange was in the wind.

The girl at the table looked very young and certainly was very beautiful. Perhaps the most beautiful woman I have ever looked at—and I have looked at plenty. Certainly she was the most dangerous woman I ever met. Yep—I rocked back on my heels as the headwaiter did his stuff.

He said: "Miss Drummond, may I present Mr. Williams? Miss Florence Drummond, sir. Mr. Brickner sent him over, Miss—" He bowed and was gone.

I stood there as the girl raised her head, extended one of those snake-like arms and gripped my sleeve.

"I didn't quite get the name," she said. "You look so dumb standing there like that. Surely you can't be *The* Mr. Williams—Race Williams? Won't you sit down?"

CHAPTER 2

THE GIRL WITH THE CRIMINAL MIND

I LOOKED DUMB all right—standing or sitting—and you'd look dumb too. Florence Drummond—The Flame—called the Girl with the Criminal Mind. No one knew her better than I did. I had worked with her and worked against her. We had

played and we had fought—and perhaps we had loved. If you don't know her, you ought to. The finest girl you ever met—at times. Then again—the woman of the night—cruel, vicious. Sometimes you could read it in her eyes as the hard lines marred her almost childlike face. Now she was the young girl drawing you to her with her youthful beauty. Tomorrow? Perhaps a gun in your stomach.

I sat down, lifted her hand, noted the ice on her fingers—the bracelet about her wrist—a hand that seldom wore jewelry.

"Well, Florence," I said, "it was a knockout to meet you here. The first bout is yours. I hope you haven't sold out for a mess of diamonds." And when she laughed, a laugh that reached only a table or two, for we were off from the other people and close to the heavy drapes that gave on a side promenade, I added: "We've seen a lot together one way or the other, so I'm warning you. The racket is dead. Malcom Brickner won't lay any more diamond bracelets. For old times' sake—get moving. I won't be crossed, and I'm on the kill."

Her eyes sparkled. She said: "The same old Race—thinks pretty well of himself and doesn't care who knows it. Don't you wonder why I'm here?"

"No," I told her. "I'm giving you a break—skip the town."

"I might"—she leaned across the table—"give you the same advice. I know why you're here—a one-man racket buster. Duncan Price hired you in. It's open season for shooting and no game laws. The job was made for you—but not for you to do alone. They never suspected

Price was bringing you into town—thought you were just another private dick." She paused a moment, placed her cigarette in a holder and let me light it, then said easily: "If you go upstairs tonight they plan to kill you."

"Is that so?" I lit a butt of my own now. "What's the lay here, Florence? Who's behind the show? Rhoden or the D.A.?" And, when she didn't answer, "Or neither one of them?"

She was startled—sat up straight—brushed the ashes off her evening gown. "What do you mean—neither one of them?"

I started to tell her I had an idea that an outside ring might be running things, but I didn't. The Flame had been startled at my question—and The Flame was not one to startle easily—in fact, not one to be startled if a bomb was chucked on the table. And I got a thought, too—one that startled *me*. Nothing impossible. The Flame had been big time—she had controlled big men. Why not? Hell, I told myself, I didn't believe it, but just the same, the thought was there. Was The Flame behind the whole racket now? Giving it the benefit of her mind, her criminal mind?

The Flame said: "So you're not interested why I came here—how I got here." She gripped my hand. "Maybe I love you still. Race—maybe I heard six months ago that you were coming—and planted myself here to help you. What would you say to that?"

"I'd say that was damned white of you, Florence." I laid the sarcasm on heavy. "You see, I only knew yesterday that I was coming."

"Well"—she didn't even redden—"you were always slow to grasp things, Race. I had a dream six months back I could help you, and that you would come here. How's that?"

"Did you dream the rings on your fingers?"

She just threw back her head and laughed. "No—they're real. My job is to entertain you. Let me entertain you with how I got an in here. It will amuse you, at least."

I could listen to that, and did. Her thin red lips quivered with mirth. "Six months or so ago when I was but a mere child," she started, "I discovered that my face and my figure and perhaps my brains would help me seek honest employment. So I came to this wicked, wicked, city. With me I brought a couple of Chicago gamblers—at least they were from Chicago, and they did gamble. The boys who have taken over the town put greed before common sense. With every percentage in their favor, the wheels and dice tables are crooked."

"It cost those gamblers some money to get you in, eh? They got rooked."

"As I said, Race, they weren't exactly gamblers. They chucked a few thousand dollars away—sized up the place—then knocked it over one night for twenty grand. Time: Four minutes and thirty-seven seconds. It was a surprise to Latimer and his friends."

"And you—didn't Latimer or Brickner suspect you?"

"Of course, but I stayed at the best hotel. Brickner came to threaten—

remained to make love. Oh—he's not a fool for women—not Brickner. I talked business, too. I told him if he squawked I'd notify every crook and murderer back in New York to come down and make easy money. But mostly I convinced him that I'd be an asset, not a liability—and I furnished him with a few good references—which wasn't hard."

I NODDED AT that one. There were few big criminals who didn't know The Flame and fewer still who wouldn't take advice from her.

"Of course, Race," she went on, "it would be silly for you to pretend not to know me—and almost suicide for me to pretend not to know you. Are we to be enemies or friends?"

"What do you mean?"

"I mean that you get out—let me handle things. I'll do you a good turn. Harvey Price will go free before morning—and without spending a cent."

"I know that," I told her. "I'm here to see that he does."

"Race"—she grabbed my wrist now—"these men are far more desperate than those you have handled in New York. They are not so clever—so suave. They were drunk with power, took what they wanted. Hoodlums went through the streets beating small shop owners. A respectable citizen was attacked. There would have been another attempt on his life—only—only—"

"Only you prevented it," I helped her out.

She didn't deny that. She said quite frankly, but after a pause: "Yes—I prevented that."

"It was bad business—you told them that." I was thinking again. Had The Flame flashed back to the past, taken control as she always took control?

"Yes, I told them that," she said. "Vice and graft and murder must be played within their own vicious little circle."

She was right, of course, I said. "And now?"

"Now they're drunk with desperation. If the Governor has Senator Rhoden take Brickner's place—it's the end. Tonight is the gang's last chance. There is one thing no public-minded citizen—no, not even Duncan Price—can shake off, and that's public ridicule."

"But his nephew won't—"

Her eyes moved, and my mouth closed tight. I turned, looked at the man standing by the table. He was a swarthy, dark-haired, greasy sort of chap, who never should have worn a dress suit until they buried him.

The Flame said: "Hello, Harry—this is Race Williams. You've heard of him. Race—Harry Largo. Race and I were good friends in New York—once."

"That so?" Harry took himself very seriously. "I have heard of him—and you. Has Brickner?"

The Flame looked at those mean little eyes for a long time. She didn't speak at once. She just slipped the diamond bracelet from her wrist and shoved it into his hand. Then she spoke.

"Harry's a wise man, Race. I like him. He's smart, like you, Race…. Give that trinket to your girl, Harry."

Harry said: "Oh—not smart like Mr. Williams." He leaned down and digging a finger against my chest said: "A knife in the back does as much damage as a bullet through the front."

NICE BOY, HARRY. I gave him a second look—noticed his ugly grin and also the finger that was still against my chest. I toyed leisurely with my fork—then moved my hand quickly. Harry hadn't seen that trick before, but he stifled his scream of pain and I damn near wrapped that silver fork about his fingers. I didn't mind the glare in his eyes.

I said, "It's the front, Harry"—and coming to my feet—"I got a girl, too, Harry. A nice girl." I leaned across the table. "Give me that trinket—or I'll push the fork through your throat."

Harry was tough. Harry was a bad guy. Harry liked to stick knives in guy's backs. But Harry had a little common sense. He handed me that bracelet, scowled and left. There wasn't a peep out of him.

The Flame said, as I tossed the bracelet to her: "What's come over you, Race? I know you never avoided trouble—even looked for it—but tonight—"

"I am playing a part," I told her. "I want them to be sure who they are dealing with. Harry, I understand, is their rottenest killer—a lad with a knife. I think if I shot Harry it would be a good idea."

"You'll only make them more desperate, Race. You would have been dead now—if—well— Latimer let himself in for it. He—" She stopped. We both turned.

A curly-haired lad whose pan was corrugated with hard living was announcing from the center of the room. He was talking about talent and he was talking about Alfred Latimer and Latimer was smiling in the spotlight.

Curly-head was saying: "Tonight, in keeping with our policy, we are introducing a little lady, known to you all—a concert singer of great promise. She will sing for you the more popular songs of the day—dance for you the more popular dances. And she will dance masked—masked until two o'clock—when she will give her final performance—of such exquisite beauty and magnetism that it will hold you spellbound. At that time she will remove her mask and startle you all with her radiance and prominence. The price we paid for this single performance is enormous. But we give our patrons only the best. And now may I introduce some of our guests—our honored guests of the evening. First, Mr. and Mrs. Ralph Holliday Johnson."

The room lights went out and a splash from the spotlight hit the table nearest us. An old toad and her husband turned red as a couple of beets—deadbeats.

I heard the woman say: "But I wanted to know if it was true. You heard what that 'Snooper' said over the radio."

So it went on. A few stood up and took a bow. The district attorney entered the back and smiled. The mayor even nodded his approval. Senator Rhoden took it without change of expression. He sat at a table with a bright-looking young man. His bulgy shirt gleamed in the light, but his hard stern face remained the same. You only needed one look at that face to know that it was going to be tough sledding for the boys if he took over. I guess

Latimer and the D.A. figured the same, for he didn't get the light for long. The sheriff simply turned his head and spoke to a judge who was with him.

It was The Flame who gave me the low down on the "notables." But when I asked her what the idea of their being there was, she just shook her head and said: "It's simply to show the respectability of the place—to the respectable people. Senator Rhoden will go anywhere to learn something. They can't faze him."

THE SHOW WAS ON. Lights, music— and the girl was there. It was a hood rather than a mask that she wore. It was tied under her chin and pulled tightly about her head. Only the holes for her eyes showed—though I think there was a black, loosely knitted place over her mouth and nose to facilitate her breathing.

Anyway, the effect of the "mask" on her singing was not so hot. If Latimer paid real dough for that voice, he'd been stuck. Her dancing was better—especially when she tossed off the black cape and her shapely figure showed.

I leaned over to The Flame and whispered: "Reminds me of the night at the fancy-dress ball—when you and I were working a stunt together. She's built like you, Florence. What's the fuss for? She isn't much."

But she got a big hand when the crowd should have been hollering for their money back. I got up and stepping through the heavy drapes to the left of the table, went to the back of the room and mingled with the folks who had come from the bar and were standing in the back. The big curtains there were pushed aside so all might see.

I heard a young bloke say: "By God, it's true, Genevieve. It's she, all right."

"Know her by her legs, eh?" the half-drunk girl giggled.

"Legs—" the man said. "That's the first time anyone ever saw Dorothy Price's legs. What a joke—for dough, too. The papers will laugh Duncan Price right out of town. I didn't believe it—" And that was all. I was strutting straight between the tables now. Straight toward The Flame. She saw me, too—raised her eyes and held them on me. I won't say she lost her nerve. I don't believe that The Flame knew fear. But anyway she came to her feet—hit for those curtains I had passed through a few minutes before—and I was after her. Yep—after her and had her— caught by the arm as she started toward the performer's entrance.

"Rotten, eh?" I swung her around. "So that's the racket. Don't tell me. I know. It's Dorothy Price and she's paying off the boy's I.O.U.s. She's been lied to. Well— " I jerked Florence to me—half raised her hand—remembered suddenly just who The Flame was and stood dead in my tracks. She had jammed a .38 so deep into my ribs that I could hear them crack.

"By God!" she cried. "No one—not even you—can talk to me like that and maul me around." No slip of a girl now— no innocent twist to her lips and childlike sparkle in her eyes. She was the girl of the night now.

That's right. My part called for a tough role. I was tough. I am tough. But no one ever understood The Flame. I'm fast and can grab guns out of poor weak women's hands as quick as the next fellow. But The Flame was a horse of seven other colors. If she was in the mood—and certainly she seemed to be—she'd scatter me all over the curtains.

I backed away—and so would you.

The Flame said: "I ought to empty the cannon into you—but you'll be killed above anyway. Besides, the boys would laugh themselves to death if Race Williams was knocked over by a girl. So I'll give you a break for a favor—a little favor."

"Yeah—" was the best I could say. "What favor?"

"Harry Largo knows too much and may talk too soon. Just shoot him to death for me."

She was gone like that—through a door toward the front of the house. Me, I turned and faced the district attorney. Maybe he saw the play. Maybe he didn't. He wanted to talk but I beat him to it. I took out my anger on him. I snapped: "Take me to Harvey Price or I'll blast this joint apart."

He whitened, hesitated, smiled.

"Come," he said. "I'll take you to Harvey Price."

CHAPTER 3

HEADLESS HARRY

WE WALKED CLEAN back around the room past the thick, ceiling-high drapes that were now pulled back and into the folds of which a dozen men could have hidden.

But they weren't hidden there, for I watched pretty closely. So down a long corridor, a turn to the right, and into Alfred Latimer's private office. Brickner opened the door, locked it after us. Latimer sat there behind a huge desk. There was an elk's head above an open fire—some golf sticks, a tennis racquet and fishing tackle in the corner. The chairs were large and soft. Latimer enjoyed his private office.

Brickner said: "We might as well convince Williams we're on the level. We'll take him to Harvey Price."

Latimer came out of his chair. "The private entrance, Brickner?" There was a question in his voice, a question which he answered himself with, "Yes—it must be the private entrance."

"Private or public suits me," I told them.

Latimer went straight to a closed door, opened it with a key from his pocket and when Brickner had entered, I followed. Latimer snapped on a light. It was a small, closet-like room. There was a high step-ladder against the wall. Plainly I could see the trap door above. A heavy steel ring was screwed in the bottom of it. Latimer put the ladder beneath the trap, climbed up the ladder. I smiled at Brickner when he waved me to precede him. Without a word he went first.

Latimer reached the top of the ladder, stretched up and pushed at the trap. It opened as if on hinges. Narrow stairs slipped down close to the top of the ladder. We all three climbed up and the trap closed. Another door and we were in a dim hall.

I said to Latimer: "What was the iron ring for?"

He turned and looked at me in the dimness. "The ring?" he said slowly. "Oh—I use that for hanging things, Mr. Williams—just hanging things."

I guess I got the point and suppose I should have shuddered, but I didn't. I felt something in my stomach, though. Well—maybe I was wrong—maybe Latimer should have shuddered.

Something was in the wind. Either these men intended to kill me and didn't want anyone else in on the know, or they intended to let me take Harvey Price away so I would be gone, too—and Dorothy Price could do her great unmasking—ruin her own reputation and make her father the laughing stock of the community.

I didn't tip my hand that I knew about the girl. I just followed the two men until Latimer threw open two great doors. Then he switched on lights. I saw a big room lit as dimly as the hall.

I won't go into the decorations except to say that they were gaudy—and expensive. Life-size statues stood in majestic dignity along the walls. If this was the main gambling-room there was nothing to show it. A few ordinary tables, long ones that might be used for private dinner parties, and chairs placed about the entire room, their backs against the walls.

Latimer pointed to a small door far down at the end, which stood out fairly well in a brighter dimness.

"Harvey Price," he said. "Two rooms and a bath. Come and talk with him."

Certainly these boys did everything to kill suspicion. Latimer was walking beside me when Brickner told him I preferred to follow. So we went down along that right wall, Latimer and Brickner just ahead of me. I didn't pull a gun but I kept my eyes peeled back over my shoulder. I was wondering if a gunshot could be heard below, and if some lad lay by a hole in a distant corner of the room and would pop me off.

But Brickner and Latimer should know their way about. If the guy missed or didn't make the shot fatal, I'd get both of them. Maybe they didn't know.

I said: "If someone takes a shot at me, why you'll both—both—"

And it happened. A statue shot out of one of those niches. Understand, I didn't see it—just saw the shadow of it—saw the shadow of a knife—a knife that seemed to be twenty feet long sweeping across the wall and ceiling.

No, I DIDN'T see the man who jumped until I had dropped to one knee, reached, grabbed, drawn and fired. Just my right arm crossed to prevent that lunging steel which was no longer a shadow from burying itself a foot in my chest. My left hand flashed up and the story was ended. His face was almost against my gun when I closed my finger and blasted away. Blasted was right. The face was gone then—gone forever.

Only a body hurtled backward from the terrific impact of my forty-four—only the dull thud of that headless killer—and the jingle of steel upon wood.

A dead silence as heavy feet stopped

walking. A deader silence as both those men turned around. Terror crept over Latimer's face as he looked at that faceless body. He gasped and sputtered. Peculiarly, Brickner took it better. There was fear in his face, I guess. Why wouldn't there be? But he said: "What—who was it?"

Latimer gasped: "Largo—Harry Largo."

And the D.A. said: "Williams—Williams—why did you do that?"

"I just wanted to do a lady a favor," I told him, and before they could get over the shock, "Come on—Harvey Price."

You see, it wasn't so much overcaution that saved my life. It was that they were overanxious. I hadn't seen the man posing as a statue, and might not have seen him in a brighter light. The dimness helped me. His jumping body became a gigantic monster against that light.

They led me to Harvey Price without any more argument. They didn't say much, either. Latimer whispered to the D.A. and I think he said: "It doesn't matter much—she wouldn't break her word—not her."

We opened the door at the end, entered a narrow hall, opened another door and there he was. Yes, I knew him from his uncle's description. It was Harvey Price all right, and he was sprawled all over a desk writing notes or something. There were bottles and glasses on the table.

Brickner said: "Harry, this is Mr. Williams. He has been sent by your uncle to take you away. You may do as you wish. Mr. Williams, you may use the side exit. Harvey will show it to you. Is that all?"

What a hopeless three words they were. The town was in a pretty mess when you killed a friend of the D.A. and he wanted to know if that was all.

"That is all," I echoed. "I feel very humble and must apologize for such a messy job. As a rule—but I hope to show you more of my work—rather neater—and more finesse. I pride myself on it."

The D.A. tried twice to talk. Finally he said: "God in Heaven, Mr. Williams! You don't think I had anything to do with that attack on you?"

"Of course not—don't be silly." I closed the door as the two of them left.

I faced Harvey Price. Harvey Priceless it should have been, for when Harvey, the pasty-faced sot, heard I had come from his uncle he put up one terrible squawk. But I wasn't going to slap Harvey down, at least not yet. I'd listen to his indignant speeches for a while—try to find some clue in Harvey's whiskey-soaked brains, if any, to the truth of Dorothy Price's appearance at the Casino.

Harvey Price's father didn't have much money. He was running around on what his uncle gave him—and he had begun to consider it hush money—hush for his own activities. His description? Well, he was thirty and he was drunk. He stood up behind the desk—leaned on it and pointed a finger at me.

"So you're the guy, eh? The guy my father told me my Uncle Duncan was getting to make me behave. They must have laughed themselves sick—Brickner and Latimer."

"They're laughing yet," I told him. "I put on a funny show for them outside. So you got into trouble and your cousin

Dorothy is dancing here tonight to get you out of it—those I.O.U.s."

He took a laugh at that—sneered. "Those I.O.Us.—she gave them her word—and she tore them up."

My hands were itching to stretch out and grab him by the throat. But I hung onto myself. There was something too fishy about the whole thing. Common sense was hitting me. Dorothy Price was a bright girl—why would she betray her father because of this alcoholic lug's reputation?

Oh, I know people have gone a long way to save someone's reputation. But you can't save something a guy hasn't got. You just looked at this soak and knew that nothing except murder would surprise his best friend.

"So she's dancing for you—disgracing herself and her father for you. For your I.O.U.s."

"Me? My I.O.U.s? What the hell do I care about scraps of paper? I wouldn't pay the dirty so-and-so's anyway. What could they do? What can they do?" And with a drunken wave of his hand that almost spilled him, "Hell—she's dancing tonight to save her father from disgrace. I just told her where her father stood and she could do as she damn pleased. I'm no blackmailer—not me. I could have shaken Uncle Duncan down for hundreds, thousands, but me, I didn't want his dirty money. He's a big shot—a puritan—a church man—a leading citizen—and secretly meeting the most notorious woman in town."

"What do you mean?" I got a jolt.

"Pictures of him—of her—together,

meeting at a little cabin back in the mountains—a little ranch he bought cheap—and had no use for. Yeah—no decent use for. I got one of the pictures myself. I kept it to mail to him."

I gave him a drink and took one myself. Maybe he didn't need it—but I did. I tried to keep my voice indifferent as I said: "So Brickner let Dorothy tear up those pictures on her promise to dance. Where did you fit?"

"Where did I fit? Dorothy's a bright girl. She wanted to be sure she had all the pictures—every negative—to destroy in her dressing-room tonight. She wanted to know that they were not fakes—so—so—" He leaned for the bottle again. His fish-like eyes blinked and for a moment the film broke. He finished the drink, stiffened slightly and said: "So I told her."

"How did you know?" I fired it at him quickly.

"I'm a bright boy," he said. "That's how I know." He shook his head viciously, glared at me. "I've talked too much—but you won't repeat it—yet."

He was a big man, perhaps six feet three, and weighed over two hundred pounds. His hands were large and hard, though his face was flabby. I guess he was still a strong man. A strong body can stand a lot of abuse up to thirty.

Harvey Price walked pretty well as he came around the desk toward me. His knuckled right fist was closed and raised. His fish-like eyes swam in drunken rage. He had come half out of his talking drunk and was belligerent. Yes—he was a big man. But me—I know my job. Guns or fists, it's all the same to me.

I watched him carefully. Some drunks suddenly take on great strength. Then he let the blow fly. It was a roundhouse, all right, smack for my chin. I didn't paste him. I just pulled my head back and let it go by. He spun like a whirling dervish and crashed to the floor.

"Quit your kidding, Harvey." I helped him to his feet. "Why clown around?"

He was dazed and stupid and still belligerent in a sullen sort of way, but he wouldn't talk. He started drinking again and got off on another subject and finally put his hand in his left trouser pocket, felt around a bit and, pulling out a bunch of bills, tossed them on the table.

"For you, boy," he said. "Forget what I said. I was talking through my hat."

"Sure, sure." I stared at those bills—three or four hundred dollars. Then I got my bright idea. I thought I could sober him up. I said: "You're stubborn and I'm stubborn—that's the way to be. I want you to tell me something. You won't. To hell with it, you say. To hell with it, I say. Do you know Harry? Headless Harry Largo?"

"Headless Largo? All afraid of Harry, but not me. I ain't afraid of anyone—not Harry."

"And why should you be?" I opened the door. "Come on out in the main room. I want to show you the joke I played on Harry."

He was leery about it but he let me take his arm and lead him out the door and down toward the light. At sight of the body Harvey Price staggered all right. But he wasn't drunk any more. I think he went cold sober—just like that. His words were thick—but not entirely from liquor.

"That—that—what's that?" he choked.

"Harry Largo," I told him. "He was a stubborn guy like you and me. I asked him a question and he didn't answer it—so I shot his head off." And grabbing his arm, "Come on, Harvey—how could you assure Dorothy Price that she had all the negatives?"

And the words came out of his mouth slow and distinct and without a moment's hesitation. He said: "Because I took the pictures."

He put his hand inside his jacket pocket, pulled out a small picture, postcard size. "The most notorious woman in town," he said. "God, what a death!"

I was looking at a girl and a man. The man was handing her something. I recognized Duncan Price all right, but not the girl at first—nor what the man was handing her.

When I lifted a magnifying glass from the desk and looked at the picture through it I saw that he was handing her money. And then I saw her face. Oh—I guessed it, and you guessed it, although I tried to pretend I didn't. "The most notorious woman in town." The Flame—Florence Drummond—the Girl with the Criminal Mind.

After I got over that one, I said: "Some mess." I looked straight at him. "Hell, man, your uncle would have given you more money than these birds did. Why didn't you come to me? I'd have fixed the payoff without your uncle knowing."

"But I want him to know." Harvey was on his feet again, the fish-like look in his eyes. "He caused me to come here. I had the pictures in my pocket. I went straight to him. I never asked for a cent. He said I was rotten—a disgrace to his name. And hell—hell—well, if he wanted a real disgrace to his name, I'd give him one that would make the name of Harvey Price forgotten in town. That's why I laughed at the I.O.U.s—those pictures were worth plenty."

"And Dorothy has torn up all the pictures?"

He looked up at the clock. "She must have. She went out on the floor once masked. She gave her word to go on the second time at two o'clock unmasked. Sometime between those two periods the pictures would be given to her to destroy. She swore on oath to go through with it. She wouldn't break her word. Not Dorothy—the little fool."

"You'd break yours, I suppose," I couldn't help saying.

"In a second, with those crooks."

I didn't sneer. After all, he was right of course. We're all built different. I made my name good with crooks, murderers and cops by never breaking my word to any of them. But just the same, he was right.

No—I DIDN'T HAVE to drag Harvey Price from the Casino. I just had to help him a bit when we passed Headless Harry. I didn't joke then or threaten. I knew he had received big money to betray his own family. I knew he had sold out his uncle and his uncle's cause, and the innocent victim, Dorothy, but I led him to the side door—out onto the street and to his father's car. There was a great clock in a church steeple. It was exactly one a.m. Funny that. I had forgotten all about the hour—yet I was right on time.

I heard the gruff voice of Harvey's father, and back of it a woman's voice.

"My boy—my poor boy—and when we are so much in need."

I leaned in and said, as they drove away: "Not poor, madame. Your son's pockets are lined with gold."

Then I walked over to the shadow in the car across the street. It was my boy Jerry—a lad whom I picked up in the underworld when he was a kid. He'd been working for me ever since.

"Jerry," I said. "There will be a stage door—a rear entrance some place, where the help and entertainers must—"

"An alley," Jerry cut in. "Right across the street—about fifty feet down from where you came out. Waiters and cuties. Not much light, but some of them come out to smoke at the edge and they don't bother to dress much and—"

"And you keep your eye on that alley. A girl will come out soon. She'll either run straight to your car—or I'll toss her into your car. Anyway, she won't be tough to handle. Take her to our bungalow, and don't let her leave. I'll probably hop in the car and come with you, but in case I don't, hang on to her tight—understand?"

"Hell—is she tough?"

"No, but she's clever. Don't let her talk you out of leaving."

"Not me—not me. No woman could ever handle me."

"No." I was sarcastic. "But if this woman 'handles' you. I'll manhandle you,"

"Is that all?"

"Yeah—except if I don't come along I'll telephone to see if things broke right. Stay by the phone, and be polite to this girl."

"Rich, eh?"

"Money has nothing to do with it, Jerry."

"But she's rich."

I wasn't going to argue with him any longer.

"Yeah," I said, "she's rich."

I saw Jerry's stupid nod of understanding as if it were true that I take no pride in my work but think only of dough.

Then I turned and stepped back into the Casino.

CHAPTER 4

THE GIRL IN THE HOOD

THE FLAME WAS not around when I hit the bar, pulled up a chair and sat down. She had not been in the main dining-room. People were dancing now. I could see around the edge of the green sea—little groups of people were chewing the fat. All types of faces—some honest, open—some hard—and the "good" people of the town.

I heard a big man with a heavy ribbon attached to his eyeglasses, say: "Nonsense—sheer nonsense. I feel like a fool here."

Another man was shrugging his shoulders and saying to his companions: "If it's true, we should know it and see it. Duncan Price is a hard man. Understand, I'm saying nothing against his—"

And so on even to the jolly little stout citizen who put it pretty straight. "The young people wanted to come—it was

free—and you only know your town by seeing what's going on in it."

As for me, I waited until Latimer got mixing with the crowd, who either fell all over him or cut him dead. They'd eat his food, drink his wine, see his scandal—but damned if they'd speak to the man.

Then my moment came. It was where the curtains were drawn back, and I stepped from my seat and dragged the cigarette girl back into the folds with me so suddenly that she didn't even gasp.

"Quiet!" I steadied her tray, pushed a ten-spot into her hand, and spoke rapidly. "I want to get back and see the new star without anyone's knowing it."

"No—no—I can't," she half cried out.

"Listen, kid." I clapped a hand over her mouth and held her tightly. "I picked you out because you were young and your face isn't hard. This dump will close in a day or two. Get out of it. Here's a hundred bucks—two hundred—look—"

"I could go back home—I could—I can't—I can't."

I guess there was fear in her face, even if I couldn't see it. But I had the dough out, and my hand was off her mouth, and I was talking fast.

"That's two hundred and ten dollars, cash, you have now. That's for trying. There will be two hundred more for success. I just want to reach her dressing-room." And when she didn't speak, "Is there anyone guarding her?"

"No, but there's one man outside the door."

"Get the man away. Take me around there."

The girl said: "Her door's locked."

"I'll open that."

"The key's on the inside. She won't open it to anyone. I don't know—I don't understand—"

"You don't have to know—don't have to understand. I'll get in."

"They know you're here—they're afraid of you, I think. No—I—" She gripped the money suddenly, said: "Wait here in the crowd. I'll try."

I thought I was double-crossed. Time was passing. Then the girl made good in a surprising way. She was fully dressed in evening clothes when I saw her again. Evening wrap and all. She worked fast, too. In and out of hallways—she was all business now—just her voice trembled a bit.

"That's her dressing-room door there. They go onto the little stage through another door. There will be no one in front of her door for fifteen minutes. The girls use this hall to go in and out. There's the door to the alley and the street down those stairs."

"So she could open her door and walk right out."

"Yes—why not?"

"Don't you know who she is?"

"I can guess," the girl said.

"And she won't leave?"

The girl's lips curled. "Why should she leave? She's being paid plenty, I'll bet. Well—there's the door—give me the money."

I knelt quickly and looked in the keyhole. The end of the key showed plainly in the lock—an ordinary door key. I took a grin and straightening, gave the girl the money, put both hands on her

shoulders, said: "You wouldn't give me the double cross, would you, kid? And if you did—"

The girl gave me a shock. She stood on her toes suddenly and kissed me. Then she was gone—hurrying down those steps. I'm no mind reader, but I had a feeling that she was on her way back to the farm.

I GOT DOWN to business—unclipped the narrow leather set of tools from my inside pocket—drew out long, strong, steel tweezers and went to work.

There was no noise. The tweezers gripped the end of the key when I shoved them into the keyhole. A tight grip and I spun the key in the lock just as if it were on my side of the door. The girl was on her feet—the hood tightly about her head. But I wasn't watching her—I got the smell of burning film, spotted the ash in the big tray.

I wasn't there to argue with the girl, to break down resistance to that oath, to make her listen to how much better it was to save her father from disgrace than herself or his cause. I smiled as I walked over toward her, toward the hood she gripped with her little hands as she stared at me through the slits.

I said easily: "I'm Race Williams, Miss Price. I want to congratulate you on your noble spirit. Your father above you—your oath above your father. Why—"

And I did it. Just jumped her fast, slammed a hand across her mouth, twisted my coat about her body, and tucking her up under my arm made for the door. If she wanted to break her pretty legs going down those stairs, that was her business.

You see, after I whirled her through that door, I had only one arm and hand for her—and that was on her throat.

Jerry was certainly on the job. He swung the car up, tossed open the door and I threw her in. I started to climb in after her—stopped and slammed the car door. Without a word, Jerry slipped the car from the curb. And without another word, a car behind Jerry's also slipped from the curb. I recognized the driver. It was the big palooka who had first threatened to toss me from the Casino.

It was quick work and nice work on my part. There were two men in the front of that touring car. None in the back—until I stepped in, looked over the front seat and saw the Tommy gun. The play was easy enough to see. Someone had spotted me talking to Jerry—and the death car was there waiting to blast our car when I got in it. The only trouble was I got out of my car and into theirs too fast.

Charlie meant well. He had the machine gun in his hand, but the sudden jerk had made him awkward. I just leaned over, and said: "Put the Tommy gun down, Charlie—or I'll make a telescope out of your head."

"You—Williams—who sent you?"

"Headless Harry," I told him, and to the driver, "Straight ahead, brother. That car you're following doesn't need any trailer."

Jerry turned the corner.

What a night! Murderers, crooks, grafters, gamblers, politicians—why they were all like children at play. For once I had been sent down to a paradise of crime. There was no law—just the threat and the will to kill.

But Duncan Price and the friendly and honest police commissioner had tipped me off just what police precincts could be counted on, and I drove the boys to one of them, where the sergeant booked and held them on the charge of reckless driving. I didn't want them going back to break the sad news to Latimer that his star attraction had been kidnaped.

That was that. A quarter to two and my work was done. At least for that night. But I'd ring up Duncan Price. He might be worried about his girl not coming home. I found a drug store—started to call Duncan Price and gave Jerry a buzz instead. If he couldn't handle the girl himself, why I'd go over and give him some aid in bringing her home.

I called the number and got Jerry.

"Nice work, boy," I started—and stopped. And then exploded. I said: "What the hell do you mean, she stuck a gun in your side? Not that kid! But—but—"

I slammed down the receiver and looked at the clock on the wall. It was ten minutes of two. Dorothy Price was to go on at two o'clock. And Jerry had told me she had stuck a gun in his back, whacked him on the head with it—and when he came around, she was gone.

Lies? Maybe. But one thing was certain. The girl had vanished. Where? It seemed silly, but I believed it all right. The girl had gone back to the Casino to make good her word—do her dance—and unmask before crooks, murderers, and friends—yes, friends—the damned hypocrites.

Five seconds later I was offering a taxi

driver a five-dollar bill to make the Casino in nothing flat. And what's more—it looked like he'd do it.

I SWUNG FROM the cab and let go for the main door. I was too late. The girl was dancing but she still wore the hood. It was tough to get through the crowd. Even the bartender was there. Of course, I worked my way through—elbowing left and right and threatening anyone who threatened me. One guy who wanted to fight it out in the center of the mob never knew how he went down.

I got through, got right to the thick silken curtain before which Latimer was standing. His face was still white, and I noticed that he divided his attention between the hooded dancer and the man—yes, the little stocky, gray-haired man who stood there leaning on his cane. You couldn't mistake him. It was Duncan Price himself. He was staring straight at the girl. And me with just a single thought. Boy! Could that girl dance! She didn't appear worried now. She was whirling faster and faster as she tossed off bits of her clothing. This girl had talent, real talent. Certainly she was making good to Latimer and Brickner. She was giving them their money's worth.

The music crashed to the close—the girl came gracefully down to the edge of the steps—one foot behind her as she leaned forward and buried her face above a slender knee.

There was a hush. Then the fatal strike of a clock. Just two—just two o'clock.

Quiet? Why you could have heard a bead drop from a chorine's headdress. The girl grabbed off her hood and came to her feet.

There was a sort of choking intake of breath. That's right. The girl was not Dorothy Price—she was Florence Drummond—The Flame.

Too much is enough. Three times now she had turned up to knock me cold.

THE APPLAUSE CAME then. What's more, I led it. Then I stopped. The Flame faded to the back. A maid slipped a long coat over her white shoulders. Then she ran to the edge of the stage—jumped down onto the dance floor—sped across it between the tables—came straight to me, and grabbing me by the arm, pulled me over to a table close to Senator Rhoden's.

I didn't think. I couldn't think. Somehow, I knew The Flame had taken the girl's place. Somehow, I knew that Latimer was surprised. But good or bad—or why she did it, I didn't know.

Then I saw Malcom Brickner. He was standing by the senator's side. He was muttering "Not going, Senator? Not going?"

The senator turned very slowly. "I have wasted my entire evening. You brought me here with the promise of opening my eyes to the truth about—about something which seemed very mysterious. I was a fool to waste an evening. Just what was the purpose?"

"Why—" Malcom Brickner's face was a pleasant sight to me. Disappointment—confusion—yes, and rage, was there—buried beneath the surface fairly well. "Don't you understand, Senator? Why Mr. Duncan Price was here—was here a minute ago?"

The senator puffed up like a pouter pigeon, said: "Mr. Duncan Price brought me a letter and a document from the governor of our state. I have been named special prosecutor as of midnight—er—" he consulted his watch—"midnight last night. You seem surprised."

"I am." Malcom Brickner was telling the truth all right. "I had heard no such thing—had no idea of such a thing."

"Not even a rumor, eh?" If the senator meant to put levity into his words, it was not in his voice nor in his eyes. "Well— you will receive notice in the morning, no doubt. Good evening, sir. I shall call at your office at seven-thirty this morning. I am sure I can count on your cooperation in every way."

"Seven-thirty?" The D.A.'s eyes widened. "Why, it's past two o'clock now."

"Seven-thirty," the senator said again. "Because I have wasted the public's time and money tonight is no reason why I should sleep away more of it. I always begin work at seven-thirty. Good-night, sir."

And the senator was gone.

"You'd better fly back to town, Florence," I said. "I don't get the whole show. I'm rather thick that way. You did the girl a good turn. Do you know about the pictures?" And when the smile went off her face and she put her cigarette out on the tray, "Did Latimer or Brickner send you—or was it your own idea to shake the old boy down later? Did you know that they had pictures of Duncan Price and you?"

"Hell!" she flashed back at me. "So that's what the kid burned. I—" She bit at her lip, and I saw Brickner walking toward our table after seeing Senator Rhoden to the door. Then The Flame said: "Boy, do you grab up your women and treat them rough! Jerry was surprised when I stuck the gun into his side," And before I could answer, "Hello, Malcom. Sit down."

So I had tossed Jerry a wildcat instead of a helpless child!

Malcom Brickner leaned on the table. "What the hell did you do, Florence? By God, I'll—"

"Easy, Malcom." She jerked her head toward me, lit another cigarette and blew smoke in Brickner's face. "Race Williams grabbed off your prize act. Her hood and costume were left behind. It was too late to hear you and Latimer cry about it—so I did the dance to save your face."

BRICKNER TRIED TO hold himself in. He was young—he was strong—or he would have had a stroke. He killed me—cut my body up in little pieces and chucked my heart in my face—all in one single look. Then he spoke to The Flame.

"I'm sorry, Florence. I'll need a good friend now. No one knows better than you that they are trying to frame me." And turning to me, "Come, Williams, I'd like to talk to you in the bar. All hell will break loose tonight." He placed his arm about The Flame and said in a low voice: "I can always trust you, Florence."

She put those great glims on him. Glims that had ruined many men. "You can always trust me, Malcom," she said. "Always."

As for me, as I followed Malcom Brickner to the bar—well, somehow I thought that both of them had lied.

At the bar, he said to me: "I don't imagine, Mr. Williams, that you would shoot me to death before all these people—and I don't imagine you would permit yourself to be jockeyed into any unfavorable situation here tonight. I am no longer the district attorney. The morning editions will carry that word. So—from twelve on last night my responsibility ended. If all hell breaks loose now, I cannot be blamed for it. I would like you to call up Mr. Duncan Price. I would like you to tell him that without my stern hand, my stern orders, our fair city will be a shambles before dawn. Tell him he must bring to me all the evidence he has collected. Yes, The Flame told me he had it."

"I'll tell him when I see him."

"No, Mr. Williams, that will not help Duncan Price and his daughter, or prevent sudden death in the city, for the truth is that you will never see him again. Oh, you can leave here when you please. But you will never reach your residence alive. It's not one man—but hundreds."

He was suave again now. And what's more, he wasn't talking through his hat. He was a desperate man. He hadn't expected the thing to come on him so soon. And neither had I. Duncan Price had worked it wrong, of course. Duncan Price knew Brickner's men, Latimer's hoodlums, and every one of them should have been covered—arrested—as soon as Brickner was superseded by Senator Rhoden. Now—Brickner was right. He could turn hell loose in the city and not be blamed for it. He might perhaps win praise, for preserving order with an iron hand for so long.

But maybe my advice would still cover that—and there was the phone at the end of the bar.

Brickner handed it to me and said: "You probably know his private number. I don't telephone him often."

The idea was not a bad one as Brickner saw it. A death car—maybe two. Even I could not avoid that with my popguns against machine guns. But Brickner was a fool. I could have called the police commissioner and gotten a police escort of a dozen motorcycles. Still, that wasn't my way. What a laugh it would give the boys back in New York if they ever heard that Race Williams had asked for a police escort because he was threatened by a lousy two-timing, murdering ex-servant of the people!

I picked up the phone and called my own number. I said: "Listen, Jerry. Bring the car down and plant it smack in front of the Casino, even if you have to clean the fenders off every high-priced jalopy there. Oh, and Jerry, toss a couple of Tommy guns in the back. Hell—of course I'll handle both of them. Set them up on the racks on both doors."

That was all. I turned to Brickner. "Well," I said, "that about covers the whole show. Now if Miss Drummond—" I turned back. The Flame was gone, and so was Alfred Latimer.

A funny feeling that. I had intended to take The Flame with me, as a hostage to my safety, I told myself, but that wasn't true. Somehow I was thinking of her safety. Why? I don't know why. It was a long time since I had held The Flame in my arms. I took a laugh. I had held her only an hour or so ago, even if I didn't mean to.

THE CASINO WAS thinning out now and I thinned with the crowd. I stood there in the doorway until Jerry came. I want to tell you, some chauffeurs had heart disease about their highly polished expensive paint-jobs when Jerry took his U-turn and jammed the car right in front of the door.

I spotted the gunman as I moved toward the car. I watched him move, too. He was as well dressed or better than anyone in the crowd. Carried himself with the easy assurance of a gentleman that knew his way about. Only his eyes gave him away. Under the bright lights he watched me and the car, and his easy gait when he started to walk was timed nicely for us to reach the door of the car together. Horns were tooting—lights were blinking on and off—cops were clearing the streets. It would be simple to get a man there on the street, and move on unsuspected.

We reached the car almost together. His hand went up under his coat and his shifty eyes for a single second covered his get-away. In that second I let him have it. Simple? Of course it was simple. Simple for me, not for him.

I stuck my left elbow into his side. His head came down, and as he started to double up, I half swung my body so others wouldn't see, and chopped a right to his chin.

A cop was two feet from me when the would-be killer went down. Even the cop didn't see the play.

I said in my best Park Avenue manner, "Disgusting how some people can't handle their liquor," and climbed into the car.

Jerry said: "What was that talk about tossing machine guns into the car and racking them up on the door? I didn't have any machine guns."

"You didn't have, Jerry?" I leaned back against the cushion. "Well, Jerry, it's not what you have in life that counts, but what people think you have."

And I was right—for we drove straight to Duncan Price's house without even a car coming near us. Jerry was trying to explain things during the ride.

"Hell, boss," he said, "you never told me you were going to toss a rattler into the car. I tell you, she didn't give me any pretty smile. I didn't fall for her—and I wasn't just dumb. I took the car up a couple of blocks—treated her real tough. I told her if she made even a peep I'd pull to the curb, tie her up like a sack of potatoes and open her head with a wrench—did it through the side of my mouth like a tough gangster, too."

"Then what?" I didn't tell Jerry the truth. "The poor little girl half fainted and sent you into a drug store for some smelling salts?"

Jerry gasped. "Not that dame. I never seen nor heard them come any tougher. When I half turned to look at her she pasted my face around with the nose of a gun and said: 'Pull to the curb before I blast all your teeth down your throat!' "

But I wasn't listening to Jerry now. Things were certainly mixed up. And The Flame—she wasn't so bad. I don't mean about her being a criminal. That part I could understand—with her. But she had given the kid a break on the dancing angle. Certainly if Brickner and Latimer knew the truth it would be curtains. And where was Dorothy Price? Home, of course. Or was she? Was The Flame playing a deeper game than any of us thought?

Cars now—inconspicuous cars—on side streets—parked in driveways of private homes. I nodded at that. They were there on my orders. I pulled up before Duncan Price's door—hopped from the car and went straight up the steps.

CHAPTER 5

A PROMISE TO DANCE

Two DETECTIVES CAME out of the darkness, dropped back, and the door opened. The commissioner of police was there, half a dozen or more first-grade detectives, several lieutenants, three or four captains, a couple of inspectors.

The commissioner took me aside.

I said: "Well, the Governor came clean. Harvey Price is out of the dump. The expected scandal, whatever it was, didn't go through. Duncan Price has a list of these crooks. You know where they are going to be tonight."

"He knows."

"It's the same thing," I snapped in. "But what you don't know is why they have been gathered together at these different points each night lately. You were waiting for the Governor to act. Then you were to strike—hit all these hide-outs simultane-ously. Why do you think all these crooks are congregated together in different parts of the city?"

"I never understood that. Duncan Price doesn't understand that."

"They are congregated together for the same reason you have your men ready. You want to crash down on them—lock them up. Price has collected the evidence. We'll indict half the Grand Jury, impanel a new one, and the big clean-up will be over almost before it starts. That's our end. Now look at Brickner's end of it. They expected the Governor would act just as much as you did. So they have their hoodlums ready. Tonight they'll wreck the city, then scatter. Don't you get the point? The dirty newspaper that has backed Brickner and his crooked crowd already has the headlines in print. *Brickner Tossed Out By Politics.* And all about the hard-driving criminals hating Brickner—Brickner feared by all the criminals. His heavy hand is stayed by the Governor's act, and the criminals held in check by his hand alone break loose. Don't you see? They'll even say the crooks of the city helped get Brickner out. You've got to strike first. Why haven't you?"

The commissioner bit his lip. "Something has gone wrong. Something has happened to Duncan Price. He's not the same. He—he—God, man, he acts as if he hasn't got the evidence—hasn't got the list of places at which the crooks were ordered to congregate."

"What do you mean, Price hasn't got that list? And if he hasn't, he's got evidence enough to roast Brickner, Latimer and a dozen or more of the leaders."

"I don't know," the commissioner said helplessly. "I was just an ordinary citizen elected to a job that I have found difficult. You go and see Duncan Price—if he'll let you in the room." He pointed to the study door.

I rapped. No answer. The commissioner said: "He won't let anyone in."

I gave the door a pound that rattled the cement ceiling.

I got an answer. It was: "Stay out!"

"This is Race Williams, Mr. Price," and he muttered something about not caring. I gave it to him straight. "I want in. If you don't unlock the door—why, I'll bring the door in with me."

The door opened and I went in. I knew what a fiery dominating man he was, so I got my talk in first.

"What's all this rot?" I started and stopped dead. He simply locked the door behind me and went slowly back to the chair by the fire. He looked ten years older since I had seen him an hour before.

He said simply: "Latimer just called a couple of minutes ago. They're going to kill my child."

"She's not home, then—" I started and stopped. It sounded stupid. It was stupid. Plain facts, those. A plain truth, too. Before they were only playing at being tough because no one opposed them. They didn't know how to take me. Desperation is a terrible thing in the mind of a man who has gone to murder. I opened my mouth to tell him they wouldn't dare. But I didn't tell him that. I didn't lie to him. I said: "What do they want? The raid called off?"

"No—no—they don't know about that.

They want all the evidence I have against them. What do you—what shall I do?"

I BIT MY lip. I didn't like it. But there was only one answer. I gave it to him, though it hurt.

"The city didn't hire me. You hired me to protect your best interests. You brought me in at the end so that bodily harm or disgrace would not strike your family. It's for you to say."

He hesitated a long moment and then produced a paper from his pocket and handed it to me.

"That's the list of the street corners they are waiting on. The garages they are ready to leave—to strike the city with terror— kill and maim innocent people. I have been well informed. It is to be a night of terror. Take it—talk to the commissioner. Advise him—then come back to me. It may take their minds off my daughter."

I went out into the hall and talked to the commissioner. He didn't quite understand it as I gave it to him. I hate murderers. I hate criminals—I hate woman-killers. I did talk to his men— those he had there—and there were a dozen or more of them.

I said: "Boys, you're the police of this city—hired to protect the citizens. Most of you want to do it. You've been afraid. Not physically afraid, but afraid of your jobs—afraid of the future of your wives and families, or those dependent on you. It must have burned inside your guts to have to take the guff from rats you knew were killers—see them walk the streets sneering at you after you had made an arrest. To find yourself demoted—walk-

CARROLL JOHN DALY

ing beats in the outskirts until Commissioner Walker here came in.

"Tonight you have orders to get certain men. The list is here in my hand. These men are armed and awaiting orders to go out and terrorize the entire town. They have always had first crack at you. Tonight you have first crack at them. This city has been robbed plenty. It can't afford the cost of lengthy trials. To convict a man it costs thousands of dollars—to bury him, five bucks. There's no fooling tonight. Either dead cops or dead murderers. The commissioner stands behind you. Senator Rhoden stands behind him and the governor of the state stands behind the senator. I want to see you all decorated for bravery under fire—not have your wives receive medals. So that's how it is. All hell is to break loose in the city tonight. Go out and break it."

An inspector had taken my list—was calling out addresses—giving sharp, quick orders that men were answering eagerly. They were good men. They had had their first real order in years that they understood.

I went back into the library, said to Price: "Give me Alfred Latimer's private phone number—you know, the one you had tapped."

"He's changed it—I can't get it now. The law's against wire-tapping and—"

The Headquarters operator had the number for me in about five seconds. I called it.

After a moment, Latimer whispered: "Who is it?"

I said: "It's your Uncle Race—Headless Harry's friend."

That didn't throw him. He chuckled back into the phone. Things were different now.

HE SAID: "COME on down and kid us some more, boy. That was a funny one about Harry, but I got a little joke that will split your sides. Price's daughter promised to dance for us—she's going to keep her promise. She'll do the dance on the end of a rope. I'll leave her body for Duncan Price. Something to remember us by if he ever catches up with us. Like the idea?"

I bit my lip, said: "Let me have it all."

"All—it's simple. We just found out from Florence Drummond that Duncan Price wants to spring a big surprise. That he has kept his evidence against me and Brickner and The Flame private from everyone. Bring that evidence down and you can have his daughter."

I said: "Hold the wire." I set down the hand-piece and went over to Duncan Price. He looked like a broken man when I first told him what they wanted. But he pepped up considerably when I told him: "I don't believe in high-minded stuff, Mr. Price. I don't believe you have the right to sacrifice your daughter. I'll take a chance but not commit suicide."

"But—there's Latimer. He killed a young girl—killed her horribly—a girl I had planted in his office—tortured her to get information from her. I have her ante-mortem statement—and facts she gathered. I didn't bring it before the Grand Jury because the Grand Jury was packed by the district attorney. Must he go unpunished and—"

I swallowed the curse and said: "She

was a paid detective like me—like the others you hired, and they died. That won't save your daughter."

He went to his safe and opened it. He had affidavits, statements, plenty of stuff. I took it all in a brief-case. It filled it.

Duncan Price said, but his voice was weak and his words not convincing: "Could I betray my fellow citizens? Besides, Latimer may be bluffing."

"Latimer's a rat. A cornered rat." I gave him the truth. "He's got nothing left but vengeance. There has never been a state law passed that can fry a man more than once. He'll kill your daughter."

After all, I was telling him what he wanted to hear. He paid me. I didn't go into his picture business with The Flame, his own actions with "the most notorious woman in town." But I did say: "There is no evidence about Miss Florence Drummond. How come?"

"There is no evidence against her," he snapped.

"There was, and you destroyed it. Is that correct?"

"You must be—" he paused. "I tell you there was no evidence against that woman."

So the old bird liked The Flame! Well—who didn't? Of course she had given him a line about herself. Friendless in the hands of criminals—and he had told her how he was going to wipe them out—about the evidence, perhaps. Maybe she had taken him over. She had taken many men over—big men—influential men—fooled top politicians, top criminals, but looking at the stocky little figure of Duncan Price it was hard to believe he had been taken in.

I said: "How did you get such complete evidence as this?"

"Detectives—"

"They must have been damn good." I eyed him.

"They were paid enough—or rather the one was. I'll admit I got far more than I expected."

The phone was buzzing. He looked at it helplessly, said: "Mr. Williams, I place everything in your hands."

"Fine," I nodded, and picked up the hand phone, said: "O.K., Latimer, I'm coming down. You know me and should know my record over the years. Every other crook does. You produce the girl and you get the evidence. Don't try to play smart."

And after listening to him for a minute I took a laugh when I answered his question if I'd be armed, I said: "Don't kid me. I'll be sporting two rods—and itching to use them. You've got the cards—at least one card in the little lady. Play your hand straight and you have no worries. Half-hour hell! I'll be there in ten minutes."

CHAPTER 6

THE TRAP IS SPRUNG

JERRY DROVE HARD and I made it in nine. Far distant I heard the scream of a siren and the noise of guns. The boys must have started out pretty fast. We ran straight to the Casino, dashed over one block, turned the corner where the yawning doors of a dark garage faced us and drove right down past the now darkened main door to the Casino.

That is, Jerry went straight down the street. I slipped open the door fifty feet before we reached the entrance—caught my balance as my moving feet hit the sidewalk and kept running right up to the husky brute of a lad who was waiting there.

I don't know if he was there to bring me straight to Latimer or if he was supposed to shoot me down. Anyway, my mad jump from that car pounded me against his chest before he knew just what was happening.

I said: "I'm Race Williams—got a date with Latimer."

Then, in the moonlight, I recognized him as one of the bad boys who had sidled down the bar toward me—and sidled back again. He had a face on him that was built to frighten children but he didn't take me for any child. He looked rather confused.

"You remember me," I went on. "If Latimer thinks he's got anything up his sleeve and this is a trap for me, it's your own hard luck—not mine."

"Why?" was the best he could do.

"Because," I told him, "when the trap is sprung you'll be right ahead of me—and I'll make a hole in your back big enough to climb in and hide."

"There might be a hundred people here for all you know, and the first one might kill you."

"O.K., buddy. There will be only ninety-nine when you're dead. But if you want to die for dear old Latimer, it's up to you."

He grew suddenly mild, gentle and friendly. "You've got things wrong, Race," he said. "I don't know the play, but Latimer is expecting you—glad to see you and— God, what's *that?*"

And "that" was the screeching of tires—the swing of a car around the corner and the flash and roar of riot and machine guns smack into the darkened garage I had just passed.

"It sounds," I said, "like the police. And it sounds like they're having target practice."

"Gawd," he said. Then "Gawd" again as he ran his sleeve across his wet forehead. "Jake Waters and some of the boys were in a car right in that garage entrance."

" 'Were' is correct," I told him. "Now take me to Latimer."

He moved quickly to the door. His hands were fumbling for the lock. His voice shook when he spoke. "The police— they never did anything like that before."

"They're learning." I put it like a college professor. "A dead cop is never any good to anyone—least of all himself. That goes for crooks, too."

"I thought things were all right." He almost chewed his tongue off to get the words out.

"They are—but it depends on your point of view. The cops are shooting first tonight. We've had quite a laugh over it."

He mumbled something and let me into the Casino. Dark curtains a couple of feet from the door deadened all light from the street. I knew that after I passed through the curtains and saw in the dim light the green sea—the lights beyond—the bar in a dull glow—and straight ahead of me the little hall which led to that private office.

"Latimer's in there," Scare-face said. "Go ahead."

"Where's your manners?" I gave it to him lightly. "Age before beauty. Lead the way."

"Hell," he straightened. "I'm only twenty-four."

I didn't try and make him happy. "Something tells me you're going to die sooner than I am—lead the way."

"Latimer's all right—he's all right—anyway, why play me? I'm only the guy who takes orders."

"You won't take orders any more if things are wrong. You'll be too dead."

THE STACCATO NOTES of machine guns came faintly to us from behind the heavy doors of the Casino. I stuck my hand in my pocket. He licked at dry lips.

"Latimer is in his office right there." He pointed to the door. "Everything is aboveboard. You're to walk in and make a deal. That's all I know."

"The girl?"

There was genuine surprise in his face. "What girl?"

I took a long look at him. He was no actor—except a bad actor. I nodded at that. I guess Brickner and Latimer had decided to deal the boys out on the girl question—and I didn't blame them.

"O.K.," I nodded. "You're just a young man who got in with bad company." I leaned forward quickly and snapped the gun from under his arm, "Here's your break. Take a powder on the gang. The racket has blown!"

He looked at me a long time. There was not much hesitation on his face when he said: "Thanks for the tip, buddy." And as the distant ping of shots came, he shud-

dered—pointed to the door—turned and was gone.

I walked straight up to the door—knocked. Latimer's voice was clear and friendly. "Williams," he called out. "Open the door and come right in."

I stiffened. Latimer had not been cheerful or pleasant before. A trap? Of course I expected one. I couldn't see the sense in it, yet I suspected one. He knew my word would be good. He knew I knew his wouldn't. He hated my guts for the way he had been handled by me. Vengeance—the lust to kill—all might be there. Maybe he valued my death above all things except one thing—and that one thing was his life.

I turned the knob and opened the door a crack. "That's it, Williams," he said. "I'm in a hurry to get this over. I'm sitting behind my desk unarmed. You can see the whole room. So open the door slowly and be sure I'm willing to do things your way."

I asked: "You're alone?"

Latimer's voice was clean-cut, honest. Too honest. "I'm alone—just open the door slowly."

"Slowly"—that was my cue. I pushed the door open about ten inches—raised my right foot—let it go against hard wood. Did that door smack back against the wall and tear itself off at the hinges? It did not. It went half-way, stopped. Then swung back as I stepped into the room.

Latimer sat behind a desk unarmed. His face did more tricks than Ferdinand the Bull's. His eyes were bulging and I followed his glance. The man lay where the door crashed back. He had a gun in one hand and a blackjack in the other.

Nice idea—to crack me down as I came in—or just shoot me in the back. Simply a murderer's choice.

"So you'd put the finger on me, Latimer? Smart guy, eh?"

Latimer never batted an eye. I didn't like the way he looked. I didn't like the bulging eyes—the steadiness of them—nor the way he leaned on the desk. But what I didn't like most was the different picture I got of that private office. The ventilating system, perhaps? A ventilating system that was not there before. Little open squares like windows along the wall. I didn't see the faces. I didn't see the guns. But I felt the eyes—or, more truthfully—I felt the guns that those eyes followed. Latimer had read too many books. Four men were covering me with guns.

A little melodramatic, you think. Well, melodrama or no, lead kills just the same.

I never let on I had spotted those little squares in the wall. I just figured I could take no position that would protect me from them. Latimer tried to attract my attention. He spoke quickly.

"Just a bodyguard, Williams. You're rather a rough fellow. Now—let me have the evidence, and I'll see that Dorothy Price goes home."

For a moment my stomach dropped. Was the girl dead? There is just one rule of the underworld. If kidnaping with physical harm to the victim means a death sentence, it's better and much easier to handle a body than a live girl. A body will never come out of the grave and identify you in court.

I was covered from several good angles. I could turn, of course, and put a bullet in one square, or even two, where the men watched. But I couldn't get them all before one got me. It was a rather elaborate trap, but then traps are educational. A lad always learns something when he walks into one. And I'm a lad who admits he has plenty to learn.

I walked easily toward Latimer and the desk he sat behind. I watched his hands as they stayed on it. Other eyes watched me.

Latimer said: "You've got the evidence with you? Your word is good."

"Yeah—" I nodded. "I've got the evidence for you when I get the girl. Here—" I shot my hand toward my jacket pocket—let that hand ride up again, and when it came loose, I pounded a forty-four caliber revolver against his chest. I didn't just hold it there and talk tough, my finger tightly on the trigger. Not me. I pulled back the trigger—held the gun so—my thumb holding the hammer so that if my thumb slipped off—or I even let go of it—or even lost the power to hold it—Latimer took lead—just above the upper part of his chest.

I said in explanation: "I want the girl."

He let me have it then, a gloat in his eyes while he talked. It faded slightly as I listened quietly. He told me about the lads covering me—five of them—and how he wanted that evidence laid on his desk—my gun dropped—or he'd order them to shoot from different angles.

"Five?" I raised my eyebrows. "Five? You fooled me there. I only counted four ventilators." Then I gave Latimer a little talk on guns—their use and their misuse.

I said: "This gun I hold close to your chest has the hammer pulled well back. I don't have to press the trigger. A good shot from one of your men—a fatal shot—and down goes the hammer and up will go Latimer. It's an awkward position in which to hold a gun. My thumb is already growing numb. Order those men to close their ventilators—fifteen seconds."

He jerked erect, said: "You die, too."

"Are you interested in my death or yours? Come on. Ten seconds are gone."

"You'll—" he stared straight at me—then almost shouted: "Hold those shots—close those ventilators!"

Latimer was a very wise man. I wasn't bluffing. I meant business. There was a single brilliant light in that room. It was in the ceiling directly over Latimer's head. I had figured nicely. I'd plug Latimer, then shoot out the light. The big boss dead, the boys would join Scare-face in a powder.

My eyes drifted slightly as each ventilator snapped closed. I nodded as I discovered the fifth one.

Latimer said: "All right—the evidence for the girl."

I said: "The girl for the evidence."

"Brickner doesn't like that. If we're picked up later, she can appear against us."

"She won't. I promise you that. Where is she?"

"There's no warrant for me yet." He straightened in his chair. "If I'm going to die, I'll die for something real—not this evidence Duncan Price has collected. I'll make his girl scream for mercy. I'll take a knife and—"

"Headless Harry was good with a knife," I reminded him.

Latimer went into the foulest description of the abuse and torture that the girl would suffer if he didn't get the evidence first. "Duncan Price has evidence what happened to others, Williams. Wait until he sees his own girl's dead body. By God, he'll have hard work to identify her. He wants it rough—you want it rough. Well—it'll be rough enough to suit either of you. And what's more, you can't threaten me. Malcom Brickner's got her, you know. She'll ring up her father if things go wrong between you and me, Race, and he can hear her—"

Blood went up into my head—dazed my vision. But I spoke very softly. He should have been warned. I don't often speak softly. I said: "Maybe you'll tell me where she is?"

"Me?" he laughed. "You could hack me to pieces and I wouldn't tell. I'll see her—"

I swung my gun down and up and he pounced out of that chair as if someone had put a lever under his chin. He didn't get a chance to be surprised. I stepped around the desk and beat him to his knees. Then I side-swiped my gun across his face.

"God! God! What are you going to do to me?"

He looked up as he cried out.

"Cut you to pieces. It's your idea." He tried to duck the downward sweep of the gun as I turned it in my hand. Like his kind, Latimer blew too soon. Killer and torturer of women! I was mad all right when I struck him. He was ready to talk before I was ready to listen. But I held back my flaying gun. After all, it was business with me.

He was there on his knees, this killer and torturer of women. He was screaming, too—pleading and begging: "Don't hit me again—you'll kill me and then you'll learn nothing."

He was right.

I said: "Where is she?"

He didn't hesitate. He said: "Brickner's got her up in his bungalow with the Drummond girl."

"Can you get hold of her?"

He paused for a long time.

Then he said: "No—but I can tell you how."

After that, he talked—talked long and well.

"Look," he said, "the town wants a fall guy. They won't be satisfied with all these little crooks. They won't even be satisfied with me. They'll want Brickner. Look, Williams, I'll tell you how to find her—how to get her safely from Brickner—everything for your promise—your word—that Duncan Price will let me slip out of the state. Understand, I'll turn Brickner in—I'll—can you do it? Will you do it?"

I gave it a thought, then talked to him straight. "Latimer," I said, "you could have had the evidence for the girl. But you deliver Brickner and Duncan Price's daughter—and you've got a free ticket. And there is no man anywhere I'd rather see roast."

He didn't hesitate now. He said: "I'll do it."

I didn't have to ask him things after that. He went into great detail. He sketched out the house for me. The room Brickner had the girl in—the best way

to enter it. He finished with, "You're a lone worker, Williams—and aren't we all? Brickner left me here tonight—and things went wrong. I'm thinking of only one person now—myself. Did you bring that evidence against me?"

I said: "I have the evidence against you—against Brickner. I didn't bring it in here with me. I'm not a fool. But I can lay my hands on it. Are you alone here now?"

He said that he was. The phone rang then, and I let him lift it and talk. His chest sort of fell. He dropped the instrument back in its cradle, turned to me, said: "Duncan Price, with your advice, has beaten us to it. The police seem to be themselves again." And with a resigned sort of shrug, "Forty-two of the boys have been killed—shot down before they had a chance to move."

"Only forty-two?" Maybe I wasn't over-sympathetic.

CHAPTER 7

THE CALL TO KILL

WE STOOD IN front of the Casino. I lit a butt and finally flagged Jerry who was driving around and around with the evidence, brought him in with me. We all went back into Latimer's office and the sweat was running down his forehead. Little cubes of perspiration—ice cubes, I'll lay ten to one. His eyes bulged further and his hands began to rub together when I took the stack of papers Jerry had given me and laid them on the table there before him.

I let him look at the affidavits and different statements including the ante-mortem statement of the dead girl. Then I showed him another and his eyes fairly popped. It was a brutal statement—about as bad as I had ever read about any man—or even heard, for that matter. I remembered it pretty well.

Part of it went like this—

"Latimer took me into his office with Stevens and he tried to make Stevens talk. But Stevens wouldn't tell where he got his information and Latimer told him to walk across the room and open the door that led to the trap and the room above. I was standing there and saw it all. Stevens opened that door—a ladder that must have been leaning against it crashed to the floor—then I saw the woman. Not all of her body—but just part of it. Later I saw all of it. She had been alive when that ladder hit the floor. But now she was dead. A heavy bit of wire was twisted about her neck. I could swear I heard her neck crack—but Stevens was right there looking into the small closet-like room. He must have seen her face—seen her die. It was his bride of one year. I never saw Stevens again—alive or dead."

The statement was signed *Johnny Weaver.*

"It's not Weaver's handwriting," Latimer gulped, and then, "Weaver couldn't have written it. He's dead—or—or"

I asked him: "Did you ever see Weaver's handwriting?" And when he shook his head mechanically, "The experts on the stand can attend to that. O.K. Throw it in the fire."

He looked at me twice—then tossed it in.

I went on; "You know my record for keeping my word. You can destroy all that evidence there. And you have my promise of no prosecution. I want to be sure that you are going to tell me the truth—and that nothing will happen to Dorothy Price."

"That's right—that's right." He wasn't waiting to examine those papers now. He was down on his knees throwing them into the fire, making them burn. It was hard for me to talk to him the way I did—but I wanted to impress upon him what a smart man I thought he was now—and later impress upon him what a smart man I was.

"You were smart, Latimer," I told him. "That was some trick in getting rid of one enemy and impressing others with the way he died."

"It wasn't bad."

He looked at me.

"Killed many that way?" I was smiling and itching to get my fingers on his throat.

"Oh—I guess nearly a—" He stopped, looked at Jerry, realized there would be a witness, and finished: "Maybe—who knows?"

ALL MURDERERS ARE proud of their work. Latimer was proud of his. He said: "Since we've nothing left in writing we can look at it the way Weaver might have imagined it."

He crossed the room then and opened the door.

The trap with the steel ring in it was far above.

"There is no door jamb," he told me. "That folding ladder there leans against the wall—supported by the door. The door opens and the ladder falls. Now, if someone were sitting on top of that ladder, bound hand and foot, and his neck attached to that steel ring by a wire, why it would be a surprise to the man on the ladder, and also to the one who opened the door. It would also have a good moral effect on the door-opener—if it happened to a friend of his who had double-crossed me."

"That's clever, damn clever, but you'd have to hide the wire away well, or some-one—"

Latimer cut in with a proud little laugh.

"It might be a piece of wire like that one running from the wall plug to the lamp—which could be replaced at anytime."

"Smart—very smart." I patted him on the back, and though my voice was pleasant enough, I'd have patted him harder if I had had a knife in my hand. "Now, Latimer, the evidence is gone. You have my promise. I want you to tell me how to reach that bungalow and save the girl—a sure way."

"I can only tell you the best way to try—after that you're on your own, Williams. Brickner's fast with his gun—desperate now."

I said: "Do the best you can. I can't ask for more. You see our lives depend upon it."

"Our lives?" Thick eyebrows went up. "You mean your life."

"No—our lives, Latimer. You and I are going to work together tonight. If I die, you die."

"Me? How?"

"On the ladder." I gave him a real grin now—at least my teeth showed. "Yes, you'll be sitting right on top of that ladder—inside the closet. Just your own cleverness. If I don't call Jerry here at a certain time—then he'll open the door. I hope that you didn't think I was simply going to trust to your childlike honesty?"

LATIMER FAIRLY SCREAMED. "No—no—you can't do that. I've done my part. Once the ladder is set against that door, you've got to be very careful how you open the door and put your foot in the crack. I tell you—no—no—" and he went wild—jumped straight at me—his huge hairy hands at the end of those long arms gripping for my throat.

Just gripping, understand. They never got there. I let my right fist come up hard then—catching him in mid-air—and bounced him back against the wall. He sat down slowly and stayed there.

"O.K., Jerry." I pointed to the lamp wire. "Let's do our stuff."

Latimer had been a careful man. Those golf clubs, tennis racquets and fishing tackle looked natural enough. He could bind a victim up, yet a search of his room would never disclose anything that might be used for the purpose of strangling or tying a man.

We had some trouble setting Latimer on top of that ladder, and twice we nearly hung him and dumped ourselves down on the floor. But he came around—saw I was determined, and assisted us all he could.

"It must be an awful death, waiting for someone to open the door," I told him.

"Now give it to me in detail if you want to live."

He didn't seem so frightened then as he described in more detail the house—how to reach it—the best method of approach from the back—where I would find a ladder—and exactly how the rooms were laid out—where the girl would be kept—and where Brickner would be—and he told me of the two men he had with him.

"It's our lives, now," he said very seriously. "Don't forget to call that boy of yours."

"You've told me everything?" I was serious, too. "Lead in my chest tonight will be just the same as if it entered yours."

"I have left out nothing," he said. "Just hurry—Brickner is a smart man, too."

"Right." I leaned over and grabbed off Jerry's necktie—then as I swung the ladder so it held against the wall I climbed quickly up, stuck my handkerchief in between his teeth, and twisted the necktie around his face. He choked or gasped or tried to speak. It didn't matter. I had heard enough. Time meant everything now. The bungalow was not far. I had to make it before Brickner telephoned Latimer, and not receiving an answer, suspected that something wrong was in the wind.

"What did you gag him for?" Jerry asked me. "He seemed scared to death then—seemed to want to say something, Why the gag?"

"Just a precaution. He might call for help—and what would you do? But I haven't the time to talk now. Wait for my call."

"If I don't hear from you, boss—do you really want me to open the door and let that wrapped-up bundle of grease string himself?"

"Of course not, Jerry," I said sternly. "If I don't call I'll be dead. I just want you to open the door to see if he's all right."

Jerry grinned.

"O.K.," he said. "You'll probably meet him in hell."

I was at the door with the key turned in the lock—had flung it open—turned back, when Jerry spoke. It jarred me a bit in the stomach and I wondered if my attitude toward life and death had—had possibly—

And then I read the truth in Jerry's eyes.

Sure—I can drop to a knee, draw, turn and shoot in one second—but this was split-second stuff. I saw Jerry's face and started to bend and spin when the gun roared and a bullet cut across my collar bone.

It would have gone smack into my spine if I hadn't started my drop. It wasn't that shot which sent me across the floor on my face—it was the blow on the head that followed it.

WHEN I CAME to I was dazed and my guns were gone. Jerry was flat on the floor and Brickner, the district attorney, was standing over me, a gun in his hand.

"Sit up!"

Malcom Brickner kicked me hard in the face a couple of times until I struggled up—sat against the wall. Jumbled thoughts were straightening out. My vision was clearing, but what I saw didn't give me any appetite.

Brickner with a gun in his hand—and

two men watching me. Two men with guns trained right on me. I should have gotten a thrill—a proud sort of thrill for the respect they paid me—but somehow I didn't.

These men were both holding Tommy guns. With my gun gone, I don't know what the hell they expected me to do about it.

Brickner raised his foot and kicked my head back hard against the wall. He said: "Williams, eh? The great Race Williams. Strutted about the damned place tonight because Senator Rhoden, the sheriff, the people—our best people—were here. Just a common gangster—that's what you were—with a chance to shoot up a place, threaten people who'd laugh at you another time—because you knew we couldn't do anything."

I said: "There's no use in kicking me around, brother. I'm the only one who can save you. I wanted to make a deal for the girl."

"What deal? What sort of a deal— once Rhoden begins to work for himself and finds how the books were falsified— complete sets removed even from Police Headquarters? What deal—with politicians backsliding and turning state's witnesses?"

Ablaze with hate he went on.

"The Flame, Florence Drummond." He jerked a bound girl up from behind the desk and sat her in the chair. "Harry told me that she was once in love with you. Told me before he died."

"Not Headless Harry?" I said sarcastically. "You surely couldn't have believed him?"

"I did—but I didn't need to. The Flame told me herself. She's fooled me for weeks. Money—jewels—everything she's got." He laughed hoarsely. "God, what a fool that cold-blooded woman has made of men. I never got more than a warm little hand that she must have heated from a cigarette butt. She was keeping her body clean for a man—a man like me! The dirty little double-crosser. Yes—I accused her of once loving you—and she threw it back in my face. 'Why once?' was what she said. Tonight she admitted it all—admitted that she is working with you."

I was stunned into sudden speech. "That was a lie," I said.

"Race"—The Flame's voice was steady as ever—"why get mixed up in an undignified argument now? You underestimated our dear Malcom. He's only playing at being organized crime. He can't think of a way out—so he thinks only of vengeance. Yes—I gave him a line tonight so he'd be sure to trap you here."

"Trap me?" I said.

And The Flame smiled. It was that old, easy smile.

"We've been through a lot, Race. I never thought you'd be actually cornered by these mice—or undernourished rats, if you want to be kind. No business with them—no finesse. Just a riot of murder and greed—and now—nothing but vengeance."

"That's right," Brickner said. "The girl's right. I've got money. I've made arrangements to leave the country—made them over a year ago. I'm going to enjoy life— not sit and stew and break my health thinking of those who stayed behind alive—ones that should have been dead."

"Where"—I was trying to keep things going for a while—"where is Dorothy Price?"

Brickner shot out the words in a torrent of fury.

"Ask her. Ask The Flame. We thought you took her. She said she could produce her. Latimer had the Price house watched, so we know that she didn't go home."

Just one thing was hopeful about the situation. Malcom Brickner wanted to talk. And more crooks have talked themselves to death than have been betrayed in any other way. I tried to move my muscles. Not bad. I had some chance to make a fight of it if things broke right. But they couldn't.

There was no wire to a lamp socket to pull out and plunge the room in darkness. The light came from the dome above and the switch was by the door.

And hell—I was wrong about Malcom Brickner. He didn't want to talk any more. He wanted action.

He said: "I like to do things neat—and that's how they're going to be done. Personally, I don't think The Flame has a heart, or I'd let her watch you die, Race. But I think if a man once loved The Flame and—not that I ever did." And swinging suddenly, "We had your picture with Duncan Price. You sold out to Duncan Price, and you know how Latimer's enemies have died, and that's how you'll die. Do you know about that yet, Williams?"

"Give me a cigarette and tell me about it," I said easily.

Don't tell me it was luck. I never play

luck. I'm a guy who's simply ready and I was ready when Malcom Brickner strode across the room. He was saying: "Well—there's a ladder behind this door—and when Latimer wanted to know anything he—"

Malcom Brickner jerked open the door to the closet-like room. A ladder crashed to the floor. A twisted tied-up body dropped from above and spun in that open doorway. Yep—I heard it distinctly—the snapping of his neck. I saw it distinctly, too. I saw his eyes bulging with life—then they took on the filmy cover—the stony stare of death—as his neck went *Crack!*

Just like that.

Everyone in that room was thrown but me—that is, mentally thrown. Things strike people differently. Malcom Brickner, right at the closet entrance, stepped back. The two boys with the machine guns stepped forward.

It's always the same in life.

Those who see a killing in a car or on the street, run away from it. Those in the background who didn't get the same mental shock, run toward it.

That's why I say, "mentally thrown." No luck, understand. A break for me, perhaps, but only because I took advantage of it. I came to my feet. Two steps and one dive and I had the second machine gunner down and had cracked his head open with his own Tommy gun the minute he hit the floor.

I saw The Flame's eyes shine. I heard her say as she tossed herself from the chair to the floor: "Just like old times, Race."

And it was.

The first machine gunner got the idea in a vague way because he was playing a tattoo against the wall with his gun before he was fully turned around. In fact, he never fully turned around and faced me. He was too dead for that.

I'm fast, but I'm no artillery unit. Malcom Brickner had his gun out—had it free—had a shot. A shot is right. He fired once, and that was all. I squeezed lead—and the show was over. Nothing dramatic. No hero holding his chest and giving a last message to his surviving countrymen.

He was dead five times before he hit the floor.

SIRENS SCREAMED. DOORS were battered down and I said to The Flame, "Florence." I got out my knife and cut those ropes in seconds. As Jerry climbed to his feet, "Florence, get out the back way. That's the police. Not yet." I grabbed her arm. "I've got to find Dorothy Price."

She grabbed both my shoulders and although one hurt I didn't wince. She said: "The kid is all right, Race. She's up in a dressing-room three doors down from hers. I planned that she wouldn't dance before you did—and beat you to it—and damn near didn't go on myself because of your thick-headedness."

"Florence"—I was very serious—"we were pretty close once, but that criminal mind of yours is no joke. You double-crossed Brickner and Latimer—double-crossed me, maybe—then got mixed up with Price in some way. Don't explain—you never could clear that."

"I even double-crossed myself," she said as feet were heard pounding across the outer rooms, and men were shouting. "I telephoned for the police—in case you couldn't make good."

That was that.

The cops were there then.

An inspector said: "So you practice what you preach, sir." He was a lad I had given orders to up at Duncan Price's home. "Just what happened?" And suddenly, "Ah—a catch. The most notorious woman in town. I want you, Miss—" and he clutched The Flame by the arm. "Malcom Brickner's woman."

The Flame's eyes fired for a moment. Then softened. She drew her arm sharply away, raised her right hand and smacked the inspector across the face with her open palm. The inspector's face whitened—red marks stood out plainly on it.

The Flame said: "Good-night. I shall not speak to your wife about the last time we met." And damn it, she started to walk from the room. The inspector hesitated, then reached out a hand.

"Oh—" She turned, avoided his hand. "I see I forgot something." With that she threw both arms about my neck—kissed me full upon the lips and walked out of the joint. And damn it, not a person raised a hand to stop her.

The inspector said awkwardly: "Just what happened?"

"Hell," I said, "are you blind? Latimer hung himself. The others felt so bad they shot themselves."

"Tied up like that—tied himself up like that?" The inspector was trying to place just which way the swinging head faced.

"He was a smart man," I said, and then, "Take it up with Duncan Price. Come on, Jerry."

They let us go, all right. Outside that room I stalled off a couple of more friendly officers. I wanted to take Dorothy home alone. I found her. She was crouched there in a dressing-room—ran into a closet after I had pounded the door in.

"Oh, Mr. Williams," she said when I explained I was from her father. "I thought it was that awful woman back again. She said if I answered or let anyone in she'd come back and kill me."

"What awful woman?"

"She came to my dressing-room long before I was to go on the second time. She just said to me, 'Are you determined to keep that fool word of yours?' and when I said that I was, she just opened her bag—took out a gun and jammed it into my side. 'Get going, kid,' she said. 'Your father wouldn't be found dead with me—even in a picture—and maybe I feel the same way about him.'"

I didn't say anything. I simply took the girl home.

DUNCAN PRICE EXPLAINED it to me in a three-hour talk. It all boiled down to this. He had hired The Flame over six months before to gather evidence for him in the city. She set one condition—when the time came to strike, I should be called in.

I was flabbergasted, all right—nearly forgot to ask for my check—nearly but not quite.

So, after all, I had been working for The Flame without knowing it. I don't know if Duncan Price gave me secret notice, or whether The Flame had fixed it that way, but I was on the plane with her when she flew back to New York.

I said: "I'm sorry, Florence. I should have known you were straight as a die—that the old days are over—that the criminal mind is gone."

"And that I dreamed you in?"

"Sure," I grinned. "You dreamed me in—but you did a remarkably fine piece of work in collecting all that written evidence—"

"I dreamed that too."

She smiled.

"Dreamed it?"

"Yes—how would I get guys to sign all that stuff? I made it up so that Duncan Price would believe it—and get the Governor to interfere. At the end I wanted you. You don't have to have evidence against dead men. One can always count on you, Race. I called. You came. You killed."

The White-Headed Corpse

CHAPTER 1

THE GAL IN THE ERMINE WRAP

Sure, I was living in a high-class, or at least high-priced, Park Avenue house. I had the money and I liked it. But the dough was going fast. It was about three o'clock in the morning and I had gone around the corner, a few blocks down, for some of Joe's beans. The beans and coffee set me back fifteen cents, and you couldn't get better at any price. That's the difference between the rich and the poor. If the rich pay enough for food they think it's good—when the poor pay fifteen cents it's got to be good.

The underpaid, all-night doorman at my Park Avenue front was sleeping behind a potted plant. I made my way over the thick rug, and knowing that the elevators wouldn't be manned this time of night, at least not more than one, decided on the automatic lifts.

One of the larger elevator doors suddenly opened. The man holding the door said: "I'll take you up, Mr. Williams. I'm the new assistant to the superintendent."

He explained his absence of cap and uniform and his plain blue suit. Sure, he explained that. But he explained a lot more before I stepped into the elevator. His right hand was in his jacket pocket, and the jacket pocket bulged. I didn't need any fortune-teller to tell me what that hand held.

He was talking as I got into the elevator—a threatening snarl to his voice as he shot that jacket pocket forward. But the snarl left his voice when I slipped slightly to one side, knocked his jacket away a bit with my elbow so that the gun in it pointed past my left side and toward a huge but not overly expensive vase behind the door.

"Kindergarten stuff," I said. My right hand jammed my gun so far into his stomach that he gasped for breath. "Come on"—I looked at his swarthy, greasy face—"have you a last message for the little girl you loved in the sunny vine-yard far across the great Atlantic?"

His dark skin turned white. Perspiration broke out on his forehead. His knees gave slightly. His speech was different now, and the snarl had become a drool. He was blabbering rather than talking.

"Before God, Mr. Williams—don't kill me—don't kill me!"

I stretched back a hand and threw the elevator door closed.

"Why not?" I jammed the gun harder. "Why not?"

"I didn't intend to kill you, just to bring you a message. A certain party said to lay off him or he'd kill you. He means it, Mr. Williams. He kills without thinking.

Don't take any case against him. Don't try to find out who he is—no matter how much you are offered."

"Yeah." I twisted his wrist up, brought it out of his pocket, and a small-caliber automatic fell to the floor. "Who is he? When does he kill me? Where do I find him?"

"He—you—" His body was bending in agony now as I kept twisting his arm. "I don't know, Mr. Williams. I only know what he told me. You're to be paid to find him. He'll kill you as soon as you take the case. God"—he was on his knees now—"I was only to take his message to you."

"His name?" I demanded.

"Ira Lent." The man nearly screamed the words as I got ready to snap his wrist. And when I released my grasp, "Thanks, Mr. Williams, thanks. He only told me to tell you that he'll find you and kill you."

I ordered: "Take the car up to the four-teenth floor—my apartment. Come on." And when he grabbed the switch and the car shot upward, "So I've been paid to kill Ira Lent?"

"Yes, haven't you?" The car jerked to a stop on the fourteenth. "I'll tell him I missed you—then you can get out of town."

I opened the door, stepped from the car, and holding the door open looked back at him. "Tell this Ira Lent that I'll wait right here for him."

He watched the forty-four in my hand, said: "You're not going to—to kill me?"

"Nonsense." I leaned in and patted him on the head. "You've brought me good news. You're a sweet little messenger of cheer. No, I haven't forgotten the gun on the floor. If you want to use it to take a shot at me you're welcome. And, brother—"

"What?" He was stunned more than surprised.

"Don't ever stand behind Ira Lent."

"No—don't stand behind him—why?"

"A number of slugs might go through him and hit you. Slam the door and get going."

Why didn't I knock his ears back? Why didn't I turn him over to the police? Simple. Someone was bringing me money to find Ira Lent, and I wanted money. I could use it.

If this Ira Lent intended to kill me I couldn't think of anything nicer than being paid to see that he didn't. I have been paid often to protect a client's life, but for someone else to pay me to protect my own life— Well, that would be rather pleasant.

Of course I was bothered about the government job tomorrow night, or rather tonight since it was already early morning. The government doesn't pay much. But I never count my sheep before they jump the fence. Five minutes later I was in bed and sleeping like a baby—that is if a baby happens to keep a six-gun under his pillow and his finger on the trigger.

I STUCK AROUND the apartment all next day and nothing happened. But I thought plenty about what the guy in the elevator had told me and the money he said I was to be paid. There was no question that I would be needing dough soon, and it looked as if I might have to give up this elevator apartment and go back to a walk-up if things didn't pick up. Don't ask me what I did with all the money I made. The answer is I spent it. And I spent it because I liked to spend it.

My boy Jerry, the lad I had picked up off the streets of the lower city and who knew more about crime at the age of ten than most so-called authorities know about it in a lifetime, was cleaning up the place and eyeing me, all ready to break into oratory. Jerry liked high living.

At length he said: "What was the matter with that blackmail case, boss?" And when I didn't answer, "Or the lad who thought his own brother planned his death? Yeah—I know he was a little goofy, but he had dough, and the courts still let him handle it."

"They didn't interest me, Jerry," I told him.

His eyes widened. He said: "There was money in it. Since when—"

"The blackmail case was a phony and the other was a dud. Besides, at the time I didn't know I'd be so short of money." Jerry shook his head sadly, said: "I wish I was young enough to go for this G-man business. But hell, boss, is there any heavy dough working for the government?"

"Jerry"—I got up, jerked my dressing gown around me and paced the rug—"there are times when we must serve our country. Besides, if they pay expenses you and the apartment will come under that head."

"Hell!" Jerry snapped his fingers. "You can make a life's work out of it, boss. I heard it over the radio the other night. Now that the Department of Justice has cleaned up the kidnapings and most of the income-tax stuff they are going to tackle this espionage business. Spy stuff, it means. And the lad on the air said the department knew of about a thousand separate espionage cases."

"Yeah—four men to a case. But there's one big ring in the country. One big guy who—" I paused as the doorbell rang.

"That," I said, "will be the government man Sergeant O'Rourke was to bring around. Ahead of his time—yes, by nearly an hour. Well, what are you gaping at? Let him in."

I tossed myself into a chair, lit a butt, and waited. It was only ten o'clock. A representative of the government had made an appointment for between ten-thirty and eleven. Sure it seemed odd, but then my business as private investigator was odd. Sergeant O'Rourke of the New York police had fixed our meeting. There was just a suggestion that special arrangements had been made to pay outside aid a "generous" compensation. But generous to me and generous to the government and even generous to the dictionary may be three separate and distinct words.

I crossed my legs and was ready to receive the representative of the United States government. Then my right hand shot up under my left armpit and I started to my feet.

Out in the hall Jerry was saying: "If you haven't an appointment you can't come in."

The woman's voice was as clear as a bell but not loud. I heard it plainly as the front door slammed. She was saying: "I wouldn't have to make a reservation to get a front table at the Parisien Club. For your benefit, boy, that's the most exclusive place in town. Don't stand in front of me. I want to see this Williams man—and what I want I get."

SHE WAS RIGHT this once anyway. A few seconds later a knockout in ermine cracked open the heavy drapes and walked into the living-room. I was back in the chair when she did her stuff. I wasn't showing any gun but I had my right hand in the large pocket of my dressing gown, and that right hand caressed a forty-four caliber revolver.

Silly, that, for a slip of a girl? Don't you believe it. I knew that a slug of lead in the stomach hurt just as much and killed you just as dead whether a brute of a man or a vision of feminine loveliness pressed the trigger.

She said imperially as she stood before me: "You're Williams, of course. I have seen your picture in the papers. Well—are you going to stand up? You'd better fire that boy. Yes, I said fire him before you lose a client—the best client you ever had." And suddenly, when I grinned up at that fine, almost daily front-page face, "On second thought you may keep him. I imagine he's built for your kind."

I waved a hand to a chair. "Take a load off your feet, sister," I said and watched the real color flood the fake red on her cheeks. I knew her, of course. Everybody who ever read a newspaper knew her, but I wasn't going to admit it.

I looked at Jerry who stood by the curtain and I caught the shadow of another figure behind him.

"Another one, Jerry?" I asked, and before he could answer, "Not as bad as the first, I hope."

"H—er, no," Jerry stammered.

"He's to wait outside," the girl cut in. Despite the high-hat attitude her voice was pleasant. I mean the tone of it.

"O.K., Jerry," I called. "Give him a seat out of earshot, and sit with him. Now, young lady."

"You know who I am, of course."

"No"—I shook my head very seriously—"I'm afraid I don't."

She was surprised—showed it plainly—said as if she expected me to roll off the chair: "I'm Freida Stanton."

"I am sorry, Miss Stanton. I have a remarkable memory for people I have met—yet—"

"We would hardly have met, Mr. Williams."

I ignored the sarcasm in her voice, shrugged my shoulders and let the politeness just ooze out. "Then you need a mind-reader, not a detective. Won't you sit down?"

"I prefer to stand." She was suddenly looking down at the second section of the evening paper that lay by my chair. My eyes followed her glance. I saw it before she spoke—was lifting the paper when she said: "My picture is there."

"So it is." I looked from the picture to her. "I remember you now, of course. One of the leaders of New York's younger café society."

She bit her lip. "*The* leader. And you may leave the *café* part off, Mr. Williams." She drew that ermine wrap tightly about her. "I have made a mistake. I am sorry I came."

"We have both made a mistake." I stretched my feet out now and leaned back in the chair. "I make it a rule never to remain seated while a lady is standing. You may remain standing if you wish."

I felt that would be the end of it. She'd blow a fuse and—and— She didn't. She just sat down on the edge of a chair, tossed back her head and laughed.

"Spoiled brat, eh? That's what you're really saying. And I like it. Only one person dared say that to me before. Yes, I like you, Race Williams. I liked you before meeting you because I knew you could take it. Now I like you personally because you won't take it. Shake—" And she grabbed my hand.

I tried to sit tight but curiosity got the best of me. "Who called you a spoiled brat? Who had the—the good taste?"

"I did." That nearly threw me. "I stand in front of the looking-glass every morning and give myself the dressing-down that everyone else is afraid to give me because I have money. Now I find someone with the nerve to slap me down. Someone who is to get real money out of me. I am not a snob, Mr.—Race. It is just that I don't respect the sort of people I meet because they don't respect me— just my money. I can stand squarely on my feet. I never need anyone."

"You need me tonight."

I WAS TAKING a new interest in the girl. When you looked back behind her brown eyes you found real character.

"No—no." She sat down on the arm of my chair, rested a crooked elbow easily on my shoulder. "You would be a little late in pointing out to me that my set is—well, useless to America. At least I have been. Now we have formed an organization. We're all going to do something for America. It was my idea—especially about spies and their activities."

After that she was real when she talked and the dark shadows beneath her clear brown eyes seemed to disappear, and I didn't dislike her so much. But to me it was all just baloney. Then she struck a note that held me.

"You see, Mr. Williams, we all must do something for our country. There was a talk on the radio about there being a thousand different spy rings, and that there is one big ring in the country headed by an unknown man. I got an interview with an influential government official—but you wouldn't be interested in that. He had to see me, of course, with the pull my money packed. And now—I have found someone who knows the name of the man who heads this spy ring."

Did I sit up straight! So would you. The government was going to talk to me about this very thing within an hour.

I guess she took my surprise for disbelief, and maybe she was right. She went on talking.

"I'll pay you what you ask to find him, apprehend him and—"

"His name?" I asked.

"You'll learn that when you agree to work for me."

"You simply want me to work for the best interests of the government and you'll pay?"

"Yes." She nodded.

"And there are no restrictions?"

"None."

"And the price you offer me?"

"I will pay you what you ask from time to time—and a retainer immediately, of course."

"How much?"

"Whatever you wish, within reason." And suddenly, "Listen, Mr. Williams. I have lots of money." Her eyes narrowed slightly. "Shall we say ten thousand dollars?"

"We'll say twenty-five hundred dollars," I told her and could have bitten my tongue out after I said it. I'm just a country lad, I guess.

"It's not the money," she chopped in. "You're different. I have been chased around by wealthy bachelors, men whose character would forbid all suggestion that they were interested in my money. But you—"

"I'm plenty interested in your money," I told her flatly. "Now what's the name of this man?"

She got up and went to the curtains. I rose and followed her—took her arm.

"This leader's name?"

"I don't know it." She turned up tired brown eyes that somehow seemed suddenly to sparkle. "The man I have with me will tell you."

"Why didn't he tell you?"

"I—I don't know. Unless he thinks I shouldn't have such knowledge."

"O.K.," I said. "Bring him in." I didn't add my thought that he had a hell of a lot of sense.

THE MAN HAD a young face—that is he looked about thirty-five except for his hair. That was pure white without a streak of gray in it. He was slim, almost delicate, and his eyes were clear blue. There were no wrinkles in his face, no bags of dissipation under his eyes.

Miss Stanton introduced him lightly. "You are to know him simply as Bert. His hair went white overnight, Mr. Williams."

"I have never believed that kind of story—before."

Bert took a grip on my hand that was like watered coffee, said: "I have always wanted to meet you, Mr. Williams. I am going to surprise you with what I have to say. It is true that my hair turned white overnight." I liked the way he spoke to the girl—a clear, determined sort of voice as he insisted that he talk with me alone.

At length Freida Stanton turned to me. "Bert wishes to speak to you alone. I'll stay with that little pal of yours and make friends…. How about some liquid refreshment, little man?" she finished as she passed through the curtains.

Alone with Bert I said: "Miss Stanton has made some remarkable statements. She's got money. You and I can use a little of it, eh?"

His blue eyes widened, then he smiled. "It may be true, Mr. Williams, that Freida and her friends are playing at being patriotic citizens. It is true, too, that for one I want to take advantage of this mood before she changes and decides to take care of a day nursery. But I don't want her money, and you don't want her money. I have heard too much about you to believe that. I do not intend to go into my past with you." And suddenly, "The man who heads this spy ring in America is named Ira Lent."

I took that on the chin, rode with the blow and, I hope without showing anything, said: "You can locate him?"

"I can arrange for him to locate me."

"Ah." I pepped up a bit. "You have, Mr.—er, Bert, a secret that has evaded the United States government. You haven't told Miss Stanton this man's name. Your whole plan may not be one of simple duty to your government, but perhaps a personal vengeance?"

His lips set very tightly. His eyes narrowed and the kindness went out of the blue. He said: "Yes—I hold a remarkable secret. I do not wish Freida to know his name. She thinks she is playing a game, but it would be a dangerous game if Ira Lent suspected her. So the less she knows the better for her. As to whether my motive is personal vengeance—that should concern only me—not you."

"Is Miss Stanton paying you for this information?"

"Mr. Williams, I am not a wealthy man. But if Freida Stanton offered me her entire fortune for my information I would not take one penny of it."

"Vengeance, then," I said to myself.

"As I said, my hair turned white overnight. To all purposes I died that night. A doctor pronounced me dead. Ira Lent stood beside me and called me the white-headed corpse. He is the only other living person who knows that the corpse came alive and was gone before he could bury it."

"He would see you?"

"He would want to see me more than any person in the world"—he paused— "but one other."

"He would want to kill you?"

"He would want to kill me. He would want to torture me."

"You go armed?"

"Armed?" He hesitated, and then, "No, I know nothing about guns."

"Hell, there's nothing to know. You point it at a man and press the trigger. You might find it handy some day."

"Yes, yes"—he seemed to be thinking—"but, Mr. Williams, in New York City I understand you need a permit—and a reason for carrying a gun."

"Gunmen have reasons but no permits." And then giving him good advice, "Miss Stanton knows enough people to get you a license. The reason? You travel with her to protect her jewelry."

"But me—a bodyguard—a—a—"

"Suit yourself," I told him.

He seemed a peculiar guy to have such a mission and such determination.

BUT IF ALL men were able to tackle their own problems of a violent kind where would I get my business? I looked at him now and it struck me he was afraid. But I have no illusions about fear. A lad who has fear and goes on just the same is a braver guy than I am.

I said: "You tell me what you want to tell me—what you should tell me. Don't make the mistake of telling me too little."

"Well"—he pulled at his rather sharp chin—"Ira Lent is the greatest danger to our country today. His machine stretches out over the nation." And seeing my bored look, "And, Mr. Williams, if he had the slightest suspicion that you were to be drawn into this case, that you were to hunt

him down, your life would be an endless fleeing from one hide-out to another until he had killed you."

"It would?" I jumped to my feet. "You let him know, then. By God, he won't have any trouble finding me. And what's more—" I stopped, looked at the eyes of the white-haired man, and said calmly, "Are you trying to find out if I have the guts for the job?"

"No, no— But I wanted you to know the truth. That you face certain death if he suspects."

"And you?"

"I am prepared. I was brought back from the dead for a purpose. My life already has—"

I cut in there. The occult and reincarnation are not up my alley. I tried: "Suppose we find him? Does that give us complete evidence against him?"

"No, Mr. Williams—no. If that were the case I could have used the government without involving myself too much."

I looked at the clock. The government man would be trotting in pretty soon. "Better let me have all of it," I said.

"Mr. Williams"—he was very serious now—"there is evidence against this Ira Lent—evidence so complete that it will hang him. That evidence is held by a woman who hates him—and blackmails him." He paused a moment. "Yes, and fears him. She is a very beautiful woman. A woman who can tear the soul out of a man—at least she has done that. You may condemn her. You may look on her as vicious. But you are not interested in prosecuting her or punishing her. You are interested in finding this man, capturing him, and preventing his future activities for all time. This woman will trust you. I know that. And this woman will—" He stopped suddenly. Freida Stanton's voice was raised down the hall. He said quickly: "This woman's name is Cora Hentz."

"And how do I find her?"

"You'll find her," he said as Freida came into the room. "I'd give my—yes, my life to know where she is. Ah, Freida."

Miss Stanton stood between the curtains and said: " 'Ah, Freida' is correct. We have a meeting, Bert. Mr. Williams can come along. It will make a hit with the crowd. What do you say, Race?" And when I said I'd trot over later, the girl went on, "A promise, then, Race. But now, a check or cash? I want assurance that you are working for me."

"You might make it cash," I said.

She swung open her bag and pulled out a wad of bills. "O.K., Race." And she did a little dance step. "There's twenty-five hundred dollars." She slapped it into my hand which opened to receive it. "That's half the retainer. Meet the crowd at my house tonight."

Bert put those mild blue eyes on me. "Maybe," he said, "the hardest part of your job will be handling Freida. It's the hardest part of mine. Come to her house later. There would be no suspicion of our meeting there." And leaning down and whispering, "I'll see you sooner than you think."

Freida grinned impishly at me. As she stood now with her brown eyes afire she was a cute trick. She gripped both my hands, spread her legs apart, pulled at my hands.

"Come on, Race, stand up for a lady." And when I came to my feet, "I'll bet you're the only real man I ever met."

And she did it. Dropped both my hands, threw her arms around my neck, and kissed me full on the lips. Cute! Sure she was cute. Pretty—hell, the girl was beautiful! Wealthy—she was worth millions. And me—well, I didn't know just what the hell to think as she let me go.

Then she was gone.

CHAPTER 2

THAT MAN AGAIN

I HAD TWO and a half grand in cash for a job that the government had already hinted about. At least, O'Rourke had. I sat back and killed a few butts. Maybe I did some thinking. Maybe I didn't.

Almost on the minute the government man and Sergeant O'Rourke, my best friend and worst admirer on the police force, walked into the apartment.

O'Rourke smiled, introduced Frank Paine, and said, not without sarcasm I thought: "Big stuff to you, boy, and some money—knowing your little peculiarities along that line. All right, Mr. Paine, you talk."

And Paine did. He was a fat little bespectacled man of about forty with a big brief-case under his arm. He wore rimless glasses and had a jolly sort of voice. He might easily be taken as a salesman for silks and linens. I happened to know that he had recently come from the hospital after shooting to death two of the most desperately wanted criminals in the Southwest.

"Williams, Race Williams. A pleasure indeed." He was all smiles. "Sometimes I wonder if it wasn't you who started off the G-men. Yes indeed, there was a time when the Department of Justice men weren't even allowed to carry a gun, and you were shooting down your daily dozen. At all events, I know we envied you. Now"—he laid his brief-case down on the table—"we're even shooting ahead of you. You let your conscience be your guide. We let the government be our protection. May I talk freely?"

"You can talk as you please with Williams," O'Rourke shot in.

"Well"—Paine sat down and throwing his left leg over his right, let it swing—"troubled times, Mr. Williams, and we'd like to rid ourselves of those troubles that may become catastrophes if war should come. We're using some outside help, and we're not waving flags or blowing trumpets to obtain the best. We're paying our way along. So I have a certain latitude in my offer to you. Let me paint you a picture that will surprise you in my—in your—in our America today."

And he did paint a picture. And it did surprise me. He talked quickly and chose his words well. He spoke of a thousand societies spreading propaganda and how the government, his department, could lay their hands on every member of these societies at the shortest possible notice. But he talked most interestingly when he came to the main subject—the single, large spy ring—headed by an American. He said then: "Mr. Williams, the Department of Justice, in case of an international disturbance is in a position to lay its hands upon a huge number of men who, it believes, are working secretly to cripple our national defense. We don't interfere with them, of course, for others, unknown to us, might take their place. Besides, knowing these foreign agents, we are in a position to furnish them with a certain amount of false information to startle the governments for which they are working.

"But we are faced with a great problem. We have one organized ring headed by, and undoubtedly manned by citizens of our own country—the scum of the criminal world, the backwash of the prohibition era. They are men who would cut their own mothers' throats for a few dollars. And the leader of this organization goes to worse than murder to obtain information about our national secrets to sell abroad. Torture, kidnaping—nothing is beyond him. He has the soul of a beast and the mind of a genius."

I said: "In all fairness to you, Mr. Paine, and to the government—I have already been approached to run this man down. It may surprise you to know that it comes from a private interest."

He shook his head. "It doesn't surprise me, Mr. Williams. Indeed, it is not entirely unexpected. And it does not change the reason for my visit. The Department of Justice is not personal. Our object is to capture and punish this leader and destroy the organization. In plain words, Mr. Williams, we are interested in the result, not in the method of obtaining that result. But we do want proof that we have the right man."

HERE WAS A plain-spoken gent and no mistake. I decided to give him a plain-spoken answer. "Mr. Paine," I said, "you did not seem surprised that I already had been approached on this same matter. But it is quite a coincidence that someone else comes to me at almost the same time about the same matter. In plain words, I don't believe in coincidence."

"Right," he said. "It is no coincidence, Mr. Williams. I admit I thought I'd be the first to speak to you—but it doesn't really matter."

"Why did you pick me out in the first place?" I asked.

O'Rourke juggled his cigar and spoke for the first time. "Hell, Race, you're known to be fearless—willing to take chances—glad to—"

"Baloney," I snapped O'Rourke off dead. "I felt something like that about it until Mr. Paine started to talk. Then"—I grinned through the side of my mouth—"it sort of struck me that perhaps the government has a man or two of its own who isn't afraid."

"Well put, well put, Mr. Williams," Paine stepped in. "I'll give you facts, not flattery. There is a person who knows this leader, a person who is beginning to know fear, a person who would not give an address. But she notified me that under certain circumstances she would deliver this spy-ring head, and the main circumstance was that all negotiations must come through you. Rather complimentary, Mr. Williams. In plain words she placed a confidence in you above the United States government."

The government man was about to go on easily when I rocked him.

"She left here half an hour ago."

"Good God, no!" He jerked erect. "She couldn't have. She wanted me to tip you to the arrangements."

And that thick head of mine got it—at least part of it. He wasn't talking about Freida Stanton at all. I gulped. He was talking about—about Cora Hentz. I sat back and pressed the button for Jerry, ordered drinks, took it easy. Maybe I smiled a bit cleverly—shrewdly.

O'Rourke said: "Hell, Race, don't get to using that head of yours. A guy gets action out of you not wisdom."

"That's right," Paine told me. "You won't have to pump a thing out of me." And to Jerry, "No water, thank you." He downed a shot of liquor. "I'm here to tell you everything. I know the name this vicious torturer and murderer goes under."

"Does it start with Ira?"

"Yes," his eyes opened wide, "and ends with Lent. She talked with me on the phone."

"Cora?" I said.

"By God, yes!" His mild gray eyes were hard on me now. "Yes, Cora Hentz. You've met her, then?" And when I shook my head, "You know where she is?"

"No," I told him. "But I'd give a lot to find her."

He took a big smile at that. "She'd give more to find you. Mr. Williams, you are well informed indeed. Sergeant O'Rourke was hardly wrong about what you can accomplish. You have hardly been slipped a hint when—" He paused, consulted the watch on his wrist. "Cora Hentz has spoken to me on the phone. She will call you here tonight."

I WAITED, DIDN'T say anything. Paine wet his lips—finally came out with it. "She will want assurance that no one is here with you. I thought—"

"You thought wrong." I put a finger against his chest. "My word has made my reputation among criminals. She'll want my word that no one else is here, and she'll get it. And it will be good."

"I won't argue the point, Mr. Williams. Your experience has been vast. But the government is a big organization. All of it is at your service."

"Thank you," I said. "If I need you I'll call you in."

"That's a promise, Mr. Williams. We don't get personal credit in the service. We don't want it." And with a whimsical curve to the left corner of his mouth, "At least we are not supposed to want it." He picked up his brief-case. "Sergeant O'Rourke and I will be moving along. This Hentz woman will be calling you within ten minutes."

"I wonder why"—I looked straight at him—"she got in touch with you at all. Why didn't she call me directly?"

Paine nodded. "I have thought of several answers to that. One is that she has proof that she has registered her willingness to betray this Ira Lent to the government. But I believe you will find her reason deeper than that. Be assured that I have been given full discretionary power in this case to act as I see fit. With foreign affairs as complicated as they are today let me say that not only the department, but the entire criminal end of the federal government right up to the Attorney General himself considers this man

the most important deterrent to our own security."

With that Paine was on his feet. He wrote quickly on a pad and tearing off the sheet of paper, handed it to me. "A telephone number and an address. Either will get me day or night. Come, O'Rourke, I understand Mr. Williams desires to work alone. I have felt the same impulse so often. It is a pleasure to have met you."

I took his hand then and walked with him to the door. Before he left, I said: "No shadows—no tails on me. That's a go?"

"A go, of course." He nodded pleasantly. "I'll tell the men I had ready. It was for your own—convenience, Mr. Williams. Tell me sometime why she called in the government first. Interesting case, interesting woman, Cora Hentz. They say she poisoned her first and second husbands in France. Good-night."

The door closed and he was gone. Also the telephone was ringing. Certainly he played things to the minute—to the second almost. I went back into the living-room and lifted the phone. The woman's voice was soft as velvet.

She said: "Race Williams—that's a relief. I want to see you now, at once. I'm Cora Hentz."

"What about an hour from now?" I asked.

Her voice wasn't like velvet. She snapped: "What about it? I said now." And her voice getting soft again, "Listen—now you're to come to me—no government men—no shadows. Can you be sure?"

"I can be sure they're dead if they follow me."

"Dead—that's right. You're the man for me." And she went into detail as to how I would contact her. Her voice was hard and cold when she finished.

"You should shake down the government for at least ten grand for this." And after a long pause, "The password is sure stuff. Remember, it's *Ira Lent*. I'll blow your head off if you don't follow my instructions."

"O.K., sweetheart," I finished, and hung up.

Hell, what a racket. The hidden genius—the hidden beast. The man nobody knew. Even I was beginning to suspect that he went under the name of Ira Lent.

I told Jerry to hold the fort and if the landlord came around for his usual drink and to talk about guys who didn't pay their rent on time, to slap the money I left him into his hand and to give him a seidel of his own muggy water from the rusty pipes.

CHAPTER 3

WOMAN OF ACTION

HARDLY FIVE MINUTES after O'Rourke had carted away the G-man I was down the street and looking for a cab. Before I found it I found Bert. He was standing there, a bent little figure under a too-large fedora and in a long coat.

"Mr. Williams." He tugged at my arm. "I sent Freida home. She's having a bit of a party tonight. All those people!" He put real expression into "all those people," and

I saw them staggering about the place as if he had spent an hour describing them.

"Yeah," I said. "Well, what's your beef?"

"My beef— Oh, I see. You're quite right, Mr. Williams. I am afraid. That is, in a physical sense I am afraid. Mentally—well, spiritually, I could die a hundred horrible deaths if I knew that he was dead."

"Why not tell me more?" I took him by the arm and walked him down the street. The arm I held shook.

"There is no more to tell—no more I wish to tell. I have a premonition of death. Understand, Mr. Williams, I think that you are the one man who can save me and punish him. Yet—he is so far above other men—any man or men that I—"

"I have found the girl, Cora Hentz," I said suddenly.

Sure, I wanted to surprise him. Sure, I wanted him to know I was on the job, but I didn't expect him to nearly faint on my arm. But that's what he just about did.

I half carried him for half a block before he came around. Then he said: "I knew it. I knew it. She's alive and well?"

"Alive and well. Does it mean anything to you?"

"Anything?" he stammered. "I loved her above anything in life then. I love her above anything in life now."

"That's the boy." I braced him up as I fingered a cruising cab. "How would you like to see her—tonight—now?"

He nearly went rubber-legged again before I got him into the cab. And did he make excuses as the taxi drove to the all-night drug store where I was to receive a call from Cora according to her instructions. He had to be at Freida Stanton's party in honor of their new endeavor. He didn't think Cora should see him quite yet. It might alarm her. He should have time to pull himself together.

I shook him up, said: "She loved you, too, didn't she?"

"Yes, yes." He didn't seem so sure of that, but he bobbed his head in the seat beside me.

And me, I was determined. I had guessed this little secret from what he had said before. If Cora were hard to handle then Bert would be my trump card.

"Where is she?" he finally stammered.

I shrugged my shoulders, almost had to threaten him to make him stay in the cab until my return. When we pulled to the curb, I pranced into the drug store which was buried there among blocks of walk-up apartments. I sat myself down on a stool and ordered a small coke from the proprietor. A man came in with a grouch and bought some aspirin. A colored boy from some elevator apartment knocked off a chocolate soda. Then a lad did a bit of whispering and walked out with some very fine-looking cough syrup. After that I was alone in the shop. Then a phone rang.

It was my call. I knew it. But I sat tight while the proprietor rubbed down the soda fountain, looked annoyed, and finally answered the phone.

He turned to me and said: "Are you Mr. Lent?"

"I'm not President Roosevelt," I cracked and walked into the phone booth. I knew her voice the minute I lifted the receiver.

Cora Hentz said: "No one followed you as far as I can make out. Why are you keeping the cab?"

"Listen, lady," I came right back, "why are you keeping me waiting? Tell me where I can see you. I'm a busy man."

The hardness went out of her voice at once. "That's right, Mr. Williams. That's right. I know it's hard to get cash out of the government, but—I'm across the street." And she gave me the number. "Apartment Four-C. The name card reads Mrs. H. Harrington Livermore and Miss Florence T. Livermore, but I live alone. Come right over."

I HUNG UP the receiver. Bright girl, Cora Hentz. No "Miss Jane Jones" or "Mrs. Frank Smith," but a real, high-sounding name. I bought a couple of packs of cigarettes, thanked the owner, and went out to Bert.

"We weren't followed, boy," I told him. "The apartment is across the street. You drive around the block, dismiss the cab, and come back and stand here by the drug store—a little on the dark side. If I open a window, wave a handkerchief—then come up."

"Yes, yes." And then with some hesitation, "I haven't—well, just a dollar with me. I—"

I slipped him a ten-spot, dismissed it with a wave of my hand. He sure was out for vengeance. Not the price of the cab on him, so he couldn't have shaken Freida Stanton down for a hell of a lot of dough. Not over two bucks, anyway.

The cab drove away. I walked over to the apartment, ducked to one side, and watched for a full minute. But I knew I hadn't been followed. Guys don't do that to me anymore. Then I went inside, pressed the bell of Four-C where the fancy names were, and pushed open the door when the latch from her button above snapped it open. I took two steps at a time to the fourth floor and found her door almost directly across from the mail-chute.

A minute later I walked in on Cora Hentz and saw her snap the chain in the bolt after she closed the door behind me.

She was a swell-looking dame—and "dame" was right and no mistake. Her hair was dark and her eyes were green and not only able to give a direct look but even a prolonged stare. If it is true that your past life is written on your face, then Cora had lived for a hundred years and lived hard. I don't mean the outside of her face, I mean the things that lay back of her eyes. She started off abruptly enough.

"Don't mind this dive, Williams. It's simply a tough living for a girl who's got real big dough socked away, and can sock more. Sit down, have a smoke, have a drink. I don't drink myself—at least for the last few months. God knows I need it, but I need my head more."

"You have been getting money from this Ira Lent?"

"That's right." She nodded. "I am shaking him down plenty." She lit my cigarette and when I refused the drink and stood before her, my legs far apart, she continued. "I'm not going to play any baby act with you. I worked with Lent. I was paid well. I stomached some pretty horrible stuff." She threw back her head and I saw

her long neck, her graceful white throat. "He went for me in a big way. He used to kiss my throat—"

I didn't like the dame at all. I said: "Why bring in the sex interest? My business is crime."

"Crime it is." She flipped ash on the rug. "I knew Lent. He trusted people just so long, then he killed them and took on someone else. The day came when he looked on my throat in a different way. Oh, he still wanted to caress it, but he wanted to caress it with a sharp knife. Sure, I saw it in his eyes at least a month before I left."

"Is Lent his real name?"

"No, but what does it matter? His real name isn't worth a bit more than the Lent is. Me—I knew him. I was collecting evidence that would hang him even before he trusted me so much." She leaned forward then. "Laugh this one off. I saw him practically boil a woman alive for information—information she didn't have. Now I've got evidence that will hang him. I won't feel safe until he's dead."

"Hung, eh?"

"Dead—I said *dead*. I don't care how he takes the dose."

I nodded and asked her: "Why didn't you deliver this evidence to the government? They'll fix him quick enough."

"Because," she said slowly, "I want Ira Lent dead before I furnish the information. You can have what the government will pay as soon as he's dead—as soon as you kill him."

I STRAIGHTENED ON the chair. There was no use to kid along with her. "Do you expect me to murder him?"

"Kill him," she snapped. "The evidence I'll furnish you will be grounds enough. What's more I'll furnish you with the list of people that work for him all over the country. One hundred and twenty leaders of men. Has there been an attempt on your life?"

"Just a minor attempt," I said, "which I didn't pay much attention to. I was warned last night not to try and find Ira Lent. Why?"

Green eyes widened. "I sent him word I'd use you if he tried to trap me again. It's the money, Williams, the money he has to send me. You see, I don't use crooks. I use an honest young lawyer. The dough comes in a sealed box and he thinks it's alimony. He's just a sap. Honest and starving until I threw him my business. He sends it to a sister in Kansas. She mails it back to me under the name I use here. I'm hitting Lent hard. He's afraid to push his search for me too much or I'll come down on some of his lieutenants as a warning. But he's got a brilliant brain. He'll kill me sooner or later unless he's too—too dead."

She was hard as nails, as cruel as women come, I guess. But she was business.

I said: "If the government put the finger on him through you, you'd be safe. Why bring me into it, and why bring me into it through the government?"

"Well—" She paused, not thinking what she'd say but if she'd say it at all. Finally she did speak. "The government wouldn't guarantee to kill him. I figured if I brought you in through the government I'd have registered an honesty of purpose."

"Miss Hentz," I said, "I can't guarantee to kill a man." And when her eyes glared and she broke into foul language about my "killing enough men," I added: "Suppose I find him, hold him prisoner, you produce the evidence that will hang him—"

"You've killed others," she flashed in. "Your business is death. He wouldn't be taken alive. He's not just a criminal and murderer. Look—I have information that will hang him. Do you think he'd just shoot me to death if he had the opportunity? He would not. He would make my death horrible. Hell, I stood beside him one night, the evidence, papers I had stolen from him, hidden in my dress, and I watched a man so horribly tortured that— yes, his hair turned completely white before he died." She paused a moment and then, "But Bert had the guts—yes, and he loved me."

It tossed me for a moment, but only for a moment, and I don't think it showed on my face. Then I said: "And you loved Bert?"

"Bert was a sap to die like that for a woman."

"Bert," I said, "didn't die." And when her green eyes shot wide, "I talked to him—tonight."

"No, no—" She clutched at both my arms. "That's not true. I was there. I saw him die. I felt his hand—his—his—" Her eyes narrowed. "I loved Bert—loved him madly."

Somehow I didn't believe that. Couldn't believe it of Cora Hentz. But I said: "Ira Lent thought him dead, too. Bert escaped. His hair turned white as you said. A living dead man, he walks again. A white-headed corpse."

"The white-headed corpse." She hardly breathed the words. "Yes—that's what Ira Lent called him when—when he died." Strong fingers burnt like thin hot bands into my arm. "I tell you he died."

I shook my head. "Do you want to see Bert"—and before she could get in on that—"now?"

"Now—now— He's here? In the neighborhood now?"

"Yes, in the neighborhood now. Do you still think he was a sap?" I walked toward the window.

"He was the bravest man I ever knew. He didn't know the meaning of fear. He died for me." And in a far-away sort of voice, "He'd die again."

"I think things have changed with Bert," I told her. "He knows the meaning of fear now, but he's the braver for it. He seeks vengeance on Ira Lent." I stood by the window, the curtain back, my handkerchief in my hand as I looked out into the night.

"Have him up. Have him up." She clutched at her breasts in a—well, I thought a theatrical way.

I WAVED THE handkerchief and peered into the darkness beside the all-night drug store. No figure was there. I turned, "Listen, Cora. Bert lost his nerve. He loves you very deeply yet—perhaps doubts your love for him. He'd die gladly in this room fighting to save your life. But perhaps it is best that he's gone. You don't love him."

"I do, I do," she said with emphasis but without enthusiasm. "But I felt his hand, his head—saw his eyes. God, I've seen

death enough. It seems impossible that he came to life again."

"He did. He never knew where you were and didn't try to locate you through fear that Ira Lent would find you through him. He evidently hasn't got the information that you have."

She snapped into life then, cursed. "You bet he hasn't." Her mouth twisted. "It doesn't seem like Bert to run away from anything—let alone me. I think you're kidding me that he's alive." Then seeing the seriousness of my face, "Well—I don't care how Lent dies. If you want to pass the killing off on Bert it suits me. I'm getting worried now. You'd be worried, too, if you knew Lent. He'd take real pleasure in seeing that you died the—the hard way. Understand, the hard way."

"I am here to get this Lent," I told her.

And stopping to think, and remembering one of the things Bert had told me, "Listen, Miss Hentz. I can't promise murder, but suppose I took Lent prisoner, held him for the government—there, don't smile—I'm in a position to do just that. Then would you produce the evidence that would hang him for the government? Understand, I'd bring you to him to prove that he would never be free to bother you."

"And there, Mr. Williams"—she pointed a long, steady finger at me—"we come to the reason why I informed the government agent but insisted on seeing you. This evidence I have against Lent would convict me myself of many crimes against the government. Get the point? I want absolute assurance from the government that they won't prosecute me."

Her tone softened as she came close to me. "You get me that assurance, get it in writing. Then capture or kill Lent, let me see him dead or alive, and I'll produce all the evidence the government needs against him and his men. Names, dates, specific crimes."

I walked toward the phone on her desk. She caught at my wrist.

"You can't get written evidence over a phone."

"But I have the government's assurance that anything I do—"

"It's got to be written. The evidence I will produce will link me up with—well, with things as bad as Lent."

"Not murder and torture?" I tried to he pleasant for after all she was the one to produce the stuff.

"Yes," she said, putting those green glims straight on me. "Murder and torture." And she didn't help the sick feeling in my stomach when she added, "He's smart this Lent, Race Williams. I'll dump five—yes, ten grand in your hands for working fast. I want action—I'll pay heavy sugar for action."

I was on my feet now. She was beautiful, or at least an exotic woman. I ducked the hands she stretched out to me and moved toward the door.

"We all want action, Miss Hentz," I said. "I'll see what I can do. My belief is that I can satisfy your request that you will not be prosecuted. But the money—keep it. I'm being paid by one client already."

"Good." She watched me at the door, held the chain ready in her hand. "I must live alone here, Mr. Williams. I have a gun and can shoot. But there are times when I must sleep. I don't think I acted too late. But I am not sure that I acted any too early."

"I am sorry I can't stay with you," I said.

She gripped my wrist then—her green eyes swam slightly. I didn't like her voice when she said: "I am sorry you can't either—or maybe you can."

I left her then and heard the chain click in its bolt. I don't know when I disliked a woman so much. But after all, she was my bread, and was in a fine position to butter that bread. So I didn't tell her that Bert today was not the Bert she knew. But after all, a guy coming back from the grave must have his limitations.

Downstairs the street was deserted. I thought of hailing a cab from the drug store, but the distance to Broadway wasn't great. I slow-footed it down the block, came back again on the other side. No Bert was in sight, no one was watching Cora Hentz' apartment. After that I hoofed it over to Broadway, flagged a cab and drove to Freida Stanton's house.

CHAPTER 4

THE WALKING DEAD MAN

FREIDA STANTON'S SHACK was a big place on Fifth Avenue that had belonged to her aunt. Sure Freida's father had dough. Her mother had dough. Her aunt had had dough and had left it all to Freida including this ranch-house on the Avenue.

CARROLL JOHN DALY

Her party was a success if liquoring and staggering and flag-waving is a success. American flags decorated the entire room. Things they called "snap mottoes" were going off like fire crackers. Boys and girls of all ages were standing on chairs and making speeches—and when I say all ages I mean from eighteen to sixty. This was the younger set and big money pulls your age down plenty.

They were wrangling over a name for their society. Anti-this and anti-that ran riot, but they hit on a name almost the minute I got into the main ballroom. The ballroom? Right. It was that kind of a house. They called themselves All American Youth, Incorporated. All American Youth, Intoxicated would have been better.

The first guy I spotted was Sergeant O'Rourke. He didn't look as if he were enthusiastic and certainly his wide, honest mouth that hung open looked surprised enough.

"You're a one-man spy ring, eh?" I accused him.

"Me—me?" He fairly blew the words out. "You're kidding, Race. I hate the stuff. But this Freida Stanton is a bright girl. Ringers get in on her parties, guests get robbed, or used to. I have three or four boys circulating around. Often I come up myself. She's no snob, my lad. She's given more to police benefits, widows and orphans of men who died on duty than any single— Good evening, Miss Freida."

Freida Stanton had grabbed both my hands, but she turned at once to O'Rourke. She seemed annoyed, then surprised, and finally tickled to death.

Boy, she went through his family in no time as if she were recalling the offspring of some crowned head in Europe. She knew the kids' grades, their marks even, the one that went to college, and the one about to be married. She dragged me off finally, leaving O'Rourke about as soft and gooey-looking as a Welsh rarebit.

In the little curtained room where the dance-floor riot was dimmed to the soft murmuring of a boiler factory she went to work on me—both hands on my shoulders, eyes eager. I was beginning to like the kid despite her ravings.

"Have you found this spy?" she asked. "Is he dead? Did the government get him? How about the woman? Oh, Race, tell me—"

I smiled. "I told you once before that you wanted a magician, not an ordinary detective. But I found the woman. So you know about that?"

"Yes, yes—something. Bert is very reticent. He should tell me everything. Oh, Race, you may be going to your death. He's very grave."

"Don't worry yourself about my death. All I want is a private wire to phone, and—" She pointed to a phone on a table in a corner, went over and closed the door. "Is Bert here?" I asked.

"Yes, yes, he came in—or maybe he was here all the time. But he is here."

"He came in," I told her. I lifted the phone, nodded toward the door. "I'll want to see Bert." I gave the number Paine had written down for me.

Freida Stanton started toward the door, paused, came back and gripped my hand as I waited.

"There's danger to you, Race—I know there is." And when I half shook her off, "I want to be with you if there is. After all, it's my case. I'm your client, and—"

"Hello, Paine?" I jumped the words into the phone. "Hold it a second." I clapped a hand across the mouth-piece and whispered hoarsely to the girl, "Go find Bert, Freida—it's important."

Maybe I put melodrama into my words. I wanted to get rid of her for a few minutes. She liked the melodrama, so I laid it on thick as she sped quickly from the room.

Then, "Listen, Paine." I let him have it fast. "I've seen Cora Hentz. She'll blow the works, but she's evidently into it heavy herself. Do you want this Ira Lent bad enough to give Cora a clean bill of health? Something definite—something she can read and keep, saying that she won't be prosecuted?" And when he gave his quick assurance that he did and that he would, "Well—it's a sure thing on Lent then, but the girl can't be fooled. I'll have to stake my word on it—and I can't be fooled either. And we should work fast."

Paine came right in with, "That's right. We don't want her to turn up dead. Don't worry, Race. Her request was anticipated. I have it in writing straight from the Attorney General. For services rendered the United States and all that. You'll have to guarantee that she will give us all—"

"Sure, sure. How soon can I come down and—and—" The door was opening. I saw the white-haired man entering. "Listen, Paine, bring it to me here. Right now. Freida Stanton's house." And I gave him the number on Fifth Avenue. Then I pronged the hand-piece.

Bert came across and clutched my arm. He said hoarsely: "Ira Lent will be delivered to you within the hour."

"What do you mean?" I said. "What happened to you?"

"I mean that I have just made arrangements to meet Ira Lent. Yes, Mr. Williams, I have a phone number where I can leave a message for him, and he calls me back. It's from—from other days."

"He'll trust you? He'll see you?"

"He'll see me. You see I plead fear of him—need of money. He's to meet me within the hour—up in the Bronx—and he's to pay me one hundred thousand dollars for Cora Hentz' address."

"You found that address tonight."

"I told him that. He wants to kill me, but he wants to find her more because of the evidence she has against him."

I said: "What happened to you tonight?"

His head lowered slightly. He half muttered the words.

"I was afraid, Mr. Williams. I am not the man Cora used to know. She's a peculiar woman. I would like to see her when I can look straight into her eyes and say, 'Don't be afraid of Ira Lent any more. He is dead and I—I—'" He stopped. I could hear the gulp in his throat as he swallowed his swallow. Then he said, "'And I—arranged his death.'"

"Another offer of murder," I told him.

"No, not murder, Mr. Williams." And coming closer to me he said: "Did she— did she— Did you tell her I was alive?

Is she the same? Does she care about—What did she say of me? How did she impress you?"

It was on my tongue to tell him the truth, but he looked so pitiful standing there. His clothes a little too big for him, his white hair above a face that seemed just as white. You could still see it in his eyes, the determined chin, and you could believe the stuff was there that had made him face death for Cora before.

And the truth? Hell, I would have told him the woman was no good—that she was cruel and selfish and no doubt had played him for a sucker before and would again. But I couldn't. Business was business. This lad was playing a part—playing a man he used to be, and he was playing it for a woman who never was—truth is truth—never was a damned bit of good.

But I put a hand on his shoulder and said softly like a fine, upstanding hypocrite: "She wanted to see you, Bert. Was shocked when she knew you were alive. What made you take a run-out powder on me?"

"I don't know. I don't know." He raised his head now. "He—Ira Lent loved her, too. She—she—but he wasn't fit to touch her hand. I saved her then. I am only the shell of the man I used to be, but if I went to her—as the same man who saved her before— Yes, I was afraid to face her as I am."

I put an arm around his shoulder. "Don't you worry about her, boy. I'll see that you get full credit for capturing Lent. Yes, or killing him if he wants it that way. She'll think a lot of the lad who freed her from—"

"You mean, you—Race Williams"—he shook my hand off his shoulder, then leaned up quickly and placed both his hands on mine—"you'll kill him if you have to kill him to save your life?"

I almost took a laugh but didn't. I spoke in pretended seriousness but what I told him was the truth all right. I said: "I'll blow his head off his shoulders if I'm in the least danger—or if you are in the least danger."

"I can count on that?" He breathed the words in a choking sort of way.

"Better still, Bert—Ira Lent can count on it."

Slender white hands fell from my shoulder.

"Ira Lent," he said, "will not be taken alive. I will deliver him to you in thirty minutes."

After that Bert talked well—talked like a man who had faced death before, planned things before. He didn't tell me he had worked for Ira Lent, but I could guess that. He spoke of the house he used to meet him in. Of the room on the second floor and how he would wait there for Lent to come. How Lent's feet would pound slowly up the stairs. How Lent had killed men in that room. Fingers bit nervously into my shoulders.

Finally he said: "Those slow feet—those pounding feet. They have struck fear into men, Mr. Williams."

"Don't you worry, Bert," I assured him. "I'll be interested in his hands and what he carries in them. I never heard of a first-rate detective being kicked to death yet."

"Do not underestimate this man, Race Williams. If he suspects you are with me, he will come into that room, and he'll come in shooting."

"If he does"—it was certainly hard to cheer this guy up—"he'll come in dead."

On the level I was anxious to meet Ira Lent and to see just how bad he was.

I thought we'd have trouble with Freida Stanton wanting to go with us and wave a flag and help bury the dead. But we didn't.

Bert said: "She's a wonderful girl, Mr. Williams. We can't go in your car if you have one here because it might be recognized. We can't go in mine because—I haven't got one." Which was good logic, I'll admit. "But Freida has several cars. She has one parked far down the side street for my convenience. I asked her to have one ready for me."

"You told her we—"

"No, I didn't tell her anything," he cut in, "except that I would need a car. I want to be frank with you, Mr. Williams. I am fighting off fear, but I wanted the car if I could no longer fight. If I had to run away and—"

"Listen, boy." I gripped his hand as he led me down the hall and back through the servants' entrance. "You have more guts than I have. A man who knows fear and goes on is made of real stuff. Don't you ever be ashamed of yourself, Bert." Yet as soon as the pinch or the death of Ira Lent was over I was going to tell Bert the truth. Cora Hentz wasn't worth her weight in mud—and wet mud at that.

CHAPTER 5

THE INVINCIBLE IRA

SOME GUY IN the ballroom was shouting that he had but one life to give for his country when we did a turn by the servants' dining-room off the kitchen and wandered out into the little garden. Garden, get that, on Fifth Avenue, and you'll have an idea of the Stanton's dough.

Bert hurried down the street now and stopped by the car. It was a long, slick, gray convertible coupé, and Bert looked at the closed rumble seat.

"Do you think, Mr. Williams, you should be sure? We could open this seat so you could stop some place and— Do you have a machine gun?"

"I have army tanks," I told him sarcastically as I took his arm and led him to the door by the wheel—yes, and guided his fingers as he took the key Freida had given him and waved it over the lock.

"But I don't use those army tanks," I said when he was behind the wheel. "Want me to drive?"

"No—no," he said as he jerked the seven-thousand-dollar boat from the curb like it was a jallopy. "I'll drive. You watch to see that we are not followed, and that no one is watching the house in the Bronx when we reach there." And sort of grimly, "It was nice of you to say what you did, Mr. Williams. You give me confidence in myself. And I have to keep my nerve up."

With that he proceeded to try and run down my nerve. Oh, not consciously, perhaps, it was just that the thing was on his mind. This Ira Lent must have put him through hell.

He said as he drove: "Mr. Williams, I admire you greatly. You are without fear. Yet—I wonder if you know what manner of man you are going to meet. You will wait with me in the room above. He will open the door below. You will hear it close. Then you will hear the steady pounding of his feet. He always approaches so steadily, with such assurance. And he always kills."

"Always—up to now." I nudged him in the ribs.

"You are a remarkable man." He looked at me in the dimness of a passing street lamp. "But you do not know Ira Lent. He has a brain that no criminal has ever equaled."

"I know enough about him," I said impatiently. "If he's half the lad you say he is, why your worries are over."

"What do you mean?"

I was getting annoyed. I said: "I mean I'll scatter that brain of his all over the Bronx and give you a chance to study it." And as he swerved, missed the curb, and straightened out again I asked him a vital question.

"Now how do you know this isn't a trap for you—and what Lent thinks is a trap for me?"

"I told him over the phone," Bert said, "that if Cora Hentz didn't hear from me within half an hour after our appointment she would send all the evidence she has on him to the government man."

"Not bad, Bert." I took another look at him. He wasn't so dumb. "You know your way about. Cora said you were some lad in your day."

"What did she mean—my day?"

"I don't know." I slipped over that one. Somehow I felt he was building up all this courage for Cora. Later I'd have to tell him the truth about that dame. And what do I mean by the truth? Why I mean that if I were playing poker with Cora I wouldn't even turn my head to spit.

She had loyalty for one person only. And she thought of that person day and night. And that person was herself. I couldn't tell him the truth yet. But Ira Lent was right. He knew his women—at least he knew Cora Hentz. The man was a criminal, murderer, yes, and torturer, but I could understand why he might spend sleepless nights while Cora lived. I'd hate to have that girl having unpretty thoughts about me—and evidence that would hang me. Yep—Ira Lent had a natural boyish desire to put a bullet in her head. At that, I don't blame him.

We hit Harlem, swung for the bridge, and passed into that section of the city which is known as the Bronx. I had Bert do a few side streets, up and down, then told him: "No one is getting our smoke." And when he seemed to miss that one. "I mean we haven't been followed."

"It was hardly likely we could be," he said. "Ira Lent has no idea where I was or am. Mr. Williams, what do you suggest I do—in entering this house?"

"Hell," I told him, "drive by it first. Let's get the lay of the land. Until he's sure of Cora he can't hammer you."

"You think he'll meet me as he always has met me—alone?"

"Why not? And if he doesn't—you've got me."

"You don't think—he might have others, take me prisoner and because of Cora's love for me—or at least what I did for her, think that she would give him all her evidence to save my life?"

"No." I put that in emphatically. "Cora—" And I let that part go. After all, it was my opinion only, and that opinion was that Cora would let her now white-haired boy friend be torn to pieces before she'd dump over her big hold on Lent—perhaps her big hold on life in that evidence.

I was going to feed him another line when he said: "We'll pass the house now."

We did, and the house had been a natural for Ira Lent's purpose and was now a natural for my purpose, whatever that was. It was in the great city of New York, yet in the country. At least, despite the towering apartments and the closely-put-together one-family houses, it stood alone, far back from the street. It was an old house that had been partially remodeled. At least the garage was alongside of it and really part of the house. The house was dark, the garage doors closed.

Bert said: "I have always driven into that garage and entered by the kitchen."

"Were the doors generally open or closed?"

"They were closed. Like they are now."

"O.K.," I nodded and was a little apprehensive of the way he handled the wheel as we sped by. But I would have been more apprehensive if I had been driving because I wouldn't be in as good a position if it were a trap. Sure—I expected a trap. I always do.

Bert could easily be a sucker for one.

Yet traps teach you a lot about danger, and often, too, when you walk right into them you eliminate that danger. Besides I am never averse to a little loose shooting if the boys want it that way. It may not be fancy brain work, but then it's so damn final.

Bert followed my instructions after I studied the street in front of the house and the street behind it. We drove around the back. I spotted the empty lot in the rear—the space on both sides of the place. As we hit that front-street again I had Bert swing the car into the driveway and straight toward the closed doors of the garage. I was crouched low in the seat. Impossible to see me from the house, or from the outside, for that matter.

There was a slight, cold fog, and certainly there was no moon. Bert said: "You open the door, Mr. Williams, and I'll drive in."

I remained crouched low in my seat and said: "No, Bert, you have to carry on. Someone may be watching—may recognize your figure. Get out, step right in front of the headlights, and open the doors. Come on, man. You've gone this far. Suppose I did it and were shot dead. Who would protect you then?"

"Yes—yes." He seemed to have trouble with the car door. "I'll do it, Mr. Williams. You're not afraid?"

"Not much," I told him, if that cheered him any. "Open the garage doors, come back to the car, and drive it in. You're supposed to be alone."

"Yes—yes." He was doing well on that "yes" stuff. And what's more, as Bert got slowly from the car, my gun dropped into my hand. I was beginning to like Bert.

He had no stomach for the job, yet was going through with it. If you're a stickler for words, you can have your choice. Love, hate, vengeance, call it what you like— something inside of Bert must have been conquering fear.

He pulled back one garage door, then the other. The dimmers he had left on the car didn't show the inside of the garage. And me, I didn't dare switch on the bright lights. Bert was supposed to be alone. A nice picture it would make if I changed the light and set his figure with its white, shining hair off in that light.

Bert was for going into the garage first and looking around. I saw him hesitating. Then he turned and came quickly back to the car. There was an apologetic note in his words—a shake in his voice.

"I thought it better to let the lights go on bright when we entered."

"That's the stuff, Bert," I told him as he closed the car door. "Remember you're supposed to be alone."

"And you—you'll act later?"

"Sure, Bert. If this Lent leads with his king, I'll put an ace on it."

"You will," he said without seeming to hear me, and treating that expensive job as though it were a hunk of tin, he gave a couple of jumps and hopped it into the garage. The garage was just an oblong cement-covered shed, and the car filled up most of it. We were there alone. The blazing headlights made no mistake about that. The damp cement walls gave the place an eerie atmosphere. At least to Bert it did. I could feel him shaking beside me. Could feel his arm close to mine.

"You're doing swell, Bert." I gripped at his arm with my left hand as my right held my gun in the tiny glare of the dash-light to give him courage. "I see a small door there by the rear. Remember we've got to find it in the dark. Yep, Bert. You have to close the garage doors, too."

I turned in my seat, my gun raised, as I watched him climb from the car again. The front of the garage and half-way back was a blaze of illumination from our lights. The rest of the garage was not so clear, but I could make out the figure of Bert at the door as I hung over the front seat and guarded him with a forty-four.

The house was silent! The street beyond the house was silent at that time of the morning—or most any other time, I guess. If a quick death was to come, it would come now. But what could I do? Suppose I had closed the door and someone opened up with a machine gun? Could Bert protect me? Could he even—

And I let that thought die. Bert had closed the doors and come back to the car. He seemed just a bit dazed—waited for me to advise him. Or if he didn't wait, I advised him anyway.

I said: "Turn off the car lights and use a flashlight. Then I can follow you in the darkness. Do we go through the rear door here?"

"Mr. Williams," Bert said, "the door in the back gives on a yard and the side entrance to the house. Inside the house a flight of stairs leads to this room above. That is the way I always came—some time ago. That is the way everyone must come. He—this Ira Lent—has sworn to me that I will enter the room first, and he will come by the front stairs as he always did. What do you think? I feel—I feel sick."

We passed through the small garage door to the cement yard beyond. I followed Bert closely—a gun in my hand. We turned and reached the five or six steps which led to the kitchen of the frame dwelling.

He opened the back door at the top of the steps and said, as we entered the kitchen: "Ira Lent won't be here yet. But we'd better be safe. Look—the door to the back stairs is still here." I gripped his arm and tossing on my flashlight for a split second saw the door.

"Not the light," Bert warned me. "I don't think Lent would double-cross me with the fear of Cora sending that evidence—but don't show a light."

He opened the door, paused, and contradicted himself the very second I stood on the lower step beside him.

"Let the light flash up here—around my arm—up the stairs at the curve. It used to be a hall but since Lent bought the house the hall is now part of that single room." My fight showed the stairs dusty but empty of life. "All right, Mr. Williams. Keep your gun out anyway."

"You're telling me," was on the tip of my tongue, but I didn't crack it out. I simply preceded Bert forward. Oh, I still admired the courage that drove him on, but I was annoyed, too. I told Bert of that annoyance when he tripped on a step.

"Listen," I whispered as I gripped his arm and straightened him up, "from now on I'll take charge." I opened the door and we entered the room at the top of the steps.

I PUT ON my flash—found that the room was without windows and that the only other entrance was the main door which was closed. I closed the other door and used my flash to find the light button. The button worked. A hundred-watt bulb did its stuff from the ceiling, and a huge, three-globe floor lamp brightened up the dirt and dust of the rest of the room.

I went over that room very carefully. There was no other entrance. There was a single closet, narrow and empty, with no windows. There was also a ventilating system high up on the walls and a couple of radiators for heat. The furniture was sparse—a long wooden table like you find in kitchens, and four or five stiff-backed kitchen chairs, one in the corner of the room beneath a wall ventilator.

Bert locked the door we had come in and put the ordinary long-barreled key in his pocket.

"No—no," I said as I made him hand over the key. "Where that door might be used for a surprise entrance against us—and I'd like it if it were, because we'd surprise someone else—it is also a method of escape. A lad shooting from the top of the stairs would have no advantage."

"Whatever you say, Mr. Williams." I could see that his legs were trembling, but his hand when it touched mine in forking over the key was neither cold nor clammy.

I didn't like the lay exactly as Bert gave it to me. We were to open the door to the main hall and wait in that room—with the lights out if we preferred it. I certainly preferred it, as I'd rather shoot at someone from darkness into light than be shot at from the darkness. We were to leave the light on in the hall outside that door—the hall that gave on the front stairs which led directly to the front door below.

I said: "As far as you know, Bert, there might be ten gunmen hiding in the hall downstairs."

"Yes—as far as I know. But there never was anyone in this house when I met him before. He always comes alone. Oh—I know that he invariably met only friends here, but Cora Hentz can—"

"What Cora can do won't help you or me if we are dead. I never could get any satisfaction in feeling that a lad was going to kill me and that then he would hang or roast for the crime afterward. However, the set-up is not so bad as soon as we put the lights out in here and kick the one in the hall lit. How soon will he come?"

Bert consulted his wrist watch, whispered: "He will come at three o'clock exactly. He always comes at three exactly."

"You have waited for him here, before—often?"

"Enough," Bert nodded. "We have about ten minutes to wait. I didn't calculate the time too carefully."

"O.K." I gave him a grim nod—a determined one, too. If things went as Bert expected, the feared and much-wanted—too-much-known and too-little-found—Ira Lent would be taken or dead within ten minutes. I snapped out the light at the switch by the main hall door.

The door opened easily under my grip. I stepped aside for a fusillade of shots, but none came.

"Where's the switch for the hall light?" I asked Bert.

"Right there." He leaned an arm around me in the dead blackness. Click—just like that—a light in the hall—a dim, yellowish forty-watter burning over the stairs. Maybe I'd have preferred a hundred watts, but there was enough light to shoot a man to death and no lad could ask for more than that.

I BACKED INTO the room again, feeling Bert's body falling away behind me as my gun bumped against his ribs.

I said: "We're to wait—just like this—and when he comes you want me to take him dead or alive. Right?"

"Dead—yes, dead or alive."

"It seems too easy to be true."

"Don't feel like that. Don't be overconfident. I'm afraid. Let me feel your arm, Mr. Williams, I can't see you in the darkness. Your presence makes me—"

He stopped dead. His breath went in and out. I heard his feet move—then remain silent. I am not sure, but I thought I could see Bert far to my right now, and certainly out of line of fire from even a side shot from that doorway.

We stood so for several minutes. There was no imagination on his part. Certainly none on mine. I couldn't be sure that I heard the front door below open. But there could be no doubt that I heard it close. Heard it close with an ominous thud.

I had made my entrance to that house unseen—but whether unguessed I didn't know. What's more, I didn't care. Slow, steady, even feet were coming up old, worn stairs.

I liked it. I won't admit that I know fear.

But I do know emotion. I got a thrill now. Ira Lent, the great desperate Ira Lent. He wasn't a fool. Yet—yet—if he were the killer he was painted he was coming to his death.

That was my point of view. Perhaps Ira Lent had a point of view of his own. Perhaps he felt, maybe knew as well as I knew the opposite, that he was coming to—to my death.

Those feet beat steadily and easily. Bert edged near me in the darkness—his fingers clutched at my right arm, the hand of which held one of my forty-fours.

"It's he—it's he," he said when I tossed off his hand, sent him staggering into complete darkness. "He'll kill you, Williams, and I—I—yes, he'll start shooting and I'll be to blame for your death."

"Don't kid yourself, Bert." I lowered my voice. "If we must have a corpse, it won't be mine, and it won't be yours."

"His steps—his steps—" Bert's voice was barely audible, but there was an hysterical note in it just the same.

Feet—slow, steady feet on the stairs. Thrilling? Sure, I suppose it was. Awe-inspiring? Well, perhaps for Bert— But for me Ira Lent was just another killer looking for a bellyful of lead.

I stood there and waited.

And he reached the top. There he was under the dim hall light. Long and gaunt with his greatcoat turned up over his throat and chin. His big fedora was pulled down over his eyes. I shook my head. Ira Lent was a little too dramatic for my way of thinking.

But he had one thing that interested me—and that was the heavy-calibered revolver he held in his right hand. It was raised slightly and the nose was still coming up as he took two steps forward and paused right in front of that door. Then he spoke.

"Bert," he said slowly and I felt the dramatic turn to the melodramatic as he got off his lines in a deep, hollow voice like an actor playing a part.

"Bert," he went on. "I have come for you. One way or another I have come for you. Put on the light."

He started to walk forward, and I spotted his long coat, his gaunt figure, and the slightest whiteness of his chin and part of his face. I got a better look at the gun—the gun that was ever rising and by luck covering me there in the darkness.

Ira Lent was bad. Death was his dish. I could have shot him to death then by just the pressure of a finger. Why didn't I? I don't know. My finger half tightened as I spoke.

"Stand still and drop the gun, Lent. Drop it."

He pulled a laugh then, coaxed it up from some place way down in his stomach. His words sneered at me.

"You never went in for guns, Bert," he said, "I'm coming in to talk to you."

His feet moved forward, his gun on a level with me now as I stepped aside. But the main thing was that he was moving when he was told to stop. He was still holding a gun when he was told to drop it. If he wanted it that way it was his hard luck, not mine.

I said simply: "Freeze. Drop the gun and reach for the ceiling." And when his gun came up the last inch to put it on a level with my body and its nose hovered to left and right I added: "Race Williams talking. And I'm paid to kill."

His knees shook, his gun dropped. I got a thrill of pride at what my name meant even to the feared Ira Lent. But he was right. I was through playing. I was ready to deliver the goods. And the goods were wrapped up in little steel jackets.

"So you're Ira Lent." I stepped toward the light. "The most feared, desperate, and—"

It happened, just like that. Bert's shout should have warned me, and maybe it did. But the pain from the bullet seemed to hit me almost the same time that I saw the flash of the gun. The flash didn't seem to come from the trembling lad in the hall who was reaching for his gun on the floor. The flash was just there—a million lights before my eyes, the buckling of my knees as the guy jerked up his gun.

Yep, he jerked it up—his hat back now, his mouth hanging open. I closed my finger on the trigger. Don't tell me where I hit him. I knew. He swallowed two forty-fours before he pitched back and spread himself out at the top of the stairs.

Another terrific pain in the head—and another flash before my eyes. I knew the truth then or thought I did. It wasn't a gunshot, the blow came first and the flash second, and the flash was the stars I saw when someone hit me with a black-jack. This time my knees buckled so that despite the spread I gave to my legs I wasn't going to stay erect.

Then I didn't know if I was shot or not. Plainly I heard the crack of a bullet, another and another—a shrill voice calling from below.

Clearly the words reached me. They were: "O'Rourke—Mr. Paine—"

Peculiar, that. The voice was a woman's voice—a girl's voice. I recognized the voice, too. Recognized it just as I sank to the floor. It was Freida Stanton.

I don't think I took another wallop. I think I went down then—and I went down with a single thought. If Bert could open that door in the rear of the room, so could someone else. And don't believe I didn't think of that before. What got me as I collapsed was that anyone could open that door on me—or any other door for that matter and I wouldn't hear it.

CHAPTER 6

THE MOOD TO KILL

FREIDA STANTON HELD my head in her arms—sitting there right on the floor beside me. The lights were bright. I opened my eyes. The government man, Paine, was saying: "It should have broken his skull like an eggshell. I would say it was that length of lead pipe. Any other man—"

"You don't know that thick skull of Race's," O'Rourke said. "You couldn't dent it with a sledge hammer.... Oh—so you're coming around."

And I was coming around. Nice friend, O'Rourke.

I sat up, knelt, then staggered to my feet, and patted the girl Freida on the head and ruffled her hair.

"How the hell did you get here?" I asked. "And Paine and O'Rourke?"

She had a nice smile. It was a little worried, but it was nice, and I liked the way she used it. She explained: "I was in the back of the car with you—underneath the closed cover of the rumble seat. I telephoned O'Rourke from a bean wagon around the corner. Mr. Paine had just come in my house and the sergeant brought him along. They really burned up the streets getting here."

"Why did you telephone O'Rourke?"

O'Rourke said: "Don't you know even now, Race? She hired a sap like you. Ah—your white-haired friend is beginning to get up."

And I saw Bert. He was holding his head. Blood ran down his forehead and into his eyes. He wasn't such a bad lad. He said over and over: "I should have thought of you, Mr. Williams. But the door behind you, the one we came in, opened so quietly. I tried to shout my warning and—"

"Just who," asked O'Rourke, "is the white-haired boy?"

"Assistant," I snapped. And straightening somewhat, "I suppose Miss Stanton told you the truth. She is my client, and Ira Lent is dead."

"Great! Where?" Paine asked.

O'Rourke seemed surprised. He said: "Yes—where?"

"In the hall. I killed him before—before whatever happened."

"God," said O'Rourke. "God, Race. That guy you shot in the hall is Dumb Benny Ikes. Yeah, you know him—take a look. Wanted for killing his wife. Cheap stuff."

I staggered out into the hall and took a look at him. I knew Benny—at least I had seen him often. Paine followed us.

I said: "So you don't think it's a crime any more to kill your own wife, O'Rourke. Have a free corpse on me."

Paine took me aside. He was more serious and less sarcastic.

"You are a very active man, Mr. Williams. I have the documents you wish which should satisfy this Cora Hentz. Here's my statement guaranteeing her freedom from prosecution by the government, and here's the letter from the Attorney General giving me power to act in her case. We expected she would demand something like this. But this tonight. Is it connected with the Ira Lent case? I just came along with O'Rourke as I was approaching the Stanton house when he received Miss Stanton's message. Just now you said something about Ira Lent being killed. Did you really think that you killed him?"

"Nix," I told him. "I was riding O'Rourke." I put the two separate letters for Cora in my pocket. "I'm going to see her—now."

"Now?" He seemed surprised. "You got a couple of pretty raps on the head. I'd say they required stitches. You have your own doctor?"

"Sure, sure." I was still trying to clear my head. "I'll have Ira Lent for you before—well, I'll have him tomorrow morning."

"Fine, fine." He nodded and his mouth and eyes opened pleasantly. "I took a look around. The door behind you was open. Someone or more than one walked in and crowned you from behind. Found the hunk of lead pipe at the bottom of the stairs—those rear stairs."

"Yeah—yeah." I looked at him. "And you figure?"

"I went down the stairs. They escaped that way after socking you and your assistant. He said he half turned and saw two before he was struck."

O'Rourke horned in: "You'd have been dead in another minute—maybe less."

"Not me," I told him. "I had two guns. I could have sprayed the room all over with lead before I dropped out."

"Then you'd have killed your assistant."

"Is he your brother?" I asked O'Rourke.

"Oh, come, Race." O'Rourke quieted down a little. "The front door was open. Miss Stanton was on the steps when we drove up. She swung suddenly in the door, started firing and shouting before we were fairly on the front steps. Admit that a lady saved your life."

"Miss Stanton," I said, "is my client. When I save—"

I stopped, squeezed the arm the girl put through mine as I staggered a bit, then said: "Come on, Bert. You need rest."

"I'm sorry, Mr. Williams, that I—"

Bert stopped there. I put a hard eye on him and shook my head. We started toward the rear stairs. I was taking the girl's arm.

"The body, you know, Race," O'Rourke said. "You can't just kill people without an official explanation."

"I'll see the D.A. tomorrow," I told him. "Unless you want the body for your-self. And, Mr. Paine—come around and see me in my office in the morning. I'll put you onto Ira Lent then. Good-night."

"I'd have a doc sew up my head if I were you, Williams," Paine said. "Those are deep cuts. O'Rourke and I will look the place over. You, Miss Stanton, and your assistant run along. That's a nasty crack on the head he got."

"You, too, Race," O'Rourke put in. "It's lucky it was your head and not your elbow, boy."

The door closed and we were down the steps. In the garage the three of us piled into the seat.

Freida Stanton said: "What happened, Bert? I thought you were so sure tonight. And—" She seemed to exhale unpleas-antly as she thought of the dead man. "It turned out to be someone else, eh? And Mr. Williams nearly—"

"Close only counts in horseshoes," I said. "Don't blame Bert, Miss Stanton. Ira Lent no doubt hired a fall-guy for the front entrance and tried his own killing from the rear stairs. I should have heard the knob turn. Never missed anything like that before. But I heard Bert shout and—"

Hell, she just backed right out of the garage jamming open the doors. But at that neither of us had thought to open the garage doors. My head had stopped bleeding. Bert's hadn't. The handkerchief he held against his forehead was soaked and red.

"You can drop me any place, Freida," Bert said. "I'm sorry my promise to deliver this—this man Ira Lent to Race Williams didn't work out."

The girl turned and started to snap at

him, but I cut in. "Don't jump on Bert. Take him to your place. That is if you put guests up for the night."

The girl made a grimace. "I'll put up at least twenty tonight." She backed the car over on the hard ground, leaving the garage doors on busted hinges, swung around and shot toward the street. "I'm sorry, Bert, but you endangered Race Williams' life."

"I'm sorry, too, but—but—but Mr. Williams is—"

"Is used to having his life endangered. You're a great girl, Freida. It was my fault tonight. We'll have a big catch for All American Youth, Incorporated in the morning. Take care of Bert tonight at your house."

After all, I had the documents that would make Cora Hentz talk and I didn't want to be bothered with Bert. The brakes screeched before Freida's house and Bert jumped out. He seemed all right, and then staggered slightly on the street as he went around to open the door for her.

"He'll need a doctor," I said. "He's got courage, Freida."

"Yes." She opened the door and told Bert to go inside. Lights still blazed in the front of the great mansion. When Bert had gone, she said: "I wish I had saved your life tonight, Mr. Williams."

"Maybe you did. Why?"

"I'd like—oh, Race—you're such a different man. I'd like to go on saving your life—at least helping you to live for the rest of my—"

"Great." I leaned over and opened the door. "I'll get my car and—"

"No—" She stepped in front of me as I started out. "Use my car. I'll come to your office in the morning when—when the others do." She leaned back in and gripped my arm as I slipped behind the wheel. "Oh, Race, Race," she said, "I'm willing to chuck it all now—just—just so nothing will happen to you."

"Nothing will happen to me," I told her grimly. I was a bit mad now. Oh, not at O'Rourke. I knew he always rode me when he wanted to push me on to results. But I was pretty damn griped at myself.

Cora Hentz was one tough baby who was able to take care of herself. But at that I made sure I wasn't followed. I wasn't in what you'd call a friendly mood. Cora Hentz and Bert had me in the mood they wanted me in, though they had nothing to do with it. I could have shot Ira Lent to death now without batting an eye. I felt stupid about that house-in-the-Bronx fiasco. I couldn't blame Bert. I never blame anyone in gun-play. That's my business. I couldn't understand it yet. Imagine me allowing someone to open a door I knew about and then smack me down.

Sure, my head felt funny. Even a thick skull like mine can feel a vicious attempt on my life by a strong man with a hunk of lead pipe. And—and—I pulled the car up just a few apartments below Cora Hentz', climbed from the car and slipped quickly up the street toward her apartment. I had what she wanted and in return she would give me the evidence against Lent and the place where he might be found. After that—I'd either slap a warrant into his hand or a couple of bullets into his stomach and walk or drag him down to Paine.

I stood for a while in the vestibule of the walk-up, but no one came in and no one came out. Somewhere a distant clock knocked off five strokes.

I got ready to lean on Cora's bell there above the tiny mail-box on the side. She would be expecting me. Then I saw the door. Someone had entered the apartment and had not closed the door tight. It meant a drunk of course, for those walk-up apartment doors closed themselves and were hard to leave open. The stew must have tried to let the door close softly behind him.

But no thinking now. I opened the door, shut it silently behind me. There was no reason for it, but I slid down the hall beside the stairs that led to the rear door. No one there of course. Why should there be? There shouldn't. Yet—I had been taken from behind once tonight. And I didn't feel in the mood to be shot down from behind later the same morning.

A dim light shone above. I'm not a lad to creep upstairs and tell you of the thrill I had on each step. I just made the steps fast. My gun was hanging low in my hand. Anyone who wanted to dispute my dash to the fourth floor and to Cora's apartment was welcome to dispute it.

Sure I was mad. Anyone who stuck a gun at me and wanted to talk, well—he just wouldn't talk. Unless you believe in mediums and heard his voice from the vast depth for half a buck.

I made Cora Hentz' door, reached for her bell and rocked back on my heels. Her door was open a thin, long crack. The brass chain she had to release to let me in before was caught in the door jam.

I gulped. I didn't like it. Cora Hentz had fled in a hurry or—

And "or—" was correct. But I wasn't any gum-shoeing detective then. I put my gun in the door first and my body afterwards. The hall was dark. I sprinkled it with light from my pocket flash with my left hand. My right hand was held high. All quiet—terribly quiet—deadly quiet.

Then I was inside and clicked the lock behind me, though I didn't put the chain in place. I wanted it that way for a quick exit.

Unpleasant going down that hall to the living-room. Sure it was. I didn't feel so good. I reached the end of the hall—the curtains that led to the living-room.

Darkness inside that living-room as I peered in. But I have an eye for detail, and had spotted the light-switch before. With my flash back in my pocket now, I shoved my left hand through the curtain and found the switch.

Why hadn't I rung the bell before I came in? Why didn't I call out to the woman now? The answer is simple. Cora Hentz was not one to leave her door open. She had either taken it on the run, or—or she hadn't—she couldn't—

My finger clicked home the button. The living-room was flooded with light. And I was through those curtains, a gun in either hand. No more head-work now. Nothing but action. The living-room was a sight.

EVERYTHING IN THE room had been torn apart. Pictures were jerked from the wall, their paper backs torn off. Pillows cut to ribbons, their stuffing on the floor.

The couch and the seats of the chairs treated the same. The rug snatched from the floor, lying in one corner of the room where it had been tossed. Books ripped apart. The back knocked out of a Chinese cabinet and—and—

I should have searched the kitchen and the dinette and the bathroom first to make it safe for myself. But I didn't. I went down the little hall to Cora's bedroom—opened the closed door, let my flash hit the disorder in that room and finally light on the bed. Yeah—on the bed and on the thing that was on the bed.

My light covered the room—the window from which there was no fire-escape. Then I pulled myself together. That's right. The hard-boiled Race Williams had to pull himself together. My head cleared—not a dull thought nor a pain in my head now.

Then I left the bedroom and went through the rest of the apartment without missing a spot a man could hide in. Closets, behind drapes, the shower curtain. Yep—I covered every place big enough to hide a man. I didn't have to go through places big enough to hide something small—like an envelope, like documents—like evidence that would put the finger on Ira Lent. No, I didn't have to do that. Someone had done it before me. Had done it thoroughly, but done it quickly.

There had been no attempt even to return the contents of drawers—to stuff the filling back in the mattress or the pillows. Sure you guessed it. Someone else had looked for that envelope. Whether he or she or they had found it or not I didn't know. Since nothing was left undisturbed it was a sure bet they hadn't found it in any room but the bedroom. I hadn't covered that room yet.

I straightened and walked back through the living-room and into the bedroom again. It wasn't a pleasant job. But then, I'm not one to shirk any kind of a job. I found the main switch and flooded the room with light.

I didn't look on the bed then. I looked under it—in the closet, behind the calico curtain where rows of dresses and such stuff was hung. Then I turned and did my job—looked straight down on the bed and the woman who lay on it.

The woman was Cora Hentz, and she was dead. Someone had dragged a knife across her throat and dug it deep. Though she had been tortured horribly before she died, death had come quickly enough. The man was in a hurry then—and from the appearance of her rooms had not found what he wanted.

Her green eyes were horrible in death. Her folded hands that were stretched up as if—as if—

But to hell with that! It was as brutal a bit of murder as I have ever seen—and I have seen plenty. What was my guess about the evidence? Well, my guess was that he didn't get it. And who was he? Ira Lent, of course. This was not a plain murder, but where a man, after torturing his victim, finally slashed out in blind fury. Well, maybe not blind, but certainly in fury from the appearance of her throat.

There was a phone by her bed. I stretched a hand toward it and then drew back. After all, where did O'Rourke fit?

He was a cop. He should know about murders without being told. Maybe that was a childish thought, for I like O'Rourke and he likes me. But I had another brain-flash. I was the only one who knew of Cora Hentz' death. All but the man who killed her. And the man who killed her was Ira Lent, and he had taken advantage—made sure through Bert that I would be at that house in the Bronx while Cora Hentz was killed.

How did he know where she lived? How did he know I was going to be with Bert? Hell, I didn't know the answers to those questions. But I did know that Ira Lent had been threatened by Cora Hentz that she would see me. And Bert—well, perhaps he knew Bert had seen me—knew that I would go to that house with Bert and—and—

Understand those were my ideas. You can like them or leave them alone. Personally, I decided to leave them alone. It would mean that Ira Lent must have followed me—Bert and me, to Cora's apartment. And it was some years since anyone got my smoke when I was watching for someone on my tail.

But I was the only one who knew that Cora was dead. If Ira Lent didn't know I knew he would strike quickly at me figuring I'd think he wouldn't do anything until he had killed Cora. Fine. Ira Lent couldn't strike too soon for me. But how had he found Cora? How?

I turned and walked out of the room, out of the apartment, and down the stairs. My head did a few tricks, but I didn't have much to worry me any more. There were no high-minded ideas in my head about justifiable homicide or turning Ira Lent over to the government men. I had looked at the girl's throat and made up my mind. I'd blow Ira Lent out of the picture the first time I saw him. I was in the mood to kill.

Sure I looked over the balustrade of the apartment porch when I left it. Sure I expected to see a death car dash down the street before I left the curb. Maybe I even expected to see the nose of a Tommy gun stick from behind drawn curtains. I was on the kill this morning.

If Ira Lent wanted it that way, why so did I.

The morning was cold—the street deserted. No gunmen suddenly jumped into life. My head was big and dull. I found Freida's car and drove straight to my good—and silent—doctor.

DOCTOR ADAMS TOOK a good look at me and brought me into his private office. He had gotten out of bed, but already seemed wide awake.

He said: "Your eyes are bright, Race. Don't tell me you've been walking around with lead pellets in you. Strip and we'll—"

"No bullets," I said. "I was hit on the head with a hunk of pipe." I sat down and bent my head forward. "And I haven't got much time to fool with it."

Doctor Adams didn't waste time. He leaned over, brushed back my hair, hummed softly.

"Let's say a dozen stitches even. It's lucky—"

I cut in with: "If you say it's lucky it was my head instead of my elbow I'll blow a hole in your middle."

"It's like that, eh?" He went to work. "It's going to hurt a bit."

"Do your stuff. No conversation."

You'd think I was a pillow the way he handled my scalp. I only squawked once. I said: "I'm going to kill a man shortly—don't make it two."

"Most people come to me and plead, not threaten. Well"—I could have shouted with the pain, but I didn't—"it's a tough skull you've got."

He finished his job, went and poured out a huge drink of dark-colored liquor. "On the house," he told me.

"Whiskey?" I asked.

"It's not sarsaparilla." He smiled.

I waved the glass away, said: "I'm on the kill tonight, Doc. And I never do my shooting through the mouth of a bottle. How'll I stand up?"

"O.K." He was putting things away and looking at my head. "I've pulled lead out of you, Race, but that's the first time someone walked up behind you and knocked you on the head. A length of pipe, I'd say."

"I said that," I told him.

I got up and put on my coat and vest. "What's the charge?"

"Nothing—nothing, boy." He patted me on the back. "I don't like your humor tonight. When you kill the man, come around cheerful-like to have me take a few bits of lead out of your chest. I'll stick it all on the one bill."

"I may get killed. Better take a century-note."

He shrugged his shoulders. "Leave it to me in your will, Race." And as he helped me on with my coat and grabbed at my arm, "You're not sick, understand. But a shot in the arm might—"

"I don't need any courage." I grinned at him. "Sell that dope to the other guy. I simply want a steady hand and a clear head."

"Fill your stomach with coffee then," he said, "and your lungs with cigarettes. Good luck, boy. I'll read the papers."

And I was down the steps and driving straight to Joe's Beef House.

JOE KEPT OPEN day and night. It was daylight when I rolled in. I took ham and eggs and lots of coffee, felt better. Then I leaned back, killed a few butts.

The smoke shot into the air like you see in paintings, but I didn't think. I just sat. I'd been doing too much thinking. In a dazed way, perhaps, I figured that Ira Lent had found out where the girl was—tortured her to find out where the evidence against him was—had been unsuccessful—had killed her and searched the apartment.

So what would he figure? He'd figure she gave it to me. And—and— I got up and paid my bill. Ira Lent would come looking for me—to torture me for that evidence—to kill me. I set my teeth a bit grimly. I was never more pleased in my life about a guy wanting, perhaps even now looking for me, to kill me. Well—I'd go to my office. That should be the first place he'd look. Who was I to stand in the way of the tough Mr. Ira Lent? I pushed out into the brisk morning air. No fooling now—I'd stretch Ira Lent so cold you could skate on his chest.

CHAPTER 7

WISE AND DEAD

I WAS SURPRISED to find that other people went to their offices as early as seven-thirty in the morning. I shot up in the elevator, approached my office door and spun the key in the lock carefully. Understand, I was simply a determined man—not a silly one.

I was covering that office with a gun when I closed the door behind me and left the morning mail lying on the floor. There was the reception-room with Jerry's desk. I didn't go in for a girl. Sometimes lads came to my office who weren't too nice with their language or the way they died on the floor.

I covered the room to my left. A tiny office that I used to slip into from my own private office so I could pass back through the outer office when Jerry showed me someone I didn't want to see. There weren't many places to hide, but I searched them all. I'm not of a nervous disposition, in fact I always claim I haven't any nerves, but I did have respect for this Ira Lent. Understand, I was going to kill Ira Lent—he wasn't going to kill me.

Twice I nearly picked up the phone on my desk to give Freida Stanton a buzz and tell Bert his girl friend had been knocked off. Not much of a loss to the community, not much of a loss to Bert, but that was my point of view only. Bert might look at it as if an angel had been killed.

I went back for the mail. There was quite a bit of it being that time of the month. A couple of envelopes weren't bills, though one long, thick manila envelope looked heavy enough to contain folders and descriptions of a steamship company that wanted someone—preferably me, to go around the world.

I lifted the mail and saw the shadow and heard the knock on my stained-glass door. My eyes widened slightly. Had someone—well, why beat around the forest—had Ira Lent seen me entering the building and decided to move quickly? Silently I slipped the lock off the door, backed into my private office and sat down behind the desk, placing the mail beside me. The knock came again.

I hollered out pleasantly enough: "Come in."

I opened my jacket to make both my shoulder-guns handy, with one eye on the door, and started to open the mail. I chose the big envelope. I didn't feel like reading much, anyway, and felt that the envelope would have fancy pictures of strange places in it. I was just about in a state to enjoy pretty pictures.

The knob turned. My right hand slipped up under my left armpit and felt pleasant around the butt of a forty-four.

The door opened slowly. I half lifted the gun, then dropped it back in the shoulder-holster. White hair and a white face was plainly visible beneath the gray fedora. Bert turned his back to me as he closed the door. It gave me a chance to recover. Bert turned and said: "I tried the door before, and it was locked." He walked into the room and stood looking at me. "I couldn't sleep. Why didn't you call me? I'm worried, and—and so are you."

"That's right, Bert," I said kindly as I jerked a thumb at a chair and moved myself into a position to watch that outer door. Then I tore open the big envelope—trying to be nonchalant. I knew what was coming next.

"Cora—Cora—" He walked toward the desk now and stood across the broad, flat surface from me. "You saw her. What did she say?"

"I didn't speak to her, Bert." I had the envelope open now and my eyes bulged. There weren't many pages, an affidavit, and a letter. Yes, a letter from Cora Hentz which began—

Dear Mr. Williams:

Death seems very near. I feel it. I know it. I am sending you the evidence you wish and taking your word that it will not be shown to the government until Ira Lent is dead. Your word is good until he is dead.

"You saw her, though—you did see her?" Bert cut in.

I turned my head, said: "Bert, I thought I was followed and decided not to—" And it struck me that Bert was entitled to the truth. It would knock him, of course, but it would give me a chance to finish that letter. I had seen something in it which read—"I will slip this envelope in the mail chute in the hall."

But I said: "Bert, you might as well take it like a man. Besides—and I'm the last guy to knock a—a live or dead woman—this Cora Hentz had no use for you. She thought you were dead. Wouldn't believe—"

"She's dead, then. She's dead." He leaned far over the desk. "I knew that. I dreamed it. Well, Mr. Williams, you don't have to find Ira Lent now. You don't have to kill him now. I'll do that. I'll—" I looked up at Bert as his right hand went fumbling under his left armpit. "I bought a gun—got a gun just as you said I should, Mr. Williams."

HE NEEDED A search warrant to find his weapon but finally got it out in his hand. It was a thirty-eight. He handled it like a cheer leader would a football. His hand shook, his eyes bulged. I was looking at the letter again.

I read on.

I should have known at the time, but I knew as soon as you left that Bert was dead. I had seen him dead, and the dead do not come to life.

Bert was saying: "You said, Mr. Williams, that I didn't have to know anything about guns. I'd just have to point it in a man's stomach—like this"—he jabbed it against my ribs—"and press the trigger."

"Sure—sure," I started soothingly and then felt the gun in my side. "Hell, Bert, it might go off, and—and—"

And I knew. Knew as I tossed my chair back and crossed my hands one under each armpit, the left cracking against Bert's gun hand as I toppled my chair back and over.

Bert fired all right. I felt the coldness, the icy cold of the hot lead as it steamed a ridge across my cheek. And that was where Bert made his mistake. He was a little too cocky in juggling that gun in

　　　　　　　　　　　CARROLL JOHN DALY

his hand, and a little too assured in leaning far over the desk as he drew a bead on me before my chair even struck the floor. And like other great criminals he had his failing. He wanted his victim to know the truth. In plain words he talked.

He just leveled the gun out with all the assurance in the world, tightened his finger on the trigger and said: "Race Williams—meet Ira Lent."

As for me, I closed the finger of my left hand—a split second and the finger of my right hand closed. A forty-four is a heavy gun. Bert didn't fire again. Before I hit the floor he had picked himself up in the air, clawed at his chest with both hands, and gone hurtling back across the room.

"You *were* Ira Lent," I said as I hit the floor and came to a kneeling position almost at once.

I staggered to my feet and brushed the blood off my cheek with my coat. No one had to tell me the story of Ira Lent's death. It wasn't very fancy shooting, but I knew that I had laid two slugs in his chest and you could have driven an army truck through the holes. But I did walk around the desk and kick the gun from his hand. Yes, he still gripped it, and his fingers twitched when I toed it over in a corner.

He wasn't dead. The blue of his eyes was beady and mean and his eyes were more alive than they had ever been.

He whispered: "Water—just a little water."

"Water!" I gave him a laugh. "Did you give that woman water? I—" And I turned and swung up my gun. Paine and O'Rourke and behind them Freida Stanton were crossing the office and coming into the room. I held up my hand, made the words "Wait and listen" with my lips. Then I took the water that Freida got from the cooler, walked over to Bert—alias Ira Lent.

"If you want a drink, talk—before I lay another slug in your chest."

Lent tried to turn from his side to his back. I helped him a bit, and he said: "You got a break, Williams. I was a fool to let you shoot. It's all in the letter that Cora sent you. I knew it last night. Well, she's dead. I didn't leave the apartment last night. I followed you in, waited on the floor above. Five or ten minutes after I saw you leave I went to her door. I was afraid you might come back, and she thought it was you and let me in. I didn't have much time or she would have told me the truth—that the evidence against me had been mailed to you. I searched the place and killed her. Wise girl, Cora. She saw this lad Bert die and knew he didn't come to life again. I simply impersonated the dead Bert."

I looked to see if the others were listening. O'Rourke was out at the phone. Paine stood silently writing in a little book. Thorough men, these government lads. Freida Stanton had the stuff too. She stood there with a surprised look in her ever-widening eyes, her mouth wide, too, I guess, but she had her hand across it, and I couldn't tell. Bert went on, his words slower now, his voice gasping. Bubbles of red formed on his mouth.

"Cora Hentz wrote me that she was going to turn me over to—to you. And I got my idea. I dyed my hair white—mixed with this—this cheap society crowd of Freida Stanton's. Sure—I told her she must pretend to have known me for a long time or—or you wouldn't take her case. One thing I had to do—I had to—to kill Cora Hentz. And since Cora was getting in touch with you I had to—to fix it so you'd lead me to her."

He gurgled deep in his throat and I suppose it was meant for a laugh. A little line of red ran down his chin.

"You played it all the way—led me to her—put yourself in a position to get killed last night. Of course I—I couldn't kill you until I had found and killed Cora. Things—things went wrong last night."

O'ROURKE WAS BACK looking at me now. And the full picture of last night got me. Bert, well, Lent, had taken me to that house—then simply arranged to kill me there. But I'm a stubborn guy, and I'm willing to take it for knowledge. He struck me with the pipe, of course, hit himself on the forehead when he heard shots below, then threw the lead pipe down the stairs.

"About the man I shot and killed in that house in the Bronx."

"Oh, that—that." Lent repeated his words but not because he was gaining strength. He was beginning to wander, a film was coming over his eyes. "You mean Benny Ikes—well—I thought it might be easy if—if I fixed it so you'd kill him. You see—he—he thought, too, that Bert was in that room—Bert—a man who had lost his courage—lost it even before he died. It would have worked, too—I—I—" He started to ramble then, asked for water. Then he seemed to pull himself together

with a tremendous effort and cried out in a rattling voice: "I hired that cheap gunman to threaten you—I—I—I was afraid you wouldn't take the case of a woman like Cora unless—unless you felt a personal threat. You're so—so conceited and so dumb, and I needed you to—to lead me to Cora."

"Give him a drink, Race," O'Rourke said.

Yeah, I gave him a drink. I splashed water down his face and it turned crimson in his mouth. O'Rourke gave me a look, opened his mouth to speak but didn't say anything. Maybe he didn't like the look on my face as he went to the cooler outside for water. But then he hadn't seen the body of Cora Hentz.

"Nice job, Williams," Paine said. "There'll be some money in it. What's this talk of the Hentz woman giving you evidence? Remember, the names of smaller leaders of this spy ring and all that?"

And I remembered Cora Hentz' letter. No evidence was to be turned over to the government until Ira Lent was dead. Sure—I knew that Cora was dead, but that wasn't mentioned in her letter. I said: "What the— Oh, hello, Doctor."

Doctor Barkley, the medical examiner, came into the room.

"Good morning, Sergeant," he said to O'Rourke. "This is the stiff, eh?" He knelt by Lent. "Why, he's dyed his hair white. Look at the roots, they're black."

"Yeah"—O'Rourke came to his feet— "we know all about that. We want to know what his chances are of getting well."

"Well—well"—Doctor Barkley dropped his bag and knelt at the man's side—"I'm a medical examiner, not an interne, Sergeant." And turning up his head, "Your job, Race?" He caught my nod. "Not like you, boy. Very messy—very messy indeed. By God, if I hadn't had my breakfast, I'd—I'd— Why Sergeant O'Rourke. Must have your little joke, eh? The man's deader than a mackerel." He laughed hollowly. "Deader than a mackerel but not quite so stiff."

"You say he's dead?" I asked.

"Dead." The coroner came to his feet, brushed off the knees of his trousers, and lifted his little black bag which he had not opened. "Let us say just dead enough to bury." He drew a little pad from his pocket, wrote on it hurriedly, handed the slip to O'Rourke.

"Permission to remove the body, Sergeant. There will have to be an autopsy, I suppose. Well, I'll give you Race's bullets then." And poking me in the ribs as he hurried out, he finished, "I always spoke of the nice, clean work you do. This is a disappointment to me, boy. But I'll back you up if you try to get money out of the city for the ruined rug. Some stiffs bleed like pigs. Good day, gentlemen. Good day, miss."

And Doctor Barkley was gone.

"Dead," I said to Paine and picked up the envelope Cora Hentz had sent me. "It's your job, Paine, but it looks like a list of names and addresses. I couldn't give them to you until Ira Lent was dead. As for you"—I turned to O'Rourke—"there's another corpse for you and Doc Barkley if the government doesn't want to be mixed in it." And I gave him Cora's address. Then I went straight to the girl—to Freida Stanton.

"It's terrible, Race." She tossed both arms around my neck and didn't seem to mind the tiny trickle of blood from my face. "I never suspected Bert. That is knowingly. But I must have suspected him when I hid in that car—then telephoned Sergeant O'Rourke. And—well, I was watching Bert. He was listening at the curtains when you telephoned Mr. Paine last night."

"You're all right, kid." I ran a hand through her hair as she half clung to me. "I had the set-up all along. I was just waiting for the breaks."

O'Rourke laughed. "Even Ira Lent—alias Bert—said you were dumb."

"Sure"—I nodded back—"but Ira Lent is dead—and I'm alive."

"You've got something there, Race," Paine said. "It's the result that counts."

I GUESS HE was right. Ira Lent was dead. I had made some dough and a bit of dress goods hanging on my arm telling me to name my own figure for the job.

"Maybe we'll do some more work for this All American Youth, Incorporated stuff." I tried to smile and felt the cut start to bleed again.

"No, no"—she daubed at my face with her handkerchief—"the meeting sort of changed as the boys and girls warmed up last night. Or so I heard. We're going to buy horses and ride in a rodeo for the homeless Chinese."

Her eyes were bright as she looked at me. Maybe mine were bright as I looked at her. But all I said was: "You'll have to do a lot of riding. There are a hell of a lot of Chinese. As for me, I don't ride—at least I don't ride a horse."

Cash for a Killer

DEATH VS. DOLLARS

THERE IS NOTHING tonier in the city of New York than the Berkeley Apartments. Johnny Slattery had a showroom on top of the building. He called it a "penthouse." So did the management for that matter, but Johnny had made a world's fair out of it. He had collected his idea from the movies. It had many rooms and too many baths. It was modernistic except for his library-office, which was the real thing. I knew that now as I sat down before his ornate desk and let my eyes wander about the room.

Maybe there were tricks in that room, for Johnny had been full of tricks all his life. But the only place to hide a man was behind the heavy drapes before a series of windows. If they were windows. You got the impression of windows all across because you could see the wainscoting and part of a window on each side of the curtains.

Johnny was big time now. He was smooth. He was polished. None of the filth of the gutter had stuck to him, and he didn't go out on the kill any more, or maybe I should say not much any more.

To the public Johnny kept himself respectable—except for a dirty dig in one of the newspapers that maybe a certain society man and banker had not exactly jumped from the window of his office one night a few months back.

But no one could prove that Slattery was at that office, and I guess Slattery could easily prove he wasn't there. Slattery had learned in his early days to prove most anything he wanted to prove. That he didn't sue the paper which had hinted pictorially that Joseph T. Foster had had some assistance in his fall was put down by many as Slattery's desire to get the whole unpleasant incident out of the public mind.

Johnny ordered influential politicians around. He was reputed to be worth plenty, but in these days who can tell. Guys think I've got truck loads of dough sunk away, too. So what?

So JOHN SLATTERY was talking—his piercing blue eyes straight on my face. He said: "I sent for you, Race, because—"

And that was as far as he got. I cut in with: "Nobody sends for me. Not even the D.A. I came because I wanted to hear what you had to say."

"All right, Race. All right, Williams. You're still the hot-headed lad you used to be. We'll just let it go that I begged you to come and you came. You're a business man. So am I. I like things done quickly. I've got ten thousand dollars for you the day you find Mary Ann Foster."

I sat up a bit straighter then.

"You mean the society girl whose father was tossed from the twentieth floor of his office window?"

There are few men who could make Johnny Slattery's face change like I did. It flushed crimson—to turn almost milky white the next second and stay that white with a few patches of yellow in it. He half moved from his seat, then slid back in it again.

When he didn't speak I tried: "What do you want with the daughter?"

"Well"—he stroked at his chin, held it tightly as the yellow patches disappeared—"I knew her old—her father." He came to his feet now, pounded a hand down on the desk. "Hell, her old man died broke. In fact he died owing dough. I want to find the girl. I'm going to marry her." And he pulled that last line as if it were the noble moment of his life.

I laughed right in his face. "Do you know any more jokes, Johnny?" And when he just stared at me, "Where are you going to hold the ceremony? In a sewer?"

And the great Johnny Slattery—gangster, racketeer, controller of politicians and high officials did more tricks with his pan than a movie comic. That highly touted calm was gone now, and his clear blue eyes were ugly and dirty. But he got himself in hand before he spoke. His words didn't get away from him.

"I'm no hood, Race Williams. I'm far out of your class. I made you an offer. You don't want it. There's the door." And when I didn't move—just sat back in the chair with my left hand deep in my jacket pocket, "Well—do you get out while you can get out?"

"Listen, Slattery," I told him. "I won't say you haven't got the nerve for it, but I thought you had more sense than to try and pull me into a trap like this. Don't look so blank." I lifted my forty-four easily from my pocket and pointed it at his chest. "Tell that gunman you have behind those curtains to come out and drop his gun. Or I'll blast a hole right through your chest."

"Precaution, Race," Slattery muttered, "simply precaution. Come on out, Gunner, and drop— Damn it, come out, I say!" This as I played with my gun, letting the hammer ride up and down.

The curtains parted. A tall, massive figure stepped out. There was a heavy automatic in his right hand. I half swung my arm and his gun dropped to the soft rug with a plump. I just stared at the man—at the great, pudgy, bear-like hands.

" 'Gunner,' eh?" I would have gotten my second laugh then, but I was too surprised. I knew him, of course. And what's more, I knew why his gun shook before he dropped it. It was because he couldn't face me with a gun in his hand.

They had called him Gunner Snyder a few years back. And I guess he had done in a few boys in his day. But he liked to shoot lads in the back in an alley—from behind an ash can—or from the inside of a closed car. He was coming along in the underworld even faster than Johnny Slattery when he first threatened me—let it be known he was out to kill me. And what's more he had tried. The flat nose spread all over the center of his face was my work. The ugly scar running up to his

ear and nicking off a bit of it was my work, too, when I gun-whipped him one night.

Now when I thought he was through, here he was behind a curtain ready for another session.

JOHNNY SLATTERY WATCHED us both, and I watched them both. But Slattery spoke first. He said: "All right, Snyder." I guess Slattery saw the ugly look in my eye because when it comes to mussing it up—back room, Marquis of Queensbury rules in a professional boxing ring, or just plain out-and-out gun-play—I can be twice as ugly as any of them. Rough stuff is my business. Slattery knew that and finished: "Go out the door, Snyder. And stay out."

Snyder was an ugly brute of a man. His small pig-like eyes were on me nervously as he swung to the right and pushed his huge bulk between us.

A nice move, that, since I was covering Slattery and had to watch his hands. A man could have some respect for Slattery. Oh, I don't mean in an upright, honest sort of way, but as a killer. A lad with guts but without too much sentiment or feeling. If he had asked me to come over for the purpose of killing me, he wouldn't mind taking a shot at me while Snyder was between us and got killed by my shot.

His hands never moved from their position on his desk, but his eyes shifted suddenly just as Snyder passed me. I caught Snyder's movement out of the side of my eye. His right hand flashing under his left armpit—his body swerving so as to put him on my side and not facing me as he shot.

I could have swung and fired. And it

wasn't respect for Slattery's soft, luxurious, expensive Oriental rug. It was simply disrespect for Snyder. Oh, I swung all right, had plenty of time to see that his gun was only half out of its holster, then I let him have it. This time I nearly drove his ear into his head. That's right, I cracked him with the nose of my gun.

Gunner Snyder tossed himself up in the air like a circus performer, landed on his face, skidded across the rug, and brought up against the wall in a silly sort of position.

I was feeling better now. I turned to Slattery. "Well," I said, "do you sweep him out or do I nail him to the floor with a few pounds of lead?"

"You mean—" Slattery's blue eyes lost their sudden hate.

"I mean I'd like to hear what you have to say alone."

He pushed his hand toward some buttons on the desk, hesitated, looked at me. Then the tension was broken. Snyder was through with his contortionist act. He unwound himself and staggered to his feet. He was muttering over and over: "I'll kill you for this, Race Williams. I'll kill you for this."

I crossed the room and opened the door for him.

"O.K., Mr. Gunner Snyder," I said. "I wish I had a dollar for every punk who tells me that." And when he was still muttering threats as he went out the door, I added: "Be a good boy, Al, or sometime I'll stick a gun between your teeth and—"

And he was gone.

I closed the door, and Slattery said: "I thought you'd plug him. I never heard of you clowning around with a killer before."

"Slattery," I told him, "I've been in the business a long time. I'll give you a bit of advice. Gunner Snyder is washed up. He was always a back-alley man. As a bodyguard"—I shrugged my shoulders—"you'd better examine the suicide clause in your insurance policy."

Slattery grinned pleasantly. "I'm glad you want to talk alone, Race, want to listen to me. I'm no fool. If you had knocked over Snyder they would have held you for homicide at least. If he had knocked you over— Well, getting rid of bodies isn't so hard today."

"And if I had knocked you over?"

"Then you would have knocked over twenty thousand dollars in hard cash." He sat down now, leaned over the desk. "I've doubled the ante, Williams. Twenty grand for finding and producing the dame."

I shook my head. "She wouldn't marry you, Slattery."

"Well, she happened to be considering my offer just before her father died."

"Her stomach would turn over and do tricks on her."

He DIDN'T LIKE that, but he took it pretty well. "I'll give you twenty grand to tell me where she is." He was eager now. "Just your word, Race. That's always been good. That's what you've built your reputation on. Come on." He dug into the desk drawer, took out a check book, wrote rapidly with a fast hand and a light touch. Then he simply waved the check in the air to blot it, handed it to me. "There—ten thousand dollars cash for simply looking, and ten more for telling me where she is. You know my check is as good as my word."

I was playing cagey now. If his check wasn't any better than his word, I wouldn't even be looking at the signature. But there it was. Ten grand—right in my hand—and just for looking.

I asked him that and he said: "Ten grand just for looking. Ten grand more for finding her."

I kept my eyes on the check and said: "What makes you think I could find her? I want to be on the level with you, Slattery. I'm not a clever detective. I wouldn't know a clue if I saw one."

"Never mind that, boy." He came around the desk and put a hand on my shoulder. "I play hunches. Last night I had a hunch that you would find her. I'm betting ten thousand dollars on that hunch. Easy money for you. You can cash the check as soon as you leave here. All I want to know is that you are working for me. Not for anyone else. Hell—I'd never even know if you looked or not. Ten grand more if you find her. Nothing to lose—not a thing to lose. Pretty soft money."

I didn't see his play. I didn't get the whole show. Maybe I didn't get it at all. Ten thousand is a lot of jack. You'll admit that. I could do as much with it as you could—perhaps more because I know more places to spend money.

I was trying to put the thing together—tie up the loose strings. Here was Johnny Slattery, the biggest crook and murderer in the city of New York, talking fancy, grabbing my hand, trying to close the check in it, almost cooing in my ear.

"You'll be well paid for doing that girl the biggest favor she ever had anyone do her. You'll find her sure, Race, and—and—What the hell are you doing?"

I was tearing up the check. I knew it was a good check. I knew that Slattery could put his name on an oblong bit of paper for ten times that amount, even more and the check would be good. But I stood up facing him now as I tossed the scraps on the desk. I was mad—really mad. And I guess that was because of temptation. It was easy money—too easy.

"Sorry, Slattery," I said. "I never take any man's money for a deal I can't pull off."

"Don't look at it like that." He was talking fast now. "Forget the job. Go where I tell you. I'll advance you twenty grand, pay you another ten. I have an idea the girl is in Miami. Go down there and I'll advise you where to look and—and—What are you looking at me like that for?"

Maybe I played the fool then. But I said exactly what was on my mind.

"Slattery," I told him, "I think you killed her father."

He snapped back on his heels. His words just choked out. "You've—you've seen her and—and—" And suddenly his voice was soft and low. "It will be worth your life to see or talk to that girl. Remember that. This is not Snyder talking, but Johnny Slattery. It will be worth your life."

"That's what you think." I walked to the door, swung it open, and closed it behind me.

Then I sauntered out of the place—not a gun showing. Maybe some of the lads around that apartment that I passed had orders not to bother me. Maybe they didn't. Take it any way you want, none of them wanted any part of me—Race Williams.

CHAPTER 2

THE GIRL IN THE ALCOVE

I POUNDED MY way back to my office wondering just what was on Slattery's mind. I know I should have been a slick, calm, smoothly efficient listener. But I'm not built that way. When I have something on my mind I like to say it. And I don't like lads hiding behind curtains listening to what I have to say and perhaps with instructions to shoot me dead if my words don't fit the music as written.

The elevator took me to my floor. I hoofed it to my office door, turned the knob and nearly put my face through the glass portion above the wood when the door didn't open. Just like that my gun sprang into my right hand. My door had never been locked before in business hours, and certainly not against me. I stepped to one side to avoid the possible shell fire through the glass, then damn near shook the door apart before getting ready to kick it in.

A voice inside chirped like a canary: "Who are you? What do you want?"

Relief? Yes. It was Jerry—the kid I had picked up and who knew more about the underworld than any fence. Relief and surprise. Jerry usually had a deep voice.

I said: "Why the mocking bird, Jerry? Open the door."

The key turned, the door opened. Jerry was trying to tuck a gun under his arm and another in his jacket pocket at the same time. He wasn't making a good job of it. He must have turned the key with his teeth—or chanced shooting himself to death.

"What the hell?" I asked him. "Was there an air raid?"

"You'll see, boss. You'll see. Lock the door"—his voice was pleading—"lock the door. I've been sitting here for an hour guarding it!"

"Guarding what?" I locked the door and followed him into my private office. I had never seen Jerry so excited before. His hand trembled as he pulled open the center drawer of my desk.

Then he stood back, eyes bugging out, and said: "Look!"

I looked. Maybe my fingers didn't do any gymnastics, and maybe my voice didn't crack like cock robin. But I did gasp, and my eyes did bulge as I sat down behind the desk and drew out the money. Thousand-dollar bills—all but two of them.

"How much, Jerry?" I asked.

Jerry shook his head, stuck a finger under his collar, finally gasped: "I don't know. I don't know. The express man brought the package. I opened it when he was gone and saw the money. Just saw it. It fell on the floor, boss. Money—money—money— It gave me a funny feeling in the stomach. No guard with it. Nothing. Just the package—and the letter—there." The pointing finger meant to direct my eyes to the envelope, but he might just as well have been pointing that finger at the Statue of Liberty down the bay.

For the moment I ignored the letter, grabbed out the money and counted it. After that I rubbed a handkerchief across my forehead. It came away a little damp anyway. Oh, I'm used to big money, but this added up to exactly—hold your breath—to exactly forty thousand dollars. Count it. I did.

Jerry ran over and closed my office door. He was breathless.

"Hide it away, boss. Every thug in the city would be around here if they knew—"

I lit a butt, blew smoke toward the ceiling, and leaned back in my chair.

"Jerry," I said, "you're wrong. If there's any man who thinks he can get that much dough away from me he's welcome to a try at it."

After all, it wasn't my money. I snapped an elastic band around each bunch of ten thousand and placed it all back in the drawer. Then I opened the letter.

Dear Mr. Williams:

Please subtract from the enclosed forty thousand dollars twenty-five hundred dollars for your service. This service which I wish you to perform may or may not be very dangerous to you at the time or afterwards. And again it may cost you your life.

You will take the money to Fitzroy and Jordan, Bankers and Brokers on Broadway. It is to pay a note contracted by the now deceased Joseph T. Foster. You will get both the canceled note and a statement from Mr. Jordan that it has been paid in full.

You will take with you Mr. George Campel of Campel, Rice, and Campel. Mr. Campel is senior member of the firm. Telephone him at once after making arrangements to see Mr. Jordan as soon as you get this letter.

Do not under any circumstances permit Mr. Jordan to know who you are or what your business is until you are in his private office.

That part I will leave to you.

I need you very much. You will hear from me shortly.

Your business is facing death and making enemies. In doing me this service you will later face death and at once make a terrible enemy. Be in your office at five o'clock.

Your Admirer,

The Girl in the Alcove

That's most of the letter. The telephone numbers and addresses were unnecessary, as I knew both the parties. Fitzroy and Jordan were brokers who lent money. A little on the shady side perhaps, but big business and nothing to lay a finger on. Campel, Rice, and Campel were, of course, one of the biggest estate and trust law firms in the city of New York.

I BUZZED CAMPEL first, got George Campel, Senior, on the phone almost at once. He didn't like the business, didn't ask my name, apparently expected the call, and was pretty nearly as nervous as Jerry about the whole thing. But his time was mine, as he put it, so I told him I'd call him back in a few minutes.

Jordan of Fitzroy and Jordan was my meat. I knew how to handle him all right. I got his number and went into my act before his secretary could tell me what a busy man he was.

I'll admit I slurred over the words a bit,

left her with the impression that I was one of the vice-presidents of the First National Bank, and when I got Jordan on the wire, I didn't go in for any introduction but just knocked away at his ear drum.

"Ah, Mr. Jordan," I said. "I've been made a director of the institution now, and I want to talk to you at once. A little matter concerning money." And when he would have said something, "No—no—the matter brooks of no delay." A bit of irritation in my voice then. "I must see you now—at once."

I kept talking until he said he would be glad to see me. Then I hung up. Who wouldn't be glad to see the Vice-president of the First National Bank who had just been appointed to the Board of Directors? After all, it was Jordan's line of business—lending money. And doing business with a vice-president of a big banking institution would help his standing in the financial world.

"O.K., Jerry," I told my vice-president, office boy, secretary, or what-have-you. "Get my black satchel, dump that dough in it."

"Boss—boss—" He almost pleaded with me. "You're not going to walk the streets with that dough on you?" And when I grinned, "I'd better come along."

"You're scared stiff now," I told him.

"So much jack sort of knocked me," Jerry said very seriously. "But if you should be killed I'd be myself again and blast the guts out of—"

I cut in on him there with a raise of my hand while I called Campel back and made a date to meet him some place

right away. He couldn't understand my not coming to his office to meet him, and didn't seem to tumble why the lobby of the Waldorf Hotel wasn't an ideal place. Finally I picked a place for him—a saloon just off Broadway and near his office. I could tell by his surprised voice that no one would ever think of looking for him there. But that was why I wanted it that way. And then I gave him the number, told him to wait at the bar for me, and smacked down the phone.

It was then I got my idea about Jerry. He was a great boy, so I told him: "Jerry, grab the old car and follow me. I may need you at that. Make it snappy. I'll wait five minutes, flag a taxi, and be on my way."

Jerry didn't want to leave me alone with that bag of heavy sugar, but he never argued on orders. He was gone like that, and I sat and looked out the window at the clock across the street. I didn't do too much thinking. As I said, rough stuff is my business, and I never got anywhere lying on my back trying to figure things out. I want action—and what I want, I get.

Six minutes by the clock in the old church tower and I came to my feet. I let my right and left hands flash up under either armpit, took a bit of a snort if not exactly a full laugh as I thought of Jerry being worried about all that dough, then grabbed up my brief-case and trotted out into the hall.

I haven't any nerves. I've always said that, and I say it now. But having nerves and being keen are two entirely different things. Certainly the lad trying to sell a towel service by going from door to door in the outer hall came as near to losing his life as any guy I know. So near, in fact, that I stopped and spoke to him.

"Have you life insurance?" I asked.

"No"—he said—"no. And I don't want any. I don't need any."

"Boy," I told him just before I rang for the elevator, "you don't know how much you needed it—just a few minutes ago."

With that I swung my thirty-seven-thousand-five-hundred-and-seven-dollar satchel under my arm. The left arm, understand. Like Jerry I was feeling the responsibility. And I was feeling something else, too, as I flagged a taxi.

The Girl in the Alcove had not once said a word about trusting to my honesty. She had just shipped the dough. Sure—I had a nice feeling toward that girl.

Call it tavern, bar, or hotel, but I swung into that Broadway saloon after catching Jerry parking across the street out of the corner of my eye, and looked the length of the bar. I didn't need to see or hear any of the argument to know the lad I was to meet. Heavy glasses, black ribbon, gray fedora, white carnation, gray hair, if I saw correctly. He was leaning against that bar, and you could see how uncomfortable he was in such surroundings. But then, it was a hard joint at that.

I came up alongside of him as I heard the bartender crack wise.

"You take beer or nothing, understand. We don't serve celery tonic here. You take beer or get out."

And that was my cue. George Campel, Senior, was a big man. Oh, I don't mean in size, I mean in the legal world, and in the social world, too, for that matter. What a break for me to show my stuff. I just sauntered up to the bar, crashed down the treasury, and said: "If the gentleman wants celery tonic, he gets celery tonic. Send out for it."

It wasn't a nice place. The bartender wasn't a nice man. He turned his round face on me, swore, and said: "If he don't get it—what?" He showed a nice set of teeth in a smile that was a bit nasty.

"So you swallow all those teeth," I said, and I said it loud.

The bartender looked surprised. Then his eyes raised. His mouth turned at the corner, and the hand on my shoulder turned me around.

"Tell it to the manager," the bartender sneered.

I faced tough Billy Rankin, owner of the Neptune Bar. What's more, he faced me. Surprise, shock, alarm—all ran over his handsome face.

I said simply: "So he gets celery tonic, eh?"

Rankin knew me, of course. The threat died on his lips. His face broke into smiles. He fairly bellowed at the bartender.

"Send out for some celery tonic if the gentleman wants it. What the hell do you think—" And as the bartender banged on the counter for a waiter he bent forward and whispered: "No trouble, boy. Nothing wrong, is there?" His eyes shifted up and down the bar uncertainly. "Hell, Race, all regular guys here." And when I said nothing, "Good God, man, you're not thinking of making a shooting-gallery out of my place?"

"Nuts," I told him. "You need a bit of

manners in your place. On your way. My friend and I want to be alone."

I LIKED IT. Truth is truth, I was flattered, and so would you be. It's nice to feel that you've built up a name along the home-town streets that makes you respected. You never saw a bottle of celery tonic appear from nowhere so fast. You never saw teeth change from a snarl to a smile without even the lips moving. And you never heard so many "sirs" come from anyone behind a bar before.

When he asked me what I'd have, I said: "Celery tonic."

Then I turned to George Campel, Senior.

"I'm Williams," I told him. "The lad who called you. If you have been inconvenienced, I'll rip the joint up."

He had difficulty in keeping his glasses on his nose.

"I see—yes—I mean, yes, I'm glad to meet you. No inconvenience. I—I—shall we get moving? You are different from the others?"

"What others?"

"I—I—but perhaps we should talk in the cab." And as we forgot the celery tonic and forgot to pay for it as we walked out, he said: "I understand the young lady has decided on you entirely. Is that correct?"

As we reached the street and climbed into a cab, I answered: "I hope it's correct. She couldn't do better. You mean Miss—er—Miss—"

But I couldn't fool George Campel that way. He was a cagey bird like the rest of his trade—high or low.

"To be sure," he said. "I mean exactly that."

"Smart guy" was on my tongue, but I didn't pull it. He didn't seem to be the sort of a lad who would take a bit of light humor, and what's more, I didn't want to kid around any more with so much cash on hand.

"Well," I finally said after we rode too long in silence, "have you anything to suggest?"

"Nothing. Absolutely nothing." And unstiffening a bit, if he could unstiffen, he added: "I don't wish to appear rude. But you must know the reputation of our firm, and you must understand as senior member just how far I am going. You are to pay—shall I say, rather, that you are to liquidate a note. I am attorney of record for the Foster estate. I shall protect the legal interests. The people—this person with whom you have so quickly arranged an appointment—is not one I would usually—indeed under other circumstances I would not call upon him at all."

"That," I said, "is what makes life interesting. A fresh bartender, a threatening owner of the same saloon, a respected member of the bar like yourself, and now Mr. Jordan. All in my line of business. I take life and the oddities it turns out as it comes."

It was some time before he spoke again.

"Are you perhaps referring to me as an oddity?" was all he could get off.

"One of my most treasured." I did a bit of high-hat myself. "But if you wish to leave everything to me, you may remain in the background."

"I am afraid that this time things will be hard to handle. I have gone as far as I can possibly go by accompanying you."

"That," I answered, "is far enough for me."

Five minutes later, without knocking off a fender, the taxi drew up before the great building in which Fitzroy and Jordan housed themselves.

"Now for it, Mr. Campel," I said as we stepped from the cab. Over my shoulder I gave Jerry the high-sign that things were all O.K., and that he could trundle on back to the office. At least I guess he gathered my meaning, because out of the corner of my eye I saw him pull off in the car which had been tailing our cab from the Neptune Bar.

Campel, Senior and I walked into the office building, and so far he was one up on me. No one had paid for the celery tonic. And I had paid for the taxi. These high-class lawyers are smart people.

CHAPTER 3

THE MAN WITH THE TURTLE NECK

I HADN'T SAID anything to Campel about the business of the moment, and he hadn't said anything to me, but he opened his case as we left the elevator and walked straight down the long marble hall to the big impressive double doors which read: *FITZROY AND JORDAN, ASSOCI-ATES—BANKERS AND BROKERS.*

Campel said: "You understand, sir, that I am here simply as a witness and as your legal advisor in representing—er—our interested party. I personally handled the entire business of Mr. Joseph T. Foster.

Just before—er—his unfortunate and sudden demise—he became involved in financial matters entirely on his own."

"So what?" I didn't like his airs, nor his "ers" for that matter.

He seemed startled, hesitated close to the doors, and finally said: "I don't think you will be able to buy what you came for. Mr. Jordan's business methods are, in my opinion, which of course is not conclusive, unethical."

"You'll be surprised at mine then, brother." I dug him playfully in the ribs, and if I had smacked a ripe tomato between his eyes he couldn't have been more surprised. Life must have gone along easily and pleasantly for Mr. Campel, Senior.

I opened the door and pushed him in ahead of me. Like him or not like him, I had to admit he made a good front to crash the Jordan private office.

The reception-room wasn't quite as big as Central Park. Behind a long railing with a gate on either side of it were two solid doors. I wasn't interested in any but the one which read in gold letters: *MR. HARRINGTON JORDAN.*

The man who got up so suddenly from behind a small desk was too big and husky to be a clerk. His face had not been knocked around enough for him to be a prize-fighter, so I drew my own conclusion. I didn't know him, but I wasn't sure he didn't know me. Neither was he for that matter, for his face screwed up like that of an old man—and not an over-ly-bright old man—doing crossword puzzles.

He wasn't nasty about my hand

stretching over the gate toward the little lock inside. That is, he wasn't nasty when I drew it back.

"Who do you want to see?" he asked.

I straightened and put on a bit of dignity of my own and jolted him considerably.

"I have no desire to see anyone," I told him. "But Mr. Jordan has a great desire to see me." And half bowing toward a rather cute little trick who sat by a phone, I added: "Have the young lady call Mr. Jordan and tell him the gentleman he is expecting is here. There—no names, please." And leaning forward and whispering, "The matter is of the greatest confidence."

The girl looked me over—rather liked what she saw. She looked Campel over and was rather awed. Then her face disappeared into the hooded mouth-piece attached to the phone. So I couldn't listen there.

However I watched and she smiled when she came out of the iron lung and told us to go straight in.

The big boy opened the gate for us. He was still looking at me, but he had ceased trying to operate that brain of his from the inside, and was now working in from the outside by scratching his head. But the puzzle of the Sphinx—meaning me— was still with him when I pulled open the thick door.

Behind that door was the great Jordan for anyone to see. He sat behind a desk that made Slattery's look like one from a child's set of toys. He held his seat for a moment to give us a chance to be impressed.

He was a peculiarly built man with a massive chest and great shoulders. But his neck was too long and his head too small, and his features were all crowded together. When he stuck his head forward he looked like a snapping turtle ready to snap.

I closed the door as he came to his feet, stepped around the desk peering at me, and trying to see Campel behind me.

"Good-afternoon." He moved his heavy body quickly. "You're—you telephoned me from the bank. This other gentleman?"

"My solicitor," I said, and I could see that he received that bit of news unpleasantly. He stepped backward, again shot his head forward.

"Mr. Campel, of course." He ignored me and stretched out a hand to Campel. "I had the pleasure of meeting you once before."

Campel's hand remained at his side. Not being fussy, I saved the situation by stepping forward and taking Jordan's hand, shook it a bit before returning it.

If he noticed the "cut direct" he didn't show it. He invited us to sit down, then getting behind his desk again, opened up with a chuckle. It sounded like pretended humor with hidden sarcasm behind it.

"Well—it must be important." He worked his head out and in again. "Important to bring you out of your office, Mr. Campel. I am highly flattered. It's money your client here wants to invest, of course. One would hardly wish to borrow money in these times. You want me to suggest a purchase?"

"No—" I didn't let Campel turn on his

dignity now. "It is money, Mr. Jordan, and I am suggesting the purchase." I opened my satchel, tossed the bills over to him. "Count them."

It threw both of them. Involuntarily, though, Jordan reached for the bills.

He was starting to count them when he stopped and said: "You carried these through the streets of New York—without protection?"

I bowed toward the open-mouthed Campel, replied: "Mr. Campel was my protection. No man could ask for more."

Jordan didn't speak then. He ran his fingers rapidly through the bills again—almost like a magician handles the cards—and I'm telling you I hoped that would be the only likeness to a magician.

When he had gone through them the third time and stacked them up in piles on his desk he breathed: "Thirty-seven one-thousand-dollar bills, and one five-hundred-dollar bill. Correct?"

"Correct," I agreed. "So we have thirty-seven thousand five hundred dollars which more than covers the principal sum and interest on the investment I wish to purchase from you."

"I don't understand." Jordan was not sarcastic now. His eyes and his mind were on the money.

"I want," I said slowly, "the promissory note made out to you by Joseph T. Foster."

Jordan's head shot forward now and stayed forward. His wide eyes grew wider.

After a minute he said: "I have no such note. You have made a mistake. You misinformed me on the phone."

He was getting to his feet when I left my chair, took a long stretch across the wide desk, and shoved him back in his throne-like chair again.

I said: "If you are speaking the truth, Mr. Jordan, this day will prove the most unfortunate of your life."

"You must be mad." He straightened from the lounging position he had taken—or I had given him. "I don't know what you're talking about. Mr. Campel, I am amazed that you came. I must ask you gentlemen to leave."

His fingers moved toward the push buttons on his desk, and I went into my act. I bent a little, let the gun from my left shoulder holster slip casually into my right hand.

My voice was low. I put the old-time melodrama into it, and said simply enough: "Mr. Jordan, I'll shoot your fingers off one by one as they reach for those buttons. The name is Williams—Race Williams. Mean anything to you?"

And it did. His hand shot back as fast as he could use that turtle-like neck of his. He didn't speak. He couldn't speak.

Campel, behind, spoke though. At least words came out of his mouth. He said: "God in heaven." And nothing more.

Cold beads of sweat broke out on what, for lack of another name, you'd have to call Jordan's forehead.

He finally gasped out: "You're the—the detective—who has shot so many—" He stopped there.

"So many crooks," I filled in for him. "You don't want to make it another. Get out the note—now."

He did, although I thought I'd have to come around the desk and help him open the drawer. But he threw the paper on the desk before him. Surprised, stunned, or knocked cock-eyed, somehow his left arm went out and his right hand encircled the money in front of him.

I picked up the note, glanced down at it, whistled softly. Jordan hadn't lied to me. The note was not his. The promise to pay was made to— You guessed it, of course, and you're right. To Johnny Slattery.

My gun was nested again now, and I handed the note to Campel.

"Pass on the signature," I said roughly, for I didn't want the situation to get too pleasant. "Come on, work that legal advice of yours."

Campel's glasses were off his nose, he had trouble in finding a tiny long-handled magnifying glass, and twice as much trouble trying to keep both the note and document with Foster's signature which he had brought along for comparison from slipping off his lap.

At length I placed them side by side on the desk for him. I took my own look-see.

"Well"—I had to jar him alive—"what do we want now? 'Canceled' stamped or written across the face of the note and a receipt for the money? Come—that legal advice—give."

By this time Jordan had come out of his fright, was perking up and beginning to do some threatening of his own. He wanted to know what Campel thought he, Jordan, would do the moment we left the office.

"I'll just pick up the phone and call the police," he said. "A nice mess for a man of your supposed standing, Mr. George Campel. If you don't go to jail why you'll be disbarred. The whole—"

And I laid the bee on Jordan and laid it hard.

"Listen, Jordan, one more yap out of you and I'll walk out of here with both the note and the money. If Slattery sold you the note you didn't pay its face value. If—"

"Mr. Slattery," said Jordan, "had my promise to sell that note to him. My word. He's trying to protect the name of a dear friend now dead and—"

"Do you fix things up my way, or do I take both note and money? Put a yes or a no to that."

He put a yes to it. I jabbed the canceled note and the receipt into my pocket, spun the befuddled lawyer toward the door. Then I walked back to Jordan.

"Jordan"— I came around the desk this time and put a finger hard against his chest—"you got real dough. Forget it. Don't try and glare me down. Campel is my witness that you went through with the transaction without a kick. And he's no doubt a better witness than Slattery might have to alibi him."

"Alibi Slattery? For what?"

"For murder." I threw in a wild one. "You know Slattery. Take my advice. Keep your trap closed, and closed tight. Bigger guys than Johnny Slattery have fried, and smaller guys than you gone for a long ride. There—don't tell me you're not mixed up in anything. I don't believe you are. I'm just saying—keep as clean as you can under the circumstances. Now—buzz the police if you want to."

I flung my bag under my arm, tossed

my hat on the back of my head, and strolled easily out of the office behind the already departing Mr. Campel. I saw him go out the gate and sort of wander toward the hall door. The big guy by the gate stopped me.

"Say," he said suddenly, "you're Race Williams, aren't you?"

"That's right," I agreed.

He smacked his lips. "The boss will want to know that."

"Sure—sure." I patted him on the shoulder. "Go tell him. It will amuse him, and I don't know anyone more in need of a good laugh right now."

With that I caught up with Campel, stood silently beside him in the elevator, escorted him to a taxi without a word passing between us. It was mean, of course. I'm not denying that, but I couldn't resist it. I'd ring him up later and put his mind at ease. But I gave him the final blow as I leaned in the window of the taxi.

"Don't you worry," I said. "If the cops come, sit tight. Say nothing, consult a lawyer." And as the taxi drew away I called after it: "Good-bye, George. See you in Sing Sing."

Then I went into a drug store and had some coffee and doughnuts.

CHAPTER 4

FIRST BLOOD

I'VE GOT A habit of always walking the wrong way down a one-way street. It's sort of an insurance I take out and pay nothing for, but it means that I always face the traffic—face the oncoming cars. And I always have faced the one car when it comes. I mean the death car.

I wasn't more than two blocks nor more than twenty or twenty-five minutes out of Jordan's office when the car came. Maybe I sense danger. Maybe living so close to death lets me know when it is coming. Maybe I unconsciously see things that flash warnings to that so-called brain of mine. Such as a driver who dashes suddenly forward then slows down, a driver who looks in any direction but mine, the lowering of windows in a big sedan, the glaring single eye that looks over a Tommy gun and waits. Call it what you want, take it any way you like, I saw the death car coming in plenty of time to dive for the areaway and escape the raking lead.

But I got a bad break. I was just about to duck back and drop into that areaway when I saw the kids—four or five little tots that just hopped out of noplace and were playing right in front of it. So I did the best I could.

I ran about twenty-five or thirty feet toward that oncoming car, slid another fifteen on my stomach, and opened fire on the death car before it opened fire on me. That bit of procedure was a new one for me, so I suppose it was a new one for the boys in the car. But as long as I was to take it, I might as well give a bit of it first.

Did I bless those kids. Here I had made my nose dive along the pavement to save their lives, and it looked as if they might have saved mine. At least if I had missed that basement entrance.

　　　　　　　　　　　　　　　CARROLL JOHN DALY

I was blazing with both guns before a shot ever came out of that car. I didn't have luck when I tell you I hit the driver, and the car swerved, and the machine gunner who stuck his ugly puss up over the window started spraying the buildings with lead at least three floors up.

No—I had bad luck in not killing the driver. Not that it was exactly bad shooting on my part. I never do any bad shooting. If I did I wouldn't be alive today. But I was trying to watch that lowering window and spot the machine gun when it came.

I spotted it—spotted also the face behind it just as the car straightened out and the nose of that Tommy gun centered directly on me. Then I let go—one with the right hand—one with the left. I don't know which one he took or both. All I know was that his face wasn't in the windows any more, that the nose of the machine gun had disappeared, and that the car had picked up speed and was going down the street.

Of course things were happening all up and down that block. Kids were yapping, people were hollering from windows. A police whistle blew, a siren shrilled.

I came to my feet, dusted off my jacket, and backed up the stone steps behind me. It was a brownstone front that had been turned into an apartment. The door was open. I backed inside, pulled some slugs from my pockets, and started to reload my gun. Things had happened fast. They might happen still faster. I wanted to be ready.

Something pounded into my back. I knew the feel of it all right. It was round and hard. What a bad break that was.

What a coincidence that was. Yep, a coincidence that I should walk down that street, back up those particular stairs, and after what had just happened, back right into the trap I was avoiding by facing the street. And I always said that I don't believe in coincidence.

A voice behind me spoke. It said: "Hold it me fine friend. Hold it just like that."

And me—for a moment I held it just like that. Then I swung suddenly around.

The man I faced said: "Glory be to God. It's you yourself—Race Williams." And with a slight cough, "Now, I might have known after what I seen from me window upstairs."

Blue trousers, heavy suspenders, a napkin tucked under his collarless shirt, a heavy police gun in his hand. It was Patrolman Clancy. Sure I knew him, and I knew his voice. Everyone knew Clancy. He must have been on the force for forty years—perhaps more. So I was right. I still don't have to believe in coincidence. And what's more, I don't have to be dead because of one.

"Listen, Clancy." I stuck a hand tight against his jacket as I pushed him quickly back into the hall when I heard people running on the stairs. "I don't want any report of this. I want you to shove me out the back some way, and—"

I stopped. Yes, I knew Clancy, and I should have known enough not to suggest any such thing to him, let alone wait until the kind, weather-beaten face cracked up into hard wrinkles. So I caught myself.

"I mean we'll take it up with Sergeant O'Rourke, I'll go and see him, Clancy."

"We'll take it up-with him now. On the

phone in my apartment. I should make a report."

O'ROURKE DIDN'T WANT to talk on the phone so he said he'd be over in five minutes. It was fifteen before he got there, took Clancy's report, told him he'd handle it himself, then chased Clancy out of his own comfortable living-room and into the kitchen and said to me: "I was talking to the cops downstairs, and some of the people who saw the shooting. Three of them say you fired first."

"Well, I'll be damned," I fairly exploded in O'Rourke's face. "You're not advocating that kind of kid stuff. You-hit-me-first business. I shoot first whenever I get the chance."

"Then you knew that car was coming for you. How?"

"I always suspect a car is coming for me. Come on, O'Rourke, it's import-ant that I don't get in the papers at this time. I've got big business on hand." And when he started to give me that line about being my friend, but how could a "mere sergeant" help me I stopped him with, "I know as well as you that you're a sergeant because you want to be a sergeant. Because being one keeps you in close contact with the men on the force. I know, too, that you could be an inspector—that you work straight from the commissioner himself, and take orders only from him. It's an important case. May be big for you later, O'Rourke."

His honest face opened wide.

"Big-hearted Race. Always gives a pal a break. Well, name my break—a police break—and I'll talk to you."

I shrugged my shoulders and went ahead cautiously.

"Are you satisfied that Joseph T. Foster committed suicide?"

"What do you mean?" O'Rourke jarred a little in his chair.

"I mean do you think he was murdered—pushed out the window?"

"Yes—I do."

"Would you like to know the man who did it?"

"I know him." O'Rourke was emphatic. "But knowing and proving before twelve men are—"

"Yeah—I know all that. How would you like the proof?"

"Can you produce it?"

"I can try."

"Who do you suspect? Come clean."

I had to be cagey, too.

"The first letter of his name is 'S,' " I said.

" 'L' is the second." O'Rourke leaned forward anxiously.

" 'A,' " I gave it to him.

" 'T.' " O'Rourke nodded. He seemed pleased.

" 'T' again," I told him. And then, "Does that cover it?"

"Sure, sure. Forget the shooting, boy, for a bit. Police business. You think he planned your death?"

"It might be. I left a certain building, swallowed a little food and drink, killed a bit of time. And the job seemed a hurried-ly-put-together one."

THERE WAS MORE after that, but I had to protect my unknown client's interests, and I didn't know exactly what those interests were. I pleaded with O'Rourke to tell me what he knew.

"Well," he said, "I'll tell you. I'll warn you, too. This lad Slattery had a bad start in life. He got the breaks, found the money easy and only did a short stretch. He can still draw a gun and use it, and whether he hires other people or not, he's still got murder in his heart. Foster didn't know Slattery's past when he met him. Slattery showed him how to make some easy money and then dumped some bum securities over on him, broke him, lent him money or showed him where to borrow it. Then he smacked him into debt and finally—understand, I can't prove this part, Race—finally mixed him up where a killing took place in a swanky bungalow up in the Maine woods."

"Hell, you don't mean Foster killed a man?"

"No," O'Rourke grunted, "Foster was the innocent victim of a frame-up. A woman was in it. A lad was killed apparently saving Foster's life. Understand, I have this in a hazy sort of way. None of it got into the papers. But Slattery wasn't there at the time. I'm putting things together now. So Slattery hushes things up to protect his friend's name. What's more he was—well, a columnist hinted a few months back that Slattery was engaged to the daughter. So putting things together this is the way I figure.

"Maybe Slattery wanted social position by marrying the daughter and the old man was selling her down the river. Maybe Slattery wanted the use of Joseph T. Foster's respected name to head some crooked deal. Foster was frightened to the verge of distraction, agreed to anything, then finally sent for Slattery to meet him privately in his office after hours. Or Slattery arranged the meeting and Foster decided to go to the police with the whole business—even tell about some crooked scheme of Slattery's. Anyway—pop!—like that, Slattery tosses him out the window."

"You can put a lot together with that head of yours," I said suspiciously.

O'Rourke reddened. "Hell, I got an anonymous letter hinting at some such things. Just hinting, understand. Look here, Race, I had more guts than the district attorney. I went point-blank to Slattery and asked him where he was that night. I didn't make any bones about it. Not me."

"Good for you. Did he have an alibi?"

"I suppose so."

"Don't you know?"

"Well, he told me that it was none of my damned business where he was, but he added that if I wanted to know, I'd find out. And the blankety-blank D.A. would find out if he ever put Slattery on the stand for any reason. He could alibi himself, of course, with big names. That is big names to the public who only see their pictures in the papers and hear them talk at election time but can't smell them. He added that I would lose my job."

I took a grin on that.

"Imagine you losing your job."

"Yes." O'Rourke didn't smile. In fact his face set rather grimly. "That's just what I have to imagine, Race. Oh—I know—the commissioner is not only my boss but my friend. He pooh-poohed it, too, when I first told him, but now they're putting the pressure on him. It's an election year you know." His smile wasn't very real. "The commissioner will pull me back in, of course."

"Of course," I agreed, but I knew better. "So Slattery's that big, eh?"

"That big." O'Rourke clenched a fist. "But it hasn't happened yet, Race, and before it does, I'd like to lay the finger on Slattery for murder. If I got a conviction—but he would probably beat the rap."

"I doubt it." And when O'Rourke just shook his head. "I'm after him, O'Rourke, and with a guy like Slattery—well—when I meet up with such a lad, put the finger on him—"

"I know," said O'Rourke. "He isn't alive to beat the rap then."

"That wouldn't be so bad for you," I said. "A dead man has no pull—no friends."

"It wouldn't be bad for the entire city." O'Rourke didn't argue that point out with me.

"I've got a good deal to go on," I told O'Rourke just before I left.

"I know you have, boy." He put an arm around me and followed me to the door.

"Sure—sure." I was out in the hall now. "Your information didn't happen to come from a girl, eh?" And when he just looked surprised I finished with, "The Girl in the Alcove?"

Then I was gone down the steps two at a time. O'Rourke didn't answer me. He didn't need to. I saw it in his face.

So I skipped through the yard behind the building, passed to the court back of

it, and came out on the street beyond. Just one thought as I went back to my office.

The Girl in the Alcove was writing a lot of letters.

CHAPTER 5

MY CLIENT SPEAKS

IT WASN'T YET three o'clock. I thought I had had enough excitement for one day, so I dropped into a newsreel theatre to rest my weary feet rather than my tired brain.

I rested my feet all right, but not my brain. I thought I had been busy. A few threats of death, Johnny Slattery—the man who always made good his threats—up to now—and the guy in the car with the big Tommy gun.

Big? Well, tiny now. I saw nothing but guys shooting other lads all over Europe. Maybe my day had been nice and restful at that. Then, too, to top it off, they showed some rioting plant workers. And people ask me how I can stand leading such an exciting life!

So I left that place, sat through nearly half an hour of mushy love and finally got a few belly laughs out of a cartoon. After that this theatre turned the war on again and me—Out.

I went back to my office and was opening the door when I heard Jerry say: "He's here now. Just came in. Hold the wire— PLEASE!" A "please" of that kind was generally not in Jerry's vocabulary. "It's the client," he whispered in a voice I could have heard a few blocks away.

"Man or woman?" And when he looked stupidly at me, "Or child? Don't tell me the client wouldn't tell you which. Couldn't you tell with your ears?"

"You couldn't tell boss," he shook his head. "Man, woman, or child."

As soon as I hit the wire in my private room I knew that he was right. The voice was hollow, lifeless. I knew the answer to that, of course. Someone was talking through the wide end of a funnel, or something like that.

The voice said: "Where have you been? You should have come right back. It's after five. What happened to you?"

I didn't like the coldness of the voice, and I could hardly say, "So what? I went to a picture show." But I put teeth in my return crack anyway. I said: "Your note is safe, your lawyer is insulted, and I shot one man to death for you. What more do you want for twenty-five hundred dollars. A European war?"

If there was a laugh it rang hollowly back in the contraption the voice was using. Words came in again.

"My package should be there in a few minutes. Has it come?"

"Package? Nothing has come that I know of beside— Hold the wire a minute, please."

I smacked out my gun and jammed my hand hard down on the desk, drawing a bead on the outer hall door through which three men came. Behind the two leaders I saw Johnny Slattery.

Johnny Slattery and two men. Another case of who shot first. I started to squeeze lead, and stopped. The man with the suitcase dropped it, and his hands shot into the air. He read it in my face I guess, in my eyes. But most of all, he read it in my right hand that held the gun so steadily

"Don't shoot!" he cried out.

"Don't shoot, Williams." Slattery stepped between the men. "It's not a blast-out."

"You bet it's not, Slattery," I said loud enough for the voice to hear. I motioned them along the wall with my gun and they moved in unison—backs sliding nicely— Slattery leaning down to pick up the suitcase.

Into the phone I said: "Call me back in fifteen minutes. I have very important customers." And I jammed down the phone.

Slattery spoke and I had never seen him so white before. I had never known his voice to tremble. Don't get me wrong. I'm not saying it was fear. It might have been eagerness or anger—or a deep passion.

"Was that—is that—my business?" he asked.

I answered him easily enough.

"If your husband has just run off with the French maid, it's your business. If you come to threaten, forget it. If you've come on real business—the business of death— start in now and we'll have it over with."

"You feel pretty sure of yourself, eh?" Slattery started getting hard, then changed his mind. "I came on a friendly visit."

"Then why the two hoods?" I motioned my gun at the dress parade of two who stood against the wall. If they didn't like my crack they didn't object. They didn't like my waving gun either.

"The suitcase." Slattery walked toward me, lifted the heavy bag and placed it on my desk. "I wouldn't carry that through the streets alone."

"Yeah. If you want to talk with me, Slattery, you'll have to chase the corporal's guard out…. Jerry!" And when Jerry came in, "Jerry, search the men against the wall. Toss the artillery on the couch there, and send them into the outer hall. Then lock the office door and come back. Is that the way you'll take it, Slattery?"

"O.K.," he agreed. Not too surly about it, anyway.

I waited until Jerry came back and said: "And this big lad. How about him, boss?"

"That man, Jerry, is Mr. Johnny Slattery. If he has a gun he may keep it. If he wishes to use it, that's his business."

"I'll put it straight to you, Williams," Slattery said, "and just once. How much will you take to blow the other side?"

"You mean sell out to you?"

"Exactly."

"You haven't got that much, Slattery."

"I've got plenty. And I mean plenty."

"Plenty isn't enough. What next?" Slattery opened his left hand and tossed a key over to me.

"For the bag," he said and his breath sort of gasped. "Take a look and check up."

"Jerry"—I still kept my gun on Slattery while I spoke— "stick your gun in Mr. Slattery's back, and if this bag blows up in my face, press the trigger."

Jerry wasn't any too fast with a gun, but he was dramatic. He made a long sweeping arc beneath his left armpit, stepped back a bit like it was a dress rehearsal, then pulled out the gun with a flourish. Only after that exhibition did he walk behind Slattery and jab the gun in his back.

"Still want the bag opened?" I eyed Slattery.

"Hell, yes." He let his lips part slightly. "When I want you dead I'll do it myself."

"Can I count on that?"

"You can count on that" And for the first time Slattery was himself—with real feeling in his voice.

"You didn't try it yourself a couple of hours ago."

"Things have changed in a couple of hours. Changed a lot."

"Really?" I stuck the key in the bag, turned the lock, snapped back the side bolts, tossed up the cover, and was glad Jerry was behind him with the gun. I let the top of the bag go down again, sucked in a few quick breaths, got my hand steady, then told Jerry to wait outside and close the door.

Then I took another look.

Money— Money? I thought I had seen a lot of jack a little earlier in the day. But nothing like this.

"Well," Slattery demanded, "what do you say?"

"Thanks, of course. What do you expect me to say?"

"Do you know what I went through to get that?" Slattery was pushing the words out through closed lips now. "I had to find the owners of half the big gambling houses in the city. And what will they think? That I'm on the rocks. That Johnny Slattery is—"

"Slattery," I cut in, "I'm not interested in other people's opinion of you. I have my own. Do you want to hear that?"

He didn't. He just looked at me. Then he slashed out: "It's extortion—blackmail—" He was working himself up into a fury and at the same time trying to keep himself calm, if you get what I mean. "And you, Williams, are a party to it."

"Slattery"—I laid both hands on the bag— "if you can prove that statement to me, then I won't deliver the suitcase. My business is clean. You know that."

He eyed me wondering how much I knew. Then he turned on his heel and walked stiffly out of the room and out of the office with Jerry unlocking the door for him.

My eyes followed him—my gun also. Jerry did, too, and he spun the key back in the lock when Slattery was gone to join his little playmates.

I WAS FINGERING through the money now. That was when I saw the envelope. It was a white envelope without any name or other markings on it. I held it in my hand for a moment. Then I looked back at the money.

"Jerry!" I finally called, "take this envelope out and steam it open for me." Jerry was a past master at that sort of stuff. "Remember, I'll do the reading of it."

I heard the water run in our little washroom, knew that Jerry was cleaning his hands thoroughly before he began. He was back in five minutes. I rubbed my own fingers on a clean handkerchief, took out the thick sheet of paper inside, and noted Johnny Slattery's name on the stationery. Then I read the terse note. Terse— Well, I couldn't tell whether Johnny had cried like a drunken sailor or cursed when he wrote it.

This one hundred and fifty thousand dollars is money left in trust with me by Joseph T. Foster for his daughter, Mary Ann Foster.

Signed: Johnny Slattery

And what's more, the damn thing was signed by a notary, too.

Laugh that off if you can.

I couldn't. The bag of money was open before me. I stared at it with my gun in my hand.

And the phone rang.

When I lifted the hand-piece the bag was shut tight—the gun no longer in my hand.

It was the voice in the funnel again and it said: "I heard the name. So the stuff arrived?"

"The stuff is here. What do you want me to do with it?"

"I want you to take a train and bring it to me tonight."

"What?" I guess I gasped.

"It's honest." And after some hesitation, "There should be an envelope there. Open it and read it."

A little light humor, and the chance to kill a bit of time brought me back to normal.

I tore open the letter and read it again, then explained: "I wasn't questioning the ethics but the stupidity of carting all that money some place by train."

"Let me be the stupid one. Unless you're afraid."

"I'm afraid for the money."

"You think there is real danger."

I had to choke a bit before I could answer that one. Imagine asking if it was dangerous to try and leave the city with all that dough belonging to Johnny Slattery and him knowing I had it.

I took so long to answer that the voice asked again: "You think there is real danger?"

"Sure," I said sarcastically, "the handle might fall off the bag."

A moment of hesitation at the other end then, "You may take five thousand dollars now for the danger you face or—or—you may take fifteen thousand dollars if you deliver the bag intact."

"Friend"—I licked my lips—"you will get your bag—intact."

"Good. Very good. You will risk your life."

That was a nice enough speech, but why should I take five when I could have fifteen? No one could take that dough away from me without killing me, and if I were dead what difference did it make whether I was paid five or fifteen grand. But if I came through alive—ah—then it did make a difference. You can't get away from the logic in that.

I got my instructions and strange ones they were for a lad with one hundred and fifty grand in his hand to follow. But I listened to them and let it go at that. I spoke only once and those words simply had to come out.

I just said: "Good God—summer resort like that, this time of year? Why you could be shot to death and no one find your—" And I stopped. Why? Well, it didn't seem as though I were spreading good cheer.

The voice belonged to a very efficient person. I repeated what I had been told, got ready to argue, and was cut off.

Here was the lay. We'll call the town Thorton-by-the-Sea though that isn't the right name. I was to take an eleven o'clock train from the Pennsylvania Station, get off at Thorton-by-the-Sea shortly after midnight. Across a little stretch of park I would find a curiosity shop. It would be closed. Back of it was a shed. In that shed was a car. I was to make sure I wasn't followed, then drive to 261 Ocean Side Avenue in Thorton itself, park the car far back in the driveway, enter by the back door and go straight into the house. There would be a light in a room beyond the dining-room. I would meet someone there who would give me further instructions.

As mixed up as a Chinese puzzle? Sure, but then I was only the leading man in the drama, and who was I to question the producer who was paying me fifteen thousand dollars for a single evening's performance? Besides, you might be a little cautious yourself with that amount of money coming to you.

Honestly, I'm asking you point-blank, what would you do between six o'clock, as it was then, and eleven o'clock that night if you were carting half the treasury around with you? I'm no genius in such matters, so if anyone has a better thought, why let me knew in case it should happen to me again.

Me— I could think only one thing. Keep my eye on that bag, and my hand on that bag. How did I spend the time? First off, I decided to eat in my favorite eating-place—favorite, that is, when I felt someone dangerous—well, let's say "interesting" was gunning for me. And I'll admit freely that Johnny Slattery was an interesting man.

I PARKED MYSELF in a rear booth, my back against the wall where there could be no surprise attack. I took one gun from under my left shoulder, placed it under a napkin and shoved it to the end of the table against the wall. Then with the bag held tightly between my knees I grabbed off another napkin and ate a good meal. Money or no money, Slattery or no Slattery, I was hungry.

If I was watched I didn't get it, and I generally get such things.

The meal over I called the waiter whom I knew well and said: "Here's five bucks, Charlie. Tell the boss I'm making a kitchen exit. So stand by the door and see that I'm not followed."

So much for that. Three minutes later I flagged a cab and drove to the Forty-second Street entrance of the Grand Central Station, walked briskly into the station, swung right, came out on Lexington Avenue, and got into another cab which went directly to the Pennsylvania Station. I grabbed a time-table, spotted the name of a station further down the line than Thorton-by-the-Sea and even Thorton itself and bought a ticket to that station. It cost me twenty-odd cents more, but I'm liberal-minded about money. Then I walked across the street, bought myself a big-brimmed dark fedora, sent my own to Jerry's address, and going back to the station sat in the waiting-room.

Maybe I'm fussy like an old woman but if a shadow had followed me it was a real shadow with no living man inside of it.

I cut a slit in the morning edition of my paper, sat with it before my face and looked through the slit. Money does things to all of us. I can't be nervous for I haven't any nerves, but I never saw so many suspicious-looking people in my life. The smoking-room was fairly well filled. They came and they went, but one lad was there for some time. He was tall and his clothes seemed a little too large for him. His hat, too, for that matter, and once I got a look at his face as he looked back suddenly over his shoulders. Thick lips, a large nose, and little staring eyes close to that nose.

If he had acted natural you might at first glance have taken him for a book-keeper with his bent, rounded shoulders. I didn't get the impression he was looking for someone to tail, but he seemed to expect that someone might tail him. He was only one of several, though, and I mention him only because I suddenly became conscious of him when a lad called out the ten-thirty train. He waited until almost ten twenty-eight, then hurriedly shuffled his flat feet toward the waiting-room door.

And me? I shuffled after him. Why? Because in calling the stations of that ten-thirty train the announcer had included Thorton-by-the-Sea.

So bag and money and everything else, I was across the station and through the gate in time to see him enter the rear car.

He was in the light and I was in the darkness when the conductor said: "Front car—smoker. Better get on here and walk through, sir."

But I didn't get on there. I ran along

the platform, passed my bent-shouldered friend as he eyed the different passengers and occasionally glanced back over his shoulder. So it was that I was comfortably seated in the rear seat of the smoking-car and the train had started when Stoop-Shoulders came in.

I had the same slit just where the paper folded so I saw him take a seat, jerk his hat down tighter, and crouch low as if he slept. If a gun or two bulged under that tightly-drawn-up overcoat or lay in one of its generous pockets I didn't know.

Then I studied the time-table and found out that this was a slow local and that it arrived at Thorton-by-the-Sea only nine minutes before the train I was to have taken.

Why did this train stop at Thorton-by-the-Sea? Don't ask me. It stopped everywhere else whether passengers got on or off. Habit, I guess.

CHAPTER 6

ENTRANCE CUE

THE CONDUCTOR CALLED Thorton-by-the-Sea, and Stoop-Shoulders snapped to his feet. I licked at my lips then. I was right after all. He was going my way, perhaps warning someone that I was to come. "Perhaps" was right. The train jarred to a stop. I swung to my feet and was on the car platform just as it went to start again.

There was my man standing below me on the bottom step, looking up and down the length of the train. Making sure, I guess, that no one else got off. Then as the train began to move again he dropped to the platform—his right hand deep in his coat pocket.

He heard me land right behind him. He couldn't help hearing me. With that loaded bag, and I mean loaded. I didn't land like any ballet dancer. He went to turn, did turn slightly, and I let my right fist crack out.

Mr. Stoop-Shoulders hit the wooden platform like a thousand of brick, rolled over once and lay still. He was close to a hedge that might have been far up at that end of the platform for decorative purposes in the summer. Now, even in the dull dimness, it was scrawny.

I didn't search him. I didn't even give him a second look. I just hot-footed it bag and all down to the station a good hundred feet back. Maybe he had nothing to do with my case. Maybe he was just an innocent lad who had a phobia he was followed. Maybe he was an erring husband out to meet the girl friend. I had nothing against him. I just didn't want him in my hair tonight. If he was innocent it would teach him not to go around looking so guilty.

My alarm that someone might see me bending over him was silly. No lights were lit in the station, just dull glares at each end of it and a worn-out, dirty arc in the center. So I held my suitcase in my left hand, and my right clutched a gun in my overcoat pocket.

I felt relieved, too. So far so good. I was alone in the night. It's peculiar how, when you feel most assured, trouble is just ahead. And it was ahead for me. I hot-footed it to the far end of the station, smacked quickly around the corner by the light, and jarred back. A lad stuck two guns right smack into my stomach. A lad I recognized, too. It was Barton Sheridan, the meanest murderer who ever cheated the electric chair.

He spoke before he looked.

"Come on," he snarled as if he were talking to a common pickpocket, "tell me where that girl's hiding before I blow you apart." Then he raised his eyes and looked straight into my face. "God—Race Williams," he said, and his fingers tightened on the triggers of twin guns.

So I shot him twice right in the chest.

He fired all right. I couldn't shoot that fast. But my bullets had picked him right up and tossed him into the air when his guns went off. Perhaps he put out a star or two—but not me.

Though there wasn't a sign of anyone, and the distant train shrilled its whistle in the night, I didn't take any chances. I kept to the shadow of the bare trees as I crossed the oval park, the street beyond, and was in complete darkness going by the curiosity shop and to the little shed behind.

Two minutes later I was driving a speedy little coupé toward Thorton three miles away. I made it in ten minutes—a little town where all the stores were closed and few people on the street. I found Ocean Side Avenue, the house, and was ready to hit up the driveway. Then I changed my mind and flashed by.

After all, my instructions had been to come on the later train. Someone might time my arrival and it was quite possible that if I arrived early someone might put a hunk of lead in my head as I strolled in the open kitchen door.

So I figured it out, killed enough time to make it a natural for the next train, and bounced into the driveway and far back beyond the red brick house.

I found the back door easily enough. It was open. I went into the kitchen, listened, didn't try my flash until I was sure, then just enough to show me it was an old house. The kitchen was big, a swing door, wide open and held back with a brick, led to the butler's pantry.

The swing door, which gave on the dining-room, was closed. I ducked out my flash, pushed the door gently, then even more gently.

Yes, I saw the light through the thick drapes that led to the room beyond where I was to meet my client. But what's more I heard voices. One, a high shrill one. The other, loud and threatening. I took advantage of the loud voice to cross the dining-room and reach the curtains and peer in.

The shrill voice was saying: "I tell you I got off the train and someone struck me. I came to, hurried to my car, and drove right here."

My eyes widened as I saw the owner of that shrill voice. He was stiff and straight in a chair—tied lightly. Those sinister eyes were wide and terror-stricken now, the thick lips quivered, the sharp nose didn't look so sharp, and the shoulders were more stooped than ever. They almost surrounded the head of iron-gray hair.

Yes, it might have been funny, but I couldn't laugh. He was not a young man. He was not a strong man. Hell—truth is truth. I had struck my own client a clout behind the ear.

The two men who were there were both of the old gang that Slattery used to head before he became respectably crooked— by that I mean with official influence behind him. He used scum yet, but wasn't seen openly with them.

Dan Evers, the stockiest of the two I knew and the other I had seen. Stack or Stoke or something like that.

But the old man was saying, as Evers held a knife close to his throat: "I know—I suspected I was followed. I have felt that for some time now. I shan't live much longer. But I won't tell. Kill me. But it means her death, and I won't tell."

"Kill you?" Dan Evers laughed. "So you expect to be treated like a gentleman, eh? Well"—and as the bound man turned white—"you haven't got much blood, but I'll drain it out of you drop by drop. Now. Where's that girl? Race Williams was going to her. Where's Race Williams?"

You've got to admit that if I had written the part myself I couldn't have thought of a more dramatic entrance. It was my cue, and I took it.

I said: "Right here behind you, Mr. Evers. There, don't turn. Both you boys empty your pockets and put all your hardware on the floor."

Evers gasped, but he'd been around too much to turn. He dropped a gun and the knife on the floor. The other lad dropped two guns. The man in the chair gasped as I stood there, my feet straddling the bag.

"You're Race Williams? They followed me. There was a man at the station. He struck me, and—"

"I know," I cut in. "I put a couple of chunks of lead in his chest."

"He's dead?" Both lads gasped together. They weren't so tough now.

"That's for the medical examiner to decide." I took a grin. "I only do the shooting. I'll be searching you two. If either one of you held out a weapon you'll have a chance to find out if two forty-fours finished Barton or not."

Evers dropped another gun to the floor. Stoke or whatever his name was just stared at me—wild-eyed, face drained, fear in his whole trembling body. That kind knows me. Knows I won't drag them off to jail so they can have their pictures taken snarling defiance at the police. They know how I work and they don't like it— not worth a damn.

"Pick up the knife and cut him free," I told Evers. "And if you so much as scratch his wrist I'll drain the blood out of you all in one spurt."

Evers was an obliging fellow. His hand trembled a bit, but that wasn't his fault. He knew I wasn't kidding.

Funny how a face I had pictured as hard and cruel could appear so quickly as pleasant, worried, and kind. But the man in the chair wanted to talk, and I wanted action. What's more I'm a lad who gets what he wants. Clothes line, cord, and even wire was finally produced by Mr. Stoop-Shoulders. I had the bad boys lie down on their faces and didn't waste much time. Hands behind their back, wire and rope, and my foot on each back for leverage when I bound those hands and feet. Then I wired the foot knots and the hand knots together.

They didn't talk. They didn't complain.

When the job was done, I brushed the loose strands of rope from my hands, took Stoop-Shoulders and the suitcase and went into the kitchen.

I locked the back door and said: "Now, you're my client, eh? Here's the bag, and the show is over. If you don't want those birds turned over to the police for any reason I'll drive them down the road a bit and toss them into some bushes. They can do their own explaining at some later time."

"Good lord!" He let his mouth hang open. "I'm not your client, sir. I'm just taking orders. I'm Philip Blackmore, sir—Mr. Williams. I was Mr. Joseph Foster's bookkeeper for years."

"Bookkeeper." I couldn't keep that in. I had been right in my first guess at the Pennsylvania Station. "Then who is my client?"

He shook his head, rubbed at his eyes, stroked the back of his ear where I had pasted him, finally said: "Great heavens! You didn't think I had the brain for this, sir? Mr. Foster helped me a great deal. I am independent today. I had to help his daughter get back some of the money that was stolen from him. I rented this house at the end of the summer—shortly after Mr. Foster was—Mr. Foster died, sir. Miss Mary Ann had to have some contact with the outside world. I am that contact. You see, I always leave the train at the station below and come here in my car. I thought I had been followed tonight. I—well, you saw what happened."

"Yeah." I lit a butt, offered him one, cut him short when he started to explain

that Mr. Foster had been against cigarette smoking so he had never "indulged."

"Tell me"—I didn't want to make social or moral small talk—"where does this bag go? Where is Miss Foster?"

"That"—he came very close—"I didn't know until tonight." He almost whispered the words in my ear. "You see, I was here and they were there. Miss Foster could telephone me—or she could come here to the house. I arranged to send the money. You know about the different amounts I guess. His debts—Mr. Foster's that is, sir. Don't ask me how it was done—I know nothing except that I received it and expressed it to you. I have taken this house under the name of Bartholemew Redman. The money just came to me in the mail."

He wasn't very interesting.

I TRIED: "You said 'they.' Who else is in it?" And when he began to tremble and his knees to shake, "O.K., don't sit down on the floor about it. What now? You must have something to tell me."

"I am to tell you where to take the money. Miss Mary Ann Foster is in the house farthest down by the rocks and breakwater in Thorton-by-the-Sea. It's a really fine summer colony, but no one lives in any of the houses now. She's been—hiding there. I am to take you to her tonight—now."

"What's in it for you?" And when that brought his shoulders up, "You're paid, aren't you?"

"I receive a little money—quite a little on each transaction I make according to my instructions. I was glad to take it.

You see—I am keeping it for Miss Mary Ann—if things go wrong. I have no one of my own. All I have will be hers some day anyway. I have known her since she—"

Yes, he was the real thing, but I wasn't interested in sentiment then. I had money to deliver. He wouldn't be a help.

I cut in with: "I'll go alone. Take your car and get out of here. Drive to New York. Pick a family hotel. Give yourself a new name, and stay out of things." And when he would have talked, "If they have located you, they will locate Miss Foster. Don't you see, they'll think of the beach houses. It will take time, but Slattery—"

"He'll kill her. He'll kill her."

"He won't if I get there first. And he won't have other men working on this job. Come on. I'll watch you drive off, follow you a bit to see that you're safe, then find this beach house. That girl should be out of there."

"They plan to leave tonight. There's a big car. You can take them to safety."

"They," he had said again, but I let it go this time.

I made Stoop-Shoulders give me a good description of the cottage. And he did.

He finished with: "You are to park the car just off the beach behind a great bare tree, sir." And then he even drew a picture of that tree. "I passed it this morning," he explained. "From there you go to the breakwater, along the stone drop to the beach, and you'll see the large bungalow with heavily boarded windows. You won't take—"

"No, I won't take you."

That finished that. I sat crouched by the wall near the driveway while he backed both the cars onto the road. There was no other way. I had to watch to see if the bound lads inside had a friend waiting in a car. Besides, there was the bag of dough between my knees. But at length he had the cars out. And we were away.

When I left him far down the road away from town I was sure he wasn't followed. And I was more sure that I wasn't. So I hit the ocean highway, and sped back toward Thorton-by-the-Sea.

Poor old guy. I felt sorry about hitting him on the head. Certainly he didn't belong in any such business as this. And how easily he fell for my story that Slattery would suspect where the girl was and start hunting for her. His voice had shaken when he told me to forget him and go for the girl.

And I got thinking about that story I made up about Slattery. And it didn't seem so made up. It hit me between the eyes suddenly. What better place could there be to hide out than a summer resort in winter time—especially down on the beach. Slattery wouldn't think of it, of course—until he found out that the man who had been handling the money got off at that station. Then it would hit him, too. But the dough had been sent to Thorton and Slattery had a keen mind. My brain was no better than his—and that's how I'd figure. So I speeded up the car, spotted the tree and drove right smack beneath it, winding in and facing out again ready for a get-away. And what's more I spotted the man who leaned against the tree—hat, heavy sailor's jacket, and rifle.

I was proud of that handling of the car.

The figure had to jump to avoid being hit I came in so quickly behind that tree. And then I was out of the car—with a single word.

"Freeze!"

CHAPTER 7

THE BUNGALOW
ON THE BEACH

THE FIGURE FROZE, laughed, dropped the rifle, and turned around. I put my flash on its face, and a small white hand came up and tore off the cap.

The man was a girl. The overalls were slacks, and she needed that sailor's jacket against the cold. I stuck my gun back in my overcoat pocket and lifted my own hat and gave her a sweeping bow.

"Good evening, Miss Foster," I said. "I'm Race Williams—here intact."

"You could do it." She nodded, then picked up the rifle. "We'll go down to the bungalow. We'll be glad to get out of it. At night we kept warm and comfortable but there were days when our huge oil heater in the living-room gave off smoke and we had to put it out until night."

"We?" I asked.

"Yes. I'm not Miss Foster."

My hand went into my pocket. She laughed again. It was not a very pleasant, nor a very musical laugh.

"I am your client," she told me. "That should be enough. But it is over now or nearly over. I am Mary Ann's friend. I was her father's secretary. I, Mr. Williams, am the Girl in the Alcove."

"You mean—you saw—"

She shot right in. Her voice was hard and cold. "I mean that I saw Johnny Slattery hurl Mr. Foster to his death."

"And Slattery knows this?"

"He doesn't know who saw him. He thinks it was Mary Ann. He thinks that poor, innocent, grief-stricken kid disappeared right after her father's death to collect retribution from him in the form of hard cash. I know what the need of money means. I know what it would mean to her. I know how Mr. Foster felt about his daughter—the disgrace—the money he owed."

Her voice got harder and harder.

"I was flung around all over the city because— Well, you might as well know the truth. It will come out in court when I stand up in the witness chair and put the finger on him for murder. No—Slattery doesn't know who saw him. But he had misgivings that someone did. For I looked from the alcove when Mr. Foster struggled with him, and Slattery heard me, gave Mr. Foster a blow in the stomach, turned toward the alcove, and as Mr. Foster regained his balance he had to turn back.

"In the moment that he turned back I ran from the alcove, reached the door, opened it, and over my shoulder I saw Mr. Foster hurled from the window. Don't you see? Slattery wasn't sure then. He only thought he heard someone—imagined the swish of a dress, perhaps. But when he got my first note some weeks later he knew he was glued to the electric chair. Mary Ann had disappeared. He thought the letters came from her. He knew that all his alibis would collapse if the daughter of the man he had murdered stood up in court and said, 'I saw him do it.' "

"What do you mean you were flung around?" I asked. "And what will come out in court? And why such—not that I don't admire it—but why such loyalty to your employer?"

"Some people I worked for found out later. Mr. Foster knew when he hired me what secretarial college I had graduated from. I don't mind telling you, Race Williams. It was a state prison for women—and unlike many other prisoners I was guilty of the crime I went there for."

"And the crime?"

She shrugged her shoulders.

"Being a poor shot. The state called it attempted murder." And after a pause, "And that ends your interest in me. What happened to the man who was to come with you?"

I told her what had happened and my idea that Slattery might be combing the beach—that we had better get moving.

She said simply: "Look."

SHE TOOK ME by the arm and half directed, half led me to the breakwater, directed my feet up the steep stones. There was a peculiar shelter of rocks where you could sit down and look through the wide openings between the stones and see up and down the beach. The bungalow was just below us, and the ocean pounding a good distance away.

"Sit down here. You wouldn't be afraid of Slattery if he came?"

"No." I shook my head. "But what of Mary Ann Foster?"

"She's asleep in the bungalow there below us. Rocks formed on the breakwater in queer shapes further down—and further back. The sea, of course, has never reached this far. I made this shelter. It is mild tonight compared with the other nights and days that I have watched—when Mary Ann slept."

"Watched with a rifle in your hand? For the coming of Slattery?"

"Yes—for the coming of Slattery."

"You know him then? You met him at Mr. Foster's office?"

"No, Slattery never visited Mr. Foster's office when I was there. Mr. Foster dealt in high-class bonds. I had been with him three years when he said I was overworked and sent me to Europe. I was one of the thousands stranded there when the war started. When I returned, Mr. Foster was hopelessly involved. I had his confidence. He permitted me, at my request, to investigate Slattery. Naturally I would have to see Slattery or even apply for a job in his so-called brokerage house. So we agreed that he must never see me at Mr. Foster's office."

"It should not have been hard for you to find out about Slattery."

"No," she said, "it was rather simple. But Mr. Foster did not like my report. He began to avoid me where once he sought my advice. He told me that Slattery was going to straighten out his affairs for him—that he was going to head a company for Slattery—and finally hinted that in some way Slattery was protecting him. He kept saying in a loud voice that Slattery was his friend—in a voice that let me know full well that he knew that Slattery was anything but his friend."

CARROLL JOHN DALY

That was getting along on O'Rourke's line.

I said: "Don't you think we'd better get Miss Foster out of that bungalow and leave? She may wake up and become nervous."

"Do you see that chimney?" The girl pointed between a large square opening in the stones. "That is how she signals me. If she is nervous she turns the oil heater a bit higher. I will see the smoke. As for anyone coming to the bungalow, we can see moving figures long before they get anywhere near it. I want to talk to you now."

"My advice—"

She snapped in quickly then: "I am paying for service—not advice."

"You got it, lady." I shoved the bag toward her. "There it is intact."

"Race"—she grabbed at my arm—"let me be the judge of what is best. Suppose Slattery is hidden some place around. Shouldn't we wait and be sure—rather than be shot down leaving the bungalow?"

What could I do? After all there was some sense in what she said. Besides I couldn't see myself standing up and going through that bag of money for my fifteen grand with my flashlight in my hand. But I had an uneasy feeling. I put it into words.

"Lady," I said, "it seems to me that you have a feeling against this Slattery. Understand, I'm not saying that you would want him shot to death, but I am hinting that you wouldn't feel too bad if he were."

"It would save me going on the stand and having my past thrown in my face. It would save frightened little Mary Ann from going through the ordeal of a murder trial. Poor kid—she thinks she suggested hiding out at the shame of her father's suicide, which I have promised to prove to her was deliberate murder. She's trusting me implicitly."

"You're pretty loyal to Mr. Foster."

HER SMALL BODY stiffened. I could see her white fingers close and her fist clench. She said: "He was the finest man I ever knew—the only fine man I ever knew."

"O.K." I moved my shoulders. "You're the doctor. If you've got to get it off your chest let me hear the rest of it."

"I won't paint Mr. Foster's name black. I half did that in a letter to Sergeant—to a police officer. But I wanted him to question Slattery. I wanted Slattery to know that the Girl in the Alcove was on to him. I wanted him to feel that the chair was close. But the truth is that this Slattery jockeyed Mr. Foster into an embarrassing position—scandal—a woman—a killing. Hell"—she almost spat out the word—"as soon as Mr. Foster told me the truth I saw through the whole thing. I told him it was a fake, extortion. I told him to make Slattery give him back the money that he robbed him of. I told him to make Slattery give a written statement that he had planned the thing or threaten Slattery's crooked scheme with exposure."

"And that's why he had Slattery come to his office that night? And why you waited in the alcove?"

"Yes. I was to take down their conversation. I have it down, all right. I'm ready to use it now. Mr. Foster died honest. His conscience was clear. He spoke to Slattery like the man he was. When he was dead I waited to tell the truth so that his daughter would not be penniless."

"You did a good job," I told her. "And what about Mary Ann Foster? How much does she know? About this money—the paying of debts?"

"She knows only that the debts are being paid—that there is some money from the estate coming to her. Poor kid, she has been nearly frozen at times."

"And you?"

"I have not felt the cold."

Clouds had cleared in the sky now. The moon was coming through rather brightly. I took a stretch and a good look. It was damned cold just sitting. There was no one on the beach. No one back along the road. The night was very clear.

"It looks," I said, "as though Slattery's brain was not as good as mine. Or as though he went off in the wrong direction." She didn't speak or take my hint, so I asked: "How did Slattery happen to send for me—suspect that you might use me?"

I could see her teeth shine white. I could see, too, that she was older than I had thought.

She said: "I wrote and told him that later I would not be without protection. That I would use you if he continued his attempts to locate me."

"I see. And—" I stopped.

Black smoke was curling up from the large square chimney of the bungalow.

The girl was on her feet at once.

"Come"—she grabbed my arm—"that's Mary Ann. She's awake—and alone and frightened."

We hurried down across the stones, onto the sand, around the back of the bungalow, and along the other side to the front door. That let us know for certain that no one was outside the place. And so we reached the front door—the only window or door which was not boarded and nailed up.

The girl knocked.

"It's well bolted—" she started to say, but I could hear the bolt being drawn back, the door being opened. A white face appeared as a blur in the flash from the oil burner set in the fireplace. I pushed the girl in ahead of me—followed her into the darkness.

Then I grabbed the door behind me—went to close it—felt it swing back and heard it smack against wood.

The next moment there was a blaze of light and something hard and round dug into my back.

A voice said behind me: "We came in almost the moment the girl left. We've waited a long time for you and that money, Race Williams. But I'm a patient man. Don't turn around."

I didn't need to turn around.

The voice was the voice of Johnny Slattery.

CHAPTER 8

SLATTERY DOES HIS STUFF

THINGS MOVED QUICKLY after that. At least they moved quickly for the boys on the other side of the fence. Sure—I was caught flat-footed. Then I staggered slightly from the blow of a gun beside my ear. Spreading my feet apart and still clutching the bag tightly I stared at the white-faced girl and at Slattery, gun in hand, standing before me now—his coat collar high about his neck.

The lad who lammed me said: "I tossed the dame's rifle over in the corner. Frisked her, too. Nothing dangerous on her, but I think she's ticklish." A nasty laugh. "I'm to do the killing, Race. Me—Gunner Snyder. Laugh that one off."

I said, stalling for time: "You'd better tie me hand and foot first."

I saw the shadow of the gun come up to strike me again, and pause right there.

"Get his guns, Snyder," Slattery said, "and quit talking." And jerking his head at the girl in the slacks, "So you're the Girl in the Alcove—Foster's secretary. I didn't think the little Foster kid had the guts or the brain for it. Come on—why hang your head in shame?"

"I'm sorry, Lyla—" the delicate, white-faced girl started. Then she stopped, looked at me. "I'm sorry, Mr. Williams. I thought I was brave. I thought I wasn't afraid to die after my father—after— But I told him. I had to—" She clutched her hands together, wavered slightly. "He hurt me terribly."

Mary Ann Foster spoke her piece, folded up slowly, and sank almost gently to the floor. If you didn't see it in her face—in her wide blue eyes—you'd think she had practiced that faint for years.

The girl she had called Lyla ran across the room—was down beside Mary Ann Foster. She held her head up from the floor.

Snyder searched me thoroughly enough. And Slattery kept his gun trained on me while he talked.

"Tough on the kid, eh, Race? If it wasn't for the wise secretary with the cap over her eyes—and you—she would not have to die. But when she let me in—thinking it was her girl friend who had just left—I burst out with the truth. I told her I had killed her father, and I was going to kill her. But first I'd make her pay in a way she wouldn't like for the trouble she had given me. Hell, she screamed with the pain and told me everything. Now you all have to take the dose."

So Slattery's entrance had been simple enough. He came at the time the girl Lyla was up on the road behind the big tree. He had been there while I sat with Lyla and listened to the story of her life and how safe things were because we could watch the whole beach. Sure—we watched it. After Slattery and his pal were inside.

"How did you find the place?" I asked.

"Easy." Slattery nodded. "That is after it finally entered my head that it might be some place along the beach. I had guys up talking to the lads that follow the beaches looking for stuff that might be washed in—guys from town who come down to gather wood. I had a lad at the station tonight to question that buzzard Philip Blackmore—her father's bookkeeper who lived in town under another name. I've had him followed and finally located his house. But I got my own break tonight and came out from the city by auto. A couple of lads had seen a girl leaving this bungalow. I tried my luck, tapped on the door, and the Foster kid let me in just as if I were an expected boy friend. When I saw her I knew." He paused, then said: "All right, Snyder, put a bullet in Williams' back."

"Don't like the job yourself?" was the best I could get off. Yep—my wisecracks were gone. Not that I was afraid to die. I'll admit I always expected to go out shooting, but with a lad or two on the floor before I died. But I was thinking of the girls. Of Lyla, yes, but mostly of the little Foster girl. She wasn't like me. She wasn't like Lyla. She hadn't much to give—but she had given what she could.

Slattery was saying: "I remember your saying, Race, that most guys want to talk—and talk themselves to death. Well—I'm through talking. I'm killing you by proxy. Let him have it, Snyder."

PANIC? NO. TERROR? No, not that either. Not even the slightest fear. Just a terrible, horrible, nauseating feeling down in my stomach. I had a job, and I had failed. Talk. Talk. Talk. And when the big moment came I couldn't talk or shoot my way out of it. I wanted action. I was getting it in a way. And all I could do was just shout. "Wait!"

I had nothing on my mind when I bellowed that "Wait!" At least nothing on my conscious mind. But it came to me just like that—just as Slattery was getting ready to give the nod again to Snyder. My ace in the hole.

I said: "And what about the money, Slattery? The dough?"

"In the suitcase. Where you so nicely kept it for me. No more talk. Let him have it, Snyder."

"The dough," I cut in quickly, and since I knew Snyder's gun was close to my back it took some effort to smile, "is not in the bag. You don't think I'd bring it with me? Hell—I've got it hidden."

"Wait!" This time it was Slattery who shouted the word. "Where did you put it? What the hell made—" And more calmly, "It's the same bag."

And I got ready to play my ace. Oh— I guess I'd take the dose all right, but there was a chance. And while Slattery had the loss of that money on his mind was the time to do it.

I said: "Same bag—but loaded with books and magazines." And as I saw the uncertainty in his eyes and figured he was thinking if I'd put it away in some bank he'd never get it anyway, I added: "It's buried down the beach."

"By God—we'll find out where if I have to take you apart and—I don't believe it. Snyder—"

And that was the big moment. Before Snyder could grab that bag I had to act. And before Slattery could have me killed he had to be sure what was in that bag.

I said: "Look—"

I dropped the bag to the floor, half turned sideways from Snyder, snapped the catches and flung it open—letting the bills spill out on the floor.

"Money—thousands—" Snyder shot toward the bag and for a moment was between Slattery and myself. And I went into my act.

Yes—I think Snyder saw the gun the moment I reached for it as it spilled out right in the center of those bills. Sure—I had put it there. That was what I meant when I said the suitcase was loaded. But Slattery had seen the gun, too. He fired wildly, blindly scattering the bills in the air.

And I had the gun—had it just as Snyder turned and thrust his gun against my stomach. The shot came. Came before I could get my gun up and fire.

Yet I felt no pain. Felt no— And I knew the truth as my eyes looked into Snyder's eyes—his dead eyes. Sure—Slattery was a cold-blooded murderer. He didn't have anything against Snyder. Perhaps he even liked him. But he didn't have any trust in him, and he didn't know—couldn't see from behind Snyder that Snyder had the drop on me. So—he just shot him straight through the head to knock him out of the way for a shot at me.

Slattery had not figured too well. The big dead body of Gunner Snyder pounded down on me all right. And where for the moment it kept me from getting a direct shot at Slattery, it also kept Slattery from plugging me—at least plugging me out of the picture. He shaved the skin of my shin and scraped the bone a bit, but most of his shots pounded into the dead body of Gunner Snyder.

For once I didn't make fun of Snyder's huge, bear-like figure—the great thickness of his body.

I dropped to one knee—Snyder's body still partly protecting me—and I put a bullet through Slattery's gun arm. Just as he fired ten feet to one side of me I laid another bullet across his heart. It spun him like a top, and I came to my feet.

He had a gun in his left hand now. His eyes were dazed. Mine weren't. Even though my shin bone was making itself evident.

I'd give him the office just before I made the kill so I said: "Bring the gun up, Slattery. You're going out anyway."

I heard a woman suck in her breath fleetingly, and I heard Lyla repeat my words as though they were a prayer, "You're going out anyway."

Then I tightened my finger slowly on the trigger, hesitated. Slattery seemed to smile. Then he opened his left hand and let his gun fall to the floor.

"I'm unarmed," he said. "It's worse than murder, Race. And both girls can witness it."

My finger tightened again. I thought of O'Rourke—what he had said. Slattery meant his job—alive. Dead—dead— Hell, killing rats like Slattery isn't murder. My finger—

I dropped my hand to my side. I guess I was like the kid. When the moment came I didn't have the guts for it. My right hand fell to my side. Blood trickled down from under the cuff of Slattery's trouser leg. He sort of smiled as he swayed.

"It's like this, Race. I deny everything I said." He looked at Lyla now who stood up facing him—her cap in her hand. "I've got an alibi. I'll beat the rap."

"If you thought you could beat the rap why did you send so much money?"

"Because—things were different." He had hard work talking. "I thought Mary Ann was going to put the finger on me. She'd swear it— They'd believe it if she said she saw me. But she couldn't—she— she—" He pointed at Lyla, called her

Muriel as his voice grew slightly thick. "Muriel, there—won't be believed. I'll see to that—to that with a good—with a good—mouth-piece."

Then he fell straight forward on his face.

"He's dead?" Lyla had a question in her voice.

"He doesn't think so—and he should know." I shrugged my shoulders. "There—take care of the kid. She's coming around."

"But he must be dead." Lyla put emphasis on "dead." And when I looked at her, "Surely you—won't leave him there like that?"

I went across to Slattery and turned him over on his back. He was still bleeding, and still had that silly grin on his face. I turned back to the girl.

"He'll do all right."

"He'll live?"

"Sure—" I said and not liking that peculiar look on her face added, "Listen, I saved his life. I could just as well have shot him and called it self-defense while he had the gun in his hand. I've done enough for Slattery."

She was across the room, down on her knees beside him. I watched her open his overcoat, pull back his jacket and vest. Yes—and tear his shirt and undershirt open. She could take it all right from the way she looked down at the wound.

She turned furtive eyes toward me, and I mean furtive and no kidding. They had been nice brown eyes—wide, real eyes—and now they were narrow and— She saw me, came to her feet, and spoke.

"He's not dead. He'll live." And when

I just stared at her she walked to a tiny chintz curtain, pulled it back. There was a low window-seat made into a bed which I guess one of the girls used.

She said: "We can't let him lie there on the floor." And when I still stared, "I tell you it's not human."

Hell—I helped her. I don't know why except that she would have tried to drag Slattery across the floor and place him on that low, couch-like bed herself. I lifted him up and put him there. Found another gun and took it. Women were hard to understand. When I turned around she was just getting up from beside the double-, triple-dead Snyder. Her right hand was under her heavy pea jacket as though she held her heart. She sure had a yen for finding out if guys were dead or not. Maybe later I'd get her a job at the morgue.

"You watch Mary Ann, please," she said. "I have a pencil and paper in my pocket. I'll try and make Slattery believe he's going to die. Maybe he'll make a statement—that he killed Mr. Foster."

"He won't."

"I can be very persuasive."

"I hope so. You have a phone here? That's connected? I suppose so, since it was you who phoned me."

"Yes. Over there on the far table. What do you want to do?"

"Call the police—Sergeant O'Rourke," I told her.

"The police? Must they come?"

"Now lady—" And I cut out the sarcasm. I saw that the girl Mary Ann was sitting up in the chair, smiled at her instead, and went straight to the phone.

CHAPTER 9

I THINK OF A NAME

I GOT O'ROURKE out of bed at once. "I've got Slattery," I told him. "He killed Foster all right. Admitted it to Slattery's daughter and—"

"Is he dead?"

"Why does everyone want Slattery dead? Just because I shot a lad once or twice—" Then I stopped and gave O'Rourke the directions and how to get there. "After all," I told him, "it's within the city limits. Your authority extends everywhere. Come with your own men. Bring the local precinct in later." And when he wanted to know how I got out there I hung up on him.

I felt kind of bad, too. It's seldom I have a case that—well, you know how most of my cases end. O'Rourke always belittled me for shooting it out, and now when it would have done the most good I had to lay down on him. O'Rourke was above all lads. The finest guy who ever wore a uniform of the world's finest police force. And—

It struck me just like that. Mary Ann needed her lawyer. She understood me all right, and she knew his number. I even got her as far as the phone, pulled up a chair for her. From behind the partly drawn curtain of the window-seat a low hum of voices came.

I thought I heard Slattery say: "No—I won't make any such statement. Or sign it. I know I'm not going to die."

And the girl with him answered: "And I know you are going to die."

But me, I was busy on the phone. George Campel lived out a bit in our direction so I connected him without trouble. Mary Ann Foster's name was magic. I gave him the directions how to reach the place. Mary Ann's plaintive voice brought a prompt response that he would come at once.

"At once," I said. "No fooling—she needs you."

"Mary Ann is my god-child," he said with that dignity of his. "I have done things for her quite unethical. To go out in the night like this is nothing. I hope she is ready to return to her aunt's apartment in the city."

"She is." I finished up with, "Get going."

Mary Ann told me then that her aunt was worried about her leaving, but she had promised not to say a word. Mr. Foster had charge of her aunt's money. Slattery had gotten it, but Lyla had seen that most of it came back to her.

"Lyla has been wonderful to me. She was wonderful to my father. She was—"

The girl stopped talking. I came to my feet—my gun in my hand.

There had been the shrill scream of a woman. As I turned Lyla was backing away from that curtain.

She cried out: "He's got a gun. He's going to kill me."

Then she lifted her right hand. I saw the gun in it. I heard it go off once—twice—a third time before I was across the room and had grabbed the girl.

"He said he had a gun," she cried out as I took the gun from her, recognized it at once as my own, and knew she had taken it from the coat pocket of Snyder where he had put it when he frisked me.

Then I walked over and looked down at Slattery.

Was Slattery dead? Both the girl and O'Rourke wanted an answer to that question. I wanted an answer to it myself now. I'll say this without fear of contradiction. I have seen a lot of dead men in my day—but I have never seen any deader than Johnny Slattery.

Three minutes later I put both my hands on Lyla's shoulders and backed her over against the wall.

"He's dead," I said, "and he didn't have any gun."

"No? No?" She looked straight at me. "He fooled me then. He stuck something against my side, said, 'Give me that gun—or I'll kill you.' I knew that would mean not only my death but Mary Ann's and yours. So I shot him."

"He didn't have any gun."

"He told me he did."

"That's your story and you're going to stick to it?"

"That's my story," she said defiantly. "And I'm going to stick to it."

So we waited and I paced the room.

Finally Lyla said: "There is no use for me to sacrifice myself by saying I saw Slattery murder Mr. Foster. Slattery is dead. Mary Ann and you both heard him admit it. He's not alive to dispute your testimony! I've done a job for my friend Mary Ann Foster. I've done a job for the finest man in the world—her father." She turned and looked toward the window-seat before which I had pulled the curtains

tightly. "And I've done a job for you, Race Williams."

"So what?" I asked.

"So—I'm leaving." She was at the door and had it open. "I don't care if you shoot me or not." She sort of choked. "I wanted to go on leading a normal life, but I thought—he wouldn't be alive. I had to kill him to save you all. But my killing him— Well—I have a record. I—"

"Just a second," I told her as I licked at my lips. "You are excited. Your imagination is running wild. You didn't kill him. I did. It was my gun. It was my duty to save Miss Foster. Beat it along, kid. Wait for Miss Foster at her aunt's apartment. And come and see me at my office tomorrow."

She backed toward the door, paused, ran suddenly forward, and throwing both arms around my neck kissed me. Then she dropped to her feet, ran out, closing the door behind her. I shoved the bolt into place, wiped the wet tears from my face—no, they weren't my tears—and turned to Mary Ann.

It took the best part of an hour to fix up her story even though it was a simple one. She had a hunch Slattery had killed her father. She was afraid of him and hid out, hiring me to try and prove him guilty. He had discovered her. Then I had come in. After that she could describe the gun battle just as she had seen it—or not seen it since she was in a faint most of the time. No one would press her or question her story. O'Rourke would see to that—not to mention her high-class lawyer. We had both heard Slattery admit the killing of her father.

After that I spent my time picking up bills and putting them in the suitcase. There was a little more room to get them back in. There was no gun there now—and the suitcase contained fifteen thousand dollars less in United States currency.

The money was intact. I was intact. Slattery wasn't.

O'Rourke came. The cops came with him. The lawyer, George Campel, Senior, followed on their heels.

O'Rourke said: "It's Snyder. And he's dead."

The fat detective right behind him repeated: "It's Snyder. And he's dead."

Then I pulled back the curtain, and they saw Slattery lying there in state. O'Rourke took one look at the job and turned to me. It was the first time I ever knew him to lose his head. After what I said to him on the phone he should have questioned me privately. But now he just blurted words out.

"I thought you said he wasn't dead?"

I looked O'Rourke straight in the eyes. My eyes were hard. His face flushed slightly. He read my message all right. And that message was that he wanted him dead. But I said stiffly and without emotion: "I was just kidding you, Sergeant—just kidding you."

Is THAT THE whole show? Just about, except that the girl called Lyla walked into my office the next day just as I was going to lunch.

"You didn't think I'd show up," she said. "Well—I don't know if you did it for me or for Mary Ann. And you'll demand an explanation."

"I did it for myself," I said. "And I don't demand any explanation."

"I had a sister," Lyla said. "The story's not a very nice one."

"Don't tell it then."

"No questions?" Her brown eyes opened in surprise. Clear eyes now. No haunted look in them.

"No. I'm going out to lunch."

She placed a hand before me as I started toward the closed office door.

"Would you take me to lunch with you?"

"Why not?" I said. "I've got a strong stomach."

She gripped my arm, looked straight into my eyes.

"Isn't there anything you want to know?"

I said: "Well—did you go to jail the first time for shooting the man you—the man whose name I'm thinking of right now?"

"If you're thinking of the name of Slattery—I did," she told me flatly—but not viciously.

That's the name I was thinking of. So what?

So I took her out to lunch.

Victim for Vengeance

CHAPTER 1

WASHED UP?

I DIDN'T LIKE Inspector Nelson and he didn't like me. I said to him:

"Put your dirty feet on the newspaper. That's what I tossed it there for. The rugs are Persian—if it means anything to you."

"They're Persian in the lease." He grinned at me. "So you've turned yellow, Race Williams. That's a laugh."

I just smiled at him.

"If I thought you meant that, Nelson, I'd slap all your teeth down your throat." And when his face got harder—if it is true that cement hardens again every so many years—I added: "You want me to walk out and shoot a guy to death for you; or maybe you just want to try and hang a murder rap on me." And walking forward and glaring eye to eye with him, for Nelson was a big lad, too: "Maybe you'll turn into a witness for me for self-defense. Is that why you've come to tell me about these threats? Do you expect me to pull your chestnuts out of the fire?"

Nelson shook his head. His hard gray eyes bored into mine. Then they drifted to the decanter and glasses on the tray on the table.

"I could go for a drink, Race," he said.

"That's the only way you'll get one." I stretched out a hand. "And I mean go for it—go outside for it."

Nelson slammed on his hat, jerked the brim over his forehead. He snapped out his words.

"So I give you a break by telling you things; then you want to get mussy because the law's on your side in your own home. Keep your bum liquor. A guy like you will need it. I always thought you were a dumb private dick, but I wasn't sure about your color until—"

"You can let it ride there." I slid close to him as he was about to turn. "You haven't got a warrant. No one would believe I'd invite a political plum like you into my place, and if—" He swung back. "Come on, if you want new teeth at the expense of the city."

Some day I'd clout Inspector Nelson's head in or he'd clout mine. But this wasn't the day.

The hall door opened and closed. Sergeant O'Rourke, the whitest guy on the force, walked down the hall and into the room.

The coppers who didn't like O'Rourke—and they weren't among the patrolmen, motorcycle, or plain clothes men—called him the commissioner's pet. With his rank of sergeant, he gave orders that his superior officers took, even though he did slip them out in the way of suggestions. He could have been an inspector, himself, but he didn't want that. He felt the rank of sergeant kept him

nearer to the cop on the beat—the man from whom nothing is hidden in his own little world.

O'Rourke slapped Nelson on the back, gave me a pat on the shoulder.

"You boys should come down to the gym and put the gloves on." And almost off-handedly to the inspector, "McDonald wants to see you down at Centre Street. He's got some fingerprints on the truck killing."

Nelson sneered:

"I've been twenty-three years on the force and never saw nor heard of a fingerprint, picked up like that, that was good for a conviction."

"The boys have to play," O'Rourke grinned, ran a hand through his gray hair and, when Nelson had gone, helped himself to a drink. "You shouldn't ride him, Race. He hasn't any sense of humor, but he's a shrewd, steady, determined man-hunter. It's more than just a job with Nelson. As a good cop, he hates all criminals."

"I'm no criminal."

"I know." O'Rourke tossed down a hooker, belched his appreciation of good liquor, and said: "He hates you on his own time, Race— It's not bad stuff, boy. Have a snifter."

I hesitated, said:

"I'm not sure."

"Ah"—O'Rourke poured himself another drink, "you never hit the liquor if something big is brewing. So you're undecided whether to go to bed or go down to the Silver Slipper Night Club and shoot a man to death?"

"Amazing, my dear O'Rourke." I

wouldn't be drawn out. "I guess I'll have the drink and go to bed. I'm not in the mood for killing tonight."

"Listen now, Race"—O'Rourke blocked my reach for the bottle—"you probably know all about it, but I'll lay it out for you, anyway. Eddie Athens is back in town. He's sporting a new moniker. They call him the Admiral. He got the name on the West coast because he started in to make a pile of jack shaking down the gambling ships. Now, they aren't around any more to be shaken down. He did plenty of dirty stuff out that way, and the boys don't like him; so he came back East. You remember Eddie Athens?"

"Sure," I nodded pleasantly. Eddie and I had had it out nearly two years back. He had told me that the city of New York wasn't big enough for both of us. He made three attempts at my life in three days, then found himself in the hospital for seven months with high-paid specialists picking lead out of him. He had been right. The city wasn't big enough for both of us. He left.

When O'Rourke waited for me to say something, I said:

"I remember him. You tell me."

"Of course." O'Rourke got it off his chest as if he had figured it out, himself, and not as if half of the underworld had talked about it. "I only know what I hear, but they said you chased him out of the city. Now he's back. But the run-out you gave him has lingered in the memory of criminals great and small, and they didn't want any part of the Admiral. Didn't, I said; not don't. They are listening to him,

now. And why? Because in the last few nights he's been hitting all the high spots, threatening you and telling politicians and everyone that you don't dare face him. Maybe not exactly an open threat of violence, but some think you're afraid to face him. Others—well, they think worse—that Eddie, the Admiral, has something crooked on you."

I took a laugh.

"You wouldn't believe that guff—any of it."

"It's not what I believe." O'Rourke shook his head. "But every criminal and every crooked politician can easily believe it. Why not? They think well of themselves and can't remember the day when no one had anything on them. So Eddie's building himself up by his derision of you, and they can all see that you're doing nothing to stop it. It isn't like you, boy. Everybody on the Stem knows your record. You had—*had,* understand—a reputation for plugging the mouth of anyone who made threats against you. That was your big asset as a private detective. Big crooks don't fear the police because they can hire high-class criminal lawyers. But"—he paused and licked at his lips—"no crook can climb out of a hole in the cemetery and get himself a mouth-piece."

"Why speak of me in the past tense?" I refused to get mad.

"Oh, I know you're not afraid of him, Race, but I'm thinking of you, boy. Nelson was just hoping you'd drive him out of town again or—"

"Plant him here?"

"That's right. Eddie Athens is too

CARROLL JOHN DALY

clever to lay a finger on. There is something big stirring; and, if he can get back the confidence of big crooked money, he'll handle it. Besides, Race, it's not entirely business with him. Do you remember Frankie Collins? You know, the big life-insurance-murder scandal."

"Yeah," I nodded. "I remember. I sent him to the chair."

O'Rourke said solemnly:

"That was over a year and a half ago. He fought the case up and down the courts. He burns tomorrow night."

"That's right," I agreed.

"Well"—O'Rourke put steady eyes on me—"it's more than a rumor that Eddie Athens was deep into that insurance racket and took well over a hundred-thousand-dollar loss on the deal. That puts something personal in it." And when I still refused to get excited: "There's more to it, too, Race. I think he actually means these threats. He's desperate for money and power. He had just got his racket working on the West coast when the law chased the gambling ships off the seas. The racketeers out there hate his guts. He's got to build up his reputation here— get big shots in with him—or some of those lads will come East and blow him apart. And he's building up that power; building up a new and great danger to the city. He's building it up by trampling you down! Why don't you do something about it? He's got brains."

"I've got brains, too." I took a smile, "Eddie Athens knows me. Why should he lay himself open to get himself killed? The answer is that someone has fooled him. Someone is trying to get me mixed up in a mess so I won't be able to handle a big case that's coming my way. And Nelson wants me to pull his official chestnuts out of the fire—even before they are fully roasted. I'm changing a bit. I'm using my head, now."

O'Rourke's laugh grated.

"Don't kid yourself, Race. That head of yours is to hang a hat on—nothing more. Eddie's no cheap murderer. He means what he says. Did you see Fletcher's column today?"

I started to say, "No," when O'Rourke jerked the newspaper out of his pocket and slapped it in my hand—folded neatly to the right spot. I read where it was blue-penciled.

—It may be news to a certain private detective, whom this column has always upheld even in his most violent methods of subduing crime, that the majority of opinions in the night spots mark him as washed up. We don't agree, but we must admit that we don't know how to argue in his favor, either. But we like to believe that it's a big case that keeps him busy and not the jitters. It is inconceivable to your reporter that this well-known private investigator, who has been pretty rough in dishing it out, can't take it when the time arrives. Oh, hum, we'll stick to our guns even if he doesn't stick to his and bet a very small bet that when he gets over his sulks he'll take a certain criminal apart and see what makes him tick—

But that was all I read, and it was enough. Sure—things were under my skin, now. My reputation was becoming public property.

O'Rourke looked at my face and said:

"The Admiral is down at the Silver Slipper. Good-night, Race."

And he left me there with the newspaper still clutched in my hand.

CHAPTER 2

MEET THE ADMIRAL

THE SILVER SLIPPER was doing a good business. Yet, Charlie Thompkins, the owner, spotted me as soon as I hit the place. His jolly laugh and booming, friendly voice were all there when he greeted me. But he smiled only with his mouth; his eyes had a worried look as he tried to make his words nonchalant.

"How ya, boy? How ya?" Wrinkles rolled down from his bald forehead and settled over his worried eyes. "Not business, I hope. Just pleasure, eh?"

His mouth laughed again, and his eyes studied me.

"Pleasure it is," I told him as I started toward the main room. He grabbed at my arm.

"Listen, boy, listen. I hate to do myself out of any business, but confidentially— not a word, understand—my best talent is up Harlem way. Actors' benefit, you know. Here, I've got a couple of tickets for it. You can just catch the midnight show." He hunted through his low-cut vest. "I know how particular you are. We've got a bum floor show here tonight."

"Never mind, Charlie," I nodded as I stepped past him. "I'll put on a floor show for you that will knock your eye out."

"Come, boy, come. I—"

I was gone—straight down that room to the big table right on the edge of the open dance floor. They saw me coming, one by one. First the stalwart, well-preserved, white-haired Ralph Fittsgibbons, big political boss. He nudged the man beside him who was thick-set, squat and with a collar up around his chin, since he didn't have any neck. He turned slowly, both his elbows on the table as he looked at me. Nothing showed on his thick-skinned, weather-beaten face. Beady eyes took me in appraisingly. Today he was Michael Fairchild Stein. I knew him when he was called Flat-faced Mike. Both these men had influence; both had money, and both knew where to get more.

There were two other men at that table. Harry Jackson was one. He was big; he was strong. He was considered reliable and had been bodyguard for some big racketeers up and down the Stem. A few years back he had beaten the rap in the Vanort-Mason murder down Florida way.

The fourth man was the one I was looking for. And if he told the truth, which I doubted, he was looking for me, too. He wore his soup and fish as if he were born in it. You wouldn't take him for a waiter. He was slouched in a chair with the side of his face toward me. Like Harry Jackson, he had a big cigar in his mouth; but, unlike Jackson, he wasn't using it as a simple decoration. He'd put it in and out of his mouth, roll it around in his fingers, and enjoy the smoke. This man was Eddie Athens, the Admiral—and my meat!

There had been a fifth party. A woman who had pulled a chair up with its back to the table, and with one knee on it was joshing with the men. She was Cathleen Conners, of course. Cathleen had come up the hard way. She wasn't young any more, but she was setting Charlie Thompkins back a couple of grand for her little singing act. What did she have that younger women didn't have? She had beauty; she had the figure; she had legs. But above all, she had talent. Charlie Thompkins got his money back double, or she wouldn't have been working there.

I said there *had* been a fifth party. And I was right. Cathleen had been along Broadway since she was eighteen. She hadn't much to learn. Her head raised as I came into the room; gorgeous brown globes settled on my face for a single second. She wasn't any Arab; but if she had a tent, it was folded and she was gone.

Fittsgibbons and Stein turned slightly and watched me come down that room between the tables. But they didn't tip Harry Jackson or the Admiral off. Maybe they thought I wouldn't like it. Harry and the Admiral were both watching the departing figure of Cathleen when I reached that table.

I grabbed the Admiral's chair, swung it around, and stood looking down at him. He had a face that was sharp and cruel, and lips so thin that they weren't more than a couple of strips of red below and above his mouth—a mouth that even in repose didn't hide the whiteness of straight, even teeth. And his eyes. Despite what people tell you, this lad's eyes were black—a hard, polished sort of ebony. If it wasn't that he sported a tiny mustache, you'd take him for the handsome villain of an old-time melodrama. He was a man

who would strike fear into you as soon as you looked at him. Understand, I said fear into you—not into me.

Those black eyes set on mine. He half-waved the cigar in his hand toward Harry, who had turned now and was facing me. Then he stuck the cigar in his mouth and looked up at me. He said:

"Don't bother, Harry. I'll handle this."

At that I leaned forward, stretched out my hand, and pulling the cigar out of his mouth, reversed it quickly and slapped the lighted end of it back into his mouth again! After that I spoke fast, acted fast. I jerked loose his bow tie and, slipping the front of it above his collar, twisted it about his neck.

"I've been hearing what a bad man you are," I told him as he spit fire like a cheap performer at a county fair. "Stand up when you speak to me!" And, twisting the tie more, I jerked him to his feet. He spluttered smoke, live ashes and high-priced Havana tobacco. "Stop kidding the boys along that you're tough. I mightn't like it, and next time I'll let you do your fire-eating tricks with short steel-jacketed cigars."

Pain and anger and madness were all in his face, but I wasn't any too good-natured either. He said:

"I'll kill you for this, Williams. I'll kill you for this!"

I took a laugh, saw that too many people were in on the show and dropped him back in the chair with the heel of my hand against his chin. And I mean against his chin!

"There's no time like the present, Big Chief Smoke Eater," I told him. And when he just sat there gulping the water that helpful Harry held to his mouth, I turned to the other men.

"Fittsgibbons and"—I let the Flat-face go—"Stein. Fine bums you hang out with." Spotting three waiters and one bouncer just behind, I turned and added: "Well, you got something you want to show?" I ran a hand up under my armpit and stroked my chin.

THOSE LADS FADED as if they were in a marionette show and invisible wires had pulled them back. Helpful Harry was patting the Admiral on the back. Me—I had done my duty. I walked right down to the little table at the end of the dance floor. The single table, and the chair across from the man who sat at that table. The chair that was forbidden to all but the favorite few who were invited to sit down. It was the private table of New York's greatest columnist and America's greatest he-gossip—Fletcher.

Fletcher didn't go in for cigars, but I got a smile out of the way he dunked out his cigarette in the coffee cup, hesitated a moment, then dropped it on the floor. He spoke quickly—loudly enough for the hovering waiters to hear when I neared him:

"Sit down, Mr. Williams. Sit down, Race. It isn't often I have the opportunity to have such a guest. I think I'll pay for your drink." He picked up his milk and sipped it, watching me over it with his thick-rimmed glasses hardly hiding the brilliancy of his great brown eyes.

You think perhaps that there should have been some excitement because of my little by-play with the Admiral? None at all. The regulars saw little in the incident other than a petty misunderstanding or a row which might take place a dozen times a night. Outsiders—they liked it. It was to them a part of New York's night life. But at that, the little altercation could be figured only in seconds—minutes, perhaps, if you're a stickler for accuracy.

I sat down and said:

"Well, what do you think, Fletcher?"

Fletcher pulled out a cigarette, stuck it into his mouth, started to strike a match, then tossed the match back on the tray. He smiled—all right, but not so good. At length he said:

"To be perfectly honest with you, Williams, I can't think of a man I'd be less pleased about being threatened by than you."

"I never threaten," I told him. "I act!"

"That," he said, "is taken from my column. May I smoke?"

I grinned, said:

"Go ahead." Fletcher had never done anything to me except for these cracks in the paper tonight. In fact, when the commissioner and the district attorney were riding me for some bit of shooting, he often came out in his column and gave me a boost. Fletcher finally lit his butt, said:

"Have a drink?"

"Maybe." I shrugged my shoulders. "I never drink when I have business, but I guess I settled my business for tonight." And as Fletcher beckoned a waiter who was hovering not too far away with an eye like an eagle, I said: "I could go for a little straight rye. I never want it said that any of my actions came through the neck of a bottle. When things are toughest, I drink Vichy."

"Very well," he grinned at me. It was a sickly grin and the face he turned to the waiter was a greenish-white. But his voice was clear enough when he spoke to the waiter. "A glass of Vichy—a small glass—for Mr. Williams."

I didn't argue. I just turned my head and looked. Eddie Athens was walking slowly toward our table. And he was alone. Now, what was on his mind? He had said something about killing me a few minutes before. Now—I just shrugged my shoulders, lifted the napkin quickly, and shoved a gun under it.

Ridiculous to shoot a man to death in a night-club? Sure—I'll agree to that. But it has been done. Ridiculous or not, it wouldn't do me much good if I were dead. So I left the gun beneath the napkin and continued my talk with Fletcher, while out of the corner of my eye I watched the slowly approaching Admiral and his hands—his white empty hands that swung at his sides.

"Trouble, Race," Fletcher whispered without moving his lips, "The Admiral."

I TURNED NOW and looked at the Admiral as he leaned on the back of an empty chair. There was no anger in his black eyes—no sardonic curve to the thin gash that was his mouth. He said simply:

"You are a remarkable man, Mr. Williams. But I am of a forgiving nature. Because of the people who were with me and the good name of the house, I will treat the matter as a joke. May I sit down? And may I caution you not to wipe your mouth with that napkin? It might explode in your face."

I said:

"You've got good eyes and evidently a tough mouth. Oh, I don't mean for words; I mean for chewing lighted cigars. No, you can't sit down."

"Really?" He pulled back the chair and dropped easily into it. "You see, if I didn't deem it advisable to handle you roughly at the other table, you could scarcely shoot me to death here. Let me assure you, Mr. Williams, if your little display of bad manners had happened at another place, you would not be so fortunate."

He was smooth, polished. You'd think I had swallowed the cigar. But a look down the room showed me his political pals and racketeer friends had left. I took the cigarette Fletcher offered me, I took the light, too, blew a couple of rings, and said:

"I haven't got your manners, and any place suits me. If you want to return the compliment and shove this butt down my throat, go ahead and see what happens to you."

A little tough, that? Perhaps. But then I'm a little tough and willing to admit it. Here, this guy had shot his mouth all along the Stem about what he'd do to me, and, now, he was trying to impress on the customers that it was simply a joke. He threw back his head and laughed. It was an annoying laugh because it seemed free and easy and not forced.

"On the level, my dear Williams," he said, and the "my dear" got under my skin and burned me up. Was it the way he said it? I guess so. Don't ask me why. I don't know. But his next words were worse. "I didn't know there were such characters left in New York. You remind me so much of the rats that come in on boats from the Orient."

I half came to my feet and then sat down again. A good fighter in the prize ring never loses his head or his temper. A good lad in my business never loses his temper, or he's apt to lose his head. Yet, I'll admit that the Admiral had my goat. I guess he read it in my face—in my eyes. And me, I could see nothing but his gleaming white teeth. And I had one thought only—to make all those white teeth disappear somewhere, preferably far back in the Admiral's mouth.

I'll admit it. I was mad. Damn good and mad! Here he was smiling and talking and undoing the nice impression I had made at his table. Perhaps he'd even say later that he was telling me off. It took a lot of control on my part. He seemed to enjoy my anger. Then I said:

"Admiral, I'm particular—and not like those rats you palled around with from the Orient. So get up and leave the table or—"

"Or?" He parted his face and let the row of ivory keys show.

"Or"—I leaned slightly forward— "I'll blow a hole in your face that will positively amaze Fletcher!"

The Admiral's eyes widened in amused speculation. He waved an empty white hand around at the crowded room.

"Here in the dining-room?"

"Here in the dining-room!"

"How quaint," was all he said, but he didn't move.

I wasn't mad any more, but I pretended to be. I just clapped my right hand on the napkin and said:

"You have ten seconds to be on your way." Then I started counting, "One, two, three, four—"

The Admiral started to speak, heard me hit eight and almost knocked his chair over backward. Then he was on his way.

I liked it. I laughed. I leaned back in the chair and took a belly laugh.

"There's one for your column," I told Fletcher.

Fletcher didn't laugh.

"I'll publish it Friday if you're still alive. Listen, Race." He was very serious, now. "It was a glorious bluff, of course, but the Admiral didn't know that." He hesitated. "Even I didn't know it. But remember this. I hear things around. Your actions tonight may have taken a million dollars—yes, a full million dollars—right out of the Admiral's pocket. And that money surely stays out of his pocket if you stay alive. Don't grin. You won't always be facing him. And you'll be just as dead if the bullet goes through the back of your head as the Admiral would be if you put it through the front of his."

"Don't spoil a lad's fun." I leaned across the table and poked Fletcher in the ribs. Then with a broader grin: "Maybe you'd suggest that I'd better shoot him to death after all."

"Yes!" Fletcher didn't grin. "I'd suggest just that."

It was then that the waiter came and said Miss Cathleen Conners would like to speak to me in her dressing room.

CHAPTER 3

THE CLIENT

CATHLEEN CONNERS DIDN'T look so young, when I was close to her there in her dressing room. And Cathleen Conners wasn't the assured woman of the world she had always been. There was plenty on her mind, and her laugh was shrill when I asked her about it.

"Nothing, really, Race, nothing that should bother me." And when I just looked at her she put both hands on my shoulders. "Maybe we never knew each other very well, Race, but you've known me a long time."

"Yes," I nodded at that one, "I remember you when—"

"It's all right," she went on when I paused. "When you were a boy and I was in vaudeville. It's true enough. I am older than people think."

"You can't be that old." I tried to laugh it off, but the answering smile I got was sort of ghastly. She couldn't seem to speak; so I tried to make it easy for her.

"Listen," I asked, "did you send me that thousand dollars with the instructions that I was to be in my apartment every night until I got a call that would pay me a lot of money?"

She hesitated a long time and then said:

"Yes—I did." I let her bite her lip. After all, it was her story and her explanation, and at last it came.

"A great many years ago," she said, "when I was first in the show business, I had a roommate who married a young play-boy. But his father cut off his money after the marriage, and he didn't play any more. In fact, she straightened him out so well that when his father died, ten years later, he left them quite a fortune. My girl friend died, leaving a very beautiful daughter." She paused then, dabbed slightly at her eyes with a bit of fancy rag. "Oh, Race—that girl has been kidnaped. They'll kill her!"

"Head up, kid." I chucked at her chin. "There's no money in a dead girl. Tell me all about it."

She went to it rapidly, then, in a mechanical sort of way. The girl had been out for a walk in Central Park. It was almost dinner time, and she had not returned home. Before her father became really worried, he received a telephone call. Just a voice on the wire told him that if he breathed a word of it to the police, he would never see his daughter alive again. He immediately got in touch with her— with Cathleen Conners.

"I know a lot of people—and a lot of life," she hurried on. "I suggested you as a contact man. But there was a question if these people would accept you. We were afraid you might be called out of town. So to be sure you'd be around we sent you that retainer. Then the girl's father was telephoned again and was told that if he ever spoke to you about it, the girl would die. There was nothing for me to do then—nothing." A long pause, and finally: "Tonight, when I saw you here, I had to tell you—*had* to tell you! He isn't capable of handling things alone."

"I'll bet he isn't. What's his name?"

She reddened slightly, and I'm going

to tell you that that was something for Cathleen Conners.

"I can't tell you that." And when I just stared at her: "Can't you see? Don't you understand? He's been warned against using you."

I DIDN'T UNDERSTAND; so I said: "Then why bother with me tonight?"

"Because, when I saw you come in—when I saw the way you handled the Admiral—everything I knew and had heard about you swept back. I had to tell you. I had to have help, Race. God help me, I have found a man who knows where the girl is held captive. The girl's father will pay you ten thousand dollars for her safe return. This man who is mixed up with the kidnaping is willing to take me to the house where the girl is. He promised to free her. He doesn't like a kidnaping rap; he's afraid. In return, I will give him protection from the police and—"

"Yes?" I helped her a bit.

"And I am to give him an alibi for his confederates if he should be suspected. The alibi is that he could not have had anything to do with her escape since he was with me in my… my apartment. I'll swear to that. I am afraid to bring the police into it because they might kill the girl, then. And I'm afraid to go with him without protection for he might—I'm thinking of the girl before myself, but he might kill me."

"You bet he might," I told her. "But how did you find out who knew where the girl was?" And suddenly snapping my fingers: "I've got it, the Admiral. Listen. You sent me a note with a thousand dollars in it. I was to stay at my apartment nights and wait for a call. Then the father of the kidnaped girl told the kidnapers on the phone that he had sent me a note." She nodded. "So you and the girl's father and the kidnapers were the only ones who knew about that note. Right after that, the Admiral started talking about fixing me if he met me. He knew I'd be home by the phone, and he could shoot his mouth off. It fits—but how did you find it out?"

"It doesn't fit, Race." She shook her head. "But that is how I found out. I have known Eddie Athens, the Admiral, for a long time. He helped me to locate this man, but he didn't mean to. I gave my word to tell his name to no one. Let us call him John Smith, then. I meet all kinds of people. The moment the girl disappeared, I put my ear to the ground. I have heard a lot in my time and learned to forget it. I won't go into what people tell me or from whom I might have received a hint. But"—she went over and looked in the closet, then came back—"but as you say, it fits that the Admiral started to threaten you after you had received that note. He was in this very club when he first made his threat, and this John Smith was sitting at the table when he made it. You see, John Smith had told him that you were tied up and wouldn't be leaving your apartment for several days."

"But you can't be sure it was John Smith who told him."

"I can be sure. I am sure! I know people, and I know their friends. The Admiral hardly knew John Smith. But I invited John Smith here to my dressing room. He was flattered and pleased. That is, he was until I pointed a gun at him and told him he must tell me where the girl was or I would turn him over to the police."

I looked at Cathleen Conners, nodded my approval. As I said, she came up the hard way and knew her way about.

"It was then," she said, "that he made the deal with me. John Smith never was a big man in the criminal world. He was willing to play along with me if I would protect him. He wanted an out—nothing else. He was badly frightened."

"But Cathleen—" I started, and she stopped me.

"You know me, Race. Broadway has known me for a long time, and knows that I'm a straight shooter. Since I saw you tonight, I phoned the girl's father. You will be paid ten thousand dollars for the safe return of the girl. I can't tell you any more. I won't tell you any more. I think John Smith is absolutely on the level with me, but I want to be sure. For the girl's sake, too. You're the only man I'd trust. If you won't go with me, I'll go alone." She tried to smile, but it was not a very good one. "Ten thousand dollars and no questions asked."

Well, what would you say? The same as I said. Ten thousand dollars was a lot of money. Of course I'd go.

Cathleen Conners did talk more. But no more about the identity of the father or the girl or of John Smith. She didn't want advice from me; so I didn't offer any. I put it down to cold business. Her arrangements with John Smith were O.K.—according to whether John Smith preferred to double-cross his friends without them knowing it and save himself from a long prison term, or whether he might decide to kidnap two women instead of one. Or murder one—that one, of course, being Cathleen Conners. Frankly, if John Smith were small-time stuff, as Cathleen had hinted, he'd think only of his skin. Murder is not for small-timers. Greed gives way to fear when the smell of burning flesh in the electric chair is easily imagined.

Cathleen was to take her car, drive over to the corner of Eightieth Street and Riverside Drive at six-thirty the next evening and pick up John Smith, He would then show her where to drive, even aid her in getting the girl free and, I presume, leave the blame to fall on some lad "sleeping" in another part of the house. Nice boy John Smith.

So I arranged to meet her on a side street, two blocks down from the Silver Slipper, a little before half past six.

She got her call then to go out and do her famous, "Won't You Be My Pretty Daddy?" song and act, which she did just once a night. She told me to wait in her dressing room until she had gone, so we wouldn't be seen talking together. I gave her a start, then left. But I did stop at the heavy curtains which led from the dressing rooms to the floor and, with five or six half-dressed young things, peeked through at Cathleen Conners.

She was a great trouper, all right. If she was frightened, she didn't show it. Her heart, her body, her whole spirit seemed to be in that damn-fool song. But that song kept her in the spotlight that she was in now. She was famous for it all over the city. She was not only a good singer and dancer, she was a good actress, too.

I watched her for a bit, there in the darkened room, a spotlight on her, another that chased around the room and lit on different male guests. She danced around the one that the spot was on, then turned her back and suddenly swung around to him, patting his cheeks and ruffling his hair while she sang, "Won't You Be My Pretty Daddy?" Some of the gents were embarrassed, but a lot of lads even used to tip the man on the spot, beforehand, to shine it on them.

But it was a catchy tune. I was whistling it when I slipped out of the Silver Slipper.

CHAPTER 4

END OF THE RIDE

CATHLEEN CONNERS was right. She shouldn't go with John Smith alone, especially when someone would pay that much money for the return of the snatched girl. She hadn't told me everything. She made no bones about saying that she wouldn't tell me. A great deal of what she said was hard to swallow, but the thought of ten thousand dollars finally forced it down. I didn't try to figure it out. She probably had a good reason for not telling me the entire truth. Just one thing was certain. She was afraid of walking into a trap. Me—I like traps. A guy learns things from them.

So I was on the side street, two blocks down from the Silver Slipper, at six-fif-

teen next evening. Cathleen came in a long, high-priced but '36 model black sedan. She seemed nervous—almost at the breaking point; so I tried to cheer her a bit.

"With the money you're making you should be ashamed of yourself driving anything but an up-to-date model," I chided her. "Now, you don't have to tell me anything more, but let me know your ideas and see if I can improve on them."

"I didn't want you to bring your car and follow me, because I was afraid he might watch."

"He would," I told her. "On the level with you or not on the level with you, he'd watch and lose me in the traffic. It's possible I could stick a gun in his side and make him go to the house and—"

"No, no!" She stepped from the car and clutched me by the arm. "I put a rug in the back seat that you could lie under, and then bob up when he had brought me to the house."

"Even if he had no suspicion of you, he would look in the back of the car. Anyone would." I hesitated and then: "You have a good-sized trunk carrier?"

"Trunk carrier?" she gasped. "Yes, but I don't know if—"

But I was around back of the car looking at her trunk carrier. We talked for a few minutes more—at least, she did. I wasn't listening much. Then I said:

"I could fit in it comfortably. Well, not comfortably, but I could fit in it."

"I don't know." She was sort of shaking her head. "Wouldn't he look in it?"

"I don't think so. I think he'll hop right in the car when you drive up. But if he does look in the carrier, there will be nothing for me to do but stick a gun in his face and try to scare him into going through with taking us both to the girl."

I would have preferred to use the gun act on John Smith, but I had a good reason for not chancing it. Suppose he wasn't on the up and up with Cathleen and had a couple of gunmen watching when she picked him up? They'd see me put the gun on him; and, where I'm not averse to a little gun-play, it wouldn't be so good for Cathleen and the imprisoned girl.

"I didn't think of the trunk carrier." Cathleen shook her head. "It's full of odds and ends."

"Easy enough." I lifted up the top of the carrier as Cathleen joined me in the street and tossed the odds and ends onto the floor of the car. A dirty blanket, a half-box of dog biscuits, one silk stocking, a shoe box and an empty purse.

Some people were passing as I shook my head over the size of the carrier. Not that it wasn't extra large, but then I'm extra large, myself. Of course, you could have gotten two men in there if you had taken them apart and distributed them carefully. But who wants to be taken apart? I tried the catches on the carrier. They were worn and rusty, and it would take some manipulation to lock them.

"They don't work very well," she told me. "I don't try to lock it any more."

"I don't want them to work well." I gave her real instructions. "You're to stay behind the wheel when this John Smith gets in. If he so much as comes around back to look at the trunk carrier, blow your horn; then I'll bounce out. Don't drive into any private garage under a house. Stay out on the street. Once he has you stop the car, I'll have a gun poking out and be ready—I mean when he reaches his destination. There seems to be plenty of ventilation." I tried to stick my little finger through the holes on either end; but the holes, though numerous, were too small.

CATHLEEN AND I looked up and down the street, waited for a man to pass, then a woman. Another quick look-see, and I hopped into the trunk carrier and chucked a few loose screws out in the gutter. Things looked better. I had thought at first that the worn old carrier would fall apart. It had looked about ready to. But it held my weight, and I finally squirmed myself into it.

No matter how I worked it, I had to lie on my side. Cathleen had to help me get the top down. It didn't fit very well, but she couldn't close it any farther; so I let it go at that. If the lad she met was suspicious or had a curious turn of mind, why I'd simply poke a gun in his face when he opened the top of the carrier and start from there.

Bum job that carrier, too, considering the original price of the car. The ventilating holes were too small to distinguish anything when we crossed Broadway, even if I could have twisted my head to look out. Then I had something more important to think about. That carrier may have been lined with old beaver board and tar-paper, but somewhere a bit of sharp tin had gotten into the mess. And what's more, it was getting into my neck. Sharp? It was like a razor blade, and I had to hold my head cocked up and resting on nothing. Then a swerve, and the tin or steel or what-have-you got me.

I went after it with my left hand, finally turned into a contortionist and got my fingers on it. Sure, I knew when I found it. The blood came. But I had luck there. It twisted free in my hand. Not much size to it, but it would have been a deadly weapon to cut a man's throat with; dull on one side and sharp on the other.

A little cramped? Sure—but I couldn't expect all the comforts of home at a little over a hundred dollars a minute. That thought was not unpleasant.

I straightened, stiffened, held my gun tightly. We must have reached Eightieth Street and Riverside Drive. The car was coming to a stop.

The car stopped. I couldn't see a thing, but I could hear a voice say, from somewhere up near the front of the car:

"If you ever breathe a word of this, Cathleen, I'm a dead—"

Then there were two sudden bangs as if hammers rang on steel, and that steel was inside my head! I react quickly to any emergency, and this was a real one. I banged up against the top of that carrier, and I banged right back again. I knew then. Two blows had come together: One against the side of the carrier, one against the top—and the bolts had been snapped home!

I shot out with my feet to kick the damned thing apart, and the whole thing struck me at once. That carrier was lined with new steel; old beaver board had been put inside of it. I had been taken in like a child. Walked into a trap! Walked into it? Hell, I had climbed into it; I even laid down in it.

And the woman, Cathleen Conners? Had she known; or was she, too, taken by surprise? As the car jumped from the curb I knew the answer to that one. She had brought the car around for me. The slamming and bolting of that top had been a well-prepared—yes, and a well-rehearsed job. It wasn't her car, but one they told her to drive. Who were they? I didn't know, but I could make a pretty good guess at one of them. And I didn't like that guess.

Like a child—that was it. She had even let the suggestion that I hide in the carrier come from me. Her talk about being under the rug. The odds and ends as if she hadn't expected me to get in there.

Trapped! Trapped! Trapped! And then my head began to work again. That is as much as that head of mine ever works. I wormed my way around, got my gun close to one of the tiny holes, and had hard work holding it there as the car swayed. I tightened my finger on the trigger.

A surprise for the people of New York. A surprise for the cops, too, if they saw a car spouting gunfire. I might crash a few windows along the route. I might—

And I didn't press the trigger. The concussion, itself, would be bad enough to deafen me, but the powder would poison me—at best put me out of action. You know, gunners in the turrets of battleships wear gas masks. If they don't—*bingo*—they go out and stay out. No, I didn't fire.

Out of action. That was a hot one. What action was I in?

Traps! All my life I watch for them; prepare for them. I thought of all the trouble I have caused myself in doubting the intentions of honest clients, of all the traps I had looked for and would be glad to go in with a gun in each hand. I had said that traps are interesting. Well, this one wasn't. At least not for me.

What to do? Nothing! Nothing right then. But when that carrier was opened, they'd find it bursting lead from two guns. I had thoughts then that maybe it never would be opened. Had thoughts of the car being abandoned, shoved into gear and let shoot off a dock into the river!

I tried to kick the sides out of the carrier. I don't know how it sounded outside the car, but inside it was bad— bad in more ways than one.

Did I curse out the woman Cathleen? I suppose so, but I didn't try to figure out why she did it. What jam was she in that made her do it? I could only figure my jam. After a while I just lay there and waited.

THE CAR SLOWED, veered hard to the right, bumped a bit, crawled slowly and jarred to a stop. For no reason at all I raised particular hell with my feet, then. Surely the sound was heard. But by whom was the question. Then I stopped and listened.

Doors closed heavily, scraping across cement. Scared? Terror-stricken? No—I was mad. Damn good and mad!

There was a bright light, now, as I nearly broke my neck and peered through the tiny holes. Heavy feet sounded and a man spoke.

"Something in the box, eh? Something from the darkest Africa? Walks, talks, and is it alive?" A laugh then, and I knew the man. Cathleen Conners had certainly taken me in nicely.

The man was the Admiral!

He went on after a couple of other laughs, greeting what he thought was the height of wit.

"It's either some dumb creature—some very dumb creature—or Race Williams, himself, the great detective. Locks himself up in a box and delivers himself like a birthday present to me."

"Will I toss him a fish?" And this voice I thought I knew, too. It sounded like Jackson, the big heel who was at the night spot with the Admiral. But the next voice I didn't know, and I can't say that I was stuck on his advice. But it was almost as if he had stolen it from one of my thoughts.

"If I were you, Admiral, I'd let him go off the dock with the car. He can't be dead too soon."

"Yes he can," said the Admiral, and there was no laugh in his voice, now. "I have waited for this, planned it, and that's the way it's going to be—eleven o'clock tonight, exactly."

Perhaps my heart did beat a bit better. Close to four and a half more hours of life. A lot can happen in that time. Another thought of mine stolen. Jackson was telling the Admiral the same thing. Then the other man said:

"How are you going to get him out of the carrier?"

I set my lips grimly. I hadn't said anything; I hadn't made a sound since my first few kicks. I hoped they'd think I was unconscious and open the cover; then I'd blast away! But the Admiral's next words weren't so good.

"Give me the ether!" he said. And a moment later: "Hold that handkerchief to my nose, Jackson. I'll just spray it in like disinfectant, and we'll have at least one unconscious cockroach."

I had a sudden flash—an idea—and I went to work on it. I tried to hold my breath and work the idea at the same time. I knew Admiral Eddie Athens would be sure to give me enough ether. I knew I was going to pass out, but I wanted to be sure that I only passed out and didn't die.

"I can hear him squirming around in there," the Admiral said in a thick voice that must have come from behind the handkerchief.

And he was right. I was squirming. The ether was beginning to get me. I tried to turn around to get my breath from the holes at the other end of the carrier, but couldn't make it. The deadly fumes of the ether were creeping over me!

Maybe I was fighting off death to die a worse one. I couldn't know what was in store for me. Then the pounding came into my ears. I ducked low with my head on my arms to breathe, but the thing got me just the same. But why eleven o'clock tonight?

What was eleven o'clock tonight— What... what— Yeah—sure... eleven o'clock... tonight—I gasped for breath. I wanted to laugh. I knew—

At eleven o'clock... they were frying the Admiral's friend... former partner, Frankie Collins... to death up at Sing Sing prison. Yeah... frying... sure...

frying his old friend... to death... his friend, Collins, that I sent to... to... frying him—

After that—real blackness!

CHAPTER 5

"YOU'RE GOING TO BURN!"

THERE WAS A bad taste in my mouth, and I felt as if I had been laid out on a morgue slab. Or maybe it was just a hospital table. There was a dull light in the room and faces watching me. All sorts of faces: doctors, it seemed; then a rather sweet young face. A nurse. She must have lifted up my head, then said:

"Drink this."

Things were coming back to me slowly. All this was the effect of the ether. I was coming out of it, and had crazy ideas. Of course, I couldn't be in a hospital, or a morgue, either, and be alive. That was too pleasant an idea. But I did open my mouth, and I did—

The water was good, and it was real. I sat up. It was a real girl, and she said:

"Drink some more."

I blinked, drank some more, opened my eyes wider and took in things—at least, fairly well.

A low-ceilinged room with great beams running across the top of it. A hard cement floor and cement walls. A couple of blankets on the floor, two old kitchen chairs, a sink, a wooden flight of stairs leading some place above, and not a window. And, of course, the girl.

I got to one knee, staggered to my feet, swayed, tacked over to the wall, steadied myself a bit and made the sink. The girl helped me, I think, but the cold water over my head helped me more.

"What did they do to you?" the girl asked. "You're Race Williams. I have often read about you. You're an—"

"I'm an idiot!" I straightened from the sink, now, took the glass from her hand and filled it twice at the tap. "Who are you?"

"I'm Dorothy Nester," she said. "It doesn't matter, Mr. Williams. You came to save me. They told me that. They opened the trap door above, threw you down the steps and said: 'It's Race Williams—come to save you.' Then they laughed."

Nice introduction, wasn't it? I stood and stared at her. Young, small, slender, with wondering, childlike blue eyes, but a determined little mouth and chin. I put my hand in my pocket for a comb, then brushed my wet hair back with my hand.

"They didn't think I'd come-to so soon," I said rather stupidly. I felt for a couple of guns that weren't there. Then I ran over to the stairs, climbed up and put my shoulder against the trap door at the top. It was thick wood and didn't give an inch. The girl watched me. As I missed a step coming down and nearly slid across the floor on my face, she turned one of the chairs around and said:

"You had better sit down for a bit."

I did sit down. The girl went on talking. "There is no way to get out. I have tried. Did they take the money from you and then not let me go back to my father? Is he terribly worried? Is he sick? Father and I were very close to each other"—and very low—"ever since my mother died."

By this time I had searched myself pretty well. Everything was gone, including cigarettes and matches. My brain was clearing—such brains as I have to clear. Finally I said:

"Do you know Miss Conners—Miss Cathleen Conners?"

"No," she answered.

"A singer in a night-club?"

"Oh, father doesn't allow me to go to night-clubs. I don't even want to go. I think I have seen her picture and heard her on the radio. She is very beautiful and has a lovely voice."

"Sure," I nodded, "a fine heart and a soul that—" But I stopped there. If she didn't go to night-clubs, there was no use of her hearing language that the worst of them wouldn't stand for.

"Tell me," she said, "what happened."

"No, there is no use in telling you that. It's about you. Do you know any of the men who kidnaped you? Anything about them? Anything that you might disclose that would help—"

"Why, no," she cut in quickly. "I never saw them before. It's just money, isn't it?"

Her eyes were wide, and a sudden touch of terror that I hadn't seen before was beginning to creep in. "Aren't you afraid?" I asked.

"I wasn't—until now," she said hesitantly. "They told me that when father paid a sum of money they would send me home. I was afraid at first—terribly afraid when they grabbed me in the park. They hurt me then. But since then—until now— Oh, they can't want anything but money."

"That's right." I cursed myself for putting such an idea into her head, but I guess I hadn't straightened myself out, yet. "Don't you worry, Dorothy. Your father will pay, and you'll be free enough. They just wanted me—well, for another reason."

"But I am worried. I am really frightened. When they brought you in, it was someone else; someone worse off than I was; someone I could help." Her voice wasn't so steady, now, and her face was paler. A little hand with small, trembling fingers felt at her throat. "Why don't they get the money and let me go? What else could they want of me?"

I GOT UP and steadied her, held her, ruffled the tawny head of hair that sank slowly onto my shoulder. She was just a kid. A brave little kid who hadn't given way. And now that I was there—a man who— And I skipped that thought as she had her first cry.

I talked to her and encouraged her. I don't know exactly what I said, and maybe she didn't either. I didn't try to figure things out—that is what had happened in the past. Maybe my future wasn't going to be long enough to do anything about it. The Admiral had taken everything from me that I could use except my shoes, and I couldn't use them, now.

The girl steadied herself. After I finished my pep talk she said quietly:

"They are going to kill you—aren't they?"

"Not them," I told her. "You sit down for a minute." And when I got her seated: "Didn't you ever hear the story of Captain Kidd? After they had locked him up in a stone house on the island and he had tried every way of escaping, he thought he'd try the door to see if it was locked. And by gosh, it wasn't. I'm going to have a turn around. I never saw the spot, yet, I couldn't get out of if I wanted to."

I went to work. The room wasn't very large. There was a little washroom off it. There were heavy drums that contained oil or something. I even moved them from the wall. There were no holes behind them or beneath them. I had found a spot I couldn't get out of, all right. You could have packed twenty-five men in that cement vault, and they couldn't have gotten out.

It seemed to help the girl to watch me try. She even got up from the chair and came over to help me when I got one of the wooden steps of the stairs partly free. I'm a strong man. The work did me good. It sweated the ether out of me.

At last the lower step of the stairs was out of its moorings and in my hands— broken rusty nails and all. A weapon of defense when the boys came down? No, a weapon of offense for me, right now. I'm not a lad to wait for action. If action doesn't come to me, I go after it.

I went after it right then. First, I tried using that thick length of wooden step as a wedge against the trap door. No go there.

Then I used it as a battering-ram, but I couldn't get any force behind it standing on those steps. Finally, I knelt down on the third from the top step, held the board over my right shoulder and, with both hands clutching it, let it drive up with all my one hundred eighty pounds behind it.

It made a noise, but nothing else. No wood cracked in the trap. No hinges gave, and no rusty nails groaned. This prison was evidently well prepared.

Suddenly a tiny hole in the trap opened. A man spoke. It was the Admiral.

"Want service, eh?" he laughed. "Well, go down and press the buttons. You know—one, for ice water; two, for the valet; and three, for a punch in the nose." And when I didn't say anything: "You'll die soon enough without trying to hurry matters. And you won't be so comfortably off for the last few hours—nor with a pretty girl to amuse you. Though you'll still have the oil, even if it isn't in the barrels."

A long pause, then a voice that held no laughter.

"You're going to burn, Race, just as Frankie will burn tonight!"

The hole disappeared. Someone was very close to me. It was the girl, of course. She said:

"What do they mean, you're going to burn? The oil? The barrels? I've been afraid of those barrels. I've been—Mr. Williams—Race, they're going to burn us to death!"

And without thinking, I said:

"No, not you. Just me."

This time it was I who gave her the water to drink. This time I supported her head when she took it. I was half holding her in the chair when she spoke.

"You"—she gripped at my hand with icy fingers—"know who these men are? If you do, tell me. When I'm free—if I am free—I'll let the police know and—"

"Don't you know who they are?" She looked at me oddly. "I mean, couldn't you identify any of them again?"

"I don't think so." She shook her head. "It was so quick in the park. In the car there was a bag over my head."

"But I mean here—since they brought you here?"

"Since they brought me here, whoever visits me wears a heavy overcoat that hides his build, has his hat well pulled down and a mask over his face."

I SIGHED WITH relief. The girl was safe, then. If they didn't intend that she should live, why hide their faces? No, the kidnaping of Dorothy Nester was just a professional job for cash. Greed came first. Once they had her—or, at least, once the Admiral had her, he thought of vengeance. And that was the part I was to play. Vengeance and money! The Admiral could never operate in the city of New York while I was alive. Now— But what could possibly have made Cathleen Conners trap me for the Admiral to kill? I would have trusted her in anything. And with a curse came the thought: I did.

I looked around the place again. There had been a tiny hole in the trap door. Was there any other tiny hole? Any other place where one of these men could listen to our talk? If they could, one of them would be straining his ears, now. So I said loud enough for anyone to hear:

"I don't know who they are, either, Dorothy. And don't you try to know." She put those great, childlike glims on me. "Don't worry about me, kid. I made a mess of things. I'm just a lad who played his own confidence and conceit once too often."

She shook her head.

"You are not afraid, yet you must feel the… the danger. You tried and succeeded in keeping up my courage when inside of me I felt that I would go mad. Inside of you, you must know the horrible thing you are to face. I think you are very brave, Race Williams. Very brave, indeed."

"You should see me when—" I started and stopped.

The trap door above had opened. Feet were coming down the stairs.

CHAPTER 6

DEATH FOR TWO!

THE TIME HAD come! Coated and hatted and with faces masked in black, three men were slowly descending those wooden steps. Three guns were held steadily in three hands; those hands were slightly raised. The guns pointed directly at me!

I knew Jackson because of his great bulk. I knew the Admiral because he was giving the orders as he brought up the rear. The third squat figure I didn't recognize. The Admiral said in a low whisper:

"Under no circumstance is he to be shot to death."

I stepped back, licked at my lips and lifted the heavy hunk of wood that had been the bottom step. If what he said was true, there was going to be a hell of a mess in that room. Some broken arms and legs, maybe a head or two—mine included.

Jackson stood on one side of the stairs, the figure I didn't know on the other. The Admiral remained on what had been the next to the lowest step, but was now the lowest.

"Like a Greek god you look, Williams—Sucker Williams." He said sharply: "Come here, girl." And before I could make up my mind to speak or not: "Come here, girl, or I'll put a bullet in your leg and one in his head!"

The girl moved quickly toward him. I was going to make a play for it. But I didn't. Two reasons: One, that I was pretty certain they wouldn't obey orders if I let go with that plank as I jumped forward. Two, that the girl might get killed in the mix-up.

The next minute it was too late. The girl had passed between the two men. The Admiral had slipped back up a step and dragged her with him.

"Drop the board, Williams," he said. "You think you're a hero standing there; so we'll see if you can fill the part." He clutched up the girl's arm, swung it behind her back. She screamed with pain. "I'll break it next!" he said.

I dropped the board. The girl's eyes had closed. She sank to the step, half lay there at the Admiral's feet.

"All right," the Admiral said to Jackson and the other man as he pushed the girl's head away from the step with his foot. "Tie him up."

Did I let them tie me? Of course I did. What else could I do? How could I be worse off? Besides, I expected to find myself tied up long ago. They sat me down on a chair with two guns sticking into my stomach; then they pulled rope from under their coats and went to work on me. I strained a bit, of course. But they got the ropes tight enough.

When they had me strapped in the chair, the Admiral came over, surveyed the job and gave orders. My hands that were bound in front of me he had changed so that they were tied down to my ankles. I sat in a crouching position with no back rest. My head was jerked too far forward.

I didn't get the idea of tying me up like that. My hope was that they were going to carry me and the chair some place else. I wouldn't have a chance to escape from that room, even if I had both my guns with me. But if they took me to another room, tied just like that— I licked at my lips. That was my hope.

I was watching the girl. She was moving there at the foot of the steps. Her eyes were half open now, and she was peering through them. I could see her pulling one knee under her. Plucky little thing—she was going to make a dash for freedom.

She did. But she wasn't more than up a step when the Admiral swung, made the stairs in one leap and gathered her in his arms. She fought then for the first time; kicked and screamed as he was backed down the steps by the force of her weight and her lurching body.

"Little she-devil," he said as he swayed back almost under the light. Then quiet in that room.

The Admiral's hat had been knocked off. The girl had clutched at his mask, torn it from his face and held it triumphantly in her hand. In the dead silence that followed she looked straight into his face and cried out:

"I'd know you anywhere, now—any place! Harm Race Williams, and some day I'll point you out to the police."

Jackson and the smaller man looked at the Admiral. The Admiral held the girl's arms, shrugged his shoulders. Then he said to the smaller man:

"Take her above, Louie, and wait for Jackson. When he joins you, take her to the… the house in the Bronx."

"I won't have any hand in killing a woman. I—" The smaller man stopped.

The Admiral said calmly:

"Take her above and be quiet." Louie grabbed Dorothy Nester roughly and half led, half dragged her up the steps. I don't think she got the full significance of what his words meant. I strained uselessly against the ropes.

The girl, wanting, believing that she might be saving my life, had forfeited her own when she looked into the Admiral's face. I think that she realized it, too, as she reached the landing above. Her sudden cry of terror rang in my ears, then—and for a long time afterward.

JACKSON SAID:

"The ropes are tight, now. But if you want them tighter, boss, I can go above and get more rope."

"No-no." The Admiral shook his head. "Houdini, himself, would have trouble in getting out of that mess. Even if Williams did get free, he couldn't get out of the place, anyway. We could come back and do the job over again, tomorrow."

"Will I roll one of the oil vats over, now?" Jackson asked. "We can use it to set the box on."

"No"—the Admiral shook his head—"our box is to go on the floor. That's why I have Williams strapped over in the position he's in. Not just so he'll look more like the monkey he imitated tonight. I want him to see the hands of the clock plainly. If the box is set too high up, it will blow a hole clean through the ceiling—beams or no beams. And I want our good friend, Race Williams, to feel the heat—as my friend will feel the heat tonight. I don't want him to be crushed to death."

Maybe I didn't understand exactly what he meant then. But I knew a few minutes later. The Admiral went above; and, while he was gone, Jackson rolled a few of the big drums of oil from the wall. I think I got the idea even before the Admiral returned.

Jackson put his hand in his pocket, bent over one of the drums of oil. I didn't see the tool he used. I didn't need to. But he punctured a hole in one of them. Almost at once there were fumes like gasoline, and a bit of the slimy stuff poured through the hole onto the cement floor. He plugged it up then with a bit of cork; then he bored a hole in another.

The floor was not even. My chair was about in the center of it, and the oil trickled down toward my feet. It was then that the Admiral came back. He was walking slowly down the steps with a large oblong box that looked like a radio. He carried it very carefully as he came toward me, set it down about three feet away from me and pushed it a bit closer. I could see the alarm clock plainly when the Admiral moved it a little closer.

"It'll blow his head off for him and do a damned good job," Jackson said.

The Admiral's voice was very low as he moved the box a little farther from me.

"I wouldn't have that happen," he said. "Not to Race Williams, tonight. Go up and toss me down that package of newspapers; then go. I want to be alone with the man who is killing my friend, tonight."

Jackson paused on the steps, hesitated, then said:

"And the dame? She knows, now."

"After the alibi. We'll have to be at the Silver Slipper at least until midnight," the Admiral continued. "And don't worry about the money. We'll have both. I sort of horned in on your little affair. Kidnaping was never for me"—he looked at me—"but I like this one. I like it very much indeed. There—just the paper, Jackson."

Jackson pounded up the stairs. The Admiral pulled up the only other chair in the room and sat down, facing me. I hadn't spoken a word yet, and I hadn't intended to. There was always a chance.

"It's been almost eighteen months since you sent Frankie Collins to the death house at Sing Sing. Every penny I could make on the West coast was spent in trying to save him from the chair."

"He killed a young girl," I said. "I pinned it on him, and it stuck."

"Well, I'll kill a young girl, too. Wouldn't you like to pin that on me?"

"A couple of Oriental rats, eh?" was all I said.

His face went white. Maybe his voice trembled a little when he spoke, but it was still low and soft.

"Tonight," he went on, "I will sit in the Silver Slipper at eleven o'clock. That is the time my friend burns. And that is the time that the time clock goes off on this little machine here, and you burn, too. Not quickly, I hope, but slowly. It—" A sudden jar behind him as a flat bundle of papers struck the floor. Then his quiet voice: "Thank you, Jackson." And back to me: "Before I leave you I will pull the plugs from those drums of oil. The oil will come up around your feet."

He looked up toward the ceiling.

"It is very powerful, but I doubt if it will crash the beams down on you. But it will make a hole big enough to create a draft. Are you susceptible to drafts, Sucker Williams?" And when I didn't speak, he took out a cigarette and lit it. "I am not too unjust or unkind. Would you like a smoke? Never fear, the oil is well plugged. There won't be any fire—yet."

I guess I never needed a smoke so much before in my life, but I saw it in his eyes in time and shook my head. But I didn't set my mouth tightly enough.

"Take mine, then," he said, and, snatching it from his lips, jammed the lighted end into my mouth, "What, don't you like a little fire?" He came to his feet in sudden anger as though he couldn't continue sitting there. "So you won't cry out—now. But you will. You will!" He raised his fist, changed his mind, and started crumpling up the paper and tossing it about the room.

"Think of it, Williams," he talked on. "I came to the city and openly let people know that you dared not face me. Tonight I will sit in the Silver Slipper. A hundred or more people will see me

there. My friend dies, but you dare not come where you know me to be. Tomorrow, the next day, a month or a year later. Race Williams never comes. Many will be sure they know; more will guess; but none can prove." He went to the drums, now, and took out the corks. "You will be just another—a different name, perhaps—but just another who crossed the Admiral and was never seen again."

"All right," I finally said. "That will settle me. Why not let the girl go? She isn't apt to run across you and—"

"Apt?" He raised his voice on that word. "There isn't a chance that she will ever see me or anyone else after tonight. I play only sure things. Kidnaping—*phaw*—that is not for me. But Jackson was set on it. He had made his plans, and most peculiarly they fitted in with what I had in my mind. Everyone knows you drove me from the city. Now, they will know that I drove you from the earth. So I want to thank you for that little trick with the cigar. It'll make quite a story."

"How?" My mouth was just beginning to get over its rawness.

"The insult was public. All the gentlemen of my profession, and that includes some respectable criminals who are called politicians, saw or will hear of it. They will say: 'Race Williams came straight to the Admiral's table, stuck a lighted cigar in the Admiral's mouth, and from that night—that very hour—Race Williams was never seen again.' Ah, the oil is at your feet. Can you see the clock plainly?"

He backed away from the oil which already surrounded my chair and was drifting toward his feet.

"It is ten minutes to nine," he said as he reached the stairs. "You have two hours. But don't be impatient or even hopeful if the hands pass the hour by a little. I made sure it wouldn't go off before eleven. You know how they are sometimes slow at Sing Sing, and I have just a touch of sentiment in the things I do."

He didn't speak after that, and neither did I. Anything I said in favor of the girl would only hurt her. He wasn't even sarcastic as he looked from the slowly flowing oil on the hard cement to my face. He didn't joke as he had when Jackson and the other man, Louie, were around. He just stared at me there, studied my face with cruel contempt as he backed slowly up the stairs. Then he sat there and watched me intently.

He never moved, but his face changed as I looked at the clock. A minute passed—five—ten—fifteen. And he didn't speak; I didn't speak. He was watching for me to crack. Nine-thirty came and went. Maybe I stiffened under his eyes; maybe I didn't. Certainly my back should have ached, but it didn't. I never saw the hands of a clock move faster. Ten was gone—ten-fifteen— How long would he wait? Ten-thirty came, and I closed my eyes. I half wished the damned thing would go off and blow us both to hell.

And then a real jerk inside of me. Suppose he stayed there until the damn thing blew up, and then sneaked upstairs? But he wouldn't. He wouldn't dare.

And I heard him move; heard the stairs give slightly. I turned my head and looked. He was still sitting there, grinning at me like an ape. The rotten, vicious— Yes, he had tricked me into looking by his movement. I looked at the clock. It was ten forty-five. Sweat broke out on my forehead. I have always said I could take it. I was taking it, now.

Then he was gone, and I heard the crack of heavy metal against metal. Three times I heard it. So he must have driven home three great bars of steel across the top of the trap. No wonder I couldn't budge it.

And I was alone with death!

CHAPTER 7

ACE IN THE SOLE

ALONE WITH DEATH, eh? Don't you believe it. I had my ace in the hole. Or my ace in the sole, if you want to put it that way. My fingers felt all thumbs, and great swollen thumbs at that, as they tore at the lace of my right shoe. Fourteen minutes to go— Cold, lifeless fingers. From the ropes? I like to think that. Certainly it wasn't fear. No, not fear—at least, not fear for myself.

Why was I digging inside my right shoe and pulling at the lace which wasn't so hard to untie? Because I had hard work lacing it up in that damned tight squeeze in the trunk carrier. I have a bright thought once in a while. I had one then.

Did you guess it? Well, I had it, now; that razor-sharp bit of tin that had nearly cut my neck in two. It was slipped down in my shoe. And, now, I had it between my fingers, pulling it out of the shoe. Then I let it stay there a moment while I worked those fingers up and down. If it fell into the oil I would die. And the girl would die!

Thoughts, then—mad thoughts. How would I save the girl when I got free of the ropes? I didn't know. But I was thinking of her, and I was thinking of life.

Yes, I had been squirming around in that trunk carrier when the Admiral sprayed the ether on me. But he had said I wasn't to die until eleven o'clock. That meant that I was to live for a few more hours, and if I was ever conscious again, I expected to be tied up. And I expected to use something to cut the ropes that held me. That bit of tin that nearly cut my neck to pieces was the thing for me. It had been tough staying conscious while I found it, planted it in my shoe and laced that shoe again.

But now I was tied in a swell position to work that razor-like bit of steel, I'm not going to say it was hard work forcing the piece of steel or tin or whatever it was through that rope. It was sharper than any knife I ever saw. Although it didn't exactly cut it like butter. The difficulty was in holding it in fingers that shook—in hands that shook.

Once, it went from my fingers, slithered on the rope. A deep cut in one finger, and I had it back. And... and... hell, I was free; I was loose; I was straightening myself in the chair and unwinding and slicing the rest of the rope!

Three minutes to go—plenty of time. There was the box. I didn't know the mechanism of it. I only knew how carefully the Admiral had handled it. I wouldn't fool with it. But there was the box, and there was the sink. I had the box in my hand and was skidding on the oil.

I made the sink and stopped. Two minutes of eleven. Two minutes to go and—

What good would it do the girl if I were still alive? I'd be alive in that room—unable to get out just as I was unable to get her out before. It wouldn't do her any good.

But it would do me good. I'd be alive. Someone would come back, of course, and I might hide by the stairs and get that person as he came in—two of them—three of them. Silly? Perhaps; but I'd be alive and have time to think.

It hit me like that. Maybe it was a good thought; maybe it wasn't. That's the stuff, Race, I told myself. You and the girl alive together or dead together. Hadn't the Admiral said if the infernal machine was too close to the ceiling, it would blow a hole in it? Hadn't he said that? Sure he had!

One minute—a half a minute—I almost landed on my back as I ran to the stairs, made them, juggled the box of death and left it there. I left it there right under the trap on the top step.

What would happen when it blew up? Your guess is as good as mine. People say I don't use my head to think, eh? Well, when that explosion came, it would settle things one way or the other. No matter which way it happened, I wouldn't have to think any more.

Maybe I was excited and ran around a bit, but I finally wound up behind one of the drums, crouched like a sprinter ready to start. It wouldn't do me any good to be knocked unconscious by the blast, and it wouldn't do me any good to be burned alive before I could reach the stairs. But I chose the oil drum and stuck to it.

Everything in the one blast—the girl's life and mine.

How would I find her after the blast if I did get free? How would I know where she was? How would I figure that out with my head? Don't make me laugh. I had gone through enough brain trouble. I'd squeeze the thought out of the Admiral's throat, his black tongue, his black heart, or out of his black soul if I had to.

No more fooling if I got the break. If—if— I stuck my fingers in my ears and waited.

God how fast the time had passed before, and now it seemed so slow. And—it came!

All hell broke loose in that room, and I broke loose with it! I dashed toward the stairs—and they weren't there. Not even steps. Just a single support leading up to the trap door. Did I say trap door? But there wasn't any trap door; just a great hole in the ceiling and a couple of twisted, broken bits of metal that might have been strong steel bars a few seconds before.

The light was still hanging from the ceiling. Maybe it helped me; maybe it didn't. The whole place seemed to be ablaze! A sudden, gentle, sweeping flame turned into a roar as I made the trap, felt the single side support that had held the stairs drop from under me, and swung by my hands.

Flames licked at my feet as I chinned myself—yes, shouldered, waisted, and just about kneed myself up through that hole and onto the floor above. A warehouse; no light but the darting flame behind me.

I was free.

A few feet down the wooden floor, and I jerked off my coat, smothered the burning oil that clung to my soaked shoes, spotted a far-distant window and a street light.

After that, the screech of engines, flames leaping high in the air behind me, a taxi driver who was surprised that I didn't want to stop and see the fire, and I was on my way.

No head, eh? After all, I had gone through. And the worst I had to show for it was a hot-foot.

CHAPTER 8

FLOOR SHOW

IT WAS TWELVE o'clock when I parked my car by the side-street entrance and walked into the Silver Slipper. I had treated myself to a shower, a shave, a change of clothes all over, and, of course, a couple of guns swung in my shoulder holsters. Also, I used the telephone.

Maybe I hadn't been fried after all—at least on the outside. Inside I was right up to the boiling point. Just as I turned toward the main floor the lights went out, and I heard the rich voice of Cathleen Conners; the voice that dug into people's hearts—into their souls. And the ad writer who put in that line was correct. It dug into my soul all right.

An assistant manager back behind the tables gripped my arm, said:

"Pretty crowded, sir. You know since we have that midnight special of Miss Conners, it brings in the people. I'll find you a place after the lights go up."

I slipped a bill into his hand and said:

"Lead me to Fletcher's table. He's expecting me. First, tip the spot man to put the light on Fletcher when Miss Conners is doing her stuff. No, he won't be offended." The man squeezed my arm.

"Oh— O.K., Mr. Williams. Mr. Fletcher said to watch for you." And after giving instructions to a boy, he said: "Mr. Fletcher said to tell you we have class tonight. Did you know that Inspector Nelson is here—and Sergeant O'Rourke? Did you know it?"

I let the anxiety in his voice slide by me.

"They've got to have fun once in a while." Then I flopped down in the chair at Fletcher's table and saw Cathleen doing her stuff before a red-faced, bald-headed man who seemed confused and bewildered as the two spotlights crossed, one striking Cathleen and the other smacking on his flat, jowled face. At that, he liked it.

Cathleen was hitting, "Won't You Be My Pretty Daddy?"

I turned in the darkness, said:

"Hello, Fletcher. Did my telephone call surprise you?"

"You can't surprise me with anything you do, Williams. But I moved up to a better ringside table. What's doing? I won a hundred dollars tonight, thanks to you." And when I wanted to know how: "Oh, a ward-heeler bet me you'd never live to see the hour that Frankie Collins was electro-cuted. Forget, eh? You sent him up a year and a half ago. I put through a call half an hour back. He was strapped in the chair screaming like a yellow rat."

"Which he was. You were wise to bet on me." And to myself I thought that he should have had odds. "Cathleen Conners don't look so good."

"Pretty good." I couldn't see Fletcher's face, of course, but I got the curiosity in his voice when he spoke. "She seemed upset earlier in the evening. I asked her if she had seen you. It threw her. But she's a trouper. Nothing could kill her act."

"No?" I grinned in the darkness. "A hundred bucks says she won't be able to finish her act. Want to lose that hundred?"

"Done," he said. "But no rough stuff this time." And then, "Your boy friend, the cigar-eating Admiral, is around. At a table with the gutter-jumper Jackson and a lug called Louie—a nervous boy."

"I'll bet you—" I stopped talking. The light was swinging around. It gave me a bit of a start when I saw Nelson's face flash into the picture and fade away again. I didn't blame Cathleen for swinging in her dance and letting his puss pass. Even the spot man hurried it on. Then she got a well-known play-boy who had half a dozen giggling blondes at his table; giggling on the outside. Inside, their little mechanical hearts burned with greed as they fought for this lad's affection. And that affection ran into four figures at times.

I didn't pay much attention to Cathleen then. I was just beginning to make out shadowy forms and white, indistinct faces from the lights behind the tables. Fletcher said:

"You seem sort of strange, Race, not your easy-going self. Your voice, well, not exactly shakes, but seems full of excitement. Will you have a drink or have you had it?"

"No," I said, "I haven't had it—not yet."

"Not yet, eh?" His voice left me with the impression that he was simply thinking the question aloud and did not expect an answer. Anyway, he didn't get one.

The play-boy was getting a bit rough, trying to pull Cathleen down on his knees, and the spotlight moved on.

I HAD DROPPED to one knee and was hidden from the spotlight by the table and cloth when the sharp glare lit right on Fletcher. But I chanced a look-see from under his arm. There was a surprised look on Cathleen's face. She hesitated. But the spot stayed, and she went into her act, although there was an empty chair at our table almost between Fletcher and her.

Neither of them liked the little show. But I did, and I waited for the part of the spiel where she swung her back toward the man, buried her head in her hands a moment, then spun around and cooed: "Won't you be my pretty daddy?"

The turn came. I snapped to my feet, slid around Fletcher, and oozed into the vacant seat. There were a couple of laughs and a couple of cries of, "Hush," and Cathleen swung back.

"Won't you be my pretty—"

She got that far and no farther, I came to my feet and said grimly:

"You bet, kid."

She fell back a step, staggered, raised her hand to her mouth and screamed. Did I win my hundred dollars? And how! The spot followed her weaving, falling, lurching body for a moment. Then the guy in the light booth got wise to himself, and the spots snapped out. Both of them at once.

But just before the spots went, a shot rang out—two in quick succession! The first there at my left side, the second bringing a cry from far back of me. Then the house lights went on, and I saw the play.

Cathleen Conners was gone. A wild figure had taken her place on the empty dance floor. It was standing, partly shielding the Admiral, whom I could see crouched there at the table behind it.

The man with the gun in his hand was Jackson. He wasn't any hero. He wasn't trying to protect his friend, the Admiral. He was trying to save his own life. He was panic-stricken. There was terror in his face. He fired at me again—wildly, blindly this time! He thought I had come there to get him.

Don't blame him. He was right. He didn't hit me, I didn't fire then to protect myself. And I didn't fire simply to get Jackson, though the last wasn't a bad thought. I fired to protect others in that room from his wild shots. I didn't go in for any trick shots. I didn't go in to shoot the gun out of his hand or cripple his arm. I didn't pick out his heart or his head with the intent to kill him—not because I didn't have the time—for I did.

I put two slugs right smack in his chest! He was off his feet when the second one caught him, but a man has to be sure in life—in death, too, for that matter—so the second shot was simply precautionary.

Who gave the order, I don't know. It might have come from the manager. It might have come from any of half a dozen sources. But someone turned out all the lights, plunging the place in blackness.

I heard Nelson, then, and O'Rourke. Nelson's voice boomed in sharp, threatening command for everyone to remain where seated. O'Rourke's voice was loud enough, but with more of an assurance that the police were taking care of things. Then he called for the lights.

I guess they got them. But not right away. I ran straight across the dance floor, bumped into one or two people, swung to my left and followed my guiding star— the little red light over the entrance to the talents' quarters. Then I was through the thick-curtained entrance.

Lights were dimmed along the carpeted hall with its several little halls leading off it. I knew Cathleen's dressing room. After bumping into frightened little girls and just as frightened big men, I found her room, grabbed the knob and turned it. The door was locked.

A rumpled bit of movement inside that room stopped almost at once. I bent, putting my eye to the keyhole. I had been right about the sound. A key was in the other side of the lock. I put my mouth close to the crack, called:

"Open the door, Cathleen. Open it, now!"

No answer. No time to fool. The Admiral, if he had any sense, would come back to Cathleen. And if he had any sense, he would never have any more, if you get what I mean—or even if you don't. One light tap on the door. No sound of feet crossing the floor within. Clutching the knob, I put my shoulder to the doer—just once.

Like papier-mâché the cheap, light wood about the lock cracked, split, and gave. I was in the room, and the door was closed behind me.

Cathleen was there by the closed closet door. It was as if she had decided to hide in the closet, but didn't have time. She swung and faced me like a cornered animal, her back against the door.

I dropped my gun back in its holster.

"I'm your pretty little daddy," I said as I slowly crossed the room, stretched out a hand and, clutching her by that long, slender, beautiful throat she was so proud of, pulled her to the center of the room.

Her lips trembled. She gasped: "You're not going to… to— I'm a woman."

"Yeah," I told her. "But there's no sex in crime. I'm not going to burn you to death, if that's what you mean."

"Like they—like those other men… you'd beat a woman? You'd… I'd die before I spoke, now. I won't tell you anything."

"Cathleen," I said slow, "you're rotten. And so am I, tonight." My hands tightened on her throat. I saw her mouth open. "But it's the girl, Dorothy Nester. I've got to know where she is."

"I don't know. I don't know!" Her hands came up and gripped at my single one. I loosened my fingers slightly, but they still sank into the soft flesh.

"Then why did you say you wouldn't tell?"

"I mean, I won't confess that they took the girl. I won't swear it against them.

Listen, Race, I know, now, about you. They intended to harm you. But they swore they'd only hold you for a little time, wouldn't harm you, and then would let you go."

"You've been around too long to believe that," I told her and meant it. "There isn't a criminal in the city—or out of it, for that matter—who would ever dare treat me, Race Williams, like that and let me loose to get him afterward."

And when she stared at me.

"Jackson can't tell me," I said, "because I just shot him to death. The Admiral can't tell me because, since he didn't come in here, he's gone up to where he's hidden the girl to kill her."

"To kill her? No—he wouldn't do that! He couldn't do that!"

"He will and he can. His word against mine might be good enough before twelve men if he had a good crooked lawyer. But it wouldn't stand up in court if Dorothy Nester was there to put the finger on him."

"No"—she made an attempt to shake her head as she talked—"he wouldn't dare. Not with me alive."

"He'll kill you, then. Or he'll have an alibi. Or you don't really care if she lives or dies so long as you get the money. No, Cathleen, I don't know what it was in you, but it must have been there all along. You've got murder in your soul."

"No—no! He can't harm her and—"

My fingers tightened on her throat.

"I never handled a woman like this before," I told her, "But I like the kid. She'll lose her life because she tried to save mine. She tore off his mask and saw his face. She thought I was to die and—"

She swung from me in sudden strength. I lunged toward her again, then stopped. She was straight and stiff, and her eyes were steady. She was saying:

"I didn't know they'd kill you. At least I didn't admit that to myself. But it wouldn't have mattered. I was turning over you to take her place. You see, Race, it was her life or yours. Dorothy Nester is my daughter!"

CHAPTER 9

THE MAN WHO KNEW

CATHLEEN CONNERS NEARLY collapsed then. But what of that? I nearly collapsed myself. She was mumbling an explanation. She had married Nester under her real name when she was first in the chorus. His parents didn't like it. The baby, Dorothy, was born. Cathleen agreed to an annulment. Then Nester married the society girl his parents picked. She was good to the child, but died a few years later. Cathleen had never seen either of them until the kidnaping; that is, she had never seen them that they knew about, but she had gone places where she knew her daughter would be. She—

And suddenly it came. She beat at my chest.

"He'll kill her! He'll kill her! He'll have to kill her, now," she cried wildly. "He knows where she is. He's in there."

She pointed at the closet door.

My lips set grimly. The Admiral, eh? Well, he wouldn't kill her, now. He wouldn't kill anyone. He wouldn't— I swung Cathleen around, opened the hall door, pushed her out, said:

"Don't let anyone in."

Then I closed the door, put a chair under the knob, blocking what was left of the door, and walked to the closet. I stood to one side and, reaching out, gripped the knob.

"All right, Admiral," I said as I flung the door open. "I'm to your left. Come out shooting. I'm on the kill."

Nothing happened. Then a gun was flung out on the floor. Another gun followed it. I wasn't boiling so much, now. I had made a mistake, and he had corrected it. If he had come out firing, I would have killed him and the girl Dorothy would have—

I almost had to support the body that, with hands raised high in the air, came out blabbering for mercy. I didn't need anyone to tell me it wasn't the Admiral. I didn't need anyone to tell me it was the squat man, Louie. Mask or no mask, I knew him.

"Don't kill me, don't kill me," he squealed like a trapped pig. "I heard the shots; saw Jackson go down; saw you kill him. I didn't want to harm the girl. You heard me say that. You heard me—"

"Where's the girl?" was all I said.

Louie didn't have enough of his senses about him to lie to me and say he didn't know. He was too busy thinking of his own life. He said:

"I can't tell you. You know the Admiral. He'd… he'd butcher me before—"

"Where's the girl?" I asked again. "There isn't going to be any Admiral to butcher you."

"If you were to tear me apart, Williams, I wouldn't speak for fear—"

I jerked my gun under his chin. He straightened. His head went back.

"Where's the girl?"

He fell to his knees, and between begging for his life and pleading with me not to hit him again, he told me. Did he tell me the truth? Sure he did! He wasn't able to make up lies; he could only stammer out the truth.

After I got the street and house number, and even direction how to find the house, I handed Louie both a straw to grab at and a rock to sink himself with. I told him that if I were late and the girl were dead, he'd burn for murder just the same as if he had put the bullet in her head or the knife in her chest. That was the law, and Louie knew it. I told him if he helped me, I'd put in a word for him and maybe he'd only get twenty years instead of life. I even threw in a suspended sentence which was purely fancy on my part, since I knew the district attorney; but it sounded good to Louie. At least, the part about his not roasting to death if I were in time to save the girl.

It was hard to understand him, for he talked like a man with his mouth full of marbles. But here is what I got:

The house was in the Bronx, well up, and far down the street he gave me—even beyond the paved road, and back by itself among the trees. There were chickens in the yard, or had been, and I could find it easy by the busted wire fence and the chicken house. There was an old wooden shed used for a garage in the back.

"Mr. Williams," he said, and his teeth

went into the "Anvil Chorus." "You can jump from that garage to the edge of a little wooden balcony. The girl's tied up in that room, and there are no bars or nothing across the windows. They're long ones—French they call them—with heavy shades. She's locked in that room and gagged and tied on a bed. No one is in the house. We all had to have our alibi here at the Silver Slipper, tonight!"

"How did the Admiral get her there so quick?" I was trying to trip him up.

He licked at his lips, but told the truth, I was sure.

"Jackson and I took her there before the Admiral left the warehouse." And maybe he lied a little, now. "Jackson bound and gagged her, Maybe I helped. But we wouldn't kill her—no, not me, not even Jackson. The Admiral only intended to keep her there until after we left the club here early in the morning. Then—"

"Then?" I encouraged him with the nose of my gun against his chin.

"Then"—he gulped it out—"he was going up and do the job, himself. She's alone there, but she can't move or talk. Jackson was very thorough in his job of binding and gagging her."

"And Cathleen Conners?"

Louie didn't want to say, but he did.

"I was to get her to come with me and pretend she could take the girl away alive, in return for... for handing you over to the Admiral."

"And take her up there and kill her, too?"

"Not me, not me!" He almost groveled on the floor. "If I could get her to go with me by telling her she could have the girl—free—I was to bring Cathleen to Lexington Avenue and Seventy-first Street where he would be waiting."

A hope there. I said:

"How long would he wait?"

"I don't know. I don't know, Jackson saw you, went crazy, and started to shoot. The Admiral said: 'Get the woman, Cathleen, Louie!' And that was all the time we had for anything."

Right, I thought. And that was all the time I had for anything.

"O.K., Louie," I said as I tapped the nose of my gun down on his head. Just like that, Louie went to sleep. Unpleasant? Of course it was. But what could I do with him until Cathleen got around to telling O'Rourke?

As for me, I turned toward the door, twisted the chair away, took the knob just as it burst open, and Nelson hurled himself into the room.

"Look here, Race," he started, and then as I went to pass him: "No, you don't, my boy, I—"

He wasn't expecting it—couldn't have been—for I wasn't expecting to do it, myself, until my right hand turned into a fist and cracked against his chin! No gun that time—just the old fist. And Inspector Nelson sat down on the floor inside the room so I could close the door behind me when I hit the hall.

Out in the hall, more cops. O'Rourke was there. He grabbed my arm. I said:

"Nelson said for me to go ahead. There's been a kidnaping. I've got to save the girl. I—"

"Dorothy Nester?" O'Rourke asked.

"Yes," I was surprised, worried, too,

because they weren't far from the door; and since it was broken around the lock, it didn't shut very tight. O'Rourke nodded.

"Father telephoned. Now, Race, you can't do this alone. Do you know where the girl is?"

"A lad in there will tell you, O'Rourke," I pleaded with the sergeant. And to Cathleen, who was leaning against the wall—or at least loud enough for her to hear: "She helped me, O'Rourke. Take care of her." I saw another plain clothes man coming down the hall. "The cops would cause her death, now. I got to go."

O'Rourke said:

"Run along, Race. Nelson said so, eh?" And to the men, "Free passage, there."

NELSON BELLOWED THEN, but I was on my way. I didn't feel safe until I was in my own car and around the corner.

Feeling safe for my own get-away was all right. But what about the girl, Dorothy Nester? What about the kid who had forfeited her own life in her effort—for she did believe it—to save mine? How much of a start did the Admiral have? Plenty, I guess. But would he make speed to kill the girl? Would he chance too much speed? Also, would he have a car handy? I ate that thought—that question—the moment I asked myself it. The Admiral would always have a car handy. But Louie had told me he was to go and get Cathleen, tell her that Dorothy Nester was safe, then meet the Admiral at the corner of Lexington Avenue and Seventy-first Street.

I'd drive to the corner of Seventy-first Street. Maybe drive right up on the curb and smack the Admiral against the building. But there were objections to that. How long would he wait? He might drive on. He might be hiding in a doorway and see me come and telephone someone to kill the girl. Or since that was planned before the shooting, he might not go to Lexington Avenue at all.

I wanted to meet the Admiral, but my first duty was to the girl.

So I shot straight for the Bronx!

CHAPTER 10

BALCONY SCENE

CATHLEEN CONNERS DIDN'T seem so bad, now, though from a personal viewpoint, I couldn't exactly approve of what she did. So she didn't believe they'd harm me? She wouldn't let herself believe anything like that. Poor woman—it was my life or her daughter's. I shrugged my shoulders. There was no use to complain. I'm no authority on mother love, but from now on I'll have my doubts about mothers carrying that love just a bit too far.

This was the chase. The way I like it, especially when there is a lad who tried to roast me alive at the end of the rainbow—my rainbow. If it wasn't for the girl—and such a kid—I might even have enjoyed it. There were no two ways about it, now. The city—the entire country—there wasn't even room in life for both the Admiral and myself. I set my lips grimly. He had made that crack some time back. It was his crack, and he could lie in it.

But the girl. Would I be on time?

Would the Admiral rush right into the house and kill her? Would he take her somewhere else? Would he leave— I gulped, but I had the thought just the same—would he leave her body there or take it away with him?

Yes, Dorothy Nester complicated things all right. The Admiral's number was up, but he'd kill the girl and destroy what he thought was any real evidence against him.

I was nervous all right, but an eager sort of nervous. I remembered with tight lips how the Admiral had sat on those cellar steps and stared. I remembered, too, the sweat that broke out on my forehead. Well, we'd see now where the sweat broke.

Louie's directions were good. He needed to make them good. His life depended on my time to begin with—and my life to end with. Yes, Louie's directions were a little too good. I passed the houses on the cement road, shot by the lots and landed on the dirt road he told me about. But I landed on it too soon—and too hard. I didn't know the ruts in it. The car swerved and bounced, and I saw the house; at least the roof of it. The moonlight wasn't so bad. I could see where I was going; so I doused the lights, swung lightly up on a dirt-and-sand bank and hopped out of the car. So much for the car. That couldn't be seen from the house.

The moonlight wasn't so welcome, now. The house, as Louie had said, was well back from the road. But there wasn't much bush or trees or anything within a couple of hundred feet of it. It looked as if the place might have been used as a dump—but not lately.

Crawling up on the bank I could easily peek over and see the house, the garage and a sort of driveway that led up to it. For the garage was on another bank behind the house. And—I couldn't be sure, of course—I thought, or at least hoped, that it was the flashing metal of a car I saw just inside its open doors.

Now what to do? You can't run slightly bent and duck in and out of moonbeams any more than you can among raindrops. I had two choices. One was to try and get into the house from below. He'd hear me maybe, and if he did, would he go on with his gruesome job, or would he come down and lay for me? I smacked my lips. If I was sure he would come down and lay for me, I'd forget what Louie had told me and take the lower floor.

Understand, this wasn't conscious thinking, and it wasn't delayed thinking, and I was acting while I thought. I was running across that lot, hopping tin cans, slipping on wet papers and making my decision almost as I reached the house. It was a car in the garage. The Admiral hadn't left yet!

With that little jump in my heart came another jump that didn't make me feel so good. The Admiral had also arrived.

No time to lose, now, I was around the back of the house, up the bank on which stood the flat-roofed garage. I could see the balcony Louie had described, the French window, yes, and a light—just a sliver of light-beyond tightly drawn, dark-green shades. And the garage. The far side of its roof was almost on a line with that balcony and the lighted window beyond it; the only light in the entire house.

Get the lay? The garage was built on a bank, but the side of that garage that faced the house was propped up by a stone wall to keep the shaky structure from falling off its foundation. Between the garage and the house was a ditch. When you stood below the balcony just between the house and the garage, you couldn't reach the balcony—not by a good number of feet you couldn't. But if you went around to the front of the garage and climbed to the roof; then the garage was well above the balcony or maybe on a level with it.

AND THAT'S WHAT I was doing. There was a window on the side of the garage all right, but it didn't seem to me as good a spot as one of the open doors. I jumped, grabbed the top of one door, chinned myself, tossed a knee up and climbed to the torn tin on top of the wobbly shed. But the tin held, and there I was—a good six feet from the balustrade of the balcony, and perhaps four feet above it.

Time would be wasted. I would have to remove my shoes and leap for that balcony. If the Admiral was already in that room he might hear me. And he was there! At least someone was there. I could see the shadow cross the long sliver of light. I could see something. Yes, I could see everything; everything I wanted to see, and a lot I didn't want to see, too, through a great rent in one of the shades.

The Admiral was standing over a little figure on the bed—a figure that was struggling. The girl, of course! He must have untied her to try and force her from the house. I saw things plainly enough. I saw the girl's hair, her face, her eyes wild with terror, and the gag across her mouth. I even saw the ropes on the bed. And then I saw her sink back; saw the Admiral's black sleeve, his white hand, and the thing that was in that hand. The thing that caught for a moment and flashed into the light!

I didn't see enough of the Admiral to shoot; to shoot to kill. I didn't—

No thoughts then. One quick look; one jerk for twin guns with two hands, and I made the leap. Oh, not to land on the balcony rail and stay there, but just to use that balcony rail as a stepping stone for what was to follow.

I thrust myself from that garage roof with force. I hit the balcony rail fairly accurately. Then, letting my body ride with plenty of steam behind it, I crossed my left arm before my eyes and hurled my one hundred and eighty pounds of beef against those French windows—or doors—or what have you.

Were the glass doors locked? Don't ask me. I didn't know, then, and I never did find out afterward.

I can't say I counted on a panic on the Admiral's part that I didn't get. I can't say that I even hoped he would be tossed completely by that kind of an entrance. I simply say that he should have been startled, at least. I didn't count or hope anything when I made the leap. I didn't even think. I just went smack from the railing through those doors like a baby tank.

Those French windows split in the center as though a big gun had cracked them. Glass, wood, yes, and I went all over the floor together. That's one thing I never had a chance to practice on, and my performance was entirely unrehearsed.

Surprised? Yes, the Admiral was surprised and nothing more. I was flat on my face when he fired the first time; had lifted my head and looked into his eyes before he fired the second time! He was cool and calm and shot deliberately. The raising of my head kept the first bullet from going through the top of it.

The slug hit the floor below my chin, skidded and, for some reason, didn't bury itself in the wood. How did I know that? Because I had a bad break and felt the lead tear into my chest!

I was trying to turn and face him when his second shot came. I didn't know where it hit me. At least, I didn't know then. I didn't feel any pain. I just knew it had hit me because my body jarred, and I felt the plump of it, soft and easy.

His third shot?

Don't be stupid. He had had his full quota of shots. He was leaning slightly forward, almost bending over me when I closed the index finger of my left hand. Somewhere under the chin it caught him!

He was a great little guy, the Admiral. There wasn't even surprise in his face—in his eyes. There was nothing there. There couldn't be. He was dead!

No pain, no nothing. The Admiral had all the breaks. That is, all the breaks until the last one. Now— Hell, I told you that before. He was dead, I said. Just dead!

I THINK I came to my feet. In fact, I know I did. I remember smiling at the girl. I remember her tearing the gag from her mouth and opening it to scream. I remember her looking at me. Her mouth hung open and her eyes were wide, but not with terror; with fear—fear for me.

I remember, too, that I heard a door crash below; that there were feet on the stairs. I looked at my hands; they were both empty. Then I saw my guns on the floor, bent forward to reach for one. The girl caught my head as I pitched on my hands and knees and grabbed at my guns.

"It's the police, Race," she said. "The sirens—I heard them. I—" Maybe she helped me; maybe she didn't. But I was on my feet again as the door burst open. I don't know which one of them was in the room first, O'Rourke or Nelson, but it was Nelson who was walking toward me.

"Now, listen. Race—" He had his hand raised.

I jerked up my right hand, made a pass at Nelson, lurched forward, spun slightly, and O'Rourke caught me in his arms. That was like me, too. Sure—I had left the girl's arms to fall into O'Rourke's.

I grinned anyway, pointed to the floor, looked up at Nelson.

"There's your chestnuts, Nelson," I said. "At least, one chestnut—and burned to a crisp."

At least that's what O'Rourke said I said. I guess he was right.

Peculiar life. The bullets weren't so bad. Just a hole through my side, and a bit of lead that could have been pulled out of my chest with your forefinger and thumb. It was the glass that was the worst. It reminded me of when I was a kid, and a farmer let go with a load of buckshot when I was borrowing a few apples.

Bullets are all right. A doctor can go after them and tell you just about where you stand; but glass, it turns up later in the most unexpected places. Don't tell me, I know.

Dorothy Nester came to see me often, and one night Cathleen Conners came with Dorothy's father. The old man had been to call on me once before and stammered a bit of a speech about all the money in the world not being able to pay me for what I had done. After my fever had gone up a couple of degrees, he produced a check for ten thousand dollars.

Cathleen stood back a bit while Mr. Nester asked for my advice. He said:

"Through a great and a mutual sorrow and you, Mr. Williams, Cathleen and I have been brought happily together again. And we like it that way. Now"— he laughed sort of hollowly—"it's a peculiar question that I have to ask a man of action like yourself. Sort of advice to the lovelorn. Cathleen and I are thinking of—well—giving Dorothy a real mother. I might say a real mother and father together. But Cathleen said you were the one to decide. I don't quite understand. I suppose it's because you were her friend. She wants me to ask you if you believe she'd make a good mother."

"I'd rather she was my mother than my friend," I said just a bit viciously, and then I got what was bothering Cathleen. Would I talk? Would I toss a monkey wrench into the works? I looked at her a second or two—

"She's a wonderful mother," I said, and I let it go at that.

But I read it in Fletcher's column even before Dorothy told me about it. How did Fletcher know? Or did he know all along?

Dorothy said a few days later and just before I left the hospital:

"She's my real mother, Race, I always knew I had a real mother and wondered what it would be like to have some-one—you know—a mother who would do anything in the world for you. She would—my mother would. Wouldn't she, Race?"

I took the hand she slipped into mine and made her very happy. But what I told her was strictly the truth, I said:

"She certainly would, Dorothy. She'd even send a man straight to his death for you."

Dorothy smiled sort of sadly. Maybe she was thinking of the Admiral. But I wasn't. Not by a damned sight I wasn't.

Too Dead to Pay

ENTITLED TO ONE CRACK

I LOOKED OVER at the country doctor and said:

"Tell me about it again."

Bernard V. Jones, M.D., straightened the black ribbon that was masquerading as a tie, pulled the frayed end of one sleeve of his Prince Albert over the end of a detachable cuff, coughed behind the back of his hand, and started:

"It was a cold, cheerless night, sixteen years ago, in the little Pennsylvania town of New Madison that the child—"

"No." I shook my head. "We'll skip the weather and come up to date. Start with when you first discovered that the child who had grown into a young woman was heir to a great fortune and what you did."

He tried another cough and another cuff and got it off his chest.

"Mr. Woodman, her father, or the man I thought was her father, died of a stroke. It was on Edith's nineteenth birthday— that's the child who was grown up. Her mother, or the woman I thought and the whole town thought was her mother, had a stroke a year later, on Edith's twentieth birthday. But she lived long enough to talk to me. She believed that a mighty Providence had connected the dates and struck her down. She told me the child was not her child; that she had been given to her to take care of when the girl was four years old; that Edith was heir to a great fortune left by her grandfather." He paused, then, before adding very solemnly: "Then she died."

"But she told you the child's right name?"

"Yes—Harriman, Edith Harriman. Her mother's name was Chalmers. This woman Gladys Woodman—Mrs. Gladys Woodman—also told me that Edith's life would be in danger if any claim was made to the fortune. And I gathered—wasn't told, understand—that the child was supposed to be dead."

"You mean that this woman and her husband were supposed to have disposed of the child, murdered her, but that something good inside of them stopped them, and they kept the child alive?"

"There was nothing good inside of them," the country doctor said stiffly. "They were a brutal, superstitious couple, and I don't know why they cared if the child lived or died. But I pulled that girl through many a crisis, and they were anxious that she live."

"No doubt," I told him, "they were afraid that if the child died they would lose their grip over the person for whom they were hiding the girl. No doubt they had promised to dispose of the child, but found her worth more money to them alive than dead."

"I don't know," Dr. Jones said honestly enough. "Naturally, I did everything for her best interest. I had advertisements inserted in the New York newspapers. At the time I said nothing to the girl of her coming good fortune. I wanted to be certain first. This woman had spoken of danger to Edith; so, in the advertisements, I inserted a box number in a neighboring town."

"And you got an answer to your advertisements?"

"Yes, in a most surprising way at first. I was shot at through the post office window while I stood at the box. The bullet narrowly escaped my head. I knew, then, that I was on the right track."

"Or the wrong one." I smiled. "You were seen opening the box. It was easy to identify you. Someone was planted there as soon after your advertisement was seen as possible. What next?"

"The letter from the firm of lawyers, Hartman, O'Neil & Hartman."

Nothing fishy about that firm. They fairly reeked with stuffiness and respectability. But to get on with the main point of the story.

"I went to see these lawyers," he went on. "The senior partner, Mr. Hartman, told me that the girl was heir to a large fortune and that Mr. Arthur Chalmers was very anxious to find his niece. She had disappeared with her mother, years back. He listened to my story, spoke of identification, and I took her at once to see Mr. Chalmers."

"The lawyer didn't meet the young lady?"

"No. Mr. Chalmers was greatly pleased. He said he was holding the money in trust for her; that the lawyers and courts, no doubt, would need a formal identification; but as far as he was concerned, she was the image of her dead mother. He insisted that she stay with him. He was grave about one matter only. He said I should keep my own council until formal identification was made. He didn't say why, but he spoke of his brother whom he had not seen in years—Colonel Tobias Chalmers. And he was most grave when he heard of the attack on me."

"And then what?"

"The next day I called at Mr. Chalmers' home to see Edith. She would not see me. Mr. Chalmers was courteous enough, but in a cold manner. He said I would, in due time, receive ample reward for keeping from the public her unhappy past life; that she was to become a rich woman and take her place in society as befitted her name. Then, to the public, she would appear as having been educated abroad and would take up her position in New York from an apparent background of culture, education, and wealth."

"Go on."

Dr. Jones cleared his throat.

"Well," he said, "my practice is a comfortable one if not lucrative. My needs are small; my personal desires practically nil. What I did for Edith was with no hope of reward; indeed, I had no thought of such. I was more hurt than angry, But I left Mr. Chalmers, returned to my hotel, packed my bag and was about to board a train when it occurred to me that this was not at all like Edith. So I used the tele-phone, got Mr. Chalmers, and again he told me that Edith refused to talk to me. So I came to you, Mr. Race Williams."

"Money changes people," I told him. And when his eyes widened, "Yes, even overnight. Here is a young girl, tossed suddenly from poverty to great wealth. Did you speak to this lawyer, Mr. Hartman, again?"

"Yes, I did. He looked me over pretty carefully. Perhaps I do look a bit seedy. After keeping me waiting for ten minutes, he took me into his private office. He was very polite. He had talked to Mr. Chalmers, who, he assured me, begged 'the young lady' to see me. He even had Edith on the phone. He was brutally frank to me. I remember his final words. 'I have talked to Miss Edith Harriman, myself, Dr. Jones. You need have no apprehension about her. She refuses to see you.' That was all, Mr. Williams. Does it not strike you as very odd?"

"You think she is prevented from seeing you?"

He did the cough act behind his hand again.

"Mr. Chalmers is a very well-known man. Mr. Hartman heads a firm that is beyond reproach. Let me put it that I would like to be assured that Edith herself does not wish to see me. Did I do right in coming to you?"

I grinned at that one.

"Dr. Jones, everyone who consults me does right," I told him and meant it. "I'll see the young lady and see that she sees you—though I won't promise what she'll say to you."

"But my dear sir—how? I was quite insistent, I assure you."

"It won't be hard." I made a note of his hotel and room number and just before he left, I added: "You didn't threaten to take away some of that culture and background and education, did you?"

"Certainly not!" His mouth hung open. "I never thought of such a thing."

"Well, I'll think of it. There, Dr. Jones, don't look so alarmed. The threat itself will be sufficient, I'm sure. I'll call on Mr. Chalmers directly after dinner. Be at your hotel."

"But if he spirits her away?"

"If he spirits her away, he'll spirit her back again."

"I won't leave my room," he told me at parting.

CHAPTER 2

A SHOCK

I DIDN'T MAKE any appointment with Mr. Chalmers. I just pulled up a few doors away from his four-story, red brick home and, mounting the worn steps, rang the bell.

If Mr. Chalmers had any idea of keeping me out when I wanted in, he should have had a chain on the door. The butler was the usual bald-headed, round-faced, well-fed servant. He knew all the old jokes about not seeing Mr. Chalmers unless I had an appointment. But my foot was in the door, and the floor was highly polished. He was anchored on a small rug—one of those man traps you step on occasionally and discover too late that you are not equipped with skid chains.

I pushed the door against him and the rug moved back, and he moved with it. He was a big man, a foolish man, and he wanted to put me out. Before his hands got me, I had braced one foot, flattened my right hand against the expanse of his white shirt front and shoved. He went sailing across the floor on the rug like a kid at play. But he didn't have a kid's sense of balance. Anyway, he shouldn't have tried standing on one leg. His other leg shot from under him and he wound up at the foot of a pedestal that had supported a statue. For the first time in his life I think he was holding an undraped lady in his arms.

At least, it was the first time in his life he did it in the presence of his master, Arthur Livingston Chalmers. That's right, Chalmers had come out of a side room and was standing in the hall. He was a big, puffy man. His wide, fishy blue eyes were covering the distance from the butler to me, and he was wondering how his man managed to mix himself up like that with a good twenty-five feet between us. As for me, I stood my ground. If Chalmers wanted to keep something quiet, he couldn't do it by having me arrested. As for having me thrown out— Well, I've been thrown out of places, of course, but I'm generally about third or fourth to go; so he'd have to decorate the sidewalk first with some of his own hired help.

Chalmers blasted away at me.

"What's the meaning of this outrage? Who are you? What do you want? What do you mean by attacking Roland?"

I said:

"I want to see you on a matter of great

importance. If Roland wants to clown around, that's between servant and master and not my business."

"And just what is your business?"

"I've come," I said, "to see Miss Edith Harriman. And I won't leave without seeing her."

"Oh, you won't?" he said. "And who sent you? That little doctor who'd be willing to create a scandal? Let me tell you, sir, you can't force your way into my house at will. There's the law."

"You've got a phone," I told him. "Call the police."

"I will. Ford!" And suddenly with a smile as a lumbering figure came from behind him: "The police are here as you see."

And I didn't see. That is I didn't see the police. But I did see the broad-shouldered figure of the man who sauntered into the hall. I did see the half-smoked and unlighted cigar, the small eyes, the little mouth, the two odd chins and the closely-cut black hair. Everything was there but the derby hat. It was Gregory Ford, head of one of the largest detective agencies in New York. He was soft-spoken and knew his business.

"Now, Race," he said slowly as he walked over toward me, "let's have what's on your mind. You're a little out of your class here, you know. It's not a back room in a saloon. I hear something about your wanting to speak to Miss Harriman. Well, Mr. Chalmers don't want people to speak to her. I agree with him. I have so advised him. I am here to see that people don't speak to her. Now what?"

"I still want to speak to her, Gregory," I said.

"Well, you can't. Is that final?"

"No, it isn't."

"No?" He shook his head at me. "Surely you don't intend to shoot your way upstairs to her." There was sarcasm in his voice, and I think a little apprehension, too. But I shook my head and said very seriously:

"I came here in a friendly spirit. I'm a man of peace, not a man of violence. I'll go to the police, obtain a warrant, and have the house searched."

"Really, now. On what grounds?" Gregory's grin was broad, and so was Chalmers'.

My next line wiped the grin off both their faces as if a mop swiped across them. I said:

"On the charge that Mr. Chalmers has murdered his niece and hidden her body in the cellar!"

GREGORY GOT THE absurdity of the statement after the first wallop had passed off, but not Chalmers. It rocked him. Roland had recovered sufficiently to stick out a chair for him to drop into. He did just that. But then, we all can't have the same sense of humor. At least my wisecrack brought an interest. Gregory Ford took me into the library.

"Look here, Race." He gave me a cigar which, with my being a cigarette smoker and having once smoked one of Gregory's free ones, I put in my pocket. "Now listen, boy. This Dr. Jones sent you. I like you—always have. I don't want to make trouble for you. That's not my way." And when I didn't say anything: "Well, what will you do if you don't see her?"

"*Ah!*" I said, "we get down to business. I'll do everything that Mr. Chalmers doesn't want me to do. I'll blow the works, make the girl's return home public, send photographers out to New Madison to take pictures of the— What are you here for anyway? To protect her from something?"

He threw out his hands.

"Not at all. Not at all," he repeated. "I'm to make a private investigation to establish her identity. Hell, if I had known that little doctor runt was going to make all this trouble, I'd have let him see the girl. But why all the fuss?"

"Why not? The doctor's a fair, sincere man. He was fond of the girl. He got her into a fortune. He can't believe she's so ungrateful. Why doesn't Mr. Chalmers want her to see him?"

"He doesn't care," said Gregory Ford. "I don't know what you're getting paid for this, and I never met the doctor. But the girl doesn't want to see him. I heard Mr. Chalmers ask her to see him." Gregory lowered his voice. "She doesn't think much of the doctor."

"Well, she should. He fixed it up so she'd get the dough."

"Wait," said Gregory. Then he went out in the hall and was gone for about ten minutes. Finally, he came back with Chalmers. He was all smiles, but Chalmers was all serious.

"Mr. Chalmers doesn't understand." Gregory Ford patted me on the back. "I told him how you're one for a bit of a joke, and as persistent as they come when you're after anything. Mr. Chalmers wants to know if you'll be satisfied with seeing the girl, yourself."

I said:

"No, I have a client. I assured him he could see the girl tonight. I make good, or I make trouble."

Chalmers said:

"I'm afraid you'll have to make trouble then." He pointed at a picture on the wall. "She's very much like her mother, poor child. Determined even after all she has gone through, I won't go into our family trouble. You may see and talk to her, Mr. Williams. I must admit that I had formed a very high opinion of Dr. Jones an honest, sincere little man. It isn't often I'm fooled, but surely my niece wouldn't act the way she has unless she had good reason. But you may tell the doctor that if he rakes up her past and the whole unfortunate story of her life I will see—use all my influence to see—that he receives no money whatsoever."

"Dr. Jones," I said, "is not interested in the money. Only in the girl."

"Just what he told me," Mr. Chalmers agreed readily enough. "But Edith has a different—" And as the door opened: "But you'll meet her, now. I sent Roland for her."

I DID MEET her. And I didn't think she was the dead image of her mother, if the photograph in the old-fashioned oval gilt frame which hung on the wall was a good likeness. Despite her gentle voice and manner, there was a hardness in her face, and a cold stare in her brown eyes as she looked at me. Her nose, too, wasn't quite as straight as the one in the picture, though her mother may have had a twisted nose, too. Even when that picture was taken, photographers were already doing wonders.

Now, I can't say that I fell with a thud for Miss Edith Harriman. Maybe she had led a hard life. She certainly looked much older than her twenty years. And she certainly looked as if she could dish it out as well as take it, too. She watched me with unfriendly eyes.

"You came from Dr. Bernard Jones?" she asked. "I don't want to see him. I don't ever want to see him again."

"Tell him why, my dear." Mr. Chalmers put an arm about her shoulders.

"Is that necessary?" She looked straight at me. "I am not ashamed of anything I have done. Why should I be? I don't care what he says about me. I don't care who he tells. I will have money. People with money don't have to worry. Let him tell what he wants. I won't pay blackmail."

Maybe I flushed a little. But I said:

"It's not my business to harm anyone, Miss Harriman; least of all you. I only ask that you see Dr. Jones. I don't care what you tell him. But I don't see why you're afraid to talk to him."

"I'm not afraid." Her eyes flashed.

"I'll guarantee he won't talk about you," I said on sudden impulse. "I promised him you'd see him."

"All right," the girl said as if she made up her mind quickly, "I'll see him and I'll talk to him. But I won't see him alone." She shrank a little then. "I'll see him with you, and I'll tell him before you exactly why I don't want to see him again and what I think of him."

"You can't faze me, lady," I said, although she did faze me. Dr. Jones had seemed such an honest little inoffensive soul. I picked up the phone on the desk. Dr. Jones was my client. I had told him he'd see the girl. I called the hotel, gave the room number, and asked for Dr. Jones. The clerk seemed to hesitate, then a voice said:

"Put the call through."

I was startled at the voice that answered. It was not Dr. Jones, but I thought I recognized it. I said rather stupidly:

"I want to speak to Dr. Jones."

"Who's calling?"

I had nothing to hide and couldn't have hidden anything if I wanted to with three witnesses present. So I said:

"Race Williams."

"Oh, you, Race!" And with that smack of the lips I knew so well, "This is O'Rourke."

"Sergeant O'Rourke?" I had a funny feeling.

"Not captain. What do you want?" I said again:

"I want to speak to Dr. Jones."

"Well, come down here then. He can't speak to you, now. He just had his throat cut! He's too dead!"

I dropped the phone back into its cradle. O'Rourke wanted to say more and so did I. But I couldn't just then.

CHAPTER 3

THE DEATH CAR

I PICKED UP my hat and walked out of the house and drove straight to Dr. Jones' hotel. Not that there was anything in it for me, and not that I especially like seeing people with their throats cut, but I had called him up, the police knew it, and Sergeant O'Rourke was my friend. I wanted to keep him that way.

It wasn't an expensive hotel, and the doctor hadn't done himself proud on the cheap inside room with bath. Homicide was on the job, and the boys were picking up their cameras and getting ready to leave. The medical examiner was a nervous little man who made clucking sounds while he knelt by the body. When he came to his feet, he smiled at me. O'Rourke snapped:

"How long has he been dead?"

"*Ah!* so you noticed that," said Dr. Steel. "I was afraid you would." And more seriously, "I'd say it was a knife, not a razor, but you can't pin me down as to time, you know. Certainly before eight o'clock. Good-night. I'll have it official for you later."

"Nasty little ghoul," O'Rourke said as the doctor went clucking out of the room. "You'd almost think he liked it."

"Business with him," I told O'Rourke, "A guy's got to get some fun out of his work. How did it happen?"

O'Rourke raised his voice. "Look at his throat. He was found just like that— sitting right there in the chair. He had his dinner in his room; and, when the waiter came up for the dishes, he was sitting like that."

I went over and looked at the doctor. I hadn't been feeling so kindly toward him after the way the girl acted. Even in death, he still looked like the little country doctor. Death hadn't hardened his face any. There was no terror in the calm repose of his mouth or the wide, sightless eyes. I said to O'Rourke:

"Someone he wasn't afraid of."

O'Rourke snapped:

"How do you know that?"

"Take it easy," I told him. "I don't know. But there would be some fear in his face if he saw it coming. So my guess is that the man walked around behind him, leaned over and slit his throat!"

"Well," said O'Rourke, "that's logical figuring. Now tell me about him."

I told O'Rourke all I knew about Dr. Jones.

"So the girl gets her hand on the dough, then won't see him any more." O'Rourke was simply repeating my thoughts. "Nice girl, eh?"

"Why don't you go up and see her?"

"I will," he nodded. "What are you going to do, now?"

I shrugged. I didn't have any client, and as far as money being paid, I never did. I said:

"Nothing. It's no hair off the back of my neck. Did he have any visitors?"

"What do you care?" O'Rourke turned away. "It's no hair off the back of your neck."

I went downstairs and saw the manager. He was nervous but wouldn't talk. He said he didn't have to, and the police had told him not to.

Then Inspector Nelson stormed across the lobby. Nelson was no friend of mine, but I wasn't of his, either, and that made us even.

I used a potted plant in place of a forest, and Nelson was so impressed with his own importance that he didn't see me. He just stuck out his chest and followed it into the elevator. O'Rourke and I were both right. It was no hair off the back of my neck. I couldn't see any dough in it; so I just walked out of the hotel and down the street.

It was a dim side street, and there weren't many people on it at that time—or most any time after dark, for that matter. But it was a short cut over to Broadway, and I thought I'd take in a movie. I don't make other people's trouble mine just to kill time. I leave people alone if they leave me alone and—

They didn't leave me alone.

I won't say that the thing was unexpected because I never admit that anything in my life is unexpected. I spotted the car and spotted the trap at just about the same time. It was a big black sedan with the curtains tightly drawn. It was a death car, and I knew it!

The car hadn't more than slowed down, the curtain in the window-hadn't more than moved, and certainly the nose of the Tommy gun and the white face behind it weren't at the window before I was lying flat on my face with both guns in my hands.

The gunman fired! Lead raked the sidewalk. Then the nose of the sub-machine gun raised, one more spasmodic series of blasts shook the air, and a white face—a white face that was stained with red—disappeared from the window of the car.

The black sedan picked up speed, shot toward the corner. And me, I was dusting myself off as I ducked into the side entrance of a shabby residence, ran easily to the back yard across the square of stones, hopped a wooden fence and passed out to the street beyond. Then I made my way to my own apartment.

You wonder what became of the lad in the car with the Tommy gun and why he didn't shoot any more? Well, there were three bullets gone from one of my guns, and if you're a betting man, I'll lay you good odds that all three of them weren't just buried in the side of that car. If they were, how would you account for the red on the white face?

You see how things happen. There I was, ready to go about my own business; but someone wouldn't have it that way. Something was in the wind, and whoever was behind that something believed that the little doctor had told me more than he should. At least, that someone had a belief, and he was willing to back it up with a machine gun.

That night O'Rourke came around to see me. He was sort of fidgety and wanted to know if I was still interested in the case. He finally came out with it.

"There's something wrong with the whole thing, Race," he said. And after accepting a drink, "Tony Fenerro was shot to death tonight. They found his body in Central Park. A fine place to dump a body so early in the evening." He knitted up his eyebrows and looked at me. "It wasn't so far from the Welford Hotel—you know, where Dr. Jones was killed. And you left about that time."

"All right," I told him. "Someone opened up on me with a machine gun

CARROLL JOHN DALY

from a black sedan. I was nervous and frightened and fired back."

"You must have been pretty nervous," he smiled. "Tony Fenerro opened his mouth in time to swallow the bullet."

"You didn't expect him to catch it in his teeth, did you? Just one killer less. What's the beef?"

"No beef." He shook his head. "We can easily settle that by a little talk with the D.A." And with a wry twist to his mouth, "We just like to keep our records clean and know where our dead bodies come from down at Headquarters, but from now on it will be hair off the back of your neck if I know anything about you."

"Well," I said, "Tony may have had a private grudge."

"Can you think of any?"

"No."

"Have you got a client?"

"No."

"So guys are shooting at you for fun. Now listen, boy, we've worked together many times, and I've helped you out when an official word down at Headquarters would do some good. This case is an odd one. A country doctor, a missing heiress, a highly respectable private banker, a hired killer, and"—he leaned forward now—"a disreputable ex-army officer who has lived a quiet life for the past sixteen years. That is quiet until last night."

"And where does this army officer fit into the picture?"

"He was the lad who visited Dr. Bernard Jones' room last night. His name is Colonel Tobias Chalmers—Arthur Chalmers' brother. The newspapers will blow the lid off the city hall if they get hold of it."

"How did you know it was Colonel Tobias Chalmers?"

O'Rourke smiled, opened his hand, and showed me the picture.

"Not holding out on you, boy. I was up and had a talk with Arthur Chalmers. He's very much distressed. He didn't have any pictures of his brother hanging about the house, but I talked him into showing me some old albums. He's a much older man, now, than when that picture was taken. But the clerk thought the face was familiar."

"And the clerk only thought he recognized him?"

"Well," O'Rourke smiled, "I went to Colonel Chalmers' apartment. He and his daughter, Thesta, were out—out all last night. Now I've laid my cards on the table. What about yours?"

"I haven't any," I told him flatly.

"You're going to look into it?"

"It looks as if someone is looking into it for me. If I want to stay alive, I'll have to look into it."

"Someone believes you know something. Else, why the attempt on your life?"

"*Ah!* that was the slip," I told O'Rourke and meant it. "I didn't get a cent from the doctor. Edith Harriman gave me the impression that Dr. Jones wasn't all he appeared to be. Someone thinks he told me more than he did."

"See you some more, Race," O'Rourke said in leaving. "I've got a couple of men flying out to New Madison, now. We can check up on the doctor's reputation and Edith Harriman's identity. Don't get yourself dumped in Central Park in the meantime, boy."

CHAPTER 4

THE SECOND MURDER

The next morning I went down to Hartman, O'Neil & Hartman. Stuffy lawyers, stuffy clients, stuffy clerks. Hartman didn't think he could see me. I didn't complain. I walked into his private office when someone walked out and pulled the regular gag:

"If you have nothing to hide there is no reason for not seeing me. A man has been murdered and there is no reason you should be mixed up in it if you don't make it necessary."

He puffed and he blew, and he did the big-bad-wolf act in a dignified sort of way. But even if he pretended not to know me, he knew my reputation which, from his way of looking at it, wasn't so good. But he finally gave the black ribbon of his nose glasses a tug and said somewhat sourly: "Just what is it that you wish to know?"

"That's fine." I gave him the pleasant grin just as if he were gladly ready to tell me everything I wanted. "I always appreciate cooperation. Now, Mr. Hartman, to what sort of a fortune does Miss Edith Harriman fall heir? How does she get it and when? And who had it before?"

"Well," he said, "there's no secret about that, and as soon as I heard that Miss Edith Harriman had been located after so many years, I took occasion to refresh my knowledge at Mr. Chalmers'—Mr.

Arthur Chalmers'—request, of course."

"Of course," I agreed, since he seemed to wait for some such agreement.

"The whole tragedy of the Chalmers family is a bit sordid, and to have it revived now, after the years, is most unfortunate for Mr. Arthur Chalmers."

"Why unfortunate for him—alone?"

"Because his life has been much… er… should I say much more conventional than the others of his family. There were three in the family besides the father. Two brothers and a sister. I shall not go into the manner in which their father, Steven G. Chalmers, amassed his fortune. Business ethics back in those days were not on the same high level as our present times. But he was unfortunate in two of his children—if I may pass an opinion which I expect to go no further than this office. Tobias lived loosely; he married and had one child, Thesta. His wife died shortly after the child's birth. Father and daughter have lately been living on a small income supplied by his brother. Thesta Chalmers is a young lady, now. So much for that branch of the family.

"There was the daughter, Edith Chalmers. She eloped with the family's chauffeur, Thomas Harriman, and was disowned by her father. Her husband became a racing driver and was killed at Indianapolis a great many years ago. They also had one daughter, Edith. The old gentleman would not even speak to his unhappy daughter again, but he did take her child—his granddaughter—into his home. Indeed, he was very fond of her. Then one day her mother appeared and took the child away. It was both of them or none. So it became none. A year later the child's mother died, a suicide. But the child, Edith, was never found until Dr. Jones brought her to Mr. Arthur Chalmers."

"The old man, Steven Chalmers, is dead, of course?"

"For some years. He was not a liberal man; yet he spent a considerable amount trying to locate his daughter's child."

"And he left her a considerable fortune?"

"Yes. I drew up his will. He wished his money to stay in the family. His son, Arthur, he knew to be a confirmed bachelor. I believe that he provided for him before he died, or at least made him a partner in the business which the son inherited. The remainder of the estate— the residuary—was to be established as a trust fund to be administered by his son, Arthur, the income from which Arthur was to use until the granddaughter, Edith, was found. The interest then was to be paid for her education and support until she was twenty-one, when the principal sum would be turned over to her."

"And if she never were found, the money would go to Arthur Chalmers. Is that it? Or if she were dead, it would go to him?"

"No!" Hartman shook his head. "If and when proof of her death was established, the money was to go to Thesta Chalmers, the daughter of Tobias Chalmers, his eldest son."

"And if no proof of death were ever established?"

"Then the fund remained in possession of Arthur Chalmers until his death, when it would be payable to Thesta Chalmers."

"It was not, then, to Mr. Arthur Chalmers' interest nor to his brother's interest nor to Thesta Chalmers' interest to find the missing girl, Edith Harriman, alive?"

"No!" Hartman shook his head. "If you take into consideration the financial interest only, it was not. In fact, to find the girl alive or dead would deprive Mr. Arthur Chalmers of the use of that money."

"But to find her dead would be of interest to Colonel Chalmers?"

"To his daughter, yes, and to him, of course, if you are considering the parental satisfaction of seeing his child handsomely provided for."

"And how much is this fortune?"

"I imagine it is considerable. I have nothing to do with the fund. Mr. Chalmers was both executor and trustee and so named in the will."

"Wasn't that a bit unusual since you were Mr. Steven Chalmers' adviser?"

"No." He shook his head again. "The old gentleman often told me that his son had the shrewdest financial mind in the city. I took care of all his legal matters, and today take care of his son's, Mr. Arthur Chalmers', legal affairs." He sat back and looked toward the ceiling. "The last time I had lunch at the Financiers' Club with Arthur Chalmers, he happened to drop the remark that he has doubled that fund in these last ten years—a remarkable feat in these security-depressed times. I wish I could give such an account to the clients whose estates I am privileged to administer."

"Well," I said, "I am much obliged to you, Mr. Hartman."

"I don't see why," he replied. "The will is on file and it is anyone's privilege to go and look at it."

"I know," I told him. "I am having a certified copy made, now."

His face froze—that is, if such a face could freeze any more. He said:

"May I inquire, then, why you bothered me?"

I smiled at him and left. It would have cost me a bit to get a legal interpretation of that will, and Hartman knew his business. I was whistling when I reached the street.

I DIDN'T WHISTLE very long. It was almost midday. It was the great, crowded City of New York. People were jamming up and down Broadway; yet I walked right into the man, felt the gun jamming me from his overcoat pocket. And for a split second I got the glimpse of a face through a car window. It was a round, jowled face. It had a flat, boneless nose and a couple of round, staring eyes. Then it was gone.

The man who held the gun said:

"To the car, buddy, and inside. Understand?"

I was surprised. Such a stunt hadn't been played on me in years. I don't frighten easily. I don't go for one-way rides. At least I never have yet. I said:

"Do you know who I am?"

"It don't matter. A gent wants to see you. If you want to stay alive and see him—hop!"

"And if I don't hop?"

"It's curtains here on the sidewalk. I have the get-away car there. I'm on the kill!"

"So am I," I told him, and before he could even close his finger on the trigger, I shot him twice! He doubled up like a jackknife and lay down on the sidewalk. The car moved from the curb. I stepped back into the building, made my way through the teeming masses who were shouting hysterically and came out on the other street. Was the hood dead? I don't know; I only shot him. I'm not a doctor or an undertaker.

I took a taxi and hopped across town. The whole thing didn't make sense. Where did I fit into the picture? Who profited by the doctor's death? Who thought he had told me something? I couldn't make it out. But I was going over to Colonel Tobias Chalmers' apartment. If a guy had to leave a place in a hurry he might leave something behind. And if he did, I might find it.

Who would profit by the return of the girl, Edith Harriman? Certainly not Arthur Chalmers because the return of the girl took away a part of his income. Not Colonel Tobias Chalmers because the return of Edith Harriman dissipated forever his daughter's chance of getting that money. I couldn't figure it. Vengeance, love and hate are great things in themselves, and I've come across many people in my time who went to murder to satisfy such passions. But where there's money concerned, experience has taught me that you can eliminate all those things. If you do, nothing remains but greed. Greed it was, then. Now who profited?

There was only one answer. The girl, Edith Harriman, herself, was the only one who could collect dough on the whole deal.

I FOUND THE apartment house, and the card in the mailbox marked the apartment as 5C. It was an inexpensive walk-up and 5C would be the top floor. I did the five flights with the steady, unhurried tread of an honest householder. But the breaks were not with me. I can open doors as well as the next lad; but I'm no Jimmy Valentine, and this 5C had a trick lock.

I walked up the stairs to the door leading to the roof, went out it and looked the surroundings over. No more luck, and what's more I stumbled on a pail. I looked over the roof and along the fire-escape. If there was no apartment across from this one—

But there was. Then more tough breaks. A fellow was cleaning windows on the opposite building, two stories down. He had only to look up to see me. He had a pail and a rag and a jacket that looked as if it was simply his own coat turned inside out.

Inside out. And I had the idea. I reversed my coat, pulled out my handkerchief, lifted the pail, and swung out over the two-foot protection parapet and onto the iron ladder that led to the fire-escape landing before 5C. I don't know if anyone saw me or not, but I do know that no one hollered: "Stop thief!" I reached the landing below and looked down for the "other" window cleaner. He was going inside; opening the window leisurely and stepping right inside.

He was teaching me things, and I'm a guy who's willing to learn. I slipped my nail file between the upper and lower window, jerked it, and snapped back the catch. After that it was easy. I left the pail on the fire-escape and stepped inside.

The furnishings of the living-room were comfortable, at one time expensive and more than slightly worn. There was a door that led to a hall that gave on the entrance door and on the other side led to the bedrooms. There were two bedrooms. I always cover the ground before I take my time searching a place.

I had covered the kitchen and the bath and one bedroom and had gone down to the second bedroom. Yeah, I knew it was a bedroom because I could see the bed. Smart fellow, me.

Then I walked into the room and saw the whole bed—yes, and what was on it. I have seen a lot in my day and have a pretty strong stomach. I needed it— needed it then perhaps more than ever before. I had seen the doctor after he was horribly murdered only the night before, and I hadn't batted an eye. This time it was different. Oh, not the throat— because that was just about the same as the doctor's!

Still, there was a difference, and I had to force myself to look. It isn't easy to see a woman treated like that. She wasn't a pretty sight. I stood there by the bed and looked down at her. I didn't have to rack my brain for a motive for murder now. Here was a dead girl—murdered the same as the doctor, and in Colonel Tobias Chalmers' apartment. The motive was there, and I was right. It was greed. Who would profit by her death? Thesta Chalmers and through her, of course, her father, Colonel Tobias Chalmers.

The dead woman was Edith Harriman, the girl I had spoken to at Arthur Chalmers' house, the heiress to a fortune.

CHAPTER 5

THE DEAD GIRL
ON THE BED

THERE WAS A phone in the front room. I'd have to call O'Rourke. It would be stupid to walk out on a murder like this. I hesitated, trying to think if I had met people when I came in, where I had picked up the taxi and where the driver had left me. Yes, I hesitated. It might be just as stupid to ring up the police.

The door to the apartment opened and closed. Quick steps pounded across wood. Was the murderer returning to the scene of the crime? My eyes found the closed door; two steps, and so did I. I was inside that closet and had the door closed behind me all but a crack.

There was a hum, now, and the feet moved into the living-room. They stopped there, padded again on the rug, hit the hardwood floor and came down the hall straight to the bedroom. I was looking out the crack when the feet reached the door, and the girl reached the room.

She wasn't very big. She wasn't a runt, either. Straight and slender with an erect little figure. Pretty and composed face with curved red lips tightly set, and wide eyes.

The picture changed. She wasn't composed any more. Her lips weren't tightly set, and her eyes were still wide—wide like her open mouth. I think the scream was there inside of her. I could see her chest going up and down, but I didn't hear it. Just the whistling intake of her breath as she turned to leave the

room—a sort of staggering run. I opened the closet door and said:

"Not yet, lady; not yet."

That was that. Her knees gave suddenly—buckled from under her—and she sank to the floor. I lifted her up and carried her out of that room of horrible and gruesome death. She didn't weigh much, and although her little figure was sturdy, there wasn't much beef on it.

I put her down on the couch in the living-room, saw her eyes flicker and close again. I said out loud to myself:

"I'll get some water in the bathroom and come back to her."

I walked out of the door and toward the hall that led to the bathroom. Just toward it, understand. I simply got myself out of her sight around the corner of the woodwork. I was right, too. That game hadn't worked on me since my first case. I saw her shadow before I saw her. She was running when she reached the hall, and I stepped out and caught her.

"Let me go, please. Let me go!" she begged. "You don't know what you are doing."

"I do know," I told her. She screamed and beat at my chest, and there was wild terror in her eyes. It wasn't the dead girl in the other room that got her. It was me. I guess she thought I had done it.

My hand went over her mouth; my other hand held hers.

"Good Lord," I said, "you don't think I did that? And if you want to clear out without being seen, you'd better not screech again like that. The police will be here any minute."

She was looking straight at me, now,

and her brown eyes were rather hazed; there was the same horror in them that I had first seen in that bedroom. But she wasn't terror-stricken any more. Then I knew why.

"You're Race Williams—the detective," she said finally when I let my hand loose. "I have seen your picture in the papers."

"And you?" I asked. "Who are you? Don't lie because I know who you are."

"Then who am I?"

"Thesta Chalmers."

I was right. It wasn't a very brilliant guess at that. She nodded.

"Yes," she said. "Where's my father?"

"Don't you know?" I asked.

She shook her head. Unless she was a great actress, she had never expected to see that corpse on the bed. And she would have to have second sight to put on her act for me, for she couldn't have known I was hiding in the closet. But I said: "Would it surprise you to know that your father just killed that girl in there?"

"Father killed her?" She shook her head as if to clear her brain from the shock. "That's impossible. Why should he?"

"Because he is very fond of you."

"Me? What would I have to do with it?"

"It will make you a very wealthy woman."

"I don't understand."

"Don't you know who the girl is?"

"No! I never saw her before in my life."

"She's your cousin," I told her brutally enough, "Edith Harriman!"

I thought she was going to fold up again, but she didn't. She opened her mouth, but no words came. At last she said:

"I can't think clearly. I can't seem to think at all. That woman—her death like that—brings me my grandfather's money?"

"I guess so," I said. "Where is your father?"

She sat down on the chair and just stared at me for a long time. Then she shook her head.

"I don't know. I haven't seen him since last night." And suddenly ducking her head into her hands, she began to sob. "You can't... no one can believe my father did this." And when I didn't say anything, she looked up at me with dull, dry eyes. "He isn't capable of such an act. He wanted me to have that money—said it was my right. But—" She stopped then. I guess she didn't figure that was a good line to help her old man. Then she came to her feet and clutched my jacket.

"Race Williams—Race Williams," she said over and over. "I have thought of you before. I wish I had the money to engage you."

I stood there and waited. It looked like I might get a client, after all, and one with money; one about to have big money.

THE THING TO do was to get out of that apartment. She clasped my hand and I promised to work for her interest and help her. I never said anything about helping her father. I simply said I'd try to bring to justice the real murderer of the girl in the back bedroom. We didn't talk money any more. Somehow, I believed her when she seemed to have forgotten she was heir to a pile of jack. But I didn't forget it. I wasn't a lad who believed that the sins of the father should be visited on the children.

Murder doesn't make me overlook things. I turned my coat right side out again and recovered the pail from the fire-escape. Then we left the apartment. I got both a good break and a bad one: a good one because I took the girl up the stairs that led to the roof, so I could deposit the pail where I had found it; a bad one because when we started down those stairs again someone was coming up from the fourth floor.

Feet were pounding up the stairs. I gripped the girl's hand, cautioned her to silence, and took a look-see between the banisters. But the look-see didn't make me feel any too good. It was not my lucky day by any means. There was Inspector Nelson and a flat foot coming up. I could guess that the man with them was the janitor. Then I pushed the girl up and out on the roof.

I'll admit she played her part well as we moved over to the far side of the building, and I got her to sit on the little parapet while I looked around. The flat roof of the apartment next door was only a few feet below us. The roofs were jammed up close to each other. She made the drop and I followed her. Things were better.

One more roof and we'd be at the corner apartment, and that apartment had its entrance around the block from hers. No one saw us as we moved to the next apartment house. And then came my first bit of luck. A careless tenant had left the roof door unhooked.

A couple of minutes later we were on the street. Straight up the block then, another block over, and we piled into a taxi. We hopped out not far from Christy's Tavern just off Broadway.

I was looking for another cab for the girl when the car went by. I couldn't be certain, but I thought I recognized the man in the rear of it. He wasn't looking at me. But I thought it looked like Mex. Why did that interest me? Well, Mex was the lad in the car before Hartman's office building; the one with the extra chins and shrewd eyes and flat nose.

The car went by. It didn't stop down the block, and no one looked back. I found a taxi facing the other direction and put the girl into it.

"Go straight to my apartment," I told her. "Jerry, my boy, will be there to let you in. Get out of the cab a block away, go up and wait there for me."

She wanted to argue or know the reason, but then all women do; so I simply stepped back and went into Christy's Tavern. I called up the office, got hold of Jerry and told him to beat it straight up to my apartment and take care of the girl.

"Leave her alone in the living-room, Jerry, and if she uses the phone, listen in on the extension. Now beat it along and be there before her. I'll be up shortly."

Then I walked down to the end of the bar and talked to Christy. He had just come in and was counting money.

"I've been here about an hour, Christy," I said as I waited for a sandwich. "Remember?"

"Sure, Race, about an hour. I'll remember."

"That's fine." I ate the sandwich and hit the street. At the door I looked back and saw Christy glancing at the clock. Then he went on counting money. Nice guy, Christy. Nice to be able to count money these days.

This time the taxi left me directly at the door of Colonel Tobias Chalmers' apartment house.

The police in New York move fast. Don't let anyone tell you different. Already they were in charge of the place. I said to Detective Murray on the door:

"It's all right. Sergeant O'Rourke is expecting me."

"That's fine, Race." He grinned at me. "He's even expecting himself."

"What do you mean?"

"The sarge hasn't come yet." And with another grin as he let me pass, "Sam McHugh is on the door upstairs. You'd better tell him Inspector Nelson is expecting you. He found the body."

"Not Colonel Tobias Chalmers?" I showed surprise.

"That's right," Murray agreed, "not Colonel Tobias Chalmers."

We grinned at each other, and I went up. Murray was a good scout, and he didn't like Inspector Nelson. He knew I riled the inspector and Murray was very human that way.

McHugh was Nelson's stooge and played the part as soon as he saw me. He called in to Nelson.

"It's the gum-shoe, Williams," he said. "Is he in or out?"

Nelson closed a door somewhere in the apartment and came through the living-room. He didn't seem surprised to see me or even annoyed. He said friendly enough—which was a bad start:

"Hello, Race. Did you come to see the girl?"

"Maybe," I said.

His eyes snapped then, his words, too. "How did you know she was dead?"

"Who's dead?" I gaped up at him. It wasn't all pretended surprise on my part either. It wasn't his question that surprised me. It was the sudden way he put it as he tried to trap me into some admission. Nelson was a good, honest, hardworking cop. But he stuck to the old school. He was tough; he was hard.

"The girl," he said, "Thesta Chalmers. Colonel Chalmers' daughter."

"She can't be." I shook my head. But he turned then and, walking to the bedroom door, he flung it open and even helped me in by gripping my arm. I did a good act then, though it wasn't hard to be shocked. If I saw that body five times a day for a week it would still knock me. The dead girl didn't look any better. I said:

"Good heavens. It's Edith Harriman!"

"Who?" he gasped.

"Arthur Chalmers' niece—the long-missing heiress. Didn't you see her up at Chalmers?"

"No!" He shook his head. "O'Rourke covered that end." And when we had left the room—for even Nelson didn't have any stomach for lounging around there: "How did you happen to come over?"

"Business," I told him.

"Where did you come from? Where have you been?"

"I had a sandwich at Christy's Tavern, then came around here."

"Just now?"

"Sure—just now."

"How long were you there?"

"I don't know. Forty-five minutes, an hour, maybe a few minutes longer."

"Uh-huh." He went out and talked to McHugh.

Then O'Rourke came in. Inspector Nelson told him about the girl. Although O'Rourke was only a sergeant, he didn't have to take any orders from Nelson. He could have been an inspector, himself, long ago, but he didn't want the job. He worked straight from the commissioner, himself, and felt that he kept closer to the uniformed man on the beat by remaining a sergeant. I imagine if the truth were told, O'Rourke got better pay than any of them—a special appropriation being laid aside for him. Anyway, when it came to a showdown, O'Rourke had the final say on things.

O'Rourke went in alone to look at the body. McHugh had the phone cradled up in his arms and under his coat as he talked into it. When he was through he nodded over at Nelson. I hadn't heard a word of his conversation, but I knew just as well as if I had heard it all who he called and what he asked. Also, I knew the answer Christy would give him. Nelson was a thorough man, and so was I.

O'ROURKE CAME OUT after a bit and looked puzzled. He talked to Nelson for a while. Then he came over to me.

"Things are beginning to develop, Race," he said. "Inspector Nelson doesn't like the way you're horning in on things. I could have some information for you. But I'd like to know where you fit, and why you came here."

"I got the address from you," I told him. "I've got a client, now. It's Miss Chalmers—Miss Thesta Chalmers."

"What does she want you to do—get her father out of the country?"

"No," I said. "To take care of her—"

"How?"

"Protect her interest."

"What interest?" And suddenly, "Now listen, Race. You're no charitable institution. Oh, I know you have helped friends out, but you didn't know this girl. What is she going to pay you with?"

"I hadn't thought of that," I told O'Rourke. "But Providence seems to be taking care of me." I jerked a hand toward the room inside. "Miss Chalmers'll be worth plenty of money, now."

"How do you figure that?"

"Well," I explained, "Arthur Chalmers had the use of the trust fund until Edith Harriman was found or her death proven. If she were found, she got the money. If she died before she was twenty-one, Thesta Chalmers got it."

"That's right," said O'Rourke with a far-away look. And then, sort of dumb: "But her death had to be proven. I looked into that will, too."

"Hell," I said, "what more proof of death do you want? But the medical examiner's report should be enough for anyone else."

"I guess so," said O'Rourke and sat down. He seemed to be thinking very hard, but then maybe he wasn't. I've often given the same appearance, myself.

A couple of smart-looking young dicks came into the room and I recognized them at once as runners for O'Rourke. He was a lad who made use of the best. They all went into the room of death, and Nelson followed them. After a time, O'Rourke came out. He beckoned to me. He was very serious. He said:

"Where's your client now?" And when I didn't answer right away, "I mean Miss Thesta Chalmers."

I sensed the ominous note, even if I didn't get the meaning of it. I said:

"I don't know. She'll ring me up when she wants me." And suddenly: "You don't think she did it?"

Even Nelson shook his head at that one.

"A woman prefers a gun," he said. "It could be, though. We want to question her about her father."

"I haven't seen her," I told them. "When she gets in touch with me, I'll let you know."

"Well," said Nelson, "she won't pay you out of the Chalmers' fortune—or what she gets because of that girl's death." Then he knocked me bowlegged. "You're going to laugh your head off when you hear this, Williams. The girl in there on the bed—the dead girl—isn't Edith Harriman!"

CHAPTER 6

LOST—ONE HEIRESS!

IT TOOK ME a full minute to recover from that one. Then I said somewhat stupidly:

"Don't kid me, Nelson. Why even her uncle, Arthur Chalmers, said she was his niece."

"Edith Harriman was found and lost again," explained O'Rourke. "There was an Edith Woodman out in New Madison. From the papers my boys found in the doctor's house, she's the missing heiress, Edith Harriman, all right. But this dead girl was someone else."

"Sure!" said Nelson. "Arthur Chalmers only thought it was his niece because she looked like her mother or something; and with the doctor's proof and all, he fell for it. But this girl is dark and the real Edith Harriman was a blonde. This girl has brown eyes; the real Edith Harriman had blue eyes."

"That's right," agreed O'Rourke while I stood there gaping at him. "We'll have further identification, of course. Half the town of New Madison knew the girl and could describe her. We'll get enough representative citizens down to look at the body. But there isn't any doubt. The real girl left New Madison with Dr. Bernard Jones, all right, but a different girl reached the house of Arthur Chalmers."

"But how did she get here in Colonel Chalmers' apartment? If she wasn't the real Edith Harriman, that lets Colonel Chalmers out. There would be no point in his killing her."

"He didn't know that she wasn't the real girl any more than his brother did. How he got her here, I don't know."

"It's a screwy set-up," I said.

"Not so screwy," said O'Rourke. "Many well-known and well-thought-of and respected men lead double lives. Let us look at it this way: Dr. Bernard Jones discovers the truth from the dying woman; is even furnished the proof of

Edith Harriman's identity. Yes, the proof was locked up in his safe-deposit box, just as the woman must have given it to him. He leaves New Madison with the girl, substitutes another in her place and makes a play for the whole fortune."

"But why would he come to me?" I objected.

"That's what we'd like to know from you." Nelson stuck his chin out, and from the glare in his eyes and the tone of his voice, I nearly took a crack at it.

"Easy does it," said O'Rourke. But I noticed he didn't look at me with such a friendly eye. Then he took a picture from his pocket and held it out to me. "The real Edith Harriman," he said simply.

I looked at the picture. Under no stretch of the imagination could the dead girl on the bed and the girl of the picture be the same person. It was too much for me. I shrugged my shoulders.

"I'm going up and have a talk with Arthur Chalmers," O'Rourke said. "There isn't any use to drag him down here to see the body. He can see it at the morgue if it's necessary. Coming along?"

I was, and I did. Nelson opened his mouth, but thought better of it. I guess he closed it again; anyway, he didn't speak. His hand didn't land on my shoulder, and then O'Rourke and I were out the door and on our way down the stairs. Dr. Steel was coming up them, his little black bag in his hand. He was whistling: "Sweet and Low."

WE FOUND CHALMERS in his office. He took it pretty well; and after he got the brutal details of the murder, he didn't seem to mind having me around. O'Rourke put it point-blank to him about his brother. He told him that the colonel had been at the hotel when Dr. Jones was slain. And, of course, there was no way of getting around the fact that the girl was found dead in his apartment. Also the police were unable to locate the colonel or his daughter. Then he wanted to know when the girl who had masqueraded as Edith Harriman had left the Chalmers' home.

Chalmers was puzzled. He shook his head, said:

"I only know that it was some time during the night or early this morning. I telephoned you, sergeant, when I discovered her missing about the middle of the forenoon. Last night she said she was tired, and I gave orders that she was not to be disturbed. I am an early riser, myself, and was at my office by nine. It was about half past ten, I believe, when my butler informed me that she had gone out. But at what time I don't know."

"Could she have left your house without the servants knowing about it? I mean in the morning."

"It is possible. There is the butler, the cook and one maid. My needs are small." He hesitated. "Then, of course, there is the little private entrance to my study on the side. She could have left that way if she came into the study. I don't know. I really don't know what to think. You are wrong about my brother. Toby was always weak, yes, but never vicious."

O'Rourke got out of him that he had been supporting his brother; sending him a small allowance.

"My father forbade it," Chalmers said, "but I have been doing it for years. There was the child, Thesta, you know. Surely she was not to blame for his past wrongs."

"What kind of associates did your brother have?"

"Bad—very bad! That was the trouble. But I believe for years he has led an exemplary life. Two years ago—but that was temporary. I believe his daughter is back with him now."

"She left him then?" I put in.

"Yes, that was at the time of her unfortunate marriage. She—"

"Her marriage?" I gasped that one out.

"Yes," he said. "But I think they have since separated."

We got all we could out of Arthur Chalmers. He seemed to be wavering between the terrible tragedy of the girl's death and an uncertainty about whether he had liked her as a niece.

"She seemed a bit hard and sophisticated," he had said. "But perhaps that would have worn off. I am sorry in a way, for my father's greatest wish was to find her." And then suddenly to me: "This other girl—the real Edith Harriman—what could have become of her? You must find her." And after a pause: "Could she be dead, too?"

We didn't have an answer for that one; so we left. I didn't say anything to O'Rourke, and he didn't say anything to me. I don't know if he was thinking what I had thought. A new factor had come into the case—Thesta Chalmers' husband. What was in it for him if Thesta inherited a lot of money? There was only one answer to that. Just what there would be in it for any man who married a woman of wealth.

I WENT RIGHT back to my apartment and put it straight up to the girl.

"You didn't tell me you were married," I said. "That might explain matters. Is he the kind of a man who would go to murder?"

"I didn't have time to tell you very much," she said. And then stiffening, "He's the kind of a man who'd do anything. And I'm the kind of a girl who would do anything to get money for a divorce from him."

"Tell me about him," I asked, "about yourself—about everything."

And she did. She told it well and bitterly.

"All right," she said. "My father was weak. He was the kindest man in the world, but he didn't know how to handle money. Maybe he gambled and drank and dreamed of inventing things and making money for me to have, but he never dreamed or talked of driving people under foot to get it like my grandfather did. He wouldn't go after my Uncle Arthur—into the courts to fight against that will—to demand that the missing Edith Harriman be declared dead. We could have used the money. We needed it. Father was afraid to antagonize his brother; afraid that Uncle Arthur might cut off the small allowance we had."

"Did you ever go to your Uncle Arthur about money?"

"Yes," she said. "But he refused to do anything. Said it was my grandfather's greatest wish that Edith should be found;

that he couldn't act anyway; that it would be against every principle he had."

"He wouldn't give you any money?"

She flushed slightly, hesitated as she lowered her head. Then she raised her eyes and looked right into mine.

"He offered me money; asked me how much I wished and told me that my father would gamble anything that he gave him. He said he was a rich man and that his home was open to me. But he knew that I wouldn't take a penny from him. That was the first time I knew he gave my father an allowance. I thought it was father's right; that it came to him from the estate." She said sort of proudly then, and I liked her for it: "I have never since lived on a penny of the money that came from my uncle. I was not a reasoning woman at the time. I was very young. I married Fletcher Darrian. Later I found work and left him; and though I returned to father because he needed me, I have since supported myself."

"Tell me about last night," I said.

"What about it?"

"You weren't home. Where did you go?"

"I had dinner with a friend and stayed at her house all night."

"Can you prove that?"

"Yes," she said.

"Now—and don't lie to me, Miss Chalmers, for if you do, I'll chuck your case. I don't believe in coincidence. Did your father suggest that you stay with some friend last night?"

She looked up at me. Her eyes were frightened. But she said:

"Yes, he did. He seemed very excited. I didn't want to go."

That was a tough one to take, fearing what the results might be for my client. But I had to get at things. I was beginning to like the girl; the way she had faced things; the way she was facing them, now. I put this to her:

"When did you last see your father?"

She had tough work getting over that one. But she stood there and faced me and then she gripped both my hands.

"I know," she said very slowly, "that my father could not have done such a thing. He telephoned me last night at my friend's house. He asked me to come to the drug store on the corner and meet him. I did. He was terribly afraid. He told me he had had a telephone call, earlier. That a man told him that he was Dr. Jones and that he had proof that Edith Harriman was dead. He told him to say nothing to anyone but to come to the Welford Hotel and straight to his room. Father went and saw the dead man there. He was afraid and left; then he telephoned me. He was afraid to go back to the apartment and asked me to go there today and get his things."

"This is what your father told you?"

"Yes, and I believe him."

"Why didn't he go straight to the police? Why didn't you advise him to do that?"

"I don't know. I would have. I wanted to. But I was stunned by what he told me. He left me there."

That didn't look so good; so I switched to her husband. It seemed he had thought she was going to have money. Her father—yes, the old man had his oar in again—had spoken of her being rich;

and when she told her husband the truth, things were not so good between them. Anyway, he had lost his job—such as it was. The last time she had heard from him he was in Chicago, and he wanted money. Yes, he knew about everything connected with her estate.

Then Thesta busted up and hung there on my shoulder. She had seen enough of life; had gone through enough to be a hard-boiled woman of the world; and outside she tried to be. But, now, she was just a kid—a crying kid. I held her; I patted her head. Me—I had seen enough of life to be hard-boiled, too; yet, now, I was risking my life for nothing. Not a cent in it for me, and not the prospect of a cent to come. I was just working for nothing. For nothing? I ran a hand through the kid's hair. She was just an armful, and she was crying.

THE DOORBELL RANG.

I pushed Thesta back and into the bedroom and went to the front door. It was Inspector Nelson, and he wasn't any too pleasant. He came right to the point.

"Where's the dame, Williams?" he demanded. "Come on; no stalling. I want to talk to her."

"Just what dame are you referring to?" I could see his play; so I moved around quickly and got between him and the door, not apparently blocking it, understand, sort of lounging before it.

"The Chalmers girl—Thesta Chalmers. Her old man is hot, and I want to talk to her." He looked over my shoulder toward the door. His grin was pleasant. He said: "I want to listen to her talk, too."

"Are you arresting her for murder?"

"Not me." His lips parted, and his teeth showed. "If I pulled her in, you'd have a shyster downtown with a writ of habeas corpus to drag her out again before I got there."

"You haven't any warrant." His eyes glared, and a huge right arm half raised. "You know, Nelson, a bit of paper that gives you the right to—"

He grabbed my shoulder and with one powerful effort swung me from the door around behind him. He had his hand on the knob when I spoke.

"Nelson," was all I said, "take your hand off that door knob, or I'll remove it at the wrist."

There was something in my voice that made Nelson look back over his shoulder. There was something in my hand that made his eyes widen. He knew me and knew my reputation. His hand stayed on the door knob, but the door stayed closed. He said:

"You know me, Race. You know you can't bluff me,"

"I'm not bluffing," I told him.

"You wouldn't… wouldn't dare."

His head started to swing back; the door knob started to turn. My finger half tightened on the trigger of my gun. I said simply:

"All right, Nelson, open the door and find out."

And he didn't find out, and neither did I. He just straightened, turned and walked from the room.

So I had gone overboard for the girl. Oh had I? Hadn't I, after all, simply gone overboard for myself? I know my rights, and I never let anyone step on them. As far as making an enemy of Nelson—well, we had never been friends. He was down on me ninety percent of the time, anyway.

I had things to do outside, but I had sent Jerry for some eats for Thesta and had to wait until he came back. Besides, I thought I knew where to find the lad I wanted to see, but not until dinner time. The girl wanted to talk about her father now; convince me that he couldn't have done it. Finally, she got out what was on her chest.

"Race"—she gripped my hand—"Race, if…if we could find my father, you wouldn't turn him over to the police—would you?"

I looked straight at her.

"Thesta, you're a swell kid. I like you. I want to help you. But I'll only stick my neck out so far." And when she would have put the question again, I repeated: "Just so far. Let it go at that."

If she didn't get the point, there was nothing more that I could do. Be reasonable. There had been a sure attempt on my life, and a second possible one. Certainly there was a little piece of paper called a warrant out for Colonel Tobias Chalmers. No, I wouldn't harbor any lad who was wanted for murder.

CHAPTER 7

GONE!

I WENT OUT with the single thought that I held the key to the situation. And that key was my gun under my left

armpit—or two keys if you're a stickler for accuracy, because I generally sport another gun under my right armpit. All I needed was a lock to shove that key into, and I thought I knew who the lock would be. Mex—just plain Mex. Everyone called him that.

Tony Fenerro might easily have worked for him. And Tony had had a shot at me. Also, Mex sat in front of that office building in a car that I was to be forced into. Mex had wanted to see me. Well, I wanted to see him, too. But I wanted to see him my way, not his.

Mex was a very old man; that is, he had lived a very long time for his particular sports of robbery, arson, kidnaping, torture and murder. He had started young and must have been pretty close to forty. Twenty-odd years in the racket. Mex's number should have been up years ago. But Mex was shrewd.

Mex wasn't hard to find. He was a big man with a big head and big shoulders and a big stomach. He liked to fill that stomach with good food. He was doing just that now. After three or four other places, I walked into Phil's Steak House, ignored the two bodyguards that were eating at another table and shoved into the booth occupied by Mex. He was alone, and he was surprised. No, he didn't show that surprise on his face. It was just the way his eyes moved toward his bodyguards to see if they were watching. They were.

I came right to the point. My left hand was on the table. My right wasn't. I said:

"Hello, Mex. You had two cracks at my life today. I'm not complaining. Any hood that wants to take a crack at killing me is entitled to one crack. Understand—one crack. Two is one too many, and three is out of the question."

Mex looked longingly at the silver top that covered the rest of his plank steak and said:

"What do you mean, boy? What do you mean?"

"That you had one shot too many, Mex. I'm on the kill myself this time."

He turned white and put back the silver top that he had just started to lift. He said:

"You must be kidding, Race. You must be kidding, boy."

"You know better than that, Mex." I shook my head at him. "You've got a reputation. You've never put a guy's number up and had a failure. I have a great deal of respect for you, Mex."

"You're going to kill me?" he sort of gasped.

"I can't see any other way," I told him. "I know your methods. You put a price on my life—rather, on my death. I'm taking that price off. Any killer knows you can't pay him if you're not around to pay him."

"Not around to pay him?" Mex was just echoing my words.

"That's it, Mex. You'll be too dead to pay. Come on, get up and walk."

"You… you can't get away with it," he stammered.

"Maybe not"—I shrugged my shoulders—"but I can try!"

"It's not like you, Race; not like you at all." He was trying to digest what I told him; trying not to believe it. Yet, when he went after my life, he must have known what the end would be if he missed out.

Anyway, he knew now; and he didn't like it. I put it to him a little more logically.

"It's my respect for you, Mex. Be reasonable. It's your life or mine. What would you do in my place?"

"But, Race, you could be wrong about me."

"Could be," I admitted, "but I don't want to think of that. I'd never forgive myself after you were dead."

Maybe my reputation isn't a nice one to have. But it's kept me alive a long time. Of course, I couldn't shoot him to death in cold blood; but he didn't know that. He licked at his lips and lifted up his half-filled glass of whiskey and soda; but he made a mess out of the tablecloth and set it down again. His hand wasn't very steady. He finally said: "You know, of course, that those are my boys at the next table; that they'd even blast you out right here if I gave the order?"

"I got a gun under the table on you," I told him. "If they make a move, I'll blow you apart."

"They'd get you then, Race."

"O.K.!" I nodded. "If you can get any satisfaction out of that, it's all right by me."

HE LOOKED OVER at the men, then looked back at me. His voice trembled when he spoke.

"All right, boy, you win. What do you want to know?"

"Know?" I raised my eyebrows.

"Sure—know," he said. "I didn't want to kill you. I only wanted to scare you."

"That was the machine gun on the street last night, eh?"

"That? That was a mistake. Race. I swear it was. Look at today. I… I—" And realizing he was admitting everything, he added quickly: "You saw me today."

"Sure! Right in the car."

"That proves it then, Race. Tony was mad to try and kill you. I just wanted to talk to you; wanted you to lay off. I swear—"

"And who paid you to warn me?"

"If I tell you that, will you forget it?"

"I tell you what, Mex"—I leaned forward confidentially—"you're both a menace and an aid to society. A menace when you go after lads like me; an aid when you put the finger on some murderer for some other murder. You tell me the truth, and I'll forget it."

"You believe I won't… won't bother you again?"

"I believe you won't bother me more than once more. I'll give you some advice. You can have one more crack at my life. You'd better be successful. The next time your man misses, I'll plug you. I'll drop you like a department store dummy the first time I see you."

"It won't happen again then." He wet his lips with his tongue, leaned across the table. "I'm trusting to your honor, Race." And there wasn't any humor when he spoke of honor. "You swear you won't talk?"

"If you tell me the truth." And with a sigh, knowing the way he worked: "I suppose the police can't mix you up in any of these murders."

"It's the truth," he said. Then, with a simple statement of fact and without shame for his own double-crossing, he said: "I'm telling you this simply to save my own hide." And in a low, hoarse whisper: "The man is Tobias Chalmers—Colonel Chalmers."

I believed him, I guess, because it was what I expected to hear. But I said:

"It don't ring right, Mex. How long have you known him?"

"Sixteen years," he told me. "Listen, I don't admit to a hand in this, but he arranged to have that kid, Edith Harriman, snatched way back in 1925. I was a young man then. What don't ring right?"

"You work for money only. What did he pay you with?"

"He had money then."

"Maybe," I said, "but not now. I've got my pride, Mex. You'd want a tidy sum to put my number up."

"But, hell, Race, I told you that I only intended to warn you and—"

"I don't believe that."

"It's the truth," Mex told me. "Maybe he got to someone else. But he'd pay me with the fortune he would inherit."

"His daughter would inherit," I corrected.

"She isn't his daughter," said Mex. "He and his wife picked up the kid after they were married. They thought it would make his old man, Steven Chalmers, come through."

"So that's it," I gasped. "He intends to kill the girl and get the money and pay you."

The thought was horrible. I guess Mex didn't like the look on my face. His words stumbled out:

"I didn't know, boy, I didn't know. I never thought he'd— I've gone in for killing, yes; but not murder—not murder like that. Just men who had it coming to them; men no one would miss. You gave your word. Your word's good. The colonel changed over the years and—"

I was on my feet. Sure, my word was good whether it was given to the jury in a court of law, to a murderer facing the chair or to a hopped-up snowbird in a back alley. That was part of my stock in trade. I never broke my word to a crook. So I got plenty of information. Sometimes it was free for vengeance; sometimes poured out by a woman who was turned out for another one; sometimes for cash; and other times just like this— through fear.

Then Mex saw why I didn't wait to hear it all. It was Inspector Nelson turning into the little bar on the side. There were no two ways about it. He wasn't looking for Mex; he was looking for me. Where had he come from? From my own apartment, probably. He had trailed me down through the different eating houses to which I had gone looking for Mex. And the trail was warm. The trail was hot, and Nelson looked determined.

Had he been at my apartment again, looking for the girl? What would he do with the girl? A hundred questions went through my head, and they might all have been wrong. But one thing was to get back to the girl and warn her; warn her that—

Mex cursed beside me. He said:

"I didn't have to talk. It was Nelson, and I could have—"

But I turned; my gun was back in my shoulder holster. I walked straight and fast toward the door. It wasn't a hundred feet, but it seemed like miles. Any minute there might be a bullet in my back. But there wasn't. Nelson, the big slob who— And I took a smile as I reached the door and hit the sidewalk. Good old Nelson. For all I knew, he might have saved my life while my back was toward Mex and his hoods.

When I hit my apartment, the girl was gone. There was a hurried, scribbled line on the back of one of my cards. I read it, and read it again. It didn't make me feel any better no matter how many times I looked at it. In fact, it made me feel worse. Yes, it looked as though Thesta Chalmers had gone straight to her death. The card read:

> Race:
> I have gone straight to my father.
> Thesta.

And after what she wrote, wouldn't it be just as if she had said:

"I have gone straight to my death."

CHAPTER 8

IDENTIFICATION

Jerry was gone, too. What did that mean? When had he gone? Where had he gone? Had Nelson been there? Had he arrested Jerry? I had hurried to the apartment for fear that Nelson had arrested the girl. I wished now that that was true; that he had locked her up and kept her safe from her father—the man who posed as her father. It was a mad, wild scheme to get money; money he couldn't get no matter how things worked out. Probably he didn't know he had murdered the wrong girl. He must be out of his head.

What about Mex? No one could ever accuse Mex of being out of his head. Had he lied to me? Had he simply told me the truth and was glad to get from under? Had he known about the dead girl in Tobias' apartment?

No coördinated thinking. Just thoughts—wild, jumbled thoughts. But one thought above the others, and it didn't have anything to do with money: Thesta, the brave little kid; Thesta, the kid who had looked into my face and taken both my hands, going straight to the slaughter. A sacrifice to greed. Mad greed, perhaps, but a sacrifice just the same. I remembered the dead Dr. Jones, now, the dead girl on the bed, the sightless eyes, the gash in the throat and—and—

I took a cab straight to Phil's Steak House. Nelson wasn't there, neither was Mex. I played along the Main Stem. Mex was too hard to find. And what of Jerry? I went back to the apartment. The phone was ringing. Jerry? The girl? A break now! I picked up the phone. I was too late. No one was there.

I put down the phone, and I mean I put it down. The doorbell rang. I made the hall in long steps and tossed the door open. Sergeant O'Rourke walked in.

"Listen, Race," he said, "where's the girl? Don't stall. We want her."

"For what?"

"Well, Nelson wants her. He was here. He's peeved." And when I opened my mouth, "Yeah, he has a piece of paper. There's a warrant out for her father's arrest. That's right, murder!"

"What about the girl? Nelson didn't find her then?" And when O'Rourke just stared at me: "I mean he was here looking for her."

"Yes, I know. It's all right for you to play a lone hand, Race, but not in a murder case. Colonel Tobias Chalmers is a queer duck." O'Rourke stopped then. "What's the matter with you? You act as if you were going to jump out of your clothes. Come on, where's his daughter?"

"I haven't seen his daughter."

"Do you mean to say she wasn't here?"

"His daughter wasn't here." I stressed the word "daughter."

"So that's how it is?" O'Rourke grinned. "Making a monkey out of Nelson. But he's a good man, Race. He's going to question the girl if he's got to arrest her to do it. Maybe you won't think it's so funny if he slaps a warrant on you. He's tough!"

"I know," I said. "What's the latest dope?"

"Well, her husband was in town."

"Yeah?" I wasn't much interested. "Did you find him?"

"No, but he's been around." And after a long pause: "We found out why he came, though."

"Why?"

"He got a telephone call in Chicago. I had Chicago on the phone. The police found his boarding-house. His landlady said the phone call was Long Distance from New York. That was yesterday morning—very early."

"He couldn't have got a train it time to—"

"He could fly in," said O'Rourke.

"Listen, O'Rourke," I told him flatly, "a lot of people seemed to know about the finding of this heiress pretty fast. There wasn't much time for so much to happen."

O'ROURKE SHRUGGED HIS shoulders.

"Dr. Bernard V. Jones knew for over a week before he brought her on—at least before he left New Madison." O'Rourke seemed to think a moment. "More than that, even. The woman told him about the girl. There's no question that she was Edith Harriman. Then the woman died. They buried her. Hell, it was all of ten days after the funeral before he left New Madison. In the meantime he had to get another girl to take Edith Harriman's place. Or have someone do that for him," he added significantly.

I said:

"If we only knew where Dr. Jones fitted into the picture." And to myself I thought why didn't I stay with Mex, chance the meeting with Nelson and find out about the doctor from Mex. But that wouldn't have helped, for Mex wouldn't have talked once he had seen the inspector come into the place.

"I think," said O'Rourke, "the doctor was an opportunist. From what we can find of his past life, he'd been more than on the level. Still, he needed money." And spreading his hands: "But he has always needed money; let his bills drag. He left an unsecured note in the bank for over a thousand dollars."

"Hell, that means he was A1. Go try and get a note without security any place today."

"Someone got in touch with him. Race. Someone painted a picture of wealth. I don't think he ever thought the real Edith Harriman would be murdered—if she was murdered." And as he turned toward the door, "If you're hiding that girl, Race, there will be trouble and—"

"Thesta Chalmers?" I choked a bit. "Listen, O'Rourke, I'd give my right arm now—gladly give it—if Nelson had found her and locked her up."

O'Rourke stopped at the door, said:

"You say that like you meant it, Race."

"I never meant anything more in my life."

O'Rourke turned, let the door close again, looked at me a long moment.

"Why not come out with it, Race? We've all got to work together on this. Do you know where her father is? Do you think her father pulled off these murders?"

I nodded at that one.

"I think Chalmers did it," I said, but I was careful not to say Thesta's father.

"I don't know." O'Rourke opened the door again. "From what I hear he didn't have the build or the strength to do it—or the health. It's all as crazy as hell. You're holding out something on me, Race."

I gulped.

"Nothing I can tell you, O'Rourke. Make every possible effort to find Tobias Chalmers."

"You can be sure we're doing that. It's going to hit Arthur Chalmers hard; but he sees it our way. It's murder, after all, and a particularly brutal bit of murder. The commissioner advised Arthur Chalmers to hole up in a hotel under another name for a few days. It's going to break nasty in the papers."

"I wonder who the dead girl was?"

O'Rourke made a face. It wasn't quite a laugh. He didn't feel like laughing. He had been years on the force, years on homicide, but he never thought murder was funny.

"So the police know a few things you don't, eh?" Then he threw me completely: "Her name was Delphine Rose. She did a bit of burlesque work and had been in trouble with the police once or twice. Her picture's down in the Rogue's Gallery." Then the line that threw me just before he left: "Mex used to like her."

The door closed, and O'Rourke was gone.

CHAPTER 9

BENEATH THE LIGHT

I DIDN'T KNOW whether to go out or stay in.

Then the phone rang. It wasn't the girl; it was Jerry.

"Hello, boss," he said. "I answered the phone call from her father. He insisted on talking to her. I got in on the extension and her father said for her to meet him at 'the old house in Bay City.' Boss, Bay City is out on Long Island and—"

"Yeah, I know," I slapped in on him. "I can get a map for two bits and don't have to pay you wages to— Well, you followed her, Jerry, and you're there now and—"

"I'm at Bay City, and I followed her on the rattler all right. But when she took the taxi-cab and I hopped another to tail her, why we got a flat tire and—"

"You lost her!"

"Yeah, that's about the size of it— though I had nothing to do with it. So I'm back here at the Bay City station and I— Is she in any danger?"

"Only of having her throat cut!" I said, but I was thinking fast. Then I asked: "Did you get the cab number—the number of the taxi you were following?"

"Why, no. I was right behind watching it. Why should I get the cab number?"

Where was Jerry's training? He cleaned that up for me when I cursed him out.

"You told me never to do any thinking, boss, but to obey orders and stick to what I was doing. Well, I didn't have any orders, and I stuck to the cab."

"Where did she pick up her cab?"

"Right back off the station—half a block nearly."

"And you?"

"Why, there were three cabs at the stand. I took the second one."

"Good. Get back there and hire both those cabs. First, the one you had; and when the girl's cab come back, hire that one, too."

"How will I know which one that is—I mean, the one she had?"

"You dumb cluck, from your driver. He'll know one of his own cabs and one of his own drivers. Bring them both to the Bay City station. Keep them there until I arrive."

I cradled the phone, clamped on my hat and with a pat or two under both arms I was on my way. No, I don't have to look for my guns when I'm going any place. They're always with me. I'd be just as apt to go out without my shirt on.

I shuddered slightly as I made the subway. Thesta Chalmers was a nice kid. She had a nice-looking throat. Only time and myself could keep it that way.

Jerry was there at the Bay City station with the two cabs and their drivers when I hopped off the train. They were bright boys and five dollars apiece over their meters got them both talking at once.

The biggest of the two had driven the girl to the corner of Elm Boulevard and Rose Street. He thought she had run through a vacant lot; but he couldn't be sure because she had tipped him well and watched for him to drive away. No, she wasn't nervous or excited. A little watchful, that was all.

That would describe Thesta. Why should she be frightened? She was going straight to her father—or at least to the man she always thought was her father. Through a vacant lot didn't place her destination any too well. But the little taxi driver was more enlightening.

"Hell," he said, "I know where she went to. The old Devine house. I took a fellow out there just before her—a furtive sort of guy. He seemed nervous, all right. And the tip wasn't so good, either. He didn't act as if he had dough. Acted like a hop-head without hop."

"Can you describe him? Young, old, tall or short, stout or thin?"

"He was an old guy all right. Sort of tall, but looked taller because he was skinny. His clothes were sort of loose on him and maybe shabby. I don't know. It was dark and that was just the impression I got. Anything wrong?"

"And a good impression, too. No, nothing wrong." I grinned at the little runt and picked his cab. He seemed to be the brighter of the two.

So we were on our way. This guy had lived in Bay City all his life. I let him talk, and we got places. His description had fitted Colonel Tobias Chalmers from what I had gathered from O'Rourke. And I knew I had the right house when he talked himself out a bit. He said:

"It was and is a lonely house. Old lady Devine cursed the bank out when they sold it for her. She was thinking, like most of the Bay City folks did, that a smart operator from Wall Street picked it up because building was ready to boom there. But her daughter didn't curse them out after the old lady died. Things got bad then—money I mean—and no building went on around that house. The lad that bought it probably ran out of dough, too, because it's been just standing there."

"Must have been ten or twelve years ago."

"Maybe. Something like that. Yeah, I guess it was. I had three of my own cabs, then, but people quit riding and I lost them. Now, I drive for this company, and I tell you there are times when I'm glad it's their headache and not mine."

"You don't know the name of the guy who bought the house, do you?"

"Yeah, but I don't remember it offhand. That is, I'd know it if I heard it."

"Was the name O'Brien?" And when

he shook his head, I tried a number of names because too often guys who get five-dollar tips want to be helpful and don't mind juggling with the truth to show their gratitude.

"Billings, Chester, Chalmers, Carter—"

"Chalmers," he said sort of doubtfully. "That seems like it."

Right! It seemed like it to me, too. Colonel Tobias Chalmers had had money at one time. But we drove by the house—a lonely, dark dwelling with no other places around it. He wouldn't have needed much jack to buy that fire box.

I didn't let the taxi driver stop the cab in front of the place; I got out two blocks down, in the shadow of a small factory.

"Closed for the night?" I nodded at the building.

"Closed for good," my driver said. "I worked there, too."

I didn't go into his exciting career of closed places. I gave instructions to Jerry.

"Look, Jerry," I said. "Drive back to the station, telephone O'Rourke, meet him there and bring him out here."

"Now, boss," Jerry clutched at my arm, "you said there was death in there. I may be dumb, but I'm good at the rough stuff where a fellow don't have to use his head and—"

I said: "More than one will be too many. It's a single man I'm after. If I wanted nothing but rough stuff, I'd call the local police and have them surround the house and break in. But they'd find the girl dead!"

"She was a nice girl," said Jerry.

I watched him drive off. I didn't like Jerry's "was"; his use of the past tense. But I started for that house. There were some trees and some high grass and plenty of rocks and cans. I guess I crawled over all of them.

I had to go alone. I no longer had any idea that I was dealing with a very bright man. I felt I was dealing with a madman. But he was able to keep things to himself. Witness the fact that Thesta didn't know he was not her father. Then there was another reason for suspecting he was mad. Mex had sold him out pretty quick. Mex was never known to be dumb.

Madmen don't reason. If the cops closed in on him, he'd hear them. And, in his depraved mind, he'd kill the girl if it was the last thing he ever did. Again, of course, I could be wrong. He might be cold sane. If he had killed two people already, another wouldn't make any difference. The law hasn't found a way to roast a guy to death in the electric chair more than once.

No light showed anywhere. The moon was dead, and the clouds were low. The house was in pitch blackness. It stood out like a great, black box against the dimmer darkness. I didn't have any special plan of attack except to get in that house without being heard. There is always the advantage of quiet by coming in by way of the cellar. But, then, there is the danger of murder being planned there and the greater danger of a bolt being on the door that leads to the floor above.

I let the deep grass guide my direction, and that took me around by the back of the house. That was my meat. There was only about a twenty-five-foot run from the grass to the covered back porch where there seemed to he a much longer and much more open run to the front. Everything depended on quiet—on speed.

I took the run, had luck on missing a sharp stone and was up the steps and on the back porch. I didn't show a light. My eyes were better accustomed to the darkness, now, and I used my fingers beneath the knob. I liked the feel of the lock. It was a simple one that my skeleton key would open, unless—

I breathed easier. The key turned, and the door opened. And how it opened. Rusty hinges gave up their dead. There is no use to open such a door an inch or half an inch at a time. You simply prolong the squeak, drag it out, make it ten times as bad. I pushed the door open quickly. The squeak wasn't as bad as I had thought.

I didn't close it, though. I just stood in the hall, listening. I knew then why some people fear silence. I feared it. Blasting guns and cursing men are my dish. The silence felt like the silence of death. It could mean that. A man and a girl had gone into that house. Had the man come out again and left the girl there? Dead there—dead like those other two?

The smell was dank, musty. It got in my nose and my mouth and made me feel like coughing. But I didn't cough. I stretched out my hand and moved forward. Then I stopped. Feet were pounding above me; feet were walking back and forth. I located the sound. It was a man's feet. If Thesta were dead, I was in the house with her murderer.

There were the back stairs, but I passed them up. The footsteps were in the room directly above the kitchen in which I stood. If the door of that room were open and the feet stopped walking, I would be heard on the stairs. I didn't know, yet, if the girl were dead or alive. If she were alive, it would take him only a split second to drag that knife across her throat! If she were dead, time meant nothing.

But the feet still beat steadily above. I chanced my flashlight. Speed, now. I used my light plenty, made the front hall, was down to the stairs by the front door, was on them—on my way up. Then I snapped the flash off and stuck it back in my pocket. A gun took its place.

Stairs creaked. I could hear the feet, now, very plainly, and I timed my steps in with theirs.

THEN I SAW the light, and I was at the landing of the first floor. Well, down to the back of the hall and to the right was an open door. No need for it to be closed. No fear of being interrupted. That was where the light came from. And that was where the feet pounded. And then, they didn't pound any more. A sudden silence, an ominous silence, and a hoarse voice; a choking, almost inhuman voice, but certainly a man's voice. It said:

"It's hard, but it's got to be this way. The same—just the same."

I was down the hall on my toes, at the doorway, turning in it with my gun up. Was I on time? I didn't know. Certainly just by seconds—a second even—only a split second if I was on time at all.

Thesta was there. I saw her plainly. She was alive, for I saw the life in her eyes; the fear and terror, too. She was lying stretched on the bare mattress of a cot, an oil lamp on a table by her head. And above her with a topcoat turned up around his neck and a black fedora pulled well down on his head was a man. Nothing but the white block of the side of his face—mostly his ear and a small part of his neck before it was hidden in his well-turned-up coat collar. I saw his hand, his right hand that had been raised in the air but was coming down, now, coming down in a sweeping arc toward her throat!

I suppose I should have been a superman. I suppose I should have shot the knife out of his hand. I had seen his ear, and I had seen the whiteness below it, and I had covered it to shout out my warning. But not now. There was no warning; no time to speak; no time for anything but death!

My finger closed upon the trigger. His knife shot down, but not at the girl—not even at the bed. The distance was hardly more than fifteen feet. I use a heavy-caliber gun. Just the whiteness below his ear that suddenly became a dull purple. Then the would-be killer spun like a top, crashed against the wall on the opposite side of the bed from me and smacked the floor on his face.

Was he dead? Don't make me laugh. I'll bet in all his career Dr. Steel hadn't seen a deader corpse. I got a better picture of the girl, now, as I crossed the room, avoided knocking over the light on the table and was by her side. I ripped the cloth from over her mouth, saw the cruel marks on her wrists where the picture wire with which she had been bound had cut into them. And she spoke—or maybe shrieked the words.

"My father... dad—" she cried out. "He's dead... dead?"

He was dead, all right, and it was a good job. So he hadn't talked at the end; hadn't told her. He was even willing to drive the knife across her throat without letting her know the truth and let her die with the last thought that the man she had trusted, loved and called father, had killed her.

I was going to tell her, then, but I couldn't. She just closed her eyes. I put my gun down on the bed. I got the wire off her wrists and her ankles. Her eyes opened and she looked into mine. I smiled at her. There was a warm glow in them which was nice, but didn't last long as terror came again, and she breathed:

"He's dead! He's dead! Tell me he's dead."

"He's dead enough," I said, but I didn't say anything about the relationship, then. I knew how she felt—just frightened; so simply to assure her, I turned to the body. It was a crumpled heap, now, and I leaned down and took one of its shoulders and turned it over so that its face was directly in the light. Directly in—

I straightened, jarred back. The man was dead all right. But the dead man wasn't Colonel Tobias Chalmers!

I straightened. "It's your uncle. It's Arthur Chalmers!"

CHAPTER 10

THE OTHER MURDERER

SILLY, THAT? SURE, it was silly. But

then I had been knocked silly by the disclosure. Of course she knew who the man was.

The girl was off the bed, now, facing me. Little hands were on my shoulders. They trembled there.

"Easy does it, kid," I said. "Tell me what happened."

"I don't know. My father telephoned me. He told me to come out here to this house. My Uncle Arthur bought it many years ago when I was a little girl. It wasn't much, but he let father and me use it in the summer. I came and I met Uncle Arthur, and he told me that the Chalmers must always stick together in time of great need, and that the police had told him they wanted father for murder. He said my father called him on the phone and said that he needed money and was frightened, and he had told him to come here. Uncle Arthur said he made the police believe he was going away for a few days so as not to have to face reporters. And he told me that he knew father couldn't have done such a thing. Then he said he'd take me to father; that father needed me. And he took me upstairs to this room."

She shook violently, but she seemed to be in pretty good shape; so it was as good a time as any to hear the story.

"And then?" I encouraged.

"There was another man here; he struck me, and when I came to I was—"

"Another man?" I gasped. "But you should have told me that and—"

She saw the other man, and I knew he was there. I read it in her eyes as she looked over my shoulder. I read it in her open mouth, in the scream that never came, in the frantic arms that suddenly went around my neck. I might have turned, and I might have shot if she wasn't hanging to me like that.

The other man never spoke. I pushed the girl from me when it came, and that push saved my life. Yes, and I guess the other man's not speaking saved my life, too. If he had ordered me to drop my gun—the gun that I was reaching for with my left hand—there would have been nothing else for me to do but drop it with the girl clinging to me. But he didn't. He just blazed away!

He shot without a word as I straightened from my half leaning position from where I was pushing the girl. And that sudden straightening sent the bullet into my back instead of into my head! I heard nothing but the roar of the gun and felt nothing but that dull thud of pounding lead.

I guess I knocked the girl to the floor with me. The bullet must have caught me high up. I felt no pain. Maybe I didn't know what I was doing when I knocked the girl under the bed. But one thing I did know I was doing, that I'm always doing, that nothing can stop me from doing. I was finishing my draw. The force of the bullet swung me around. I hit the floor on my back. My gun was in my left hand.

The other murderer fired more than once, but he had nothing to hit because he had knocked me out of sight behind the bed on his first shot. He saw that at once. Heavy feet pounded two or three steps across the room, a heavy body struck the bed, and a flat face, a huge chest, a hairy wrist, and part of an arm with a wicked stubnosed automatic were all just a foot or two above me.

That was his second mistake. He didn't fire. He moved his gun up to cover my head and make sure. My teeth gritted. I didn't have much strength, but it doesn't take much strength to close a finger. I think he saw the gun that was half hidden beneath my coat, for his eyes went wide.

"One more chance, Mex," I said. Then I closed my finger on the trigger and blasted his huge body off the bed and onto the floor at the other side.

I GOT UP then and stumbled around the foot of the bed. Stumbled is right. I felt light in the feet. I felt light in the head, too, but not light enough to let things stand like that while I lay down on the floor. I knew that Mex's face had disappeared, but I had an idea that my gun hadn't been pointing at his face when I fired it. I was right.

Mex was still alive, and Mex could talk, and he did. I propped him up against the wall. His wasn't a pretty story. But then, after the events that had happened, I didn't expect a pretty story. He said:

"I lied to you tonight, Race. Tobias is her father all right. But it was Arthur Chalmers who was the real bad boy of the family. Tobias was wild, and his father knew it. But Arthur was a crook and a killer, and his father never knew it. Arthur was young when I first picked up with him; he had a woman, then, and he chucked her over. She blackmailed him and threatened to tell his father. Arthur was a bad man to fool with, and that was his first murder. I swear I didn't know what was on his mind, but he knifed her just like he did Delphine Rose in his brother's apartment the other night."

He had to take a breath then, and I'm telling you he had trouble sucking in air. He didn't have long to go; and since I had kicked his gun across the room and had my own in my hand, I could afford to listen. It came in gasps and grunts, but I got it all right. He went on:

"Arthur was afraid his sister's child, Edith Harriman, would get his old man's dough… so he cooked it up to take the child. It wasn't hard… the mother believed in her brother and thought he was taking care of the child until her father would come around to accepting both of them. I'm not sure what happened after that… I think Arthur Chalmers told his sister that the child had died. But if he pushed his sister out of that window or if she jumped to her death, I'll never know."

He gasped then, and I thought he was going out on me. I asked:

"What became of the child—the real Edith Harriman?"

He gulped on that, but finally said:

"He paid a couple to hide her. They hid her well… even he didn't know where she was. But they shook him down plenty. Things went bad for him… he juggled money around. Then his own big fortune disappeared, and he had nothing but the girl's trust fund which he had hard work making look good in his accounts. Then the people who were minding the girl died… left this Dr. Bernard Jones proof of her identity, and he advertised in the paper."

"And you fixed things up with the doctor?"

"Hell, no!" said Mex, his eyes widening. "The doctor was too damned honest. I know my check is up… doesn't matter what I say. It was all rather clever." His eyes began to glaze, now. "We nearly got the doctor in the post office that time. Maybe you think I know something about crime, but I never met anyone with a head like Arthur Chalmers'. He thought fast… acted faster. Arranged it so that the lawyer, Hartman, never saw Edith Harriman. Arranged it so Dr. Bernard Jones brought the real girl to his side door… servants never saw her. He arranged it so that Delphine Rose was there and would impersonate her; promised Delphine a lot of money she didn't get, then lured her to Colonel Chalmers' apartment and killed her."

"Ah!" I saw the light, "that's why he wouldn't let Dr. Jones see the girl again. He decided to let his lawyer and the law discover that she was really not the missing heiress, Edith Harriman, his niece, and even be surprised."

"Sure!" agreed Mex. "It was well worked out. Dr. Jones brought her in the side door of his library. Dr. Jones left. Five minutes later Delphine Rose appeared before the servants as Edith Harriman; detectives brought there to protect her met her as Edith Harriman; you met her as Edith Harriman. But when it was shown she was not the real Edith Harriman, Arthur still had the use of the trust fund. Smart, eh?"

"But he couldn't have killed Dr. Jones."

"Couldn't he? He had the side entrance that he came and went through unseen. He could telephone his brother, trap him into going to the hotel and seeing Dr. Jones dead. Just as he telephoned Thesta's husband to come on—pretending he was Colonel Tobias—and complicating things."

"But," I said, "what became of the real Edith Harriman?"

His lips hung open, his eyes blinked. He clutched at his chest. His fingers were red. I tried again: "But if Edith Harriman were dead, he wouldn't have the trust fund—only as long as she lived."

"He would have if… if Thesta Chalmers and Tobias, his brother, were dead, too."

"So it was to be a complete wipeout." I gave that a little bit of thought. "But why me?"

"You were the key to the whole business, Race," Mex told me. "He thought you knew… knew that he had killed Edith Harriman. "That's why he wanted you killed; that's why he told me it was worth half of everything he would get in cash if you were dead. Above everything, he wanted you dead."

"He wasn't so smart there," I said. "If I knew, I would have talked long ago."

"I tried to tell him that. But he wouldn't believe it. He said with so much money involved you'd try and blackmail him… get more out of him than you could from Thesta."

"The rat—" I started and stopped. Then: "But what made him think I knew, Mex?"

Mex's voice was weak now. I had to kneel down to get his words.

"He said… he said that you practically told him that you knew he killed Edith Harriman. But you put it over well… so that the detective there would think it was a joke… and… and—"

"But where's her body?" I had him by the shoulder, now, shaking him. I guess he didn't know what he was saying when he finished. But he said:

"Arthur Chalmers said you knew where Edith Harriman's body was. You told him where it was… told him… told—"

THAT WAS ALL. Just as easy as that, he passed out. Did I reverently place a clean sheet or a clean handkerchief over his face? Did I stand up and remove my hat in the presence of death? I did not. But I didn't kick him in the face, and that was something to be proud of. For I knew that even if he had tried to put it on Arthur Chalmers he had at least knifed the little doctor.

Thesta had been listening, vaguely conscious of what went on. Then reality struck home to her with a wallop.

"Father—my father—he's dead!" she screamed.

Her father wasn't dead. We found him in a room across the hall, bound and gagged. A thin, emaciated, shaky man— old, old beyond his years.

O'Rourke came with Nelson and Jerry, and pretty soon the place was alive with cops. Nelson didn't want to listen but wanted to bully the girl, and I wanted to crack him; but O'Rourke got us straightened out. I talked and they listened, and the blood ran down my back and side. And no one gave a damn, not even me.

Then Thesta Chalmers did.

"It's a mess," said O'Rourke. And whispering to me: "If Nelson thought she was heiress to a pile of jack it wouldn't hurt any."

"Isn't she?" I demanded.

"No." He shook his head. "I had a long talk with Hartman. He said that if Arthur Chalmers died, Hartman's firm administers the trust and pays out the interest to designated charitable institutions. It still takes proof of Edith Harriman's death to establish Thesta Chalmers as the legal and rightful heir. In that case the corpus delicti must be produced. Mex may have lied. Arthur Chalmers may have hidden her away again alive. Now, if you had the head for it, Race, and could find her body—"

"Her body, eh?" I said. "That would even be proof to Nelson? Head for it. Why… why—"

I WAS THINKING when we got into the big car, Thesta close to me and O'Rourke and Nelson sitting on the small seats facing us. I was still thinking when they took Colonel Tobias out at Headquarters to go through the silly formality that they call law. And suddenly I had it. I just leaned back and laughed. Then I said:

"O.K., boys, I'll help you out just once more. I'll produce just one more body for you."

"No wisecracks," said Nelson.

"Why not?" I asked. "It was a wisecrack that brought me into this whole mess, and the same wisecrack will clear it up. Come on, drive right to Arthur Chalmers' house."

Thesta stuck close to me when we went into the Chalmers' study. O'Rourke started to call a doctor when he saw the way I flopped into the big chair, but I got him to call Dr. Steel, the medical examiner, instead.

"That's right, O'Rourke," I told him. "Another body right here in the house." Then I called the butler, Roland, in. There was just one question to ask him. It was: "Is there a room in the cellar of this house that Mr. Chalmers didn't let anyone go into and the keys to which he kept himself?"

"Why, yes, sir." Roland was polite now. "The small room with the heavy door. It's just behind the wine room in the cellar. Mr. Chalmers always kept rare vintages and old brandies locked up there."

O'Rourke said later that I stood his hair on end with my weird laugh and that I shook a finger at him like a detective right out of a book. But why not? I saw the whole thing, now. Remember the wisecrack I made when Arthur Chalmers told me I couldn't see the girl? I was only joking when I said I'd accuse him of murdering the girl and hiding her body in the cellar. We were both fooled by that crack. He thought I meant it, and I thought his collapse into the chair was from indignation. But it wasn't. He was scared stiff by it—because it was exactly the truth. And now that wisecrack was to pay me dividends because I was working for an heiress.

"O.K., boys"—that was where I did the pointing finger act—"break down the locked door to the little room behind the main wine cellar. You'll find Edith Harriman's body there—also a bottle of old brandy."

And I was right. They found both, but they only brought me the brandy.

Made in the USA
Columbia, SC
12 July 2021